BBLE
VN

THE WHY-WHY'S GONE BYE-BYE

ALADDIN | New York | London | Toronto | Sydney | New Delhi

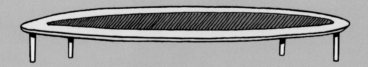

ALADDIN / An imprint of Simon & Schuster Children's Publishing Division / 1230 Avenue of the Americas, New York, New York 10020 / First Aladdin edition August 2022 / Copyright © 2022 by Stephan Pastis / All rights reserved, including the right of reproduction in whole or in part in any form. / ALADDIN and related logo are registered trademarks of Simon & Schuster, Inc. / For information about special discounts for bulk purchases, please contact Simon & Schuster Special Sales at 1-866-506-1949 or business@simonandschuster.com. / The Simon & Schuster Speakers Bureau can bring authors to your live event. For more information or to book an event contact the Simon & Schuster Speakers Bureau at 1-866-248-3049 or visit our website at www.simonspeakers.com. / Designed by Karin Paprocki and Stephan Pastis / The illustrations for this book were rendered digitally. / The text of this book was hand-lettered and set in Bodoni. / Manufactured in China 0522 SCP / 2 4 6 8 10 9 7 5 3 1 / Library of Congress Control Number 2021944661 / ISBN 9781534496149 (hardcover) / ISBN 9781534496132 (paperback) / ISBN 9781534496156 (ebook)

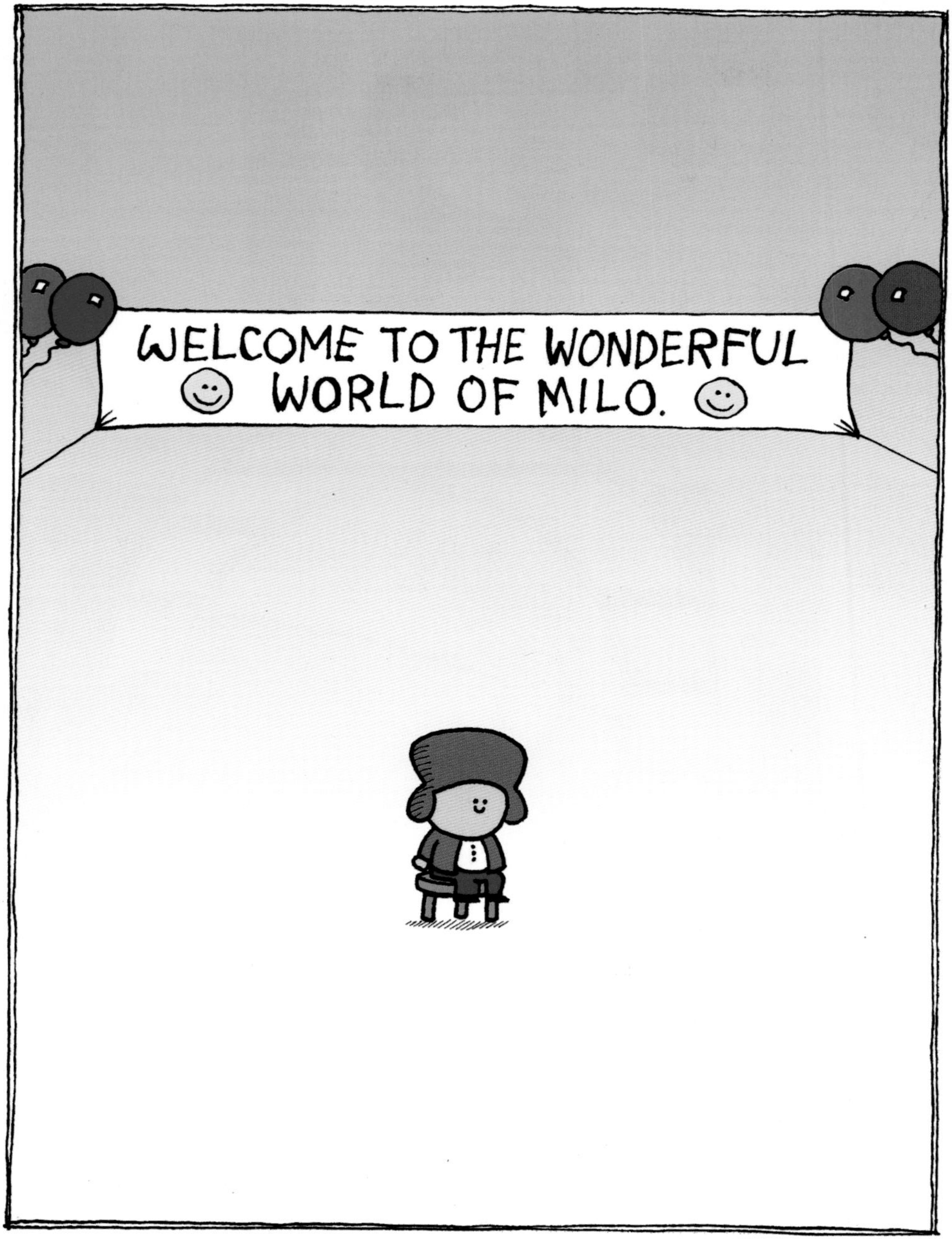
WELCOME TO THE WONDERFUL WORLD OF MILO.

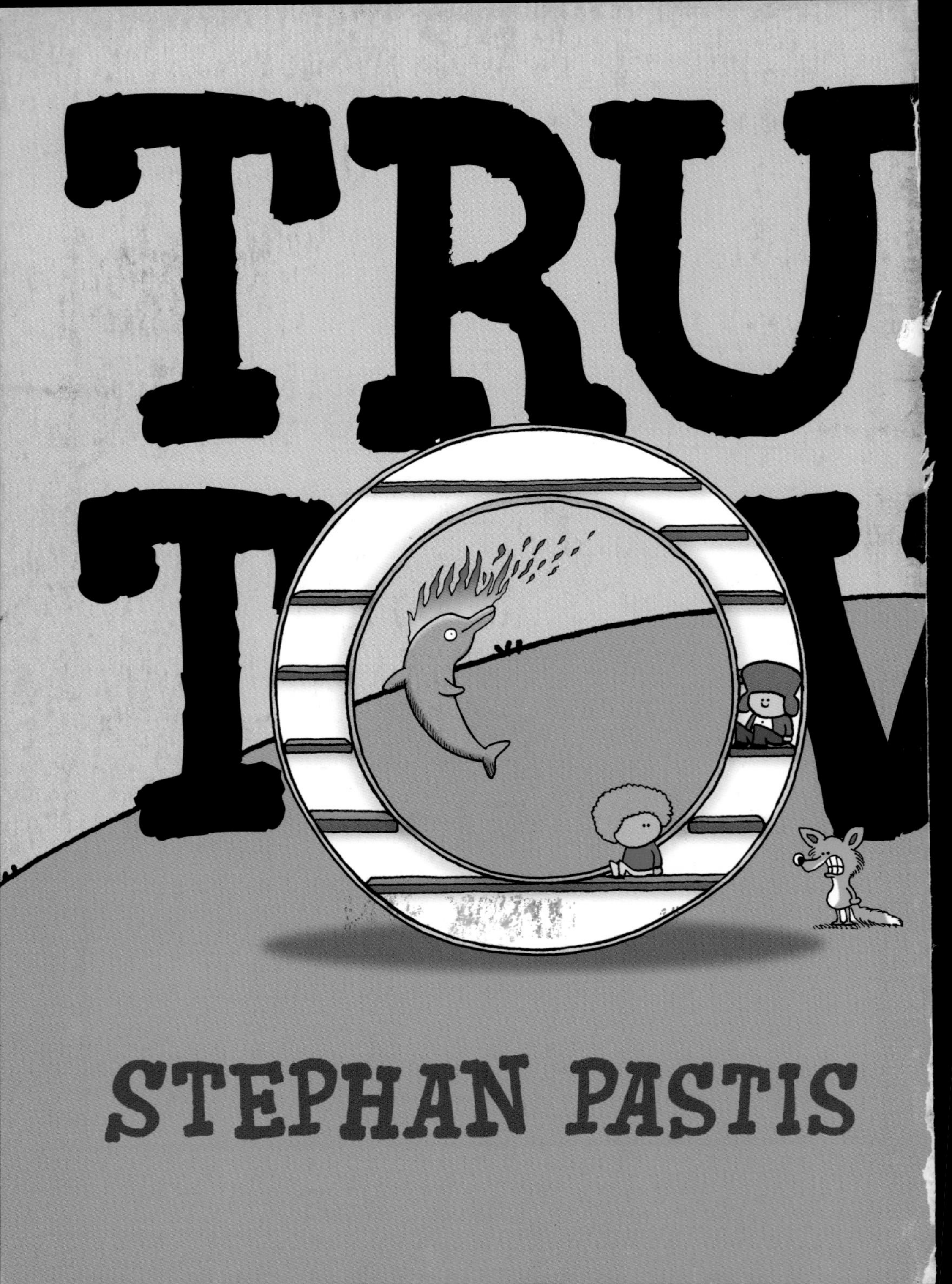
TRU
STEPHAN PASTIS

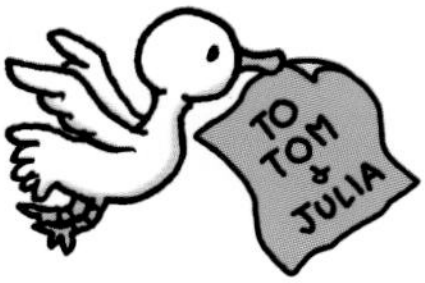
TO
TOM
&
JULIA

PROLOGUE

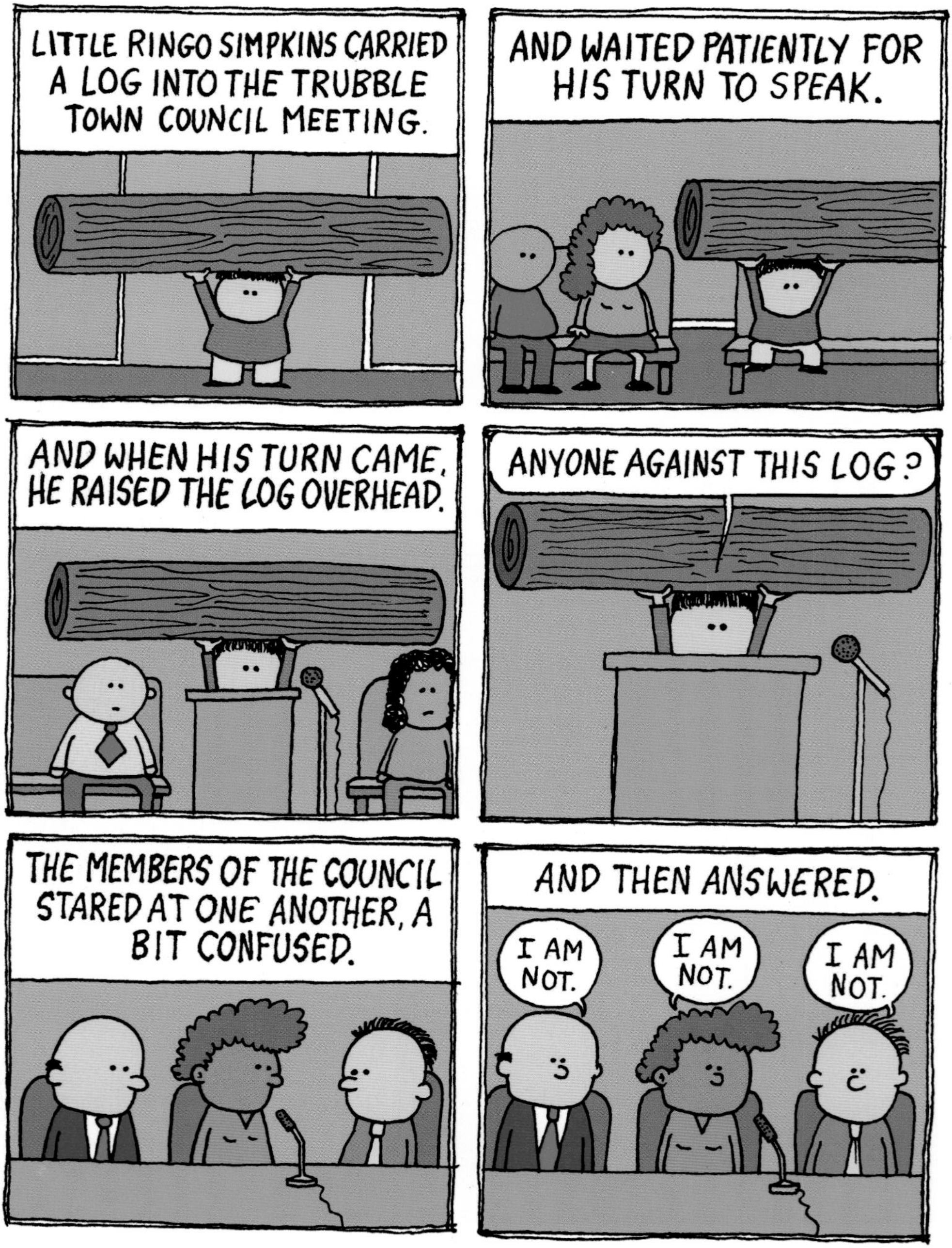
LITTLE RINGO SIMPKINS CARRIED A LOG INTO THE TRUBBLE TOWN COUNCIL MEETING.
AND WAITED PATIENTLY FOR HIS TURN TO SPEAK.
AND WHEN HIS TURN CAME, HE RAISED THE LOG OVERHEAD.
ANYONE AGAINST THIS LOG?
THE MEMBERS OF THE COUNCIL STARED AT ONE ANOTHER, A BIT CONFUSED.
AND THEN ANSWERED.
I AM NOT.
I AM NOT.
I AM NOT.

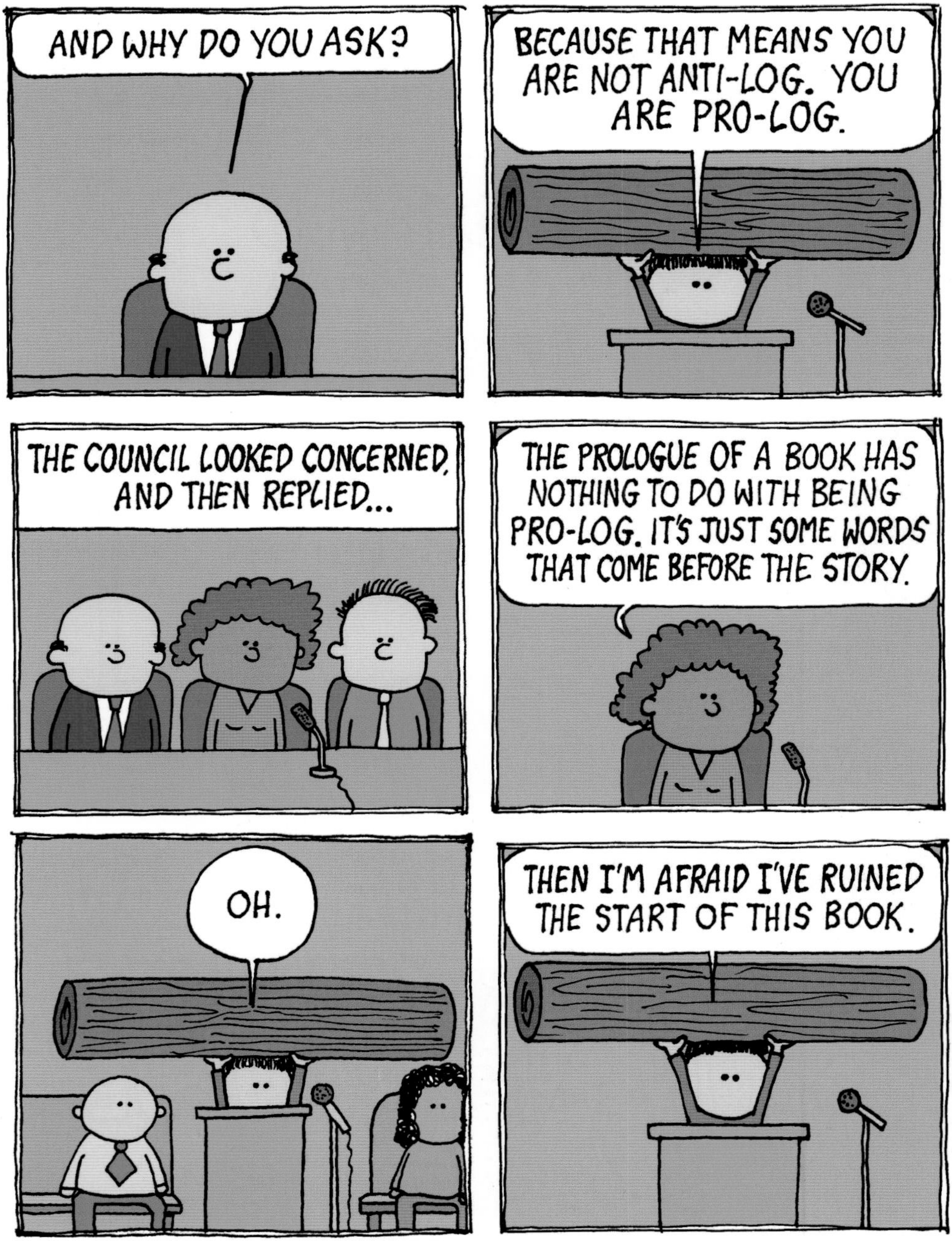
AND WHY DO YOU ASK?
BECAUSE THAT MEANS YOU ARE NOT ANTI-LOG. YOU ARE PRO-LOG.
THE COUNCIL LOOKED CONCERNED, AND THEN REPLIED...
THE PROLOGUE OF A BOOK HAS NOTHING TO DO WITH BEING PRO-LOG. IT'S JUST SOME WORDS THAT COME BEFORE THE STORY.
OH.
THEN I'M AFRAID I'VE RUINED THE START OF THIS BOOK.

CHAPTER WON

BY THE END OF WHICH...

WE HOPE TO HAVE WON BACK THE READERS WE LOST IN THE PROLOGUE

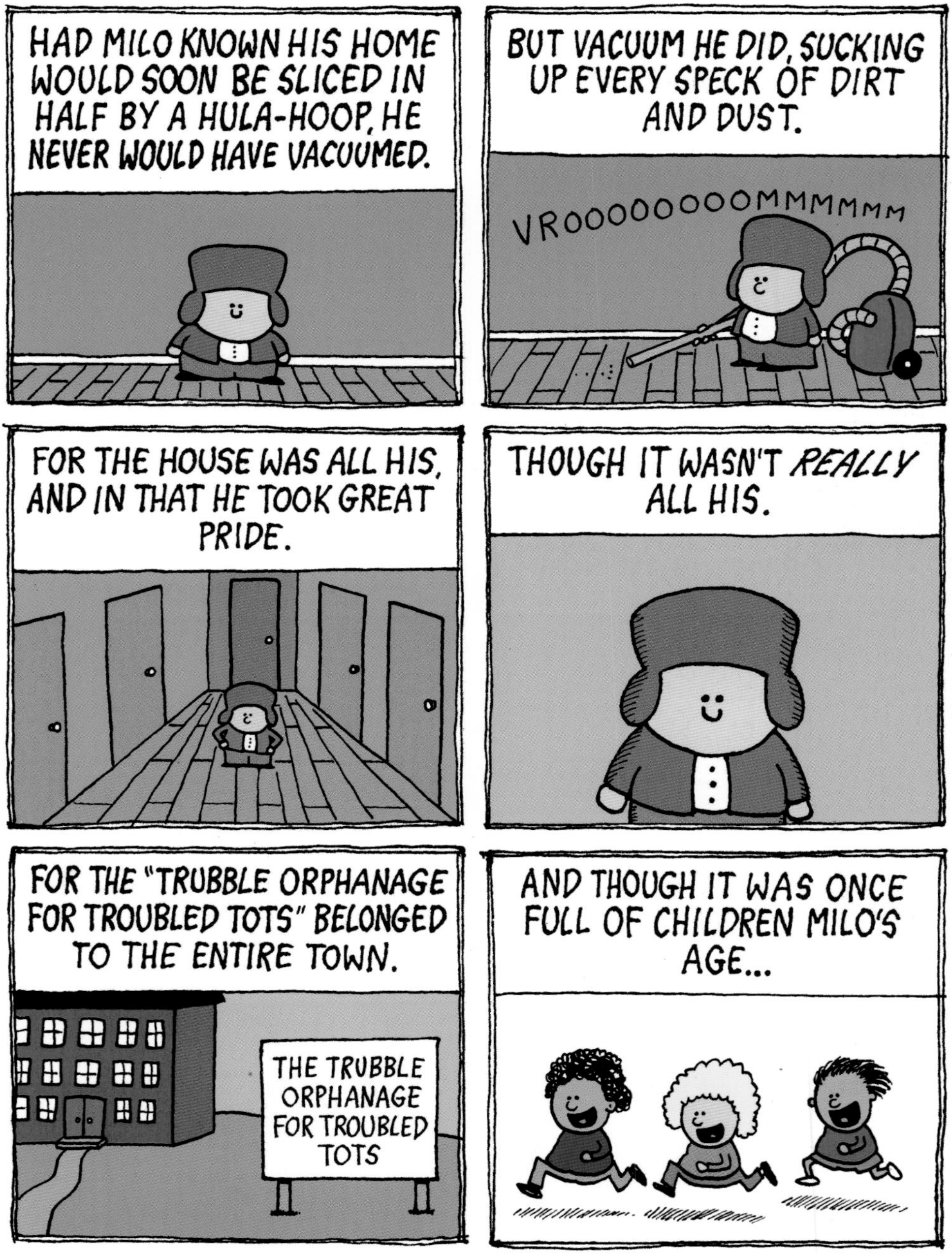
HAD MILO KNOWN HIS HOME WOULD SOON BE SLICED IN HALF BY A HULA-HOOP, HE NEVER WOULD HAVE VACUUMED.
BUT VACUUM HE DID, SUCKING UP EVERY SPECK OF DIRT AND DUST.
VROOOOOOOOOMMMMMMM
FOR THE HOUSE WAS ALL HIS, AND IN THAT HE TOOK GREAT PRIDE.
THOUGH IT WASN'T *REALLY* ALL HIS.
FOR THE "TRUBBLE ORPHANAGE FOR TROUBLED TOTS" BELONGED TO THE ENTIRE TOWN.
THE TRUBBLE ORPHANAGE FOR TROUBLED TOTS
AND THOUGH IT WAS ONCE FULL OF CHILDREN MILO'S AGE...

ALL OF THE KIDS HAD GRADUALLY BEEN PLACED WITH VARIOUS FAMILIES.

UNTIL EVENTUALLY THERE WAS JUST MILO.

AND WHILE OTHER CHILDREN MIGHT HAVE FOUND THAT DIFFICULT, MILO SAW IT AS AN OPPORTUNITY.

FOR HE SAW ITS MANY ROOMS AS A BIG, BLANK CANVAS UPON WHICH HE COULD CREATE A NEW WORLD.

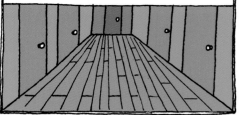

SO THERE WAS THE "ROOM OF REMARKABLE IDEAS," WHERE ONE WENT TO HAVE REMARKABLE IDEAS.

ROOM OF REMARKABLE IDEAS

AND THE "SPACE OF INFINITE SADNESS," WHERE ONE WENT TO BE SAD.

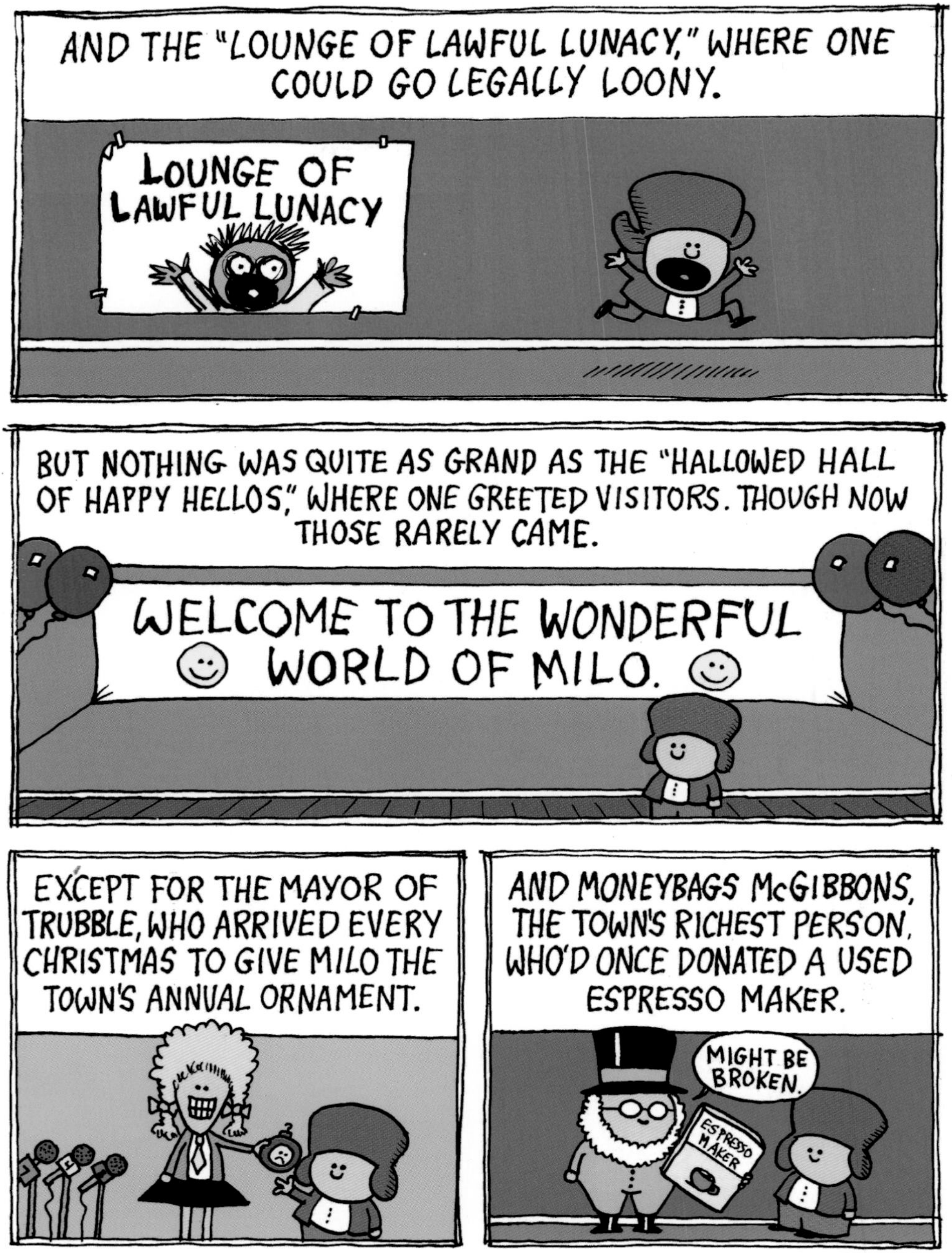
AND THE "LOUNGE OF LAWFUL LUNACY," WHERE ONE COULD GO LEGALLY LOONY.
LOUNGE OF LAWFUL LUNACY
BUT NOTHING WAS QUITE AS GRAND AS THE "HALLOWED HALL OF HAPPY HELLOS," WHERE ONE GREETED VISITORS. THOUGH NOW THOSE RARELY CAME.
WELCOME TO THE WONDERFUL WORLD OF MILO.
EXCEPT FOR THE MAYOR OF TRUBBLE, WHO ARRIVED EVERY CHRISTMAS TO GIVE MILO THE TOWN'S ANNUAL ORNAMENT.
AND MONEYBAGS McGIBBONS, THE TOWN'S RICHEST PERSON, WHO'D ONCE DONATED A USED ESPRESSO MAKER.
MIGHT BE BROKEN.
ESPRESSO MAKER

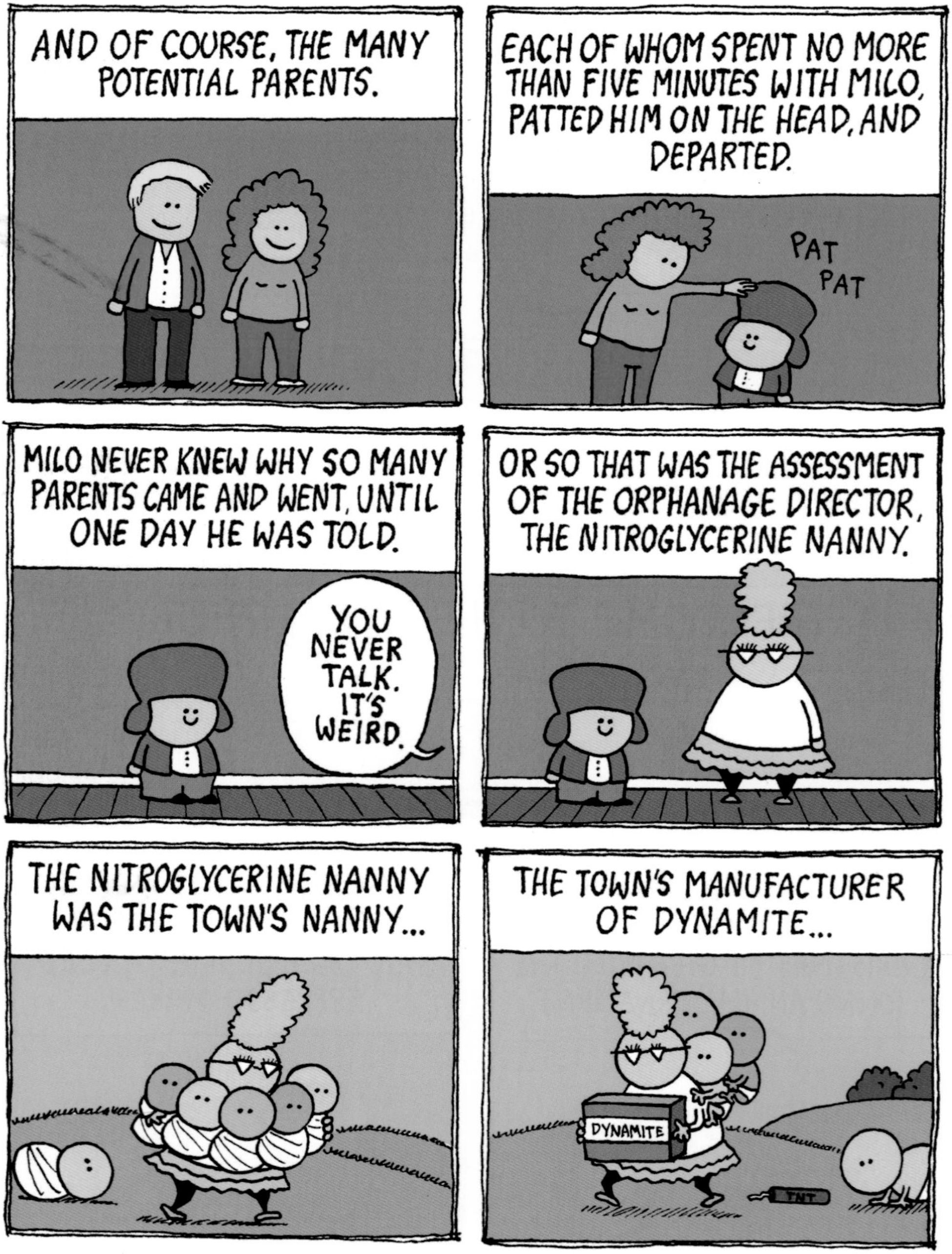
AND OF COURSE, THE MANY POTENTIAL PARENTS.
EACH OF WHOM SPENT NO MORE THAN FIVE MINUTES WITH MILO, PATTED HIM ON THE HEAD, AND DEPARTED.
PAT
PAT
MILO NEVER KNEW WHY SO MANY PARENTS CAME AND WENT, UNTIL ONE DAY HE WAS TOLD.
YOU NEVER TALK. IT'S WEIRD.
OR SO THAT WAS THE ASSESSMENT OF THE ORPHANAGE DIRECTOR, THE NITROGLYCERINE NANNY.
THE NITROGLYCERINE NANNY WAS THE TOWN'S NANNY...
THE TOWN'S MANUFACTURER OF DYNAMITE...
DYNAMITE
TNT

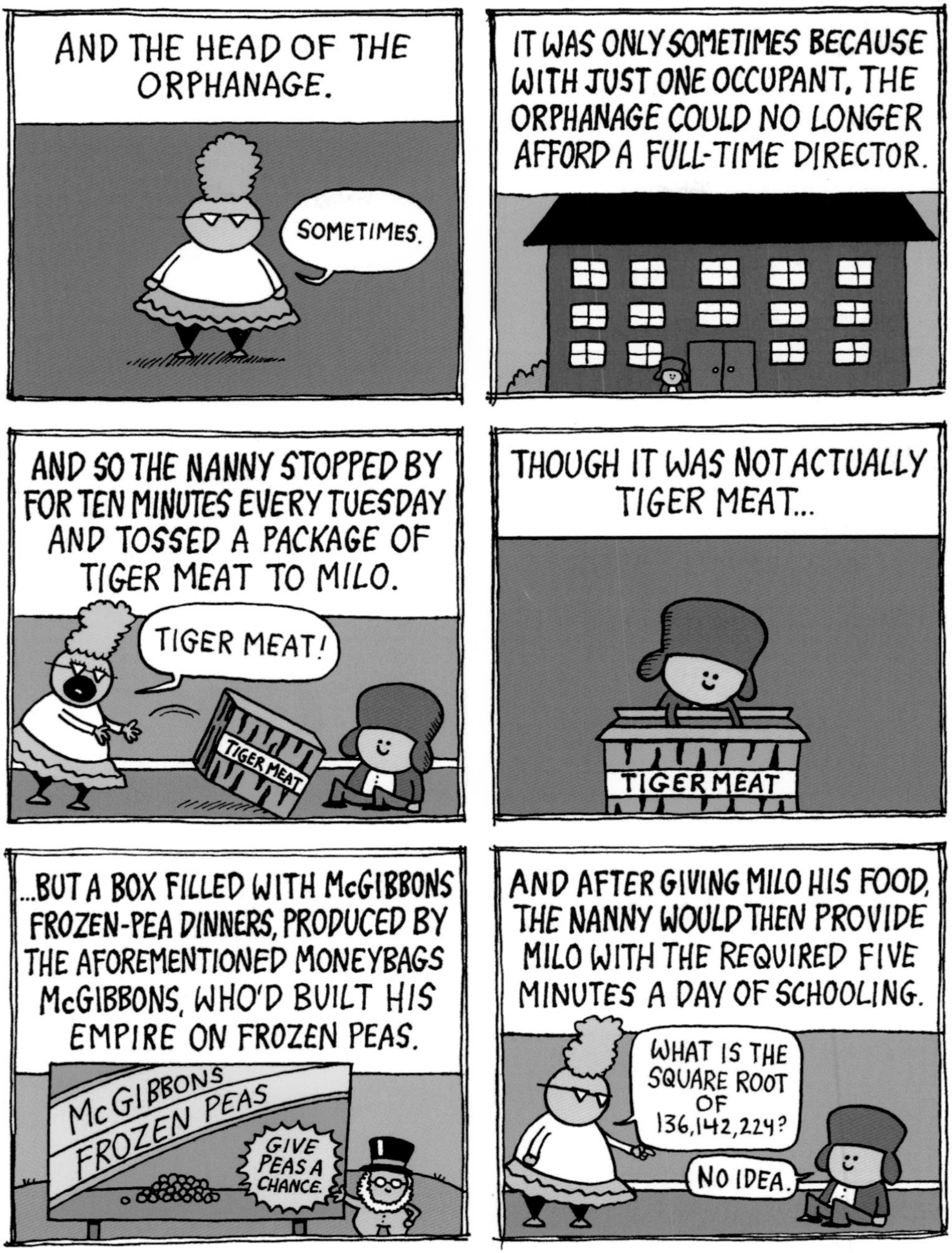
AND THE HEAD OF THE ORPHANAGE.
SOMETIMES.
IT WAS ONLY SOMETIMES BECAUSE WITH JUST ONE OCCUPANT, THE ORPHANAGE COULD NO LONGER AFFORD A FULL-TIME DIRECTOR.
AND SO THE NANNY STOPPED BY FOR TEN MINUTES EVERY TUESDAY AND TOSSED A PACKAGE OF TIGER MEAT TO MILO.
TIGER MEAT!
TIGER MEAT
THOUGH IT WAS NOT ACTUALLY TIGER MEAT...
TIGER MEAT
...BUT A BOX FILLED WITH McGIBBONS FROZEN-PEA DINNERS, PRODUCED BY THE AFOREMENTIONED MONEYBAGS McGIBBONS, WHO'D BUILT HIS EMPIRE ON FROZEN PEAS.
McGIBBONS FROZEN PEAS
GIVE PEAS A CHANCE.
AND AFTER GIVING MILO HIS FOOD, THE NANNY WOULD THEN PROVIDE MILO WITH THE REQUIRED FIVE MINUTES A DAY OF SCHOOLING.
WHAT IS THE SQUARE ROOT OF 136,142,224?
NO IDEA.

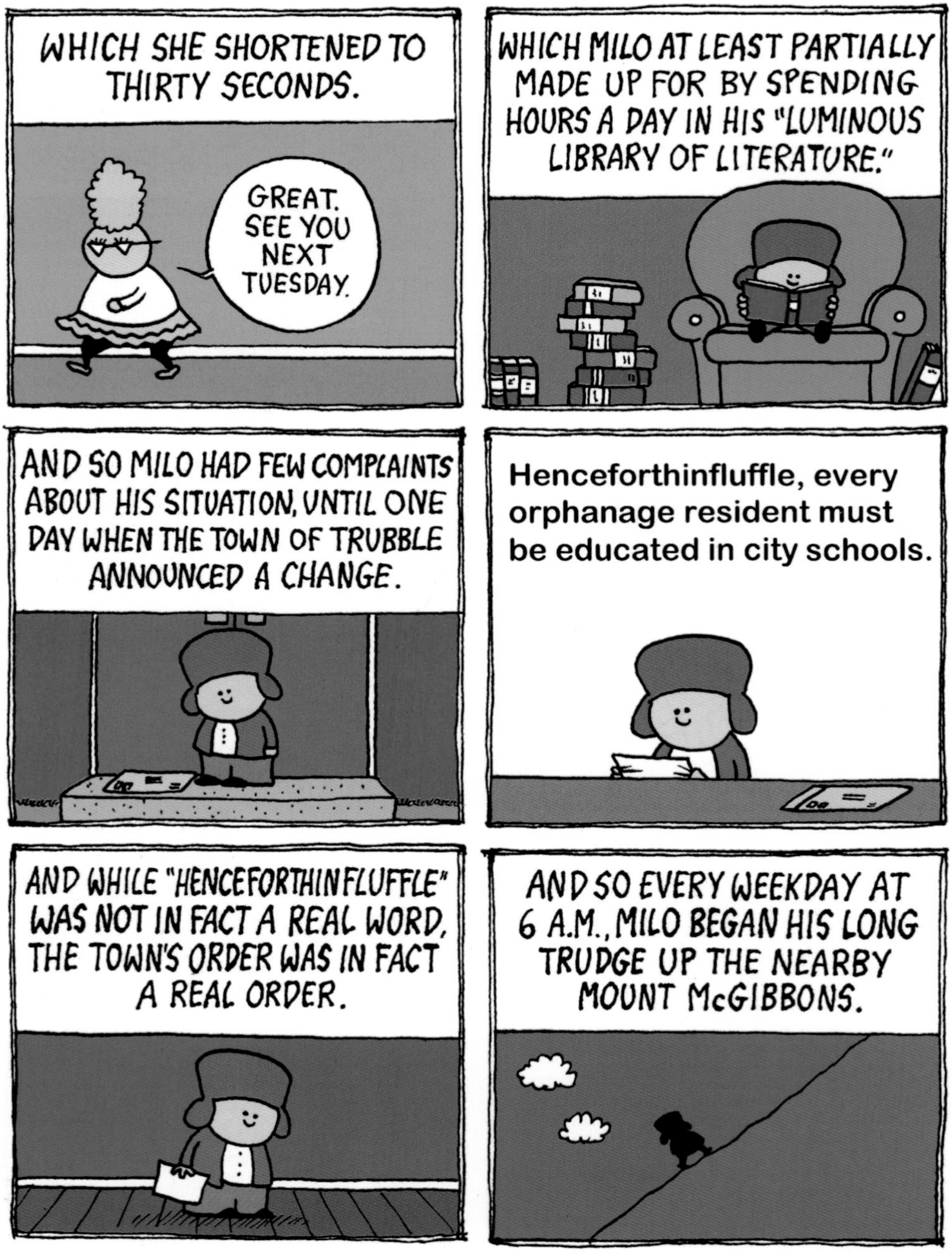
WHICH SHE SHORTENED TO THIRTY SECONDS.
GREAT. SEE YOU NEXT TUESDAY.
WHICH MILO AT LEAST PARTIALLY MADE UP FOR BY SPENDING HOURS A DAY IN HIS "LUMINOUS LIBRARY OF LITERATURE."
AND SO MILO HAD FEW COMPLAINTS ABOUT HIS SITUATION, UNTIL ONE DAY WHEN THE TOWN OF TRUBBLE ANNOUNCED A CHANGE.
Henceforthinfluffle, every orphanage resident must be educated in city schools.
AND WHILE "HENCEFORTHINFLUFFLE" WAS NOT IN FACT A REAL WORD, THE TOWN'S ORDER WAS IN FACT A REAL ORDER.
AND SO EVERY WEEKDAY AT 6 A.M., MILO BEGAN HIS LONG TRUDGE UP THE NEARBY MOUNT McGIBBONS.

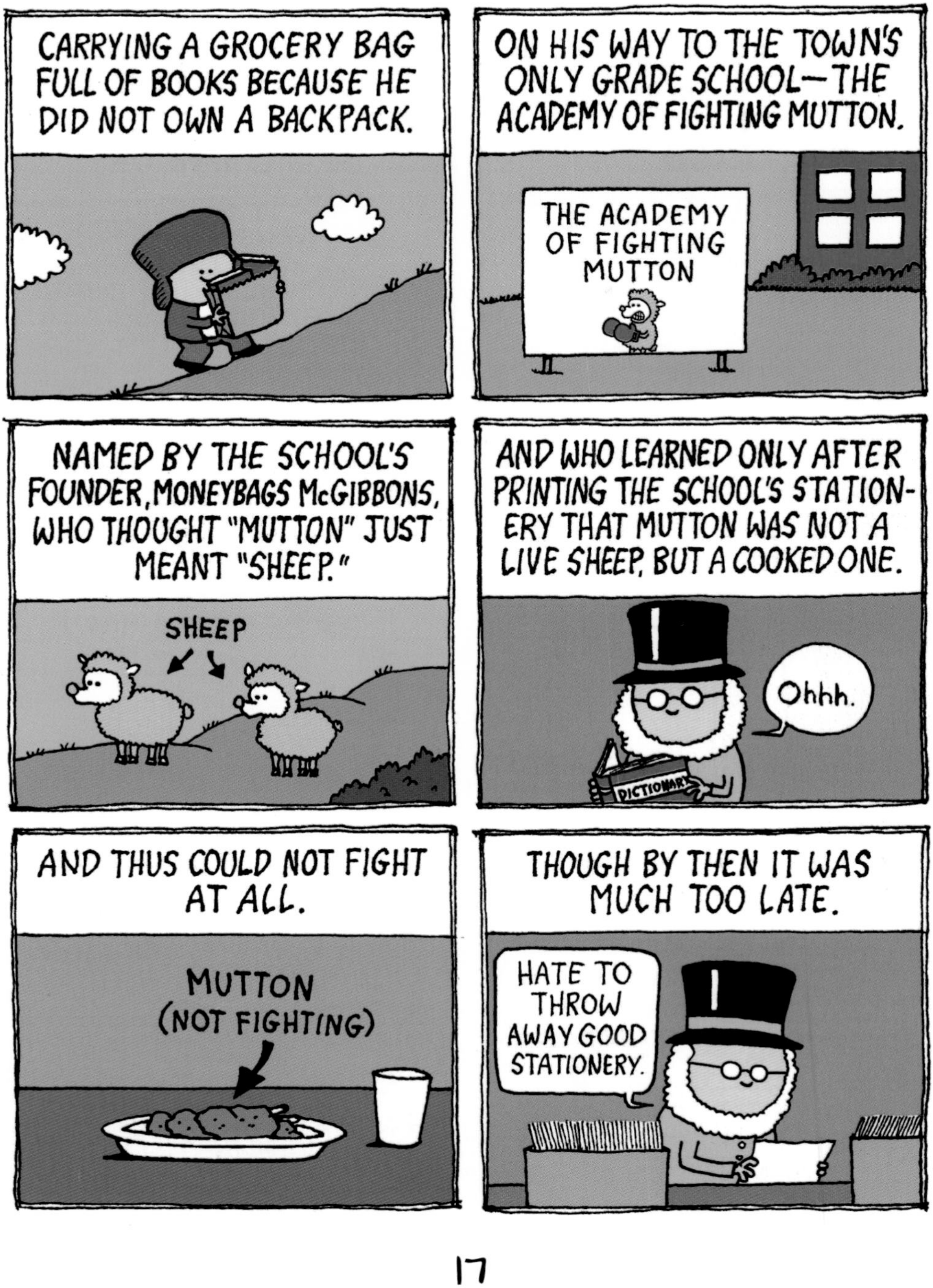
CARRYING A GROCERY BAG FULL OF BOOKS BECAUSE HE DID NOT OWN A BACKPACK.
ON HIS WAY TO THE TOWN'S ONLY GRADE SCHOOL—THE ACADEMY OF FIGHTING MUTTON.
THE ACADEMY OF FIGHTING MUTTON
NAMED BY THE SCHOOL'S FOUNDER, MONEYBAGS McGIBBONS, WHO THOUGHT "MUTTON" JUST MEANT "SHEEP."
SHEEP
AND WHO LEARNED ONLY AFTER PRINTING THE SCHOOL'S STATIONERY THAT MUTTON WAS NOT A LIVE SHEEP, BUT A COOKED ONE.
Ohhh.
DICTIONARY
AND THUS COULD NOT FIGHT AT ALL.
MUTTON (NOT FIGHTING)
THOUGH BY THEN IT WAS MUCH TOO LATE.
HATE TO THROW AWAY GOOD STATIONERY.

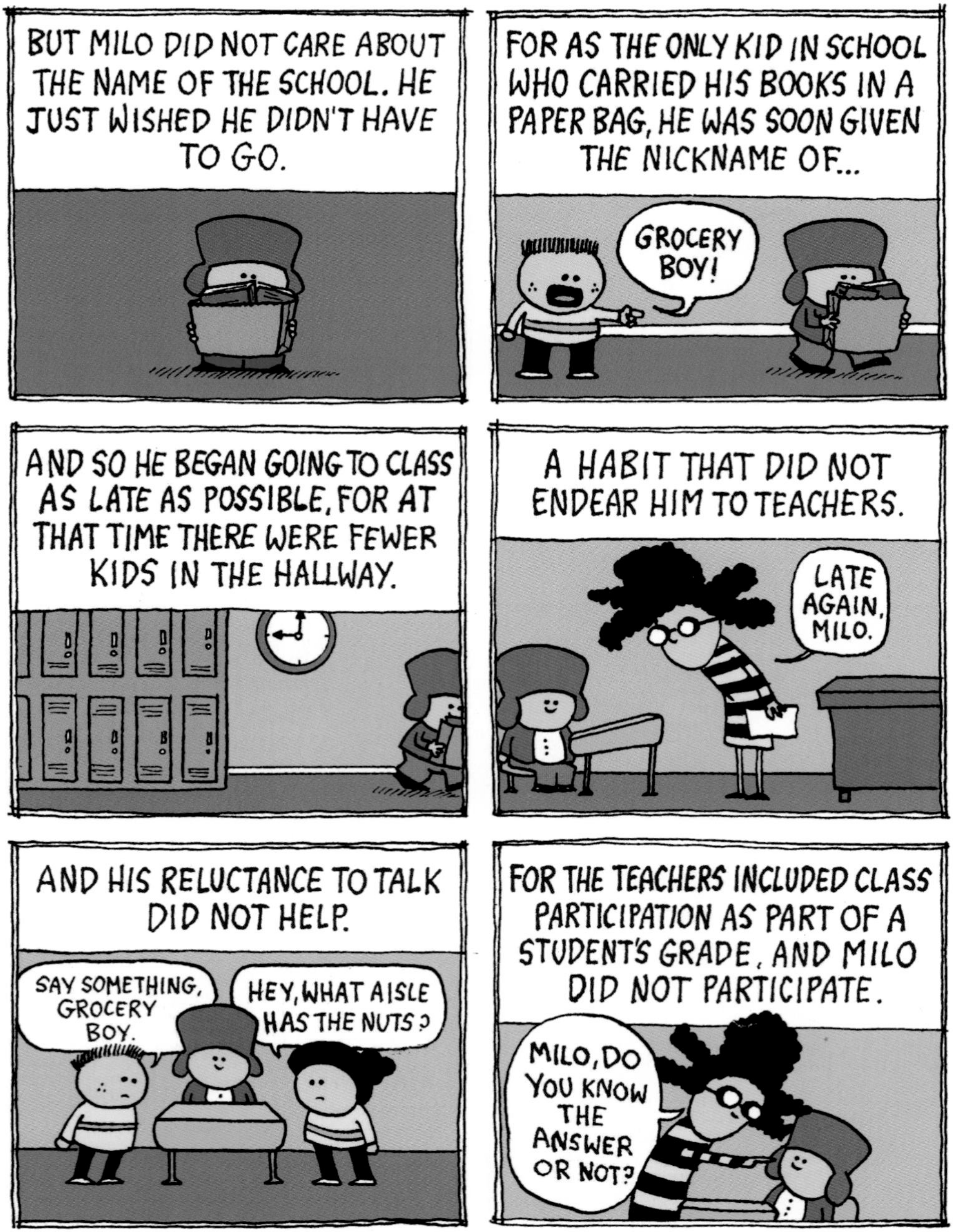
BUT MILO DID NOT CARE ABOUT THE NAME OF THE SCHOOL. HE JUST WISHED HE DIDN'T HAVE TO GO.
FOR AS THE ONLY KID IN SCHOOL WHO CARRIED HIS BOOKS IN A PAPER BAG, HE WAS SOON GIVEN THE NICKNAME OF...
GROCERY BOY!
AND SO HE BEGAN GOING TO CLASS AS LATE AS POSSIBLE, FOR AT THAT TIME THERE WERE FEWER KIDS IN THE HALLWAY.
A HABIT THAT DID NOT ENDEAR HIM TO TEACHERS.
LATE AGAIN, MILO.
AND HIS RELUCTANCE TO TALK DID NOT HELP.
SAY SOMETHING, GROCERY BOY.
HEY, WHAT AISLE HAS THE NUTS?
FOR THE TEACHERS INCLUDED CLASS PARTICIPATION AS PART OF A STUDENT'S GRADE, AND MILO DID NOT PARTICIPATE.
MILO, DO YOU KNOW THE ANSWER OR NOT?

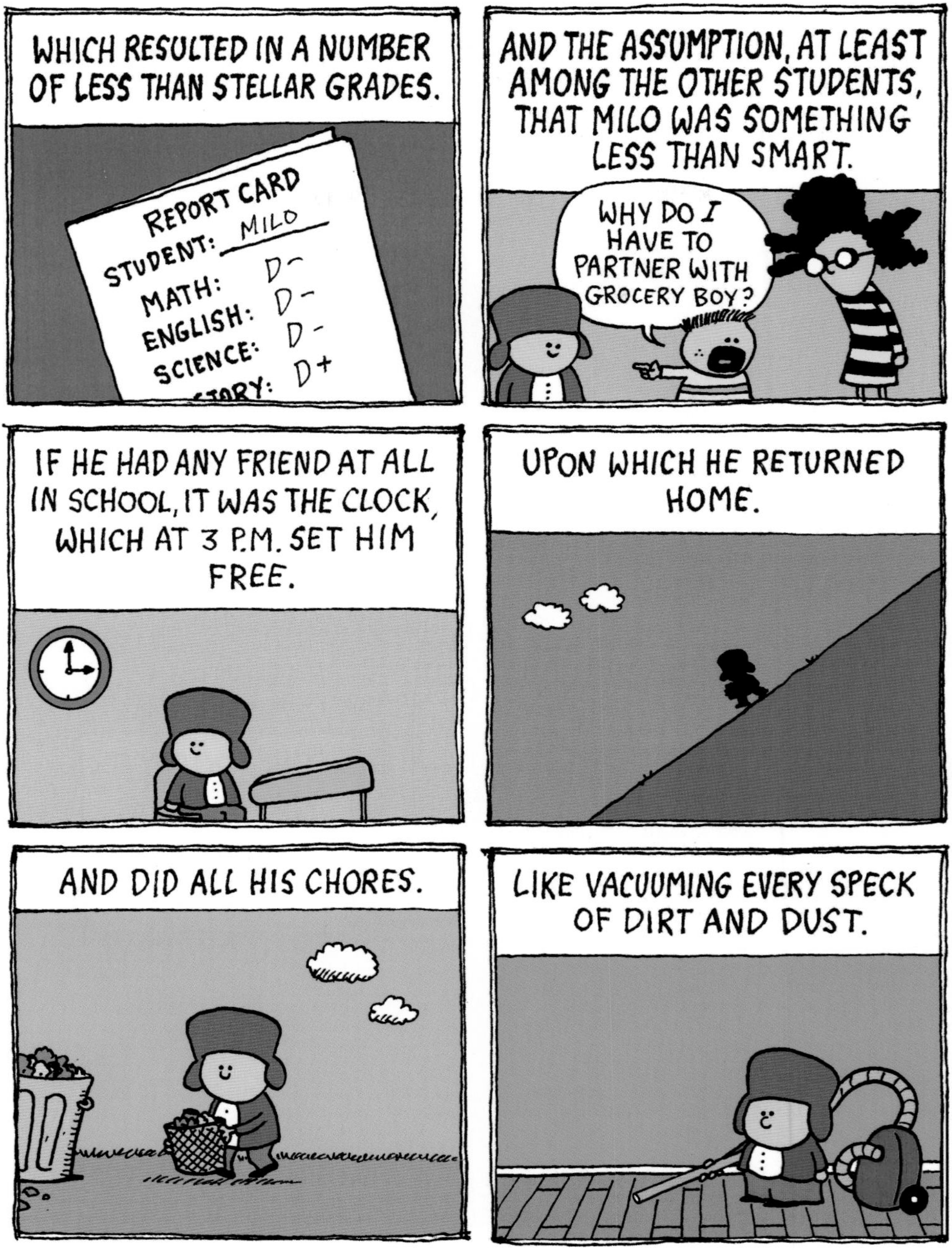
WHICH RESULTED IN A NUMBER OF LESS THAN STELLAR GRADES.
REPORT CARD
STUDENT: MILO
MATH: D-
ENGLISH: D-
SCIENCE: D-
AND THE ASSUMPTION, AT LEAST AMONG THE OTHER STUDENTS, THAT MILO WAS SOMETHING LESS THAN SMART.
WHY DO *I* HAVE TO PARTNER WITH GROCERY BOY?
IF HE HAD ANY FRIEND AT ALL IN SCHOOL, IT WAS THE CLOCK, WHICH AT 3 P.M. SET HIM FREE.
UPON WHICH HE RETURNED HOME.
AND DID ALL HIS CHORES.
LIKE VACUUMING EVERY SPECK OF DIRT AND DUST.

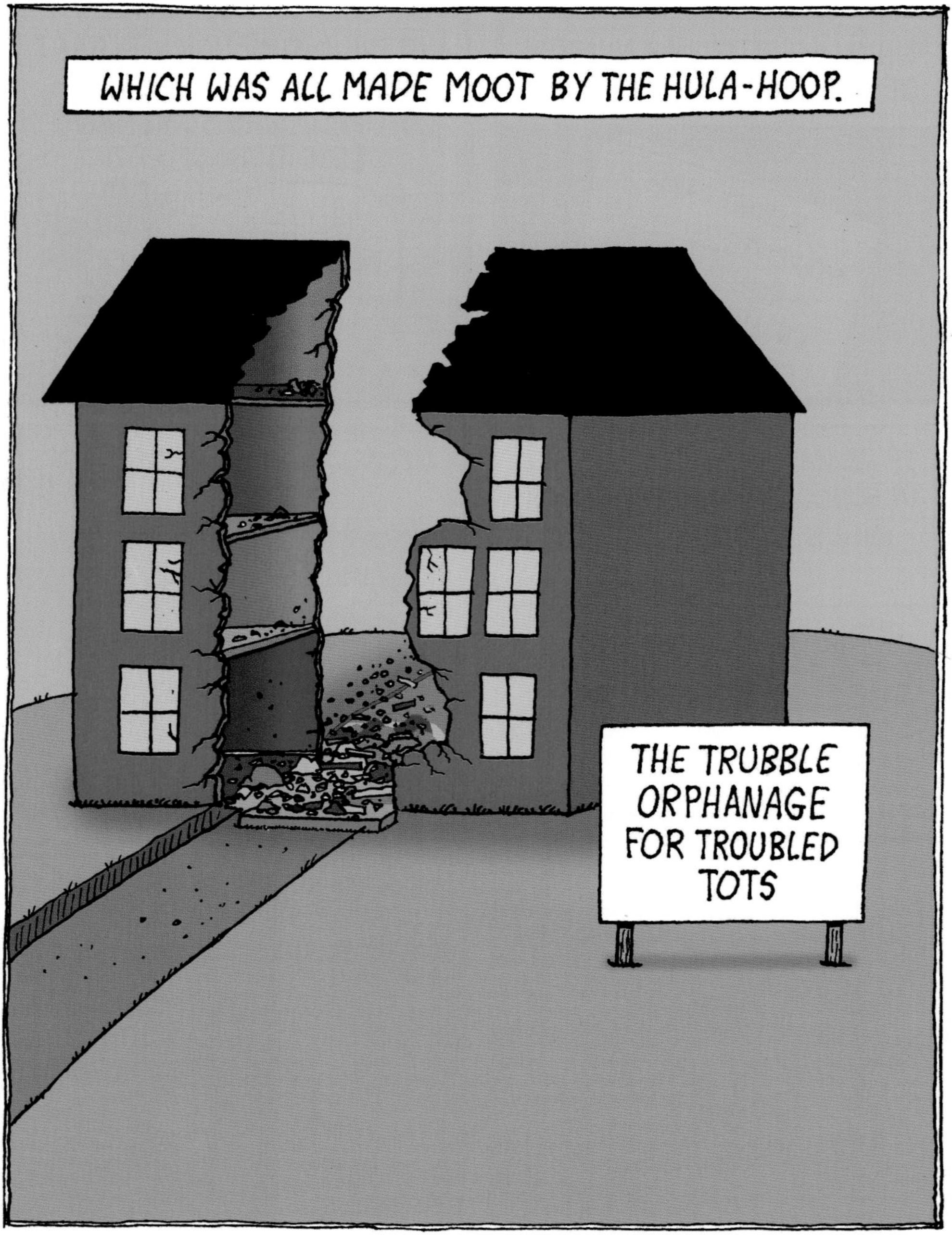
WHICH WAS ALL MADE MOOT BY THE HULA-HOOP.
THE TRUBBLE ORPHANAGE FOR TROUBLED TOTS

CHAPTER 1.5

BECAUSE CHAPTERS SHOULDN'T HAVE TO BE WHOLE NUMBERS

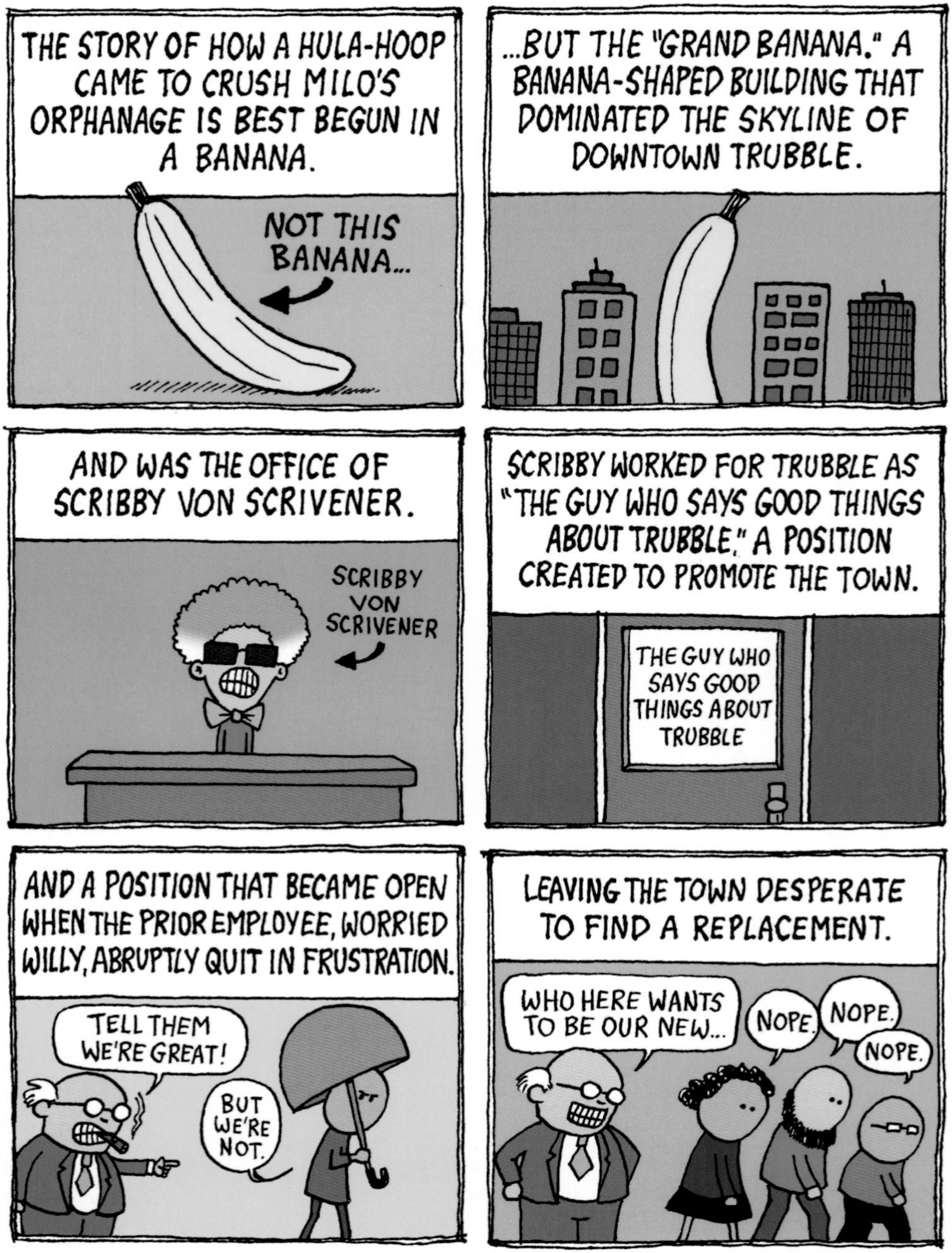
THE STORY OF HOW A HULA-HOOP CAME TO CRUSH MILO'S ORPHANAGE IS BEST BEGUN IN A BANANA.
NOT THIS BANANA...
...BUT THE "GRAND BANANA." A BANANA-SHAPED BUILDING THAT DOMINATED THE SKYLINE OF DOWNTOWN TRUBBLE.
AND WAS THE OFFICE OF SCRIBBY VON SCRIVENER.
SCRIBBY VON SCRIVENER
SCRIBBY WORKED FOR TRUBBLE AS "THE GUY WHO SAYS GOOD THINGS ABOUT TRUBBLE," A POSITION CREATED TO PROMOTE THE TOWN.
THE GUY WHO SAYS GOOD THINGS ABOUT TRUBBLE
AND A POSITION THAT BECAME OPEN WHEN THE PRIOR EMPLOYEE, WORRIED WILLY, ABRUPTLY QUIT IN FRUSTRATION.
TELL THEM WE'RE GREAT!
BUT WE'RE NOT.
LEAVING THE TOWN DESPERATE TO FIND A REPLACEMENT.
WHO HERE WANTS TO BE OUR NEW...
NOPE.
NOPE.
NOPE.

UNTIL THEY GOT AN APPLICATION FROM *SCRIBBY,* WHO DEMANDED AS ONE OF THE CONDITIONS FOR TAKING THE JOB...

...THAT MY OFFICE BE SHAPED LIKE A BANANA.

THAT DOES SOUND A-PEELING.

BUT THE JOB ITSELF WAS NOT APPEALING. BECAUSE THE TOWN OF TRUBBLE WAS HEADED DOWNHILL FAST.

TRUBBLE'S FUTURE PROSPECTS

MOSTLY BECAUSE OF THE FLAMING DOLPHIN.

FLAMING DOLPHIN

WHICH SCRIBBY FIRST LEARNED ABOUT WHEN HE GOT A CALL ON HIS BANANAPHONE.

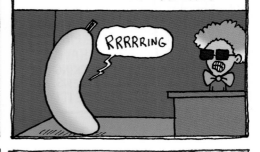

RRRRRING

GREETINGS, SCRIBBY. IT'S MAYOR WILLAMINA, QUEEN ON HIGH.

TITLE SHE SOMETIMES USED

"BANANA BANANA," ANSWERED SCRIBBY, USING HIS STANDARD GREETING.

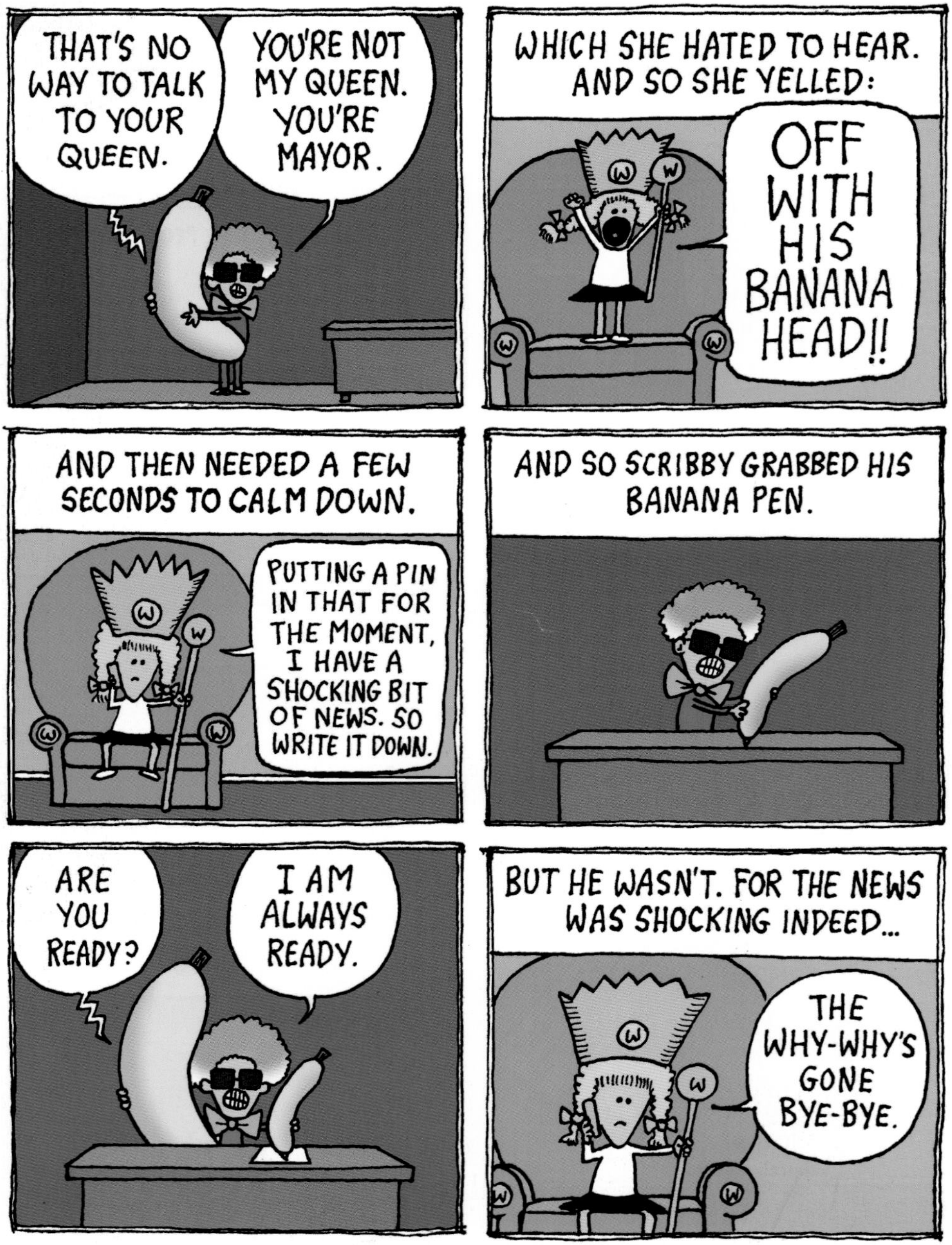
THAT'S NO WAY TO TALK TO YOUR QUEEN.
YOU'RE NOT MY QUEEN. YOU'RE MAYOR.
WHICH SHE HATED TO HEAR. AND SO SHE YELLED:
OFF WITH HIS BANANA HEAD!!
AND THEN NEEDED A FEW SECONDS TO CALM DOWN.
PUTTING A PIN IN THAT FOR THE MOMENT, I HAVE A SHOCKING BIT OF NEWS. SO WRITE IT DOWN.
AND SO SCRIBBY GRABBED HIS BANANA PEN.
ARE YOU READY?
I AM ALWAYS READY.
BUT HE WASN'T. FOR THE NEWS WAS SHOCKING INDEED...
THE WHY-WHY'S GONE BYE-BYE.

CHAPTER TOO

AS IN...

TOO SHOCKING TO BE BELIEVED

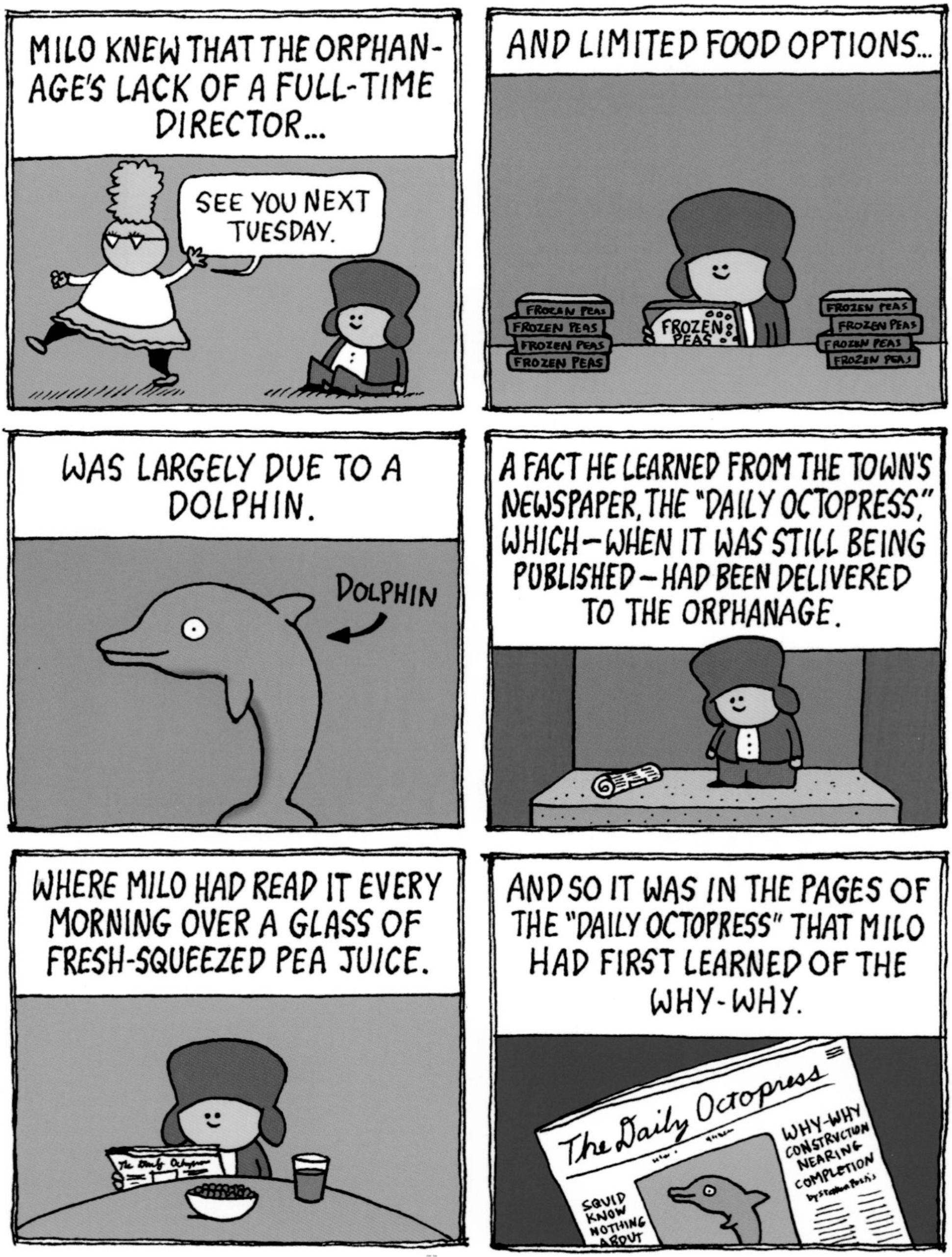
MILO KNEW THAT THE ORPHANAGE'S LACK OF A FULL-TIME DIRECTOR...
SEE YOU NEXT TUESDAY.
AND LIMITED FOOD OPTIONS...
FROZEN PEAS
FROZEN PEAS
FROZEN PEAS
FROZEN PEAS
FROZEN PEAS
FROZEN PEAS
FROZEN PEAS
FROZEN PEAS
FROZEN PEAS
WAS LARGELY DUE TO A DOLPHIN.
DOLPHIN
A FACT HE LEARNED FROM THE TOWN'S NEWSPAPER, THE "DAILY OCTOPRESS," WHICH—WHEN IT WAS STILL BEING PUBLISHED—HAD BEEN DELIVERED TO THE ORPHANAGE.
WHERE MILO HAD READ IT EVERY MORNING OVER A GLASS OF FRESH-SQUEEZED PEA JUICE.
AND SO IT WAS IN THE PAGES OF THE "DAILY OCTOPRESS" THAT MILO HAD FIRST LEARNED OF THE WHY-WHY.
The Daily Octopress
WHY-WHY CONSTRUCTION NEARING COMPLETION
SQUID KNOW NOTHING ABOUT

THE WHY-WHY WAS A THOUSAND-FOOT-TALL FLAMING-DOLPHIN SCULPTURE THAT HAD STOOD ATOP CITY HALL.

IT WAS CALLED THE WHY-WHY BECAUSE WHEN THE IDEA HAD FIRST BEEN PROPOSED, PEOPLE HAD ASKED:

WHY SHOULD WE BUILD IT?

WHY ARE WE SO INCOMPETENT?

AND WHILE THE FLAMING DOLPHIN HAD NOT BEEN AN ACTUAL DOLPHIN, THE FLAMES *HAD BEEN* ACTUAL FLAMES.

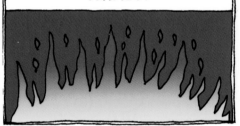

AND SO THE TOWN HAD CAUGHT ACTUAL FIRE.

AND THOUGH THERE HAD BEEN TALK OF EXTINGUISHING THE FLAMES, THE TOWN HAD NOT.

BECAUSE IT'S EXCITING!

AND COULD NOT.

BECAUSE WE HAVE NO FIREMEN!

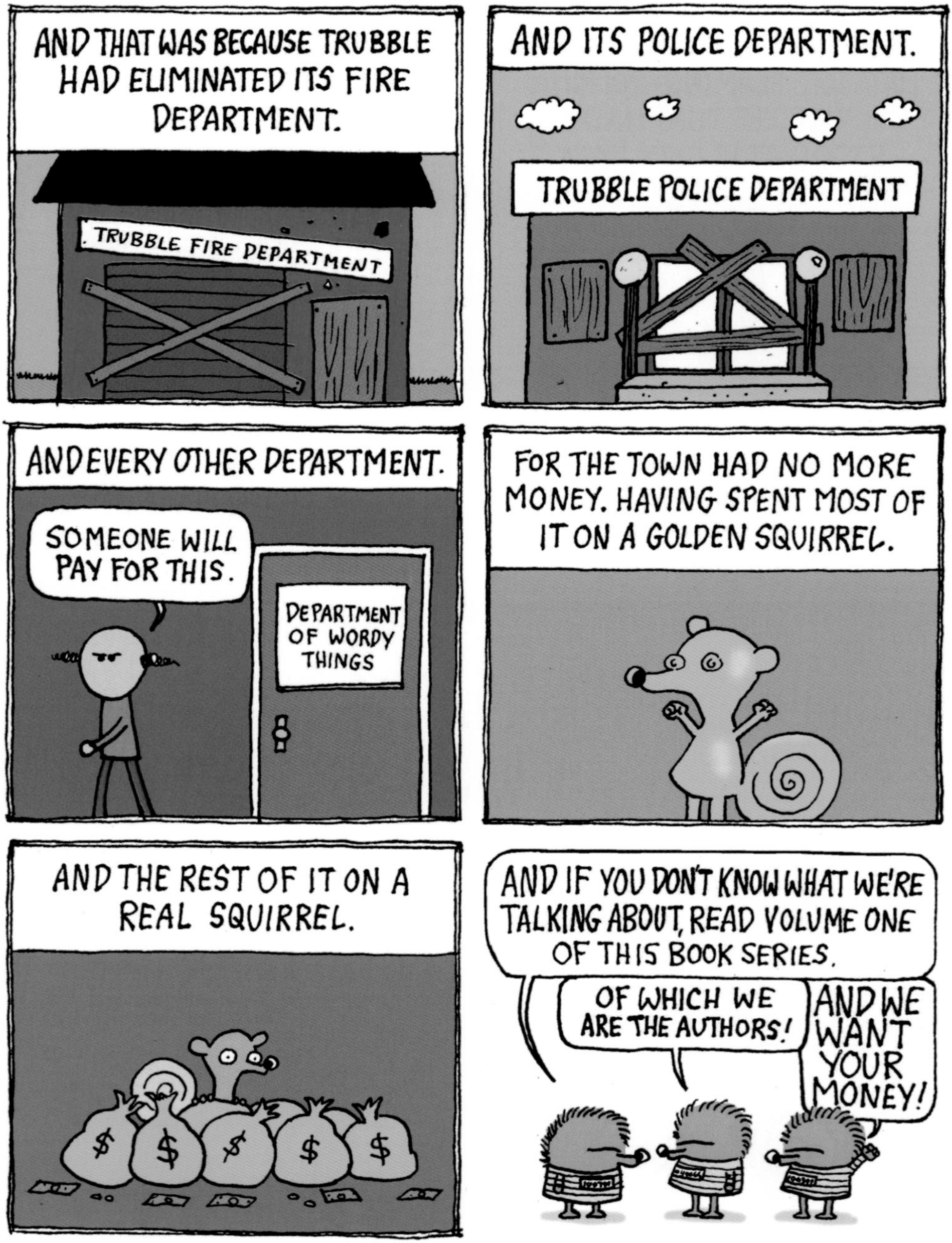
AND THAT WAS BECAUSE TRUBBLE HAD ELIMINATED ITS FIRE DEPARTMENT.
TRUBBLE FIRE DEPARTMENT
AND ITS POLICE DEPARTMENT.
TRUBBLE POLICE DEPARTMENT
AND EVERY OTHER DEPARTMENT.
SOMEONE WILL PAY FOR THIS.
DEPARTMENT OF WORDY THINGS
FOR THE TOWN HAD NO MORE MONEY. HAVING SPENT MOST OF IT ON A GOLDEN SQUIRREL.
AND THE REST OF IT ON A REAL SQUIRREL.
AND IF YOU DON'T KNOW WHAT WE'RE TALKING ABOUT, READ VOLUME ONE OF THIS BOOK SERIES.
OF WHICH WE ARE THE AUTHORS!
AND WE WANT YOUR MONEY!

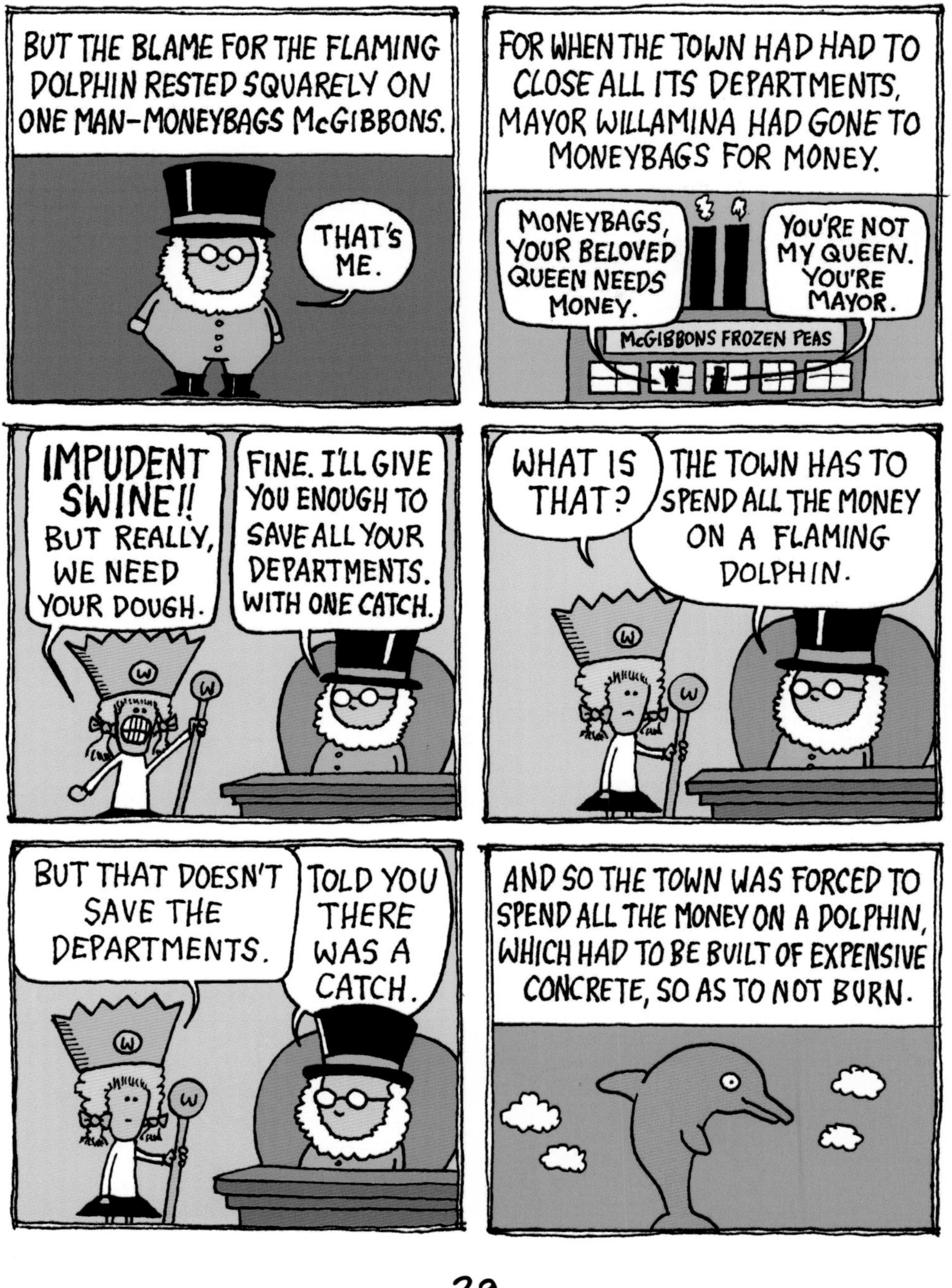
BUT THE BLAME FOR THE FLAMING DOLPHIN RESTED SQUARELY ON ONE MAN—MONEYBAGS McGIBBONS.
THAT'S ME.
FOR WHEN THE TOWN HAD HAD TO CLOSE ALL ITS DEPARTMENTS, MAYOR WILLAMINA HAD GONE TO MONEYBAGS FOR MONEY.
MONEYBAGS, YOUR BELOVED QUEEN NEEDS MONEY.
YOU'RE NOT MY QUEEN. YOU'RE MAYOR.
McGIBBONS FROZEN PEAS
IMPUDENT SWINE!! BUT REALLY, WE NEED YOUR DOUGH.
FINE. I'LL GIVE YOU ENOUGH TO SAVE ALL YOUR DEPARTMENTS. WITH ONE CATCH.
WHAT IS THAT?
THE TOWN HAS TO SPEND ALL THE MONEY ON A FLAMING DOLPHIN.
BUT THAT DOESN'T SAVE THE DEPARTMENTS.
TOLD YOU THERE WAS A CATCH.
AND SO THE TOWN WAS FORCED TO SPEND ALL THE MONEY ON A DOLPHIN, WHICH HAD TO BE BUILT OF EXPENSIVE CONCRETE, SO AS TO NOT BURN.

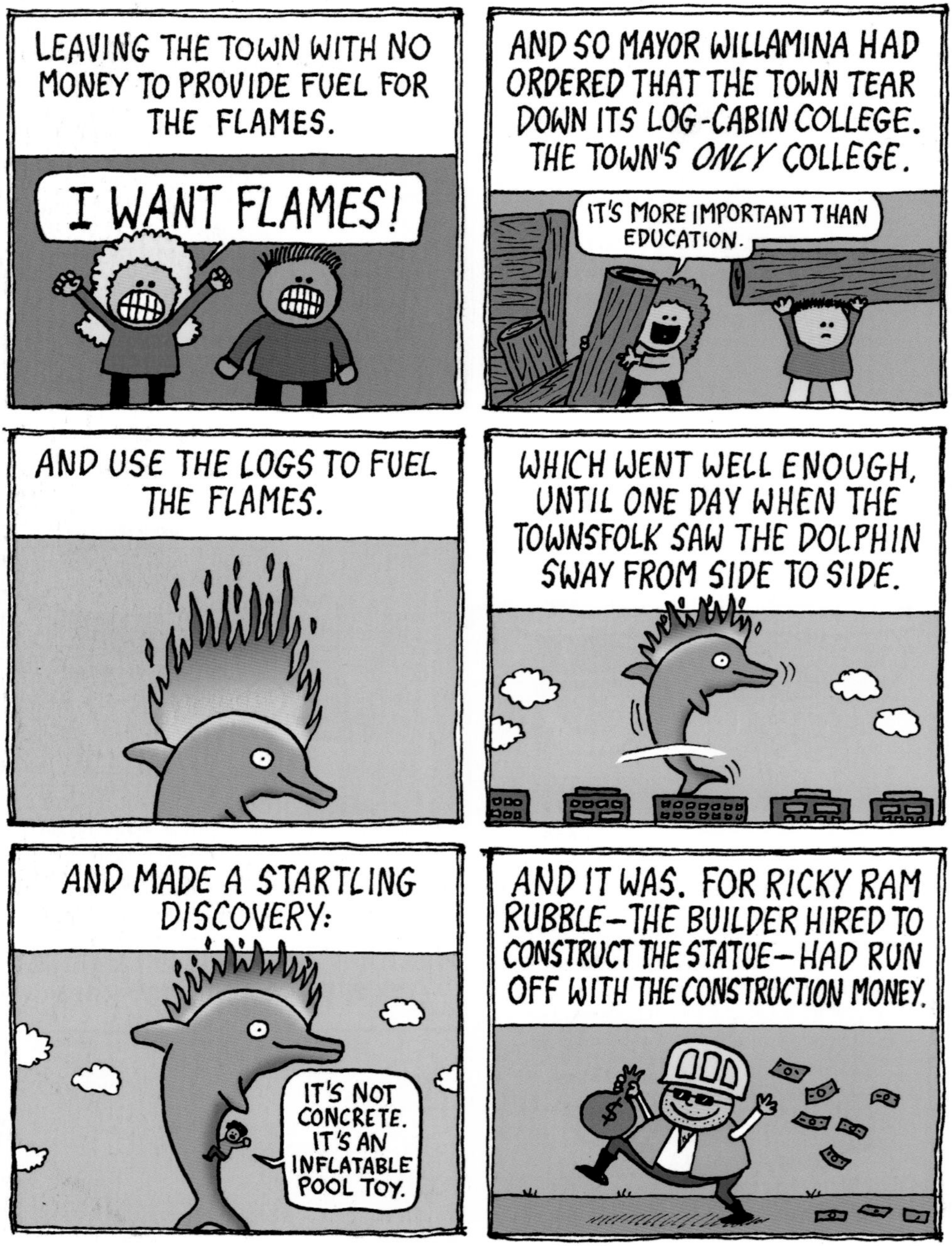
LEAVING THE TOWN WITH NO MONEY TO PROVIDE FUEL FOR THE FLAMES.
I WANT FLAMES!
AND SO MAYOR WILLAMINA HAD ORDERED THAT THE TOWN TEAR DOWN ITS LOG-CABIN COLLEGE. THE TOWN'S *ONLY* COLLEGE.
IT'S MORE IMPORTANT THAN EDUCATION.
AND USE THE LOGS TO FUEL THE FLAMES.
WHICH WENT WELL ENOUGH, UNTIL ONE DAY WHEN THE TOWNSFOLK SAW THE DOLPHIN SWAY FROM SIDE TO SIDE.
AND MADE A STARTLING DISCOVERY:
IT'S NOT CONCRETE. IT'S AN INFLATABLE POOL TOY.
AND IT WAS. FOR RICKY RAM RUBBLE—THE BUILDER HIRED TO CONSTRUCT THE STATUE—HAD RUN OFF WITH THE CONSTRUCTION MONEY.
$

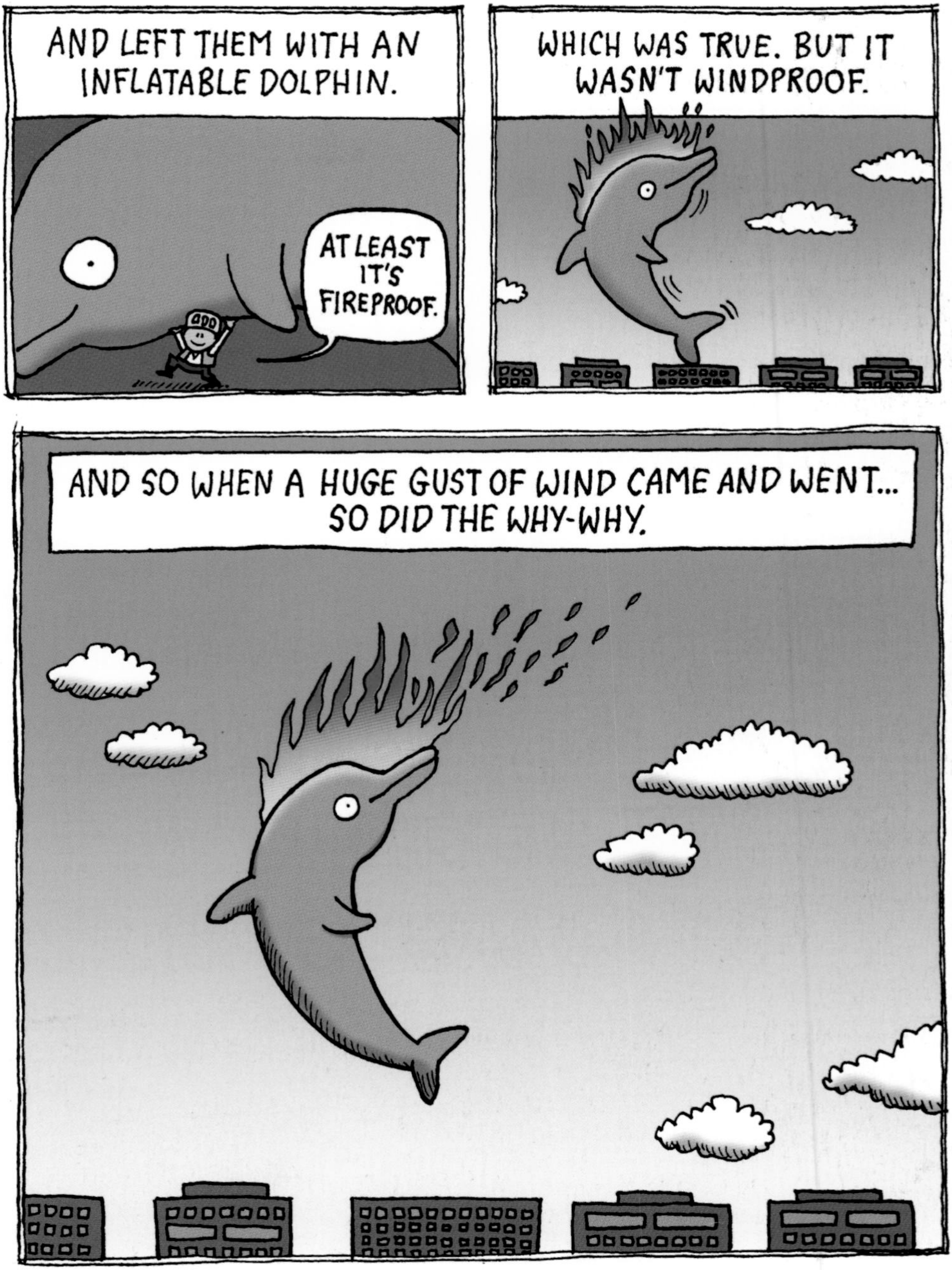
AND LEFT THEM WITH AN INFLATABLE DOLPHIN.
AT LEAST IT'S FIREPROOF.
WHICH WAS TRUE. BUT IT WASN'T WINDPROOF.
AND SO WHEN A HUGE GUST OF WIND CAME AND WENT... SO DID THE WHY-WHY.

CHAPTER THREE

WHICH IS...

THREE TIMES BETTER THAN ALL THE PREVIOUS CHAPTERS COMBINED, WHICH MAY NOT BE SAYING MUCH

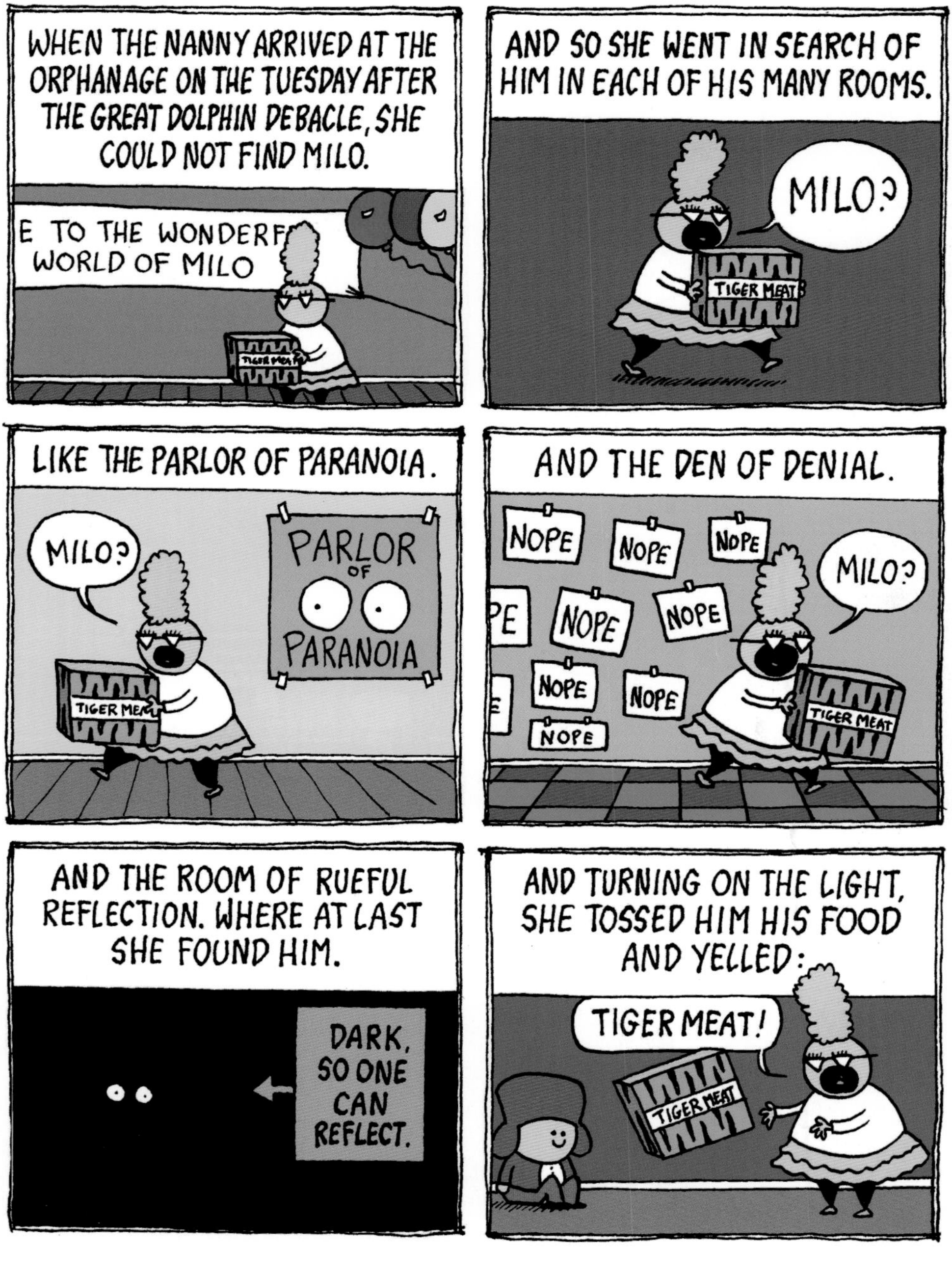

WHEN THE NANNY ARRIVED AT THE ORPHANAGE ON THE TUESDAY AFTER THE GREAT DOLPHIN DEBACLE, SHE COULD NOT FIND MILO.
E TO THE WONDERF
WORLD OF MILO
AND SO SHE WENT IN SEARCH OF HIM IN EACH OF HIS MANY ROOMS.
MILO?
TIGER MEAT
LIKE THE PARLOR OF PARANOIA.
MILO?
PARLOR OF PARANOIA
TIGER MEAT
AND THE DEN OF DENIAL.
NOPE
NOPE
NOPE
NOPE
NOPE
NOPE
NOPE
NOPE
MILO?
TIGER MEAT
AND THE ROOM OF RUEFUL REFLECTION. WHERE AT LAST SHE FOUND HIM.
DARK, SO ONE CAN REFLECT.
AND TURNING ON THE LIGHT, SHE TOSSED HIM HIS FOOD AND YELLED:
TIGER MEAT!
TIGER MEAT

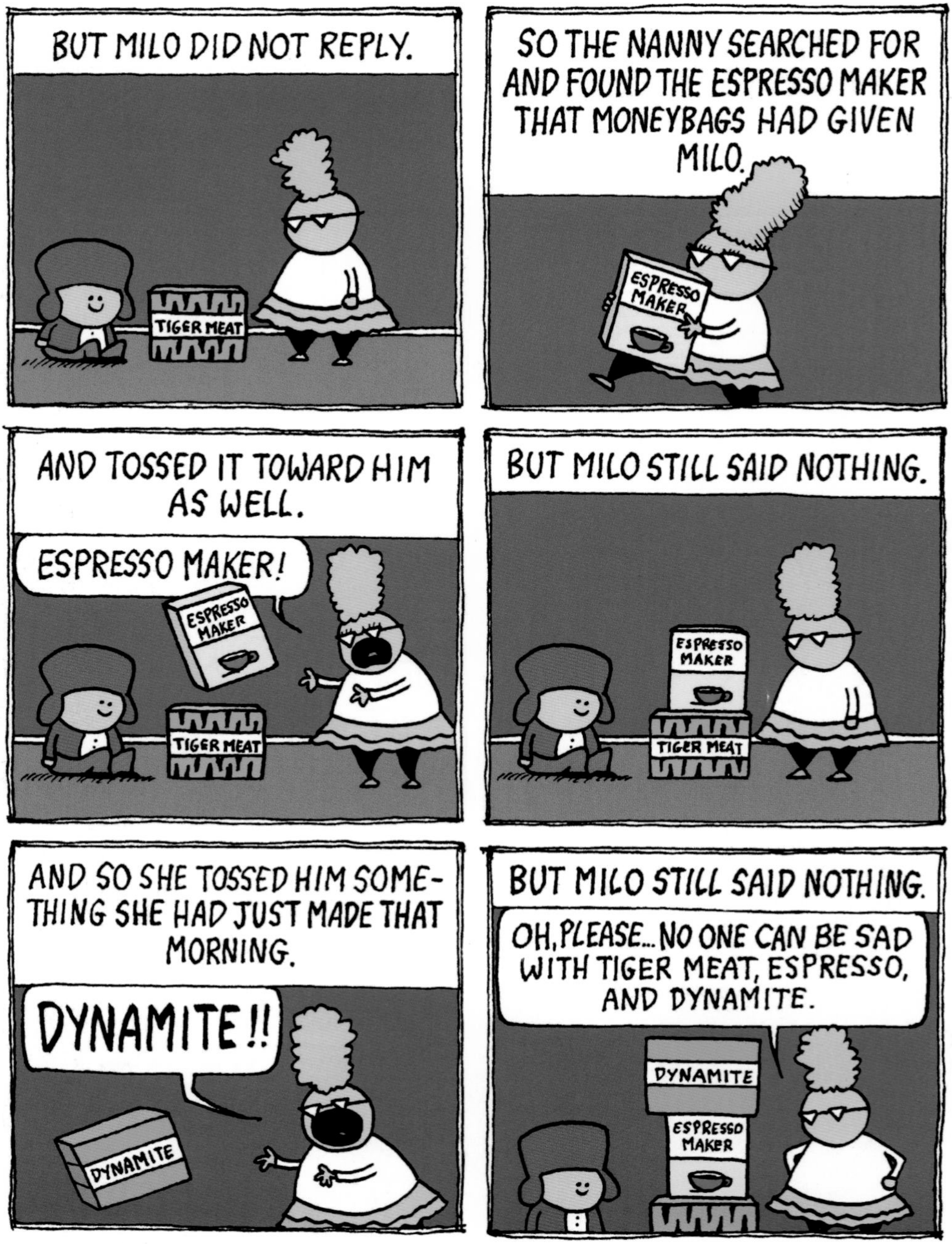
BUT MILO DID NOT REPLY.
TIGER MEAT
SO THE NANNY SEARCHED FOR AND FOUND THE ESPRESSO MAKER THAT MONEYBAGS HAD GIVEN MILO.
ESPRESSO MAKER
AND TOSSED IT TOWARD HIM AS WELL.
ESPRESSO MAKER!
ESPRESSO MAKER
TIGER MEAT
BUT MILO STILL SAID NOTHING.
ESPRESSO MAKER
TIGER MEAT
AND SO SHE TOSSED HIM SOMETHING SHE HAD JUST MADE THAT MORNING.
DYNAMITE!!
DYNAMITE
BUT MILO STILL SAID NOTHING.
OH, PLEASE... NO ONE CAN BE SAD WITH TIGER MEAT, ESPRESSO, AND DYNAMITE.
DYNAMITE
ESPRESSO MAKER

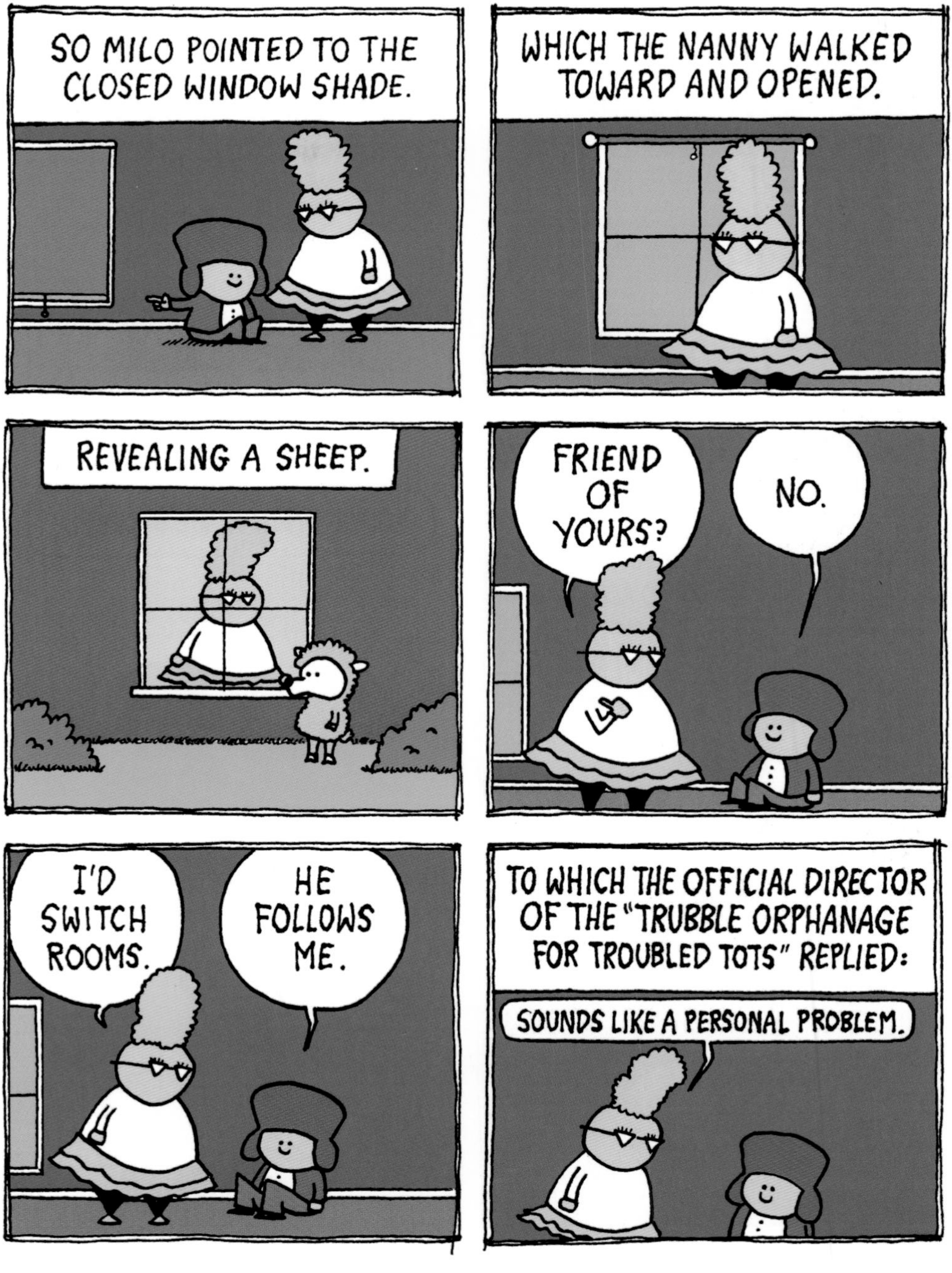
SO MILO POINTED TO THE CLOSED WINDOW SHADE.
WHICH THE NANNY WALKED TOWARD AND OPENED.
REVEALING A SHEEP.
FRIEND OF YOURS?
NO.
I'D SWITCH ROOMS.
HE FOLLOWS ME.
TO WHICH THE OFFICIAL DIRECTOR OF THE "TRUBBLE ORPHANAGE FOR TROUBLED TOTS" REPLIED:
SOUNDS LIKE A PERSONAL PROBLEM.

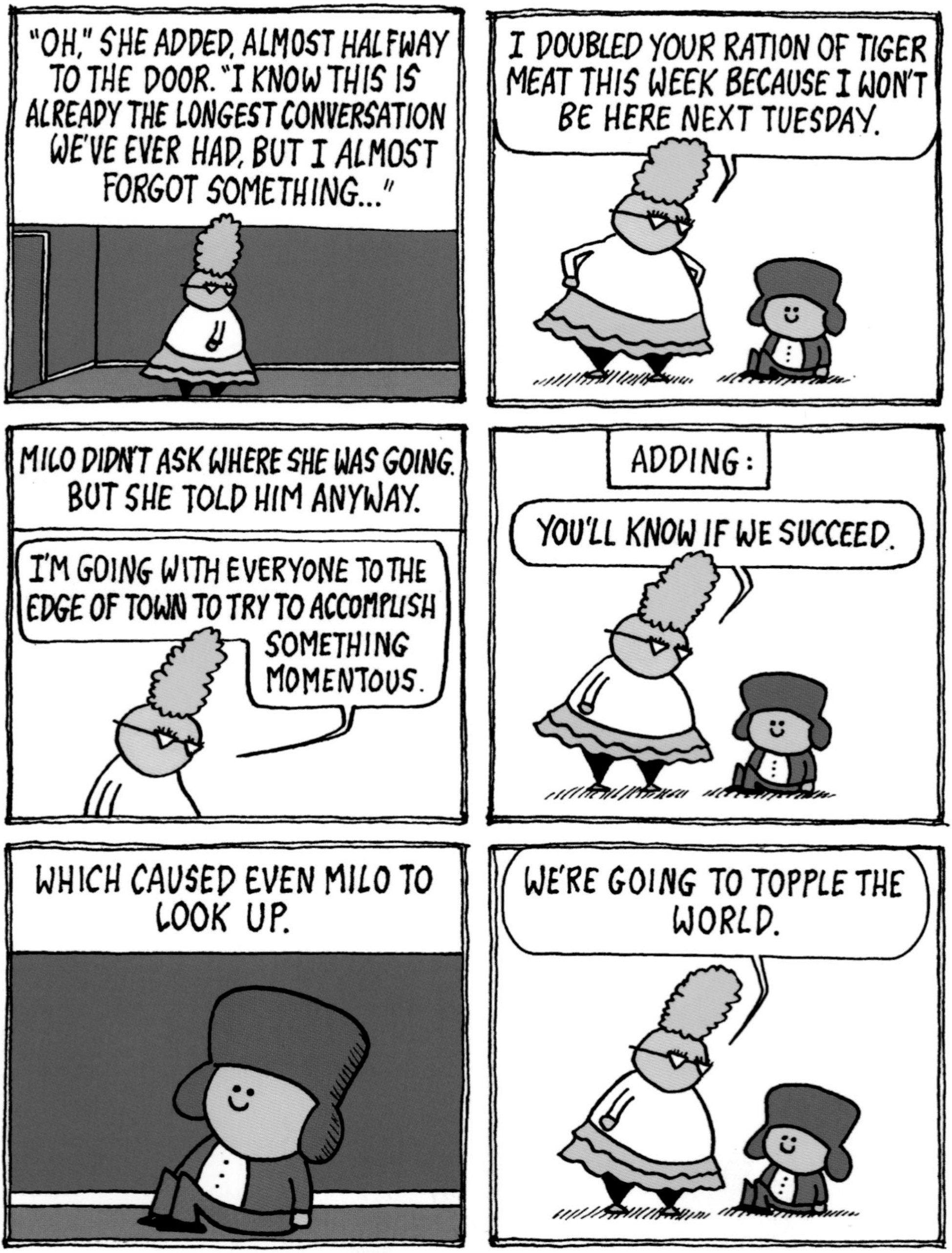

"OH," SHE ADDED, ALMOST HALFWAY TO THE DOOR. "I KNOW THIS IS ALREADY THE LONGEST CONVERSATION WE'VE EVER HAD, BUT I ALMOST FORGOT SOMETHING..."
I DOUBLED YOUR RATION OF TIGER MEAT THIS WEEK BECAUSE I WON'T BE HERE NEXT TUESDAY.
MILO DIDN'T ASK WHERE SHE WAS GOING. BUT SHE TOLD HIM ANYWAY.
I'M GOING WITH EVERYONE TO THE EDGE OF TOWN TO TRY TO ACCOMPLISH SOMETHING MOMENTOUS.
ADDING:
YOU'LL KNOW IF WE SUCCEED.
WHICH CAUSED EVEN MILO TO LOOK UP.
WE'RE GOING TO TOPPLE THE WORLD.

CHAPTER
NOT AS GOOD AS THE LAST ONE, BUT STILL QUITE GOOD

IN WHICH...

WE GET POINTS FOR HONESTY

AFTER THE GREAT DOLPHIN DEBACLE, THE TOWNSFOLK OF TRUBBLE HAD NO MONEY, NO DOLPHIN, AND NO HOPE.

AND SO, DESPERATE FOR A DISTRACTION, THEY TURNED TO "23 SQUIDOO."

"23 SQUIDOO" WAS A NEWS NETWORK NAMED FOR THE CHANNEL IT WAS ON AND ITS HANDSOME ANCHOR, SQUIDDY McSQUIDLOW.

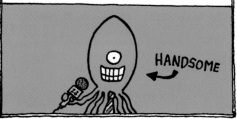

HANDSOME

WHO BECAME TRUBBLE'S ONLY SOURCE OF NEWS WHEN THE TOWN'S NEWSPAPER—THE "DAILY OCTOPRESS"—FAILED.

OUT OF BUSINESS

THE CAUSE OF WHICH WAS THE PAPER'S UNFORTUNATE DECISION TO BEGIN PRINTING ONLY THE TRUTH.

BOOOOOO, TRUTH.

AT A TIME WHEN TOWNSFOLK WANTED ONLY THE LIES.

YAAAAAAY, LIES.

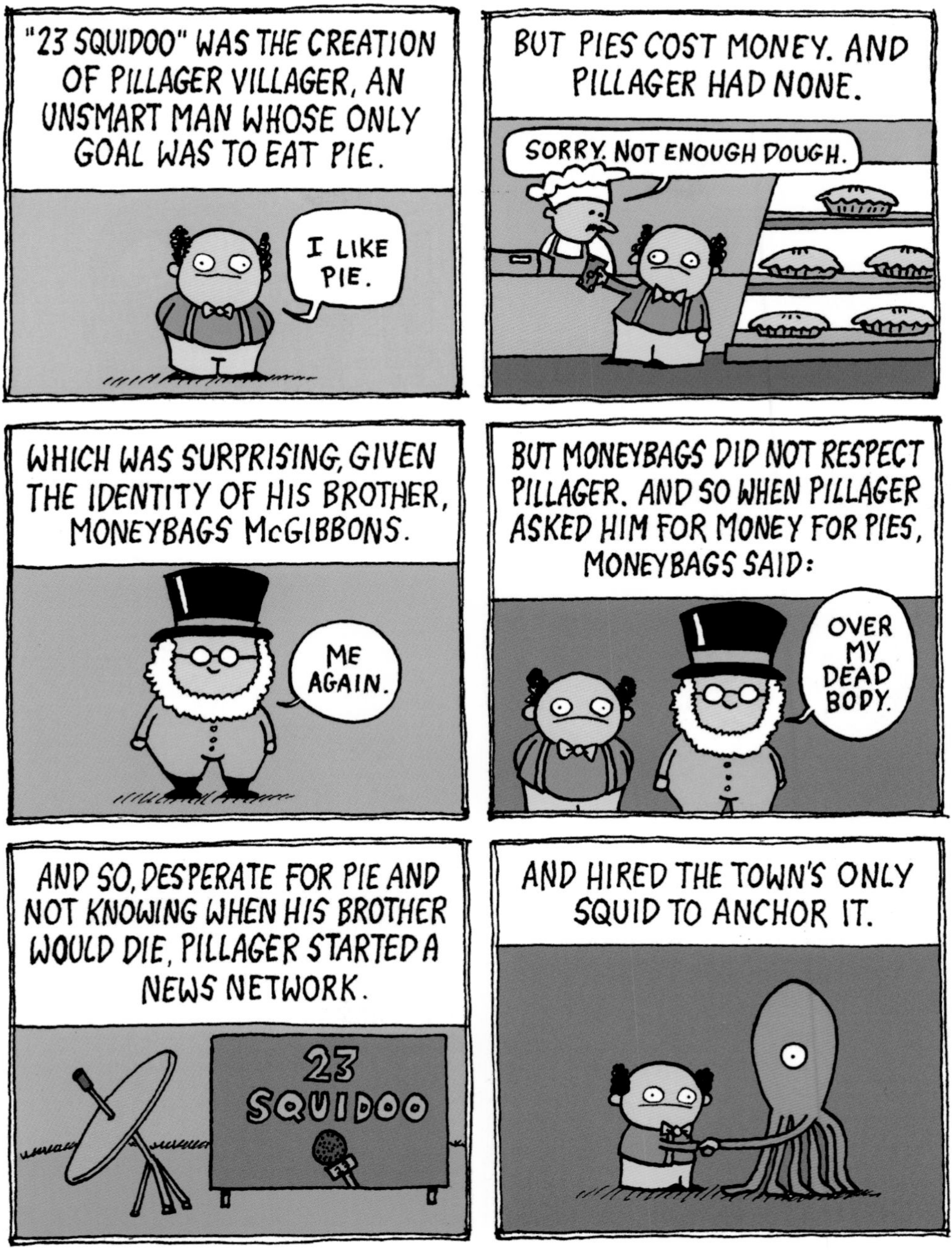
"23 SQUIDOO" WAS THE CREATION OF PILLAGER VILLAGER, AN UNSMART MAN WHOSE ONLY GOAL WAS TO EAT PIE.
I LIKE PIE.
BUT PIES COST MONEY. AND PILLAGER HAD NONE.
SORRY. NOT ENOUGH DOUGH.
WHICH WAS SURPRISING, GIVEN THE IDENTITY OF HIS BROTHER, MONEYBAGS McGIBBONS.
ME AGAIN.
BUT MONEYBAGS DID NOT RESPECT PILLAGER. AND SO WHEN PILLAGER ASKED HIM FOR MONEY FOR PIES, MONEYBAGS SAID:
OVER MY DEAD BODY.
AND SO, DESPERATE FOR PIE AND NOT KNOWING WHEN HIS BROTHER WOULD DIE, PILLAGER STARTED A NEWS NETWORK.
23 SQUIDOO
AND HIRED THE TOWN'S ONLY SQUID TO ANCHOR IT.

PROVIDING THE SQUID WITH JUST ONE JOURNALISTIC PRINCIPLE:

LIES BRING PIES!

FOR PILLAGER HAD REALIZED THAT LIES MEANT MORE VIEWERS.

WHICH MEANT MORE MONEY.

MONEY RECEIVED LOTS

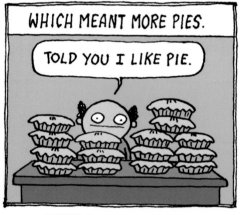

WHICH MEANT MORE PIES.

TOLD YOU I LIKE PIE.

AND SO THE TOWNSFOLK OF TRUBBLE WATCHED MORE NEWS THAN EVER BEFORE.

IF ONE COULD CALL IT NEWS.

ALIENS ARE COMING FOR YOUR CHIHUAHUA!

BAD NEWS FOR YOU.

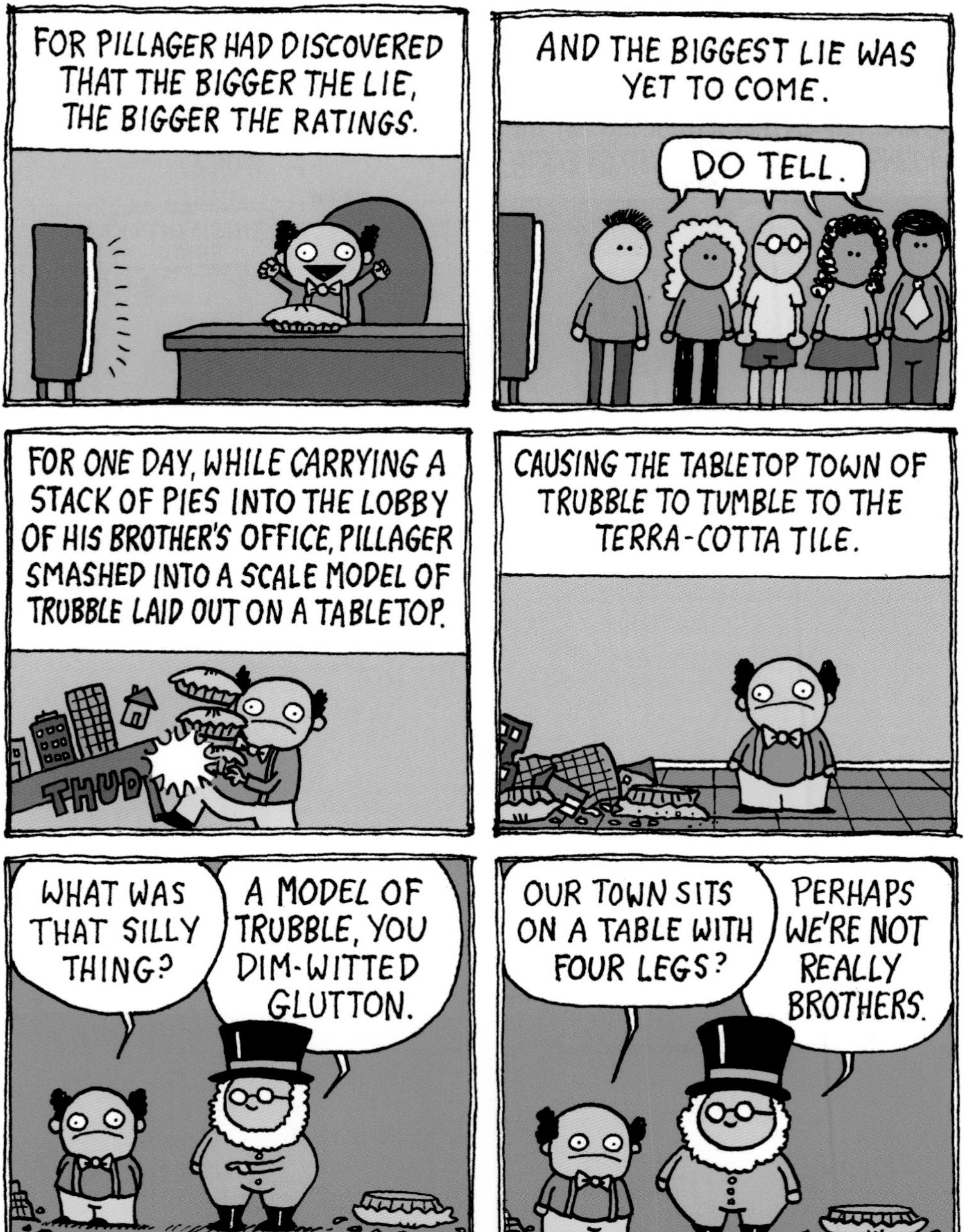

FOR PILLAGER HAD DISCOVERED THAT THE BIGGER THE LIE, THE BIGGER THE RATINGS.
AND THE BIGGEST LIE WAS YET TO COME.
DO TELL.
FOR ONE DAY, WHILE CARRYING A STACK OF PIES INTO THE LOBBY OF HIS BROTHER'S OFFICE, PILLAGER SMASHED INTO A SCALE MODEL OF TRUBBLE LAID OUT ON A TABLETOP.
THUD
CAUSING THE TABLETOP TOWN OF TRUBBLE TO TUMBLE TO THE TERRA-COTTA TILE.
WHAT WAS THAT SILLY THING?
A MODEL OF TRUBBLE, YOU DIM-WITTED GLUTTON.
OUR TOWN SITS ON A TABLE WITH FOUR LEGS?
PERHAPS WE'RE NOT REALLY BROTHERS.

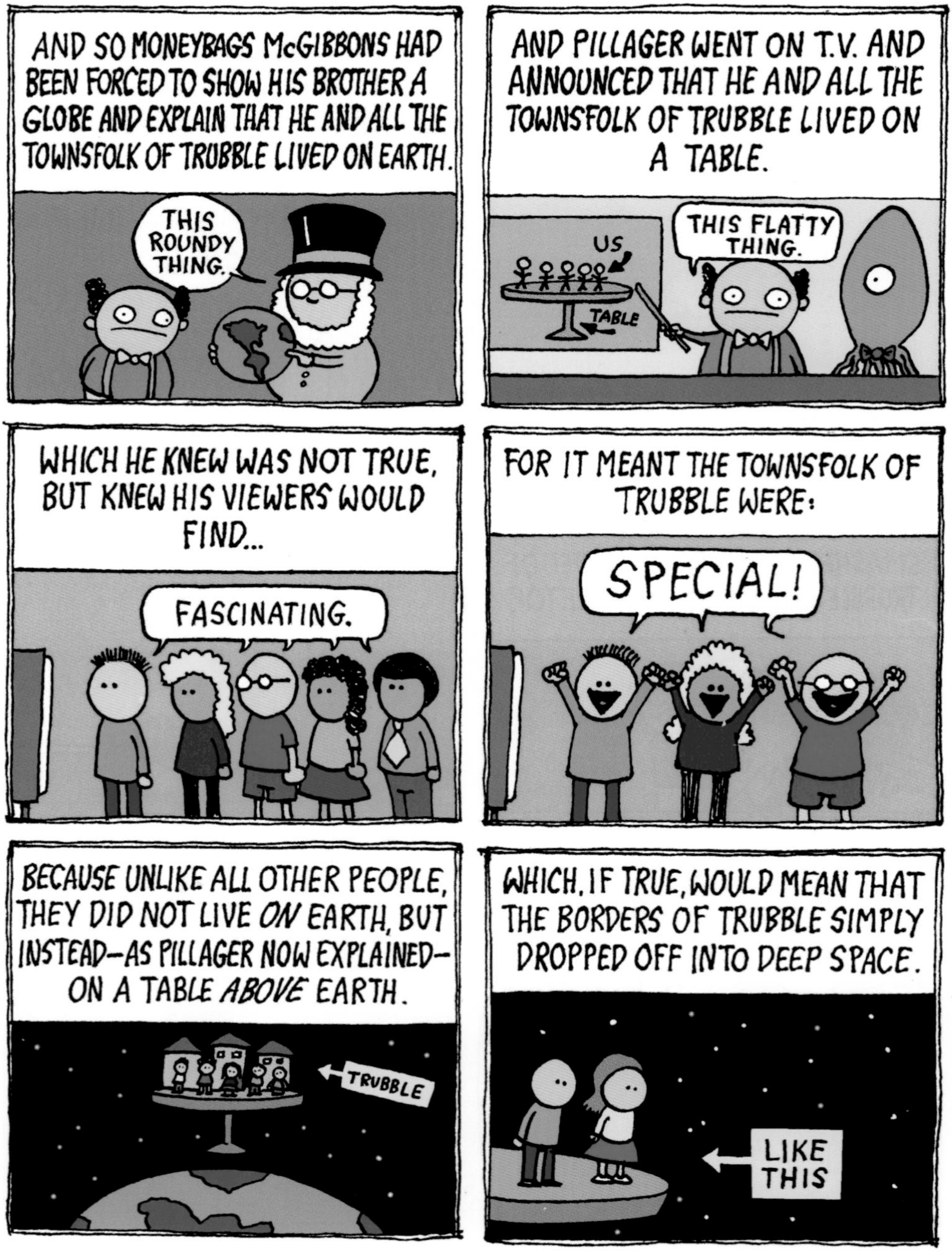
AND SO MONEYBAGS McGIBBONS HAD BEEN FORCED TO SHOW HIS BROTHER A GLOBE AND EXPLAIN THAT HE AND ALL THE TOWNSFOLK OF TRUBBLE LIVED ON EARTH.
THIS ROUNDY THING.
AND PILLAGER WENT ON T.V. AND ANNOUNCED THAT HE AND ALL THE TOWNSFOLK OF TRUBBLE LIVED ON A TABLE.
US
TABLE
THIS FLATTY THING.
WHICH HE KNEW WAS NOT TRUE, BUT KNEW HIS VIEWERS WOULD FIND...
FASCINATING.
FOR IT MEANT THE TOWNSFOLK OF TRUBBLE WERE:
SPECIAL!
BECAUSE UNLIKE ALL OTHER PEOPLE, THEY DID NOT LIVE ON EARTH, BUT INSTEAD—AS PILLAGER NOW EXPLAINED—ON A TABLE ABOVE EARTH.
TRUBBLE
WHICH, IF TRUE, WOULD MEAN THAT THE BORDERS OF TRUBBLE SIMPLY DROPPED OFF INTO DEEP SPACE.
LIKE THIS

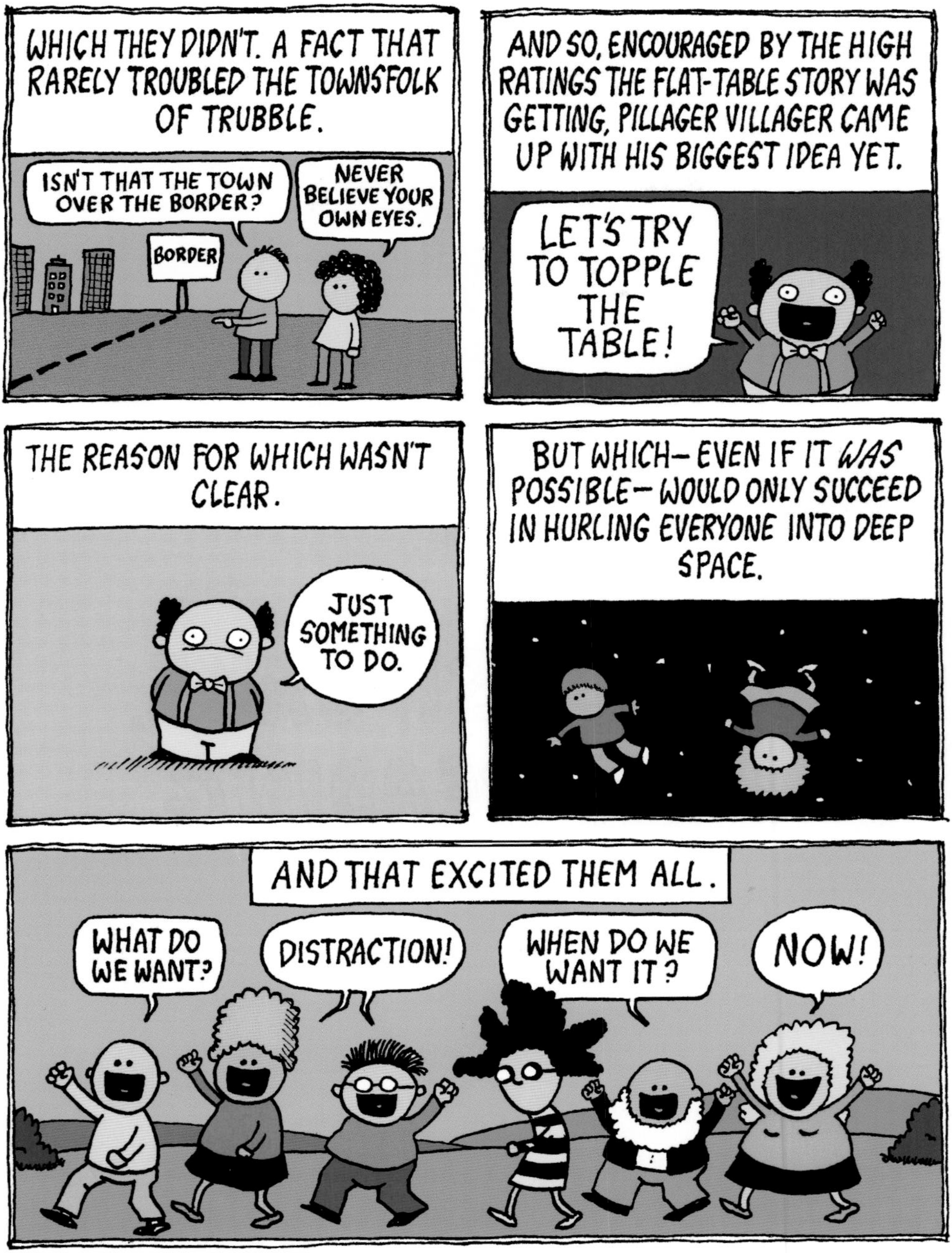
WHICH THEY DIDN'T. A FACT THAT RARELY TROUBLED THE TOWNSFOLK OF TRUBBLE.
ISN'T THAT THE TOWN OVER THE BORDER?
NEVER BELIEVE YOUR OWN EYES.
BORDER
AND SO, ENCOURAGED BY THE HIGH RATINGS THE FLAT-TABLE STORY WAS GETTING, PILLAGER VILLAGER CAME UP WITH HIS BIGGEST IDEA YET.
LET'S TRY TO TOPPLE THE TABLE!
THE REASON FOR WHICH WASN'T CLEAR.
JUST SOMETHING TO DO.
BUT WHICH—EVEN IF IT *WAS* POSSIBLE—WOULD ONLY SUCCEED IN HURLING EVERYONE INTO DEEP SPACE.
AND THAT EXCITED THEM ALL.
WHAT DO WE WANT?
DISTRACTION!
WHEN DO WE WANT IT?
NOW!

CHAPTER FOR

AS IN...

FOR GOSH SAKE, KEEP READING

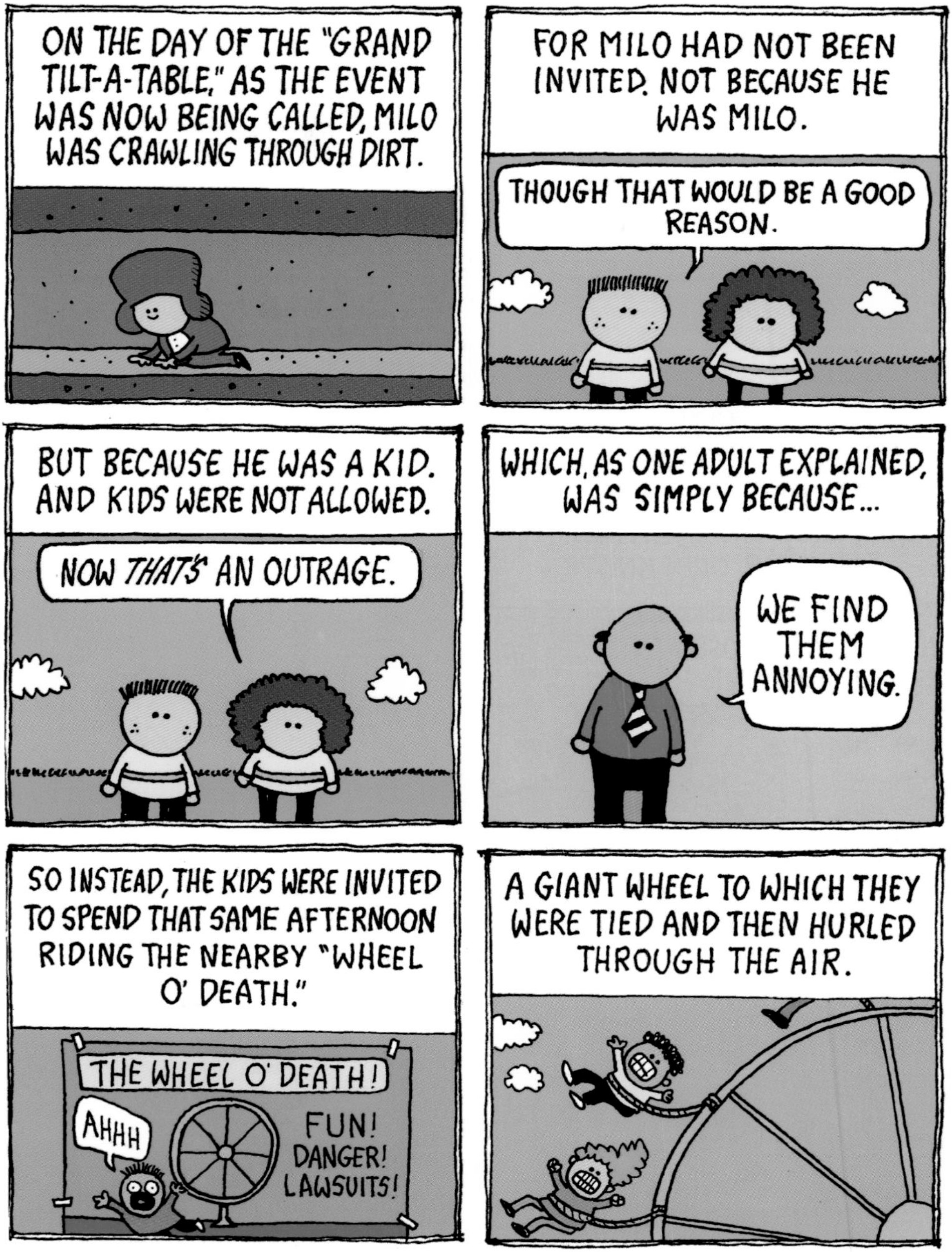
ON THE DAY OF THE "GRAND TILT-A-TABLE," AS THE EVENT WAS NOW BEING CALLED, MILO WAS CRAWLING THROUGH DIRT.
FOR MILO HAD NOT BEEN INVITED. NOT BECAUSE HE WAS MILO.
THOUGH THAT WOULD BE A GOOD REASON.
BUT BECAUSE HE WAS A KID. AND KIDS WERE NOT ALLOWED.
NOW *THAT'S* AN OUTRAGE.
WHICH, AS ONE ADULT EXPLAINED, WAS SIMPLY BECAUSE...
WE FIND THEM ANNOYING.
SO INSTEAD, THE KIDS WERE INVITED TO SPEND THAT SAME AFTERNOON RIDING THE NEARBY "WHEEL O' DEATH."
THE WHEEL O' DEATH!
AHHH
FUN!
DANGER!
LAWSUITS!
A GIANT WHEEL TO WHICH THEY WERE TIED AND THEN HURLED THROUGH THE AIR.

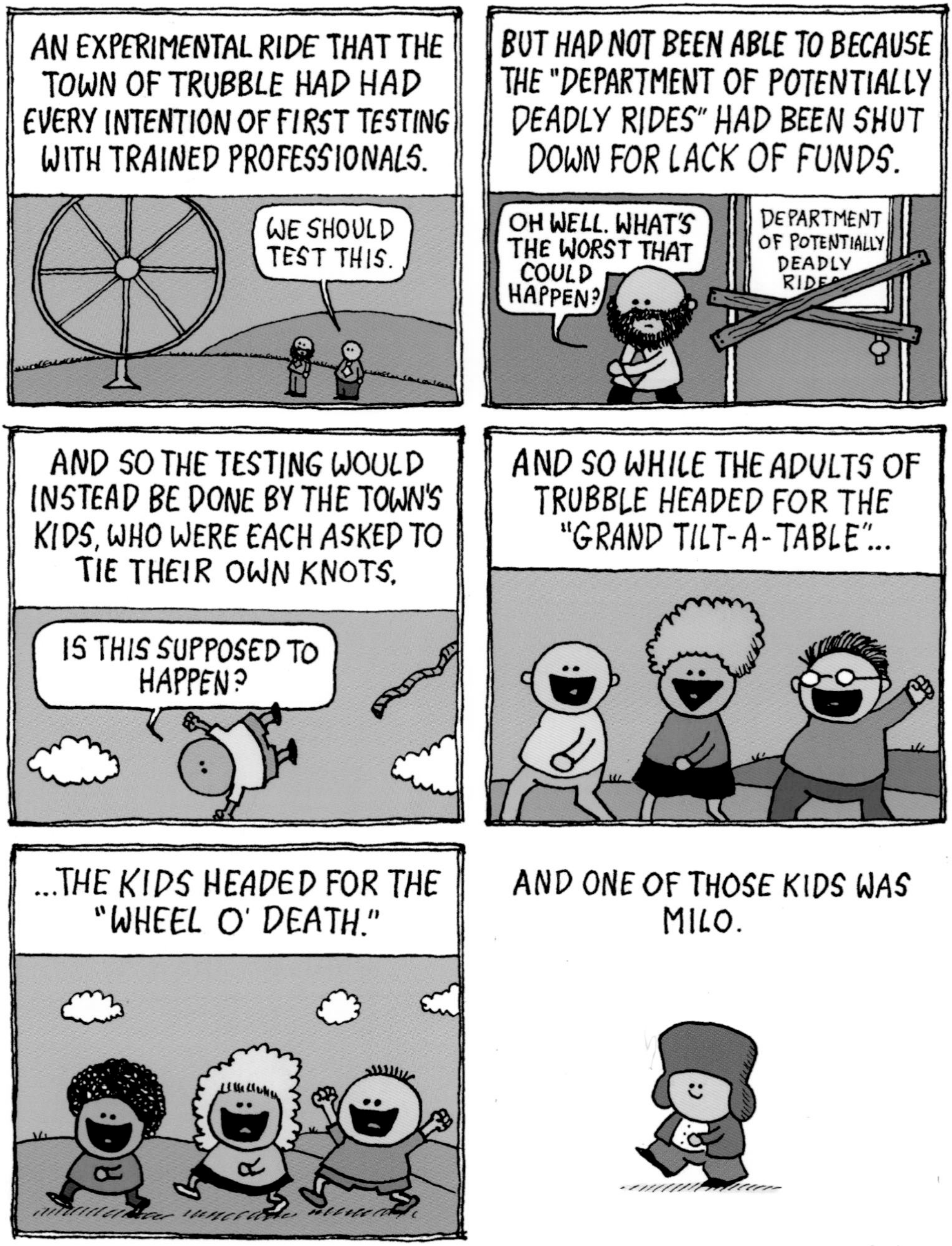
AN EXPERIMENTAL RIDE THAT THE TOWN OF TRUBBLE HAD HAD EVERY INTENTION OF FIRST TESTING WITH TRAINED PROFESSIONALS.
WE SHOULD TEST THIS.
BUT HAD NOT BEEN ABLE TO BECAUSE THE "DEPARTMENT OF POTENTIALLY DEADLY RIDES" HAD BEEN SHUT DOWN FOR LACK OF FUNDS.
OH WELL. WHAT'S THE WORST THAT COULD HAPPEN?
DEPARTMENT OF POTENTIALLY DEADLY
AND SO THE TESTING WOULD INSTEAD BE DONE BY THE TOWN'S KIDS, WHO WERE EACH ASKED TO TIE THEIR OWN KNOTS.
IS THIS SUPPOSED TO HAPPEN?
AND SO WHILE THE ADULTS OF TRUBBLE HEADED FOR THE "GRAND TILT-A-TABLE"...
...THE KIDS HEADED FOR THE "WHEEL O' DEATH."
AND ONE OF THOSE KIDS WAS MILO.

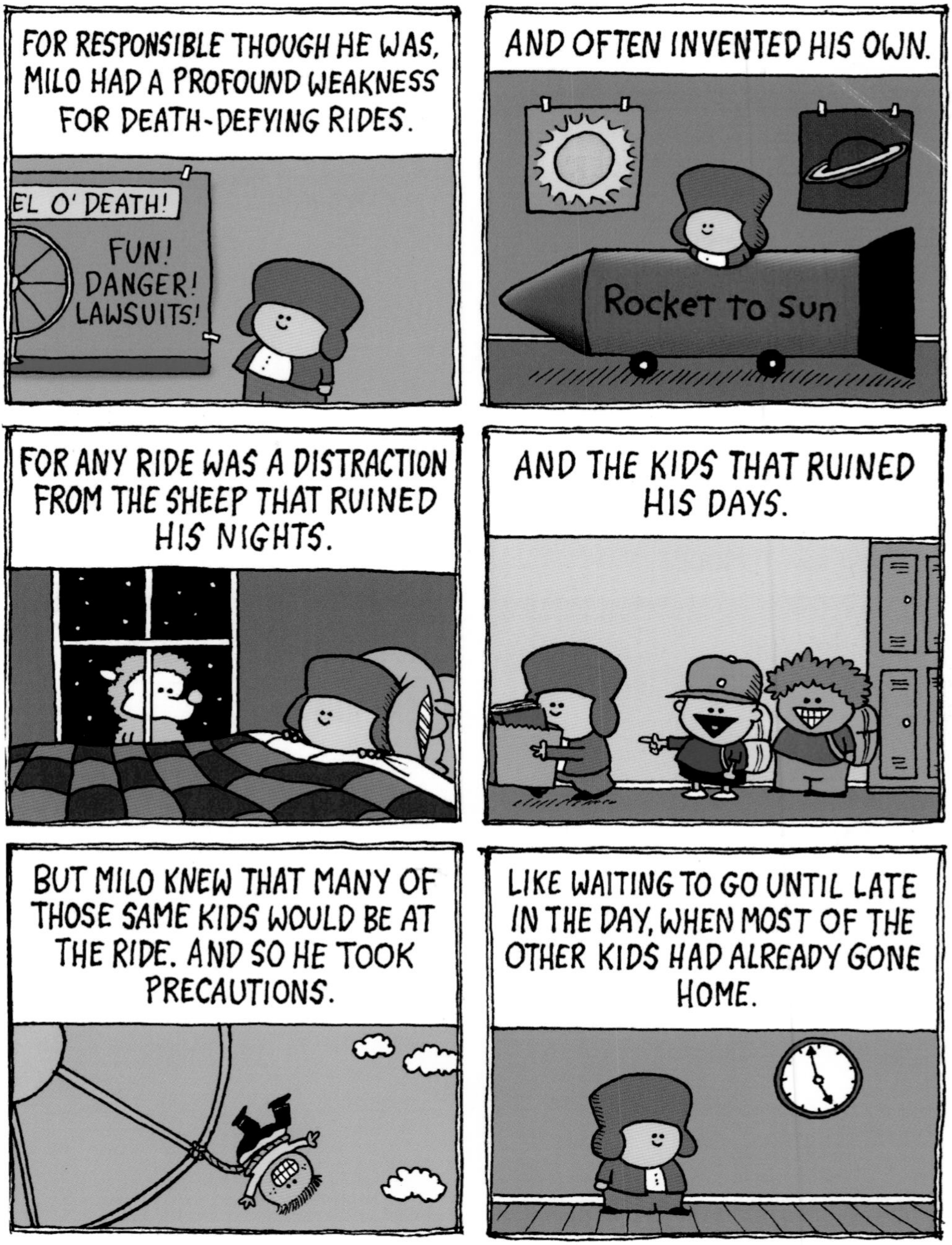
FOR RESPONSIBLE THOUGH HE WAS, MILO HAD A PROFOUND WEAKNESS FOR DEATH-DEFYING RIDES.
EL O' DEATH!
FUN! DANGER! LAWSUITS!
AND OFTEN INVENTED HIS OWN.
Rocket to Sun
FOR ANY RIDE WAS A DISTRACTION FROM THE SHEEP THAT RUINED HIS NIGHTS.
AND THE KIDS THAT RUINED HIS DAYS.
BUT MILO KNEW THAT MANY OF THOSE SAME KIDS WOULD BE AT THE RIDE. AND SO HE TOOK PRECAUTIONS.
LIKE WAITING TO GO UNTIL LATE IN THE DAY, WHEN MOST OF THE OTHER KIDS HAD ALREADY GONE HOME.

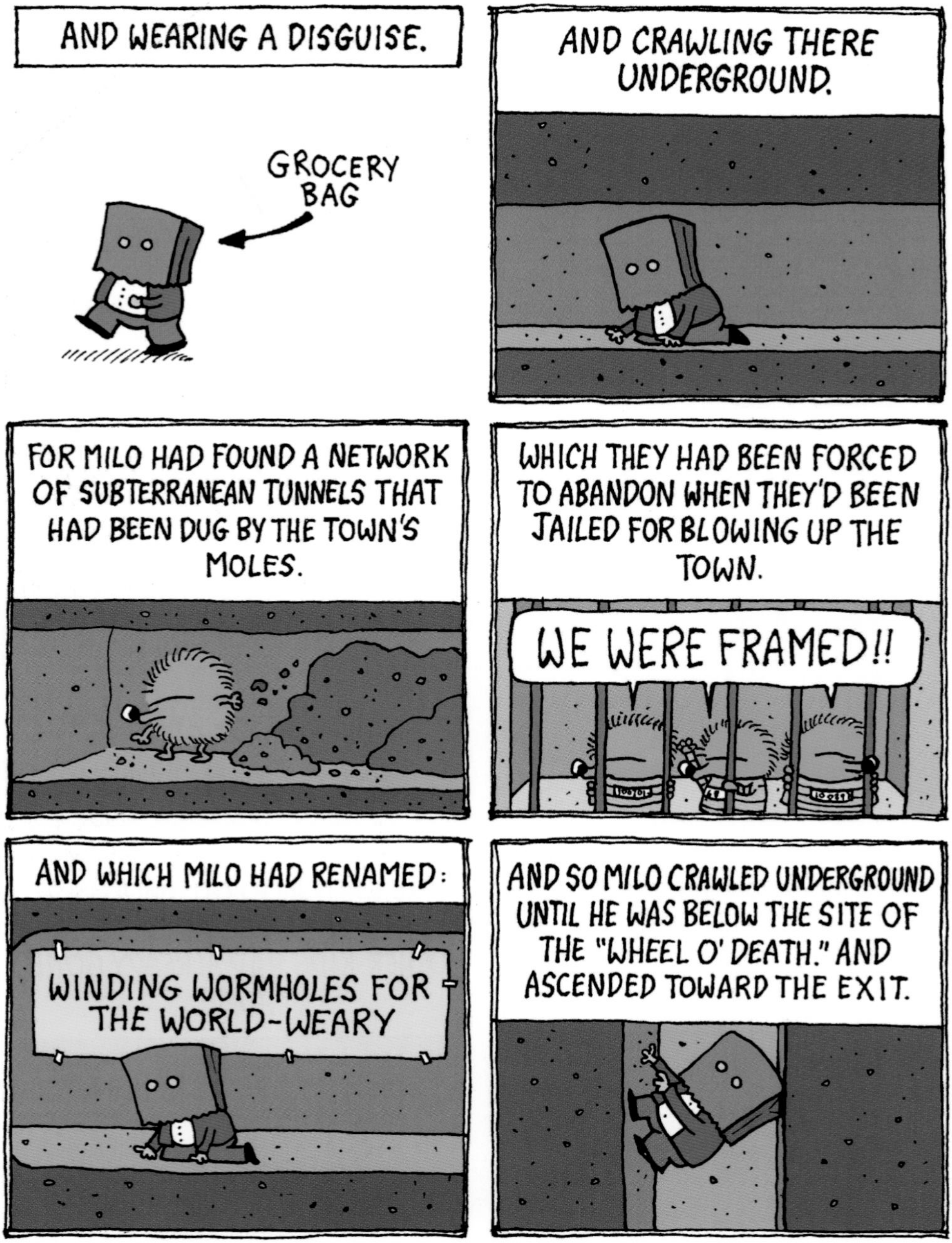
AND WEARING A DISGUISE.
GROCERY BAG
AND CRAWLING THERE UNDERGROUND.
FOR MILO HAD FOUND A NETWORK OF SUBTERRANEAN TUNNELS THAT HAD BEEN DUG BY THE TOWN'S MOLES.
WHICH THEY HAD BEEN FORCED TO ABANDON WHEN THEY'D BEEN JAILED FOR BLOWING UP THE TOWN.
WE WERE FRAMED!!
AND WHICH MILO HAD RENAMED:
WINDING WORMHOLES FOR THE WORLD-WEARY
AND SO MILO CRAWLED UNDERGROUND UNTIL HE WAS BELOW THE SITE OF THE "WHEEL O' DEATH." AND ASCENDED TOWARD THE EXIT.

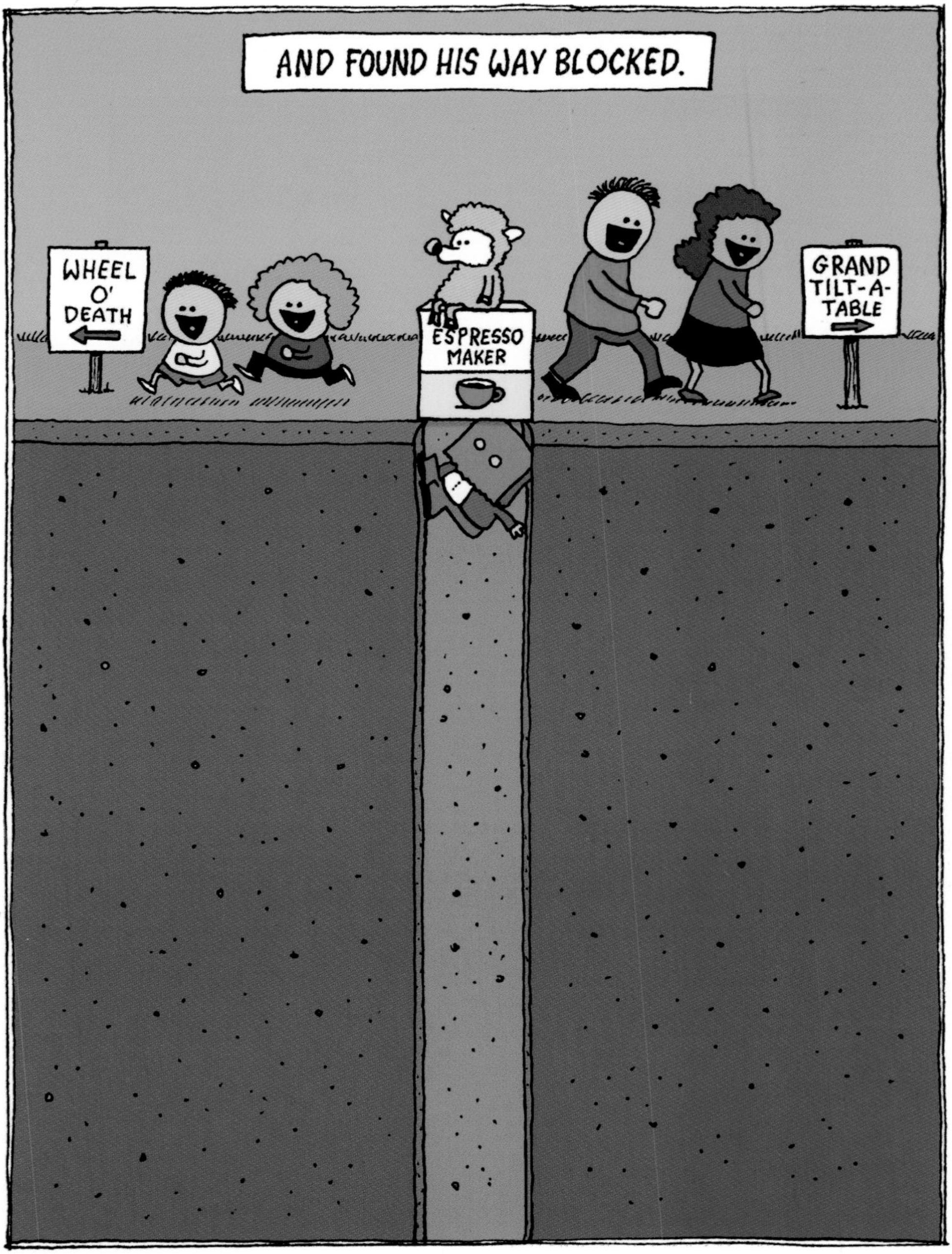
AND FOUND HIS WAY BLOCKED.
WHEEL O' DEATH
ESPRESSO MAKER
GRAND TILT-A-TABLE

CHAPTER
G

AS IN...

GEE, I DIDN'T KNOW
CHAPTERS COULD BE
LETTERED INSTEAD
OF NUMBERED, BUT
IT TURNS OUT THAT
THEY CAN

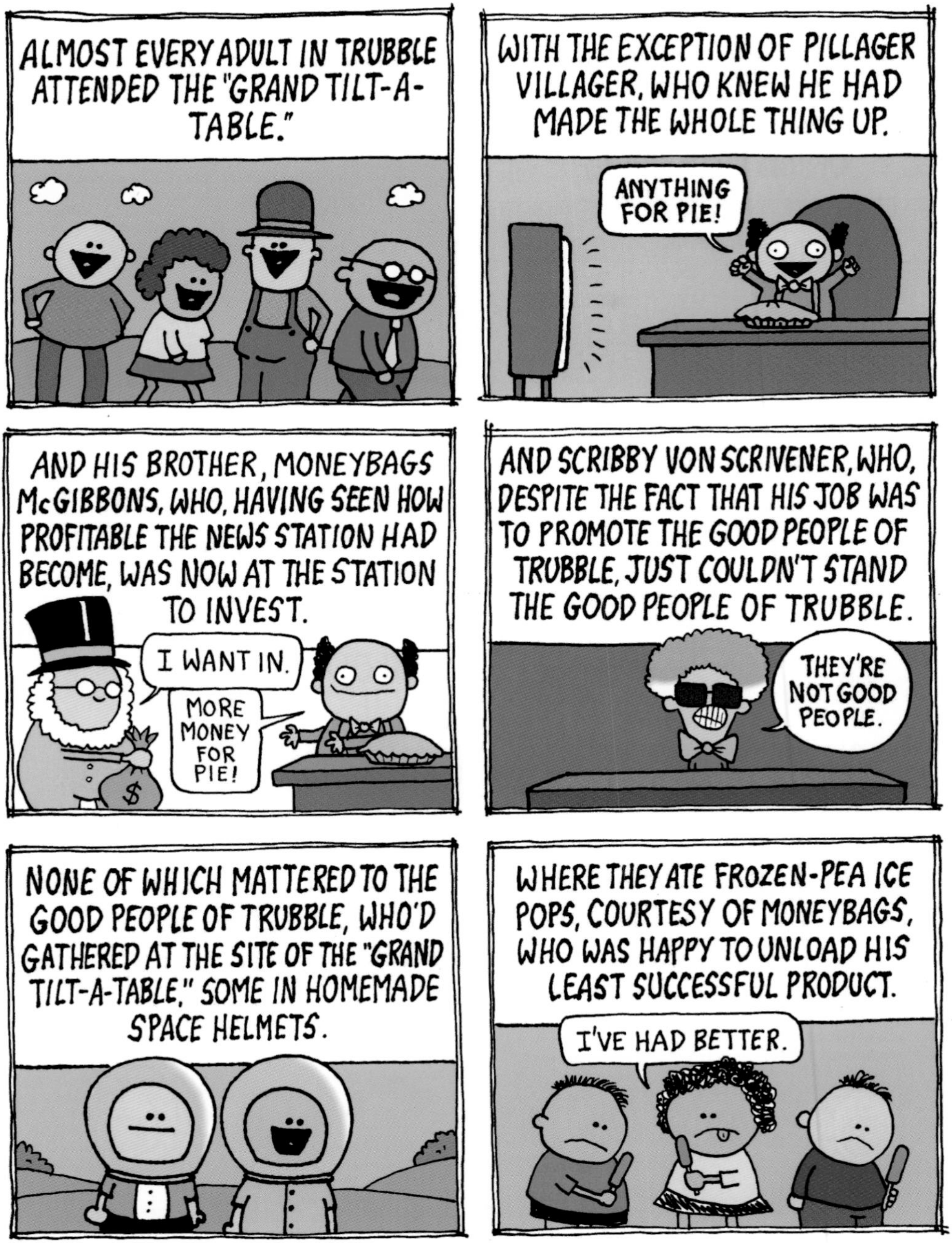
ALMOST EVERY ADULT IN TRUBBLE ATTENDED THE "GRAND TILT-A-TABLE."
WITH THE EXCEPTION OF PILLAGER VILLAGER, WHO KNEW HE HAD MADE THE WHOLE THING UP.
ANYTHING FOR PIE!
AND HIS BROTHER, MONEYBAGS McGIBBONS, WHO, HAVING SEEN HOW PROFITABLE THE NEWS STATION HAD BECOME, WAS NOW AT THE STATION TO INVEST.
I WANT IN.
MORE MONEY FOR PIE!
AND SCRIBBY VON SCRIVENER, WHO, DESPITE THE FACT THAT HIS JOB WAS TO PROMOTE THE GOOD PEOPLE OF TRUBBLE, JUST COULDN'T STAND THE GOOD PEOPLE OF TRUBBLE.
THEY'RE NOT GOOD PEOPLE.
NONE OF WHICH MATTERED TO THE GOOD PEOPLE OF TRUBBLE, WHO'D GATHERED AT THE SITE OF THE "GRAND TILT-A-TABLE," SOME IN HOMEMADE SPACE HELMETS.
WHERE THEY ATE FROZEN-PEA ICE POPS, COURTESY OF MONEYBAGS, WHO WAS HAPPY TO UNLOAD HIS LEAST SUCCESSFUL PRODUCT.
I'VE HAD BETTER.

THE PLAN WAS FOR EVERYONE TO STAND ON ONE EDGE OF THE TOWN, OR, AS THEY BELIEVED, ONE EDGE OF THE GIANT TABLE.

AND SEE IF THE UNBALANCED TABLE WOULD TOPPLE.

WHICH IT DIDN'T.

WELL, DUH.

AT WHICH POINT THE TOWN'S MANUFACTURER OF DYNAMITE GRABBED A MICROPHONE.

LET'S JUST BLOW THE WHOLE TABLE UP!

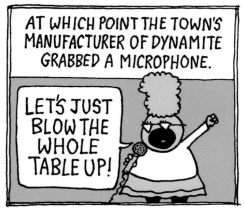

WHICH THE TOWNSFOLK CHEERED. AND THEN THEY BEGAN CHANTING:

BLOW IT UP!! BLOW IT UP!!

UNTIL THEY REALIZED THEY WOULD ALL DIE.

LEAVE IT BE! LEAVE IT BE!

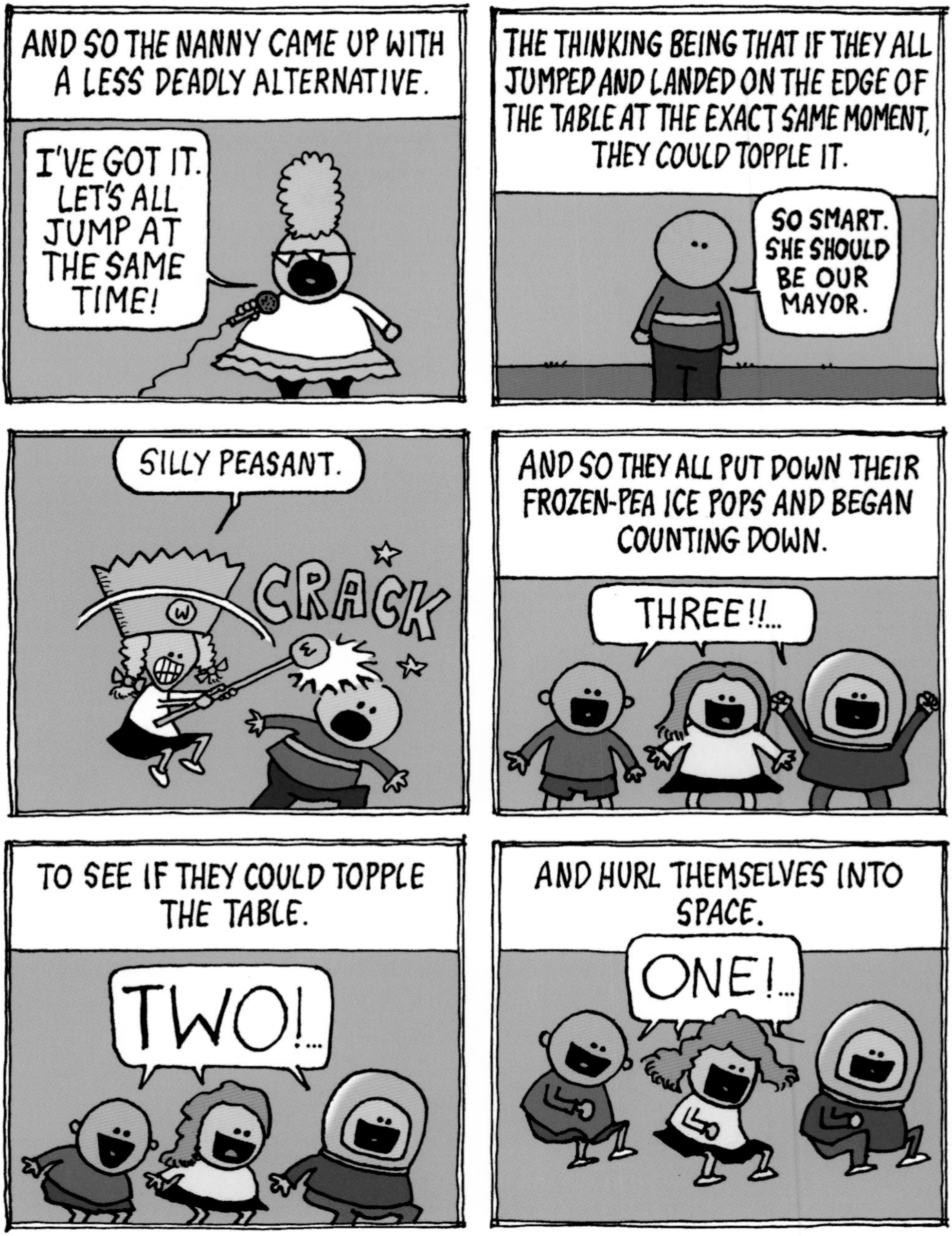
AND SO THE NANNY CAME UP WITH A LESS DEADLY ALTERNATIVE.
I'VE GOT IT. LET'S ALL JUMP AT THE SAME TIME!
THE THINKING BEING THAT IF THEY ALL JUMPED AND LANDED ON THE EDGE OF THE TABLE AT THE EXACT SAME MOMENT, THEY COULD TOPPLE IT.
SO SMART. SHE SHOULD BE OUR MAYOR.
SILLY PEASANT.
CRACK
AND SO THEY ALL PUT DOWN THEIR FROZEN-PEA ICE POPS AND BEGAN COUNTING DOWN.
THREE!!...
TO SEE IF THEY COULD TOPPLE THE TABLE.
TWO!...
AND HURL THEMSELVES INTO SPACE.
ONE!...

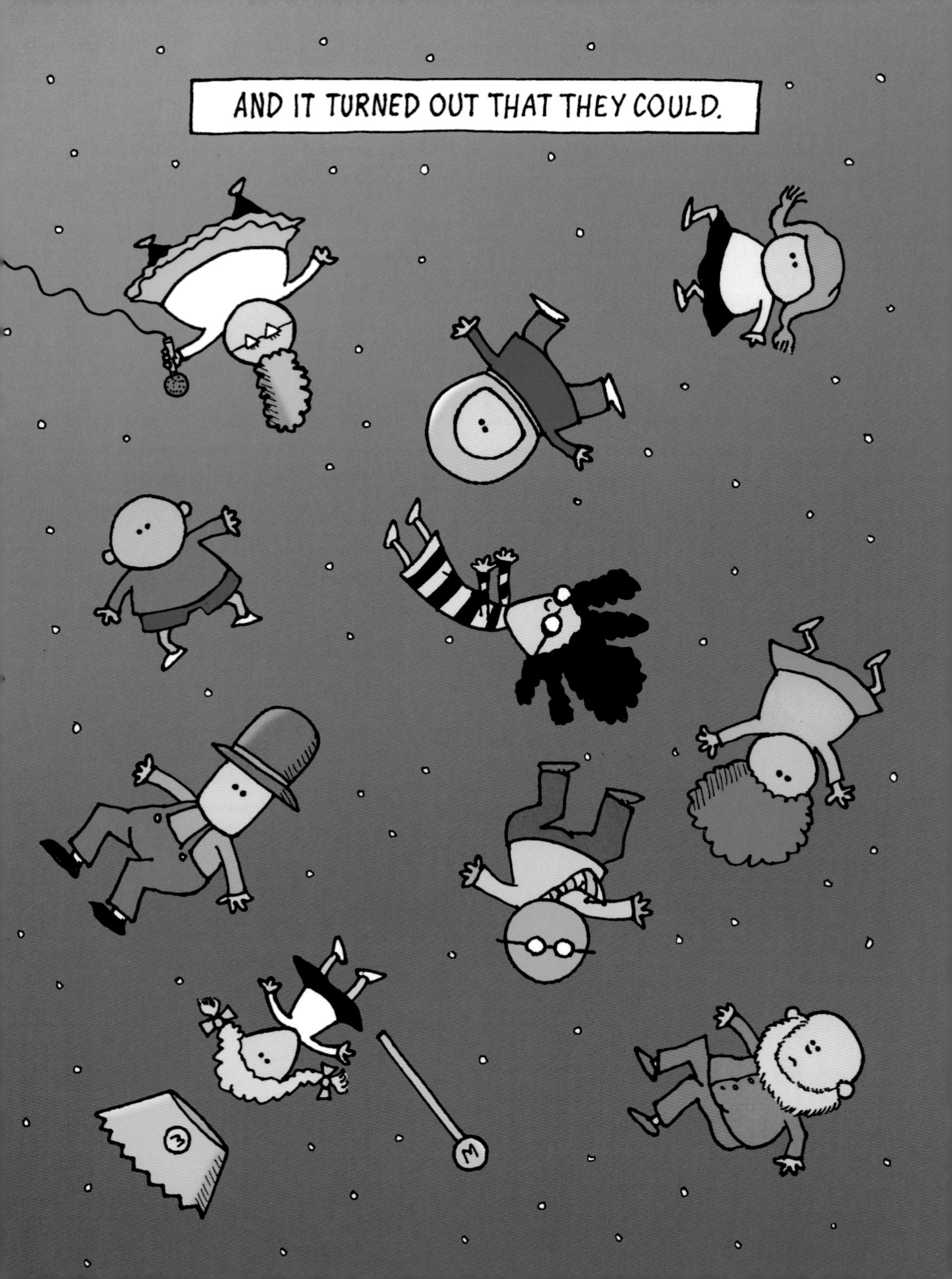
AND IT TURNED OUT THAT THEY COULD.

CHAPTER FIVE

AS IN...

HIGH-FIVE, WE TOPPLED THE TABLE

HIGH-FIVE ME, BRO.

NONE OF THE STORIES ON "23 SQUIDOO" HAD EVER TURNED OUT TO BE TRUE.

SOCKS YOU'VE LOST IN THE DRYER COULD BE FORMING ARMIES.

LOCK THE DOORS.

SO WHEN THE TOWNSFOLK OF TRUBBLE FELL INTO DEEP SPACE, NO ONE WAS MORE SHOCKED THAN THE STATION'S OWNER, PILLAGER VILLAGER.

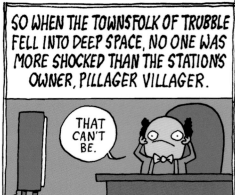

THAT CAN'T BE.

AND ITS NEWEST INVESTOR, MONEYBAGS McGIBBONS.

YOU JUST WIPED OUT EVERY HUMAN IN TRUBBLE!!

WHICH WASN'T EXACTLY TRUE, AS ONLY THE ADULTS HAD DISAPPEARED.

ONLY ADULTS

FOR THE CHILDREN'S LIVES HAD BEEN SAVED—BY, OF ALL THINGS, THE "WHEEL O' DEATH." WHICH HAD KEPT THEM TETHERED TO SOLID GROUND.

BUT HAD DONE NOTHING TO PROTECT THE ADULT OPERATING THE RIDE.

SEE YA.

RIDE OPERATOR

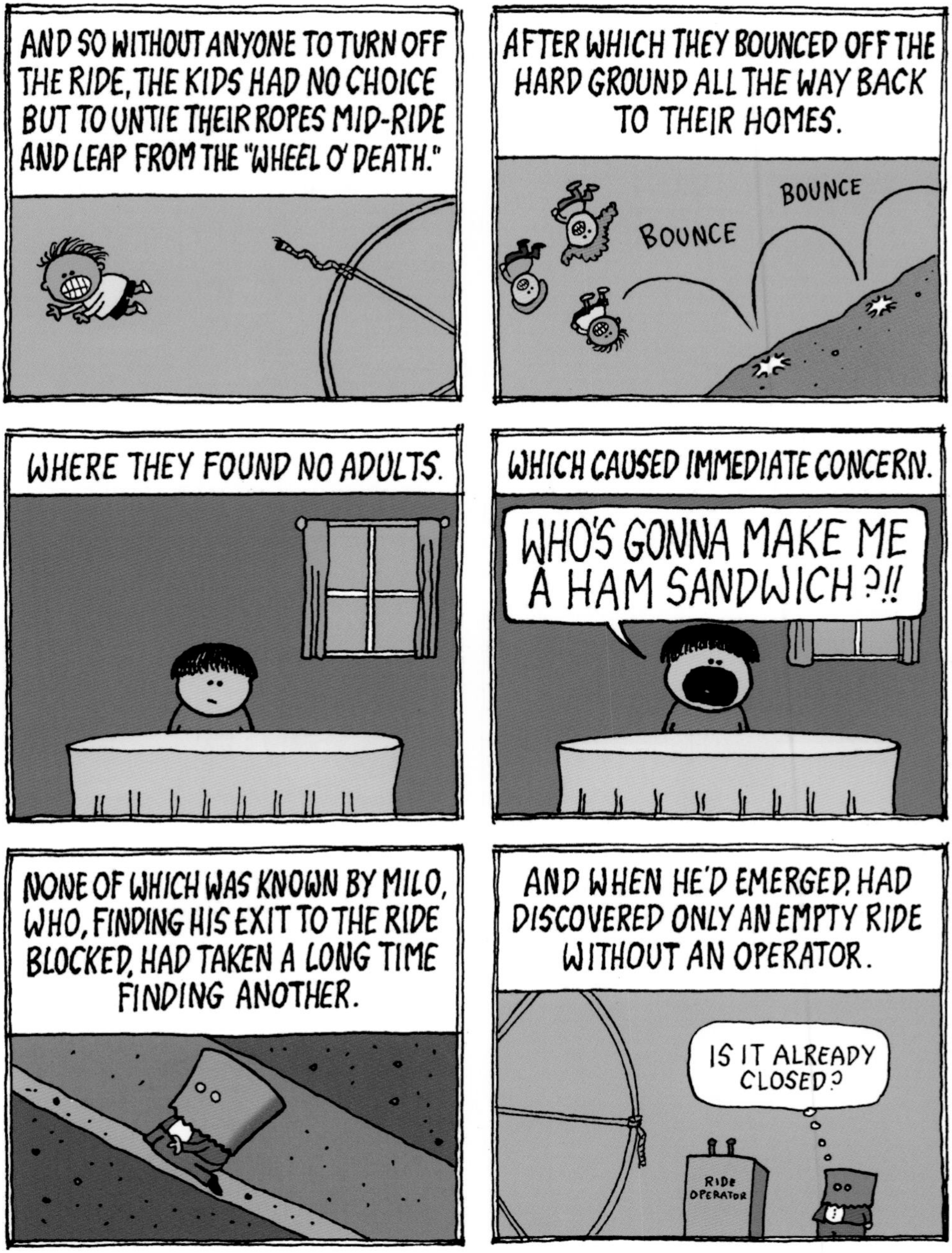
AND SO WITHOUT ANYONE TO TURN OFF THE RIDE, THE KIDS HAD NO CHOICE BUT TO UNTIE THEIR ROPES MID-RIDE AND LEAP FROM THE "WHEEL O' DEATH."
AFTER WHICH THEY BOUNCED OFF THE HARD GROUND ALL THE WAY BACK TO THEIR HOMES.
BOUNCE
BOUNCE
WHERE THEY FOUND NO ADULTS.
WHICH CAUSED IMMEDIATE CONCERN.
WHO'S GONNA MAKE ME A HAM SANDWICH ?!!
NONE OF WHICH WAS KNOWN BY MILO, WHO, FINDING HIS EXIT TO THE RIDE BLOCKED, HAD TAKEN A LONG TIME FINDING ANOTHER.
AND WHEN HE'D EMERGED, HAD DISCOVERED ONLY AN EMPTY RIDE WITHOUT AN OPERATOR.
IS IT ALREADY CLOSED?
RIDE OPERATOR

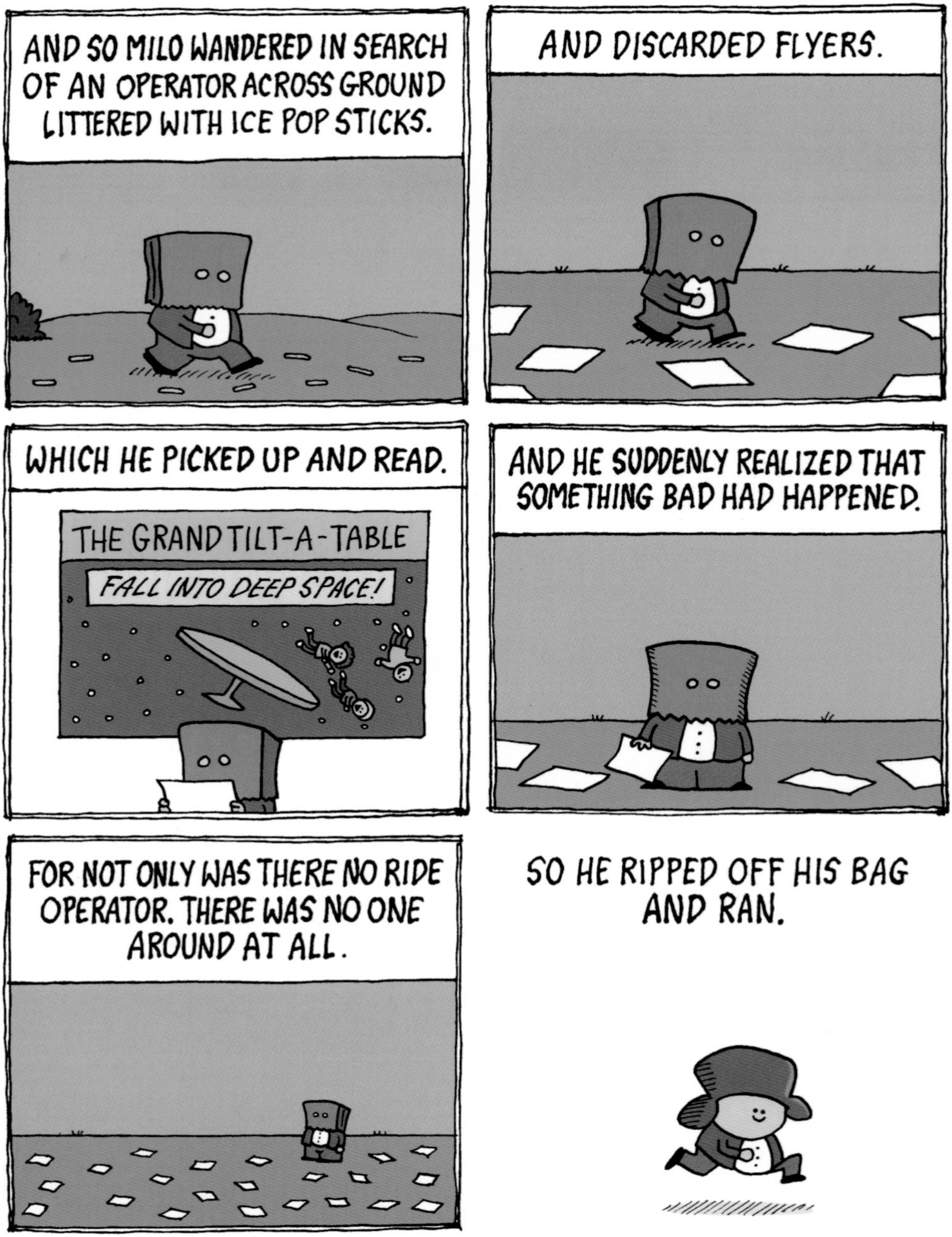
AND SO MILO WANDERED IN SEARCH OF AN OPERATOR ACROSS GROUND LITTERED WITH ICE POP STICKS.
AND DISCARDED FLYERS.
WHICH HE PICKED UP AND READ.
THE GRAND TILT-A-TABLE
FALL INTO DEEP SPACE!
AND HE SUDDENLY REALIZED THAT SOMETHING BAD HAD HAPPENED.
FOR NOT ONLY WAS THERE NO RIDE OPERATOR. THERE WAS NO ONE AROUND AT ALL.
SO HE RIPPED OFF HIS BAG AND RAN.

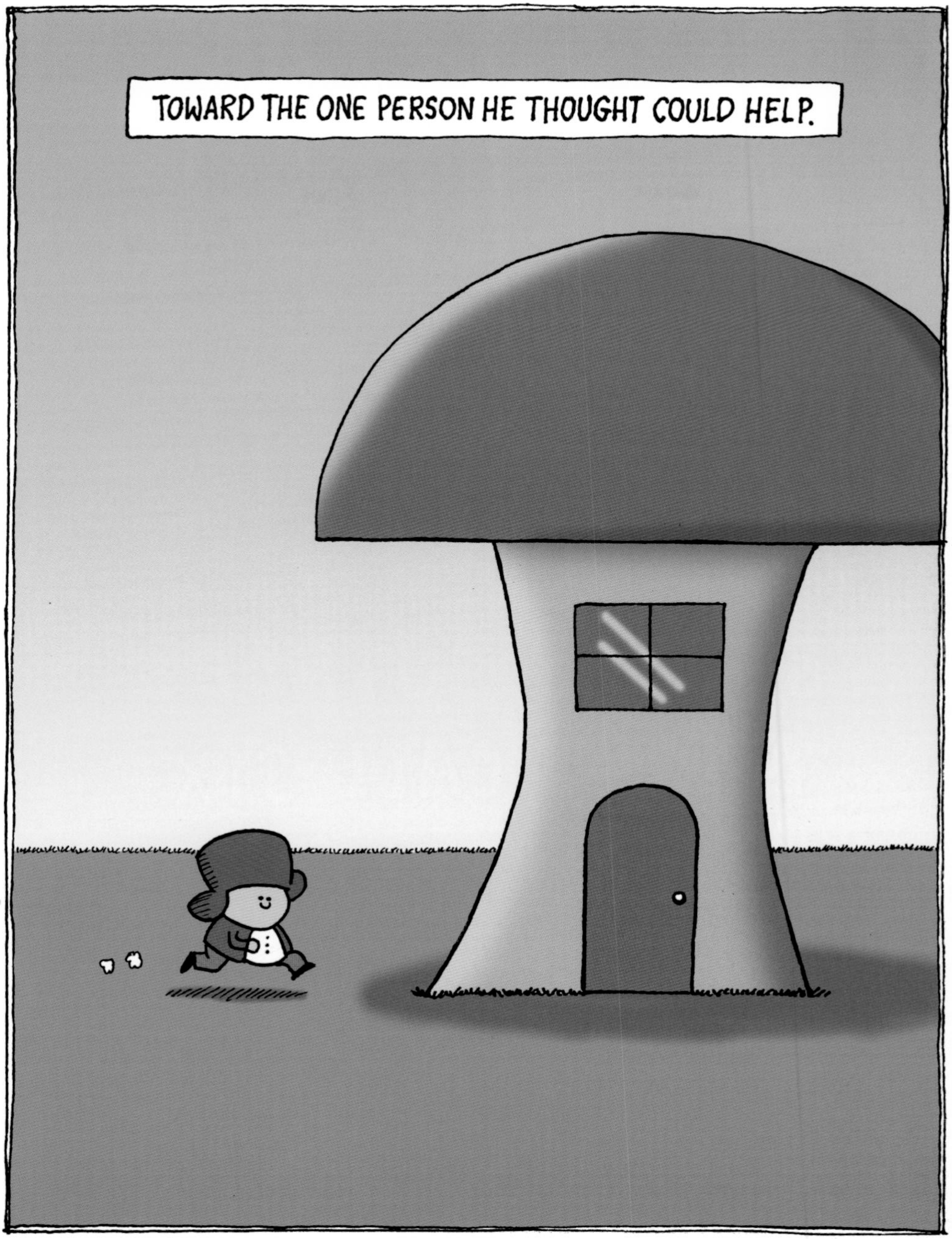
TOWARD THE ONE PERSON HE THOUGHT COULD HELP.

CHAPTER AFTER FIVE

WHICH...

BETTER AUTHORS MIGHT CALL "SIX"

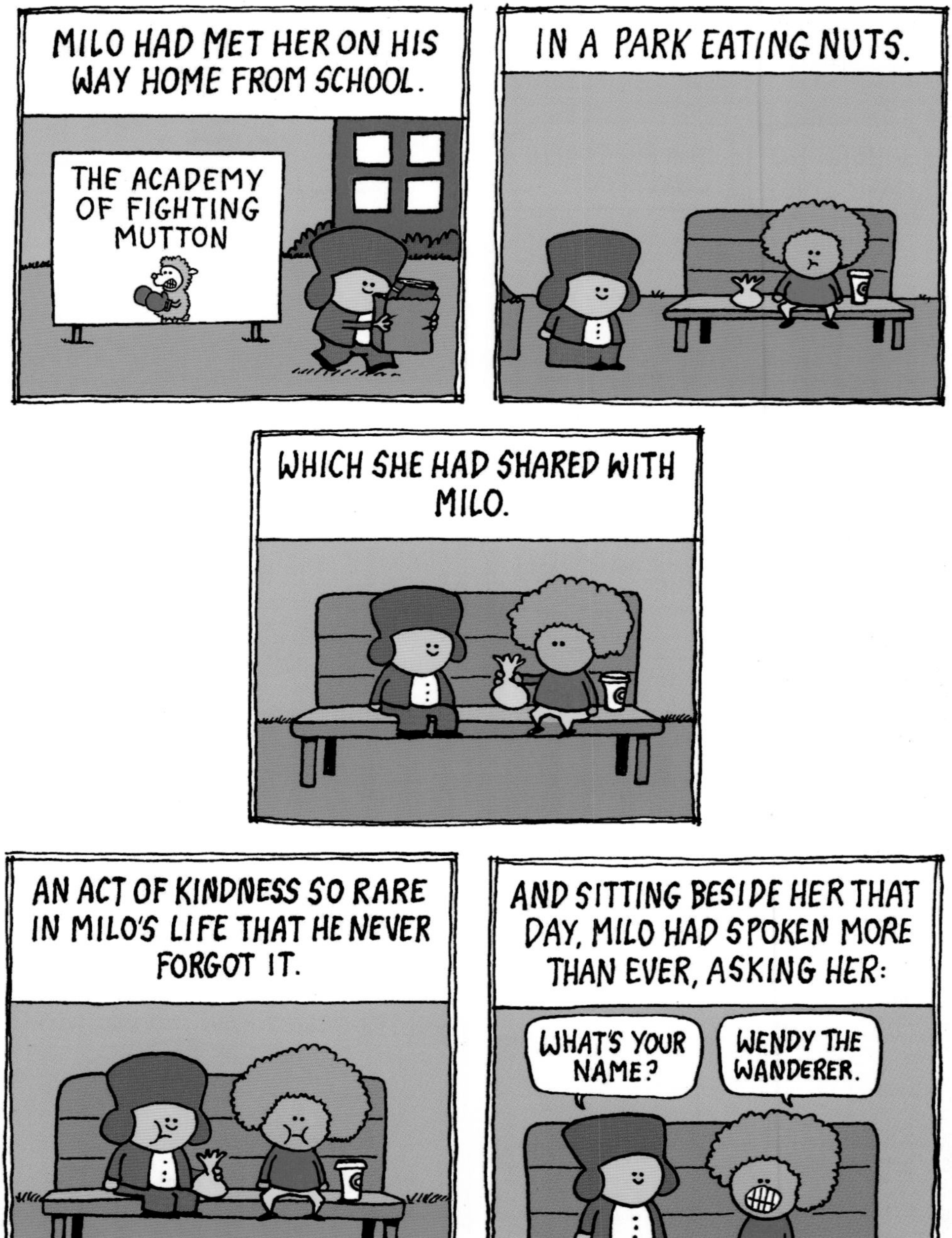
MILO HAD MET HER ON HIS WAY HOME FROM SCHOOL.
THE ACADEMY OF FIGHTING MUTTON
IN A PARK EATING NUTS.
WHICH SHE HAD SHARED WITH MILO.
AN ACT OF KINDNESS SO RARE IN MILO'S LIFE THAT HE NEVER FORGOT IT.
AND SITTING BESIDE HER THAT DAY, MILO HAD SPOKEN MORE THAN EVER, ASKING HER:
WHAT'S YOUR NAME?
WENDY THE WANDERER.

AND...

WHERE DO YOU LIVE?

IN A BIG, PURPLE MUSHROOM.

AND...

DO YOU GO TO OUR SCHOOL?

FOR MILO WAS SECRETLY HOPING HE HAD FOUND A FRIEND WHO COULD IMPROVE HIS DAYS AT THE ACADEMY OF FIGHTING MUTTON.

THE ACADEMY OF FIGHTING MUTTON

BUT HIS HOPE WAS DASHED WHEN WENDY REPLIED...

I'M HOMESCHOOLED.

FOR WENDY EXPLAINED THAT HER FATHER—WORRIED WILLY—WORRIED ABOUT RAIN, PAIN, AND THE MUNDANE.

UMBRELLA STOPS RAIN, BUT NOT PAIN OR THE MUNDANE.

WORRIED WILLY →

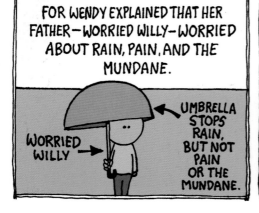

AND WORRIED ABOUT HIS DAUGHTER MORE THAN ALL ELSE COMBINED.

IT DOESN'T RAIN INDOORS, DAD.

BETTER SAFE THAN SORRY.

AND SO WILLY THOUGHT IT BEST THAT HIS DAUGHTER BE TAUGHT AT HOME.

WHICH WAS TOO BAD FOR MILO, WHO ROSE TO SAY GOODBYE.

AND LOOKING BACK OVER HIS SHOULDER, HE WATCHED AS WENDY, WHO HAD RUN OUT OF NUTS, FED A SUGAR-FILLED DRINK TO A SQUIRREL.

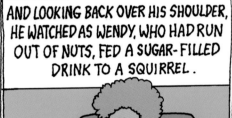

WHICH MADE SOME TOWNSFOLK ANGRY.

SQUIRRELS EAT NUTS!! **NUTS! NUTS! NUTS!!**

AND MADE THE SQUIRREL INSANE.

SPROING

AND SO MILO RAN BACK.

DON'T BLAME HER! BLAME ME! I ATE THE LAST OF THE NUTS!

WHICH THE TOWNSFOLK IGNORED. BUT WENDY DID NOT.

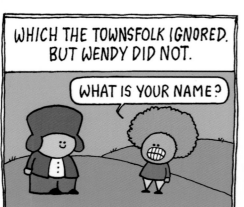

WHAT IS YOUR NAME?

MILO.

THANK YOU, MILO THE MAGNIFICENT.

AND SUDDENLY THE NORMALLY QUIET MILO WANTED TO YAMMER WITH WENDY ALL DAY.

YAMMER YAMMER YAMMER YAMMER YAMMER

YAMMER YAMMER YAMMER YAMMER YAMMER

LISTEN, MILO THE MAGNIFICENT. IF THE DAY EVER COMES WHEN I CAN DO SOMETHING FOR YOU, JUST COME TO THE PURPLE MUSHROOM.

AND WHEN THAT DAY CAME, HE DID.

WENDEEEEEEEEEEEEE!!

64

CHAPTER 711

NAMED NOT FOR THE
CONVENIENCE STORE
BUT JUST BECAUSE IT'S A
BIG NUMBER WE LIKE. THOUGH
WE HAVE NOTHING AGAINST
THE CONVENIENCE STORE.

MILO YELLED FOR WENDY UNTIL HE SAW A LIGHT GO ON IN THE WINDOW UPSTAIRS.

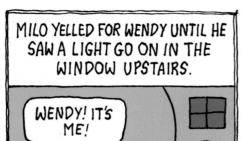

WENDY! IT'S ME!

AND HEARD A GIRL'S VOICE REPLY:

WILL YOU PLEASE SHUT YOUR PIEHOLE?!

AND SHE WAS NOT WENDY.

APOLOGIES FOR MY TEMPER. MAY I ASK WHO YOU ARE?

BUT MILO DID NOT ANSWER.

ARE YOU NOT GOING TO SAY ANYTHING?

I KNOW YOU CAN TALK. I HEARD YOU YELL.

BUT MILO STAYED SILENT.

FINE. I'LL START. MY NAME IS BLUEGIRL.

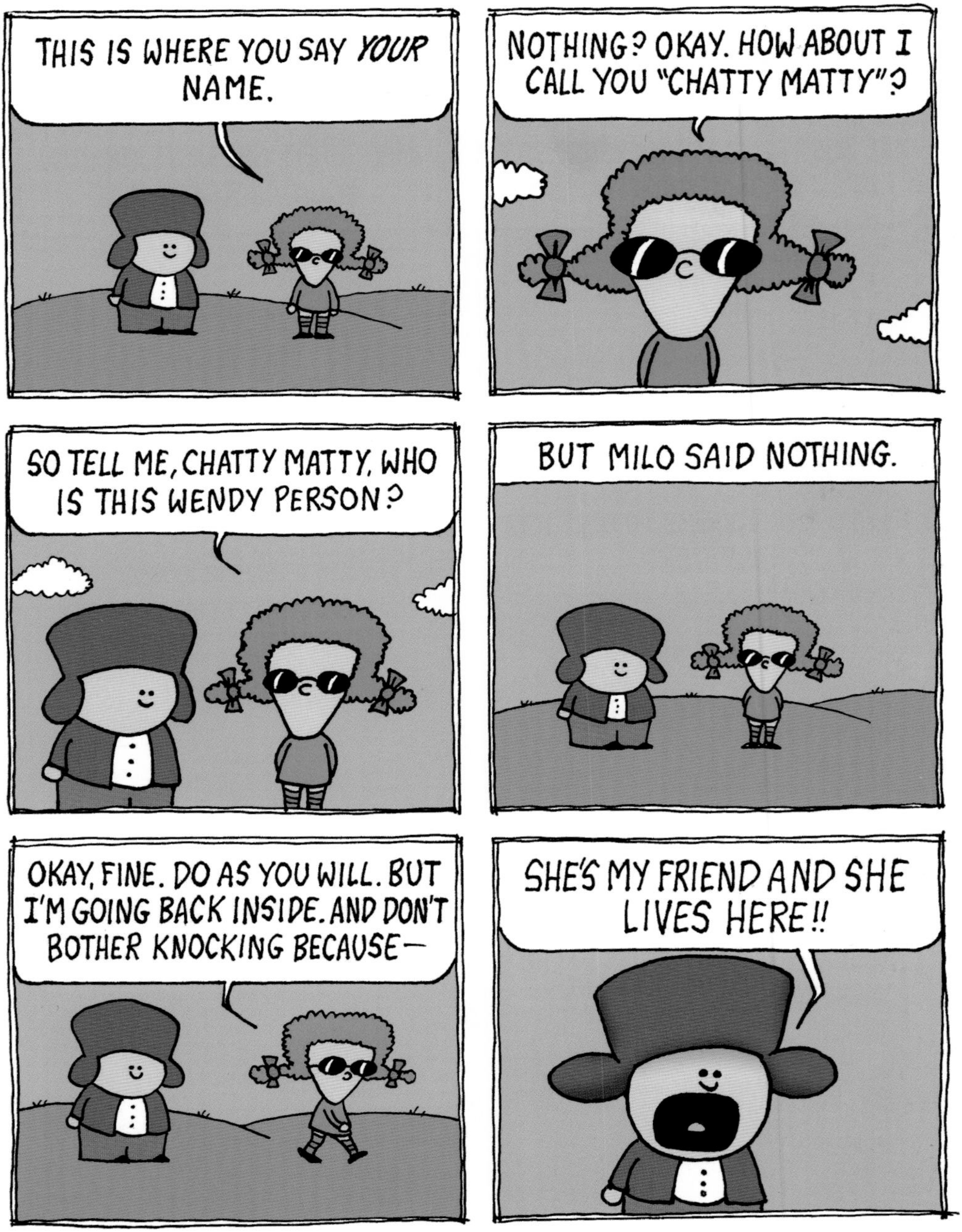
THIS IS WHERE YOU SAY *YOUR* NAME.
NOTHING? OKAY. HOW ABOUT I CALL YOU "CHATTY MATTY"?
SO TELL ME, CHATTY MATTY, WHO IS THIS WENDY PERSON?
BUT MILO SAID NOTHING.
OKAY, FINE. DO AS YOU WILL. BUT I'M GOING BACK INSIDE. AND DON'T BOTHER KNOCKING BECAUSE—
SHE'S MY FRIEND AND SHE LIVES HERE!!

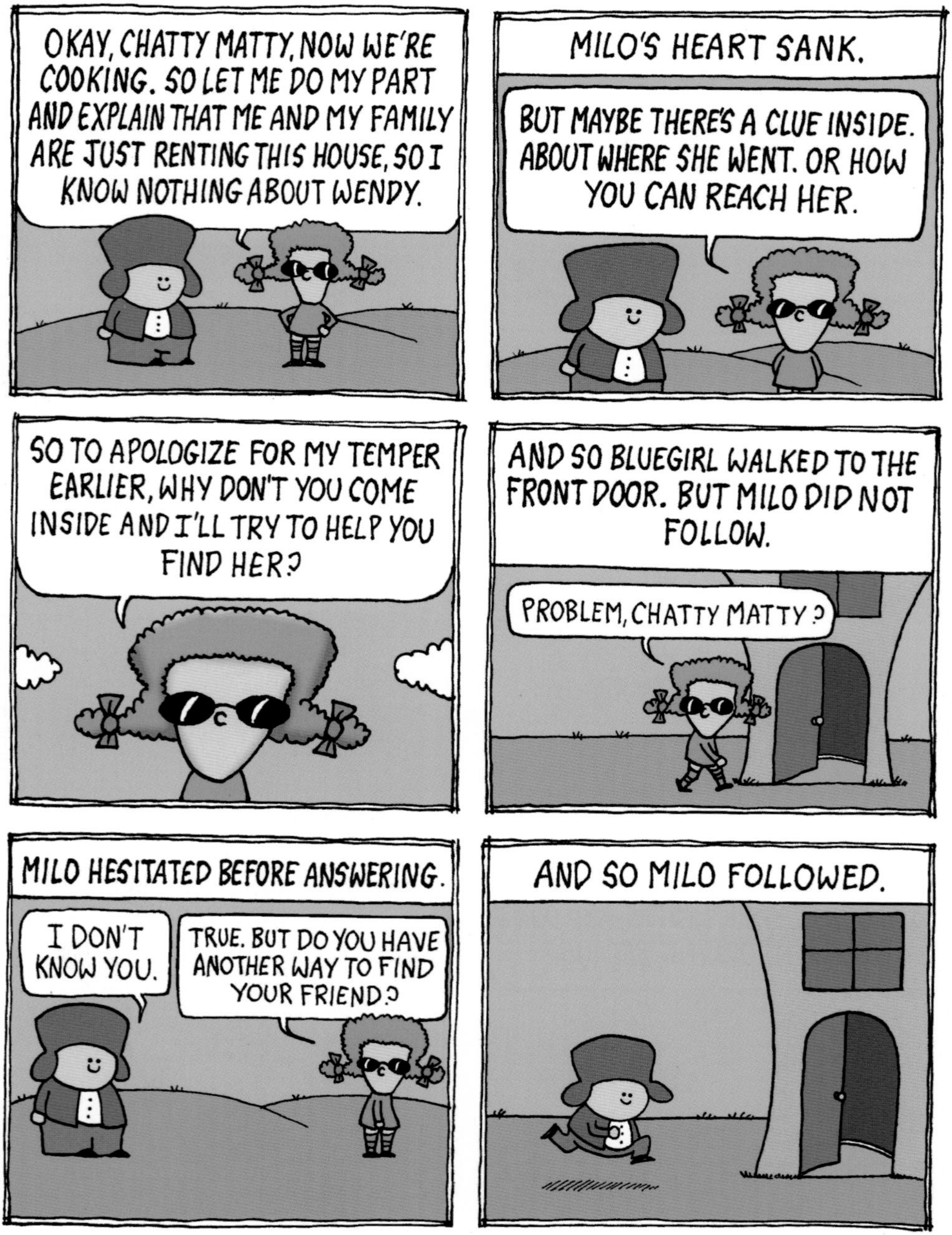
OKAY, CHATTY MATTY, NOW WE'RE COOKING. SO LET ME DO MY PART AND EXPLAIN THAT ME AND MY FAMILY ARE JUST RENTING THIS HOUSE, SO I KNOW NOTHING ABOUT WENDY.
MILO'S HEART SANK.
BUT MAYBE THERE'S A CLUE INSIDE. ABOUT WHERE SHE WENT. OR HOW YOU CAN REACH HER.
SO TO APOLOGIZE FOR MY TEMPER EARLIER, WHY DON'T YOU COME INSIDE AND I'LL TRY TO HELP YOU FIND HER?
AND SO BLUEGIRL WALKED TO THE FRONT DOOR. BUT MILO DID NOT FOLLOW.
PROBLEM, CHATTY MATTY?
MILO HESITATED BEFORE ANSWERING.
I DON'T KNOW YOU.
TRUE. BUT DO YOU HAVE ANOTHER WAY TO FIND YOUR FRIEND?
AND SO MILO FOLLOWED.

CHAPTER ATE

AS IN...

MILO ATE A DONUT, WHICH DOES NOT IN FACT HAPPEN UNTIL THE *NEXT* CHAPTER, BUT WE REALLY LIKE THE PUN

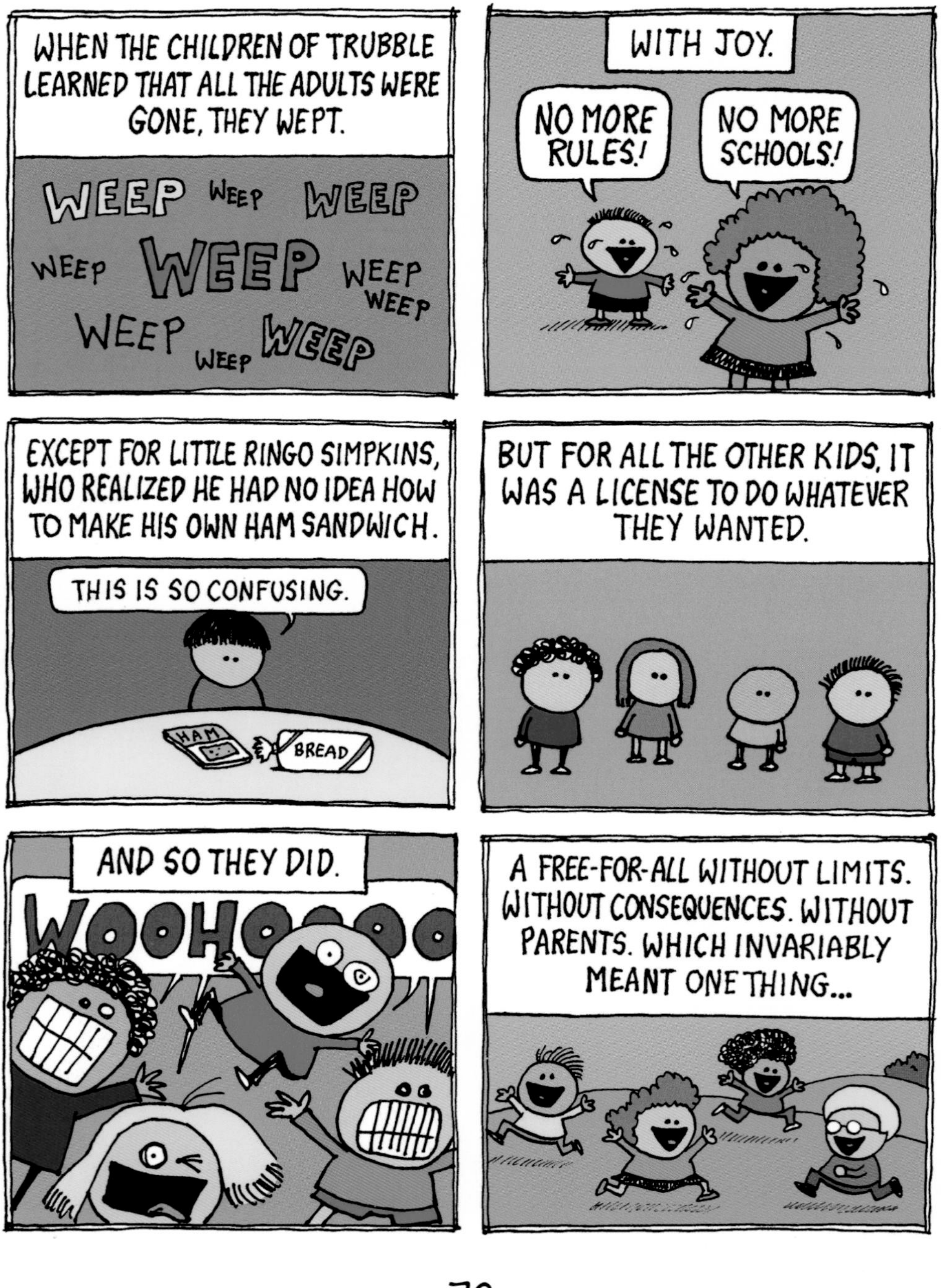
WHEN THE CHILDREN OF TRUBBLE LEARNED THAT ALL THE ADULTS WERE GONE, THEY WEPT.
WEEP WEEP WEEP
WEEP WEEP WEEP WEEP
WEEP WEEP WEEP
WITH JOY.
NO MORE RULES!
NO MORE SCHOOLS!
EXCEPT FOR LITTLE RINGO SIMPKINS, WHO REALIZED HE HAD NO IDEA HOW TO MAKE HIS OWN HAM SANDWICH.
THIS IS SO CONFUSING.
HAM
BREAD
BUT FOR ALL THE OTHER KIDS, IT WAS A LICENSE TO DO WHATEVER THEY WANTED.
AND SO THEY DID.
WOOHOOOOO
A FREE-FOR-ALL WITHOUT LIMITS. WITHOUT CONSEQUENCES. WITHOUT PARENTS. WHICH INVARIABLY MEANT ONE THING...

...EVERYONE GOT THEIR TOYS STOLEN.

THAT'S MY TRAIN.

THAT'S MY DOLL.

THAT'S MY DOG.

AND SO THEY REALIZED THAT EVEN IN THEIR KID-ONLY WORLD, THEY WOULD STILL NEED SOME SEMBLANCE OF ORDER.

SO THEY DECIDED TO ELECT A LEADER, GIVING EACH OF THE 275 KIDS IN TOWN ONE VOTE EACH.

RESULTING IN A 275-WAY TIE.

ELECTION RESULTS

JOHN: |
JIM: |
ZOE: |
MARCIA: |
PARRI: |
JOYCE: |
LISA: |
JENNIFER: |
LOUIS: |
PANA: |
PA...

AND SO THE KIDS NEEDED A NEW WAY TO BEST CHOOSE THEIR MOST QUALIFIED LEADERS.

"WHAT IF THE RULERS ARE JUST ME AND LENNY AND JENNY?" ASKED BENNY, BLATANTLY APPEALING TO EVERYONE'S SENSE OF RHYME.

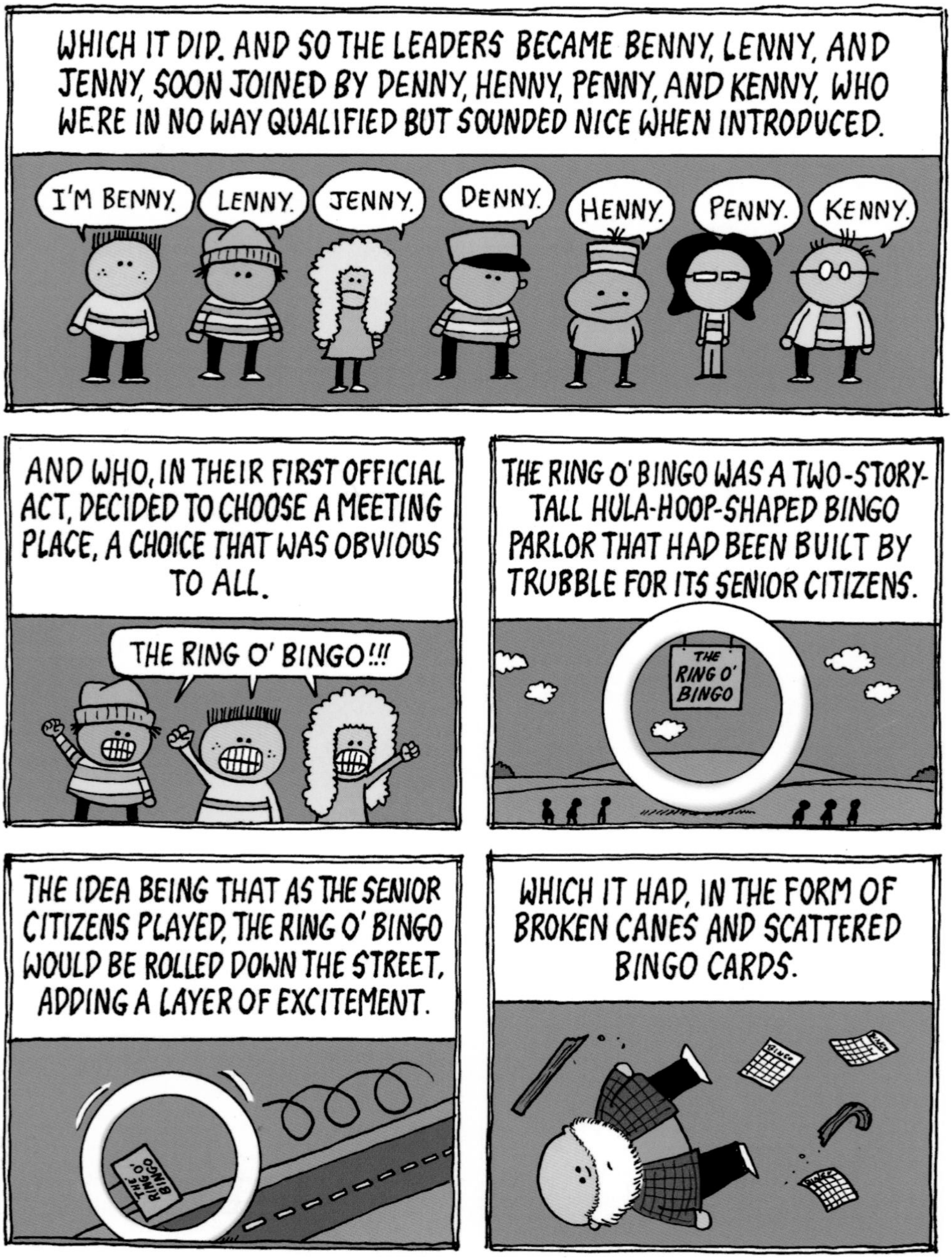
WHICH IT DID. AND SO THE LEADERS BECAME BENNY, LENNY, AND JENNY, SOON JOINED BY DENNY, HENNY, PENNY, AND KENNY, WHO WERE IN NO WAY QUALIFIED BUT SOUNDED NICE WHEN INTRODUCED.
I'M BENNY.
LENNY.
JENNY.
DENNY.
HENNY.
PENNY.
KENNY.
AND WHO, IN THEIR FIRST OFFICIAL ACT, DECIDED TO CHOOSE A MEETING PLACE, A CHOICE THAT WAS OBVIOUS TO ALL.
THE RING O' BINGO!!!
THE RING O' BINGO WAS A TWO-STORY-TALL HULA-HOOP-SHAPED BINGO PARLOR THAT HAD BEEN BUILT BY TRUBBLE FOR ITS SENIOR CITIZENS.
THE RING O' BINGO
THE IDEA BEING THAT AS THE SENIOR CITIZENS PLAYED, THE RING O' BINGO WOULD BE ROLLED DOWN THE STREET, ADDING A LAYER OF EXCITEMENT.
THE RING O' BINGO
WHICH IT HAD, IN THE FORM OF BROKEN CANES AND SCATTERED BINGO CARDS.

AND SO THE TOWN HAD HAD NO CHOICE BUT TO CLOSE THE RING O' BINGO AND PUT IT SOMEPLACE FAR AWAY WHERE IT COULD DO NO MORE HARM.

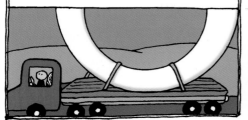

WHICH WAS HIGH ATOP MOUNT McGIBBONS.

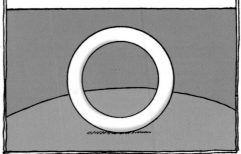

WHERE IF ONE DAY THEY GOT A "T" AND "R" AND "U" AND "B" AND "L" AND "E," THEY COULD SPELL THE TOWN NAME— THOUGH INCORRECTLY.

TROUBLE

CLOSE ENOUGH.

AND IT WAS THERE THAT LENNY, BENNY, JENNY, PENNY, DENNY, HENNY, AND KENNY NOW HEADED TO GOVERN FROM INSIDE THE OLD RING O' BINGO.

WHERE THEY FACED THEIR FIRST OBSTACLE TO GOVERNING: THEY COULD NOT FIND A DOOR.

THOUGH EVENTUALLY THEY DID. IN AN INCONVENIENT SPOT.

IT'S UP HEREEEEEEEEEE

73

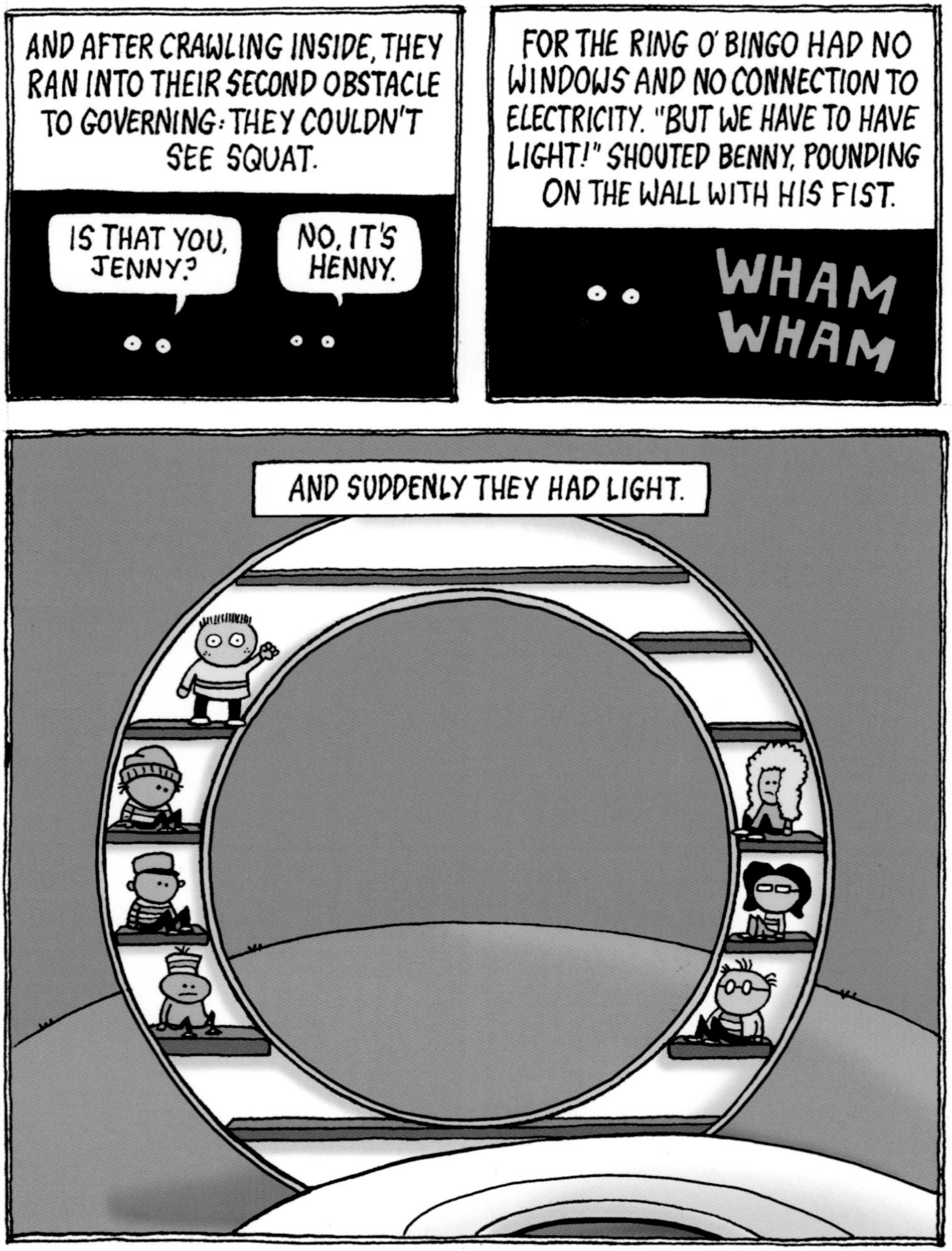
AND AFTER CRAWLING INSIDE, THEY RAN INTO THEIR SECOND OBSTACLE TO GOVERNING: THEY COULDN'T SEE SQUAT.
IS THAT YOU, JENNY?
NO, IT'S HENNY.
FOR THE RING O' BINGO HAD NO WINDOWS AND NO CONNECTION TO ELECTRICITY. "BUT WE HAVE TO HAVE LIGHT!" SHOUTED BENNY, POUNDING ON THE WALL WITH HIS FIST.
WHAM
WHAM
AND SUDDENLY THEY HAD LIGHT.

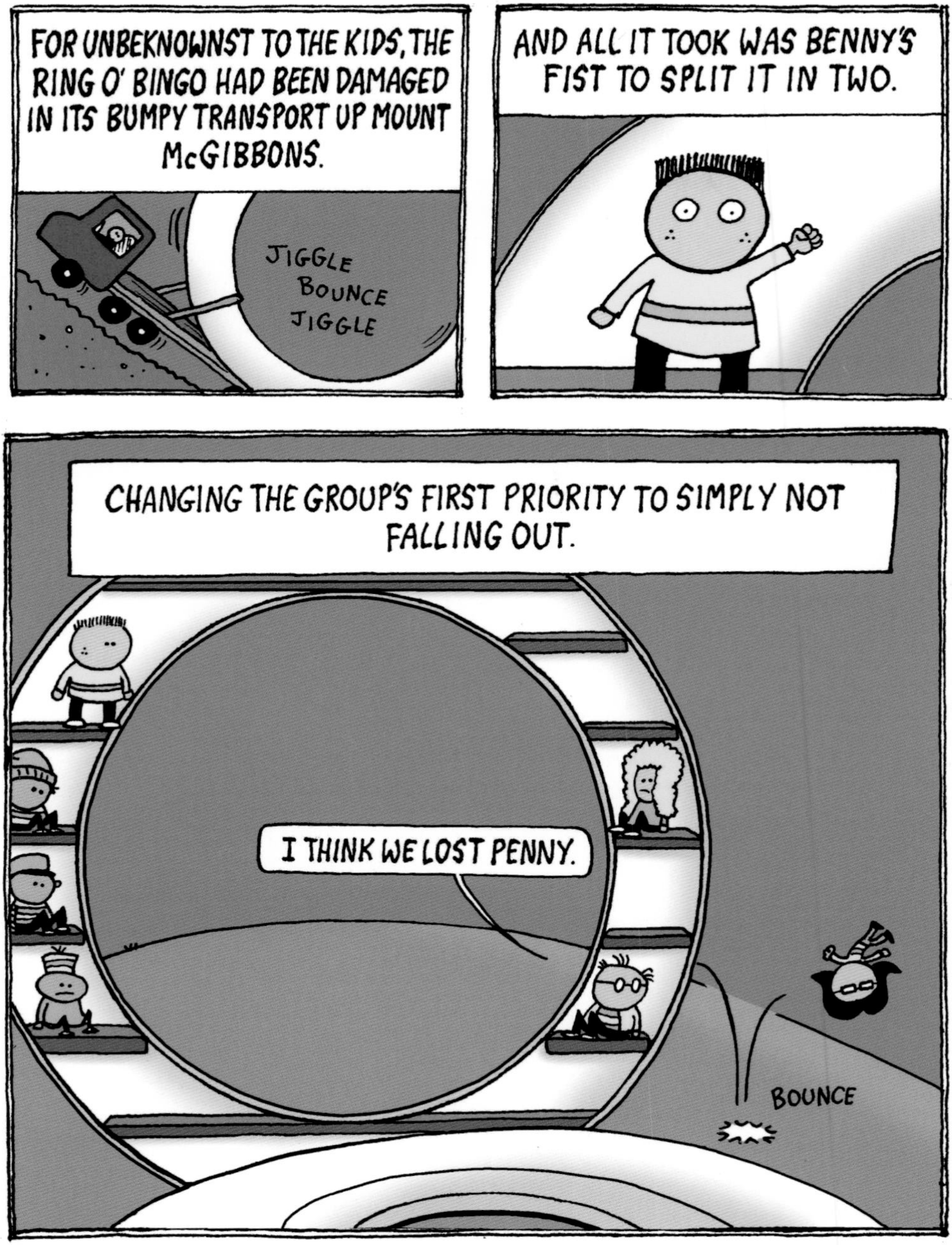
FOR UNBEKNOWNST TO THE KIDS, THE RING O' BINGO HAD BEEN DAMAGED IN ITS BUMPY TRANSPORT UP MOUNT McGIBBONS.
JIGGLE
BOUNCE
JIGGLE
AND ALL IT TOOK WAS BENNY'S FIST TO SPLIT IT IN TWO.
CHANGING THE GROUP'S FIRST PRIORITY TO SIMPLY NOT FALLING OUT.
I THINK WE LOST PENNY.
BOUNCE

CHAPTER
_____

IN WHICH...

THERE IS NO ATTEMPT
MADE TO GIVE THE
CHAPTER A NUMBER

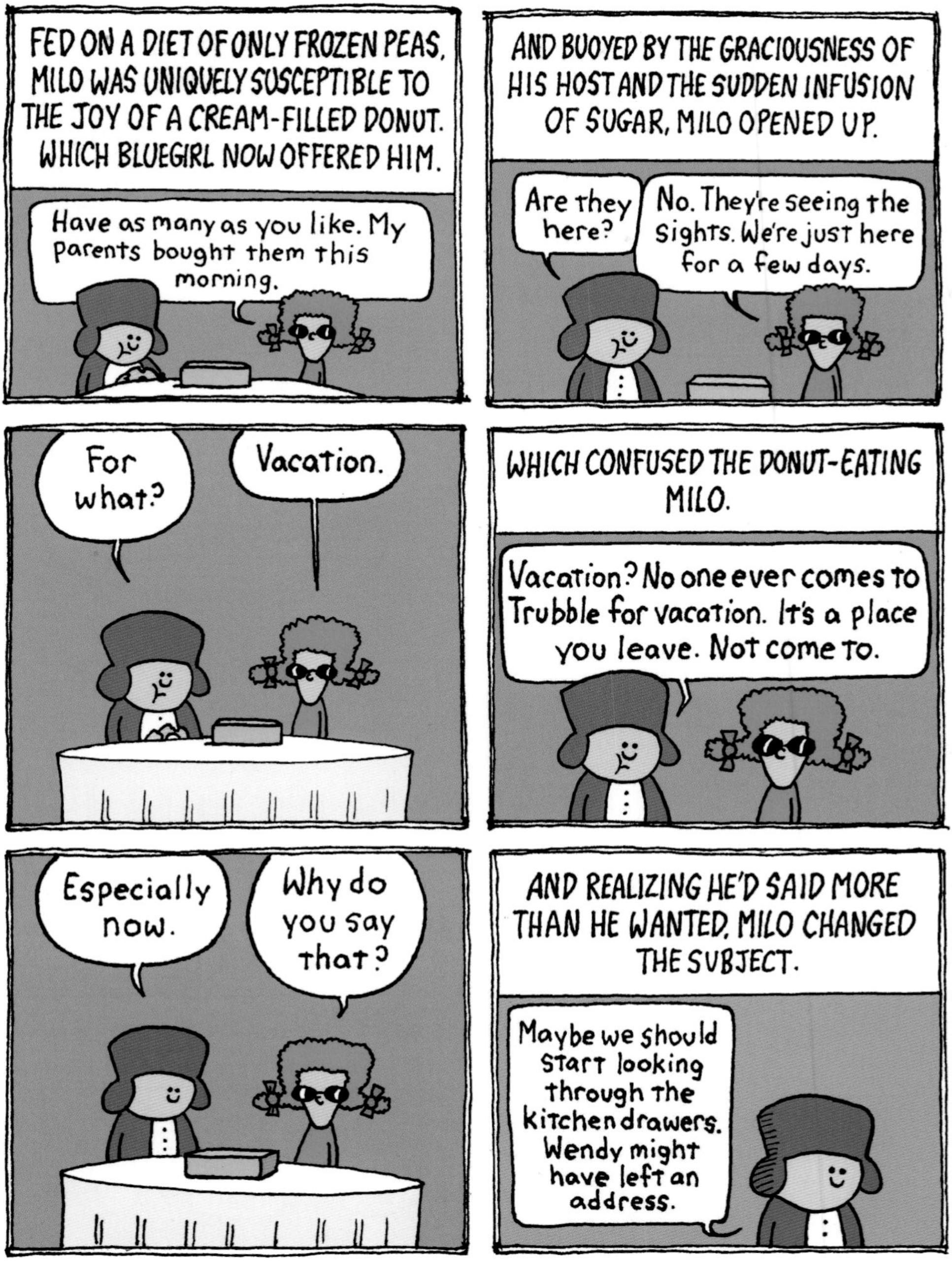
FED ON A DIET OF ONLY FROZEN PEAS, MILO WAS UNIQUELY SUSCEPTIBLE TO THE JOY OF A CREAM-FILLED DONUT. WHICH BLUEGIRL NOW OFFERED HIM.
Have as many as you like. My parents bought them this morning.
AND BUOYED BY THE GRACIOUSNESS OF HIS HOST AND THE SUDDEN INFUSION OF SUGAR, MILO OPENED UP.
Are they here?
No. They're seeing the sights. We're just here for a few days.
For what?
Vacation.
WHICH CONFUSED THE DONUT-EATING MILO.
Vacation? No one ever comes to Trubble for vacation. It's a place you leave. Not come to.
Especially now.
Why do you say that?
AND REALIZING HE'D SAID MORE THAN HE WANTED, MILO CHANGED THE SUBJECT.
Maybe we should start looking through the kitchen drawers. Wendy might have left an address.

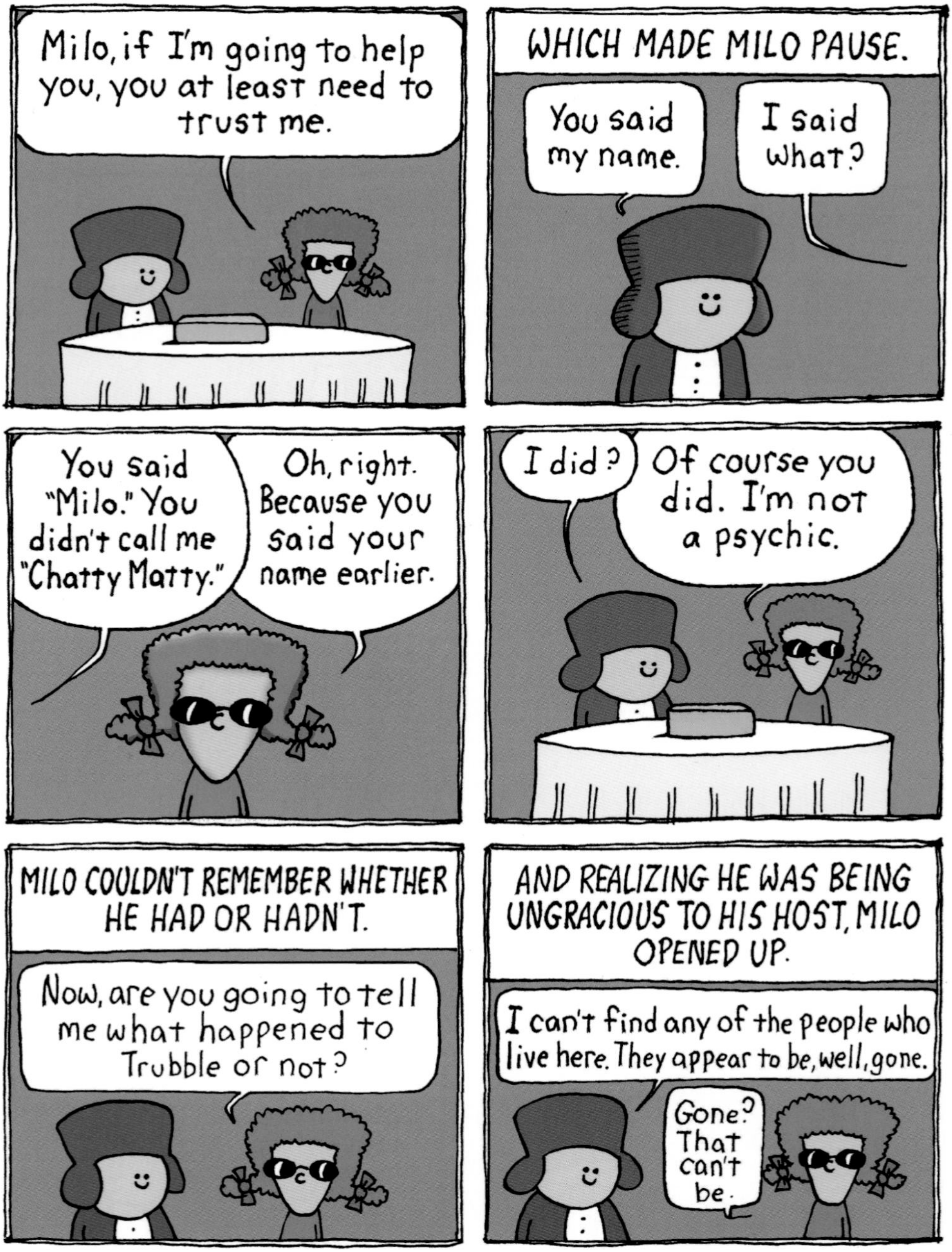
Milo, if I'm going to help you, you at least need to trust me.
WHICH MADE MILO PAUSE.
You said my name.
I said what?
You said "Milo." You didn't call me "Chatty Matty."
Oh, right. Because you said your name earlier.
I did?
Of course you did. I'm not a psychic.
MILO COULDN'T REMEMBER WHETHER HE HAD OR HADN'T.
Now, are you going to tell me what happened to Trubble or not?
AND REALIZING HE WAS BEING UNGRACIOUS TO HIS HOST, MILO OPENED UP.
I can't find any of the people who live here. They appear to be, well, gone.
Gone? That can't be.

Well, something happened to them. That's why I'm here. To get Wendy's help. And find out what's going on.

MILO ROSE TO BEGIN SEARCHING THE HOUSE FOR ANY CLUE AS TO WHERE WENDY WAS.

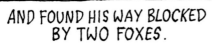

AND FOUND HIS WAY BLOCKED BY TWO FOXES.

Don't be scared, Milo. They're just our pets. You probably startled them when you rose so quickly.

Your family has pet foxes?

We're unique.

Does this one have a name?

Which.

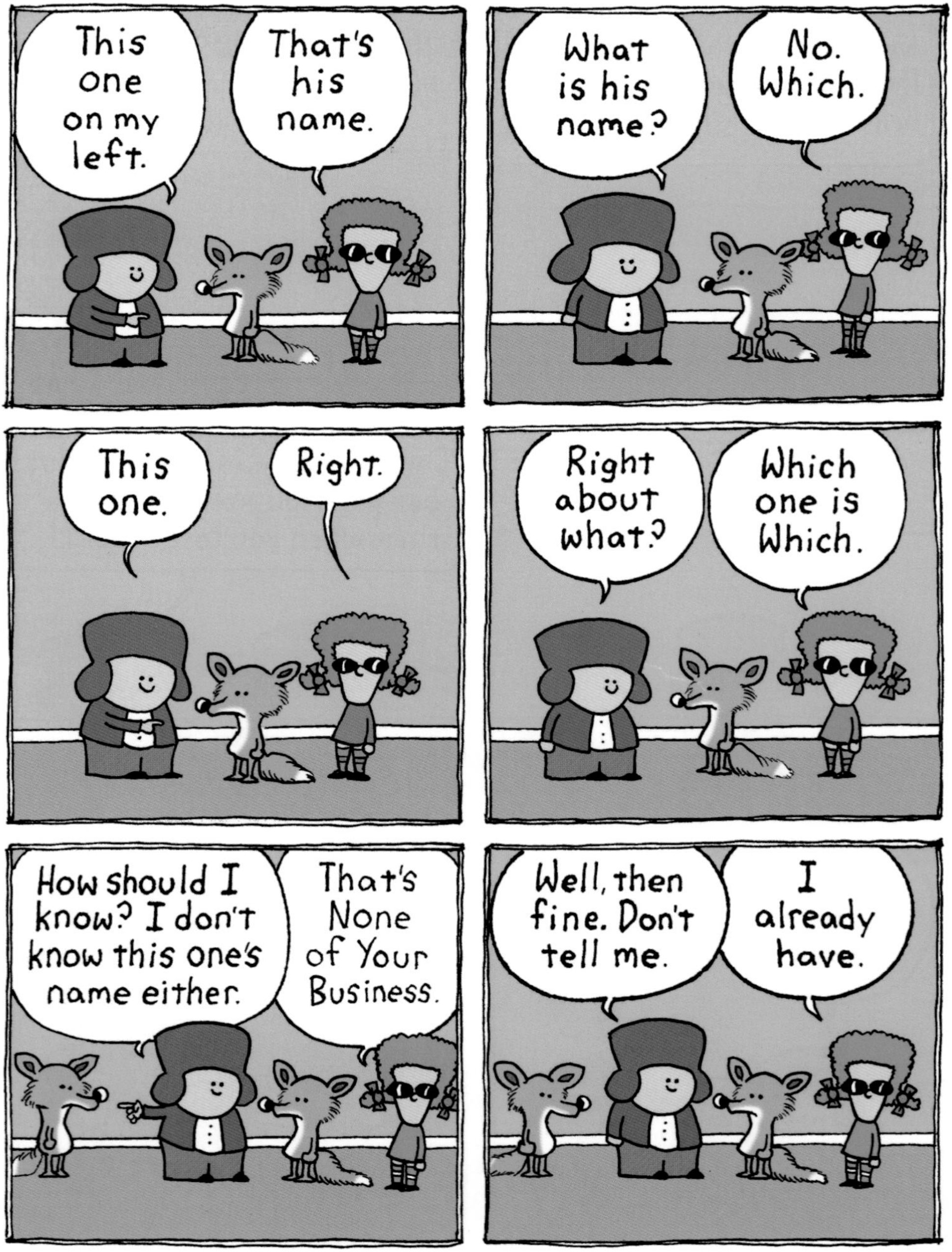
This one on my left.
That's his name.
What is his name?
No. Which.
This one.
Right.
Right about what?
Which one is Which.
How should I know? I don't know this one's name either.
That's None of Your Business.
Well, then fine. Don't tell me.
I already have.

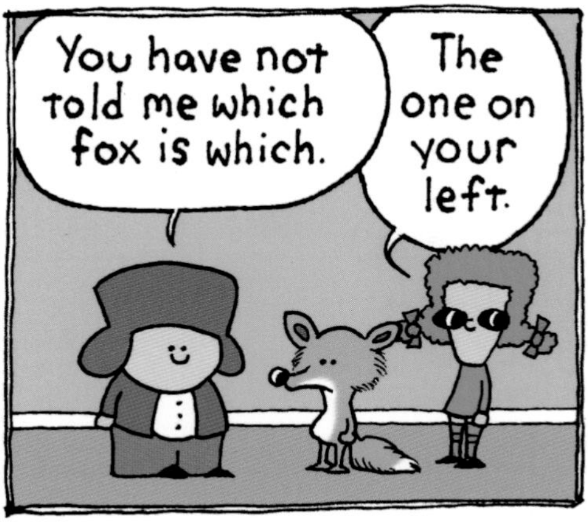
You have not told me which fox is which.
The one on your left.

IT WAS THE MOST MILO HAD EVER SPOKEN IN HIS LIFE. AND IT HAD GOTTEN HIM NOWHERE.

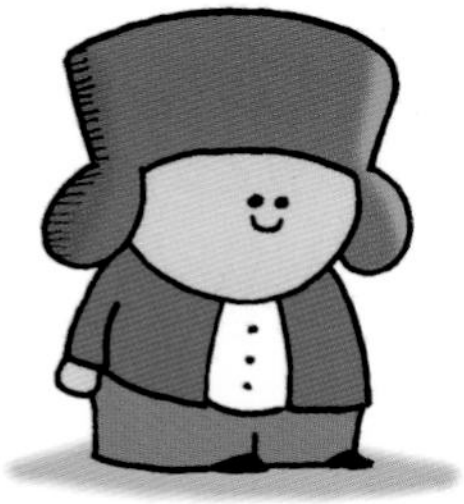

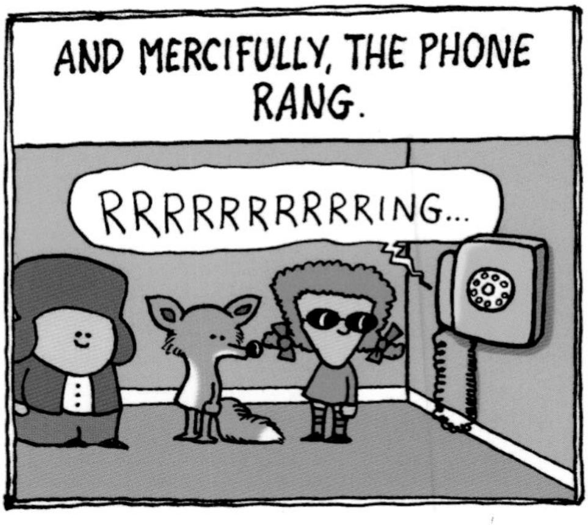
AND MERCIFULLY, THE PHONE RANG.
RRRRRRRRRRING...

CHAPTER SORRY

IN WHICH...

WE APOLOGIZE FOR THE HEADACHE WE CAUSED YOU IN THE LAST CHAPTER AND PROMISE TO DO BETTER

"BANANA BANANA," SAID THE VOICE THAT BLUEGIRL HEARD OVER THE PHONE.

Who's this?

Scribby Von Scrivener. Is this Wendy?

None of your business.

WHICH MADE ONE OF THE FOX'S EARS PERK UP.

Well, put Worried Willy on the line. Immediately.

Sorry. Don't know the guy.

BANANA PHONE

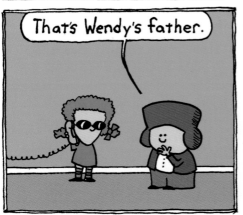

That's Wendy's father.

You listen to me. Willy used to hold the job I hold now. And I need his help. So give him this message.

83

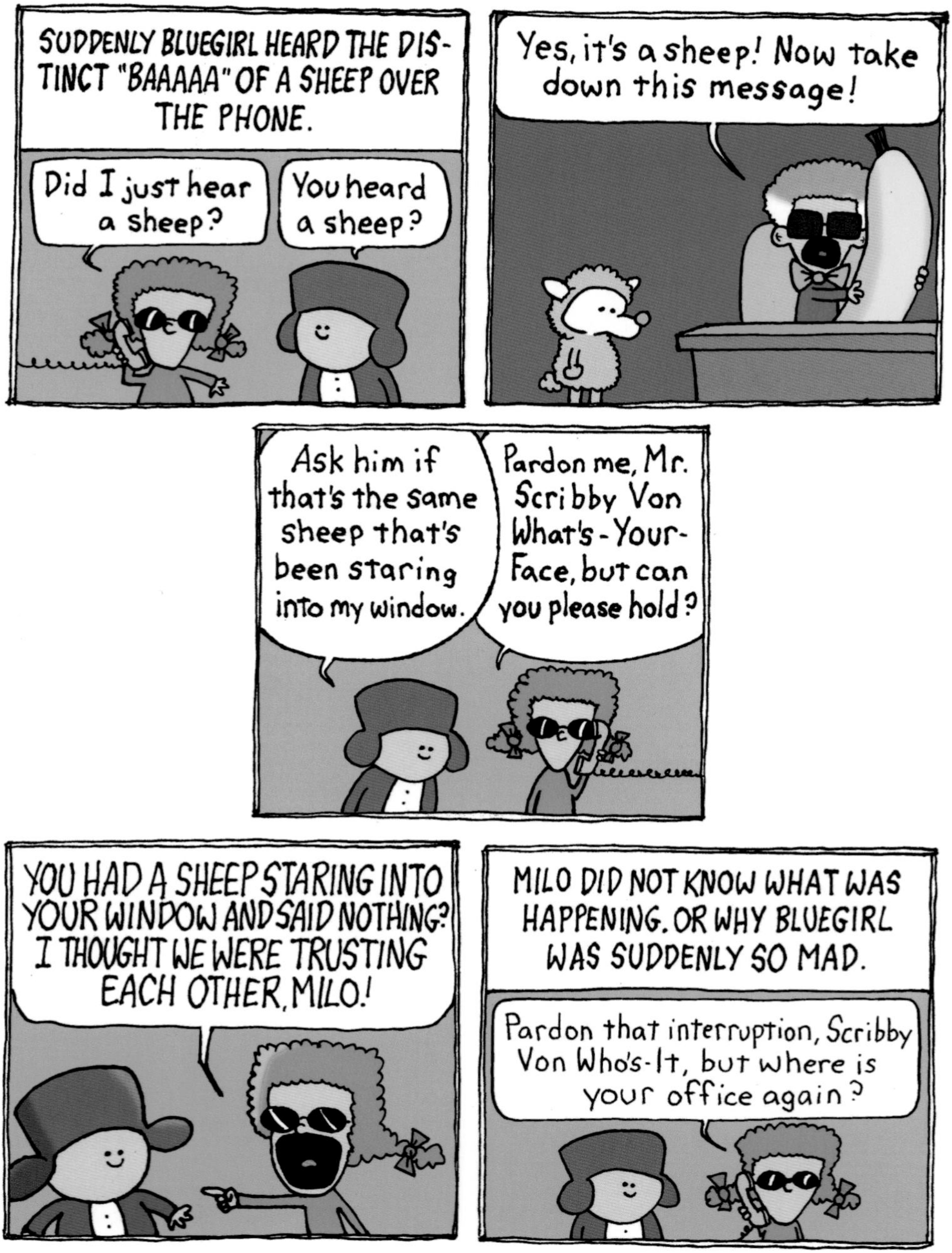
SUDDENLY BLUEGIRL HEARD THE DISTINCT "BAAAAA" OF A SHEEP OVER THE PHONE.
Did I just hear a sheep?
You heard a sheep?
Yes, it's a sheep! Now take down this message!
Ask him if that's the same sheep that's been staring into my window.
Pardon me, Mr. Scribby Von What's-Your-Face, but can you please hold?
YOU HAD A SHEEP STARING INTO YOUR WINDOW AND SAID NOTHING? I THOUGHT WE WERE TRUSTING EACH OTHER, MILO!
MILO DID NOT KNOW WHAT WAS HAPPENING. OR WHY BLUEGIRL WAS SUDDENLY SO MAD.
Pardon that interruption, Scribby Von Who's-It, but where is your office again?

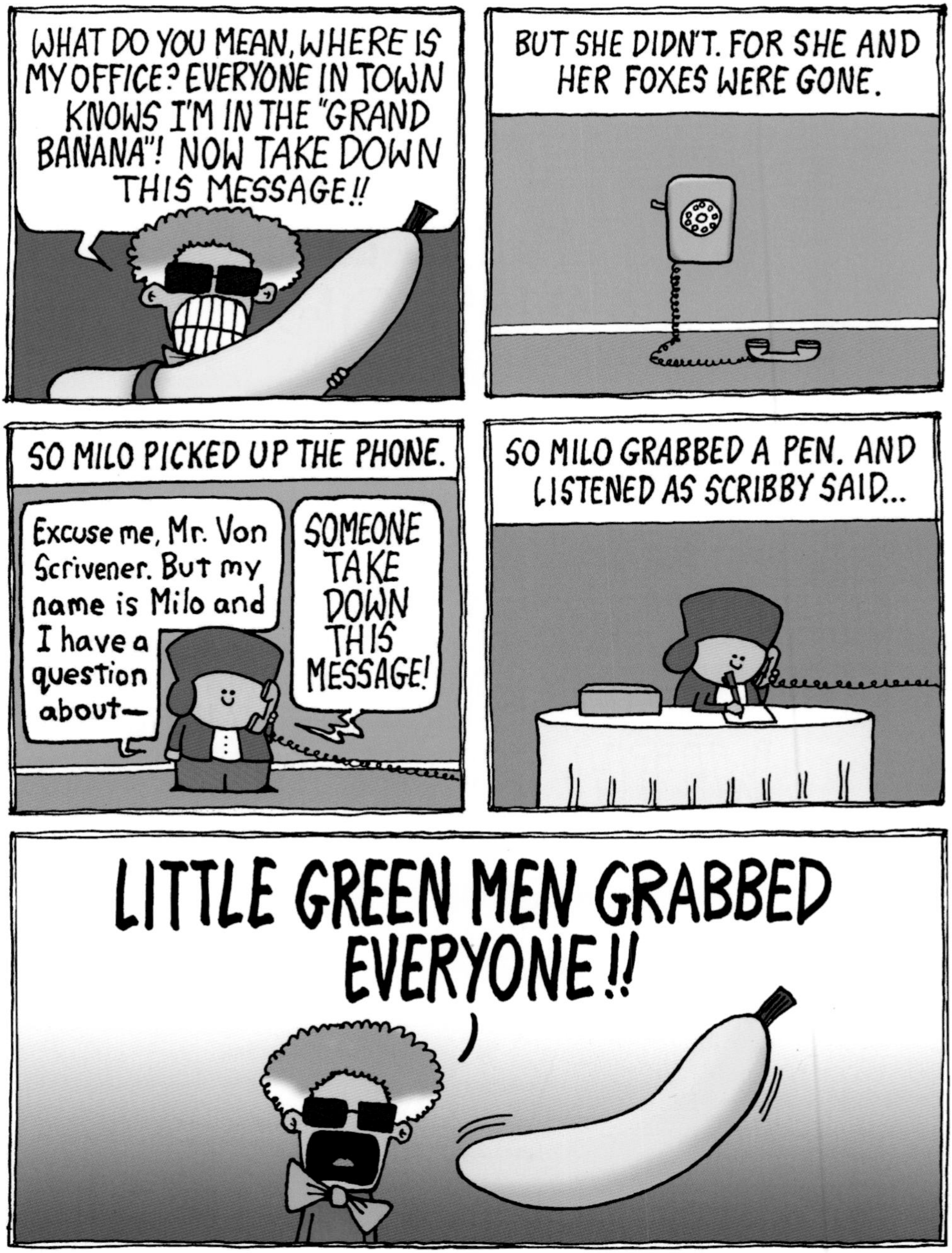
WHAT DO YOU MEAN, WHERE IS MY OFFICE? EVERYONE IN TOWN KNOWS I'M IN THE "GRAND BANANA"! NOW TAKE DOWN THIS MESSAGE!!
BUT SHE DIDN'T. FOR SHE AND HER FOXES WERE GONE.
SO MILO PICKED UP THE PHONE.
Excuse me, Mr. Von Scrivener. But my name is Milo and I have a question about—
SOMEONE TAKE DOWN THIS MESSAGE!
SO MILO GRABBED A PEN. AND LISTENED AS SCRIBBY SAID...
LITTLE GREEN MEN GRABBED EVERYONE!!

CHAPTER RAPTOR

IN WHICH...

THERE ARE NO RAPTORS, BUT NOT MUCH RHYMES WITH "CHAPTER"

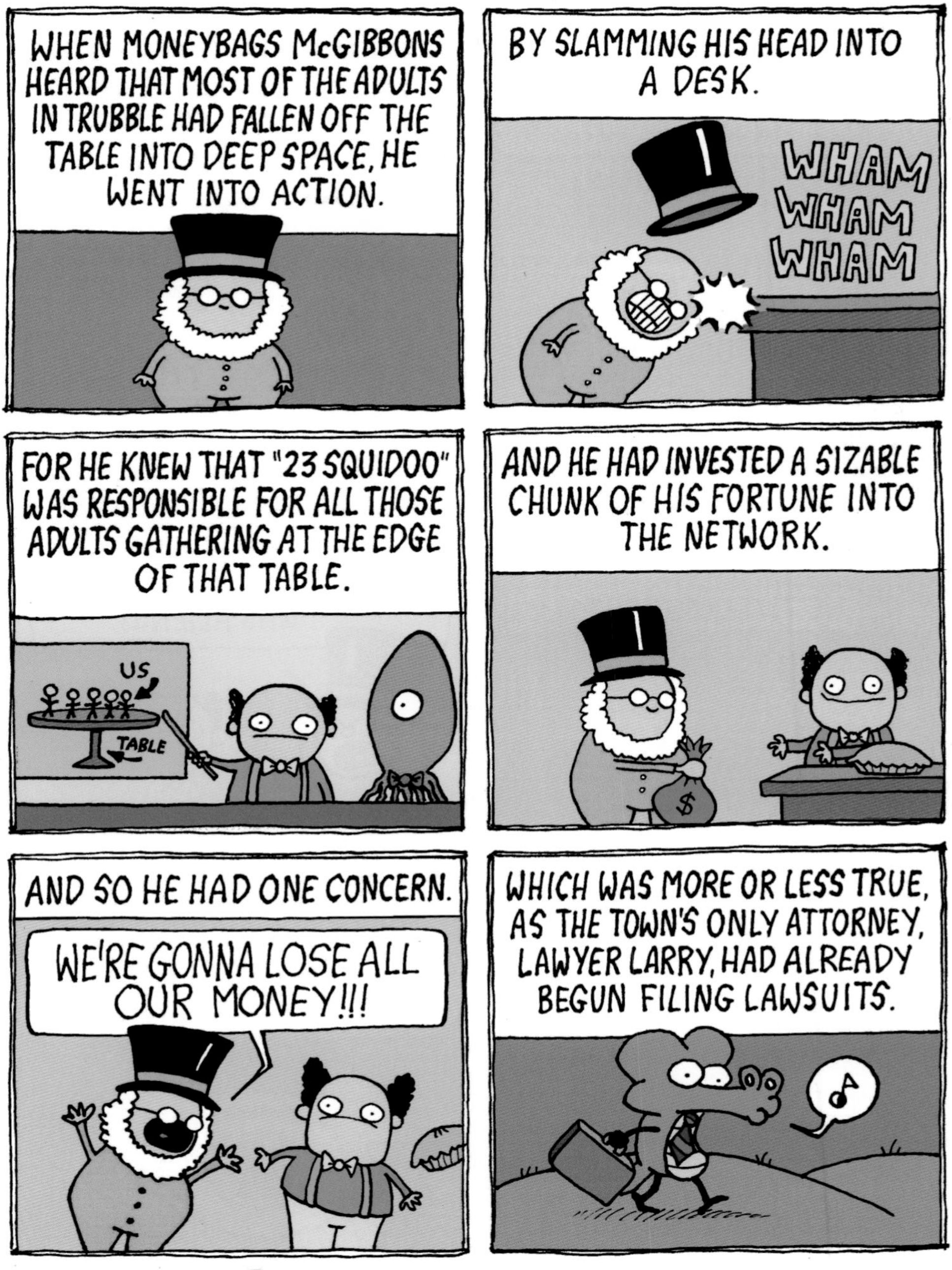
WHEN MONEYBAGS McGIBBONS HEARD THAT MOST OF THE ADULTS IN TRUBBLE HAD FALLEN OFF THE TABLE INTO DEEP SPACE, HE WENT INTO ACTION.
BY SLAMMING HIS HEAD INTO A DESK.
WHAM
WHAM
WHAM
FOR HE KNEW THAT "23 SQUIDOO" WAS RESPONSIBLE FOR ALL THOSE ADULTS GATHERING AT THE EDGE OF THAT TABLE.
US
TABLE
AND HE HAD INVESTED A SIZABLE CHUNK OF HIS FORTUNE INTO THE NETWORK.
$
AND SO HE HAD ONE CONCERN.
WE'RE GONNA LOSE ALL OUR MONEY!!!
WHICH WAS MORE OR LESS TRUE, AS THE TOWN'S ONLY ATTORNEY, LAWYER LARRY, HAD ALREADY BEGUN FILING LAWSUITS.

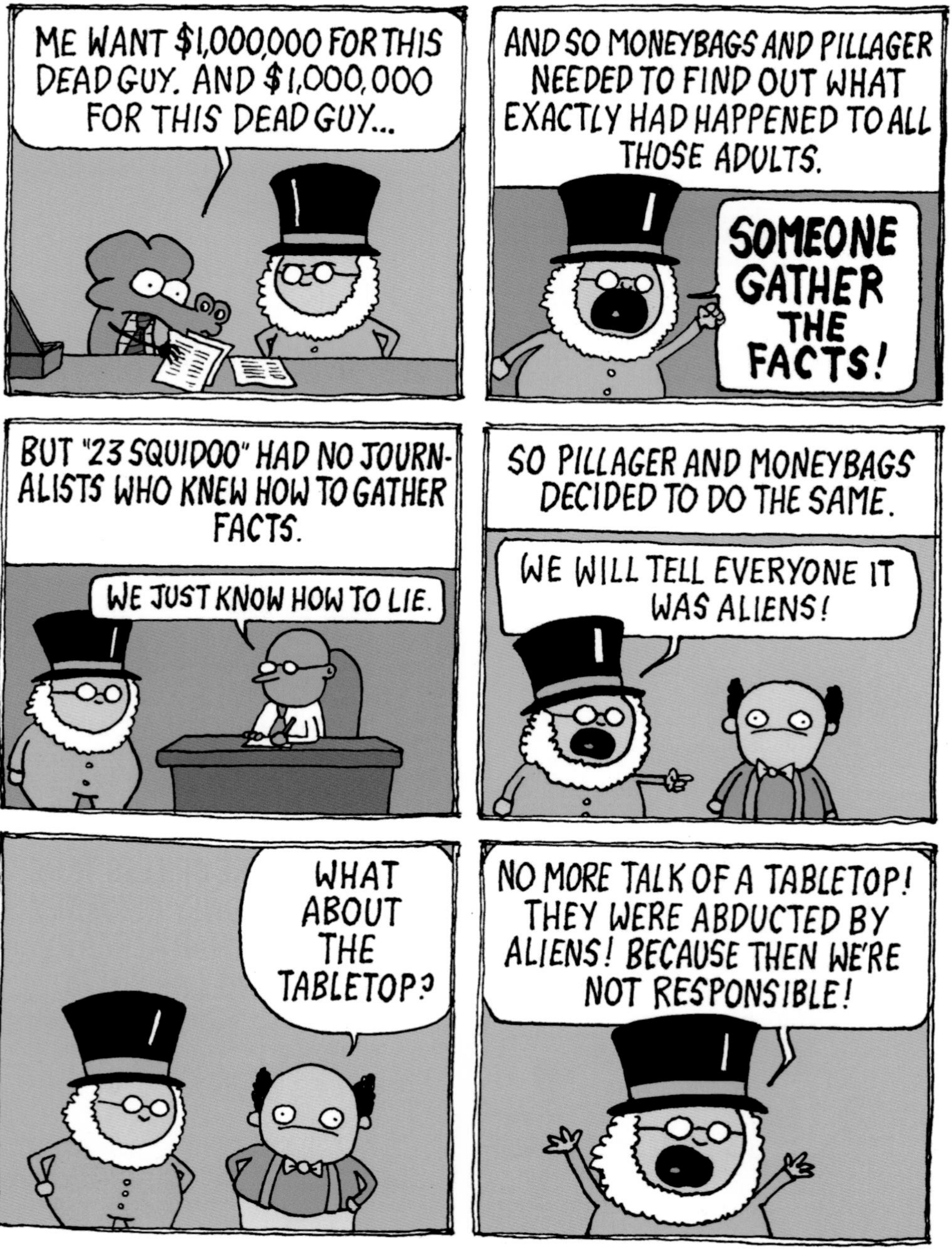
ME WANT $1,000,000 FOR THIS DEAD GUY. AND $1,000,000 FOR THIS DEAD GUY...
AND SO MONEYBAGS AND PILLAGER NEEDED TO FIND OUT WHAT EXACTLY HAD HAPPENED TO ALL THOSE ADULTS.
SOMEONE GATHER THE FACTS!
BUT "23 SQUIDOO" HAD NO JOURNALISTS WHO KNEW HOW TO GATHER FACTS.
WE JUST KNOW HOW TO LIE.
SO PILLAGER AND MONEYBAGS DECIDED TO DO THE SAME.
WE WILL TELL EVERYONE IT WAS ALIENS!
WHAT ABOUT THE TABLETOP?
NO MORE TALK OF A TABLETOP! THEY WERE ABDUCTED BY ALIENS! BECAUSE THEN WE'RE NOT RESPONSIBLE!

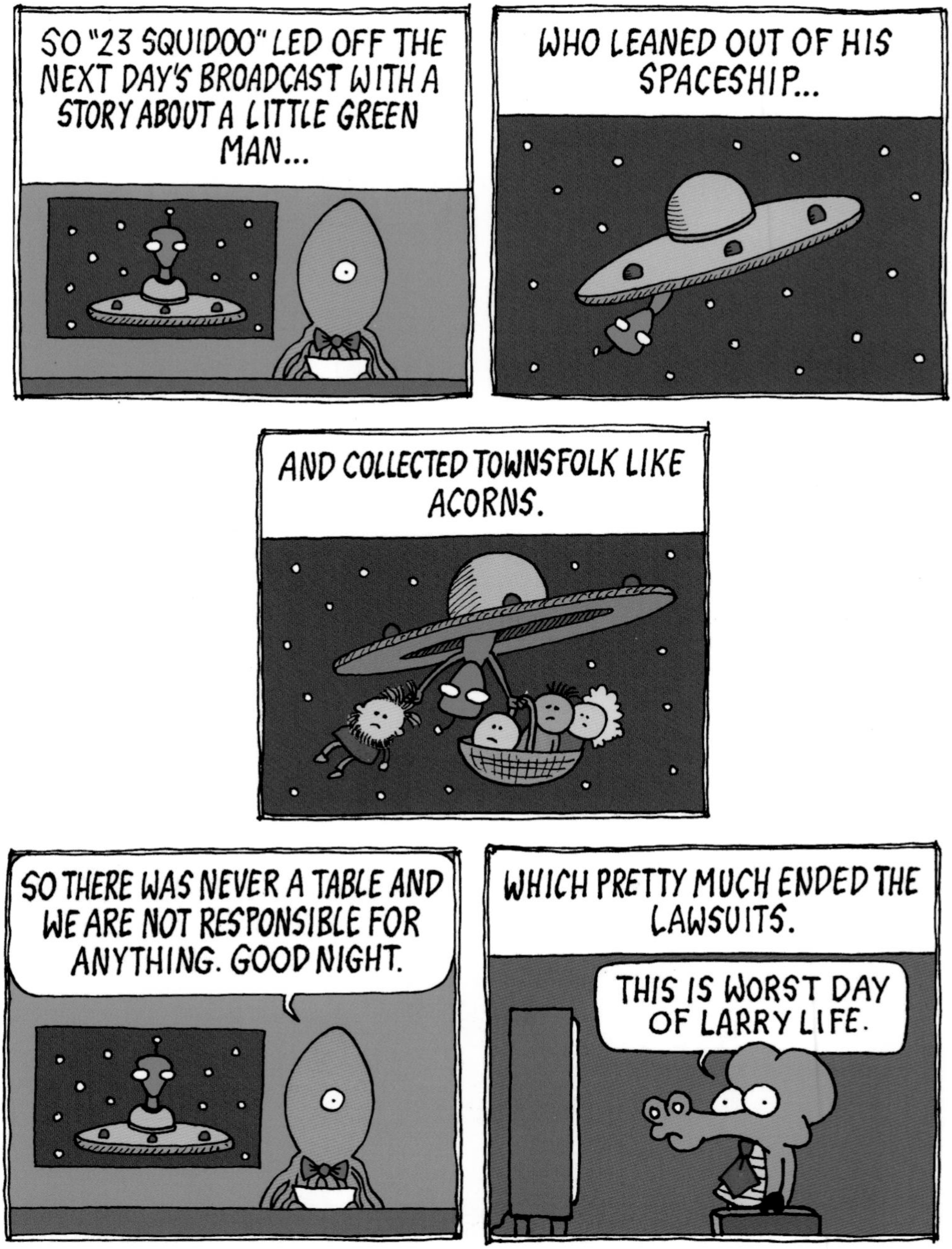
SO "23 SQUIDOO" LED OFF THE NEXT DAY'S BROADCAST WITH A STORY ABOUT A LITTLE GREEN MAN...
WHO LEANED OUT OF HIS SPACESHIP...
AND COLLECTED TOWNSFOLK LIKE ACORNS.
SO THERE WAS NEVER A TABLE AND WE ARE NOT RESPONSIBLE FOR ANYTHING. GOOD NIGHT.
WHICH PRETTY MUCH ENDED THE LAWSUITS.
THIS IS WORST DAY OF LARRY LIFE.

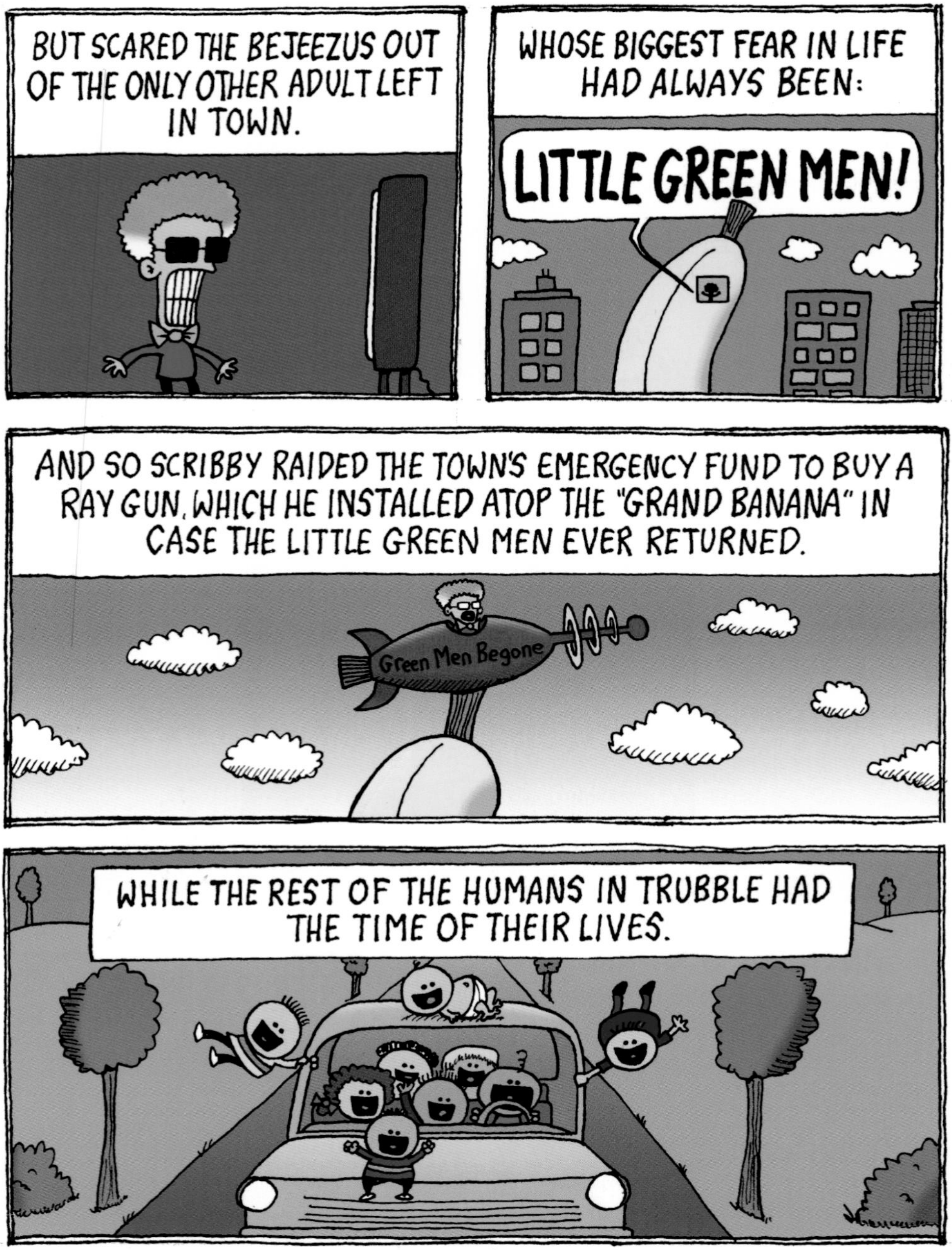
BUT SCARED THE BEJEEZUS OUT OF THE ONLY OTHER ADULT LEFT IN TOWN.
WHOSE BIGGEST FEAR IN LIFE HAD ALWAYS BEEN:
LITTLE GREEN MEN!
AND SO SCRIBBY RAIDED THE TOWN'S EMERGENCY FUND TO BUY A RAY GUN, WHICH HE INSTALLED ATOP THE "GRAND BANANA" IN CASE THE LITTLE GREEN MEN EVER RETURNED.
Green Men Begone
WHILE THE REST OF THE HUMANS IN TRUBBLE HAD THE TIME OF THEIR LIVES.

CHAP

IN WHICH...

WE GET SO LAZY WE DON'T EVEN WRITE OUT THE WHOLE WORD

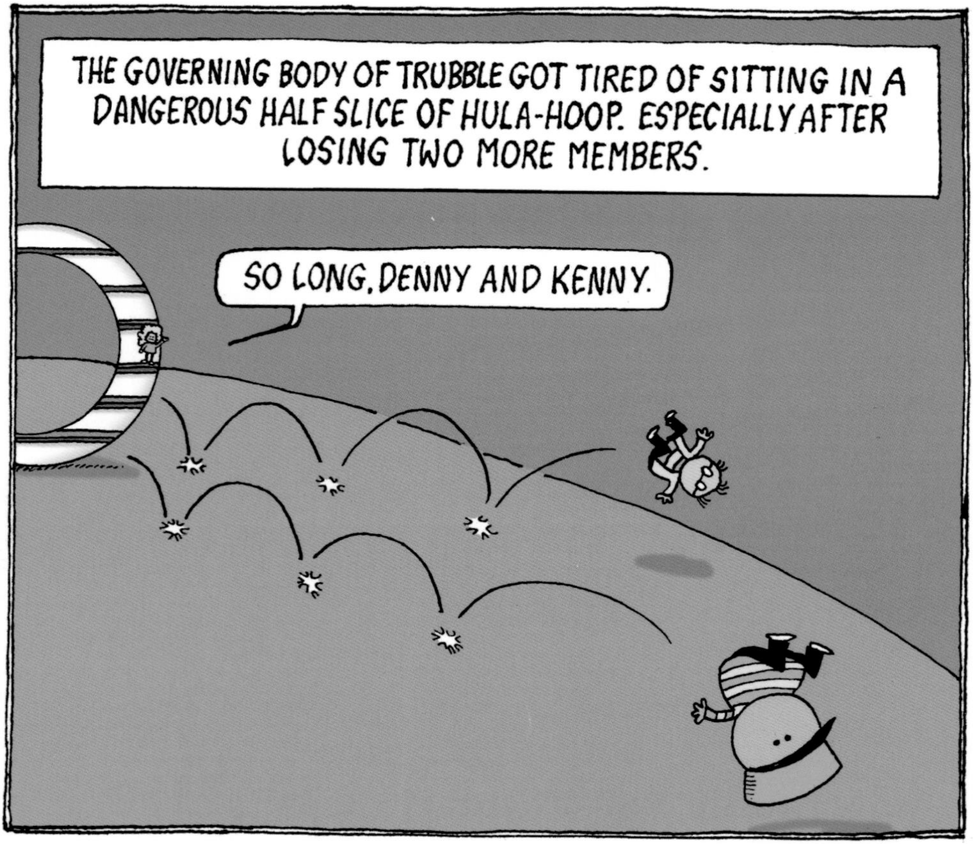
THE GOVERNING BODY OF TRUBBLE GOT TIRED OF SITTING IN A DANGEROUS HALF SLICE OF HULA-HOOP. ESPECIALLY AFTER LOSING TWO MORE MEMBERS.
SO LONG, DENNY AND KENNY.

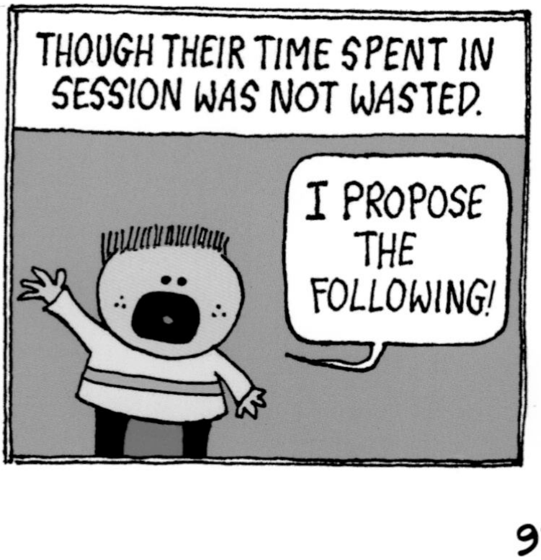
THOUGH THEIR TIME SPENT IN SESSION WAS NOT WASTED.
I PROPOSE THE FOLLOWING!

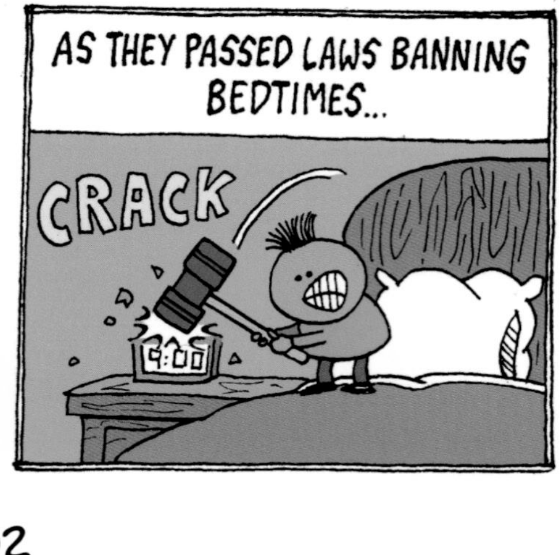
AS THEY PASSED LAWS BANNING BEDTIMES...
CRACK
9:00

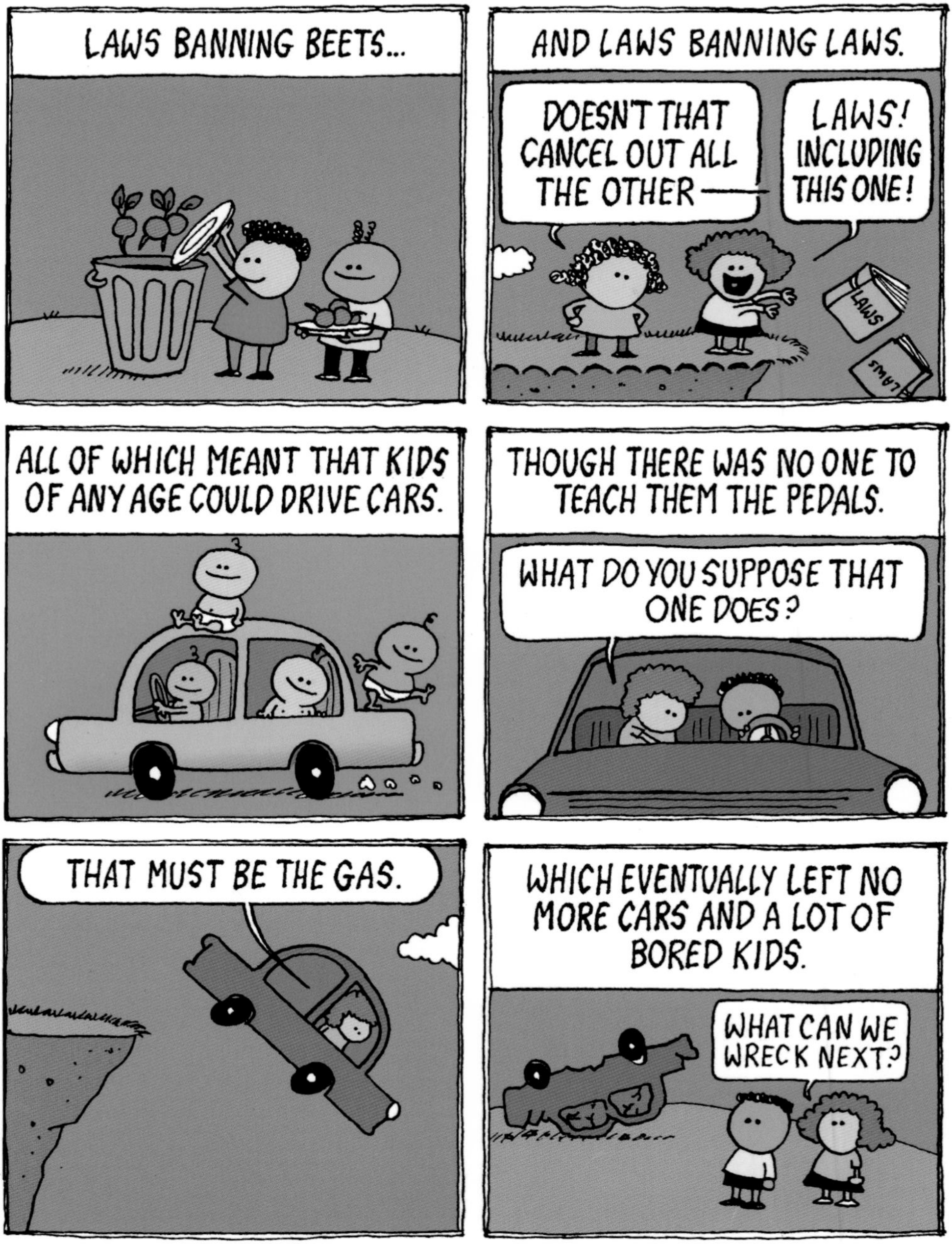
LAWS BANNING BEETS...
AND LAWS BANNING LAWS.
DOESN'T THAT CANCEL OUT ALL THE OTHER —
LAWS! INCLUDING THIS ONE!
LAWS
LAWS
ALL OF WHICH MEANT THAT KIDS OF ANY AGE COULD DRIVE CARS.
THOUGH THERE WAS NO ONE TO TEACH THEM THE PEDALS.
WHAT DO YOU SUPPOSE THAT ONE DOES?
THAT MUST BE THE GAS.
WHICH EVENTUALLY LEFT NO MORE CARS AND A LOT OF BORED KIDS.
WHAT CAN WE WRECK NEXT?

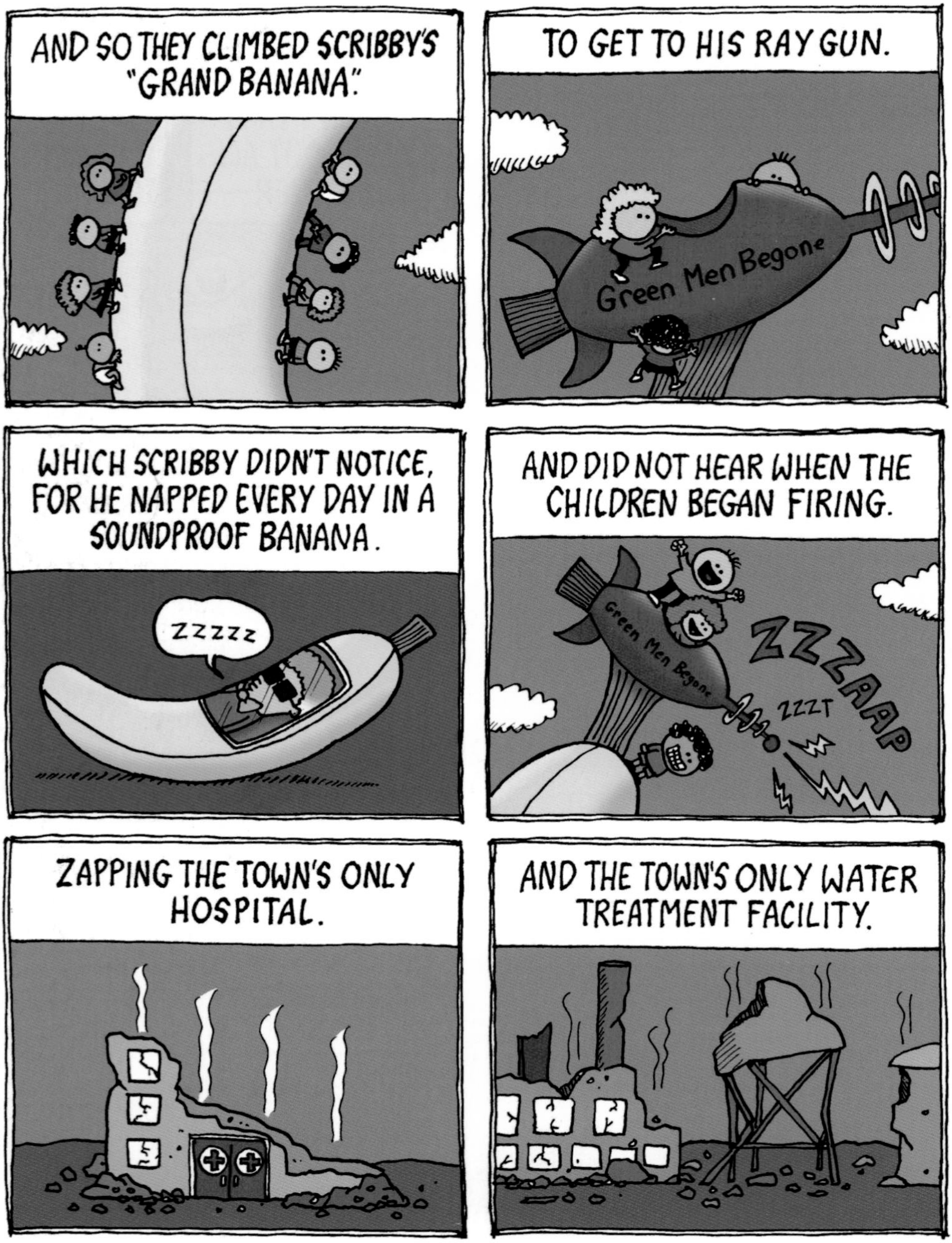
AND SO THEY CLIMBED SCRIBBY'S "GRAND BANANA."
TO GET TO HIS RAY GUN.
Green Men Begone
WHICH SCRIBBY DIDN'T NOTICE, FOR HE NAPPED EVERY DAY IN A SOUNDPROOF BANANA.
ZZZZZ
AND DID NOT HEAR WHEN THE CHILDREN BEGAN FIRING.
Green Men Begone
ZZZAAP
ZZZT
ZAPPING THE TOWN'S ONLY HOSPITAL.
AND THE TOWN'S ONLY WATER TREATMENT FACILITY.

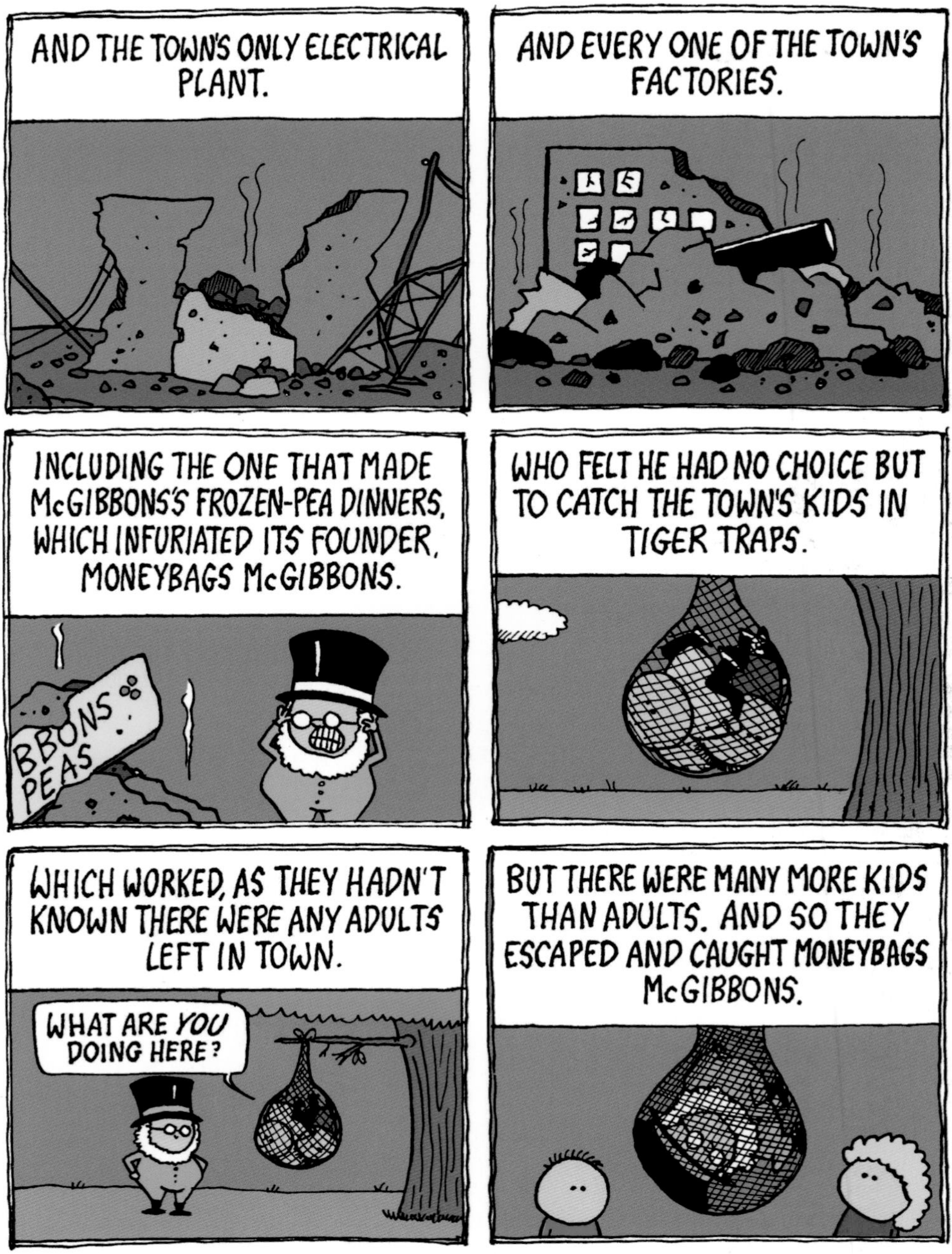
AND THE TOWN'S ONLY ELECTRICAL PLANT.
AND EVERY ONE OF THE TOWN'S FACTORIES.
INCLUDING THE ONE THAT MADE McGIBBONS'S FROZEN-PEA DINNERS, WHICH INFURIATED ITS FOUNDER, MONEYBAGS McGIBBONS.
BBONS
PEAS
WHO FELT HE HAD NO CHOICE BUT TO CATCH THE TOWN'S KIDS IN TIGER TRAPS.
WHICH WORKED, AS THEY HADN'T KNOWN THERE WERE ANY ADULTS LEFT IN TOWN.
WHAT ARE *YOU* DOING HERE?
BUT THERE WERE MANY MORE KIDS THAN ADULTS. AND SO THEY ESCAPED AND CAUGHT MONEYBAGS McGIBBONS.

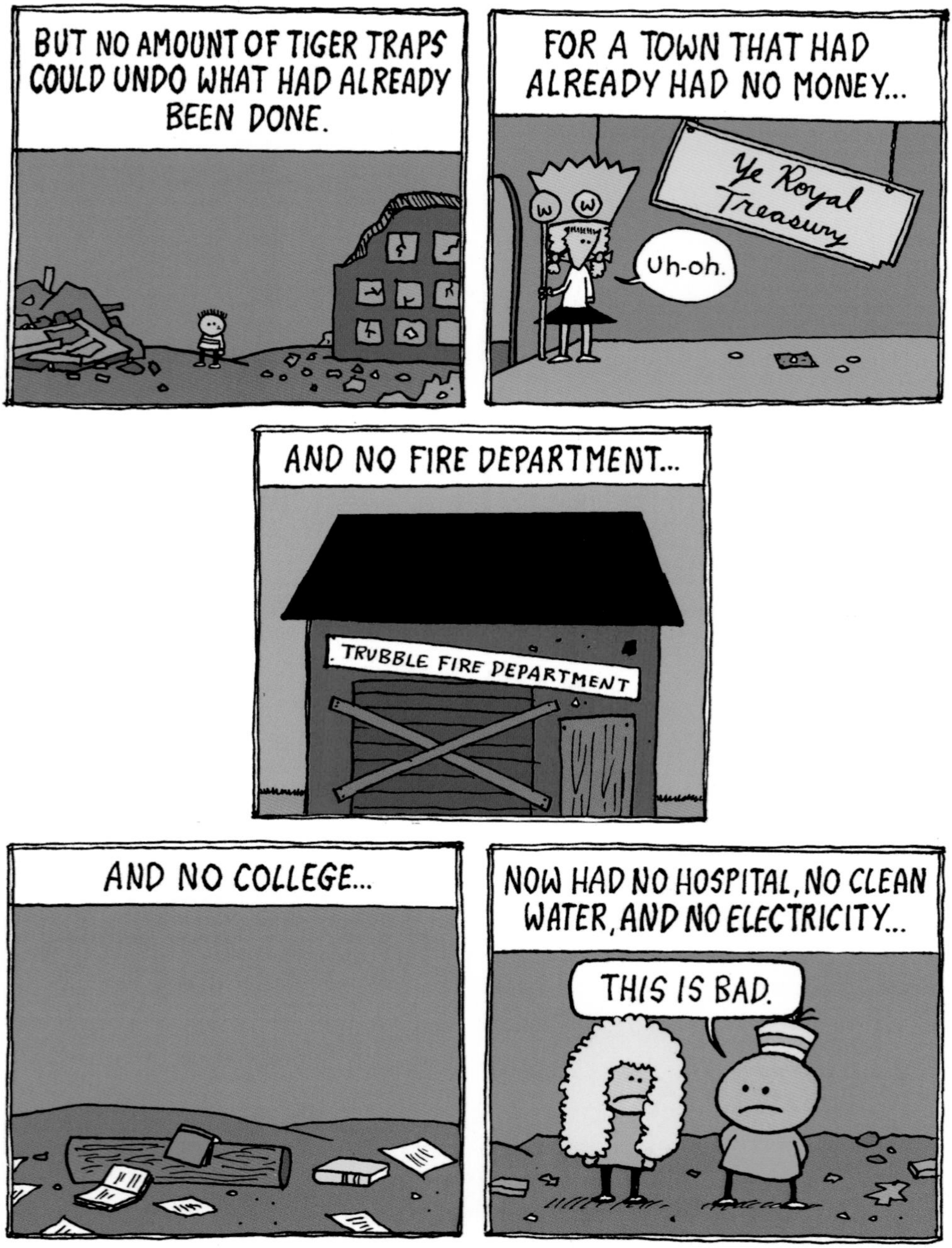
BUT NO AMOUNT OF TIGER TRAPS COULD UNDO WHAT HAD ALREADY BEEN DONE.
FOR A TOWN THAT HAD ALREADY HAD NO MONEY...
Ye Royal Treasury
Uh-oh.
AND NO FIRE DEPARTMENT...
TRUBBLE FIRE DEPARTMENT
AND NO COLLEGE...
NOW HAD NO HOSPITAL, NO CLEAN WATER, AND NO ELECTRICITY...
THIS IS BAD.

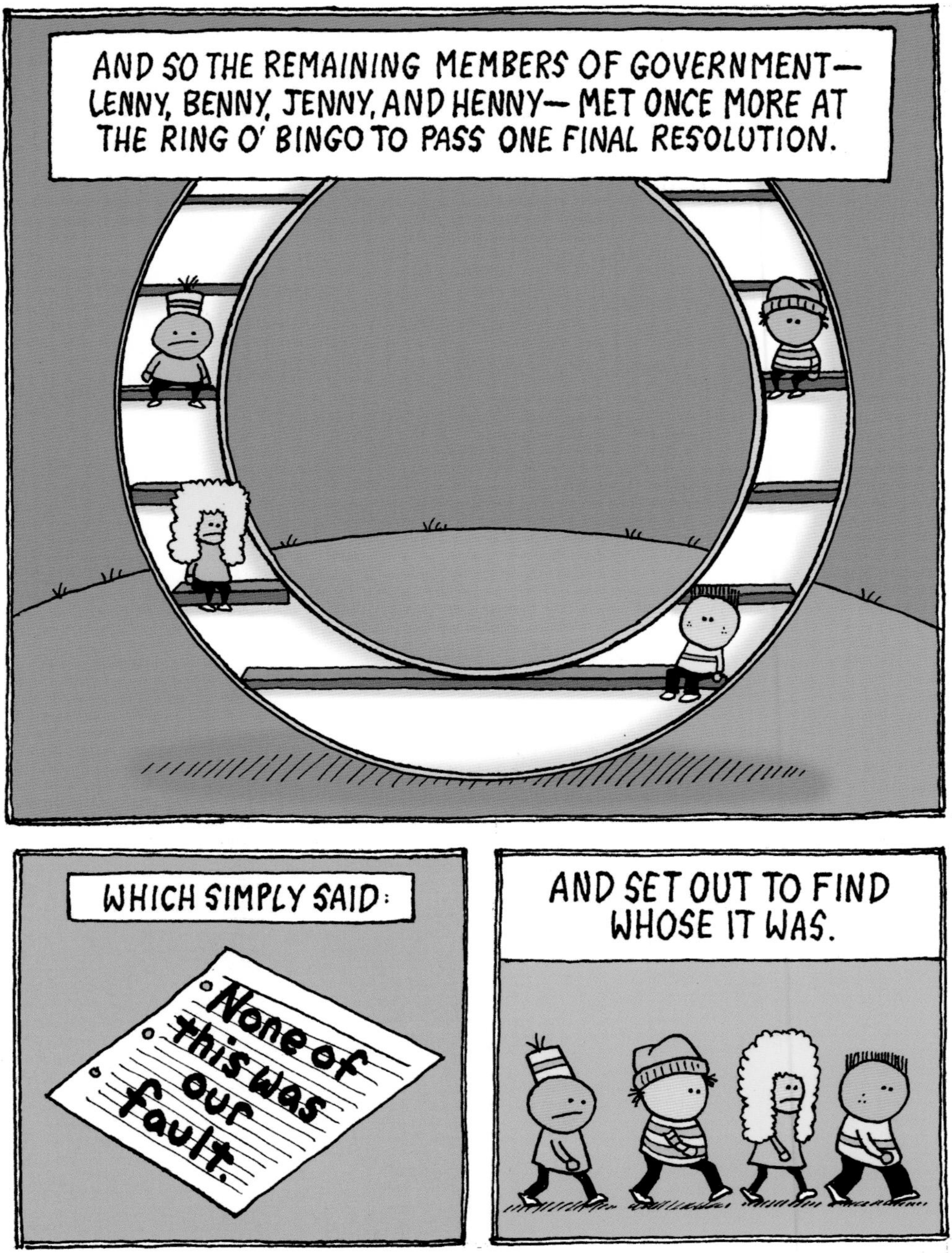
AND SO THE REMAINING MEMBERS OF GOVERNMENT— LENNY, BENNY, JENNY, AND HENNY— MET ONCE MORE AT THE RING O' BINGO TO PASS ONE FINAL RESOLUTION.
WHICH SIMPLY SAID:
None of this was our fault.
AND SET OUT TO FIND WHOSE IT WAS.

CHAPTER SOMEWHERE AROUND FIFTEEN

IN WHICH...

WE GUESS WHAT CHAPTER NUMBER THIS MIGHT BE

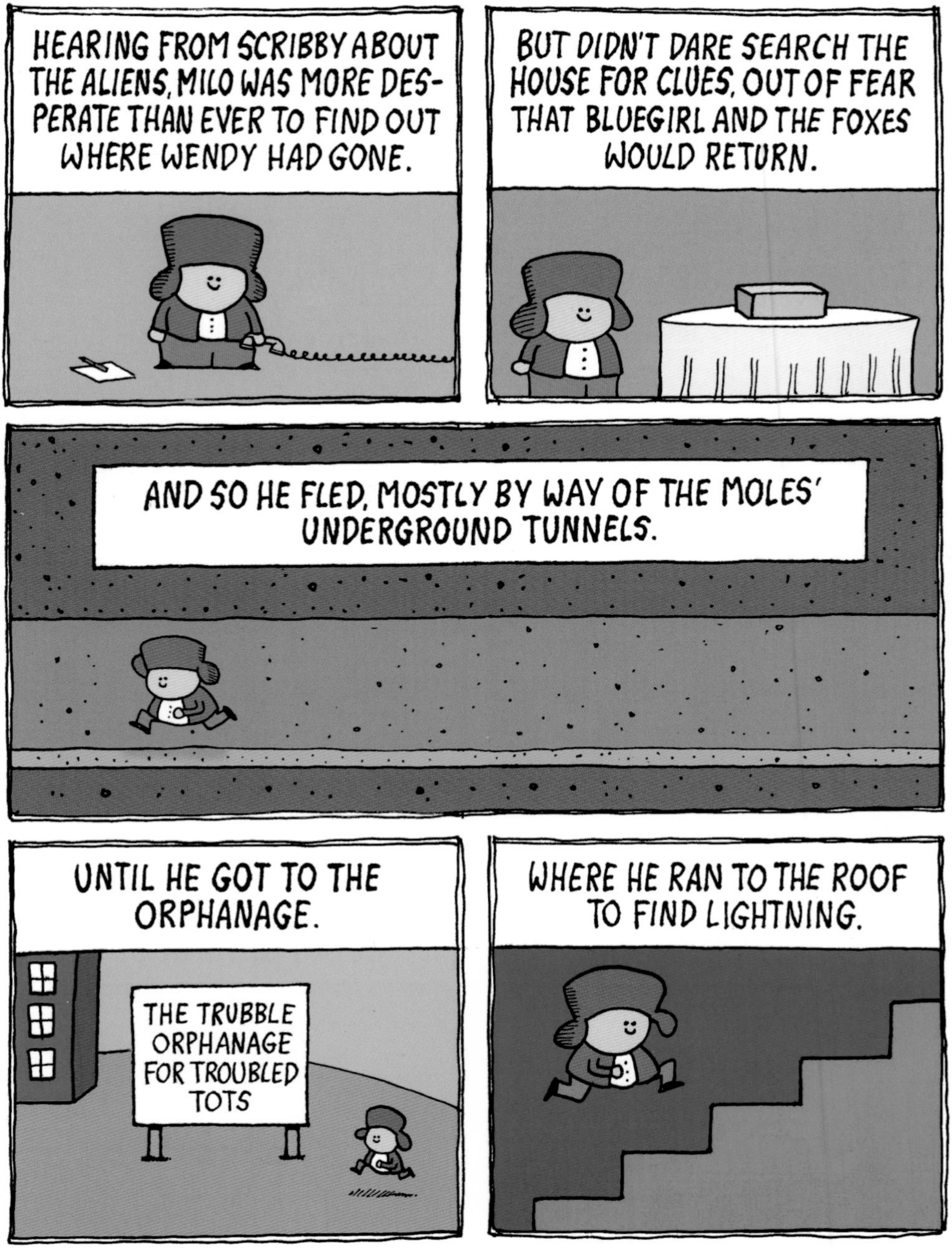
HEARING FROM SCRIBBY ABOUT THE ALIENS, MILO WAS MORE DES-PERATE THAN EVER TO FIND OUT WHERE WENDY HAD GONE.
BUT DIDN'T DARE SEARCH THE HOUSE FOR CLUES, OUT OF FEAR THAT BLUEGIRL AND THE FOXES WOULD RETURN.
AND SO HE FLED, MOSTLY BY WAY OF THE MOLES' UNDERGROUND TUNNELS.
UNTIL HE GOT TO THE ORPHANAGE.
THE TRUBBLE ORPHANAGE FOR TROUBLED TOTS
WHERE HE RAN TO THE ROOF TO FIND LIGHTNING.

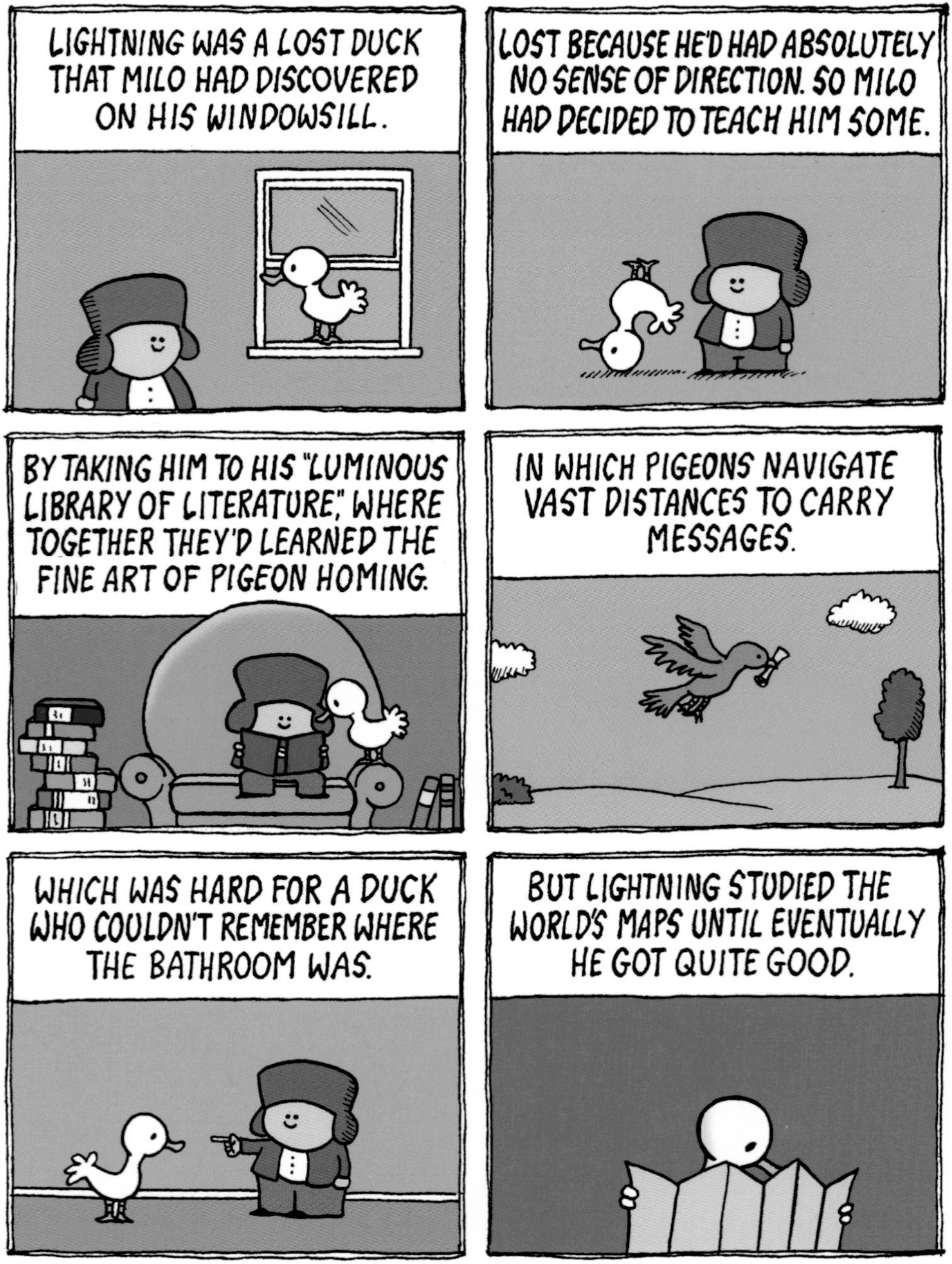
LIGHTNING WAS A LOST DUCK THAT MILO HAD DISCOVERED ON HIS WINDOWSILL.
LOST BECAUSE HE'D HAD ABSOLUTELY NO SENSE OF DIRECTION. SO MILO HAD DECIDED TO TEACH HIM SOME.
BY TAKING HIM TO HIS "LUMINOUS LIBRARY OF LITERATURE," WHERE TOGETHER THEY'D LEARNED THE FINE ART OF PIGEON HOMING.
IN WHICH PIGEONS NAVIGATE VAST DISTANCES TO CARRY MESSAGES.
WHICH WAS HARD FOR A DUCK WHO COULDN'T REMEMBER WHERE THE BATHROOM WAS.
BUT LIGHTNING STUDIED THE WORLD'S MAPS UNTIL EVENTUALLY HE GOT QUITE GOOD.

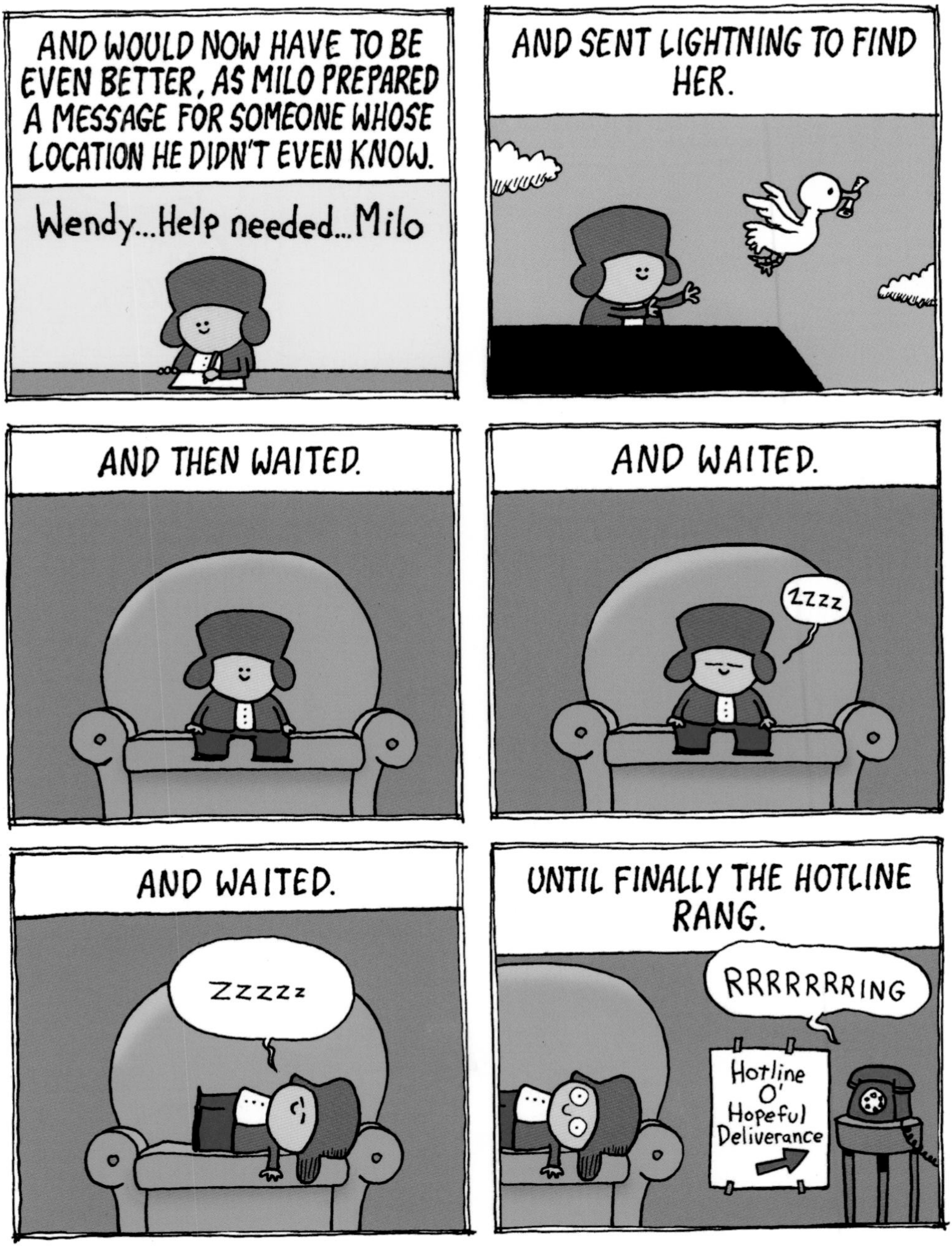
AND WOULD NOW HAVE TO BE EVEN BETTER, AS MILO PREPARED A MESSAGE FOR SOMEONE WHOSE LOCATION HE DIDN'T EVEN KNOW.
Wendy...Help needed...Milo
AND SENT LIGHTNING TO FIND HER.
AND THEN WAITED.
AND WAITED.
Zzzz
AND WAITED.
Zzzzz
UNTIL FINALLY THE HOTLINE RANG.
RRRRRRRING
Hotline O' Hopeful Deliverance

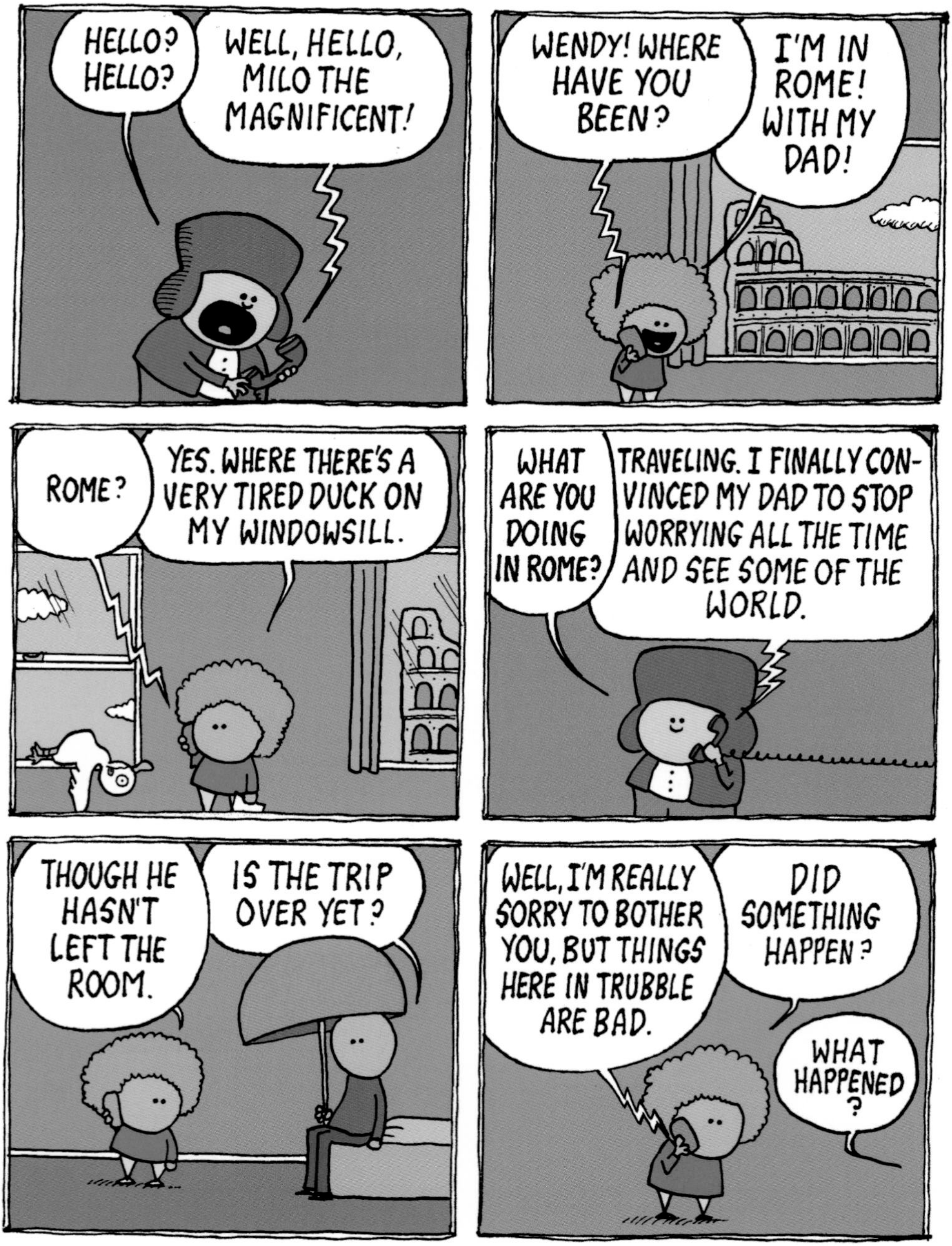
HELLO? HELLO?
WELL, HELLO, MILO THE MAGNIFICENT!
WENDY! WHERE HAVE YOU BEEN?
I'M IN ROME! WITH MY DAD!
ROME?
YES. WHERE THERE'S A VERY TIRED DUCK ON MY WINDOWSILL.
WHAT ARE YOU DOING IN ROME?
TRAVELING. I FINALLY CONVINCED MY DAD TO STOP WORRYING ALL THE TIME AND SEE SOME OF THE WORLD.
THOUGH HE HASN'T LEFT THE ROOM.
IS THE TRIP OVER YET?
WELL, I'M REALLY SORRY TO BOTHER YOU, BUT THINGS HERE IN TRUBBLE ARE BAD.
DID SOMETHING HAPPEN?
WHAT HAPPENED?

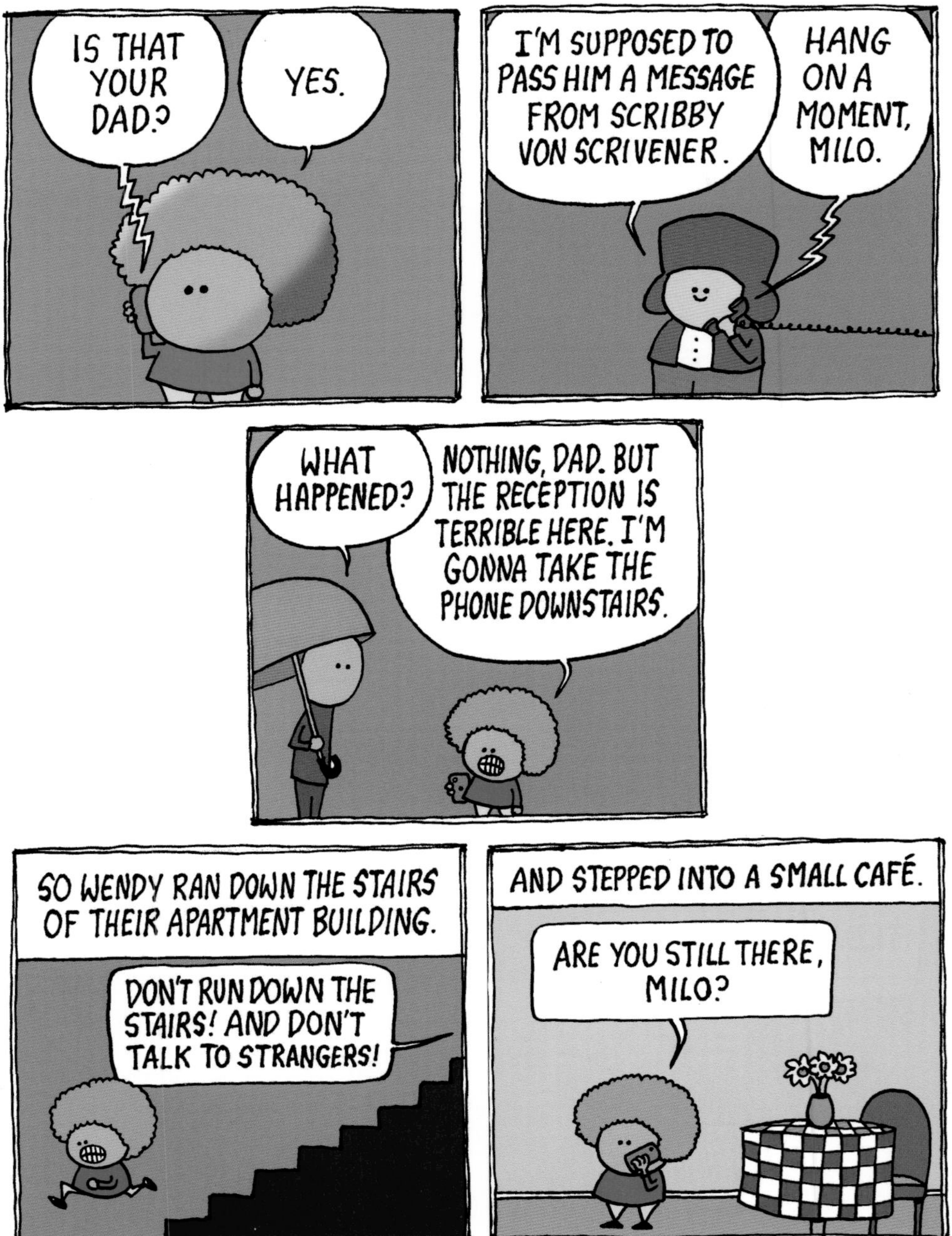
IS THAT YOUR DAD?
YES.
I'M SUPPOSED TO PASS HIM A MESSAGE FROM SCRIBBY VON SCRIVENER.
HANG ON A MOMENT, MILO.
WHAT HAPPENED?
NOTHING, DAD. BUT THE RECEPTION IS TERRIBLE HERE. I'M GONNA TAKE THE PHONE DOWNSTAIRS.
SO WENDY RAN DOWN THE STAIRS OF THEIR APARTMENT BUILDING.
DON'T RUN DOWN THE STAIRS! AND DON'T TALK TO STRANGERS!
AND STEPPED INTO A SMALL CAFÉ.
ARE YOU STILL THERE, MILO?

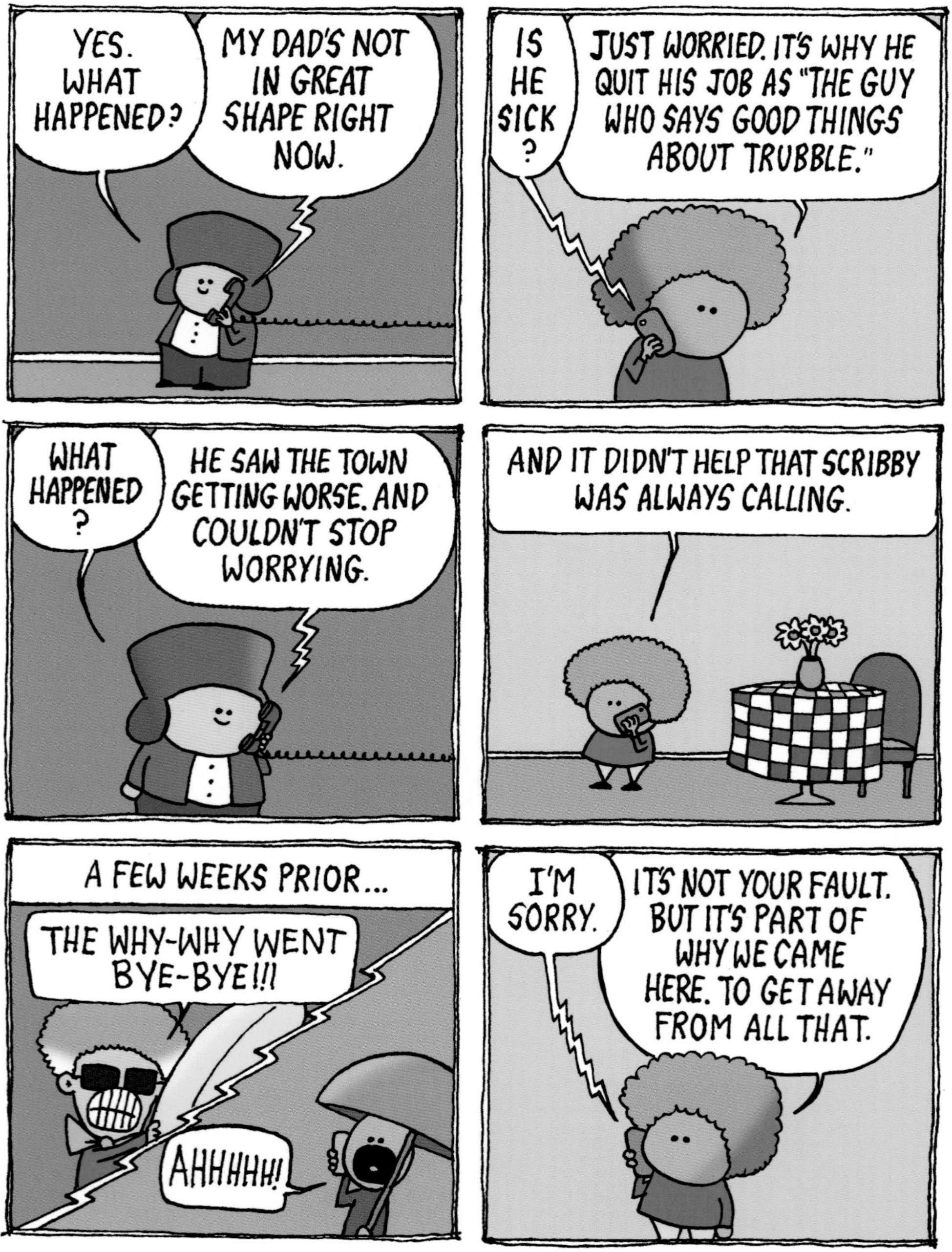
YES. WHAT HAPPENED?
MY DAD'S NOT IN GREAT SHAPE RIGHT NOW.
IS HE SICK?
JUST WORRIED. IT'S WHY HE QUIT HIS JOB AS "THE GUY WHO SAYS GOOD THINGS ABOUT TRUBBLE."
WHAT HAPPENED?
HE SAW THE TOWN GETTING WORSE. AND COULDN'T STOP WORRYING.
AND IT DIDN'T HELP THAT SCRIBBY WAS ALWAYS CALLING.
A FEW WEEKS PRIOR...
THE WHY-WHY WENT BYE-BYE!!!
AHHHHH!
I'M SORRY.
IT'S NOT YOUR FAULT. BUT IT'S PART OF WHY WE CAME HERE. TO GET AWAY FROM ALL THAT.

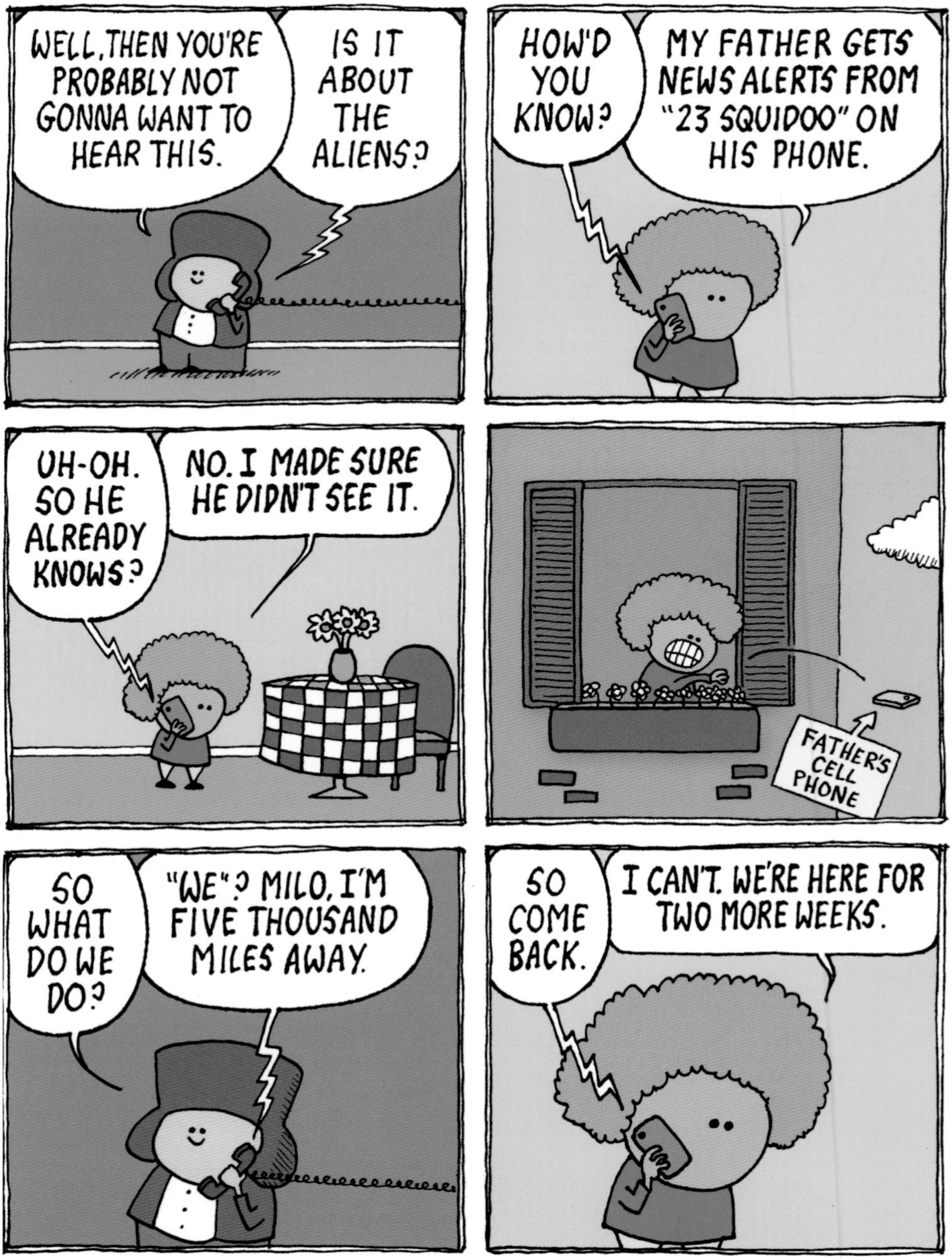
WELL, THEN YOU'RE PROBABLY NOT GONNA WANT TO HEAR THIS.
IS IT ABOUT THE ALIENS?
HOW'D YOU KNOW?
MY FATHER GETS NEWS ALERTS FROM "23 SQUIDOO" ON HIS PHONE.
UH-OH. SO HE ALREADY KNOWS?
NO. I MADE SURE HE DIDN'T SEE IT.
FATHER'S CELL PHONE
SO WHAT DO WE DO?
"WE"? MILO, I'M FIVE THOUSAND MILES AWAY.
SO COME BACK.
I CAN'T. WE'RE HERE FOR TWO MORE WEEKS.

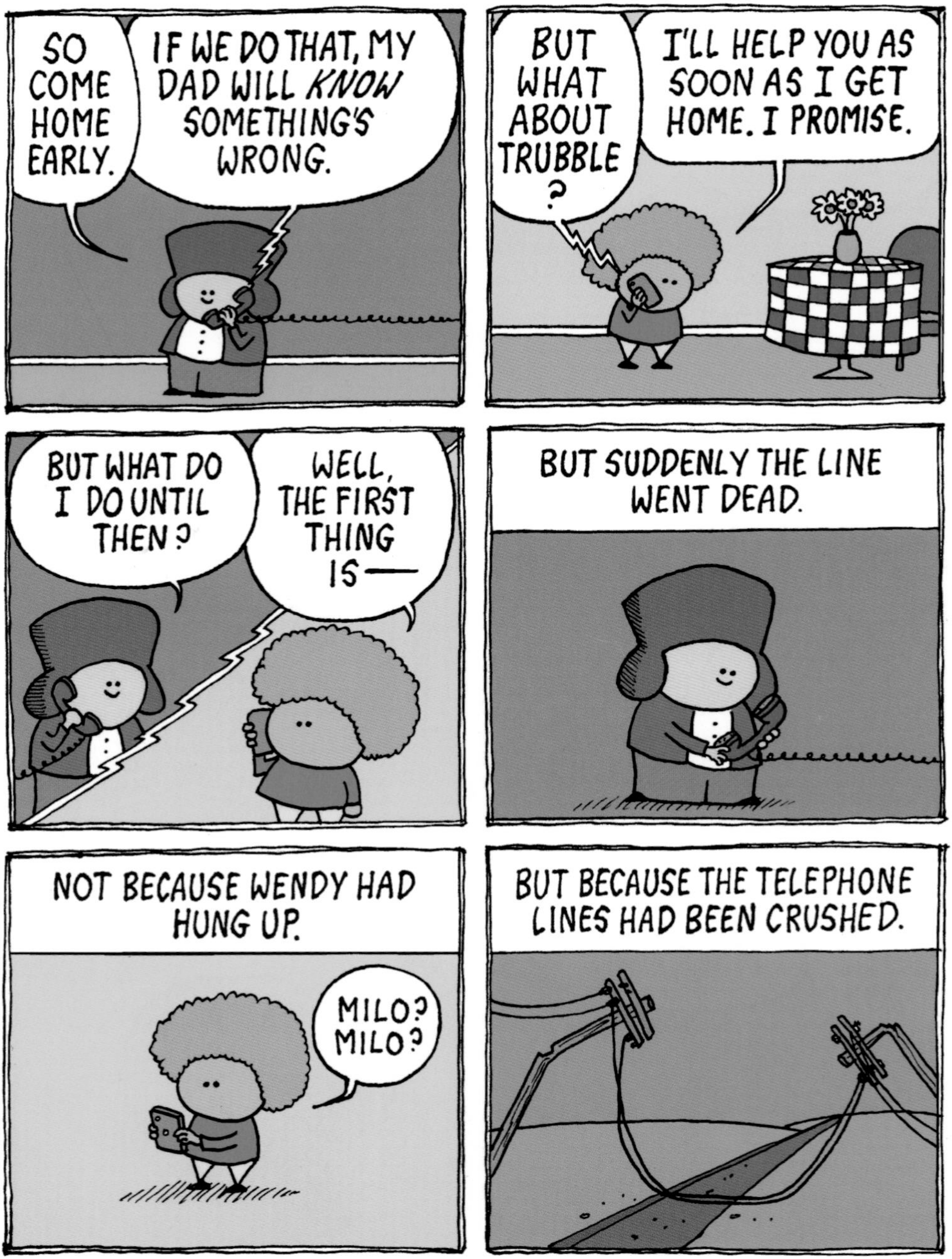
SO COME HOME EARLY.
IF WE DO THAT, MY DAD WILL *KNOW* SOMETHING'S WRONG.
BUT WHAT ABOUT TRUBBLE?
I'LL HELP YOU AS SOON AS I GET HOME. I PROMISE.
BUT WHAT DO I DO UNTIL THEN?
WELL, THE FIRST THING IS—
BUT SUDDENLY THE LINE WENT DEAD.
NOT BECAUSE WENDY HAD HUNG UP.
MILO? MILO?
BUT BECAUSE THE TELEPHONE LINES HAD BEEN CRUSHED.

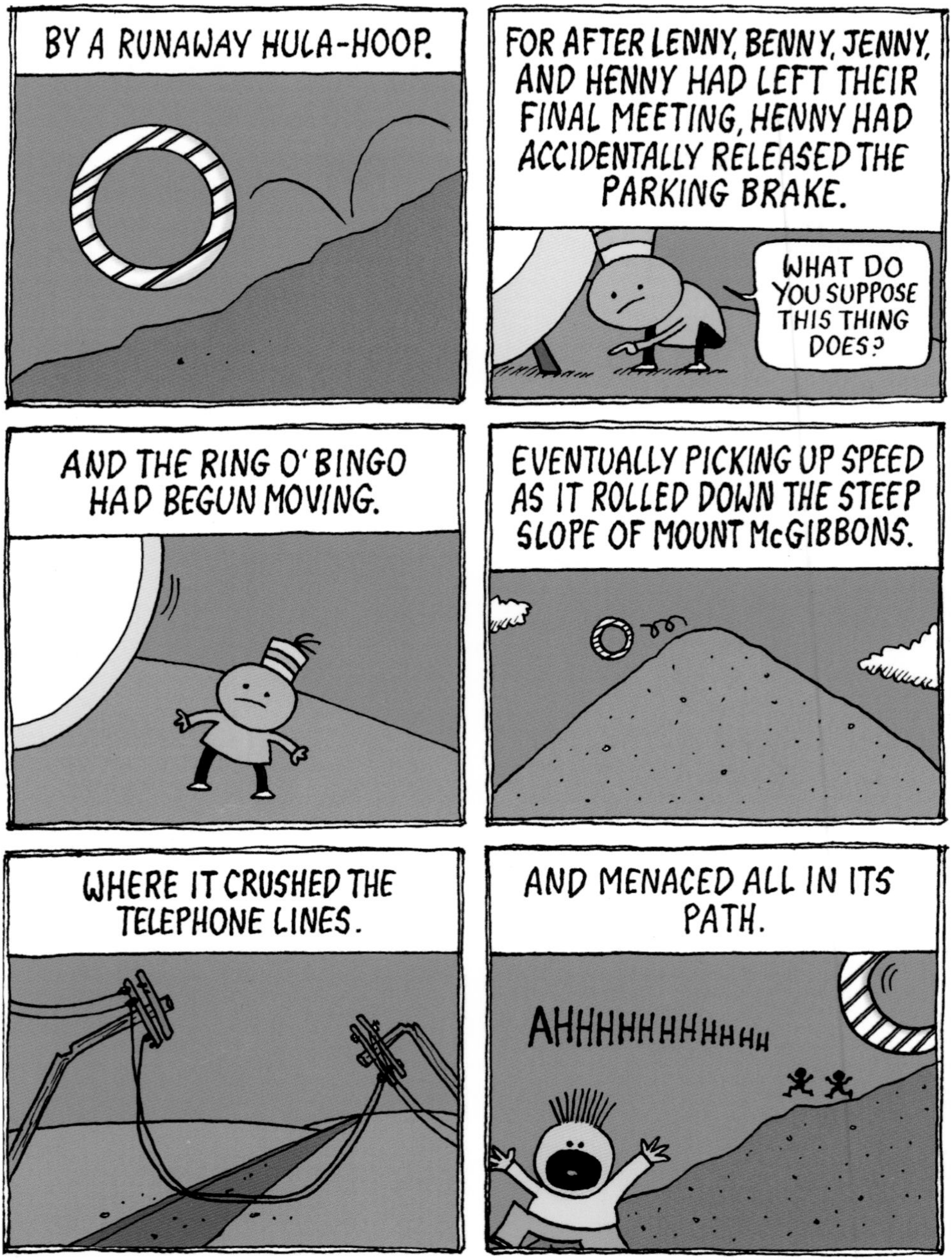
BY A RUNAWAY HULA-HOOP.
FOR AFTER LENNY, BENNY, JENNY, AND HENNY HAD LEFT THEIR FINAL MEETING, HENNY HAD ACCIDENTALLY RELEASED THE PARKING BRAKE.
WHAT DO YOU SUPPOSE THIS THING DOES?
AND THE RING O' BINGO HAD BEGUN MOVING.
EVENTUALLY PICKING UP SPEED AS IT ROLLED DOWN THE STEEP SLOPE OF MOUNT McGIBBONS.
WHERE IT CRUSHED THE TELEPHONE LINES.
AND MENACED ALL IN ITS PATH.
AHHHHHHHHHHH

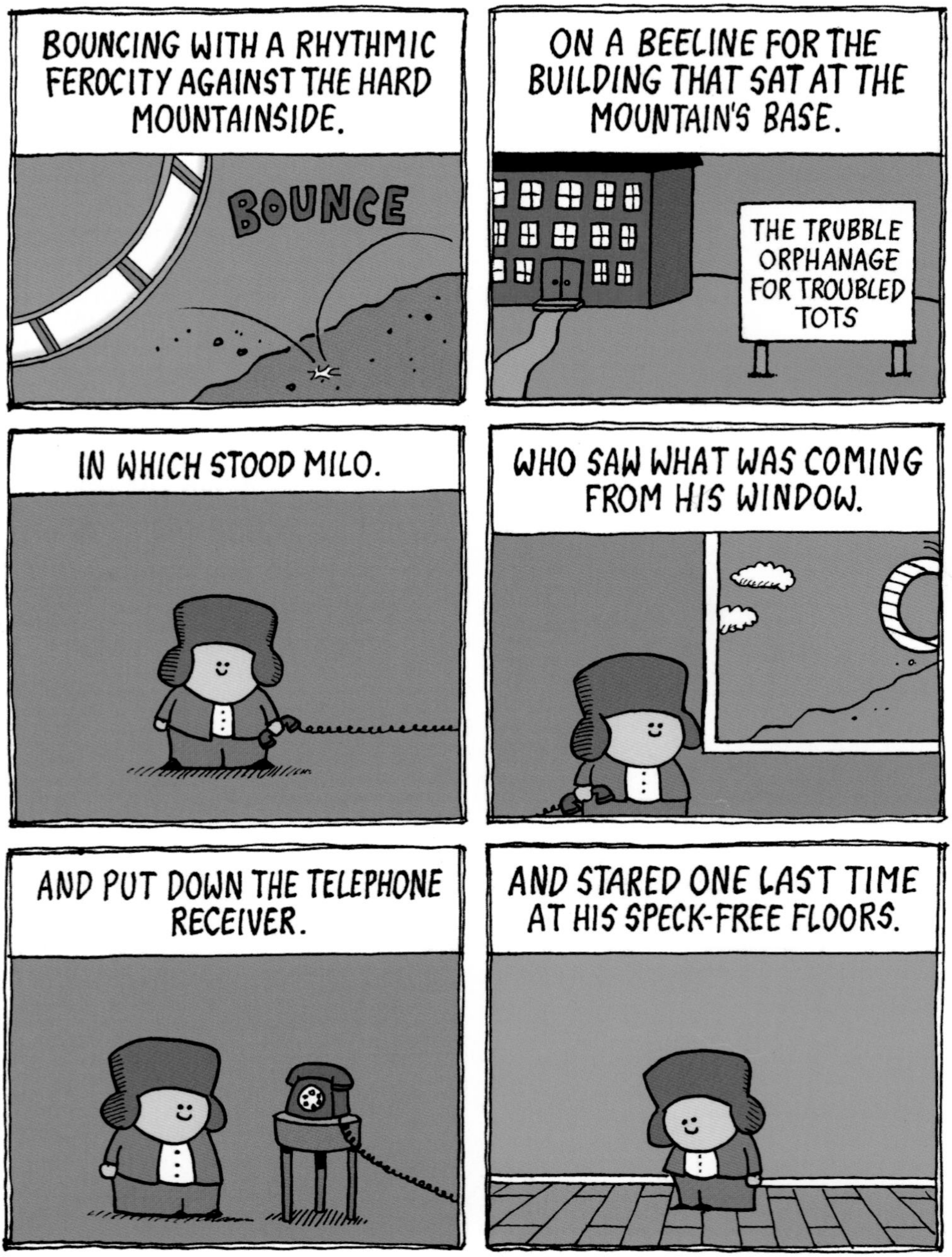
BOUNCING WITH A RHYTHMIC FEROCITY AGAINST THE HARD MOUNTAINSIDE.
BOUNCE
ON A BEELINE FOR THE BUILDING THAT SAT AT THE MOUNTAIN'S BASE.
THE TRUBBLE ORPHANAGE FOR TROUBLED TOTS
IN WHICH STOOD MILO.
WHO SAW WHAT WAS COMING FROM HIS WINDOW.
AND PUT DOWN THE TELEPHONE RECEIVER.
AND STARED ONE LAST TIME AT HIS SPECK-FREE FLOORS.

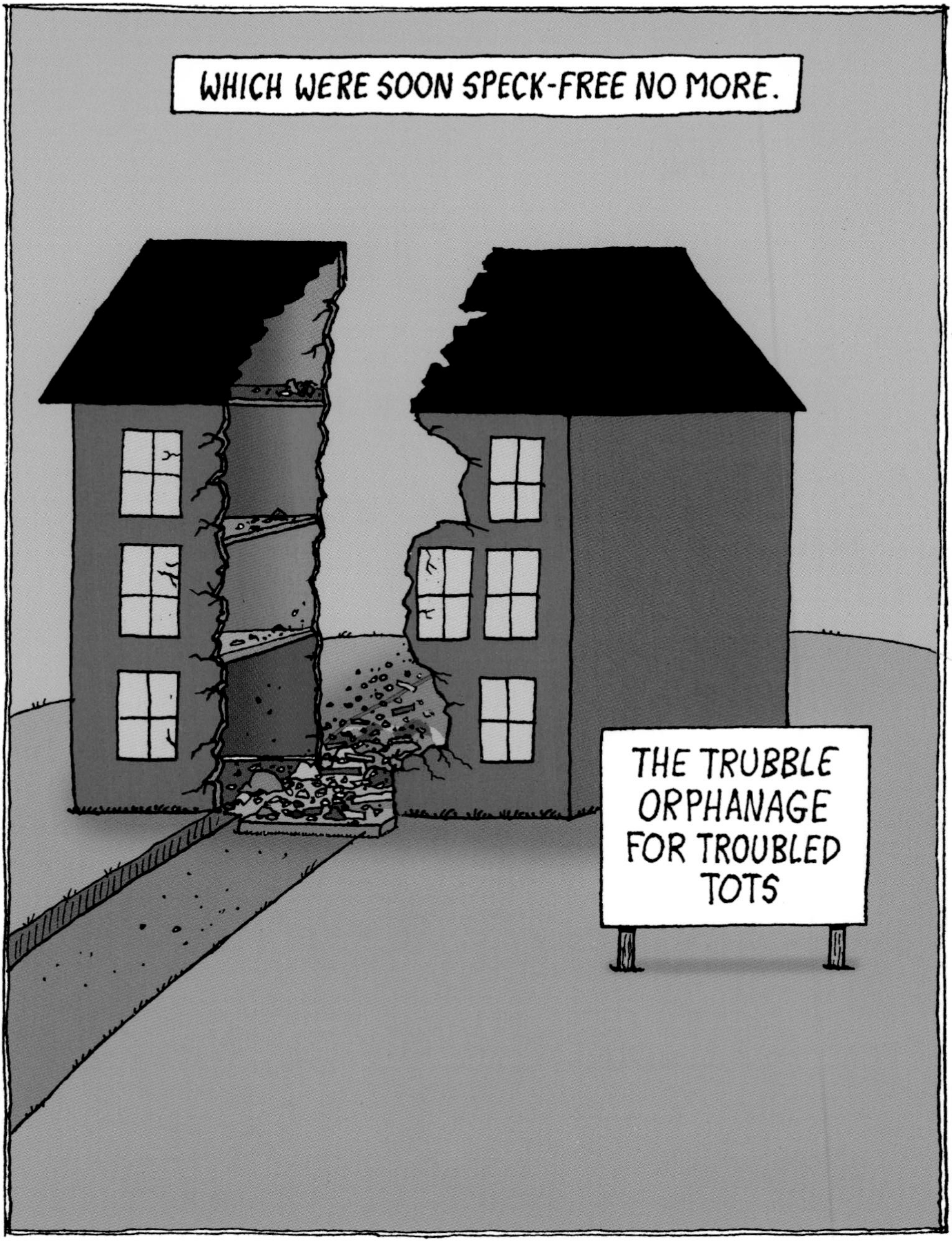
WHICH WERE SOON SPECK-FREE NO MORE.
THE TRUBBLE ORPHANAGE FOR TROUBLED TOTS

CHAPTER AFTER THE LAST ONE

WHICH IS...

AN ACCURATE DESCRIPTION OF THE PLACEMENT OF THIS CHAPTER

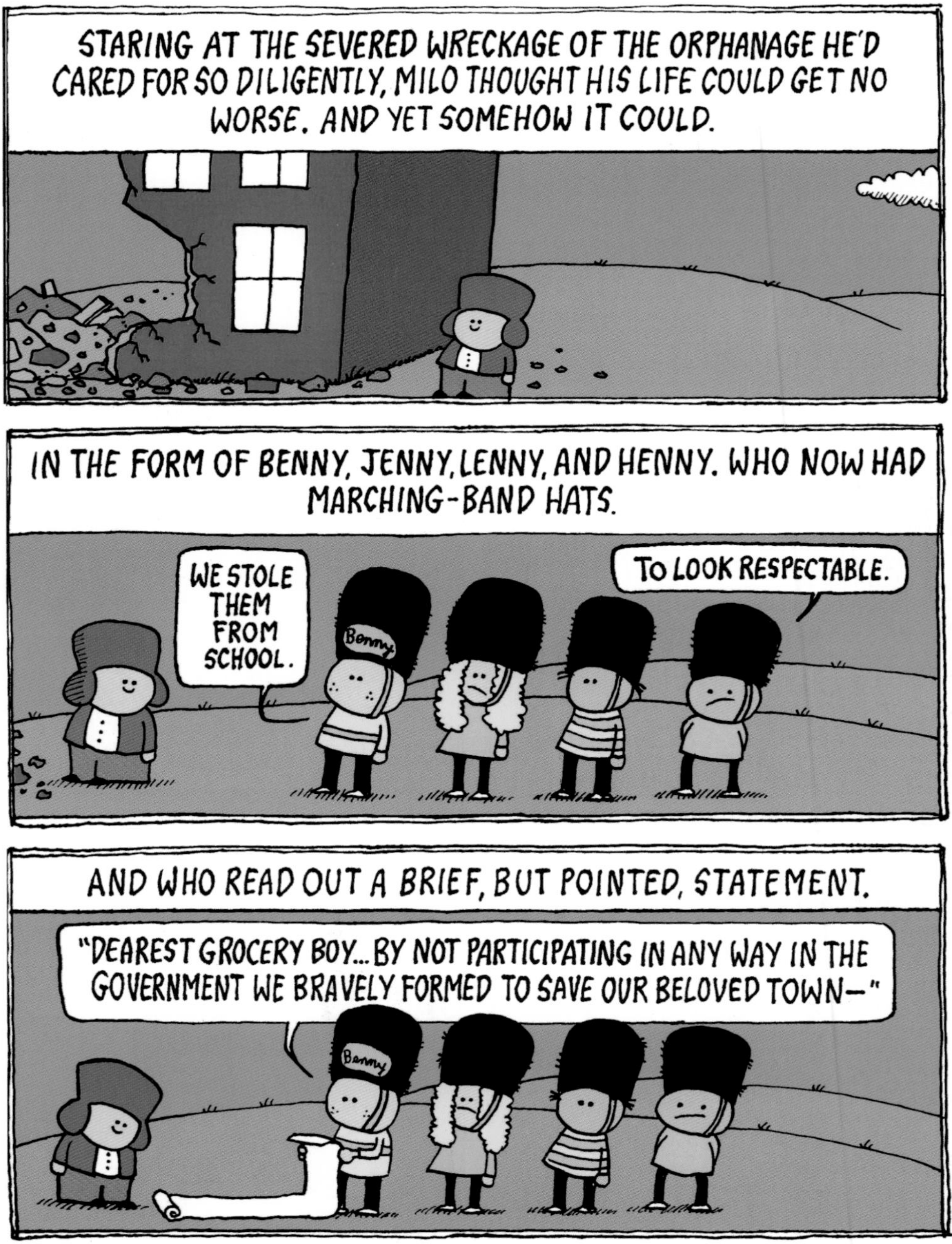
STARING AT THE SEVERED WRECKAGE OF THE ORPHANAGE HE'D CARED FOR SO DILIGENTLY, MILO THOUGHT HIS LIFE COULD GET NO WORSE. AND YET SOMEHOW IT COULD.
IN THE FORM OF BENNY, JENNY, LENNY, AND HENNY. WHO NOW HAD MARCHING-BAND HATS.
WE STOLE THEM FROM SCHOOL.
TO LOOK RESPECTABLE.
Benny
AND WHO READ OUT A BRIEF, BUT POINTED, STATEMENT.
"DEAREST GROCERY BOY... BY NOT PARTICIPATING IN ANY WAY IN THE GOVERNMENT WE BRAVELY FORMED TO SAVE OUR BELOVED TOWN—"
Benny

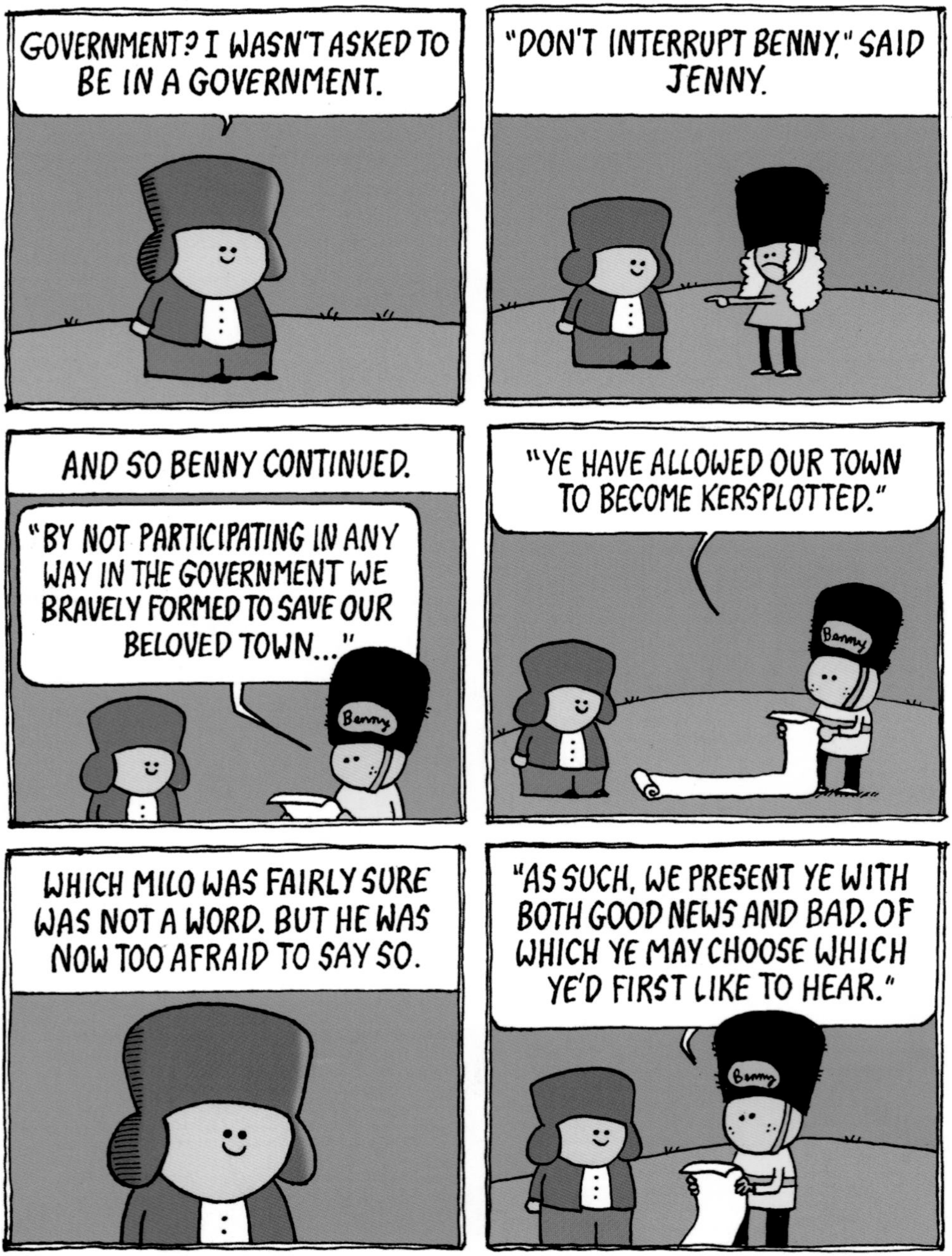
GOVERNMENT? I WASN'T ASKED TO BE IN A GOVERNMENT.
"DON'T INTERRUPT BENNY," SAID JENNY.
AND SO BENNY CONTINUED.
"BY NOT PARTICIPATING IN ANY WAY IN THE GOVERNMENT WE BRAVELY FORMED TO SAVE OUR BELOVED TOWN..."
Benny
"YE HAVE ALLOWED OUR TOWN TO BECOME KERSPLOTTED."
Benny
WHICH MILO WAS FAIRLY SURE WAS NOT A WORD. BUT HE WAS NOW TOO AFRAID TO SAY SO.
"AS SUCH, WE PRESENT YE WITH BOTH GOOD NEWS AND BAD. OF WHICH YE MAY CHOOSE WHICH YE'D FIRST LIKE TO HEAR."
Benny

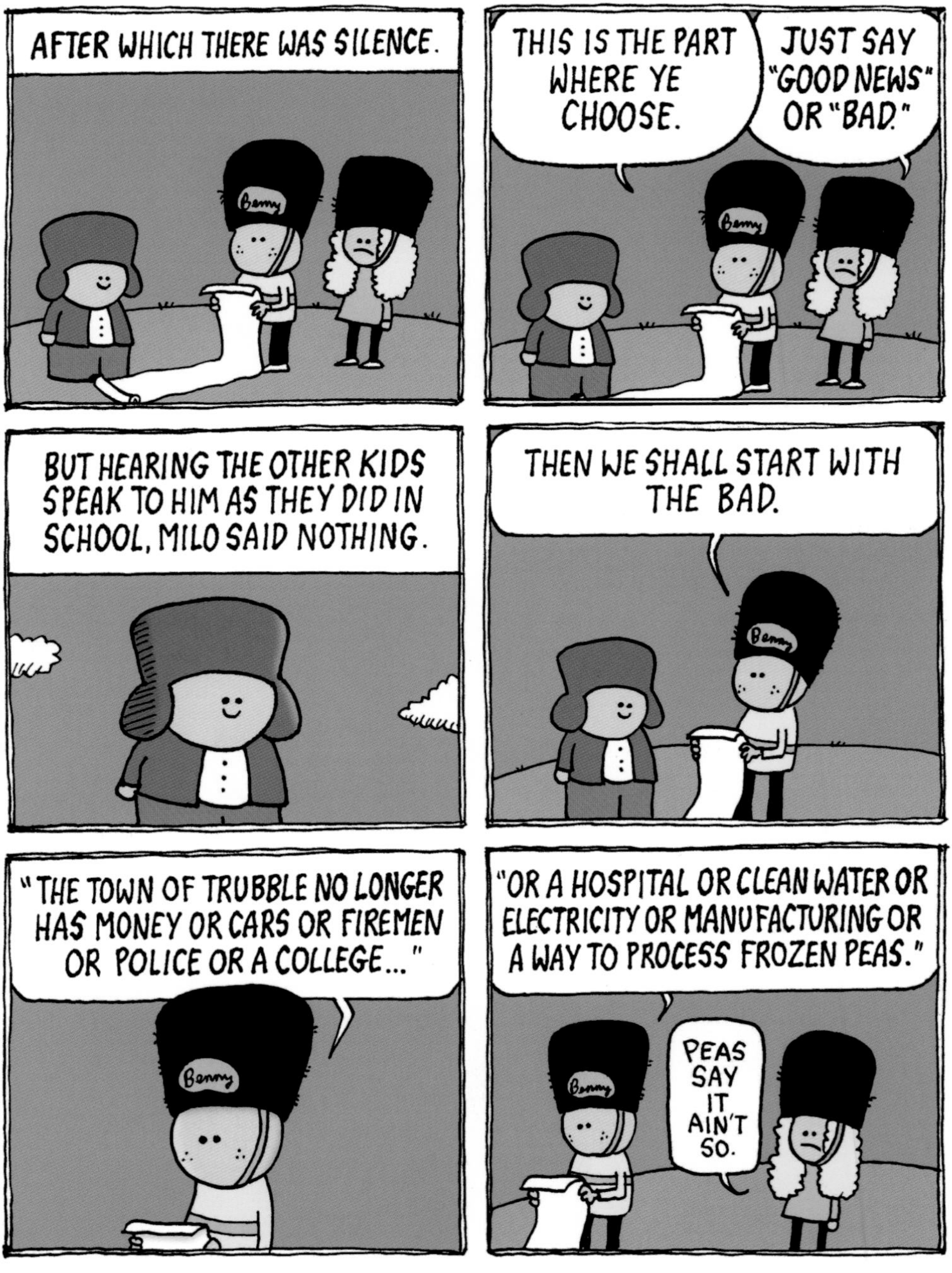
AFTER WHICH THERE WAS SILENCE.
Benny
THIS IS THE PART WHERE YE CHOOSE.
JUST SAY "GOOD NEWS" OR "BAD."
Benny
BUT HEARING THE OTHER KIDS SPEAK TO HIM AS THEY DID IN SCHOOL, MILO SAID NOTHING.
THEN WE SHALL START WITH THE BAD.
Benny
"THE TOWN OF TRUBBLE NO LONGER HAS MONEY OR CARS OR FIREMEN OR POLICE OR A COLLEGE..."
Benny
"OR A HOSPITAL OR CLEAN WATER OR ELECTRICITY OR MANUFACTURING OR A WAY TO PROCESS FROZEN PEAS."
Benny
PEAS SAY IT AIN'T SO.

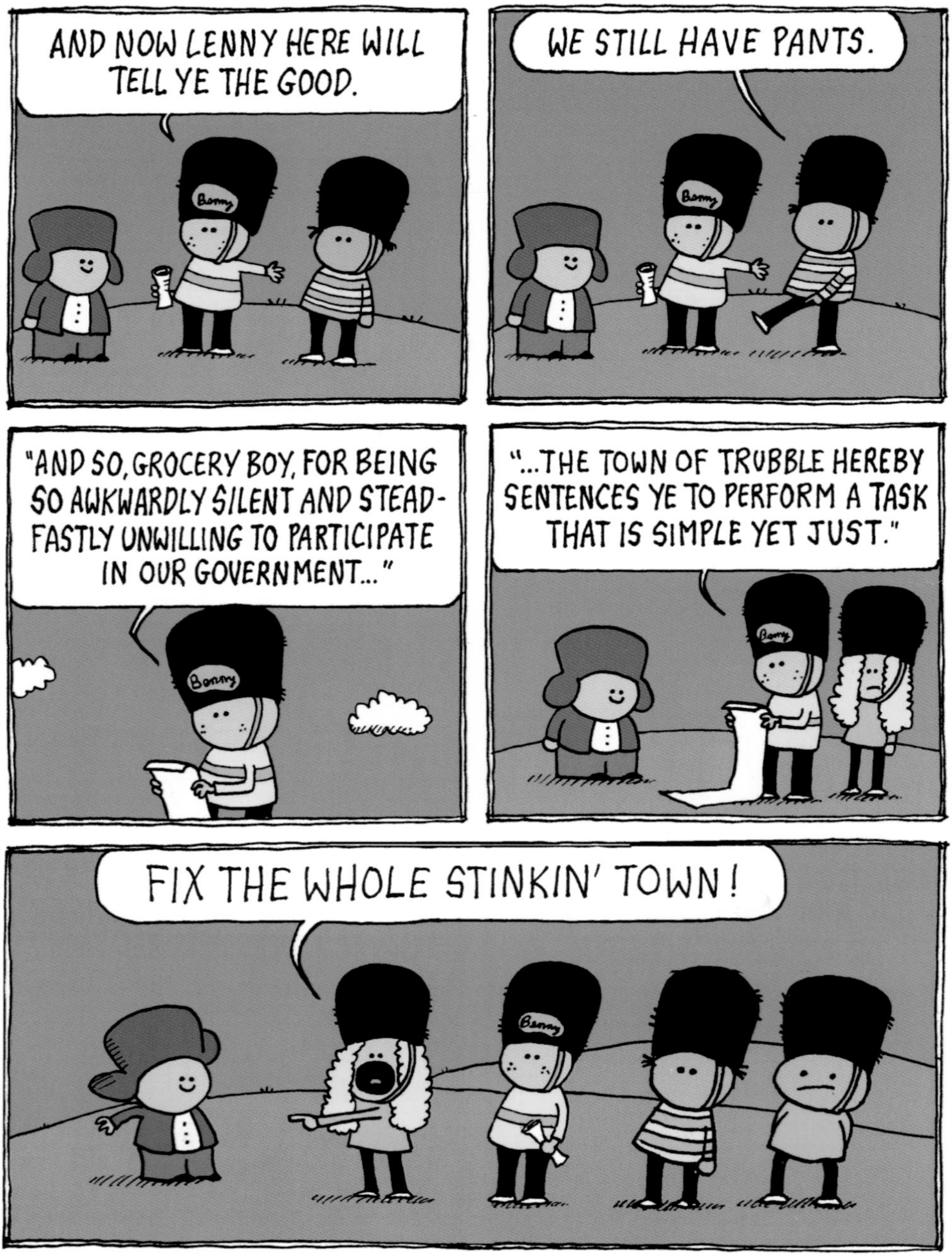
AND NOW LENNY HERE WILL TELL YE THE GOOD.
BONNY
WE STILL HAVE PANTS.
BONNY
"AND SO, GROCERY BOY, FOR BEING SO AWKWARDLY SILENT AND STEAD-FASTLY UNWILLING TO PARTICIPATE IN OUR GOVERNMENT..."
BONNY
"...THE TOWN OF TRUBBLE HEREBY SENTENCES YE TO PERFORM A TASK THAT IS SIMPLE YET JUST."
BONNY
FIX THE WHOLE STINKIN' TOWN!
BONNY

CHAPTER BEFORE THE NEXT ONE

WHICH IS...

ACCURATE IN THAT IT COMES BEFORE THE NEXT ONE

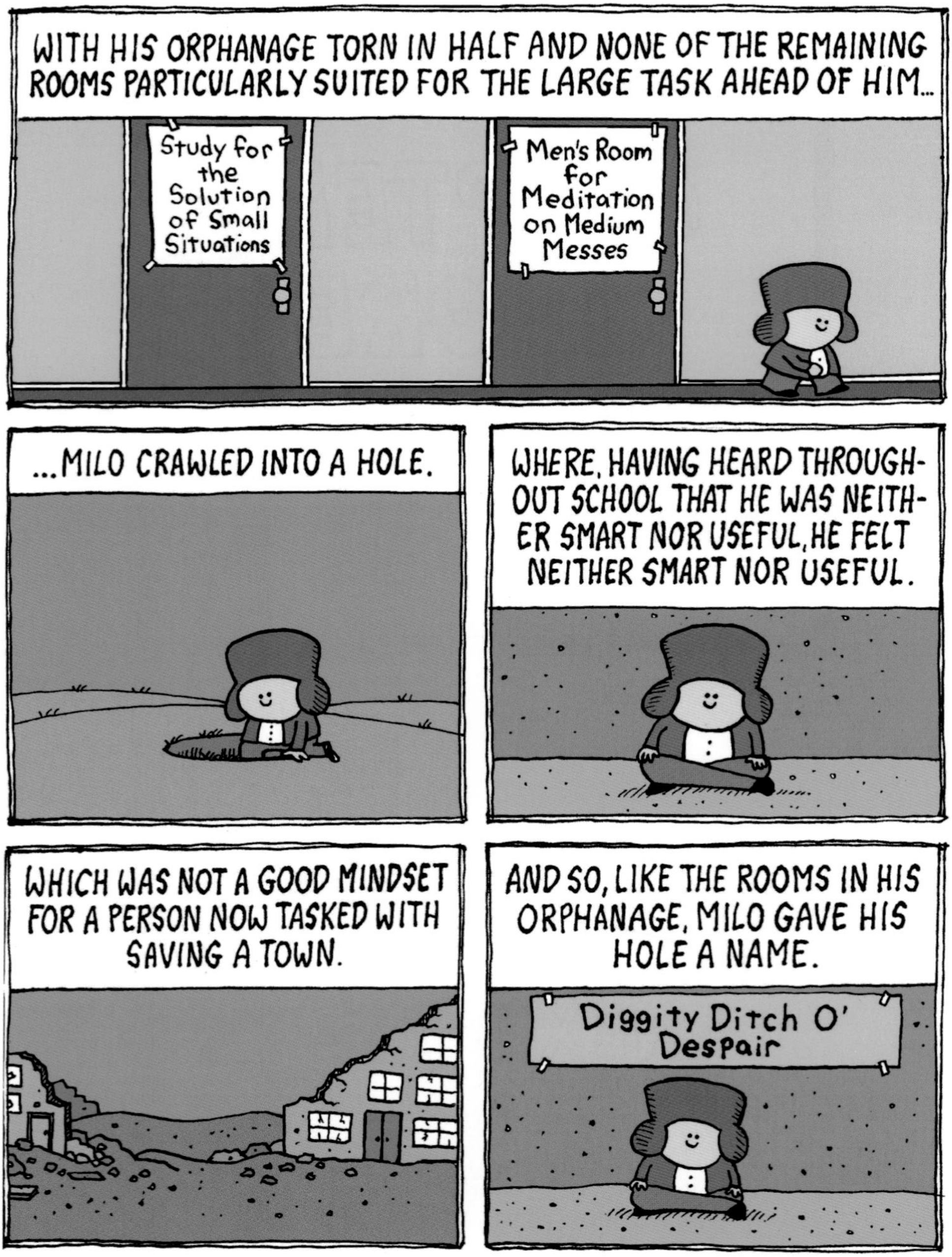
WITH HIS ORPHANAGE TORN IN HALF AND NONE OF THE REMAINING ROOMS PARTICULARLY SUITED FOR THE LARGE TASK AHEAD OF HIM...
Study for the Solution of Small Situations
Men's Room for Meditation on Medium Messes
...MILO CRAWLED INTO A HOLE.
WHERE, HAVING HEARD THROUGHOUT SCHOOL THAT HE WAS NEITHER SMART NOR USEFUL, HE FELT NEITHER SMART NOR USEFUL.
WHICH WAS NOT A GOOD MINDSET FOR A PERSON NOW TASKED WITH SAVING A TOWN.
AND SO, LIKE THE ROOMS IN HIS ORPHANAGE, MILO GAVE HIS HOLE A NAME.
Diggity Ditch O' Despair

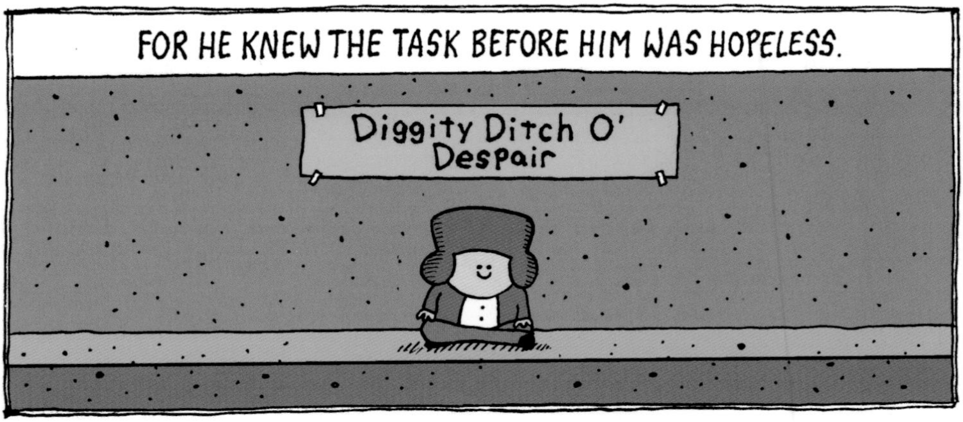
FOR HE KNEW THE TASK BEFORE HIM WAS HOPELESS.
Diggity Ditch O' Despair

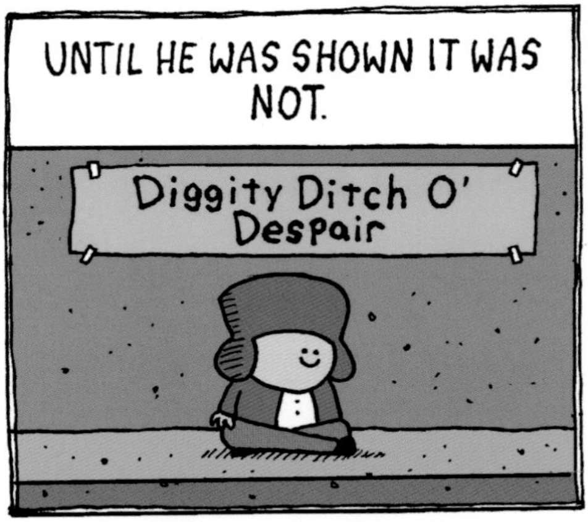
UNTIL HE WAS SHOWN IT WAS NOT.
Diggity Ditch O' Despair

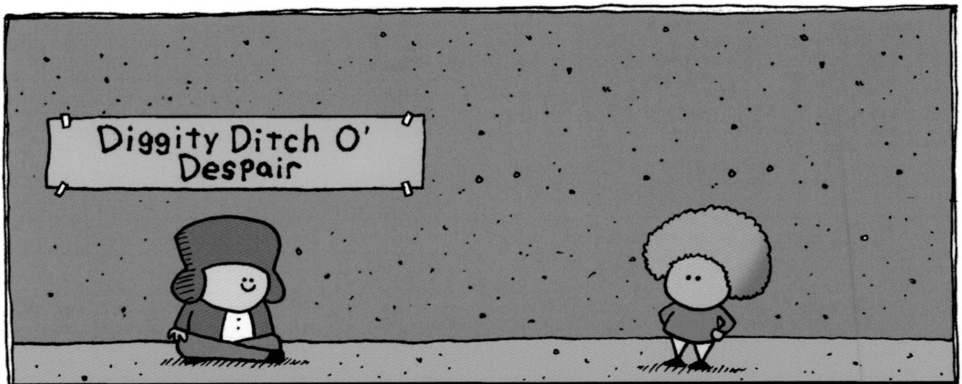
Diggity Ditch O' Despair

CHAPTER THE NEXT ONE

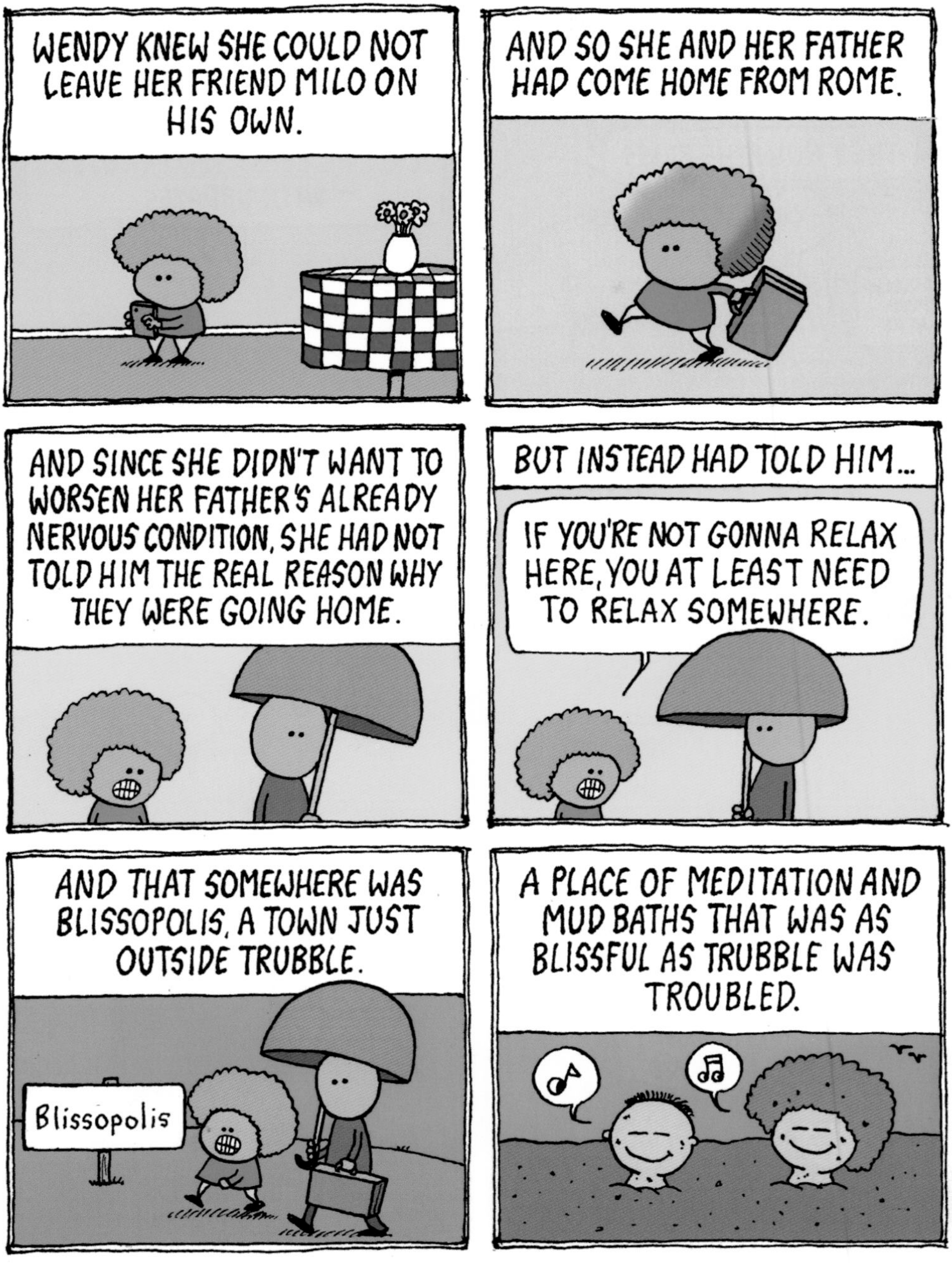
WENDY KNEW SHE COULD NOT LEAVE HER FRIEND MILO ON HIS OWN.
AND SO SHE AND HER FATHER HAD COME HOME FROM ROME.
AND SINCE SHE DIDN'T WANT TO WORSEN HER FATHER'S ALREADY NERVOUS CONDITION, SHE HAD NOT TOLD HIM THE REAL REASON WHY THEY WERE GOING HOME.
BUT INSTEAD HAD TOLD HIM...
IF YOU'RE NOT GONNA RELAX HERE, YOU AT LEAST NEED TO RELAX SOMEWHERE.
AND THAT SOMEWHERE WAS BLISSOPOLIS, A TOWN JUST OUTSIDE TRUBBLE.
Blissopolis
A PLACE OF MEDITATION AND MUD BATHS THAT WAS AS BLISSFUL AS TRUBBLE WAS TROUBLED.

AND A TOWN THAT DID NOT ALLOW CHILDREN.

THEY RUIN THE BLISS.

SOPOLIS MUD BATHS

SO WORRIED WILLY PAID A BABY-SITTER TO WATCH WENDY.

CALL ME EVERY TEN MINUTES WITH UPDATES.

AND WENDY PAID THE BABYSITTER TO NOT WATCH WENDY.

AND WENDY MADE HER WAY TO MILO. WHERE SHE GOT HIM TO CLIMB OUT OF HIS HOLE.

AND RETURN TO HIS ORPHANAGE. WHICH HE WAS HAPPY TO SHOW OFF.

Parlor of Pals

DESPITE ITS PRESENT CONDITION.

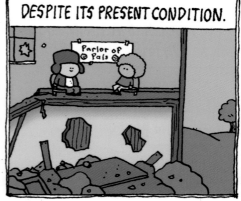

Parlor of Pals

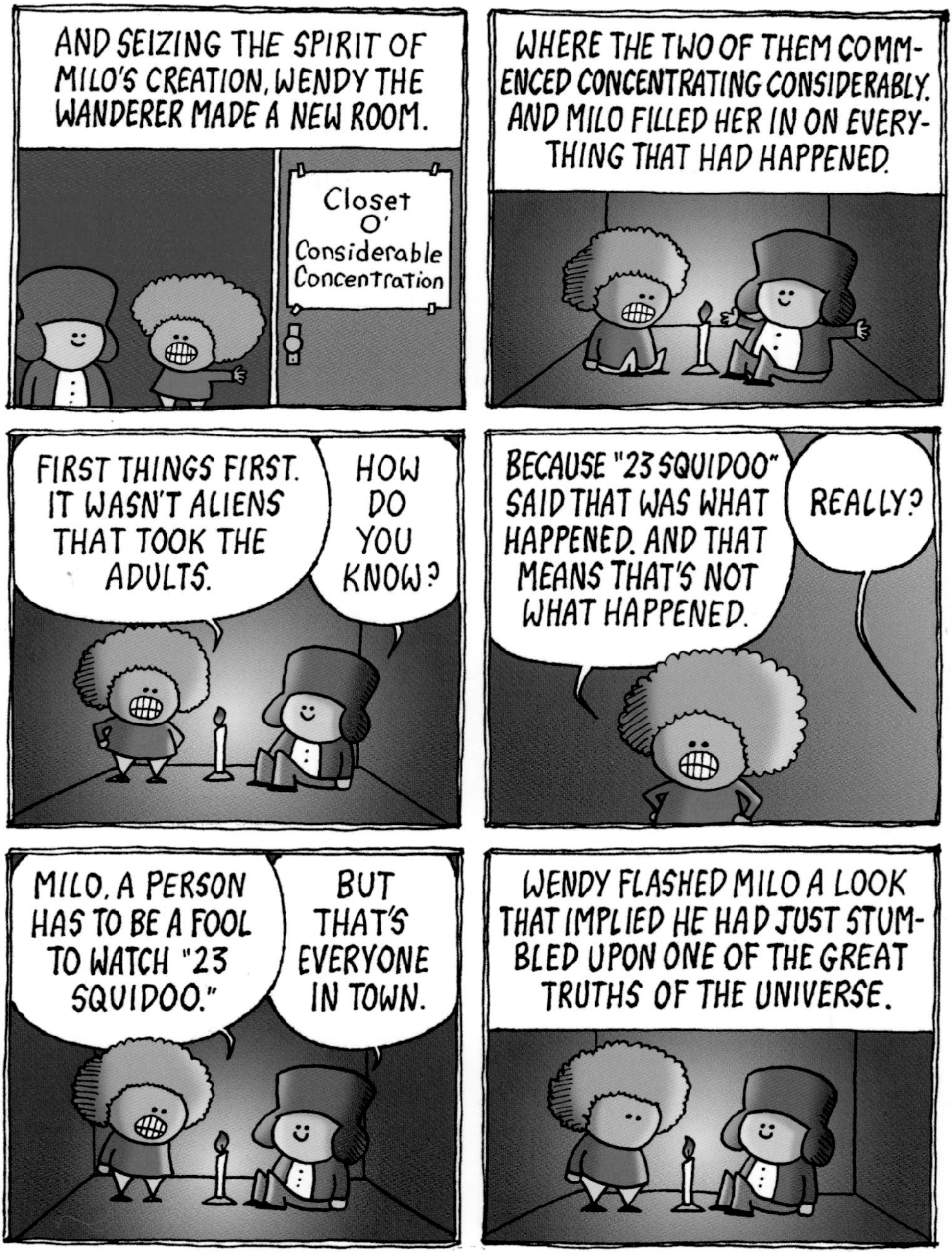
AND SEIZING THE SPIRIT OF MILO'S CREATION, WENDY THE WANDERER MADE A NEW ROOM.
Closet O' Considerable Concentration
WHERE THE TWO OF THEM COMMENCED CONCENTRATING CONSIDERABLY. AND MILO FILLED HER IN ON EVERYTHING THAT HAD HAPPENED.
FIRST THINGS FIRST. IT WASN'T ALIENS THAT TOOK THE ADULTS.
HOW DO YOU KNOW?
BECAUSE "23 SQUIDOO" SAID THAT WAS WHAT HAPPENED. AND THAT MEANS THAT'S NOT WHAT HAPPENED.
REALLY?
MILO, A PERSON HAS TO BE A FOOL TO WATCH "23 SQUIDOO."
BUT THAT'S EVERYONE IN TOWN.
WENDY FLASHED MILO A LOOK THAT IMPLIED HE HAD JUST STUMBLED UPON ONE OF THE GREAT TRUTHS OF THE UNIVERSE.

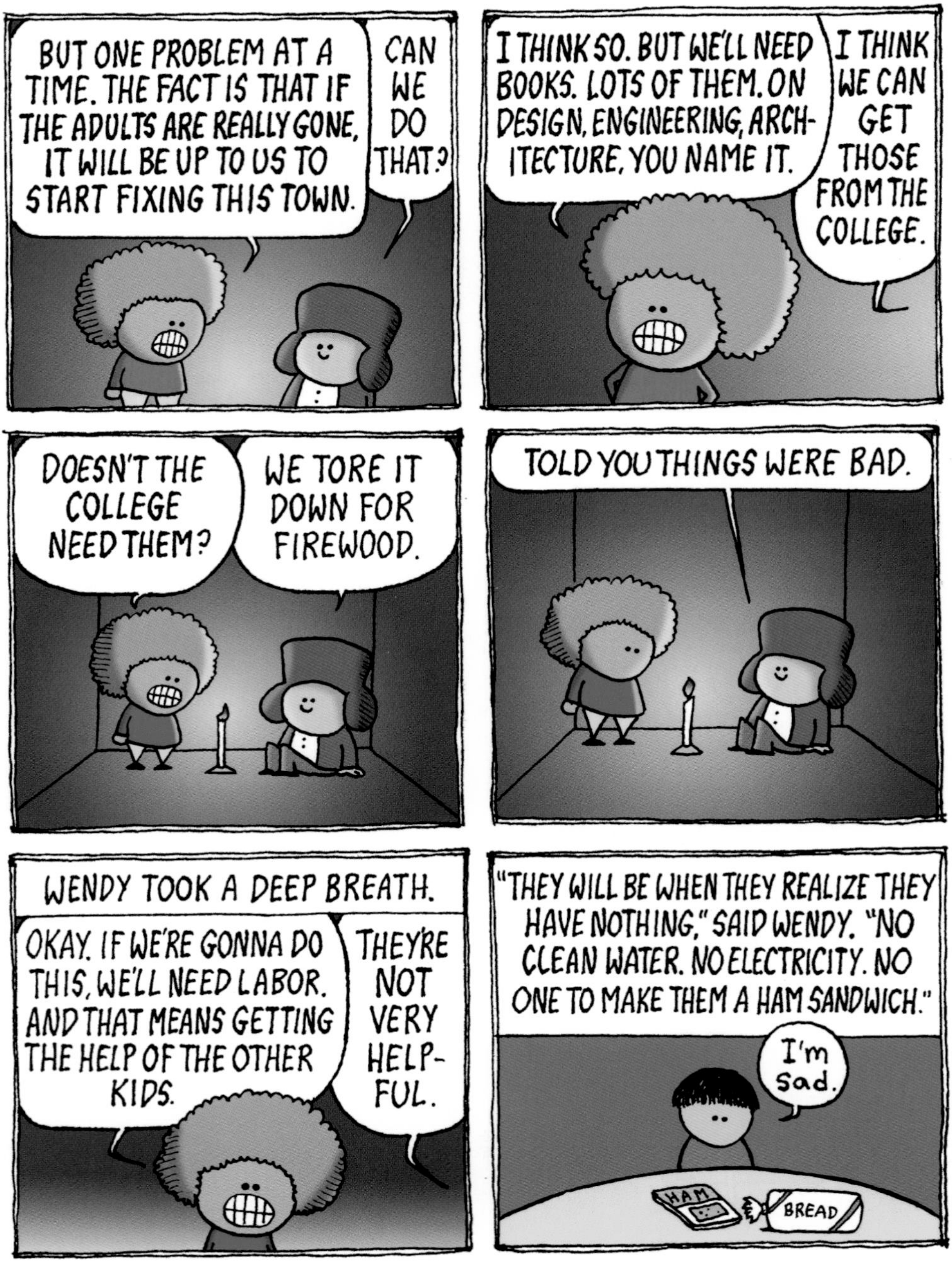
BUT ONE PROBLEM AT A TIME. THE FACT IS THAT IF THE ADULTS ARE REALLY GONE, IT WILL BE UP TO US TO START FIXING THIS TOWN.
CAN WE DO THAT?
I THINK SO. BUT WE'LL NEED BOOKS. LOTS OF THEM. ON DESIGN, ENGINEERING, ARCHITECTURE, YOU NAME IT.
I THINK WE CAN GET THOSE FROM THE COLLEGE.
DOESN'T THE COLLEGE NEED THEM?
WE TORE IT DOWN FOR FIREWOOD.
TOLD YOU THINGS WERE BAD.
WENDY TOOK A DEEP BREATH.
OKAY. IF WE'RE GONNA DO THIS, WE'LL NEED LABOR. AND THAT MEANS GETTING THE HELP OF THE OTHER KIDS.
THEY'RE NOT VERY HELPFUL.
"THEY WILL BE WHEN THEY REALIZE THEY HAVE NOTHING," SAID WENDY. "NO CLEAN WATER. NO ELECTRICITY. NO ONE TO MAKE THEM A HAM SANDWICH."
I'm sad.
HAM
BREAD

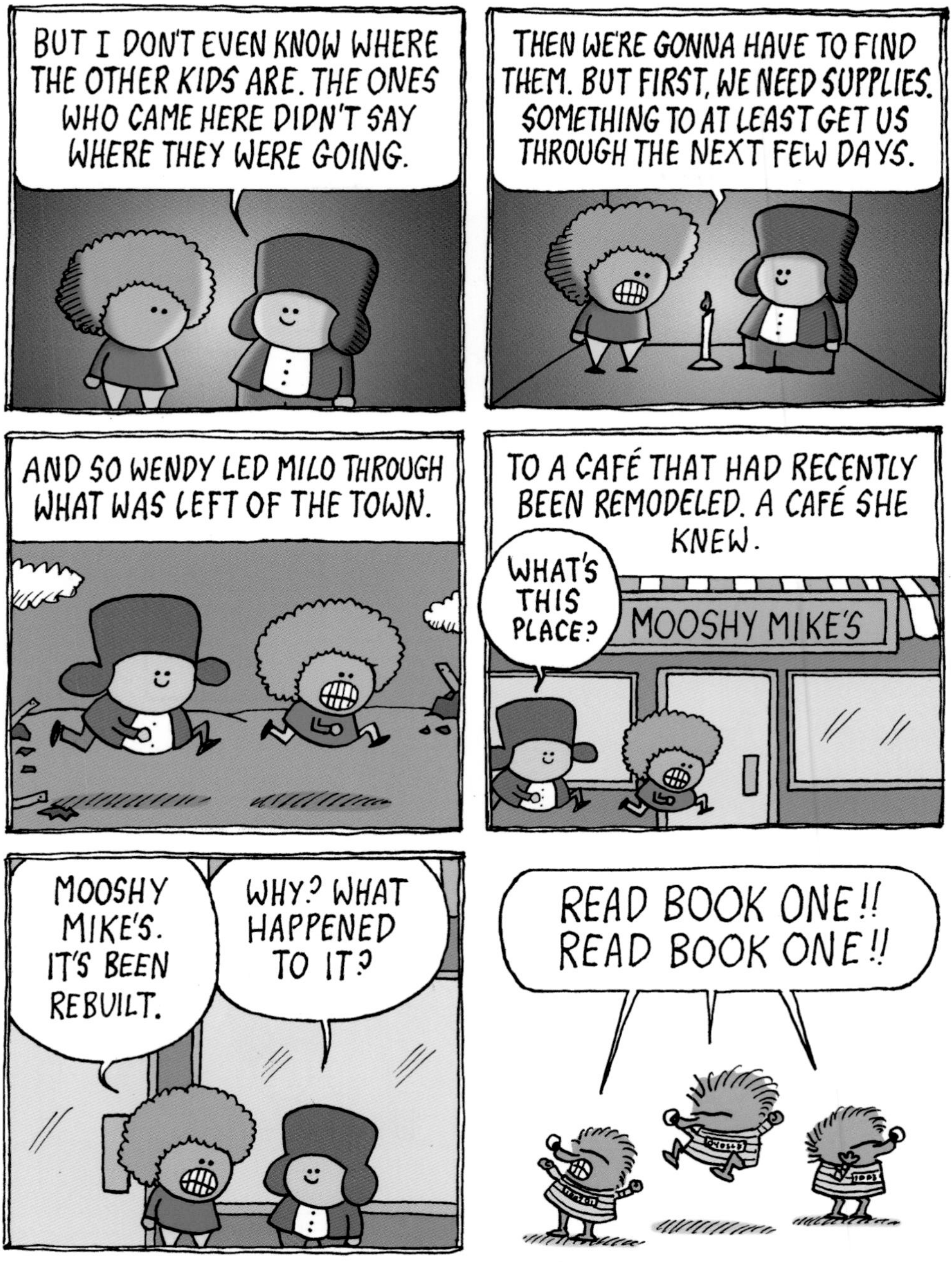
BUT I DON'T EVEN KNOW WHERE THE OTHER KIDS ARE. THE ONES WHO CAME HERE DIDN'T SAY WHERE THEY WERE GOING.
THEN WE'RE GONNA HAVE TO FIND THEM. BUT FIRST, WE NEED SUPPLIES. SOMETHING TO AT LEAST GET US THROUGH THE NEXT FEW DAYS.
AND SO WENDY LED MILO THROUGH WHAT WAS LEFT OF THE TOWN.
TO A CAFÉ THAT HAD RECENTLY BEEN REMODELED. A CAFÉ SHE KNEW.
WHAT'S THIS PLACE?
MOOSHY MIKE'S
MOOSHY MIKE'S. IT'S BEEN REBUILT.
WHY? WHAT HAPPENED TO IT?
READ BOOK ONE!! READ BOOK ONE!!

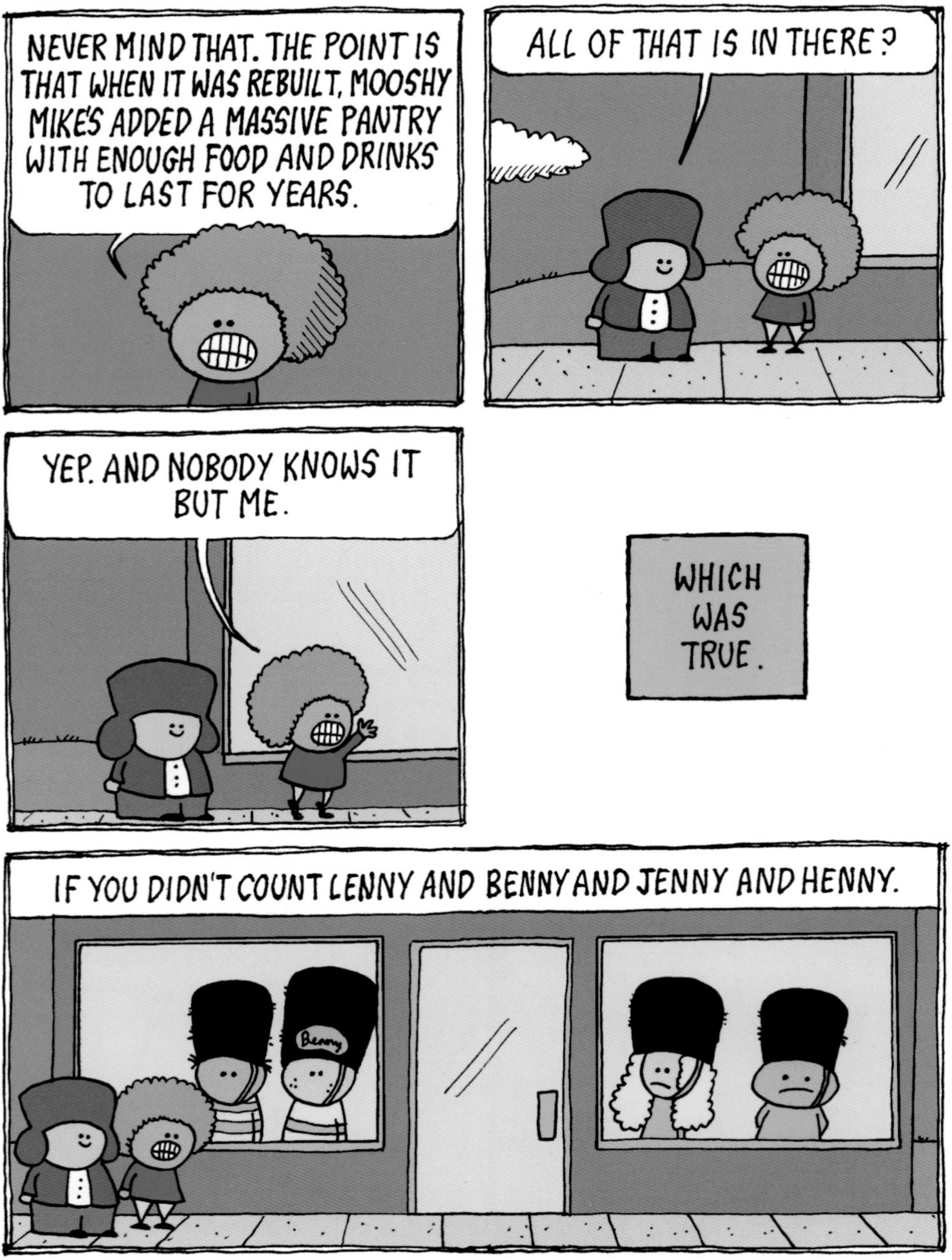
NEVER MIND THAT. THE POINT IS THAT WHEN IT WAS REBUILT, MOOSHY MIKE'S ADDED A MASSIVE PANTRY WITH ENOUGH FOOD AND DRINKS TO LAST FOR YEARS.
ALL OF THAT IS IN THERE?
YEP. AND NOBODY KNOWS IT BUT ME.
WHICH WAS TRUE.
IF YOU DIDN'T COUNT LENNY AND BENNY AND JENNY AND HENNY.
Benny

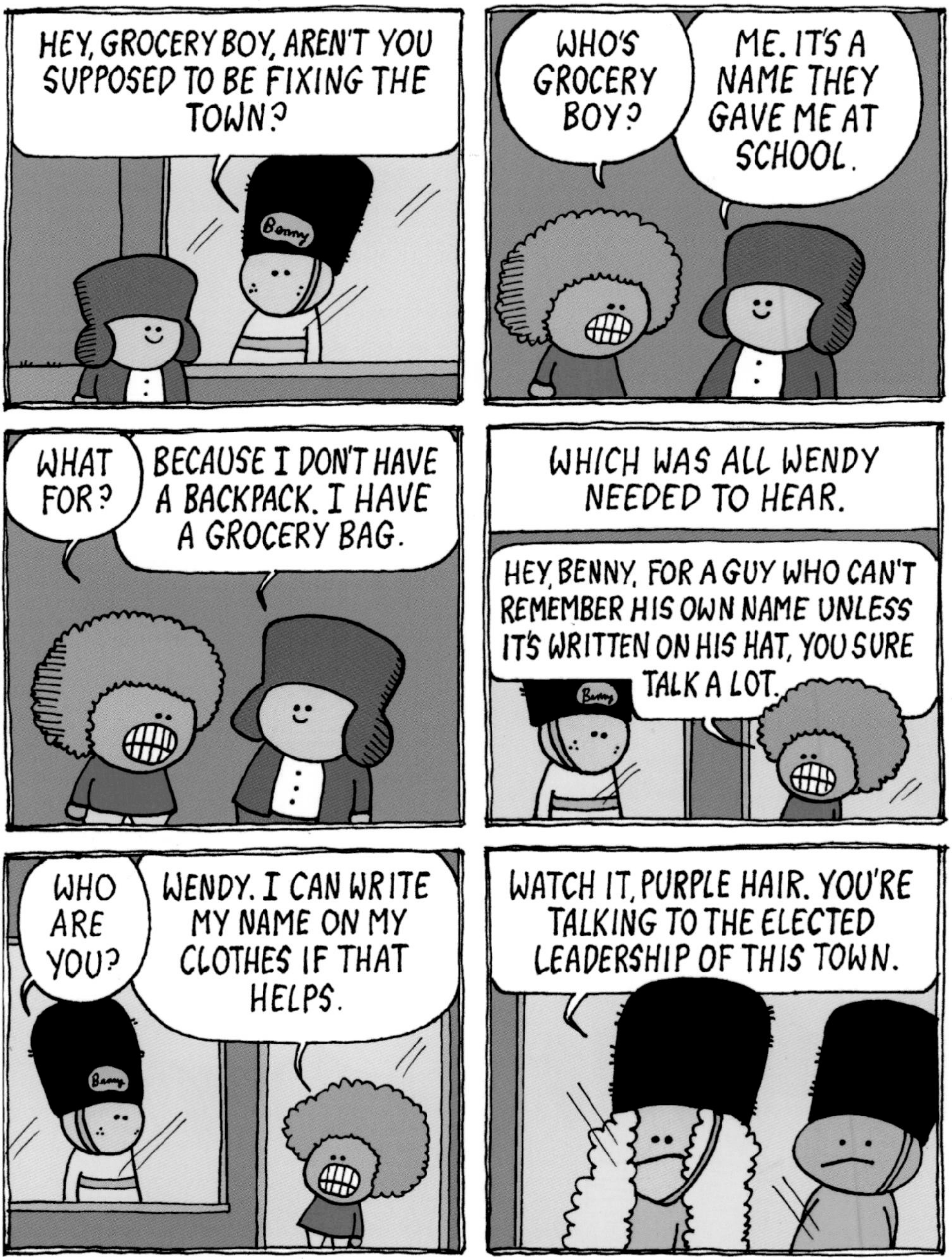
HEY, GROCERY BOY, AREN'T YOU SUPPOSED TO BE FIXING THE TOWN?
WHO'S GROCERY BOY?
ME. IT'S A NAME THEY GAVE ME AT SCHOOL.
WHAT FOR?
BECAUSE I DON'T HAVE A BACKPACK. I HAVE A GROCERY BAG.
WHICH WAS ALL WENDY NEEDED TO HEAR.
HEY, BENNY, FOR A GUY WHO CAN'T REMEMBER HIS OWN NAME UNLESS IT'S WRITTEN ON HIS HAT, YOU SURE TALK A LOT.
WHO ARE YOU?
WENDY. I CAN WRITE MY NAME ON MY CLOTHES IF THAT HELPS.
WATCH IT, PURPLE HAIR. YOU'RE TALKING TO THE ELECTED LEADERSHIP OF THIS TOWN.

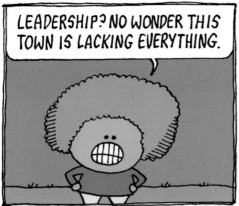

LEADERSHIP? NO WONDER THIS TOWN IS LACKING EVERYTHING.

YOU'RE LACKING EVERYTHING. WE'VE GOT MUFFINS.

AND MOOSHIES!*

* Steaming cup o' hot chocolate shoved chock-full with forty marshmallows. A Mooshy Mike specialty.

AND A PANTRY THAT CAN LAST US FOR YEARS!

HOW DID YOU KNOW THAT WAS IN THERE?

MY DAD IS MOOSHY MIKE.

ONLY REASON WE LET HIM STAY.

WHERE ARE THE REST OF THE KIDS FROM THIS TOWN?

IN THE BATHROOM. WE PASSED A LAW SAYING THEY HAD TO STAY THERE UNTIL WE FINISHED ALL THE MUFFINS.

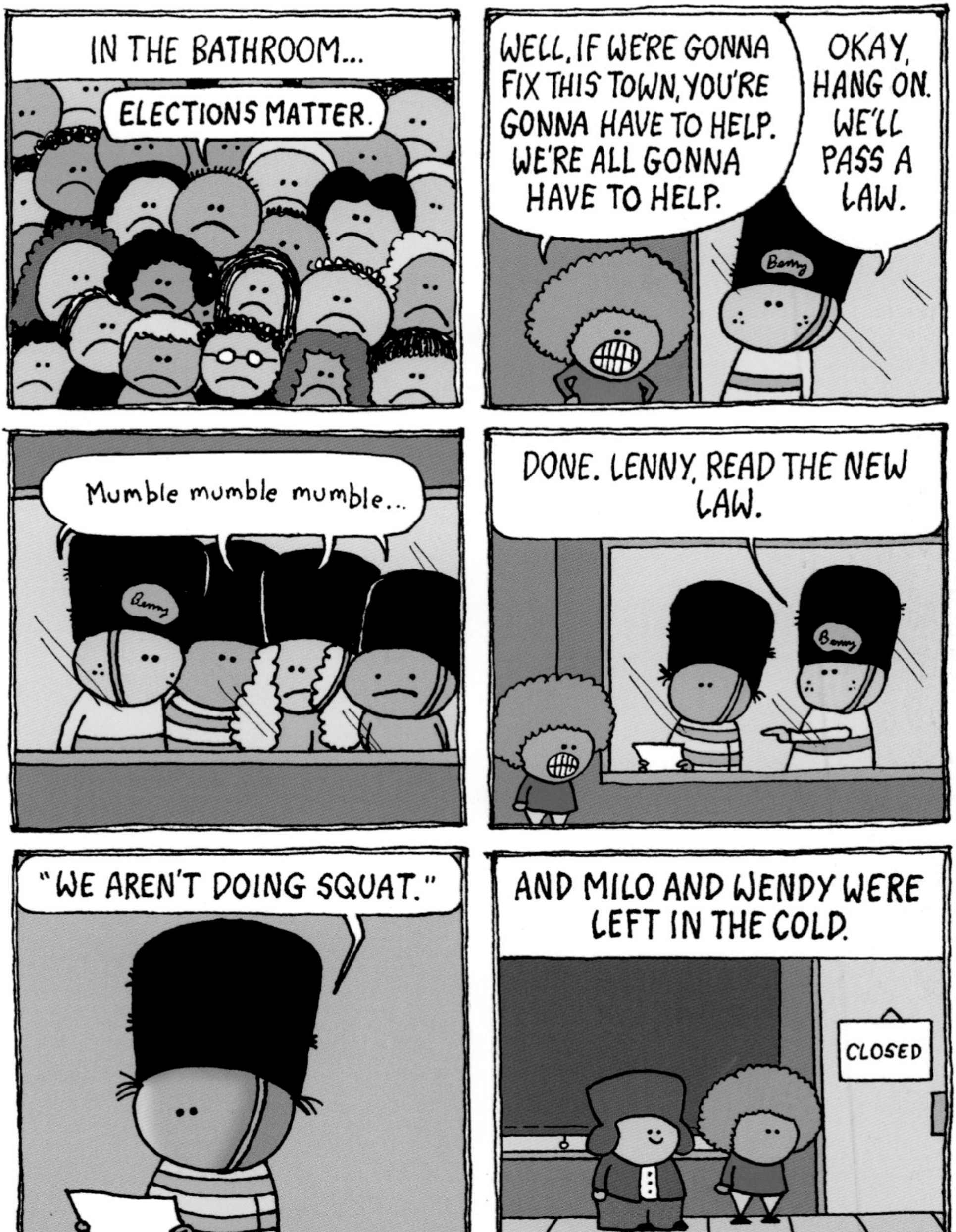
IN THE BATHROOM...
ELECTIONS MATTER.
WELL, IF WE'RE GONNA FIX THIS TOWN, YOU'RE GONNA HAVE TO HELP. WE'RE ALL GONNA HAVE TO HELP.
OKAY, HANG ON. WE'LL PASS A LAW.
Benny
Mumble mumble mumble...
Benny
DONE. LENNY, READ THE NEW LAW.
Benny
"WE AREN'T DOING SQUAT."
AND MILO AND WENDY WERE LEFT IN THE COLD.
CLOSED

CHAPTER MUCH BETTER

WHICH IS...

SO MUCH BETTER THAN THE LAST CHAPTER, IT'S NOT EVEN FUNNY

DESPERATE FOR HELP, WENDY LED MILO DOWNTOWN.

WHAT ARE WE DOING NOW?

GOING TO SEE SCRIBBY. THE GUY YOU TALKED TO ON THE PHONE.

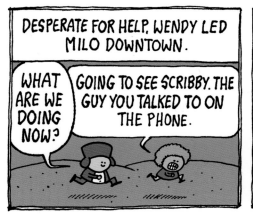

BUT REACHING THE BASE OF THE BANANA, THEY FOUND IT RINGED WITH BARBED WIRE.

WE CAN'T EVEN GET TO THE FRONT DOOR.

MAYBE THERE'S AN INTERCOM BUTTON WE CAN PRESS.

YOU SURE? HE DOESN'T SEEM VERY FRIENDLY.

HE WILL BE TO US. HE'S ALWAYS RELIED ON MY FATHER.

AND SUDDENLY, THE GROUND AROUND THEM EXPLODED.

BOOM ZAP KABOOM

AS A FRIGHTENED SCRIBBY VON SCRIVENER BEGAN FIRING RAY GUN BEAMS IN ALL DIRECTIONS.

ALIENS!!

Green Men Begone

ZAP ZZZT

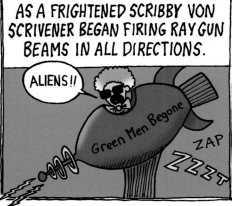

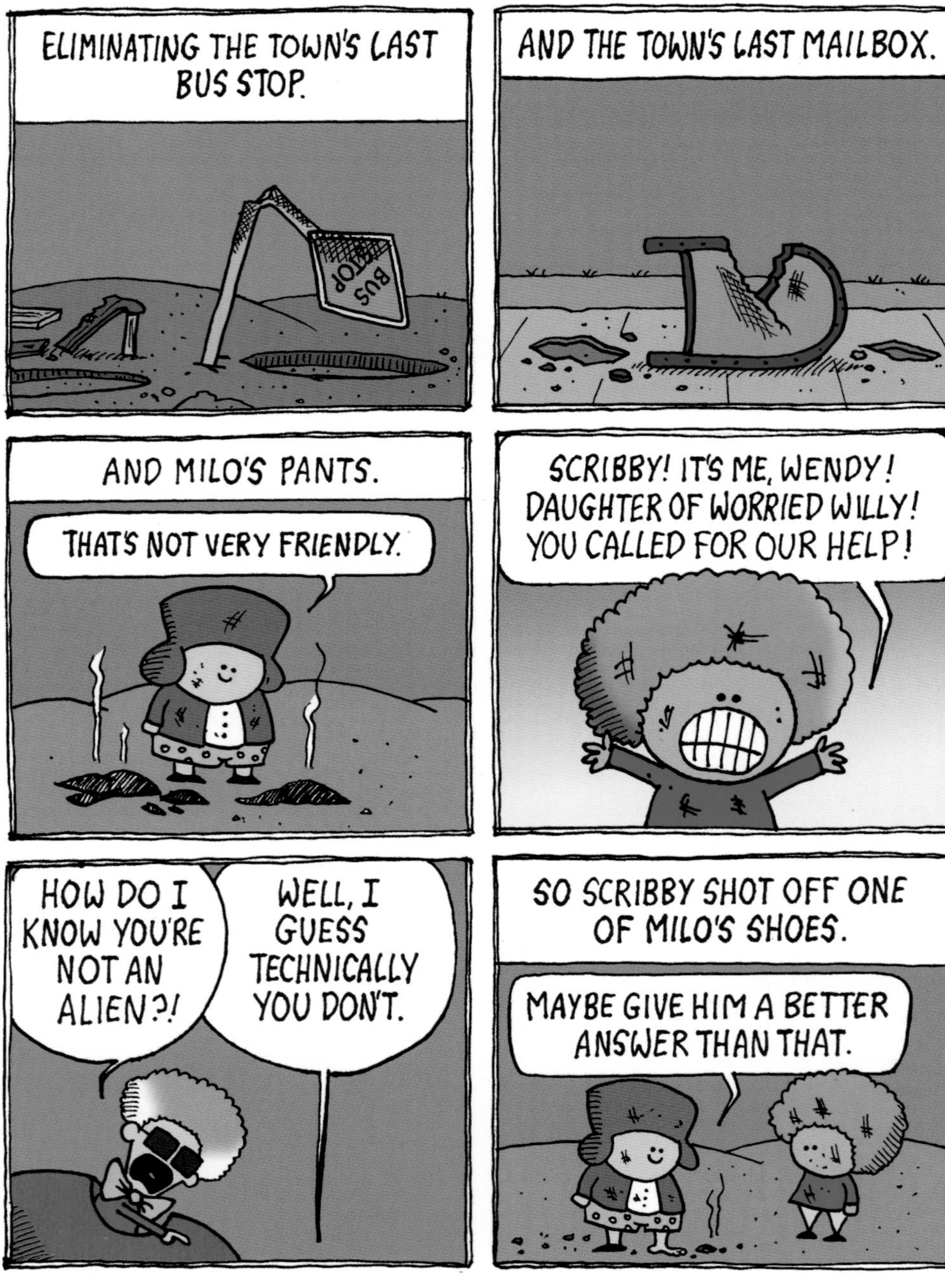
ELIMINATING THE TOWN'S LAST BUS STOP.
BUS STOP
AND THE TOWN'S LAST MAILBOX.
AND MILO'S PANTS.
THAT'S NOT VERY FRIENDLY.
SCRIBBY! IT'S ME, WENDY! DAUGHTER OF WORRIED WILLY! YOU CALLED FOR OUR HELP!
HOW DO I KNOW YOU'RE NOT AN ALIEN?!
WELL, I GUESS TECHNICALLY YOU DON'T.
SO SCRIBBY SHOT OFF ONE OF MILO'S SHOES.
MAYBE GIVE HIM A BETTER ANSWER THAN THAT.

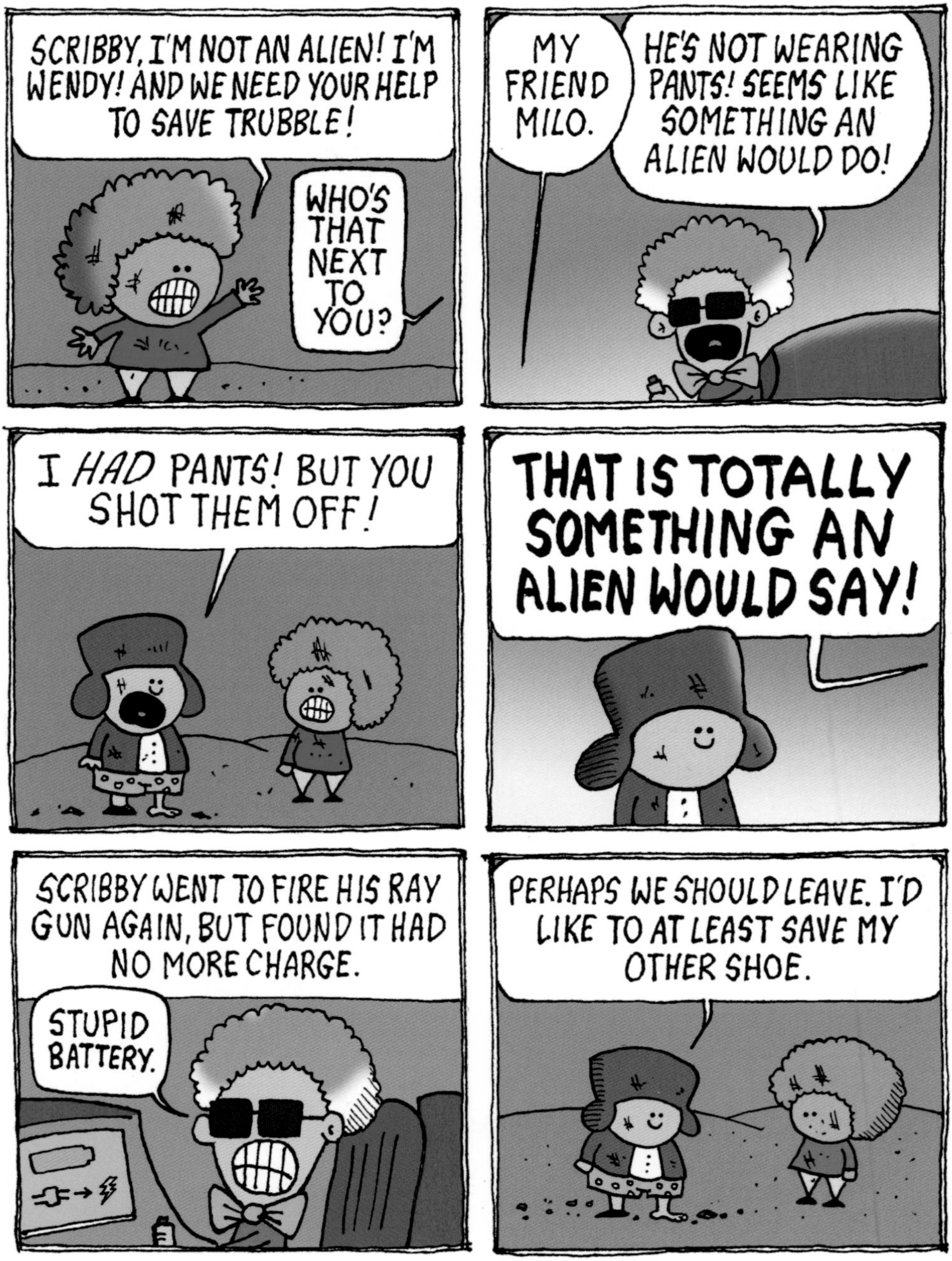
SCRIBBY, I'M NOT AN ALIEN! I'M WENDY! AND WE NEED YOUR HELP TO SAVE TRUBBLE!
WHO'S THAT NEXT TO YOU?
MY FRIEND MILO.
HE'S NOT WEARING PANTS! SEEMS LIKE SOMETHING AN ALIEN WOULD DO!
I HAD PANTS! BUT YOU SHOT THEM OFF!
THAT IS TOTALLY SOMETHING AN ALIEN WOULD SAY!
SCRIBBY WENT TO FIRE HIS RAY GUN AGAIN, BUT FOUND IT HAD NO MORE CHARGE.
STUPID BATTERY.
PERHAPS WE SHOULD LEAVE. I'D LIKE TO AT LEAST SAVE MY OTHER SHOE.

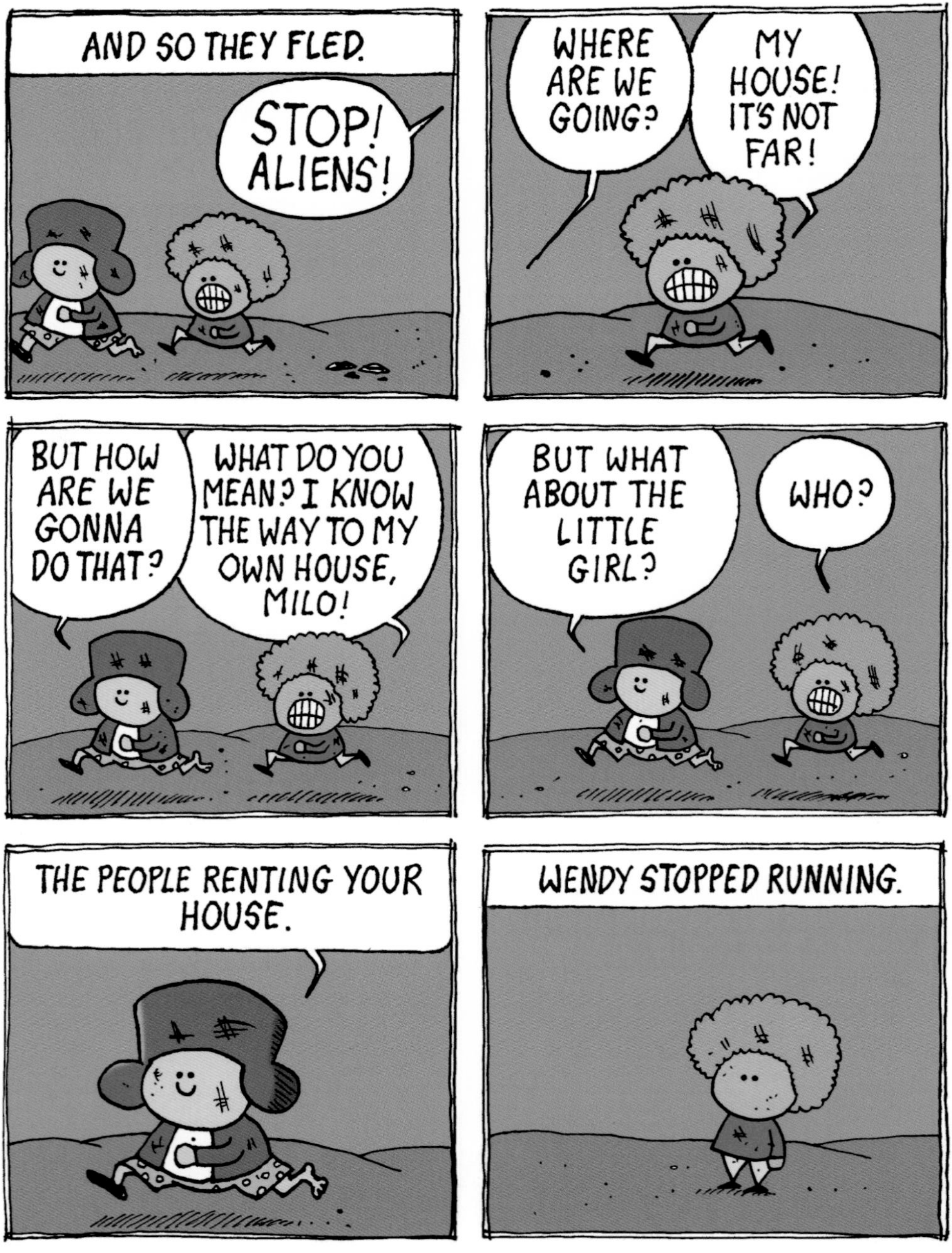
AND SO THEY FLED.
STOP! ALIENS!
WHERE ARE WE GOING?
MY HOUSE! IT'S NOT FAR!
BUT HOW ARE WE GONNA DO THAT?
WHAT DO YOU MEAN? I KNOW THE WAY TO MY OWN HOUSE, MILO!
BUT WHAT ABOUT THE LITTLE GIRL?
WHO?
THE PEOPLE RENTING YOUR HOUSE.
WENDY STOPPED RUNNING.

WE DIDN'T RENT OUR HOUSE TO ANYBODY.

CHAPTER EVEN BETTER THAN THE LAST ONE, AND THAT'S SAYING SOMETHING

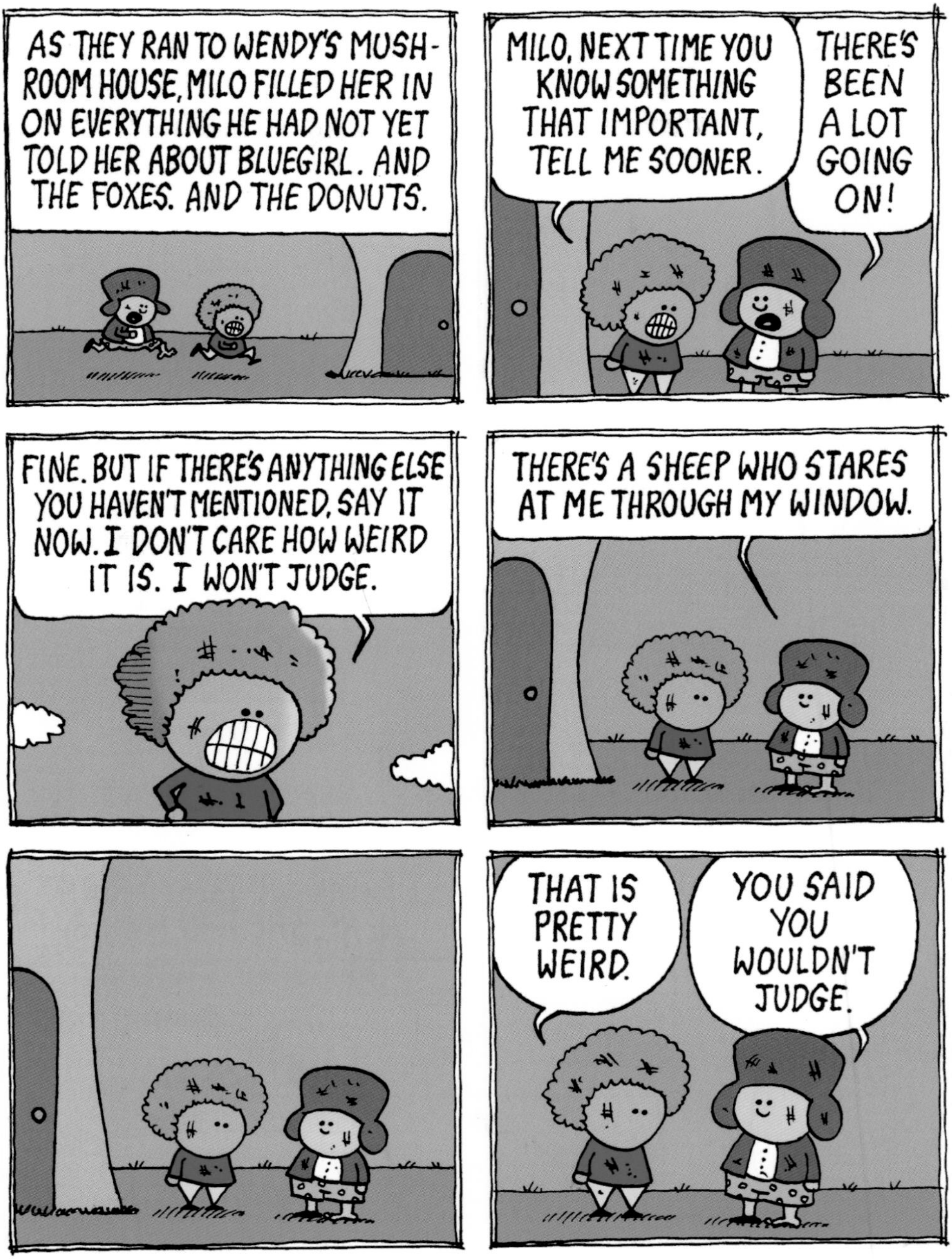
AS THEY RAN TO WENDY'S MUSH-ROOM HOUSE, MILO FILLED HER IN ON EVERYTHING HE HAD NOT YET TOLD HER ABOUT BLUEGIRL. AND THE FOXES. AND THE DONUTS.
MILO, NEXT TIME YOU KNOW SOMETHING THAT IMPORTANT, TELL ME SOONER.
THERE'S BEEN A LOT GOING ON!
FINE. BUT IF THERE'S ANYTHING ELSE YOU HAVEN'T MENTIONED, SAY IT NOW. I DON'T CARE HOW WEIRD IT IS. I WON'T JUDGE.
THERE'S A SHEEP WHO STARES AT ME THROUGH MY WINDOW.
THAT IS PRETTY WEIRD.
YOU SAID YOU WOULDN'T JUDGE.

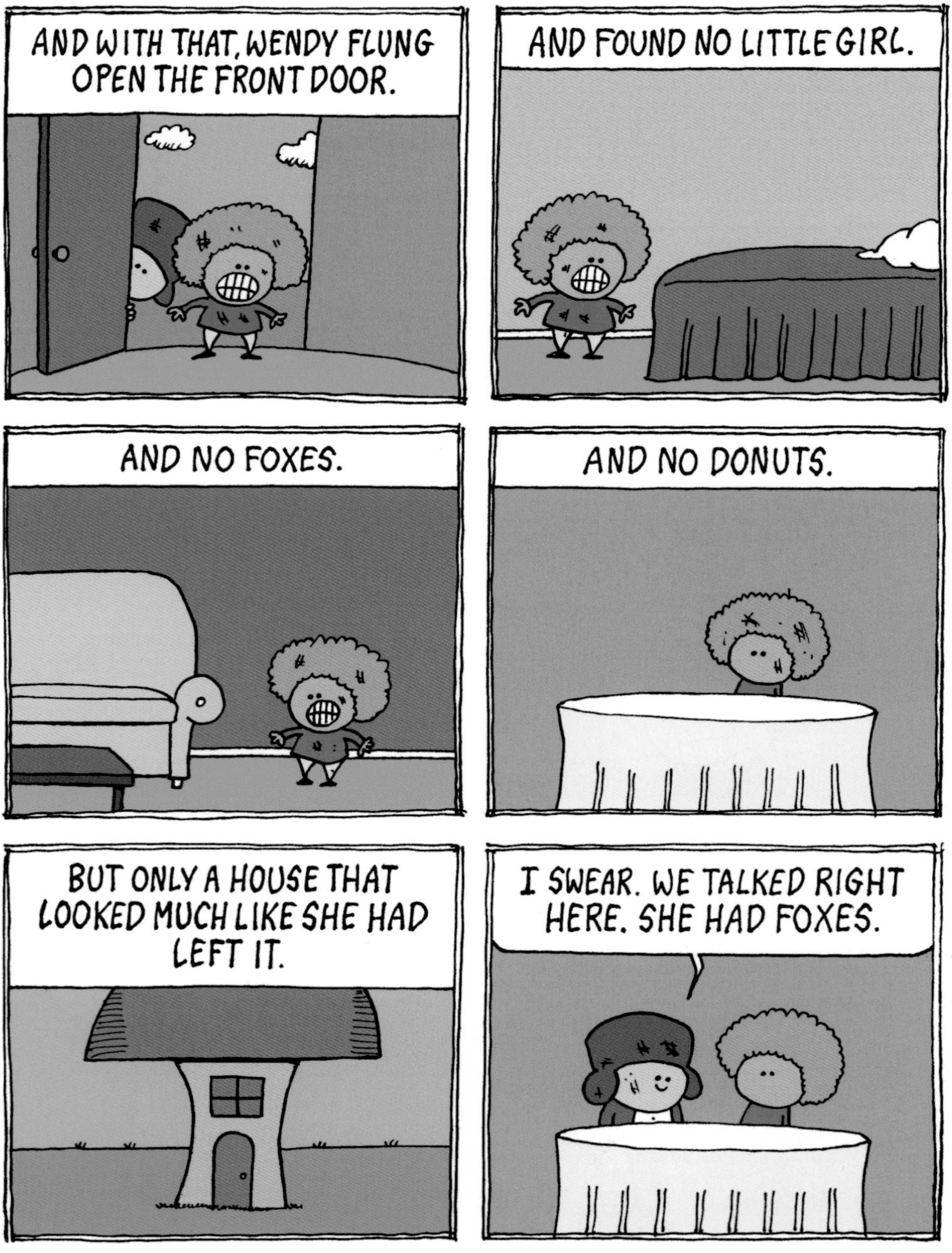
AND WITH THAT, WENDY FLUNG OPEN THE FRONT DOOR.
AND FOUND NO LITTLE GIRL.
AND NO FOXES.
AND NO DONUTS.
BUT ONLY A HOUSE THAT LOOKED MUCH LIKE SHE HAD LEFT IT.
I SWEAR. WE TALKED RIGHT HERE. SHE HAD FOXES.

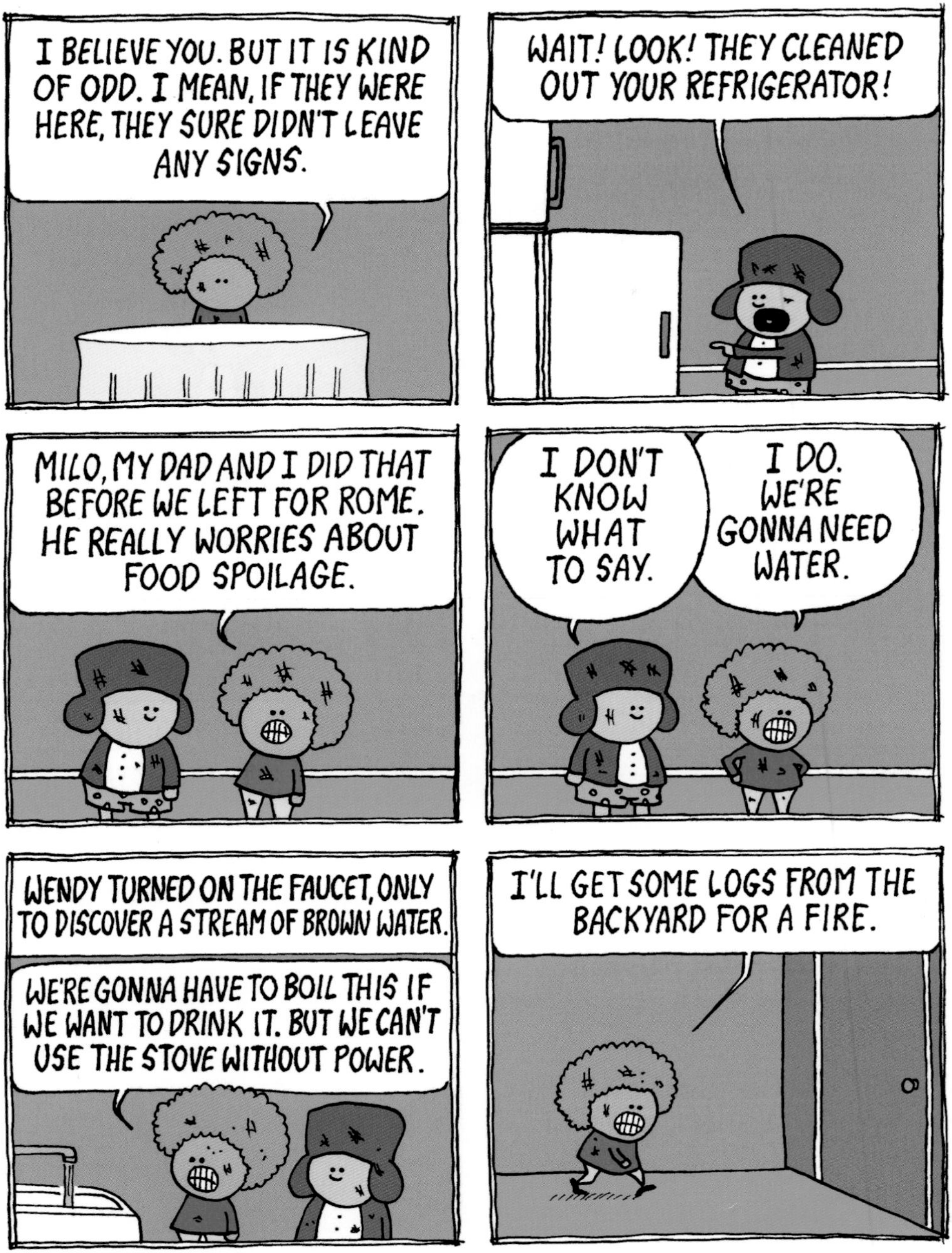
I BELIEVE YOU. BUT IT IS KIND OF ODD. I MEAN, IF THEY WERE HERE, THEY SURE DIDN'T LEAVE ANY SIGNS.
WAIT! LOOK! THEY CLEANED OUT YOUR REFRIGERATOR!
MILO, MY DAD AND I DID THAT BEFORE WE LEFT FOR ROME. HE REALLY WORRIES ABOUT FOOD SPOILAGE.
I DON'T KNOW WHAT TO SAY.
I DO. WE'RE GONNA NEED WATER.
WENDY TURNED ON THE FAUCET, ONLY TO DISCOVER A STREAM OF BROWN WATER.
WE'RE GONNA HAVE TO BOIL THIS IF WE WANT TO DRINK IT. BUT WE CAN'T USE THE STOVE WITHOUT POWER.
I'LL GET SOME LOGS FROM THE BACKYARD FOR A FIRE.

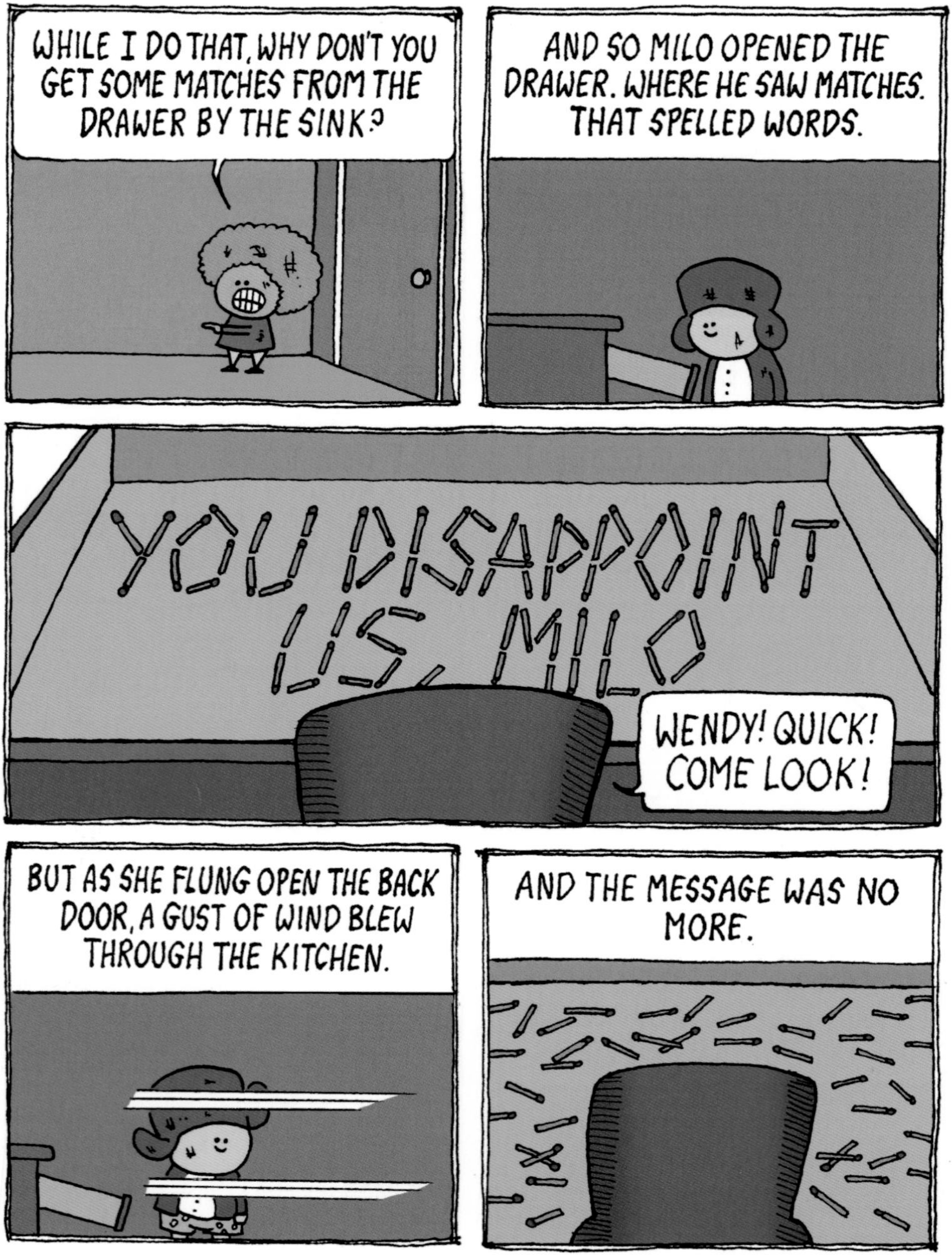
WHILE I DO THAT, WHY DON'T YOU GET SOME MATCHES FROM THE DRAWER BY THE SINK?
AND SO MILO OPENED THE DRAWER. WHERE HE SAW MATCHES. THAT SPELLED WORDS.
YOU DISAPPOINT US, MILO
WENDY! QUICK! COME LOOK!
BUT AS SHE FLUNG OPEN THE BACK DOOR, A GUST OF WIND BLEW THROUGH THE KITCHEN.
AND THE MESSAGE WAS NO MORE.

CHAPTER
27

IN WHICH...

WE RANDOMLY
ASSIGN A NUMBER
TO THIS CHAPTER

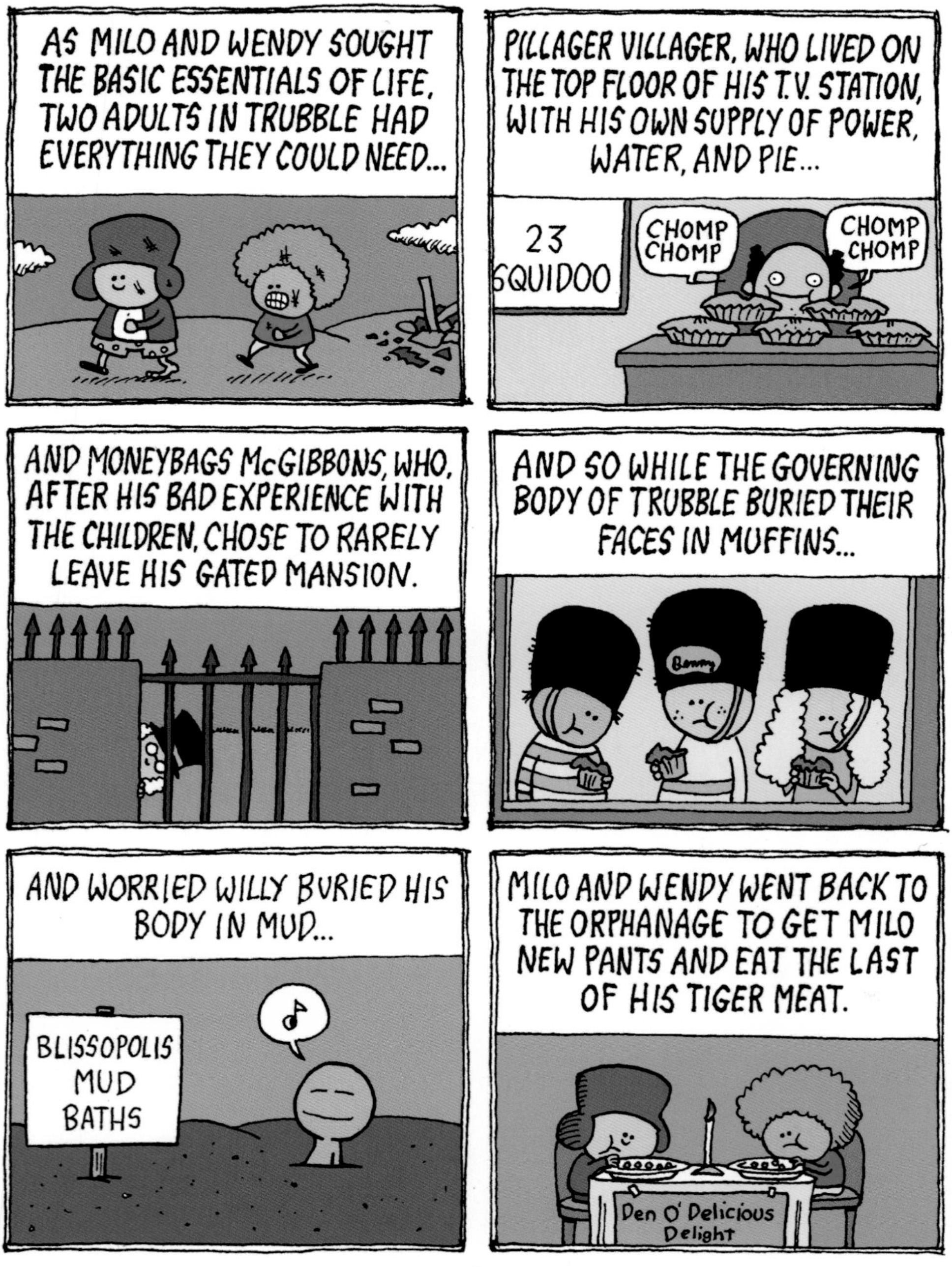
AS MILO AND WENDY SOUGHT THE BASIC ESSENTIALS OF LIFE, TWO ADULTS IN TRUBBLE HAD EVERYTHING THEY COULD NEED...
PILLAGER VILLAGER, WHO LIVED ON THE TOP FLOOR OF HIS T.V. STATION, WITH HIS OWN SUPPLY OF POWER, WATER, AND PIE...
23 SQUIDOO
CHOMP CHOMP
CHOMP CHOMP
AND MONEYBAGS McGIBBONS, WHO, AFTER HIS BAD EXPERIENCE WITH THE CHILDREN, CHOSE TO RARELY LEAVE HIS GATED MANSION.
AND SO WHILE THE GOVERNING BODY OF TRUBBLE BURIED THEIR FACES IN MUFFINS...
Benny
AND WORRIED WILLY BURIED HIS BODY IN MUD...
BLISSOPOLIS MUD BATHS
MILO AND WENDY WENT BACK TO THE ORPHANAGE TO GET MILO NEW PANTS AND EAT THE LAST OF HIS TIGER MEAT.
Den O' Delicious Delight

AND AFTERWARD SAT ON THE "BOUNCY BALLS OF BEWILDERMENT."

WHAT DO WE DO NOW?

WE THINK OF SOMETHING.

YEAH, WELL, MAYBE IT'S BETTER THAT YOU DO THAT.

WHAT'S THAT SUPPOSED TO MEAN?

I THINK IT'S FAIR TO SAY I'M PRETTY USELESS IN ALL THIS. UNLESS YOU NEED SOMEONE TO GET HIS PANTS SHOT OFF...

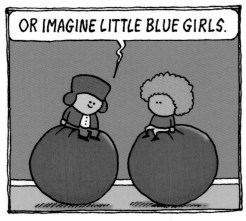

OR IMAGINE LITTLE BLUE GIRLS.

WENDY STARED AT HER FRIEND.

IS THIS ABOUT THOSE KIDS AT MOOSHY MIKE'S? I NOTICED YOU GOT REALLY QUIET AROUND THEM.

BUT MILO DIDN'T ANSWER. HE JUST GOT UP AND WALKED INTO ANOTHER ROOM.

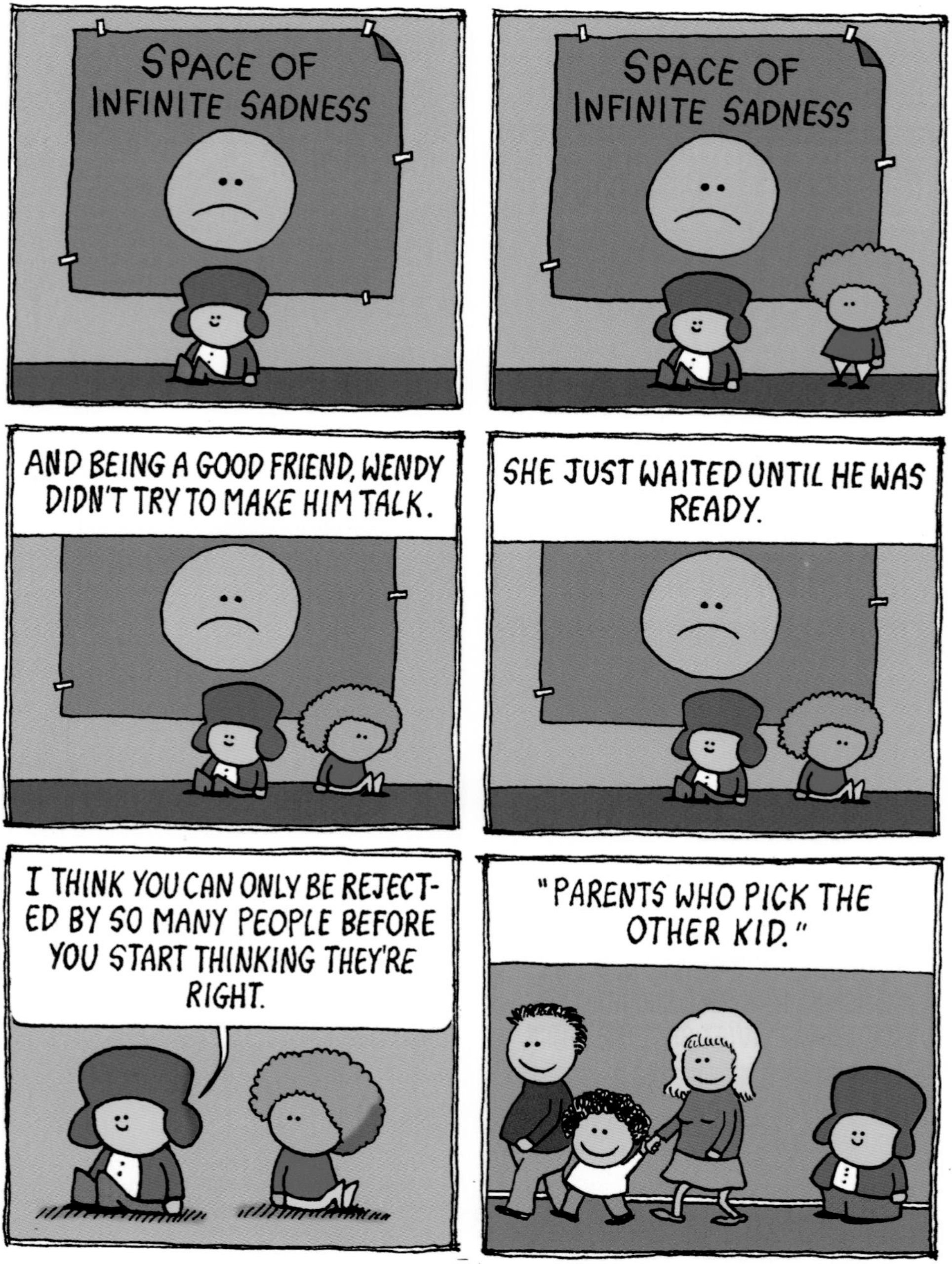
SPACE OF INFINITE SADNESS
SPACE OF INFINITE SADNESS
AND BEING A GOOD FRIEND, WENDY DIDN'T TRY TO MAKE HIM TALK.
SHE JUST WAITED UNTIL HE WAS READY.
I THINK YOU CAN ONLY BE REJECTED BY SO MANY PEOPLE BEFORE YOU START THINKING THEY'RE RIGHT.
"PARENTS WHO PICK THE OTHER KID."

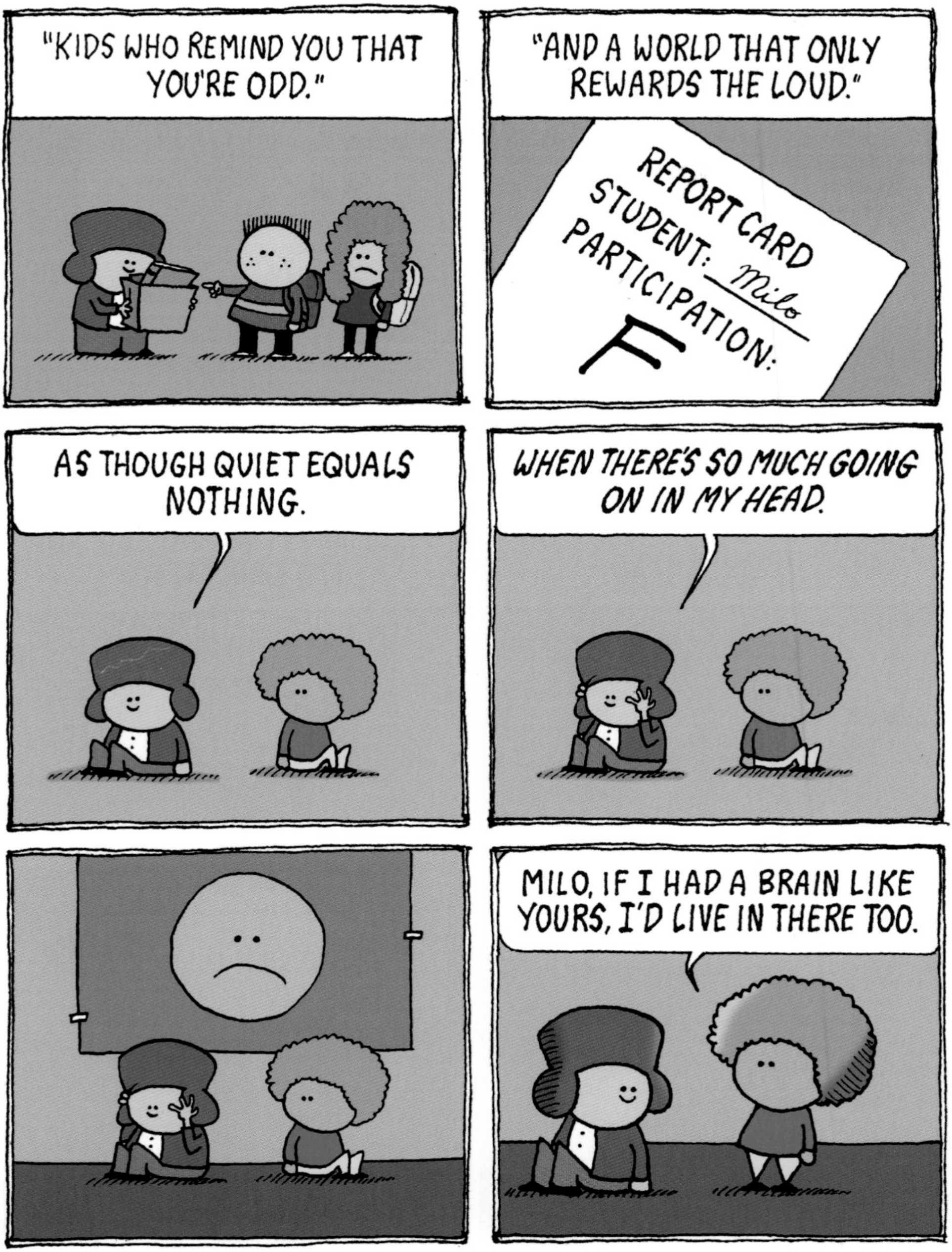
"KIDS WHO REMIND YOU THAT YOU'RE ODD."
"AND A WORLD THAT ONLY REWARDS THE LOUD."
REPORT CARD
STUDENT: Milo
PARTICIPATION:
F
AS THOUGH QUIET EQUALS NOTHING.
WHEN THERE'S SO MUCH GOING ON IN MY HEAD.
MILO, IF I HAD A BRAIN LIKE YOURS, I'D LIVE IN THERE TOO.

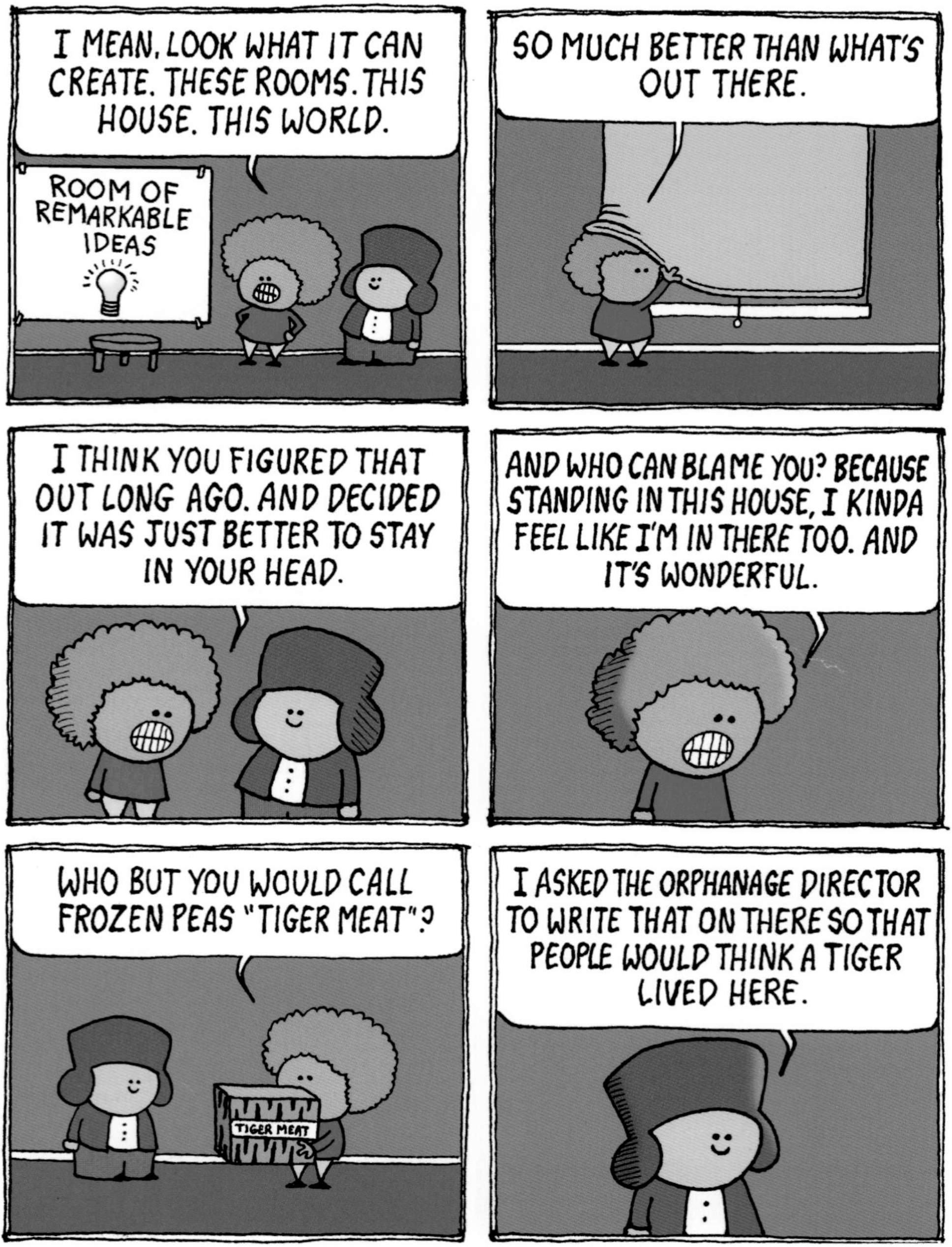
I MEAN, LOOK WHAT IT CAN CREATE. THESE ROOMS. THIS HOUSE. THIS WORLD.
ROOM OF REMARKABLE IDEAS
SO MUCH BETTER THAN WHAT'S OUT THERE.
I THINK YOU FIGURED THAT OUT LONG AGO. AND DECIDED IT WAS JUST BETTER TO STAY IN YOUR HEAD.
AND WHO CAN BLAME YOU? BECAUSE STANDING IN THIS HOUSE, I KINDA FEEL LIKE I'M IN THERE TOO. AND IT'S WONDERFUL.
WHO BUT YOU WOULD CALL FROZEN PEAS "TIGER MEAT"?
TIGER MEAT
I ASKED THE ORPHANAGE DIRECTOR TO WRITE THAT ON THERE SO THAT PEOPLE WOULD THINK A TIGER LIVED HERE.

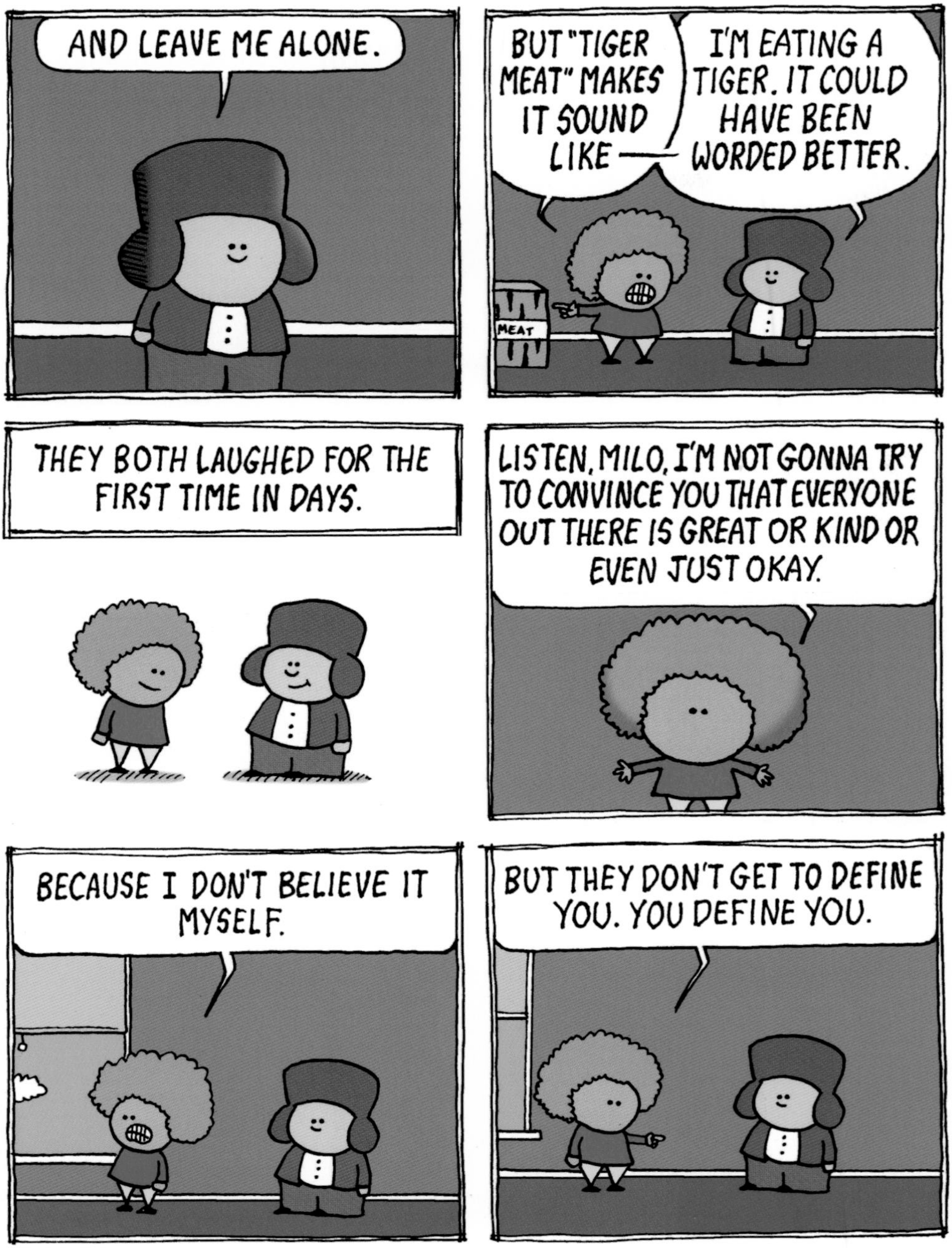
AND LEAVE ME ALONE.
BUT "TIGER MEAT" MAKES IT SOUND LIKE—
I'M EATING A TIGER. IT COULD HAVE BEEN WORDED BETTER.
MEAT
THEY BOTH LAUGHED FOR THE FIRST TIME IN DAYS.
LISTEN, MILO, I'M NOT GONNA TRY TO CONVINCE YOU THAT EVERYONE OUT THERE IS GREAT OR KIND OR EVEN JUST OKAY.
BECAUSE I DON'T BELIEVE IT MYSELF.
BUT THEY DON'T GET TO DEFINE YOU. YOU DEFINE YOU.

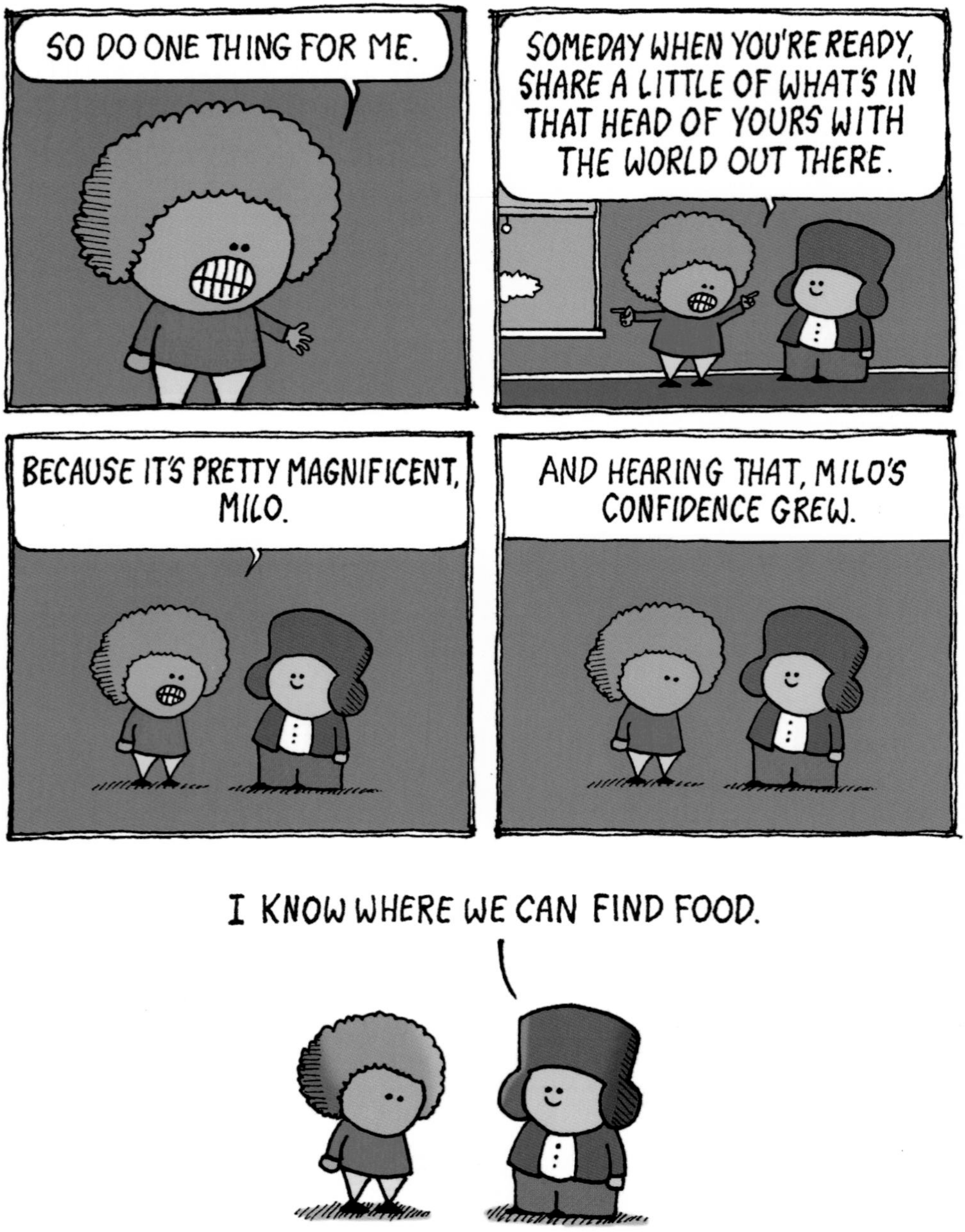
SO DO ONE THING FOR ME.
SOMEDAY WHEN YOU'RE READY, SHARE A LITTLE OF WHAT'S IN THAT HEAD OF YOURS WITH THE WORLD OUT THERE.
BECAUSE IT'S PRETTY MAGNIFICENT, MILO.
AND HEARING THAT, MILO'S CONFIDENCE GREW.
I KNOW WHERE WE CAN FIND FOOD.

CHAPTER 28

IN WHICH...

WE NUMBER CHAPTERS LIKE NORMAL PEOPLE

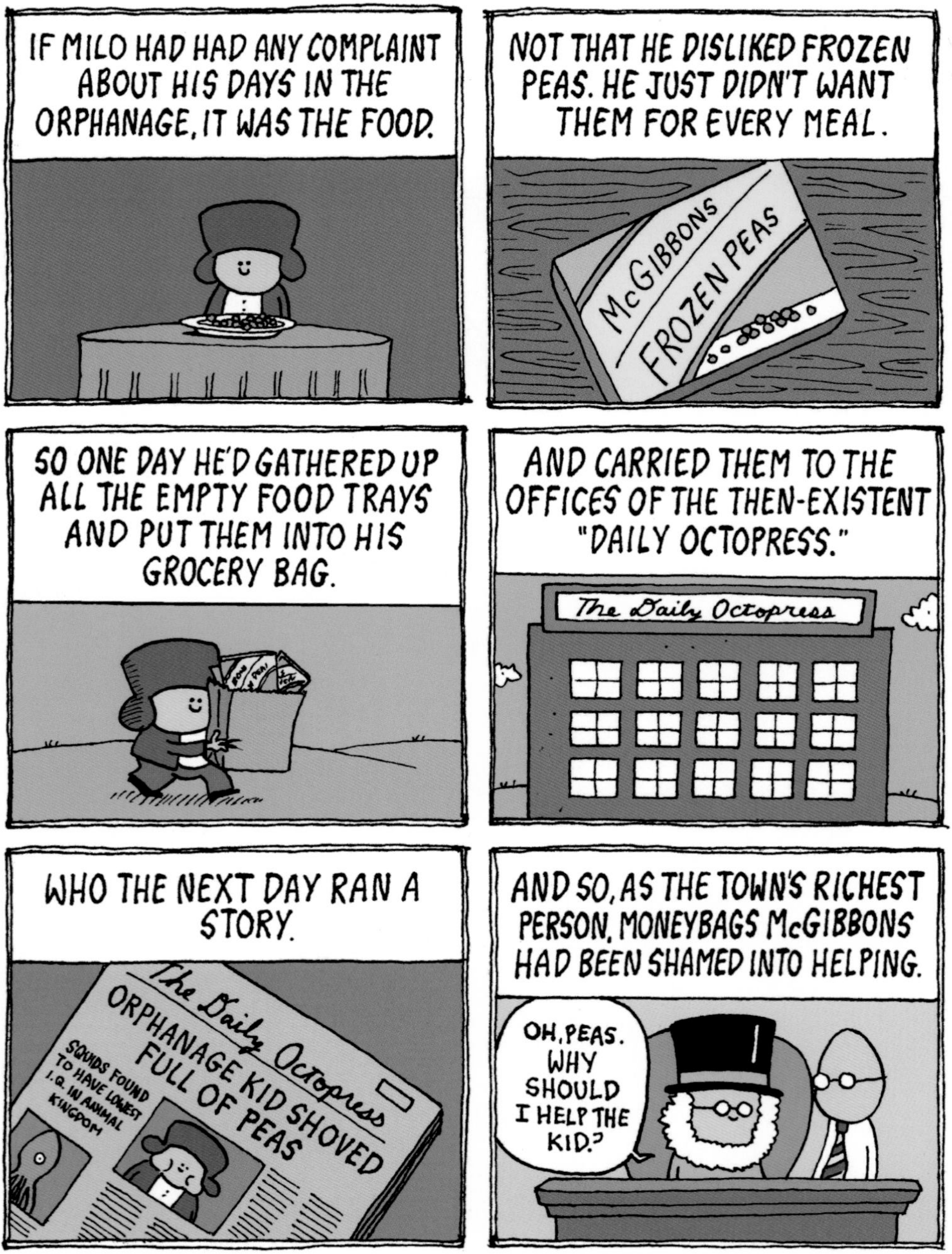
IF MILO HAD HAD ANY COMPLAINT ABOUT HIS DAYS IN THE ORPHANAGE, IT WAS THE FOOD.
NOT THAT HE DISLIKED FROZEN PEAS. HE JUST DIDN'T WANT THEM FOR EVERY MEAL.
McGIBBONS
FROZEN PEAS
SO ONE DAY HE'D GATHERED UP ALL THE EMPTY FOOD TRAYS AND PUT THEM INTO HIS GROCERY BAG.
AND CARRIED THEM TO THE OFFICES OF THE THEN-EXISTENT "DAILY OCTOPRESS."
The Daily Octopress
WHO THE NEXT DAY RAN A STORY.
The Daily Octopress
ORPHANAGE KID SHOVED FULL OF PEAS
SQUIDS FOUND TO HAVE LOWEST I.Q. IN ANIMAL KINGDOM
AND SO, AS THE TOWN'S RICHEST PERSON, MONEYBAGS McGIBBONS HAD BEEN SHAMED INTO HELPING.
OH, PEAS. WHY SHOULD I HELP THE KID?

BY GIVING MILO ONE GIFT CERTIFICATE A YEAR FOR DINNER AT ANY RESTAURANT, PROVIDED IT COST NO MORE THAN $2.75.

MAYBE HE CAN BUY A BREADSTICK.

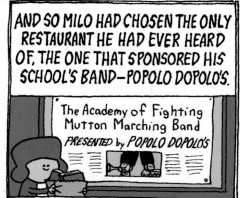

AND SO MILO HAD CHOSEN THE ONLY RESTAURANT HE HAD EVER HEARD OF, THE ONE THAT SPONSORED HIS SCHOOL'S BAND—POPOLO DOPOLO'S.

The Academy of Fighting Mutton Marching Band
PRESENTED by POPOLO DOPOLO'S

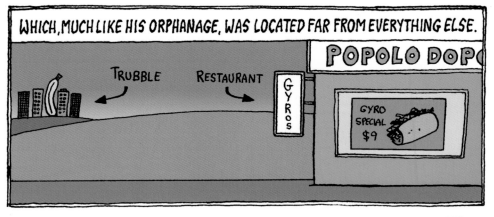

WHICH, MUCH LIKE HIS ORPHANAGE, WAS LOCATED FAR FROM EVERYTHING ELSE.

TRUBBLE

RESTAURANT

GYROS

POPOLO DOP

GYRO SPECIAL $9

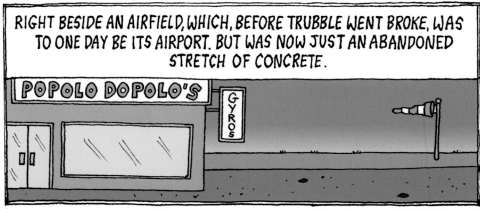

RIGHT BESIDE AN AIRFIELD, WHICH, BEFORE TRUBBLE WENT BROKE, WAS TO ONE DAY BE ITS AIRPORT. BUT WAS NOW JUST AN ABANDONED STRETCH OF CONCRETE.

POPOLO DOPOLO'S

GYROS

AND THUS, POPOLO DOPOLO'S HAD NO CUSTOMERS.

WHICH NEVER STOPPED ITS OWNER, POPOLO DOPOLO, FROM COOKING ENORMOUS MOUNDS OF FOOD.

POPOLO DOPOLO

FOR THE CUSTOMERS HE HOPED WOULD ONE DAY COME.

BUT WHO AT THAT MOMENT CONSISTED OF ONLY MILO.

WHO RECEIVED FOOD FAR IN EXCESS OF HIS GIFT CERTIFICATE.

FROM THE PROUD AND BEAMING POPOLO.

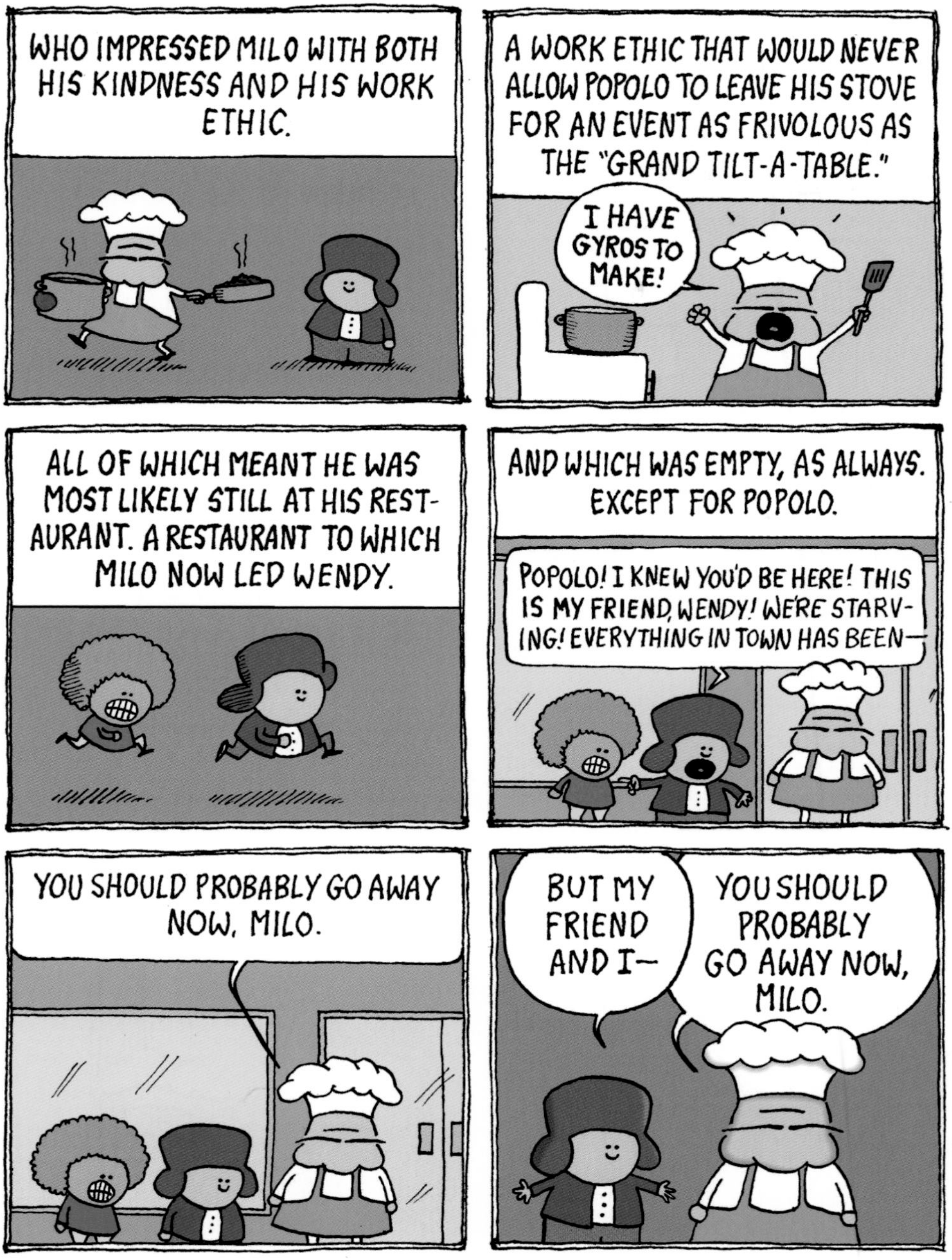
WHO IMPRESSED MILO WITH BOTH HIS KINDNESS AND HIS WORK ETHIC.
A WORK ETHIC THAT WOULD NEVER ALLOW POPOLO TO LEAVE HIS STOVE FOR AN EVENT AS FRIVOLOUS AS THE "GRAND TILT-A-TABLE."
I HAVE GYROS TO MAKE!
ALL OF WHICH MEANT HE WAS MOST LIKELY STILL AT HIS REST-AURANT. A RESTAURANT TO WHICH MILO NOW LED WENDY.
AND WHICH WAS EMPTY, AS ALWAYS. EXCEPT FOR POPOLO.
POPOLO! I KNEW YOU'D BE HERE! THIS IS MY FRIEND, WENDY! WE'RE STARV-ING! EVERYTHING IN TOWN HAS BEEN—
YOU SHOULD PROBABLY GO AWAY NOW, MILO.
BUT MY FRIEND AND I—
YOU SHOULD PROBABLY GO AWAY NOW, MILO.

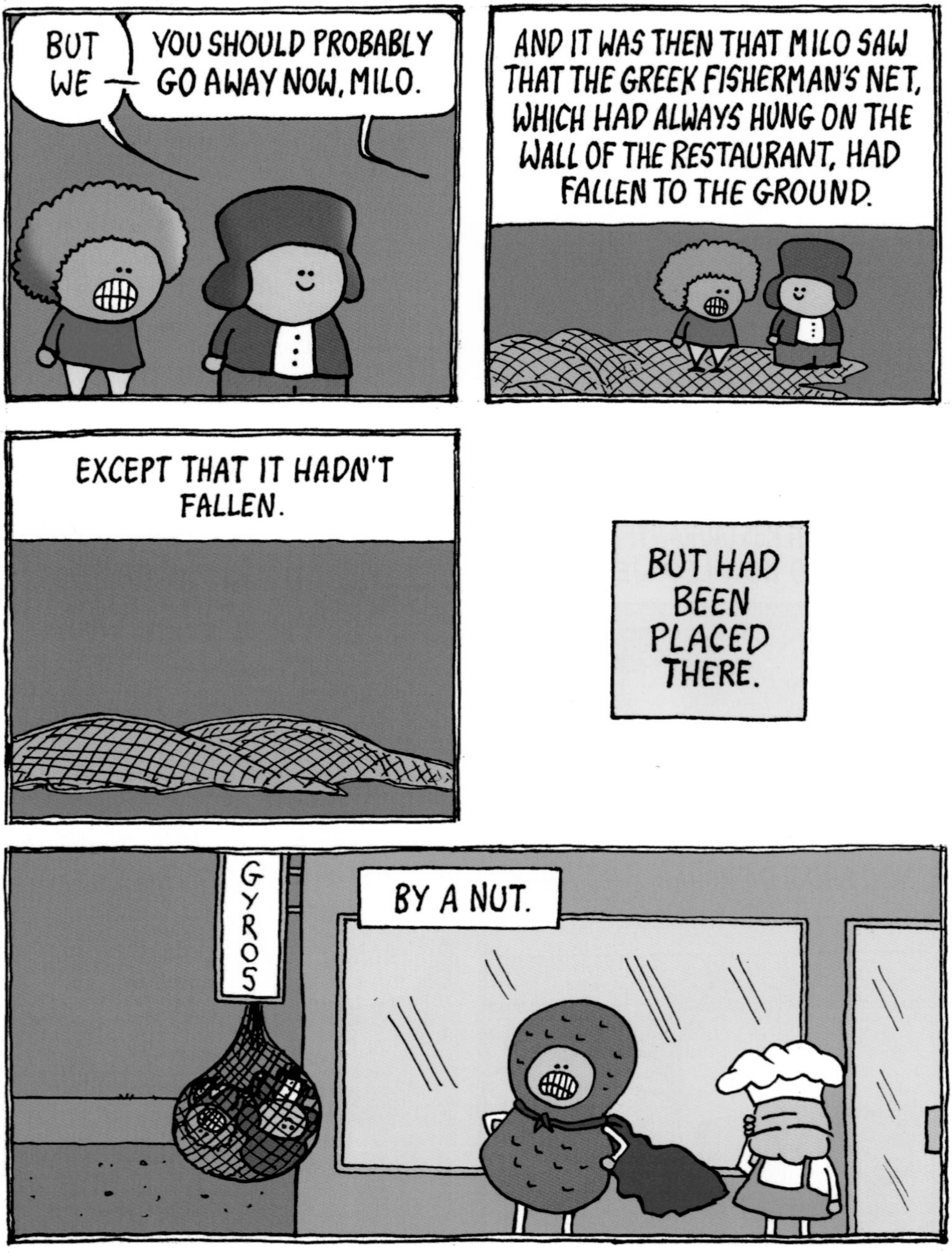
BUT WE —
YOU SHOULD PROBABLY GO AWAY NOW, MILO.
AND IT WAS THEN THAT MILO SAW THAT THE GREEK FISHERMAN'S NET, WHICH HAD ALWAYS HUNG ON THE WALL OF THE RESTAURANT, HAD FALLEN TO THE GROUND.
EXCEPT THAT IT HADN'T FALLEN.
BUT HAD BEEN PLACED THERE.
GYROS
BY A NUT.

CHAPTER GREAT

IN WHICH...

WE TRY TO BE HUMBLE, BUT FAIL

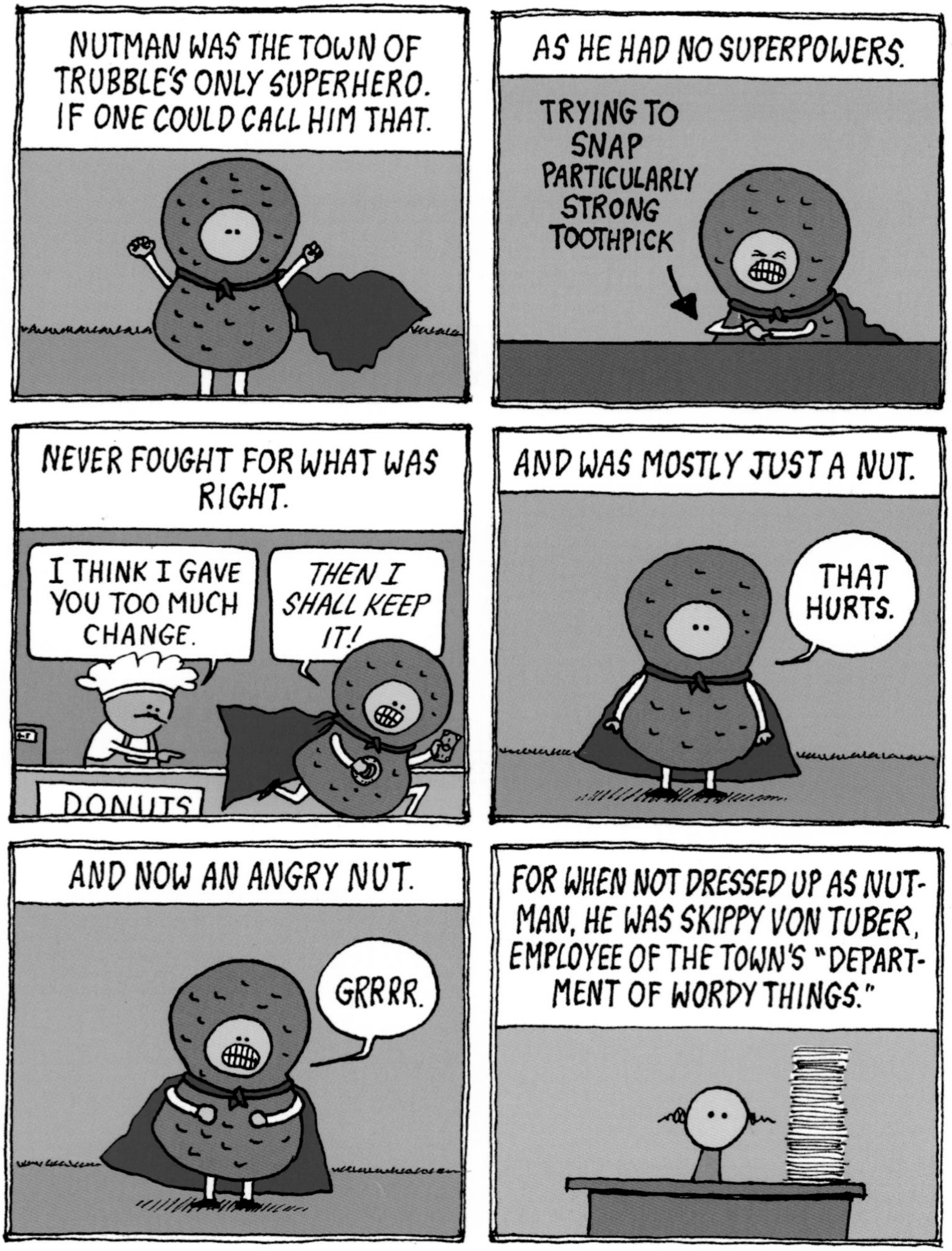
NUTMAN WAS THE TOWN OF TRUBBLE'S ONLY SUPERHERO. IF ONE COULD CALL HIM THAT.
AS HE HAD NO SUPERPOWERS.
TRYING TO SNAP PARTICULARLY STRONG TOOTHPICK
NEVER FOUGHT FOR WHAT WAS RIGHT.
I THINK I GAVE YOU TOO MUCH CHANGE.
THEN I SHALL KEEP IT!
DONUTS
AND WAS MOSTLY JUST A NUT.
THAT HURTS.
AND NOW AN ANGRY NUT.
GRRRR.
FOR WHEN NOT DRESSED UP AS NUT-MAN, HE WAS SKIPPY VON TUBER, EMPLOYEE OF THE TOWN'S "DEPART-MENT OF WORDY THINGS."

UNTIL THE BROKE TOWN SHUT IT DOWN.

SOMEONE WILL PAY FOR THIS.

DEPARTMENT OF WORDY THINGS

AND WHILE THAT EXPLAINED HIS ANGER, IT DID NOT EXPLAIN HIS RATIONALE FOR RESORTING TO CRIME.

THAT, I SHALL NEVER REVEAL!

BUT NUTMAN WAS JUST AS BAD AT BEING A CRIMINAL MASTERMIND AS HE WAS AT BEING A SUPERHERO. AND SO WHEN WENDY ASKED, HE REVEALED.

IT ALL STARTED THE DAY THE TOWN LAID ME OFF!

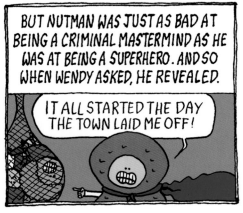

AND IT WAS ALL THE FAULT OF MONEYBAGS McGIBBONS!

"FOR WHEN OUR MAYOR WENT TO HIM FOR MONEY, HE INSISTED THAT IT ALL BE SPENT ON THAT DREADED DOLPHIN."

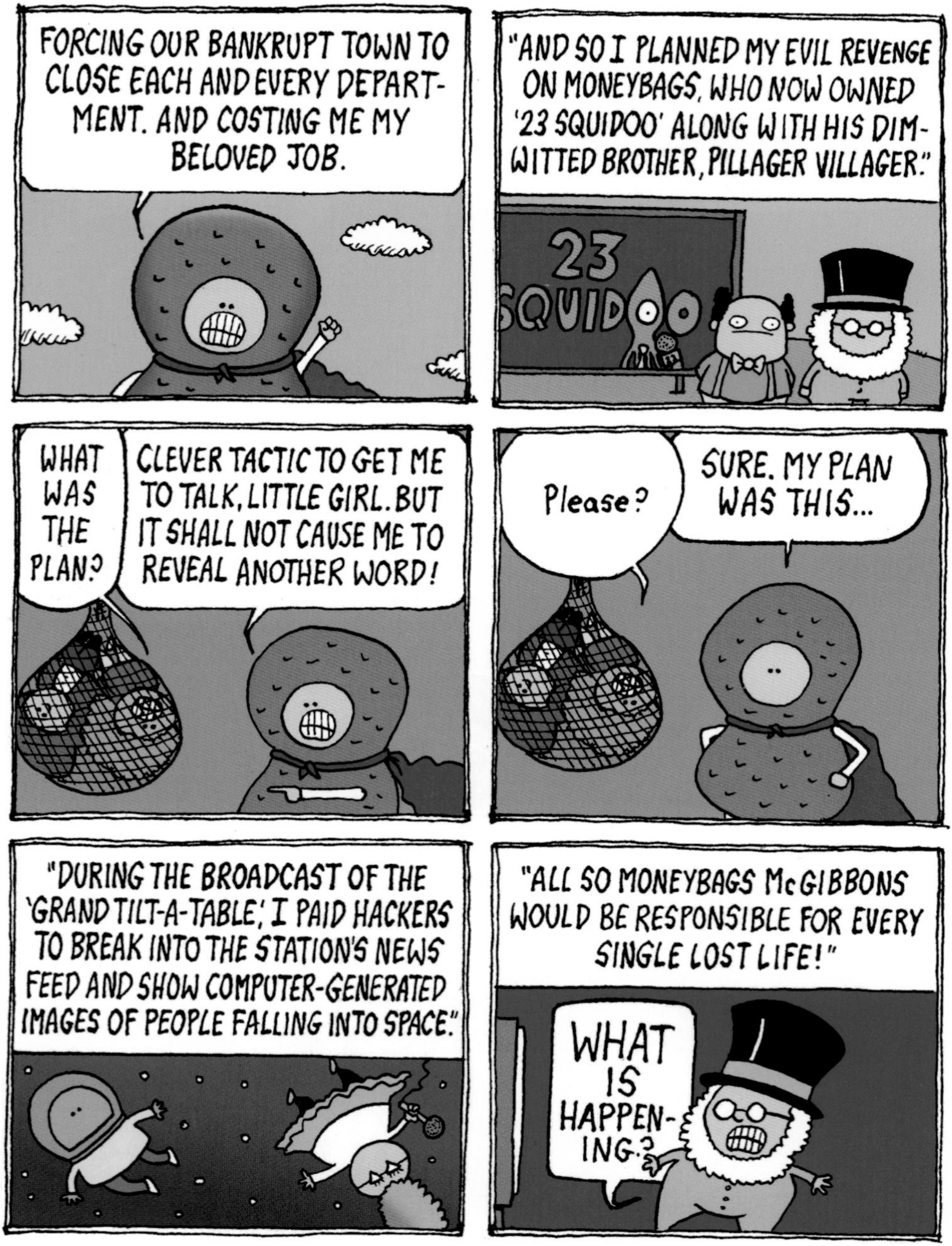

FORCING OUR BANKRUPT TOWN TO CLOSE EACH AND EVERY DEPARTMENT. AND COSTING ME MY BELOVED JOB.
"AND SO I PLANNED MY EVIL REVENGE ON MONEYBAGS, WHO NOW OWNED '23 SQUIDOO' ALONG WITH HIS DIM-WITTED BROTHER, PILLAGER VILLAGER."
23 SQUIDOO
WHAT WAS THE PLAN?
CLEVER TACTIC TO GET ME TO TALK, LITTLE GIRL. BUT IT SHALL NOT CAUSE ME TO REVEAL ANOTHER WORD!
Please?
SURE. MY PLAN WAS THIS...
"DURING THE BROADCAST OF THE 'GRAND TILT-A-TABLE,' I PAID HACKERS TO BREAK INTO THE STATION'S NEWS FEED AND SHOW COMPUTER-GENERATED IMAGES OF PEOPLE FALLING INTO SPACE."
"ALL SO MONEYBAGS McGIBBONS WOULD BE RESPONSIBLE FOR EVERY SINGLE LOST LIFE!"
WHAT IS HAPPENING?

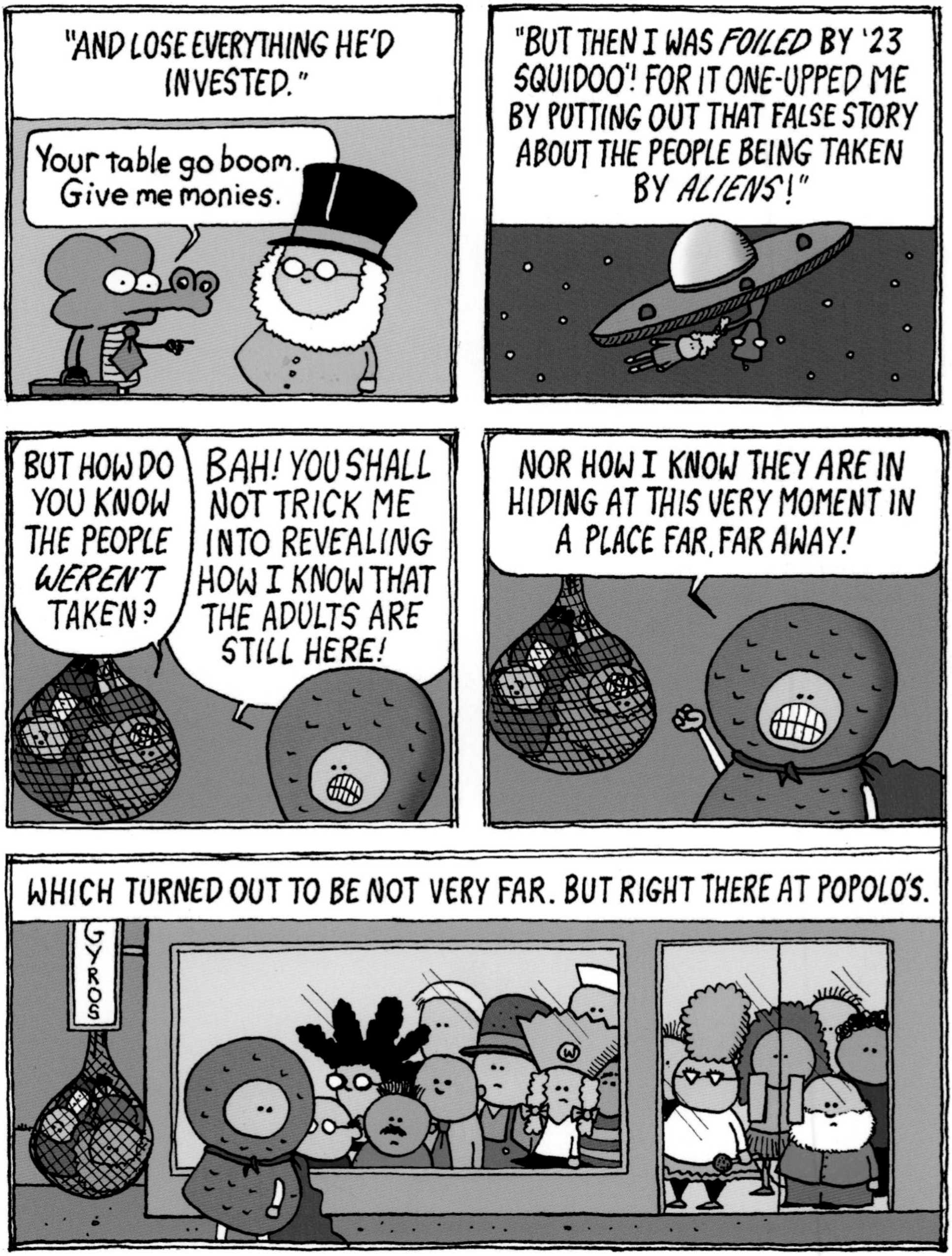
"AND LOSE EVERYTHING HE'D INVESTED."
Your table go boom. Give me monies.
"BUT THEN I WAS *FOILED* BY '23 SQUIDOO'! FOR IT ONE-UPPED ME BY PUTTING OUT THAT FALSE STORY ABOUT THE PEOPLE BEING TAKEN BY *ALIENS*!"
BUT HOW DO YOU KNOW THE PEOPLE *WEREN'T* TAKEN?
BAH! YOU SHALL NOT TRICK ME INTO REVEALING HOW I KNOW THAT THE ADULTS ARE STILL HERE!
NOR HOW I KNOW THEY ARE IN HIDING AT THIS VERY MOMENT IN A PLACE FAR, FAR AWAY!
WHICH TURNED OUT TO BE NOT VERY FAR. BUT RIGHT THERE AT POPOLO'S.
GYROS

CHAPTER WOW

IN WHICH...

YOU ARE SUITABLY WOWED, OR WE GIVE YOU YOUR MONEY BACK *

* Not true. Don't try.

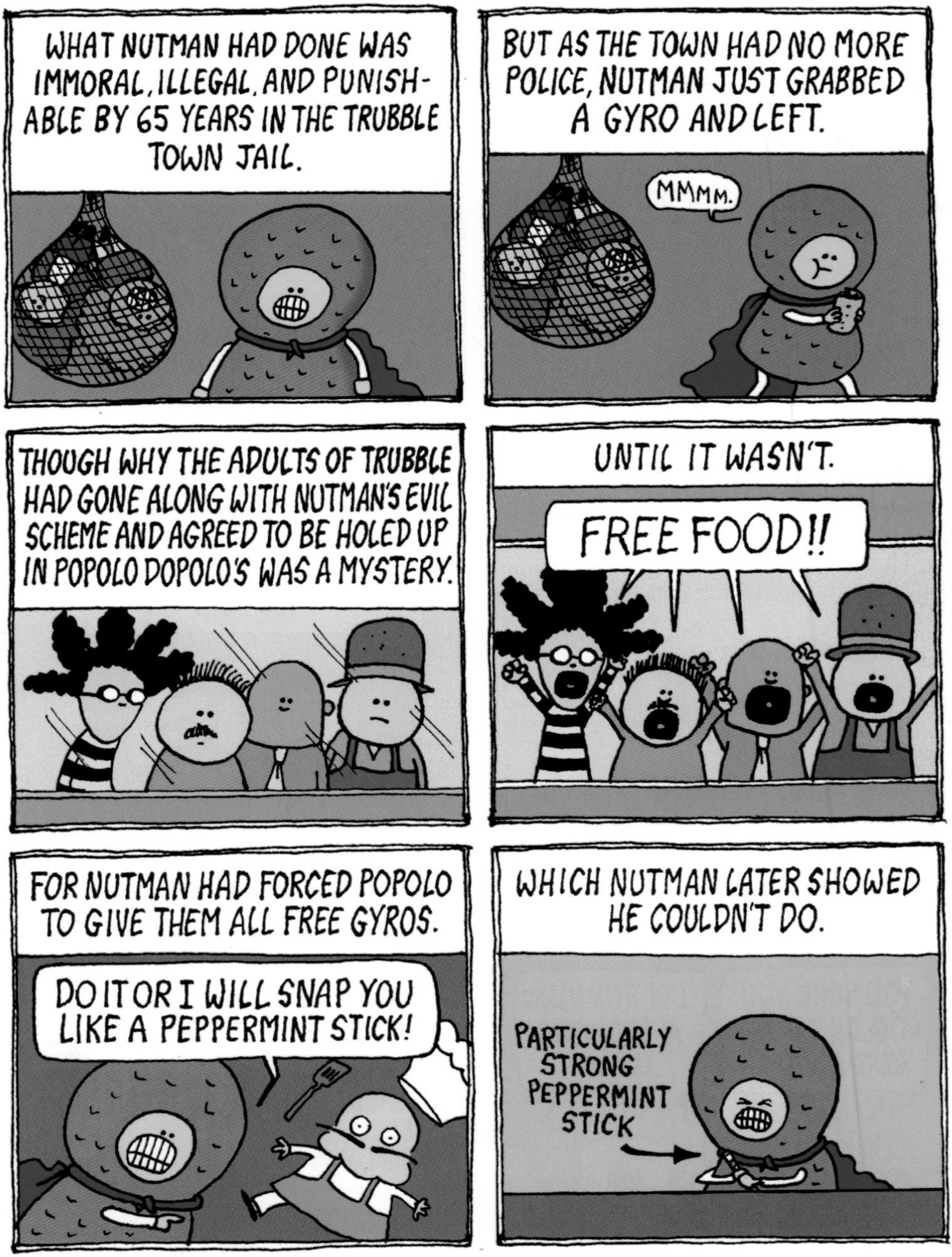
WHAT NUTMAN HAD DONE WAS IMMORAL, ILLEGAL, AND PUNISHABLE BY 65 YEARS IN THE TRUBBLE TOWN JAIL.
BUT AS THE TOWN HAD NO MORE POLICE, NUTMAN JUST GRABBED A GYRO AND LEFT.
MMMM.
THOUGH WHY THE ADULTS OF TRUBBLE HAD GONE ALONG WITH NUTMAN'S EVIL SCHEME AND AGREED TO BE HOLED UP IN POPOLO DOPOLO'S WAS A MYSTERY.
UNTIL IT WASN'T.
FREE FOOD!!
FOR NUTMAN HAD FORCED POPOLO TO GIVE THEM ALL FREE GYROS.
DO IT OR I WILL SNAP YOU LIKE A PEPPERMINT STICK!
WHICH NUTMAN LATER SHOWED HE COULDN'T DO.
PARTICULARLY STRONG PEPPERMINT STICK

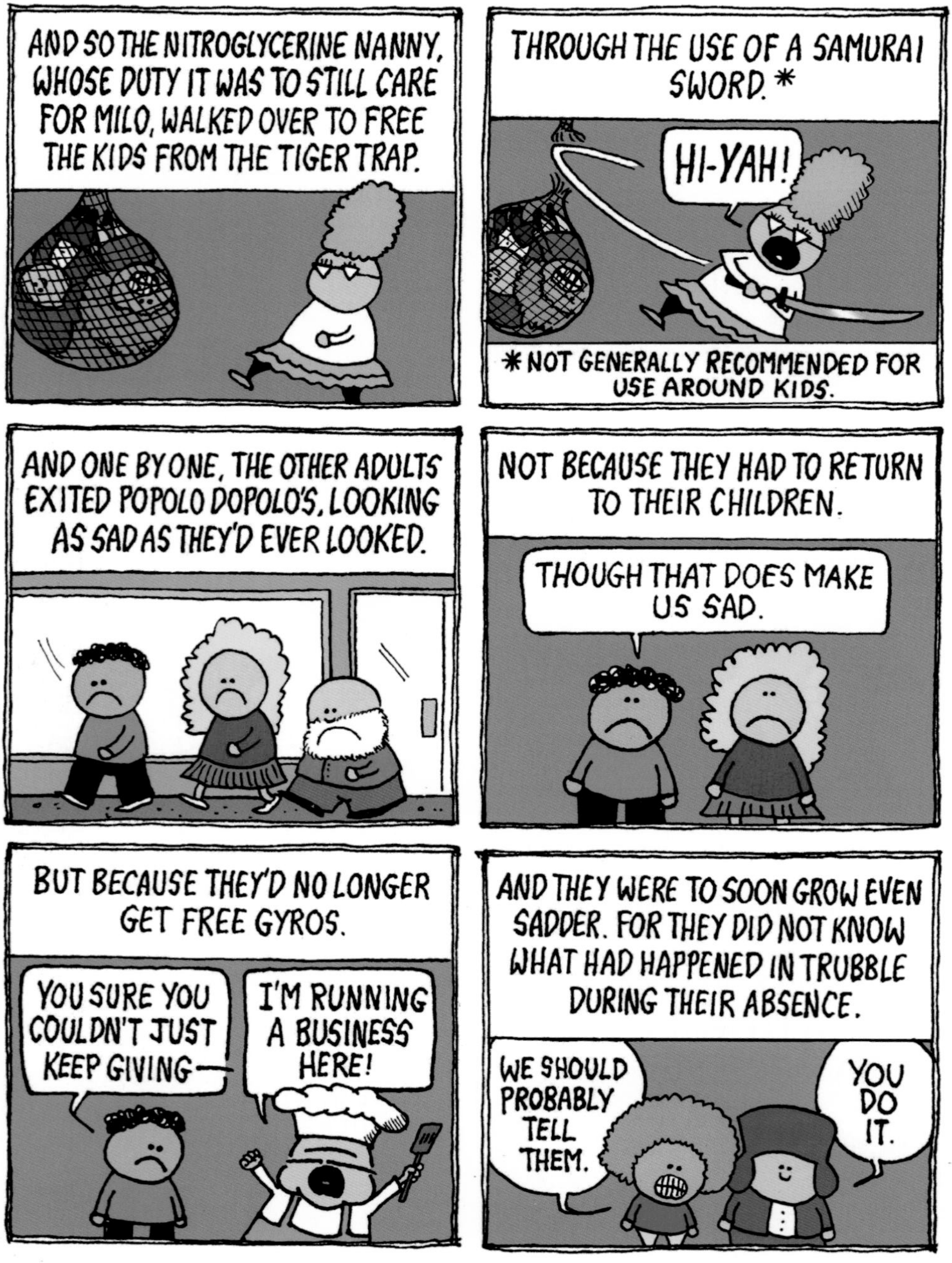
AND SO THE NITROGLYCERINE NANNY, WHOSE DUTY IT WAS TO STILL CARE FOR MILO, WALKED OVER TO FREE THE KIDS FROM THE TIGER TRAP.
THROUGH THE USE OF A SAMURAI SWORD.*
HI-YAH!
*NOT GENERALLY RECOMMENDED FOR USE AROUND KIDS.
AND ONE BY ONE, THE OTHER ADULTS EXITED POPOLO DOPOLO'S, LOOKING AS SAD AS THEY'D EVER LOOKED.
NOT BECAUSE THEY HAD TO RETURN TO THEIR CHILDREN.
THOUGH THAT DOES MAKE US SAD.
BUT BECAUSE THEY'D NO LONGER GET FREE GYROS.
YOU SURE YOU COULDN'T JUST KEEP GIVING—
I'M RUNNING A BUSINESS HERE!
AND THEY WERE TO SOON GROW EVEN SADDER. FOR THEY DID NOT KNOW WHAT HAD HAPPENED IN TRUBBLE DURING THEIR ABSENCE.
WE SHOULD PROBABLY TELL THEM.
YOU DO IT.

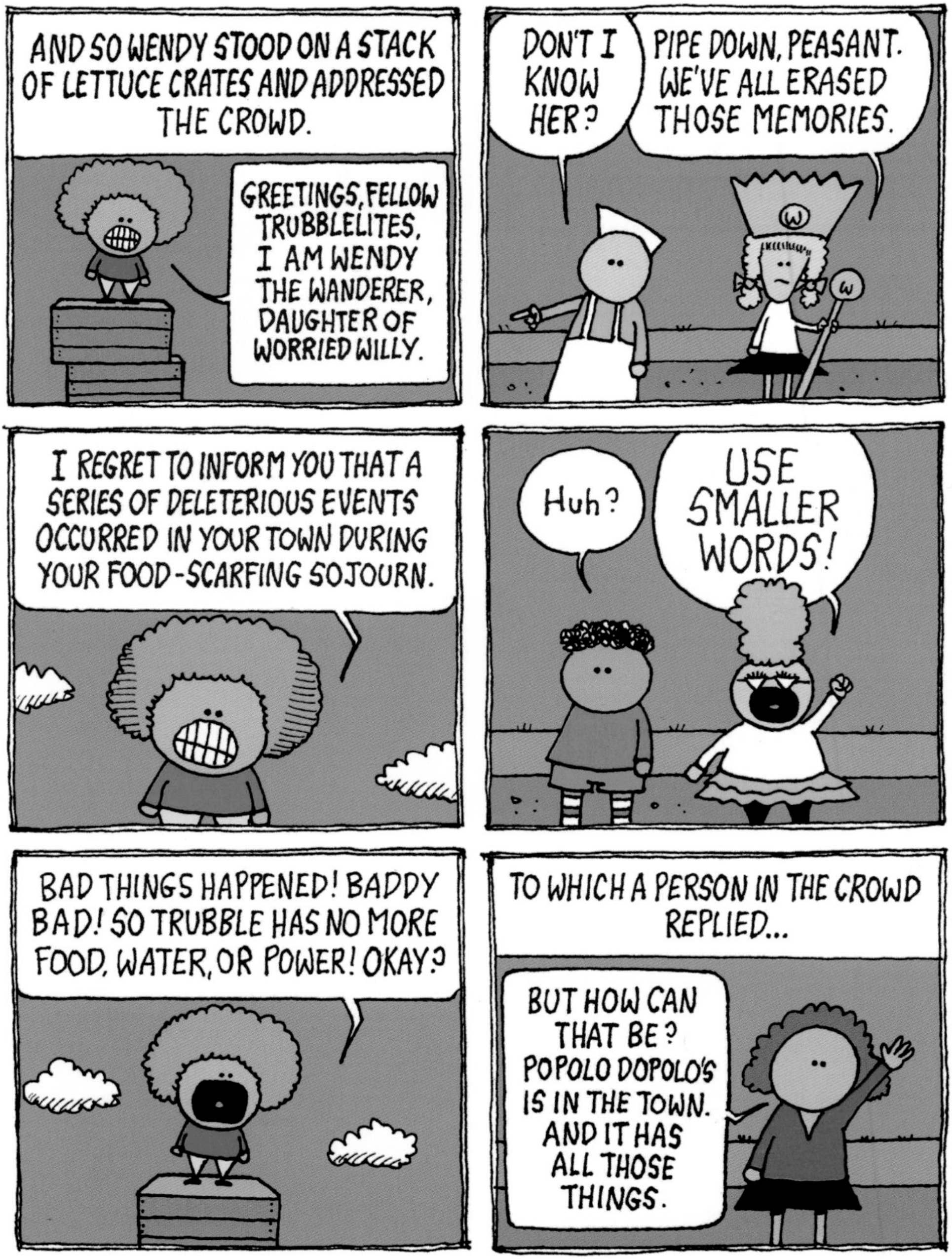

AND SO WENDY STOOD ON A STACK OF LETTUCE CRATES AND ADDRESSED THE CROWD.
GREETINGS, FELLOW TRUBBLELITES. I AM WENDY THE WANDERER, DAUGHTER OF WORRIED WILLY.
DON'T I KNOW HER?
PIPE DOWN, PEASANT. WE'VE ALL ERASED THOSE MEMORIES.
I REGRET TO INFORM YOU THAT A SERIES OF DELETERIOUS EVENTS OCCURRED IN YOUR TOWN DURING YOUR FOOD-SCARFING SOJOURN.
Huh?
USE SMALLER WORDS!
BAD THINGS HAPPENED! BADDY BAD! SO TRUBBLE HAS NO MORE FOOD, WATER, OR POWER! OKAY?
TO WHICH A PERSON IN THE CROWD REPLIED...
BUT HOW CAN THAT BE? POPOLO DOPOLO'S IS IN THE TOWN. AND IT HAS ALL THOSE THINGS.

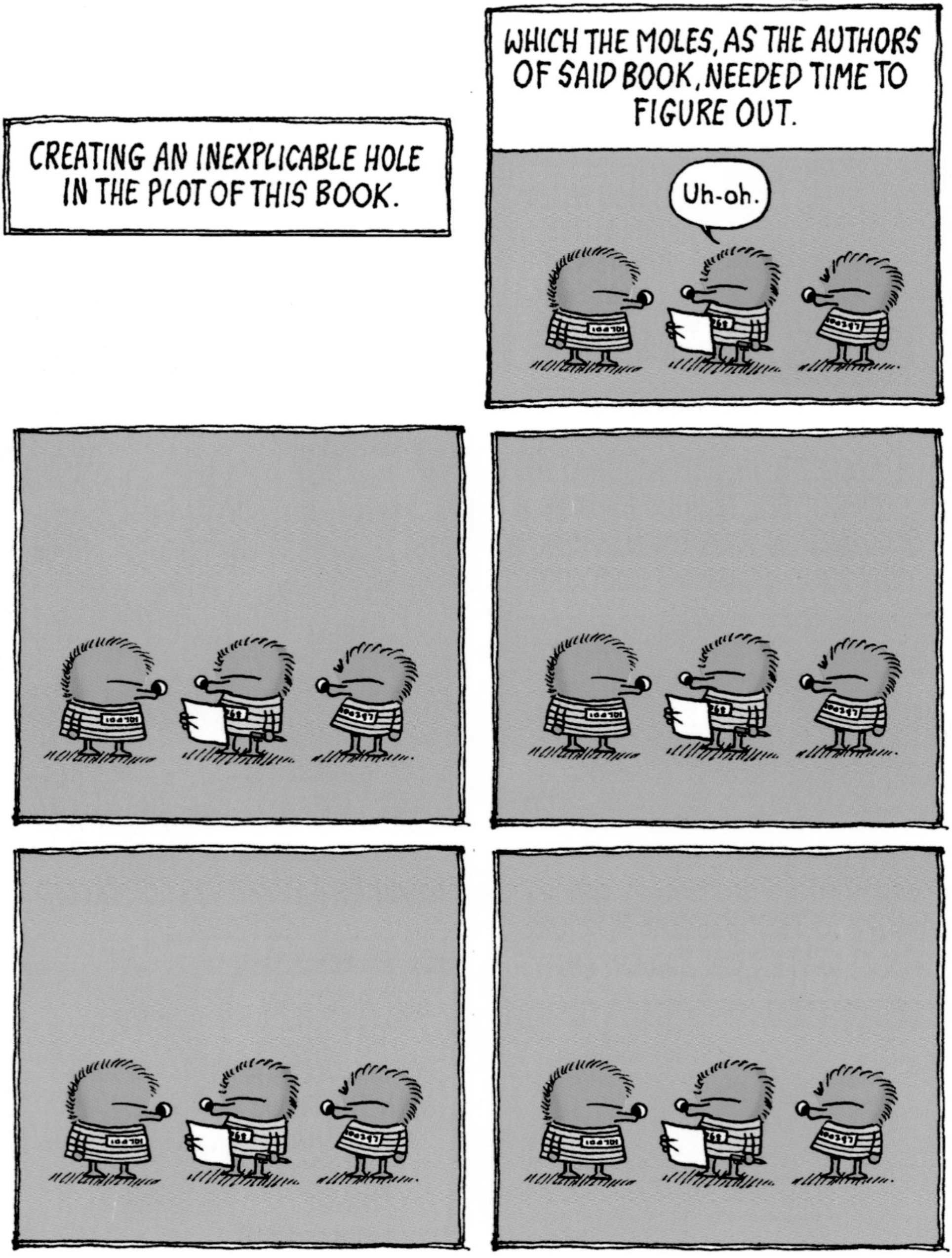
CREATING AN INEXPLICABLE HOLE IN THE PLOT OF THIS BOOK.
WHICH THE MOLES, AS THE AUTHORS OF SAID BOOK, NEEDED TIME TO FIGURE OUT.
Uh-oh.

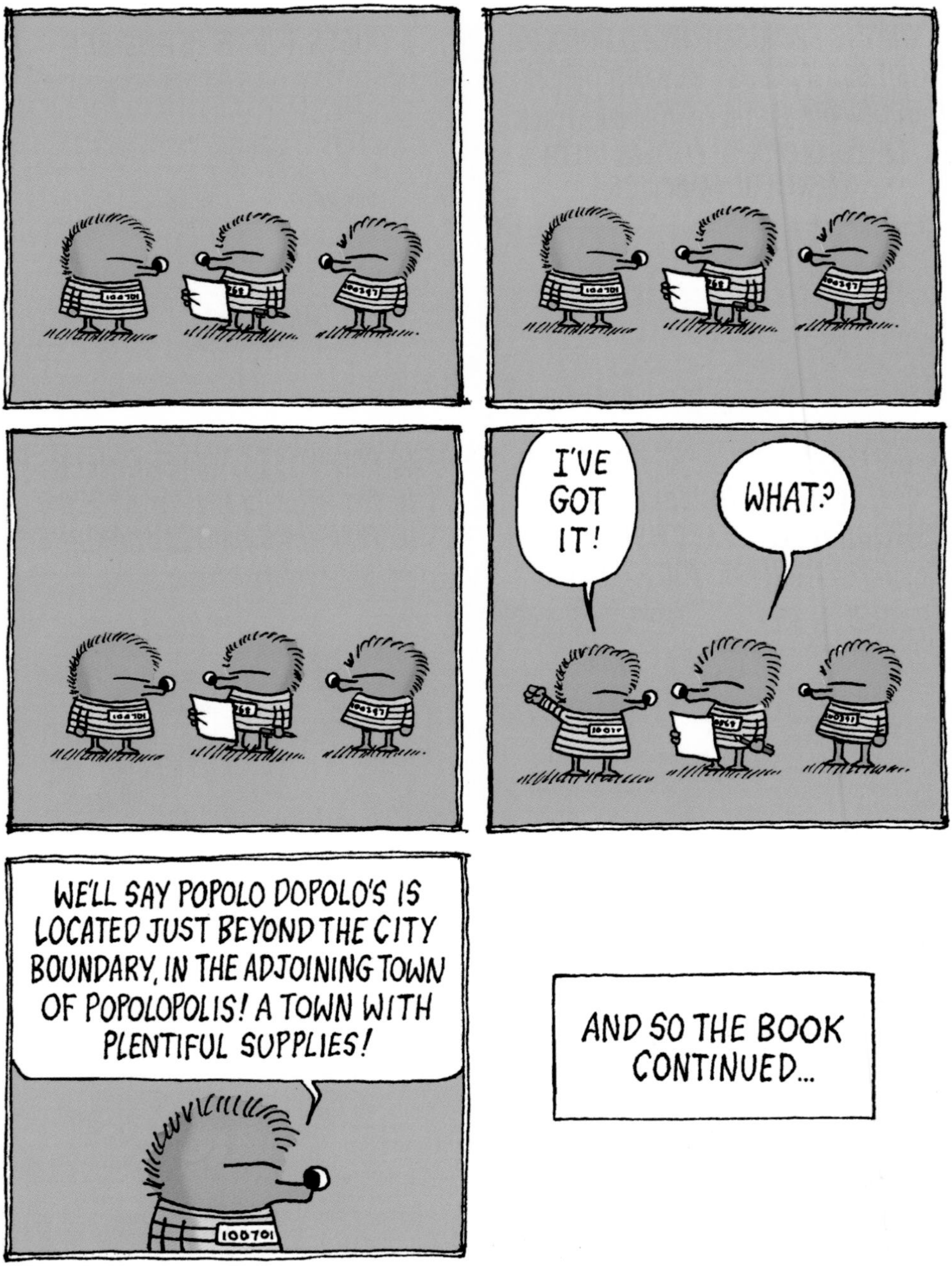
I'VE GOT IT!
WHAT?
WE'LL SAY POPOLO DOPOLO'S IS LOCATED JUST BEYOND THE CITY BOUNDARY, IN THE ADJOINING TOWN OF POPOLOPOLIS! A TOWN WITH PLENTIFUL SUPPLIES!
AND SO THE BOOK CONTINUED...

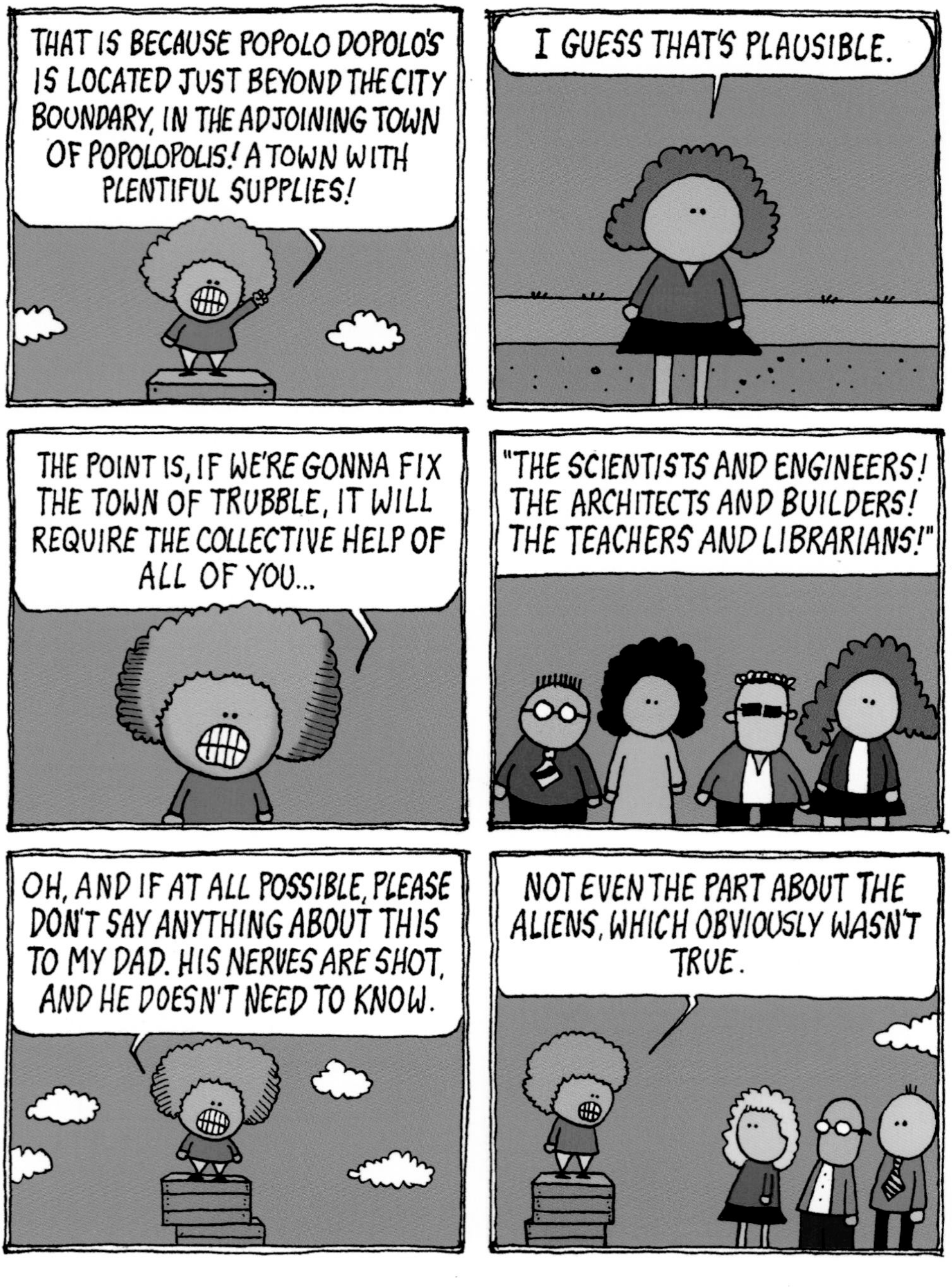
THAT IS BECAUSE POPOLO DOPOLO'S IS LOCATED JUST BEYOND THE CITY BOUNDARY, IN THE ADJOINING TOWN OF POPOLOPOLIS! A TOWN WITH PLENTIFUL SUPPLIES!
I GUESS THAT'S PLAUSIBLE.
THE POINT IS, IF WE'RE GONNA FIX THE TOWN OF TRUBBLE, IT WILL REQUIRE THE COLLECTIVE HELP OF ALL OF YOU...
"THE SCIENTISTS AND ENGINEERS! THE ARCHITECTS AND BUILDERS! THE TEACHERS AND LIBRARIANS!"
OH, AND IF AT ALL POSSIBLE, PLEASE DON'T SAY ANYTHING ABOUT THIS TO MY DAD. HIS NERVES ARE SHOT, AND HE DOESN'T NEED TO KNOW.
NOT EVEN THE PART ABOUT THE ALIENS, WHICH OBVIOUSLY WASN'T TRUE.

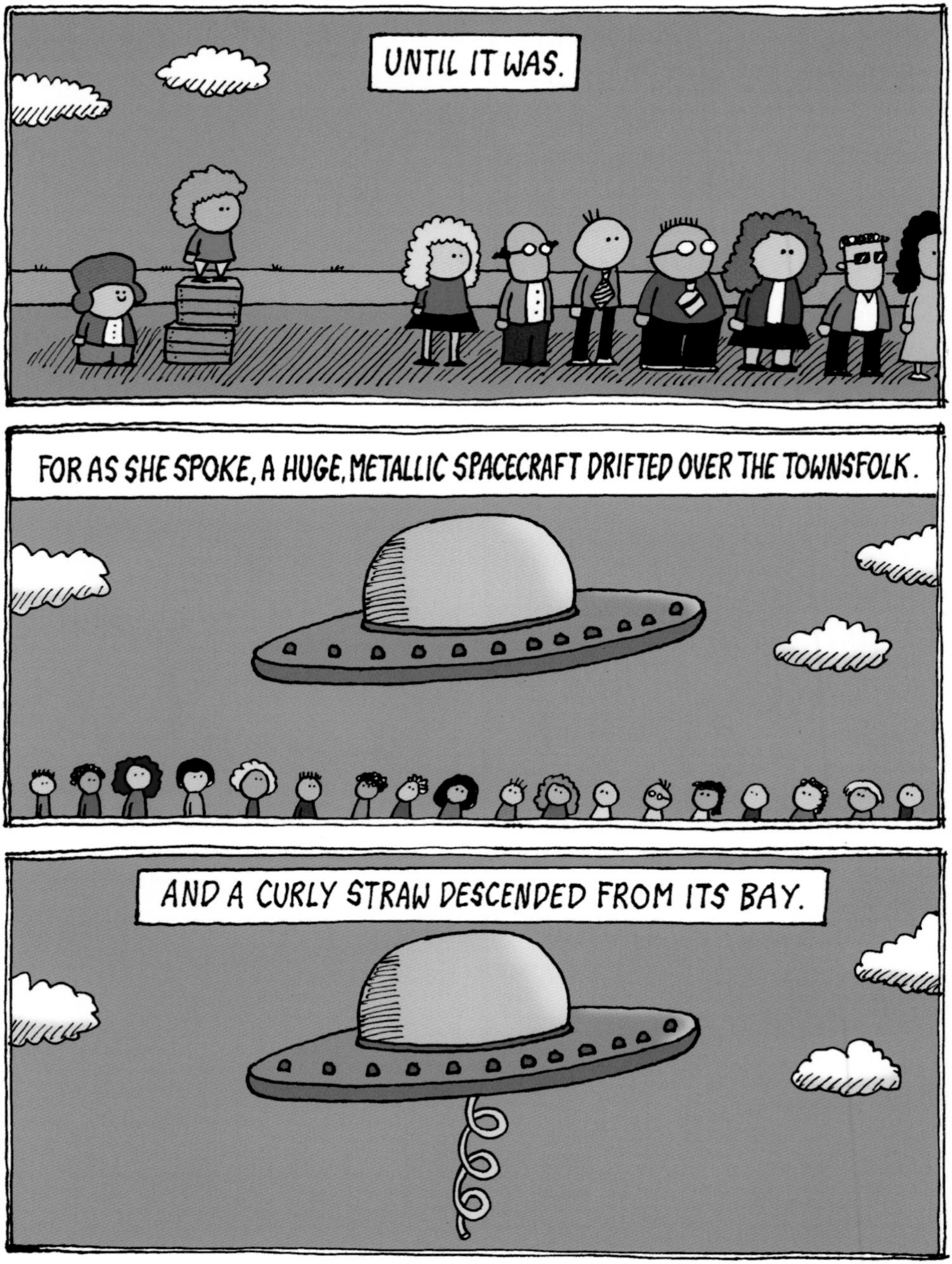
UNTIL IT WAS.
FOR AS SHE SPOKE, A HUGE, METALLIC SPACECRAFT DRIFTED OVER THE TOWNSFOLK.
AND A CURLY STRAW DESCENDED FROM ITS BAY.

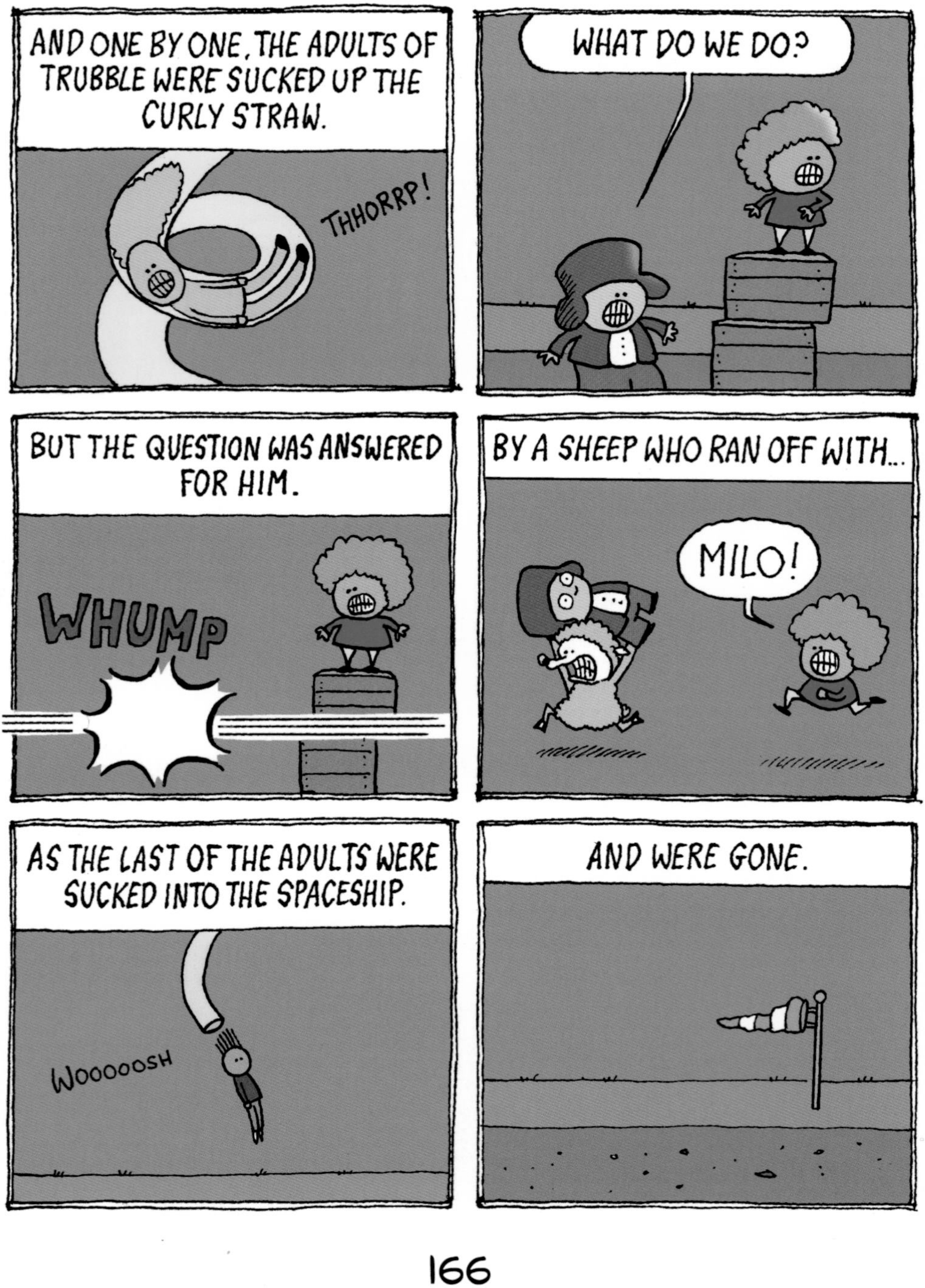
AND ONE BY ONE, THE ADULTS OF TRUBBLE WERE SUCKED UP THE CURLY STRAW.
THHORRP!
WHAT DO WE DO?
BUT THE QUESTION WAS ANSWERED FOR HIM.
WHUMP
BY A SHEEP WHO RAN OFF WITH...
MILO!
AS THE LAST OF THE ADULTS WERE SUCKED INTO THE SPACESHIP.
WOOOOOOSH
AND WERE GONE.

CHAPTER WHAT THE HECK JUST HAPPENED?

IN WHICH...

WE HOPEFULLY FIND THAT OUT

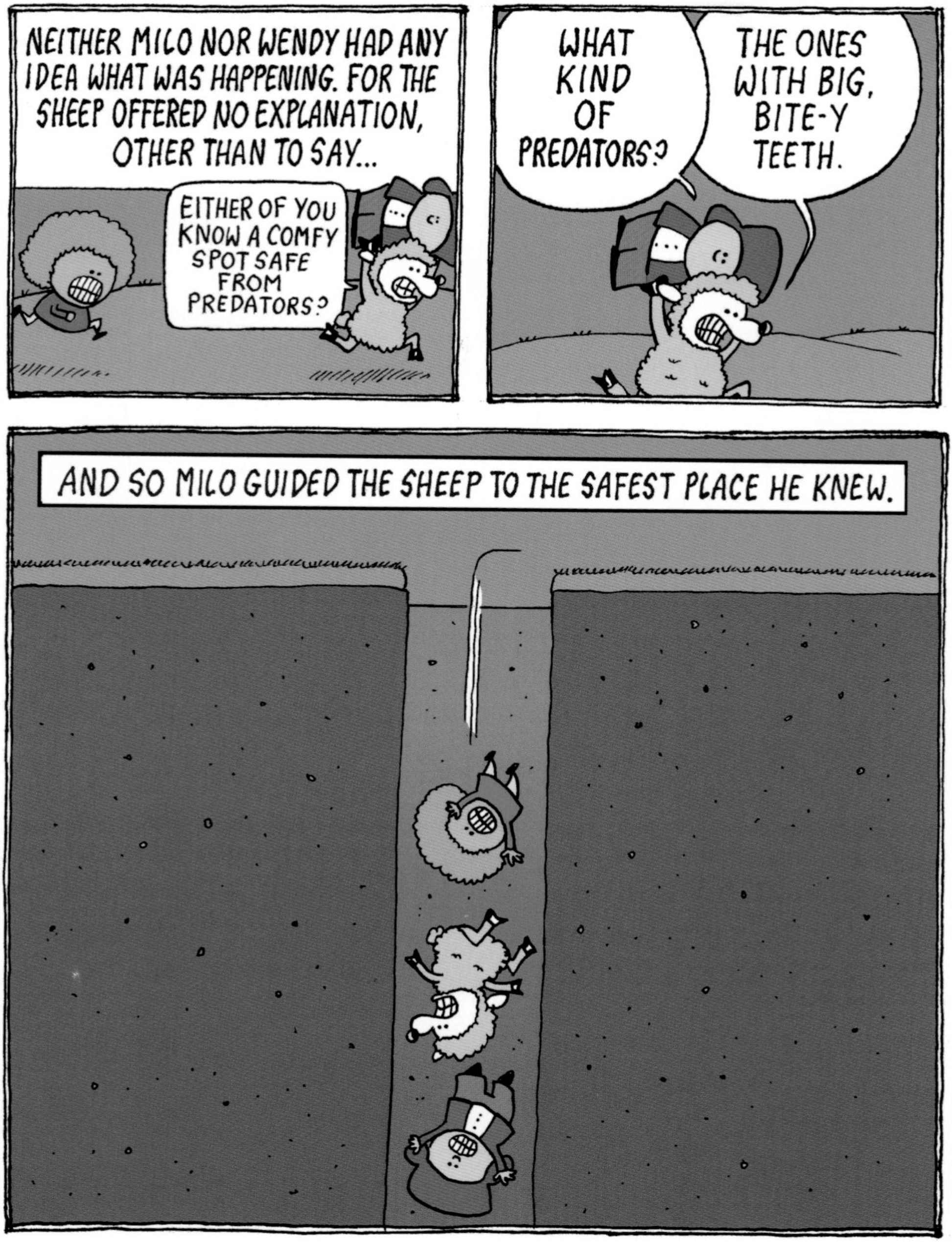
NEITHER MILO NOR WENDY HAD ANY IDEA WHAT WAS HAPPENING. FOR THE SHEEP OFFERED NO EXPLANATION, OTHER THAN TO SAY...
EITHER OF YOU KNOW A COMFY SPOT SAFE FROM PREDATORS?
WHAT KIND OF PREDATORS?
THE ONES WITH BIG, BITE-Y TEETH.
AND SO MILO GUIDED THE SHEEP TO THE SAFEST PLACE HE KNEW.

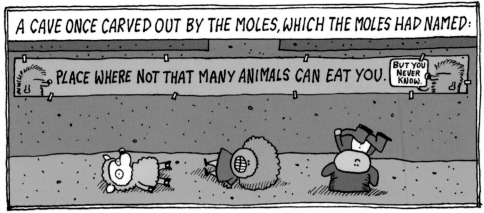

A CAVE ONCE CARVED OUT BY THE MOLES, WHICH THE MOLES HAD NAMED:

PLACE WHERE NOT THAT MANY ANIMALS CAN EAT YOU.

BUT YOU NEVER KNOW.

WELL, THAT SIGN IS COMFORTING. SPEAKING OF WHICH, ANYONE BRING FOOD FROM POPOLO DOPOLO'S?

PLACE WHERE NO / THAT MANY ANIMALS CAN EAT YOU.

BUT YOU NEVER KNOW.

WHO ARE YOU? WHAT'S GOING ON? WHAT JUST HAPPENED OUT THERE?

AND WHY HAVE YOU BEEN WATCHING ME?

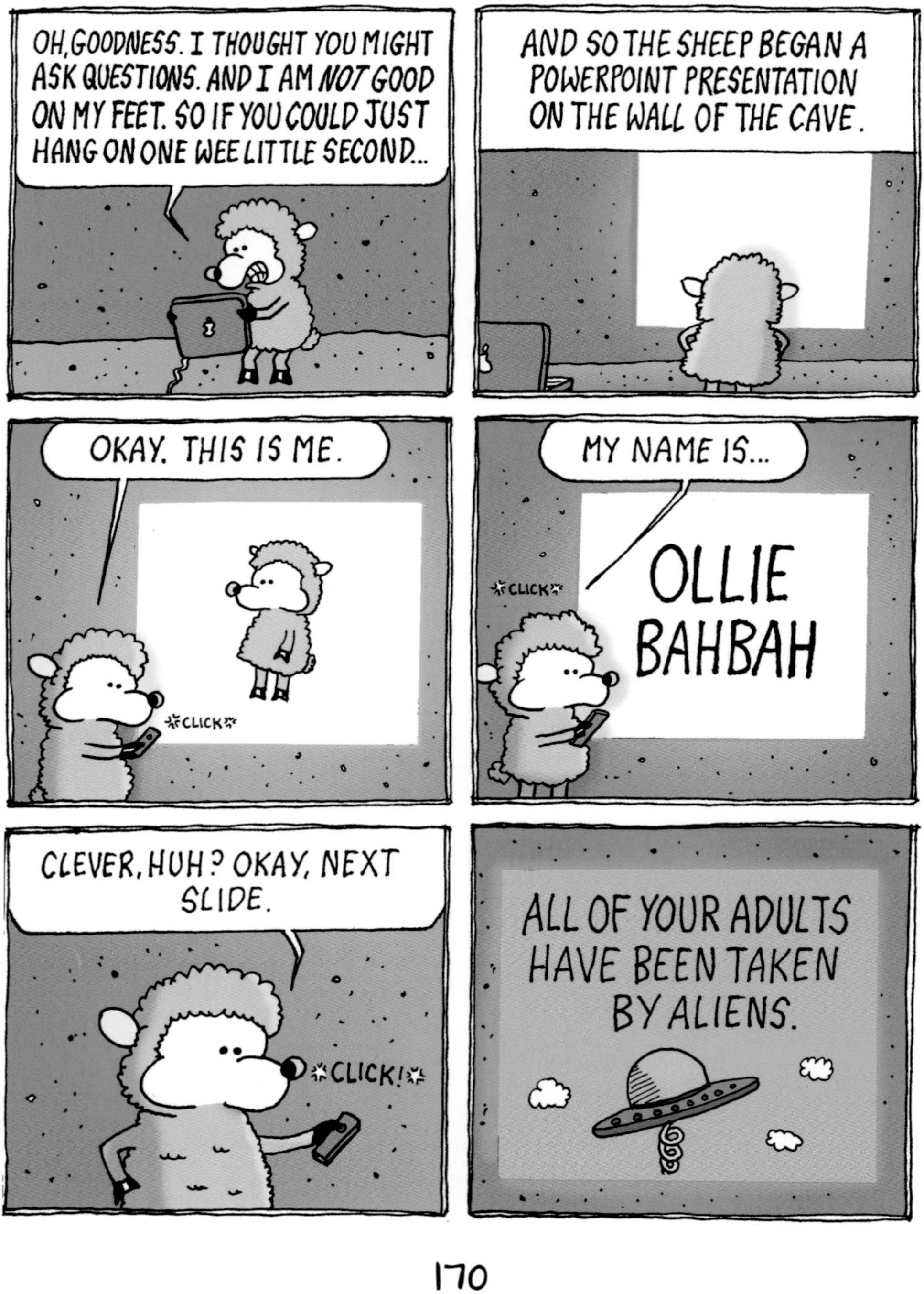
OH, GOODNESS. I THOUGHT YOU MIGHT ASK QUESTIONS. AND I AM *NOT* GOOD ON MY FEET. SO IF YOU COULD JUST HANG ON ONE WEE LITTLE SECOND...
AND SO THE SHEEP BEGAN A POWERPOINT PRESENTATION ON THE WALL OF THE CAVE.
OKAY. THIS IS ME.
CLICK
MY NAME IS...
CLICK
OLLIE BAHBAH
CLEVER, HUH? OKAY, NEXT SLIDE.
CLICK!
ALL OF YOUR ADULTS HAVE BEEN TAKEN BY ALIENS.

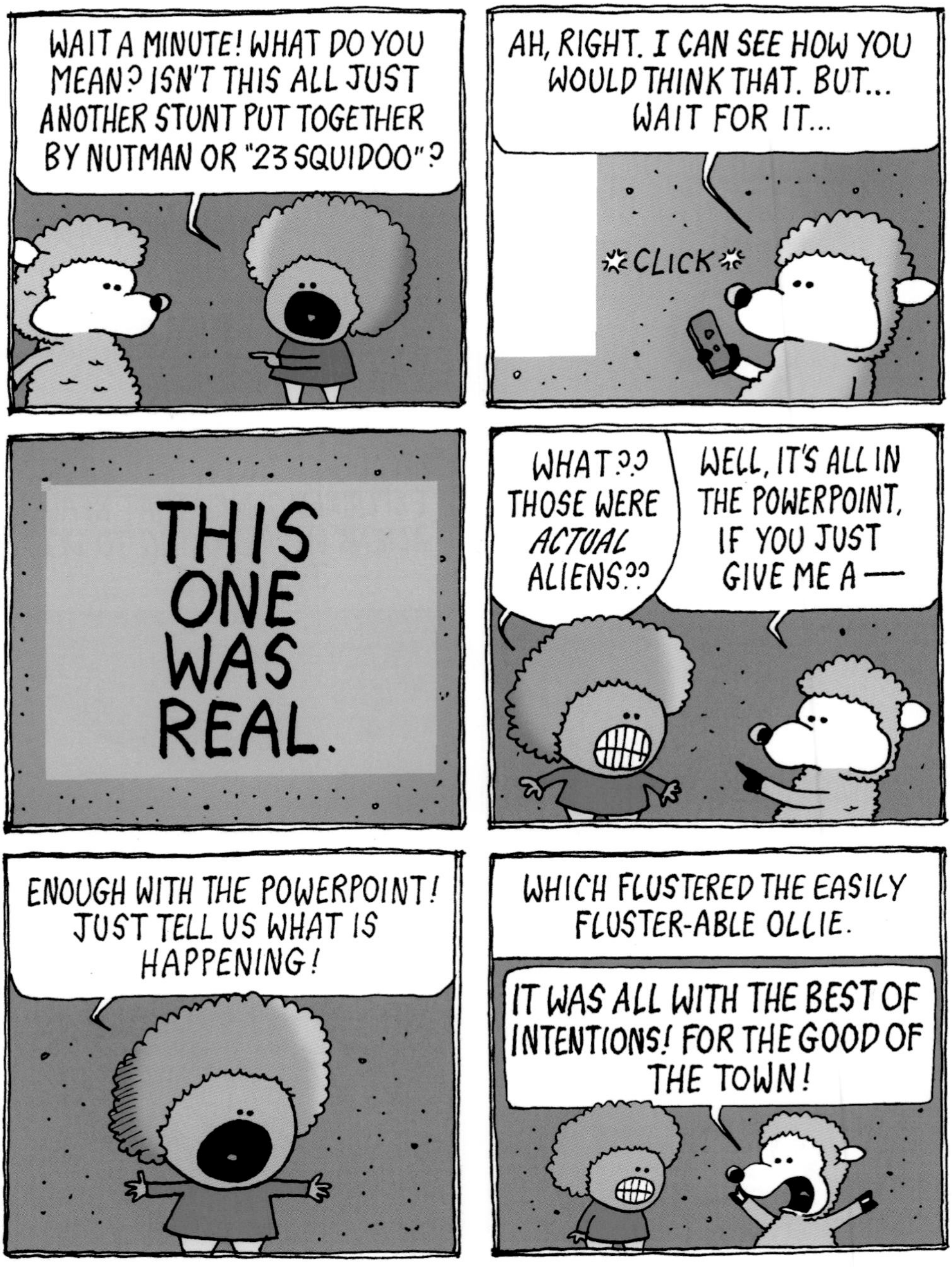

WAIT A MINUTE! WHAT DO YOU MEAN? ISN'T THIS ALL JUST ANOTHER STUNT PUT TOGETHER BY NUTMAN OR "23 SQUIDOO"?
AH, RIGHT. I CAN SEE HOW YOU WOULD THINK THAT. BUT... WAIT FOR IT...
CLICK
THIS ONE WAS REAL.
WHAT?? THOSE WERE *ACTUAL* ALIENS??
WELL, IT'S ALL IN THE POWERPOINT, IF YOU JUST GIVE ME A—
ENOUGH WITH THE POWERPOINT! JUST TELL US WHAT IS HAPPENING!
WHICH FLUSTERED THE EASILY FLUSTER-ABLE OLLIE.
IT WAS ALL WITH THE BEST OF INTENTIONS! FOR THE GOOD OF THE TOWN!

WHAT ARE YOU TALKING ABOUT?

THEY'RE AN ALIEN RACE! THE BERRYMANALOWS! AND YES, THE ADULTS ARE, WELL, BYE-BYE!

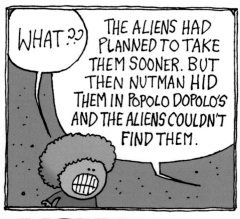

WHAT??

THE ALIENS HAD PLANNED TO TAKE THEM SOONER. BUT THEN NUTMAN HID THEM IN POPOLO DOPOLO'S AND THE ALIENS COULDN'T FIND THEM.

THEN THERE WAS THE FAKE STORY ON "23 SQUIDOO" ABOUT ALIENS TAKING EVERYONE. WHICH, FRANKLY, WAS *QUITE* THE COINCIDENCE.

"BECAUSE LITTLE DID THEY KNOW," EXPLAINED OLLIE, "THAT REAL ALIENS WERE LOOKING TO DO JUST THAT."

REAL ALIENS →

BUT WHY WOULD THEY WANT TO TAKE OUR ADULTS IN THE FIRST PLACE?

WELL, THEY'VE BEEN WATCHING YOUR PLANET AND—

AND?

AND, WELL, THERE'S NO EASY WAY TO SAY THIS, BUT...

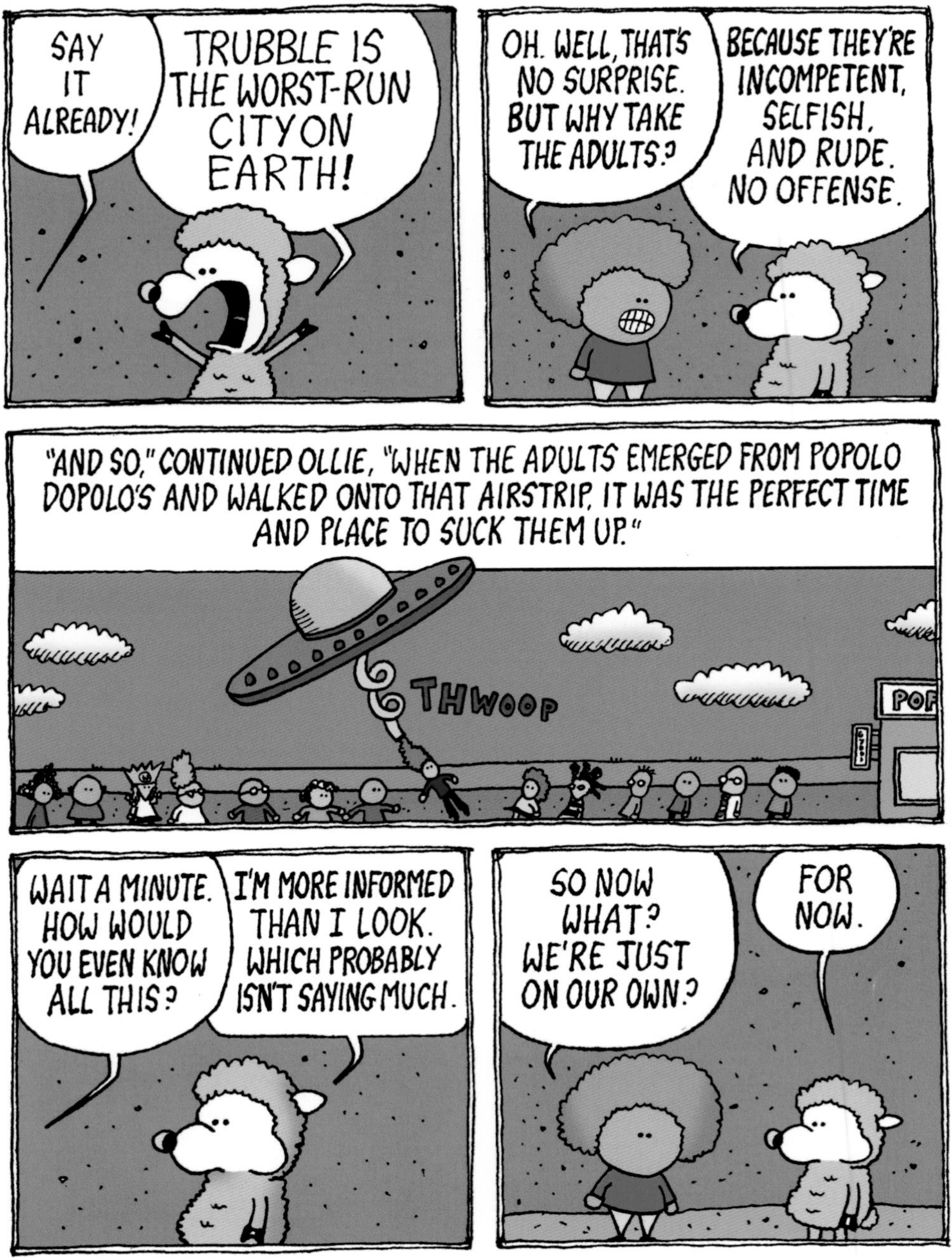
SAY IT ALREADY!
TRUBBLE IS THE WORST-RUN CITY ON EARTH!
OH. WELL, THAT'S NO SURPRISE. BUT WHY TAKE THE ADULTS?
BECAUSE THEY'RE INCOMPETENT, SELFISH, AND RUDE. NO OFFENSE.
"AND SO," CONTINUED OLLIE, "WHEN THE ADULTS EMERGED FROM POPOLO DOPOLO'S AND WALKED ONTO THAT AIRSTRIP, IT WAS THE PERFECT TIME AND PLACE TO SUCK THEM UP."
THWOOP
POP
WAIT A MINUTE. HOW WOULD YOU EVEN KNOW ALL THIS?
I'M MORE INFORMED THAN I LOOK. WHICH PROBABLY ISN'T SAYING MUCH.
SO NOW WHAT? WE'RE JUST ON OUR OWN?
FOR NOW.

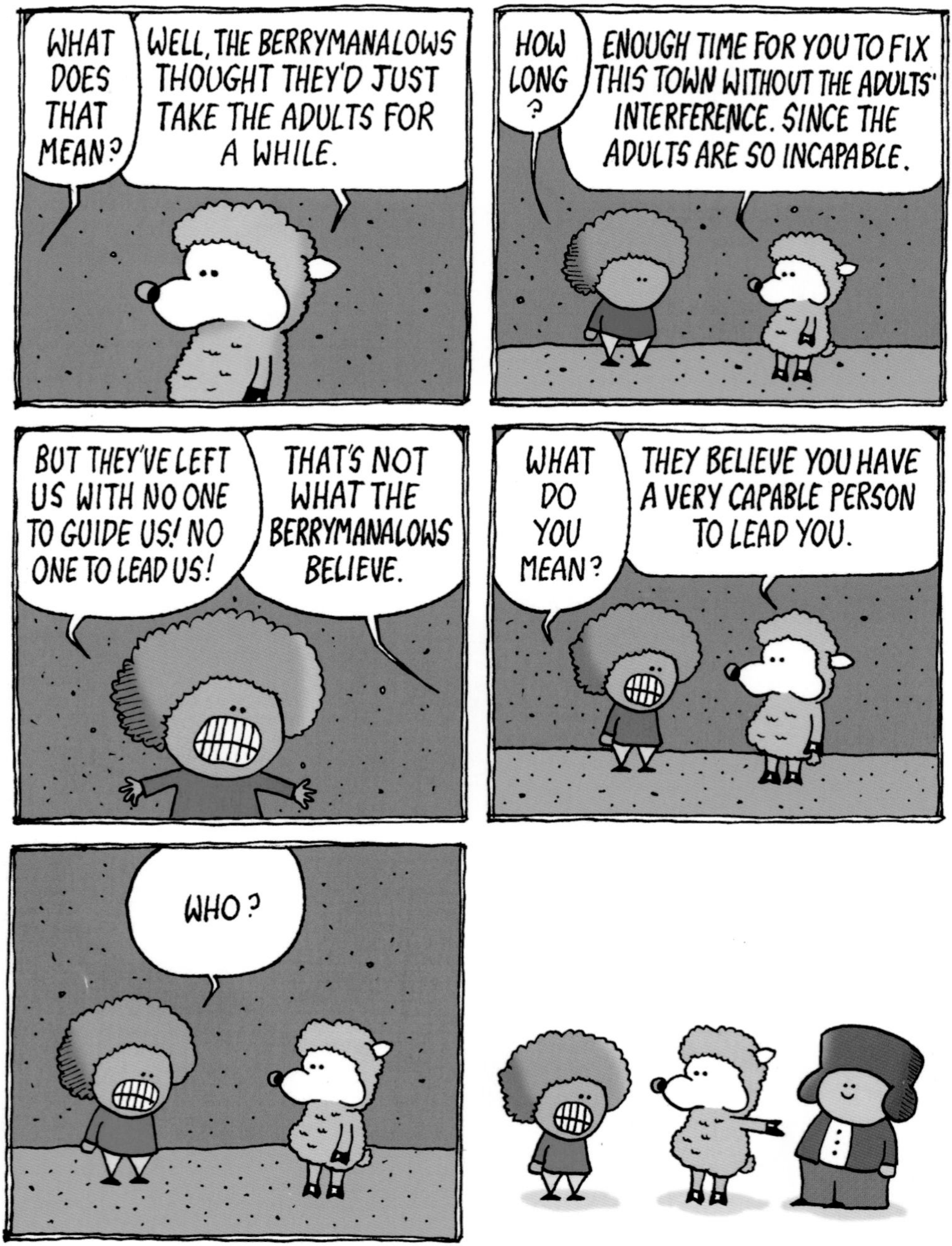
WHAT DOES THAT MEAN?
WELL, THE BERRYMANALOWS THOUGHT THEY'D JUST TAKE THE ADULTS FOR A WHILE.
HOW LONG?
ENOUGH TIME FOR YOU TO FIX THIS TOWN WITHOUT THE ADULTS' INTERFERENCE. SINCE THE ADULTS ARE SO INCAPABLE.
BUT THEY'VE LEFT US WITH NO ONE TO GUIDE US! NO ONE TO LEAD US!
THAT'S NOT WHAT THE BERRYMANALOWS BELIEVE.
WHAT DO YOU MEAN?
THEY BELIEVE YOU HAVE A VERY CAPABLE PERSON TO LEAD YOU.
WHO?

CHAPTER DIDN'T SEE THAT COMING, DID YOU?

IN WHICH...

WE CONTINUE TO AMAZE

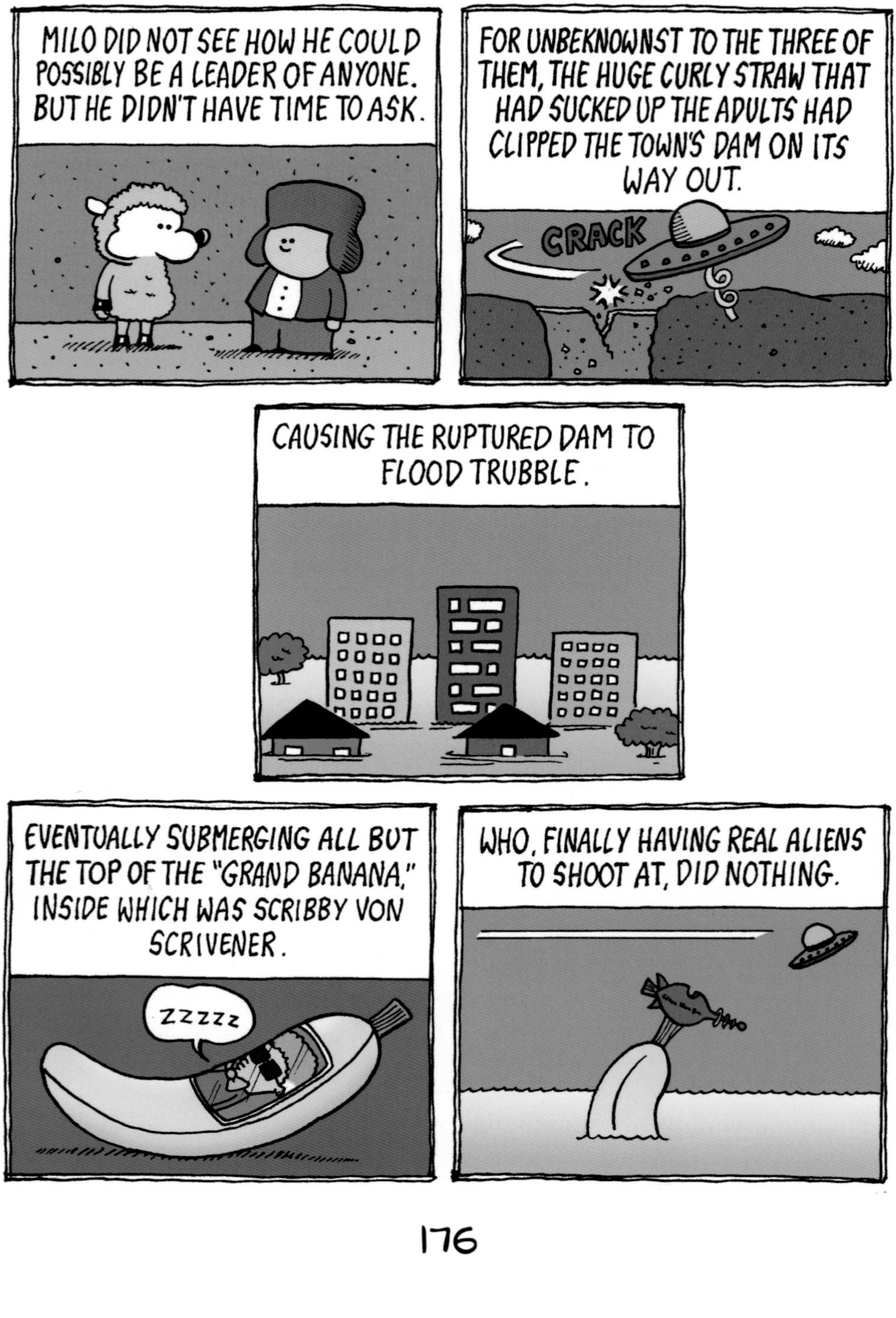
MILO DID NOT SEE HOW HE COULD POSSIBLY BE A LEADER OF ANYONE. BUT HE DIDN'T HAVE TIME TO ASK.
FOR UNBEKNOWNST TO THE THREE OF THEM, THE HUGE CURLY STRAW THAT HAD SUCKED UP THE ADULTS HAD CLIPPED THE TOWN'S DAM ON ITS WAY OUT.
CRACK
CAUSING THE RUPTURED DAM TO FLOOD TRUBBLE.
EVENTUALLY SUBMERGING ALL BUT THE TOP OF THE "GRAND BANANA," INSIDE WHICH WAS SCRIBBY VON SCRIVENER.
ZZZZZ
WHO, FINALLY HAVING REAL ALIENS TO SHOOT AT, DID NOTHING.

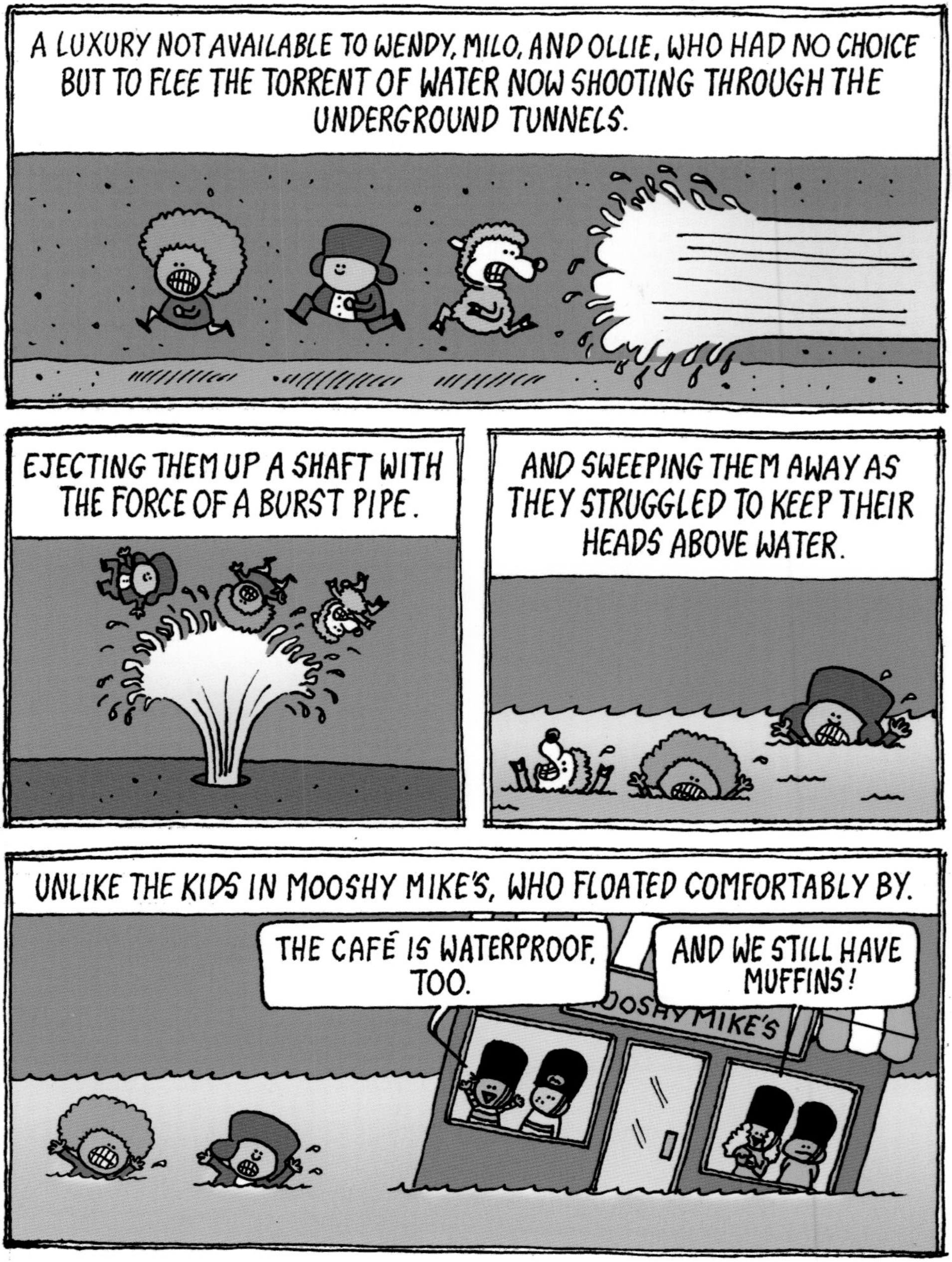
A LUXURY NOT AVAILABLE TO WENDY, MILO, AND OLLIE, WHO HAD NO CHOICE BUT TO FLEE THE TORRENT OF WATER NOW SHOOTING THROUGH THE UNDERGROUND TUNNELS.
EJECTING THEM UP A SHAFT WITH THE FORCE OF A BURST PIPE.
AND SWEEPING THEM AWAY AS THEY STRUGGLED TO KEEP THEIR HEADS ABOVE WATER.
UNLIKE THE KIDS IN MOOSHY MIKE'S, WHO FLOATED COMFORTABLY BY.
THE CAFÉ IS WATERPROOF, TOO.
AND WE STILL HAVE MUFFINS!

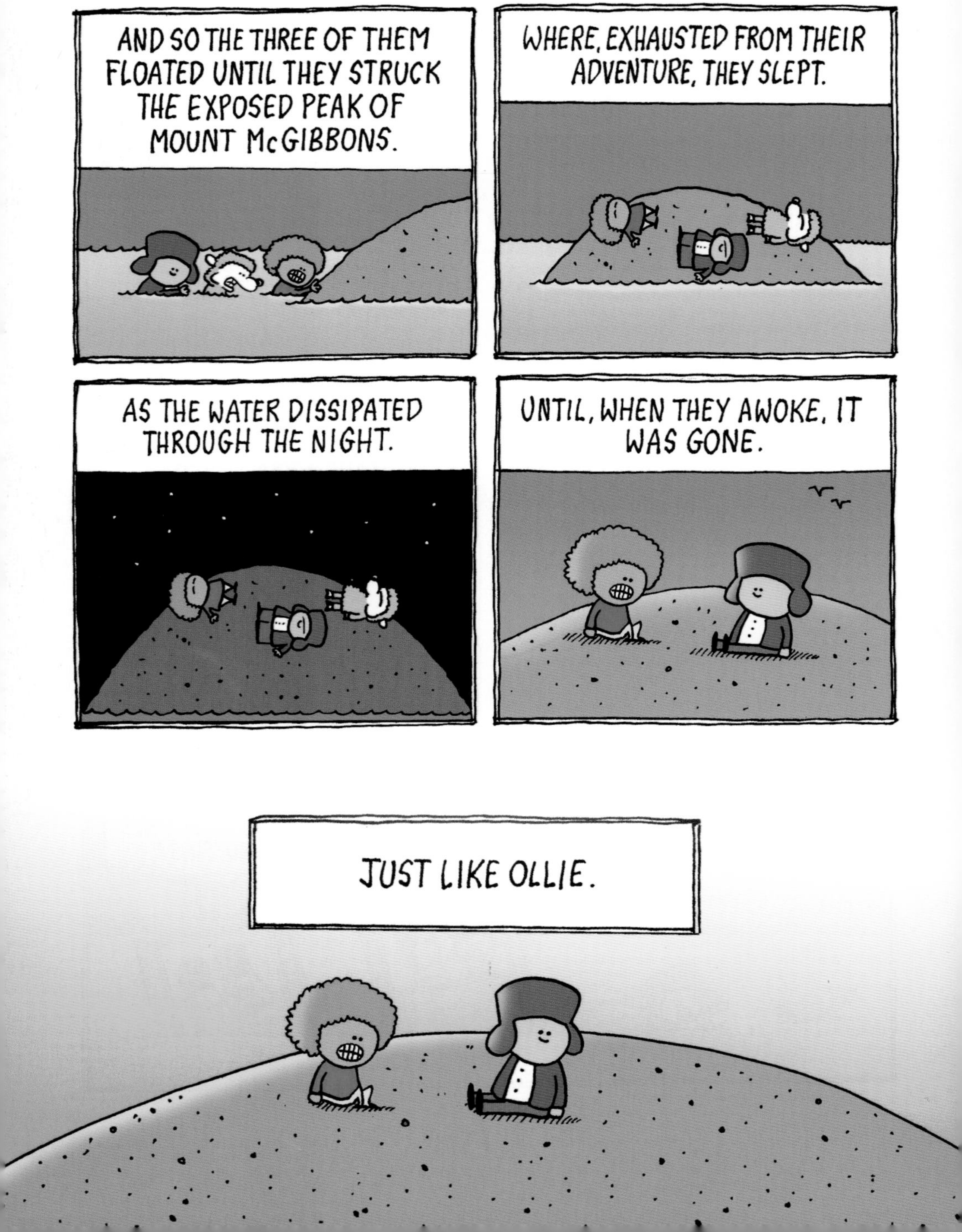
AND SO THE THREE OF THEM FLOATED UNTIL THEY STRUCK THE EXPOSED PEAK OF MOUNT McGIBBONS.
WHERE, EXHAUSTED FROM THEIR ADVENTURE, THEY SLEPT.
AS THE WATER DISSIPATED THROUGH THE NIGHT.
UNTIL, WHEN THEY AWOKE, IT WAS GONE.
JUST LIKE OLLIE.

CHAPTER 33

IN WHICH...

WE MAKE NO ATTEMPT TO LOOK BACK AND SEE WHAT CHAPTER NUMBER THIS SHOULD ACTUALLY BE

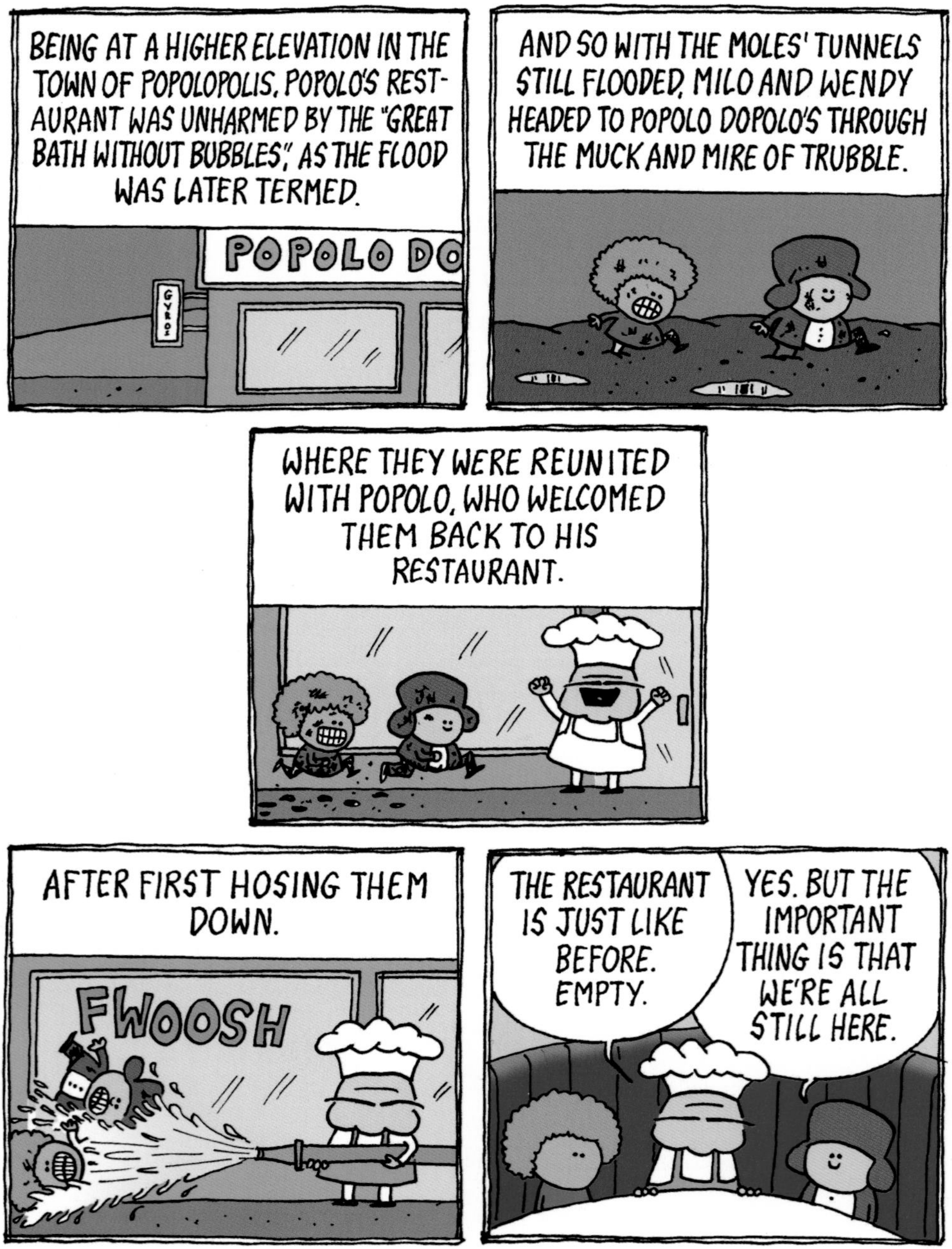
BEING AT A HIGHER ELEVATION IN THE TOWN OF POPOLOPOLIS, POPOLO'S RESTAURANT WAS UNHARMED BY THE "GREAT BATH WITHOUT BUBBLES," AS THE FLOOD WAS LATER TERMED.
POPOLO DO
GYROS
AND SO WITH THE MOLES' TUNNELS STILL FLOODED, MILO AND WENDY HEADED TO POPOLO DOPOLO'S THROUGH THE MUCK AND MIRE OF TRUBBLE.
WHERE THEY WERE REUNITED WITH POPOLO, WHO WELCOMED THEM BACK TO HIS RESTAURANT.
AFTER FIRST HOSING THEM DOWN.
FWOOSH
THE RESTAURANT IS JUST LIKE BEFORE. EMPTY.
YES. BUT THE IMPORTANT THING IS THAT WE'RE ALL STILL HERE.

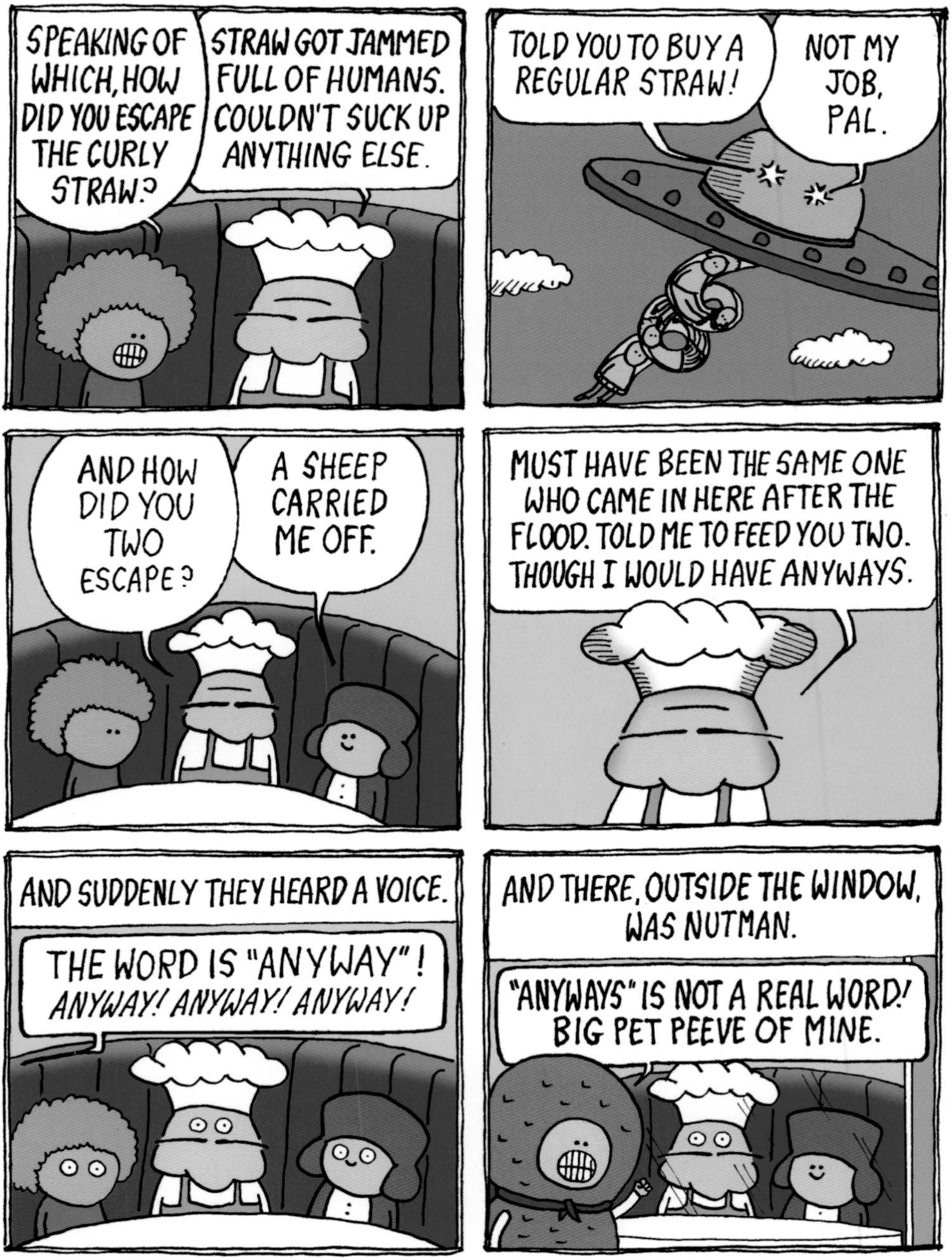
SPEAKING OF WHICH, HOW DID YOU ESCAPE THE CURLY STRAW?
STRAW GOT JAMMED FULL OF HUMANS. COULDN'T SUCK UP ANYTHING ELSE.
TOLD YOU TO BUY A REGULAR STRAW!
NOT MY JOB, PAL.
AND HOW DID YOU TWO ESCAPE?
A SHEEP CARRIED ME OFF.
MUST HAVE BEEN THE SAME ONE WHO CAME IN HERE AFTER THE FLOOD. TOLD ME TO FEED YOU TWO. THOUGH I WOULD HAVE ANYWAYS.
AND SUDDENLY THEY HEARD A VOICE.
THE WORD IS "ANYWAY"! ANYWAY! ANYWAY! ANYWAY!
AND THERE, OUTSIDE THE WINDOW, WAS NUTMAN.
"ANYWAYS" IS NOT A REAL WORD! BIG PET PEEVE OF MINE.

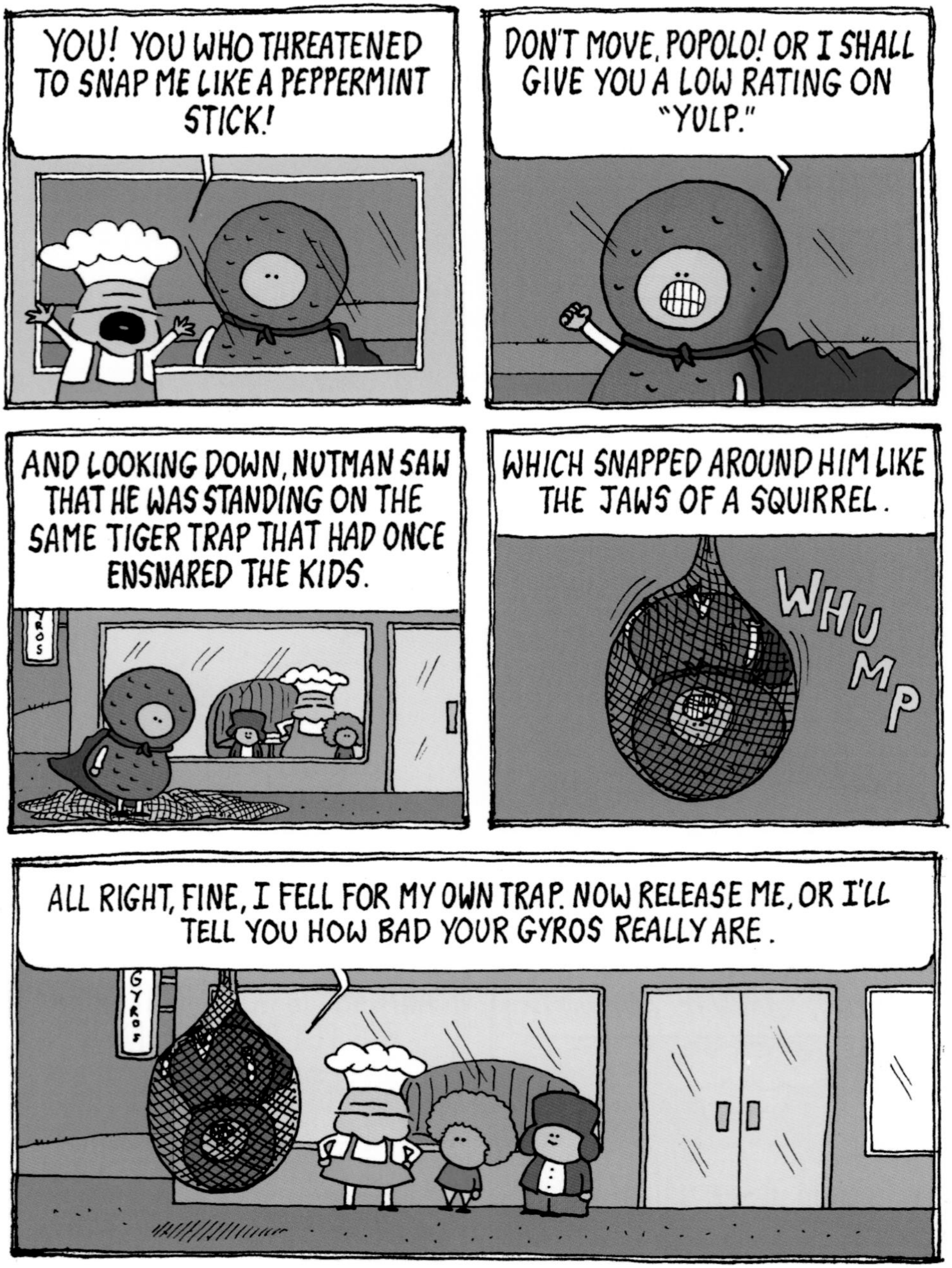
YOU! YOU WHO THREATENED TO SNAP ME LIKE A PEPPERMINT STICK!
DON'T MOVE, POPOLO! OR I SHALL GIVE YOU A LOW RATING ON "YULP."
AND LOOKING DOWN, NUTMAN SAW THAT HE WAS STANDING ON THE SAME TIGER TRAP THAT HAD ONCE ENSNARED THE KIDS.
WHICH SNAPPED AROUND HIM LIKE THE JAWS OF A SQUIRREL.
WHUMP
ALL RIGHT, FINE, I FELL FOR MY OWN TRAP. NOW RELEASE ME, OR I'LL TELL YOU HOW BAD YOUR GYROS REALLY ARE.
GYROS

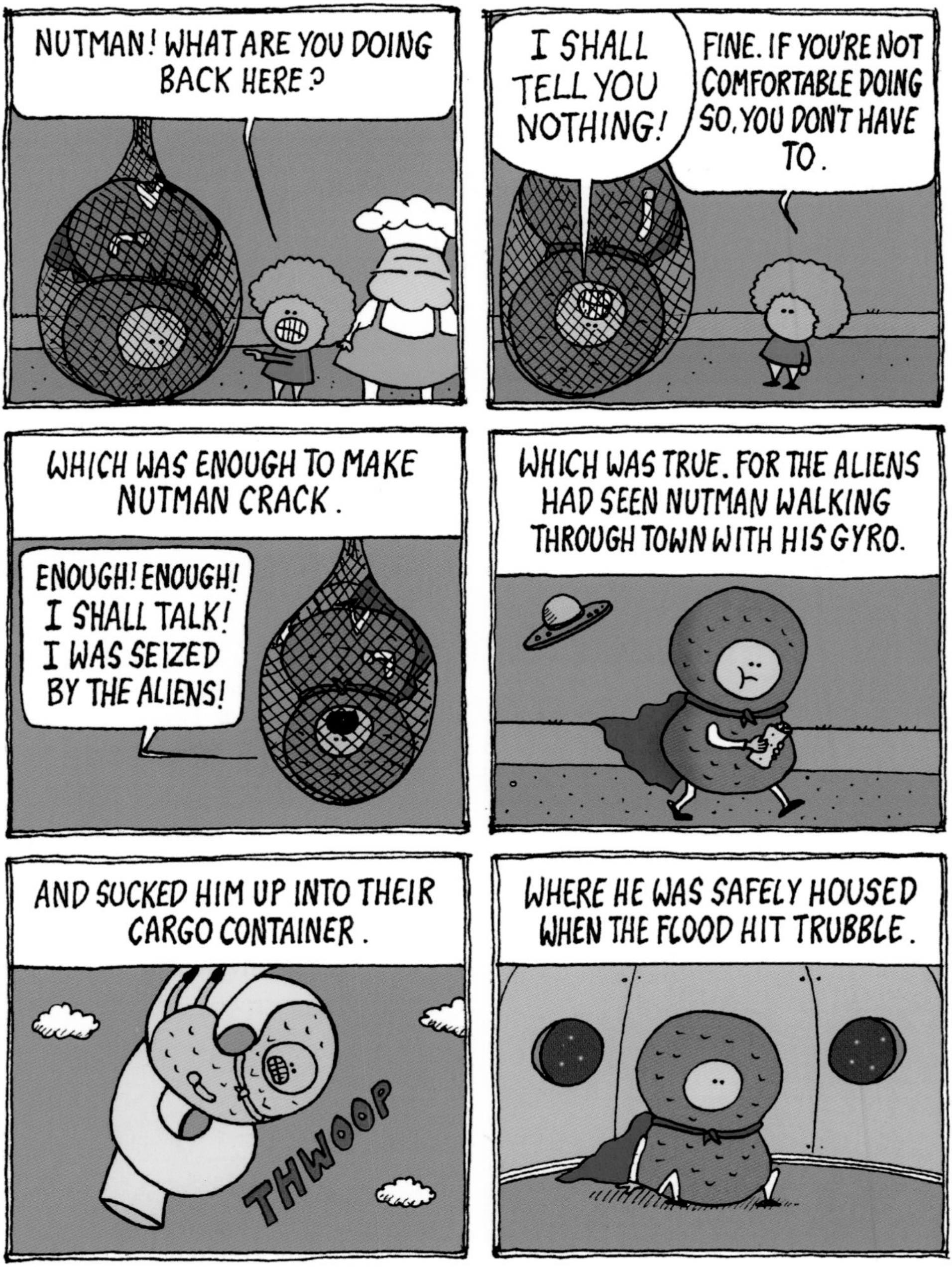
NUTMAN! WHAT ARE YOU DOING BACK HERE?
I SHALL TELL YOU NOTHING!
FINE. IF YOU'RE NOT COMFORTABLE DOING SO, YOU DON'T HAVE TO.
WHICH WAS ENOUGH TO MAKE NUTMAN CRACK.
ENOUGH! ENOUGH! I SHALL TALK! I WAS SEIZED BY THE ALIENS!
WHICH WAS TRUE. FOR THE ALIENS HAD SEEN NUTMAN WALKING THROUGH TOWN WITH HIS GYRO.
AND SUCKED HIM UP INTO THEIR CARGO CONTAINER.
THWOOP
WHERE HE WAS SAFELY HOUSED WHEN THE FLOOD HIT TRUBBLE.

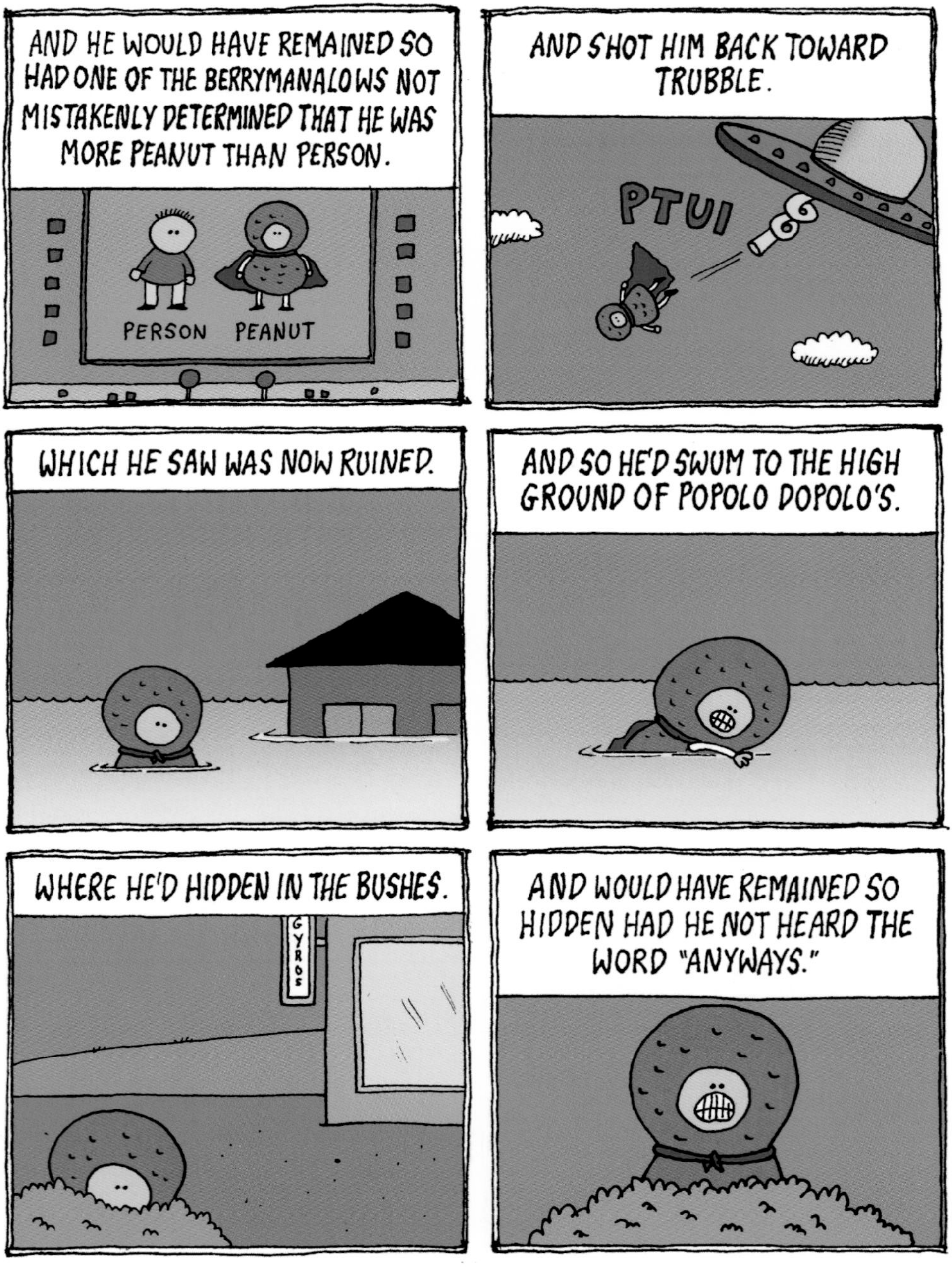
AND HE WOULD HAVE REMAINED SO HAD ONE OF THE BERRYMANALOWS NOT MISTAKENLY DETERMINED THAT HE WAS MORE PEANUT THAN PERSON.
PERSON
PEANUT
AND SHOT HIM BACK TOWARD TRUBBLE.
PTUI
WHICH HE SAW WAS NOW RUINED.
AND SO HE'D SWUM TO THE HIGH GROUND OF POPOLO DOPOLO'S.
WHERE HE'D HIDDEN IN THE BUSHES.
GYROS
AND WOULD HAVE REMAINED SO HIDDEN HAD HE NOT HEARD THE WORD "ANYWAYS."

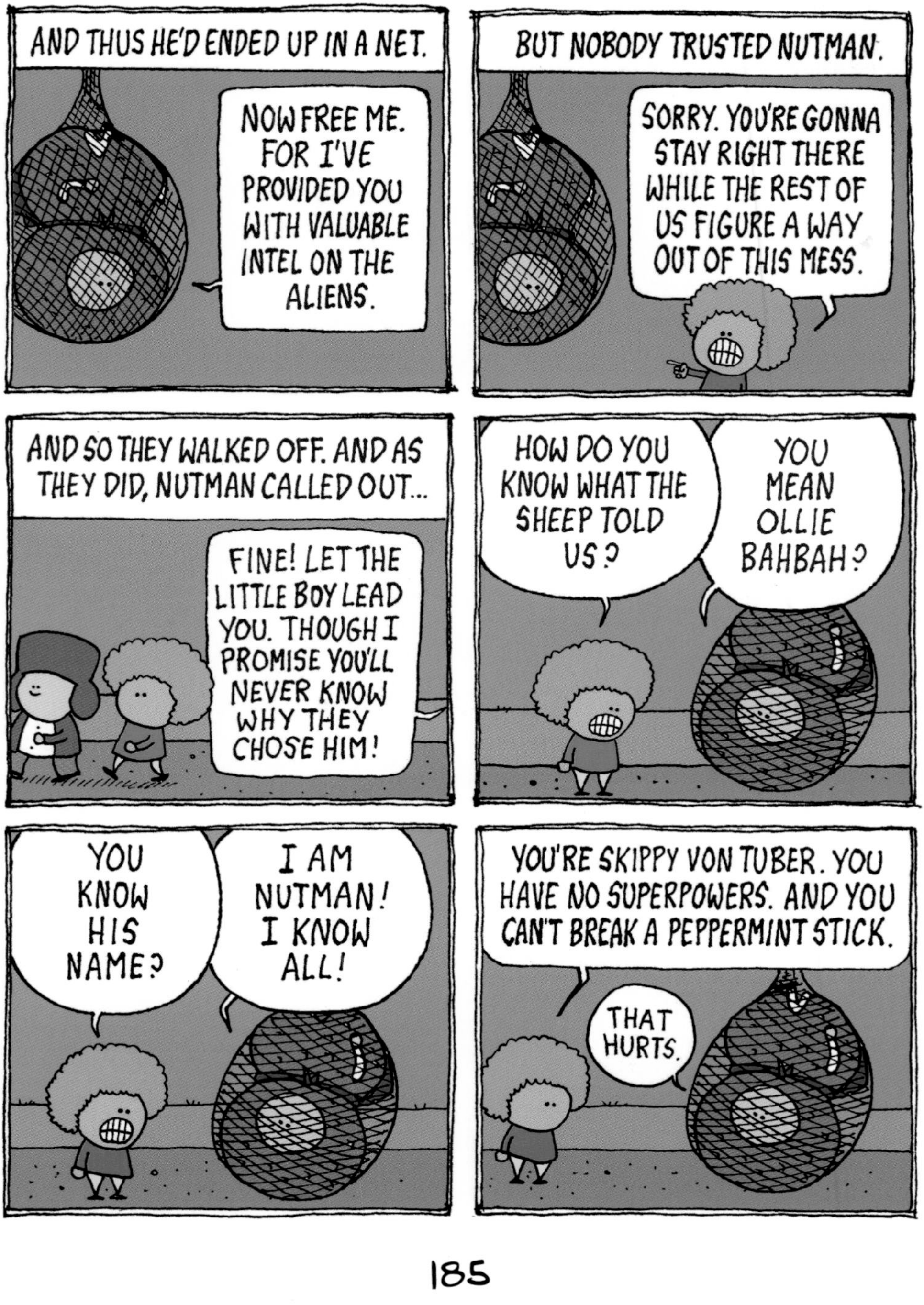
AND THUS HE'D ENDED UP IN A NET.
NOW FREE ME. FOR I'VE PROVIDED YOU WITH VALUABLE INTEL ON THE ALIENS.
BUT NOBODY TRUSTED NUTMAN.
SORRY. YOU'RE GONNA STAY RIGHT THERE WHILE THE REST OF US FIGURE A WAY OUT OF THIS MESS.
AND SO THEY WALKED OFF. AND AS THEY DID, NUTMAN CALLED OUT...
FINE! LET THE LITTLE BOY LEAD YOU. THOUGH I PROMISE YOU'LL NEVER KNOW WHY THEY CHOSE HIM!
HOW DO YOU KNOW WHAT THE SHEEP TOLD US?
YOU MEAN OLLIE BAHBAH?
YOU KNOW HIS NAME?
I AM NUTMAN! I KNOW ALL!
YOU'RE SKIPPY VON TUBER. YOU HAVE NO SUPERPOWERS. AND YOU CAN'T BREAK A PEPPERMINT STICK.
THAT HURTS.

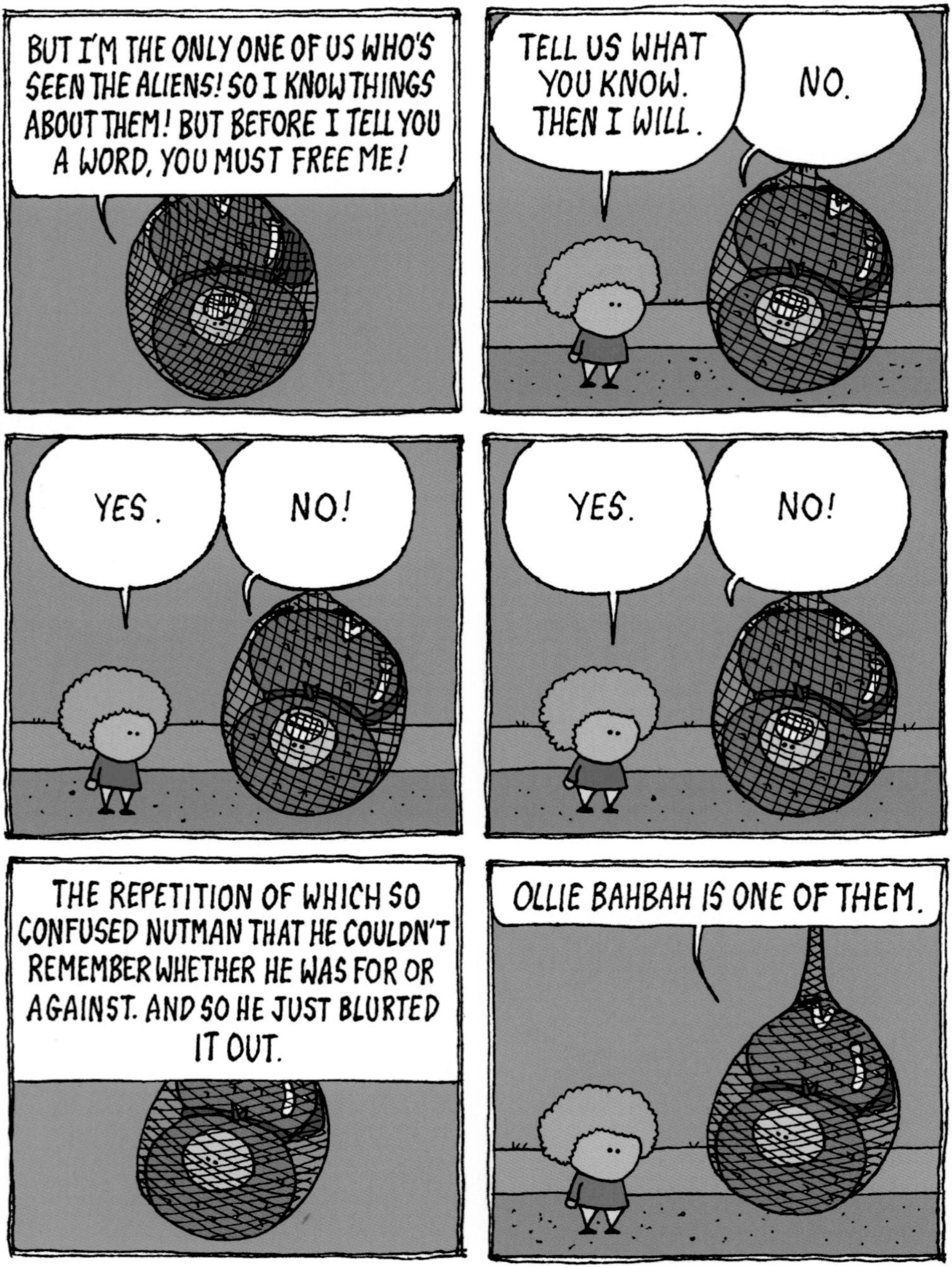
BUT I'M THE ONLY ONE OF US WHO'S SEEN THE ALIENS! SO I KNOW THINGS ABOUT THEM! BUT BEFORE I TELL YOU A WORD, YOU MUST FREE ME!
TELL US WHAT YOU KNOW. THEN I WILL.
NO.
YES.
NO!
YES.
NO!
THE REPETITION OF WHICH SO CONFUSED NUTMAN THAT HE COULDN'T REMEMBER WHETHER HE WAS FOR OR AGAINST. AND SO HE JUST BLURTED IT OUT.
OLLIE BAHBAH IS ONE OF THEM.

CHAPTER 34

IN WHICH...

WE PRETEND
THAT CALLING
THE LAST CHAPTER
"CHAPTER 33"
WAS CORRECT AND
JUST KEEP GOING

TO GAIN HIS FREEDOM FROM THE NET, NUTMAN TOLD WENDY AND MILO ALL HE HAD LEARNED ABOUT THE BERRY-MANALOW ALIENS DURING HIS TIME ON THE SPACESHIP.

SUCH AS THE FACT THAT THEY WERE A GROUP OF FORMER LOUNGE SINGERS.

BOOOOOOOOOO...

LOVE YOU, BABE.

WHOSE LACK OF COMMERCIAL SUCCESS HAD DOOMED THEM TO FOREVER LIVE IN THEIR PARENTS' BASEMENTS.

GET A JOB!

GET OFF MY BACK, MA!

AND SO THEY FINALLY HAD TO GET REAL JOBS. AND THUS WENT TO WORK FOR A NONPROFIT SPACE ORGANIZATION CALLED "S.I.N.G.," WHICH STOOD FOR:

SAVE
INCOMPETENT
NINCOMPOOP
GOVERNMENTS

THE MISSION OF WHICH WAS TO SAVE THE WORST-RUN CITIES IN THE UNIVERSE. AND THUS THEY HAD FOUND TRUBBLE.

THAT ONE IS *BAD*.

THEIR PLAN FOR WHICH WAS SIMPLE.

FIND THEM A BETTER LEADER.

AND MAYBE DO SOME LOUNGE SINGING ON THE SIDE.

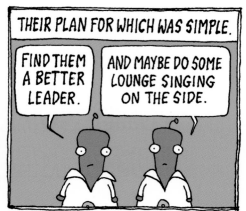

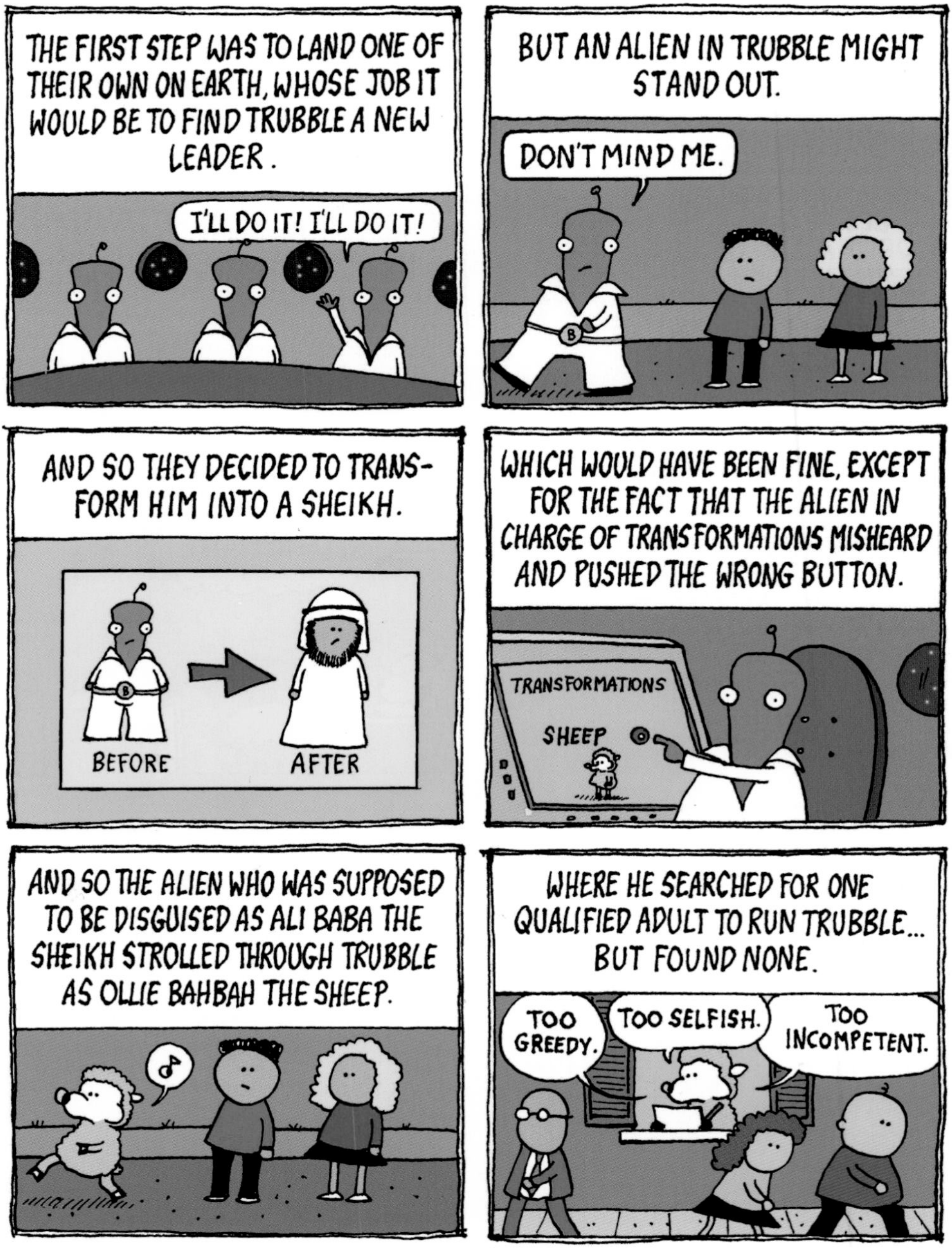
THE FIRST STEP WAS TO LAND ONE OF THEIR OWN ON EARTH, WHOSE JOB IT WOULD BE TO FIND TRUBBLE A NEW LEADER.
I'LL DO IT! I'LL DO IT!
BUT AN ALIEN IN TRUBBLE MIGHT STAND OUT.
DON'T MIND ME.
B
AND SO THEY DECIDED TO TRANS-FORM HIM INTO A SHEIKH.
B
BEFORE
AFTER
WHICH WOULD HAVE BEEN FINE, EXCEPT FOR THE FACT THAT THE ALIEN IN CHARGE OF TRANSFORMATIONS MISHEARD AND PUSHED THE WRONG BUTTON.
TRANSFORMATIONS
SHEEP
AND SO THE ALIEN WHO WAS SUPPOSED TO BE DISGUISED AS ALI BABA THE SHEIKH STROLLED THROUGH TRUBBLE AS OLLIE BAHBAH THE SHEEP.
WHERE HE SEARCHED FOR ONE QUALIFIED ADULT TO RUN TRUBBLE... BUT FOUND NONE.
TOO GREEDY.
TOO SELFISH.
TOO INCOMPETENT.

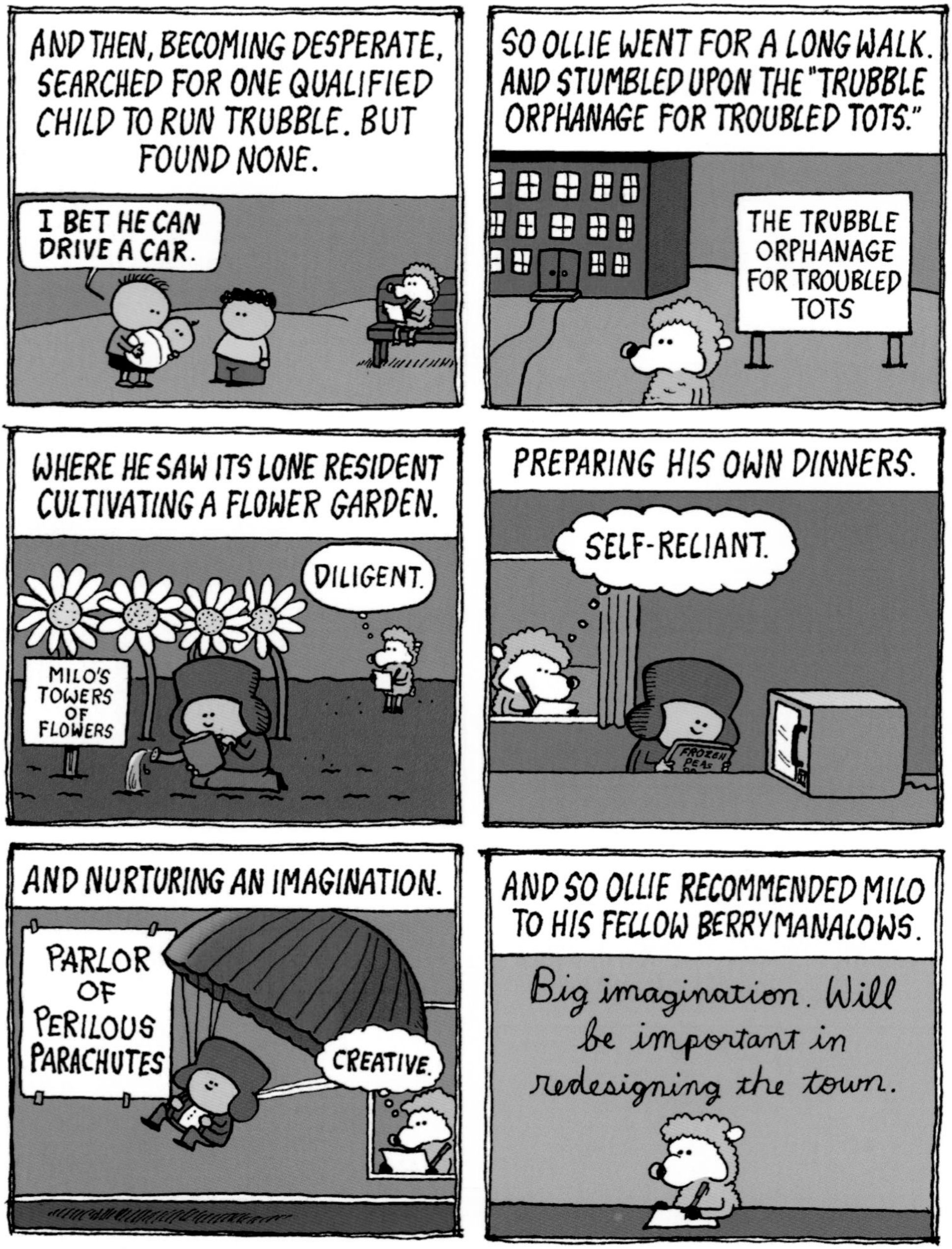
AND THEN, BECOMING DESPERATE, SEARCHED FOR ONE QUALIFIED CHILD TO RUN TRUBBLE. BUT FOUND NONE.
I BET HE CAN DRIVE A CAR.
SO OLLIE WENT FOR A LONG WALK. AND STUMBLED UPON THE "TRUBBLE ORPHANAGE FOR TROUBLED TOTS."
THE TRUBBLE ORPHANAGE FOR TROUBLED TOTS
WHERE HE SAW ITS LONE RESIDENT CULTIVATING A FLOWER GARDEN.
DILIGENT.
MILO'S TOWERS OF FLOWERS
PREPARING HIS OWN DINNERS.
SELF-RELIANT.
FROZEN PEAS
AND NURTURING AN IMAGINATION.
PARLOR OF PERILOUS PARACHUTES
CREATIVE.
AND SO OLLIE RECOMMENDED MILO TO HIS FELLOW BERRYMANALOWS.
Big imagination. Will be important in redesigning the town.

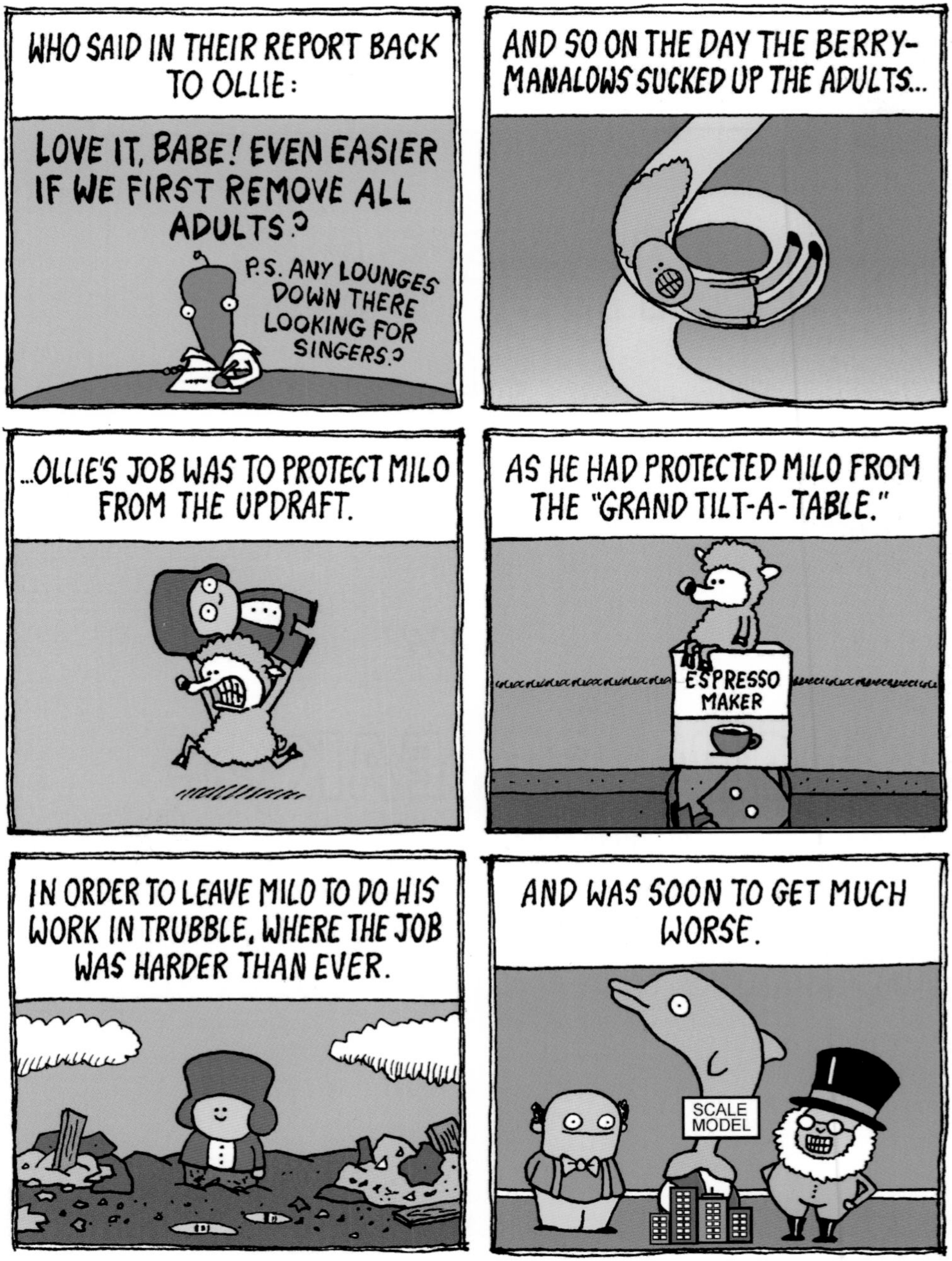

WHO SAID IN THEIR REPORT BACK TO OLLIE:
LOVE IT, BABE! EVEN EASIER IF WE FIRST REMOVE ALL ADULTS?
P.S. ANY LOUNGES DOWN THERE LOOKING FOR SINGERS?
AND SO ON THE DAY THE BERRY-MANALOWS SUCKED UP THE ADULTS...
...OLLIE'S JOB WAS TO PROTECT MILO FROM THE UPDRAFT.
AS HE HAD PROTECTED MILO FROM THE "GRAND TILT-A-TABLE."
ESPRESSO MAKER
IN ORDER TO LEAVE MILO TO DO HIS WORK IN TRUBBLE, WHERE THE JOB WAS HARDER THAN EVER.
AND WAS SOON TO GET MUCH WORSE.
SCALE MODEL

CHAPTER 35

IN WHICH...

OUR STREAK OF NUMBERING CHAPTERS CORRECTLY CONTINUES

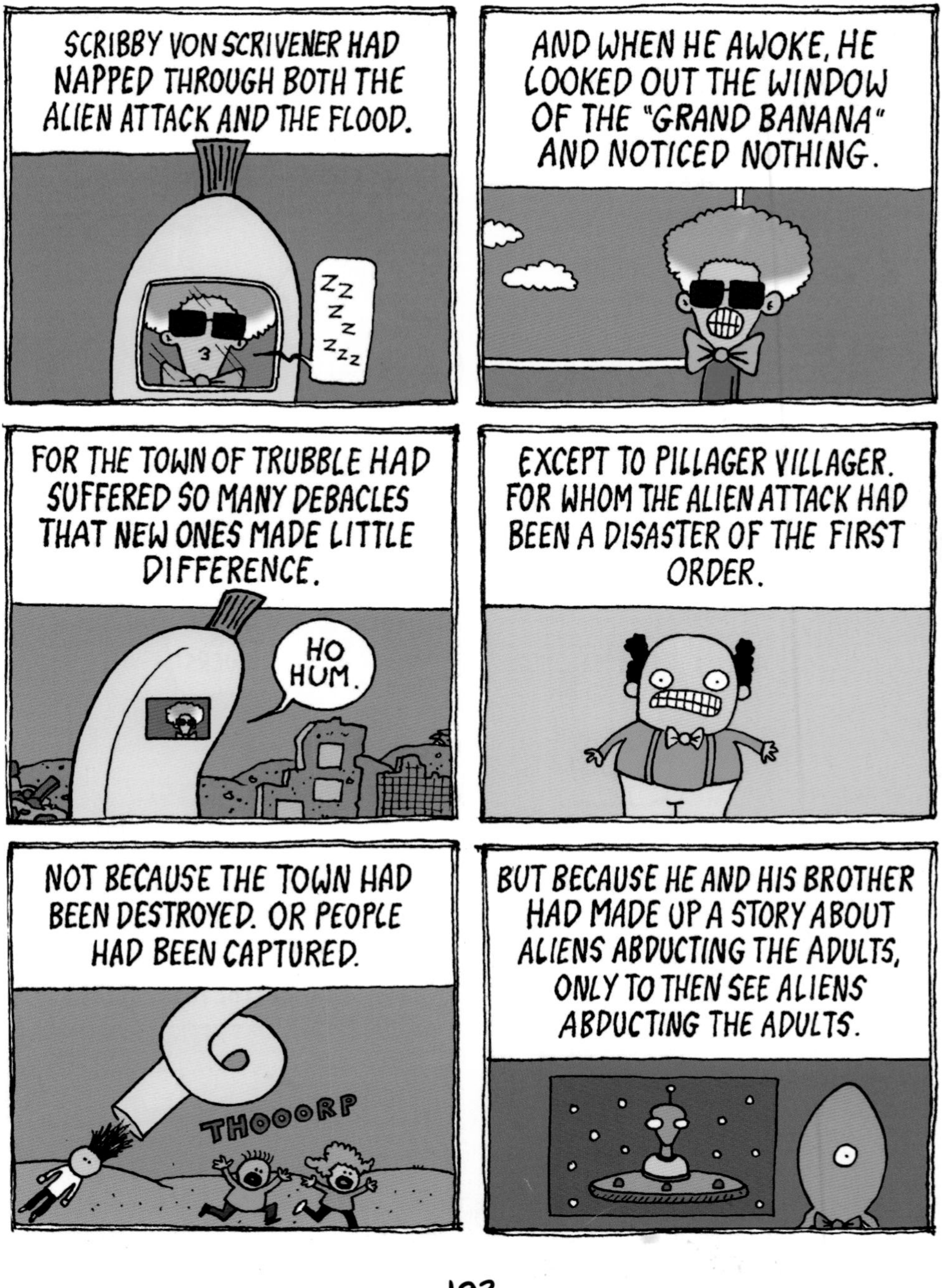
SCRIBBY VON SCRIVENER HAD NAPPED THROUGH BOTH THE ALIEN ATTACK AND THE FLOOD.
Z Z Z Z Z Z Z
AND WHEN HE AWOKE, HE LOOKED OUT THE WINDOW OF THE "GRAND BANANA" AND NOTICED NOTHING.
FOR THE TOWN OF TRUBBLE HAD SUFFERED SO MANY DEBACLES THAT NEW ONES MADE LITTLE DIFFERENCE.
HO HUM.
EXCEPT TO PILLAGER VILLAGER. FOR WHOM THE ALIEN ATTACK HAD BEEN A DISASTER OF THE FIRST ORDER.
NOT BECAUSE THE TOWN HAD BEEN DESTROYED. OR PEOPLE HAD BEEN CAPTURED.
THOOORP
BUT BECAUSE HE AND HIS BROTHER HAD MADE UP A STORY ABOUT ALIENS ABDUCTING THE ADULTS, ONLY TO THEN SEE ALIENS ABDUCTING THE ADULTS.

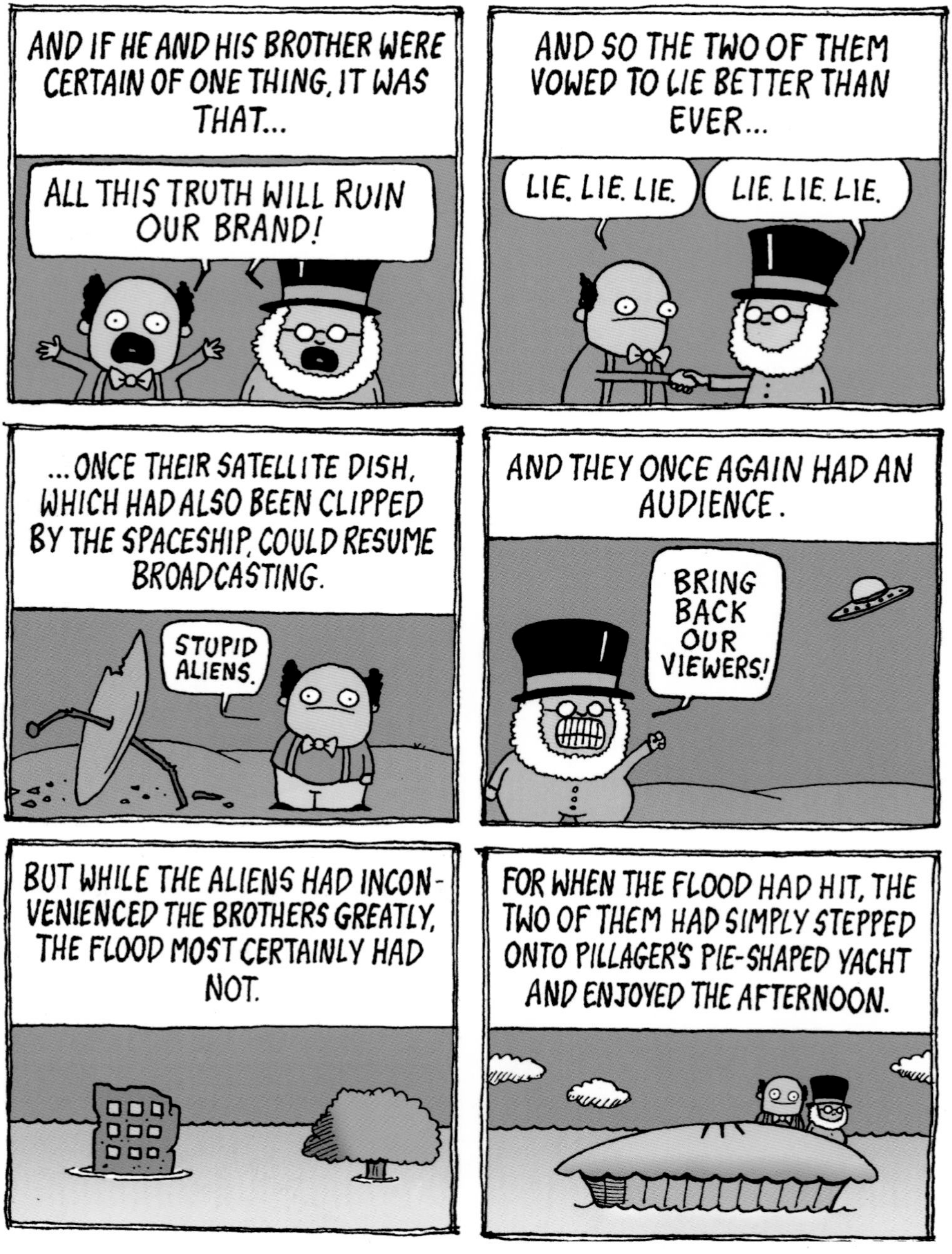
AND IF HE AND HIS BROTHER WERE CERTAIN OF ONE THING, IT WAS THAT...
ALL THIS TRUTH WILL RUIN OUR BRAND!
AND SO THE TWO OF THEM VOWED TO LIE BETTER THAN EVER...
LIE. LIE. LIE.
LIE. LIE. LIE.
...ONCE THEIR SATELLITE DISH, WHICH HAD ALSO BEEN CLIPPED BY THE SPACESHIP, COULD RESUME BROADCASTING.
STUPID ALIENS.
AND THEY ONCE AGAIN HAD AN AUDIENCE.
BRING BACK OUR VIEWERS!
BUT WHILE THE ALIENS HAD INCONVENIENCED THE BROTHERS GREATLY, THE FLOOD MOST CERTAINLY HAD NOT.
FOR WHEN THE FLOOD HAD HIT, THE TWO OF THEM HAD SIMPLY STEPPED ONTO PILLAGER'S PIE-SHAPED YACHT AND ENJOYED THE AFTERNOON.

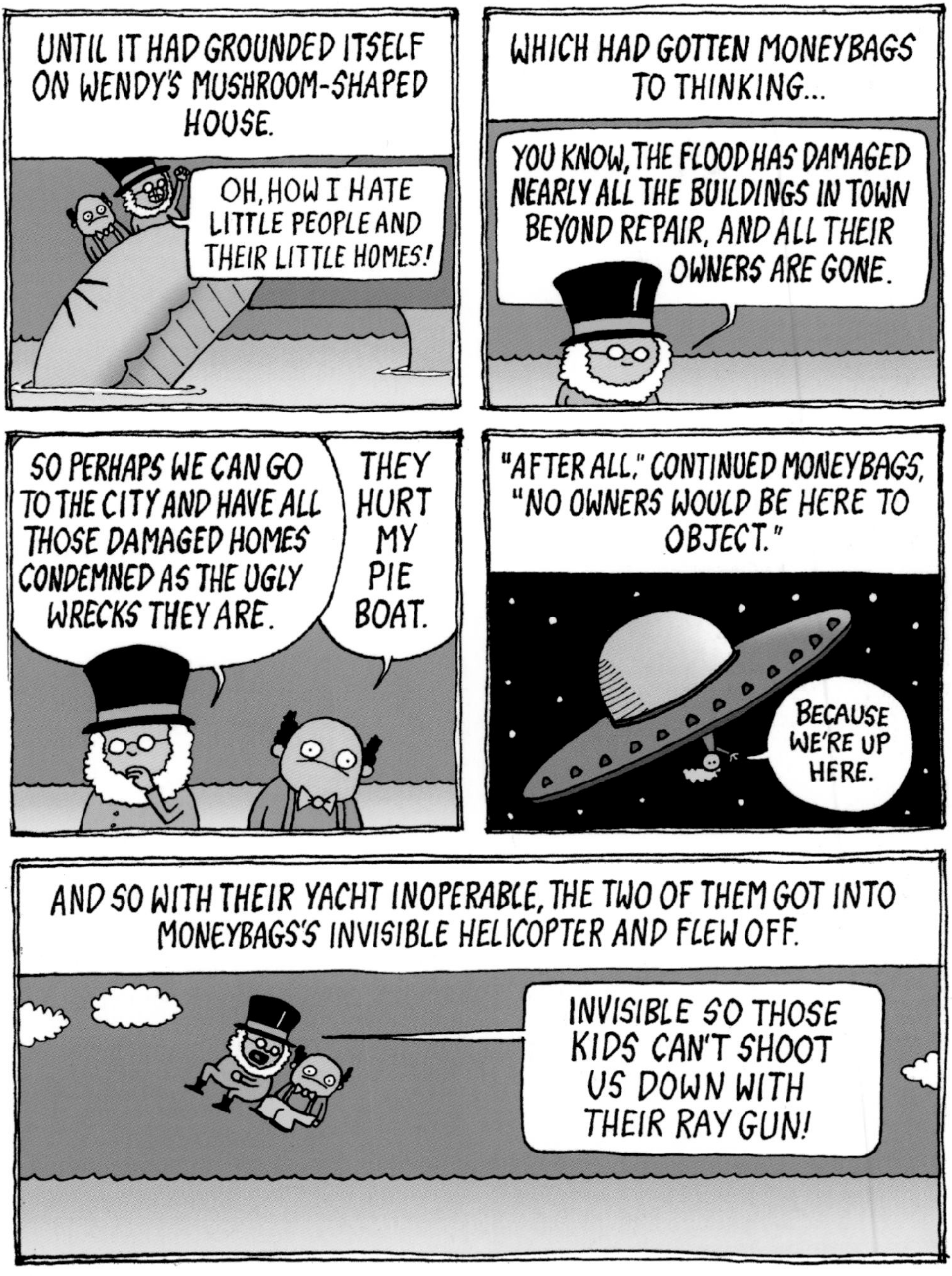
UNTIL IT HAD GROUNDED ITSELF ON WENDY'S MUSHROOM-SHAPED HOUSE.
OH, HOW I HATE LITTLE PEOPLE AND THEIR LITTLE HOMES!
WHICH HAD GOTTEN MONEYBAGS TO THINKING...
YOU KNOW, THE FLOOD HAS DAMAGED NEARLY ALL THE BUILDINGS IN TOWN BEYOND REPAIR, AND ALL THEIR OWNERS ARE GONE.
SO PERHAPS WE CAN GO TO THE CITY AND HAVE ALL THOSE DAMAGED HOMES CONDEMNED AS THE UGLY WRECKS THEY ARE.
THEY HURT MY PIE BOAT.
"AFTER ALL," CONTINUED MONEYBAGS, "NO OWNERS WOULD BE HERE TO OBJECT."
BECAUSE WE'RE UP HERE.
AND SO WITH THEIR YACHT INOPERABLE, THE TWO OF THEM GOT INTO MONEYBAGS'S INVISIBLE HELICOPTER AND FLEW OFF.
INVISIBLE SO THOSE KIDS CAN'T SHOOT US DOWN WITH THEIR RAY GUN!

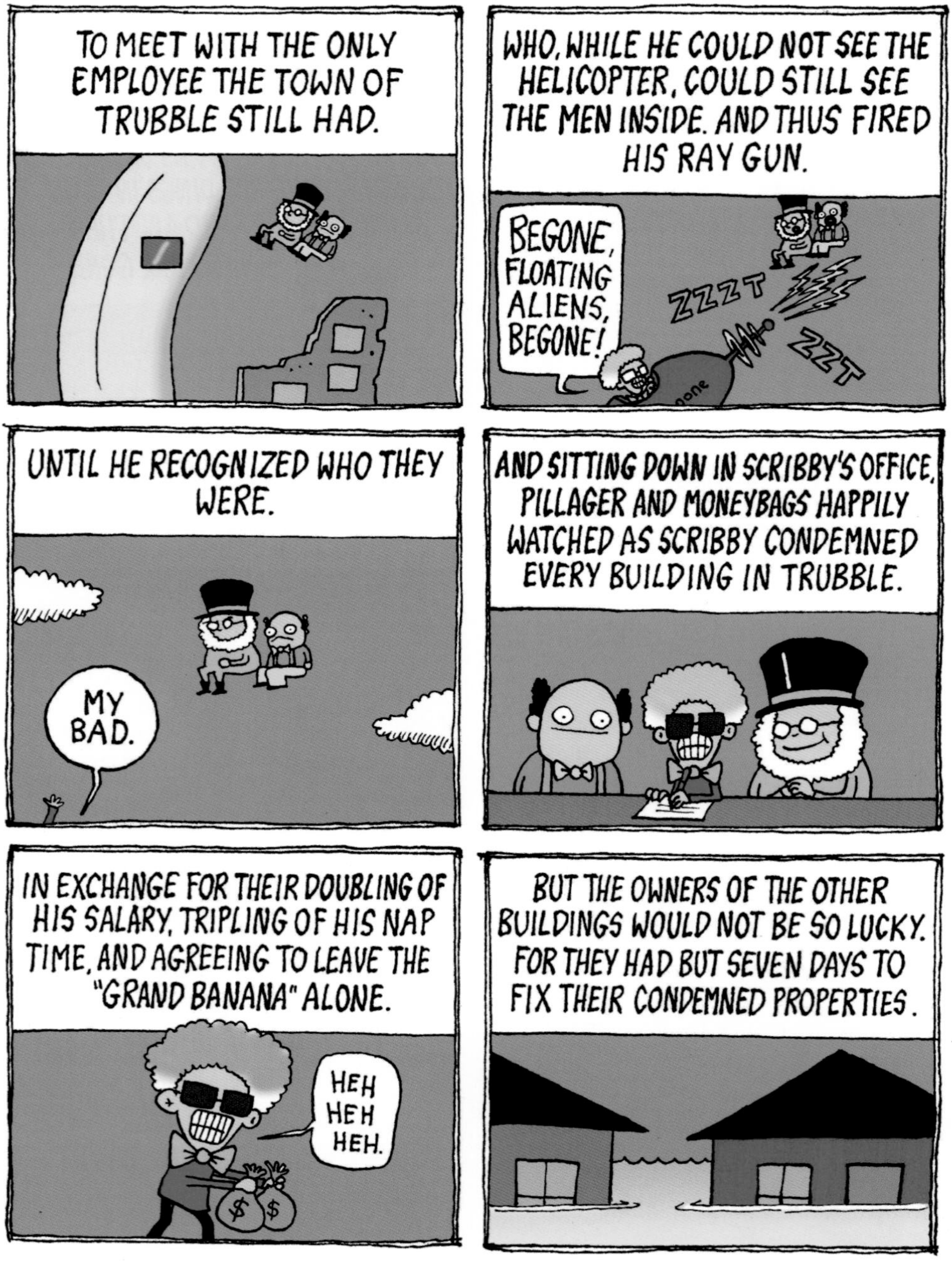
TO MEET WITH THE ONLY EMPLOYEE THE TOWN OF TRUBBLE STILL HAD.
WHO, WHILE HE COULD NOT SEE THE HELICOPTER, COULD STILL SEE THE MEN INSIDE. AND THUS FIRED HIS RAY GUN.
BEGONE, FLOATING ALIENS, BEGONE!
ZZZT
ZZT
UNTIL HE RECOGNIZED WHO THEY WERE.
MY BAD.
AND SITTING DOWN IN SCRIBBY'S OFFICE, PILLAGER AND MONEYBAGS HAPPILY WATCHED AS SCRIBBY CONDEMNED EVERY BUILDING IN TRUBBLE.
IN EXCHANGE FOR THEIR DOUBLING OF HIS SALARY, TRIPLING OF HIS NAP TIME, AND AGREEING TO LEAVE THE "GRAND BANANA" ALONE.
HEH HEH HEH.
$
$
BUT THE OWNERS OF THE OTHER BUILDINGS WOULD NOT BE SO LUCKY. FOR THEY HAD BUT SEVEN DAYS TO FIX THEIR CONDEMNED PROPERTIES.

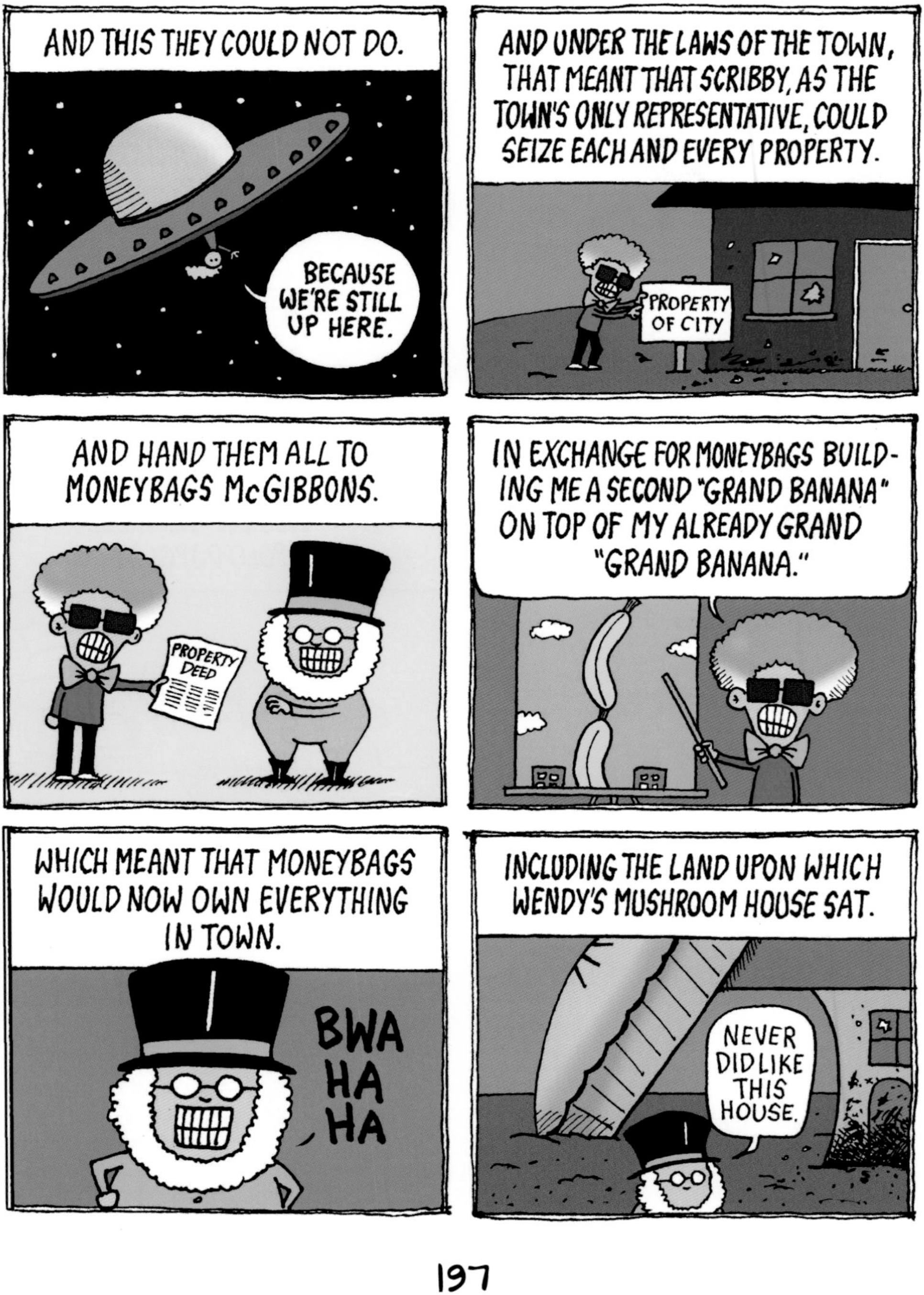
AND THIS THEY COULD NOT DO.
BECAUSE WE'RE STILL UP HERE.
AND UNDER THE LAWS OF THE TOWN, THAT MEANT THAT SCRIBBY, AS THE TOWN'S ONLY REPRESENTATIVE, COULD SEIZE EACH AND EVERY PROPERTY.
PROPERTY OF CITY
AND HAND THEM ALL TO MONEYBAGS McGIBBONS.
PROPERTY DEED
IN EXCHANGE FOR MONEYBAGS BUILDING ME A SECOND "GRAND BANANA" ON TOP OF MY ALREADY GRAND "GRAND BANANA."
WHICH MEANT THAT MONEYBAGS WOULD NOW OWN EVERYTHING IN TOWN.
BWA HA HA
INCLUDING THE LAND UPON WHICH WENDY'S MUSHROOM HOUSE SAT.
NEVER DID LIKE THIS HOUSE.

AND THE LAND UNDER MILO'S ORPHANAGE.

NEVER DID LIKE THIS KID.

AND SO MONEYBAGS CALLED RICKY RAM RUBBLE AND ASKED IF HE WOULD BE THE BUILDER ON A NEW PROJECT, THE DETAILS OF WHICH WERE NOT YET CLEAR...

BUT WHICH WOULD INVOLVE THE REMAKING OF THE ENTIRE CITY.

JUST DON'T RIP ME OFF THIS TIME.

WHO? ME?

A CITY THAT MILO AND WENDY WERE JUST THEN PLANNING THEMSELVES ON THE TABLES OF POPOLO DOPOLO'S.

BUT WAS AT THAT VERY MOMENT BEING ALTERED FOREVER.

THE TRUBBLE ORPHANAGE FOR TROUBLED TOTS

CHAPTER 4

IN WHICH...

OUR STREAK OF NUMBERING CHAPTERS CORRECTLY ENDS

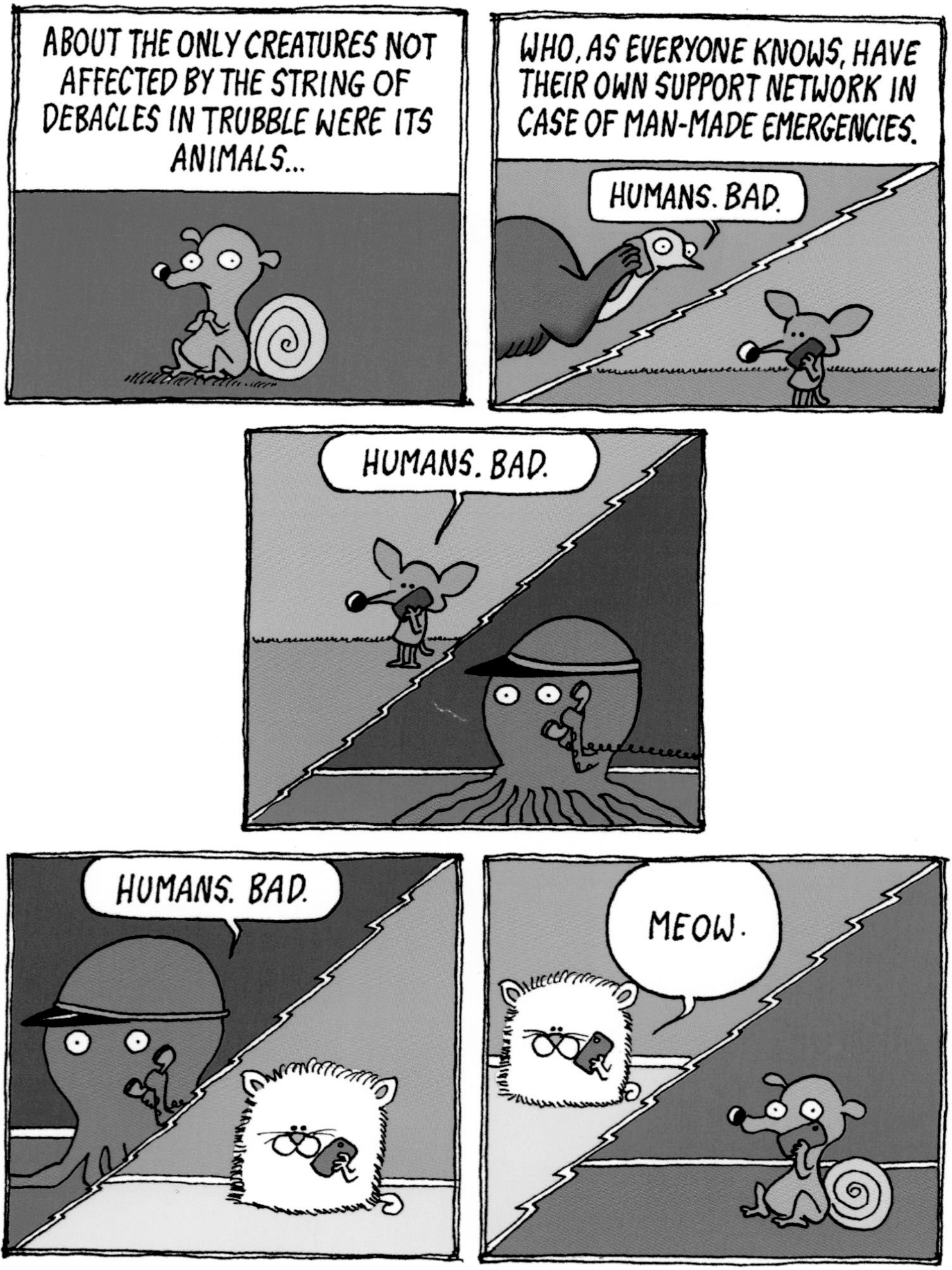
ABOUT THE ONLY CREATURES NOT AFFECTED BY THE STRING OF DEBACLES IN TRUBBLE WERE ITS ANIMALS...
WHO, AS EVERYONE KNOWS, HAVE THEIR OWN SUPPORT NETWORK IN CASE OF MAN-MADE EMERGENCIES.
HUMANS. BAD.
HUMANS. BAD.
HUMANS. BAD.
MEOW.

AND WHO HAD LONG SINCE HEADED FOR SQUIRRELY McSQUIRREL'S TREE.

WHICH WAS ROOMIER THAN IT LOOKED. AND CONTAINED THE "DIRT MUNCHER 2000," DESIGNED BY THE ANIMALS TO DRILL TO THE EARTH'S FIERY CORE.

DIRT MUNCHER 2000

WHICH IT DID. PROTECTING ITS OCCUPANTS FROM THE HEAT WITH ITS TOP-NOTCH AIR-CONDITIONING.

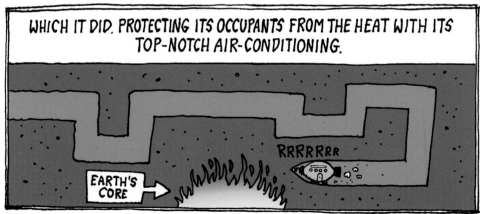

RRRRRRR

EARTH'S CORE →

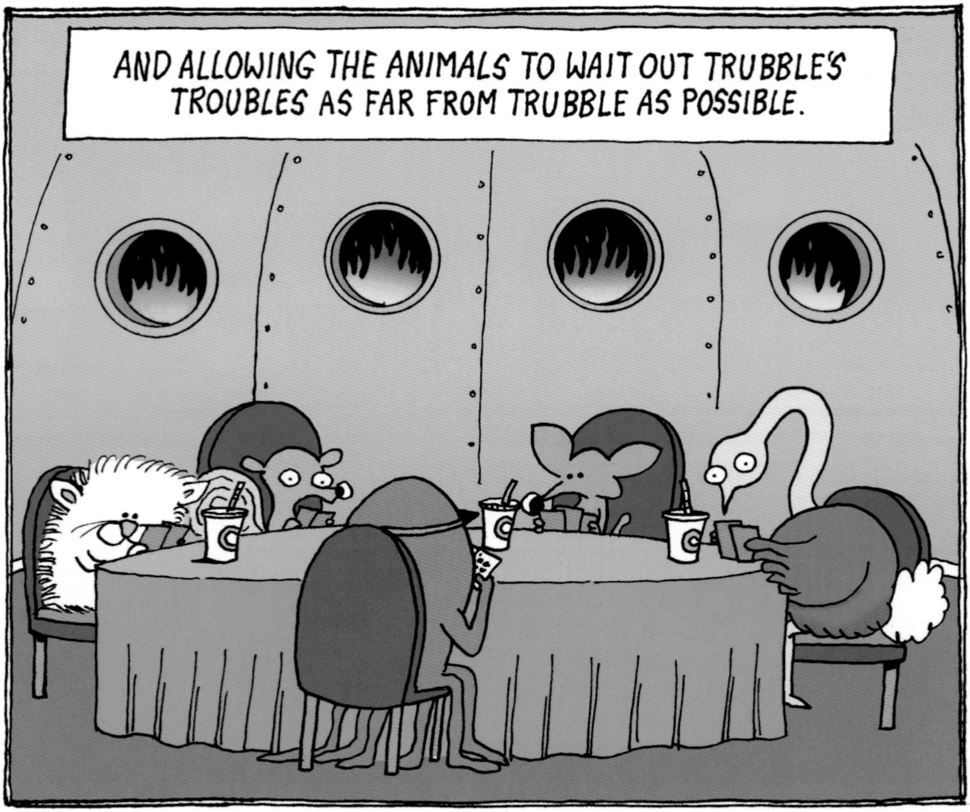
AND ALLOWING THE ANIMALS TO WAIT OUT TRUBBLE'S TROUBLES AS FAR FROM TRUBBLE AS POSSIBLE.

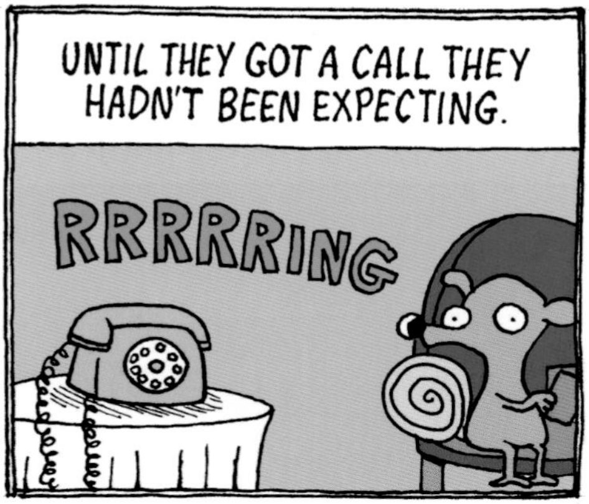
UNTIL THEY GOT A CALL THEY HADN'T BEEN EXPECTING.
RRRRRING

CHAPTER NUMBER DOES IT REALLY MATTER ANYMORE?

IN WHICH...

WE THINK YOU'LL AGREE THAT IT DOESN'T

AFTER NUTMAN TOLD WENDY AND MILO WHAT HE KNEW ABOUT THE ALIENS' PLAN, THEY FREED HIM FROM HIS NET.

SO LONG, SUCKERS!

DID HE JUST STEAL A GYRO?

YOU SAID YOU DIDN'T LIKE THEM!

AND MILO SAT DOWN TO DESIGN A BRAND-NEW TRUBBLE.

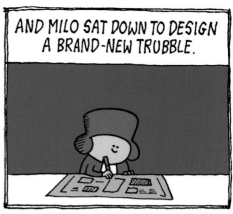

EXPERIENCING A CREATIVE BURST LIKE HE HAD NEVER HAD BEFORE.

FOR HE NOW SAW THE TOWN OF TRUBBLE AS HE HAD ONCE SEEN THE ORPHANAGE.

THE TRUBBLE ORPHANAGE FOR TROUBLED TOTS

AS A BLANK CANVAS UPON WHICH TO PAINT HIS MASTERPIECE. AND PAINT IT HE DID, FILLING THE DESIGN WITH ALL THAT HE WANTED.

LIKE GARDENS AND FLOWERS AND TOWN SQUARES AND TOWERS.

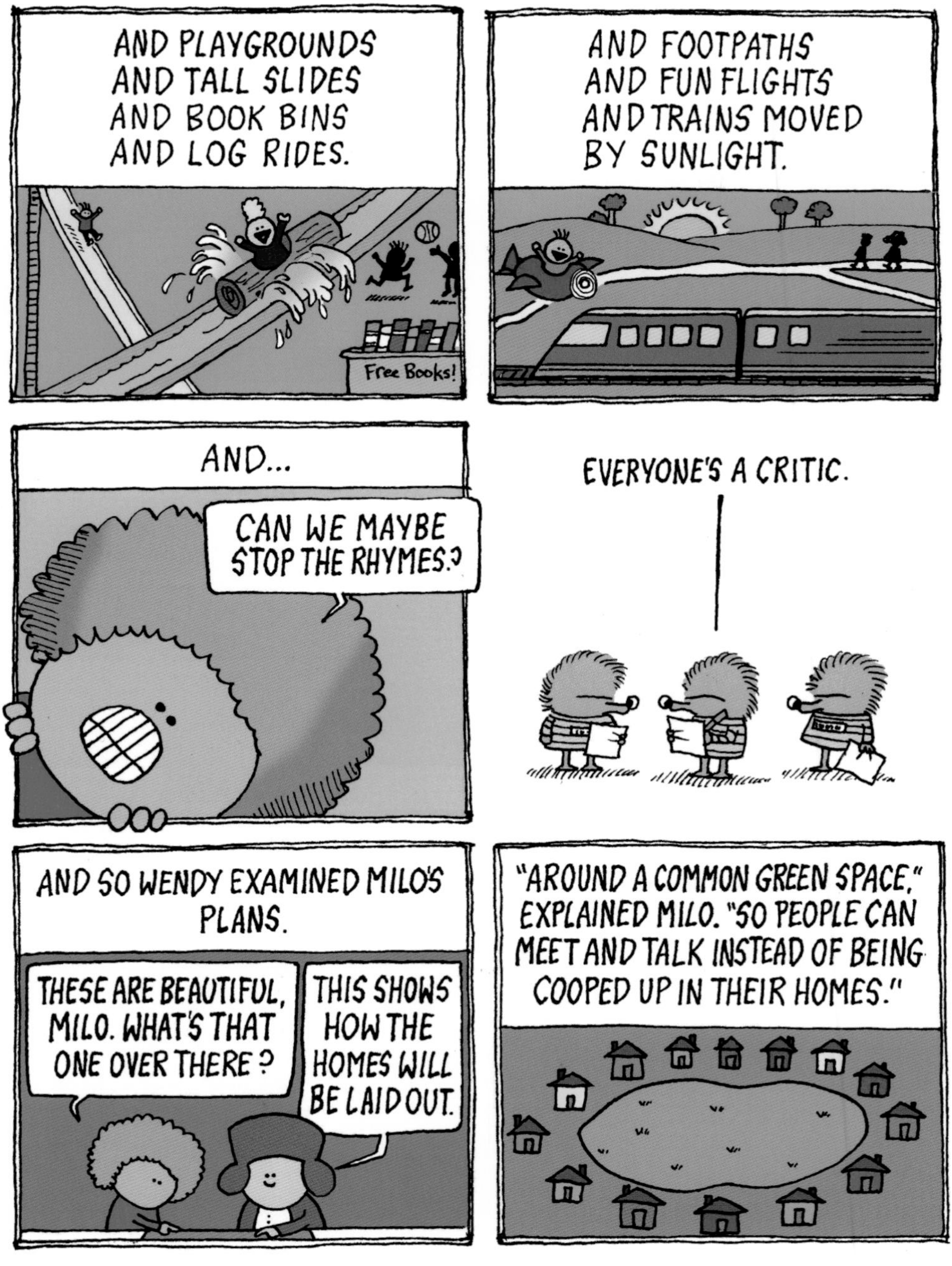
AND PLAYGROUNDS AND TALL SLIDES AND BOOK BINS AND LOG RIDES.
Free Books!
AND FOOTPATHS AND FUN FLIGHTS AND TRAINS MOVED BY SUNLIGHT.
AND...
CAN WE MAYBE STOP THE RHYMES?
EVERYONE'S A CRITIC.
AND SO WENDY EXAMINED MILO'S PLANS.
THESE ARE BEAUTIFUL, MILO. WHAT'S THAT ONE OVER THERE?
THIS SHOWS HOW THE HOMES WILL BE LAID OUT.
"AROUND A COMMON GREEN SPACE," EXPLAINED MILO. "SO PEOPLE CAN MEET AND TALK INSTEAD OF BEING COOPED UP IN THEIR HOMES."

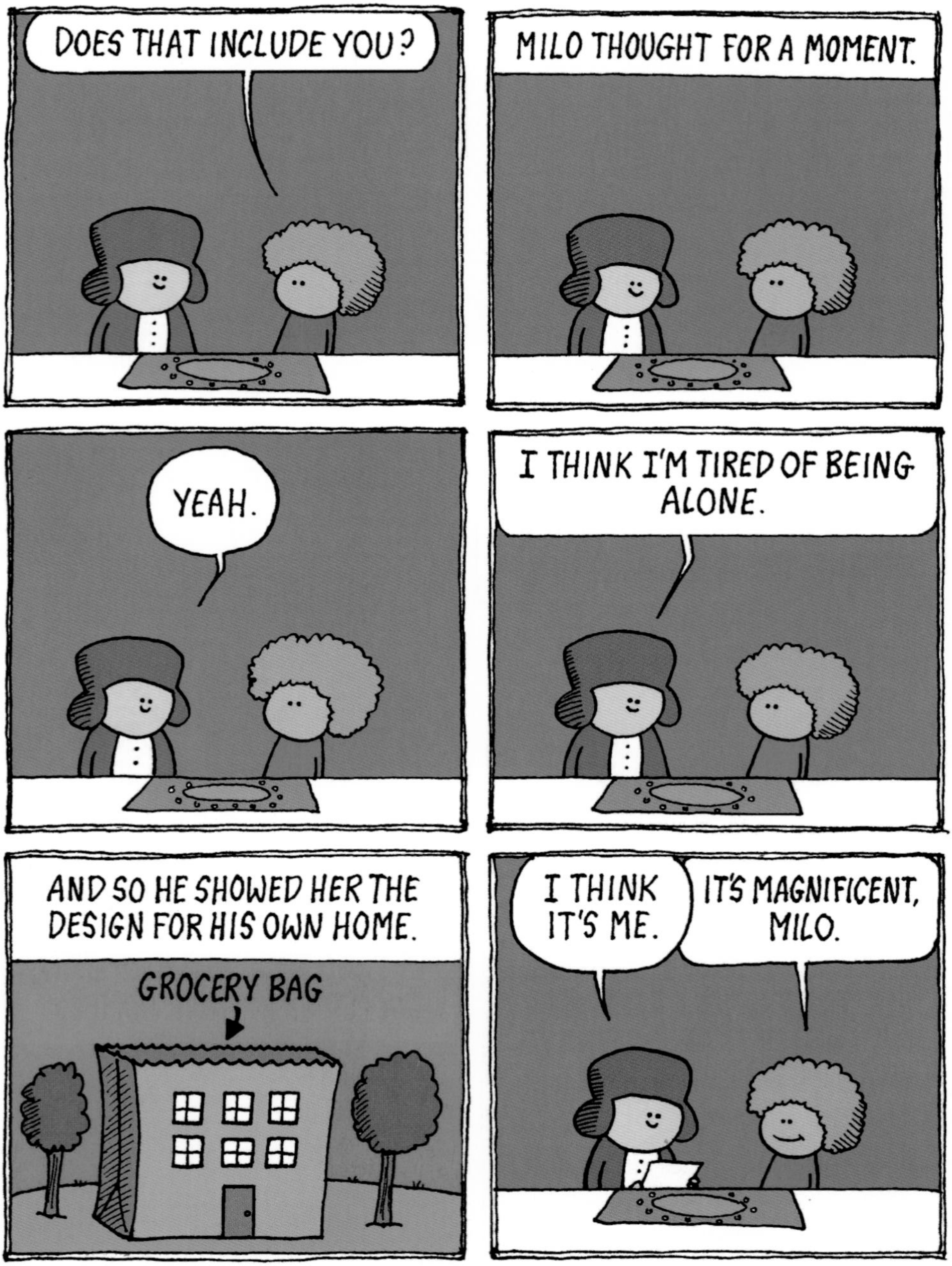
DOES THAT INCLUDE YOU?
MILO THOUGHT FOR A MOMENT.
YEAH.
I THINK I'M TIRED OF BEING ALONE.
AND SO HE SHOWED HER THE DESIGN FOR HIS OWN HOME.
GROCERY BAG
I THINK IT'S ME.
IT'S MAGNIFICENT, MILO.

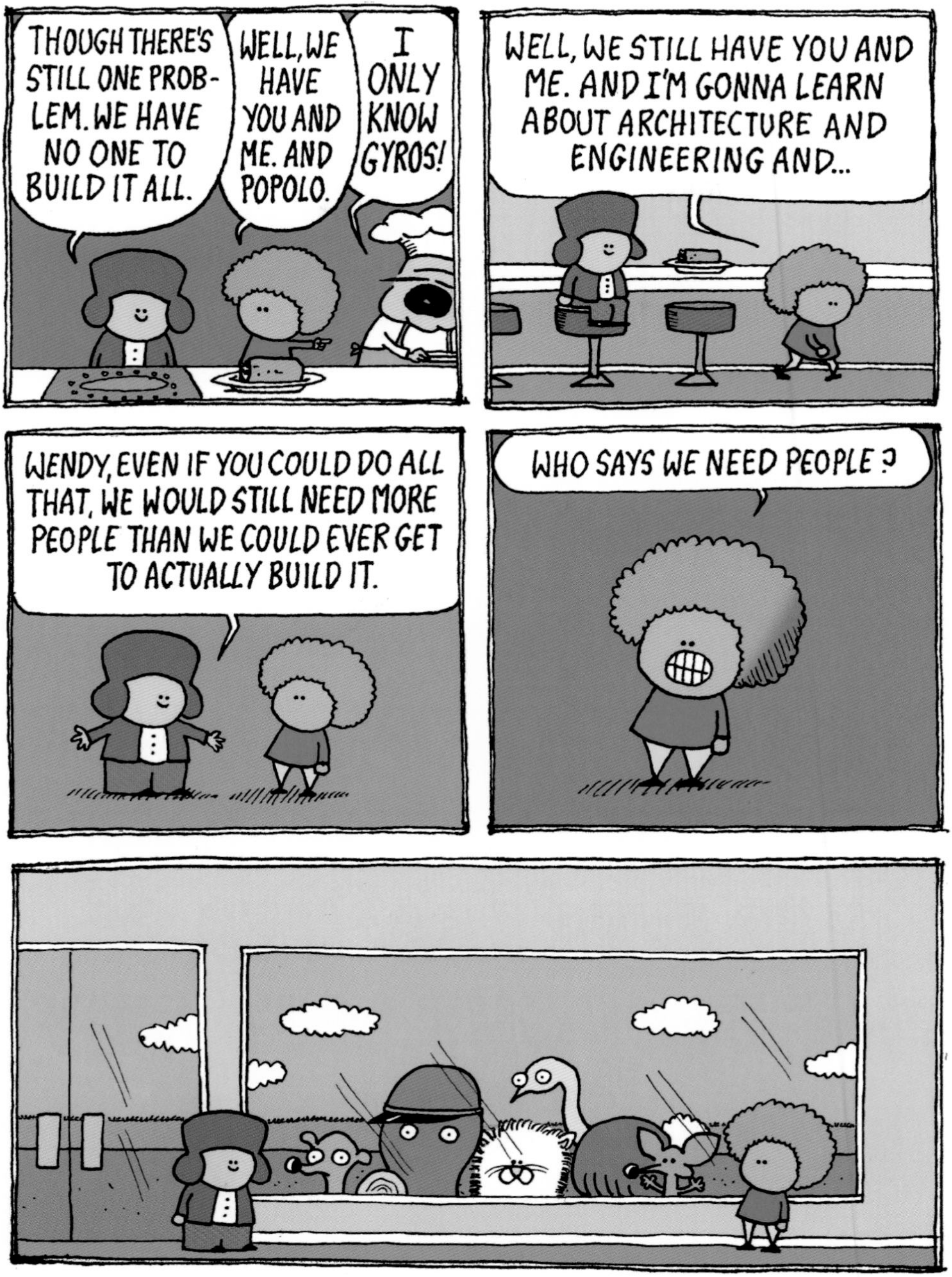
THOUGH THERE'S STILL ONE PROBLEM. WE HAVE NO ONE TO BUILD IT ALL.
WELL, WE HAVE YOU AND ME. AND POPOLO.
I ONLY KNOW GYROS!
WELL, WE STILL HAVE YOU AND ME. AND I'M GONNA LEARN ABOUT ARCHITECTURE AND ENGINEERING AND...
WENDY, EVEN IF YOU COULD DO ALL THAT, WE WOULD STILL NEED MORE PEOPLE THAN WE COULD EVER GET TO ACTUALLY BUILD IT.
WHO SAYS WE NEED PEOPLE?

CHAPTER 4,000

WHICH IS...

A CHAPTER NUMBER WE'RE PRETTY SURE NO BOOK HAS EVER REACHED, SO WE THOUGHT WE'D TRY IT HERE

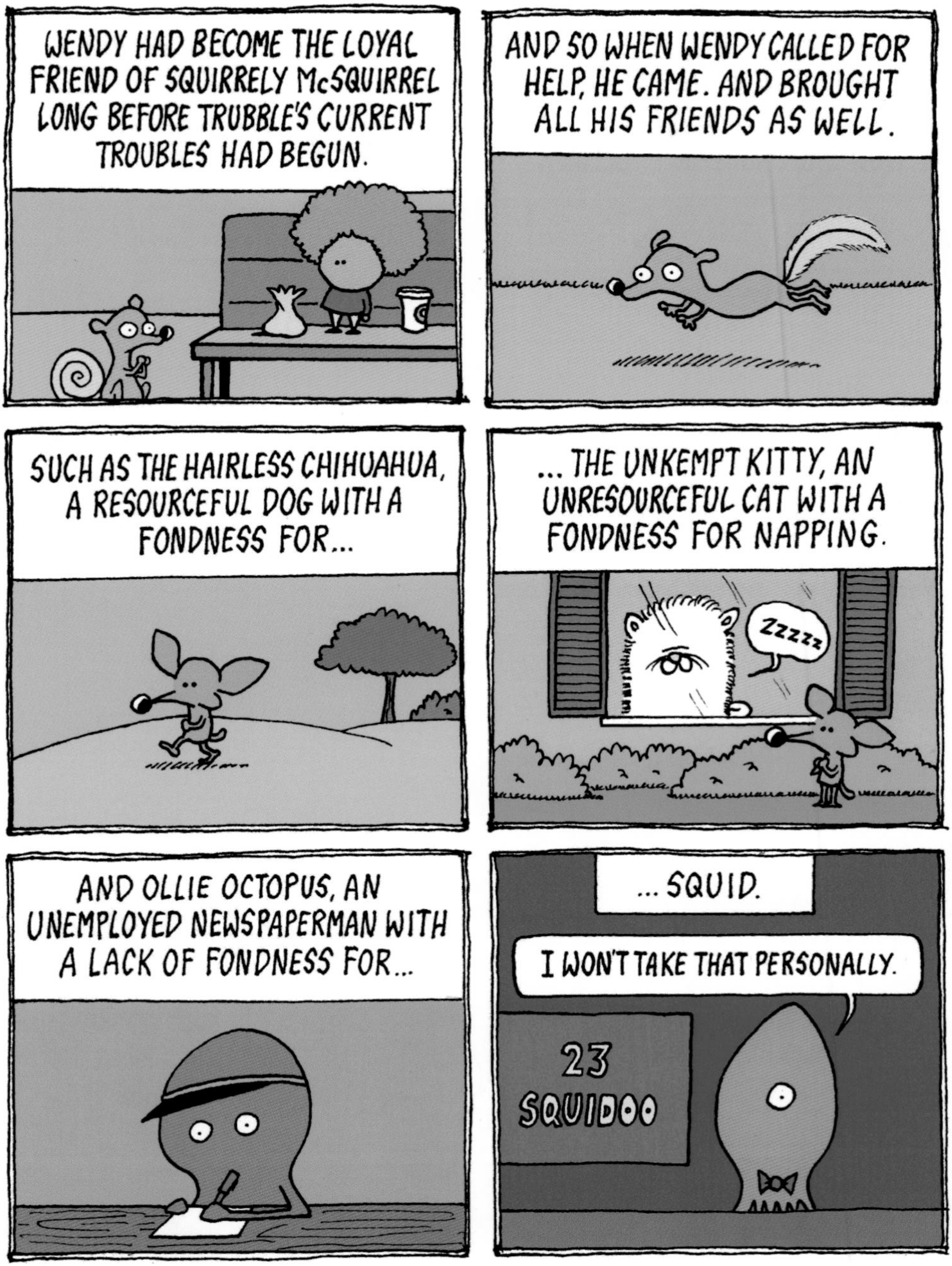
WENDY HAD BECOME THE LOYAL FRIEND OF SQUIRRELY McSQUIRREL LONG BEFORE TRUBBLE'S CURRENT TROUBLES HAD BEGUN.
AND SO WHEN WENDY CALLED FOR HELP, HE CAME. AND BROUGHT ALL HIS FRIENDS AS WELL.
SUCH AS THE HAIRLESS CHIHUAHUA, A RESOURCEFUL DOG WITH A FONDNESS FOR...
... THE UNKEMPT KITTY, AN UNRESOURCEFUL CAT WITH A FONDNESS FOR NAPPING.
ZZZZZ
AND OLLIE OCTOPUS, AN UNEMPLOYED NEWSPAPERMAN WITH A LACK OF FONDNESS FOR...
... SQUID.
I WON'T TAKE THAT PERSONALLY.
23
SQUIDOO

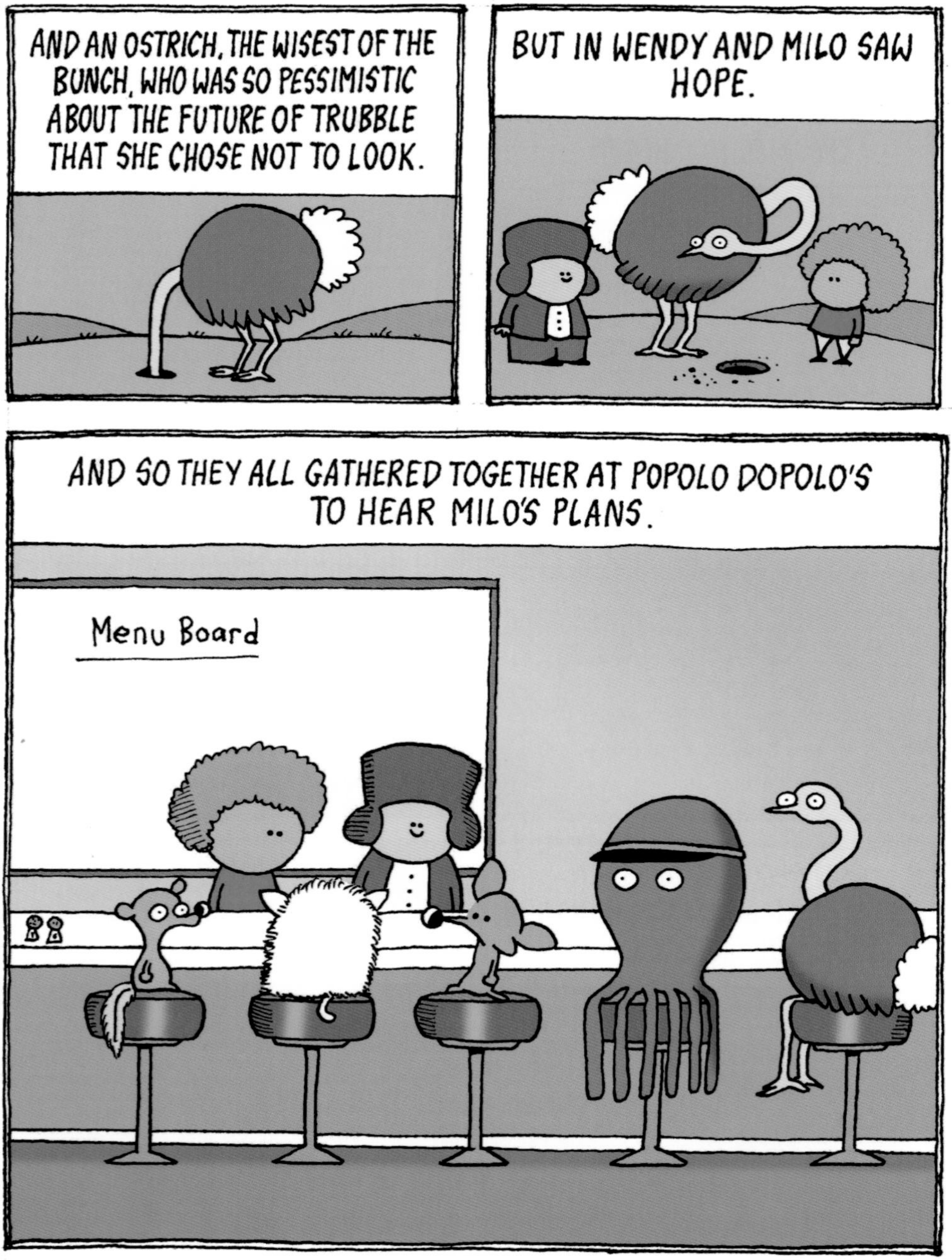
AND AN OSTRICH, THE WISEST OF THE BUNCH, WHO WAS SO PESSIMISTIC ABOUT THE FUTURE OF TRUBBLE THAT SHE CHOSE NOT TO LOOK.
BUT IN WENDY AND MILO SAW HOPE.
AND SO THEY ALL GATHERED TOGETHER AT POPOLO DOPOLO'S TO HEAR MILO'S PLANS.
Menu Board

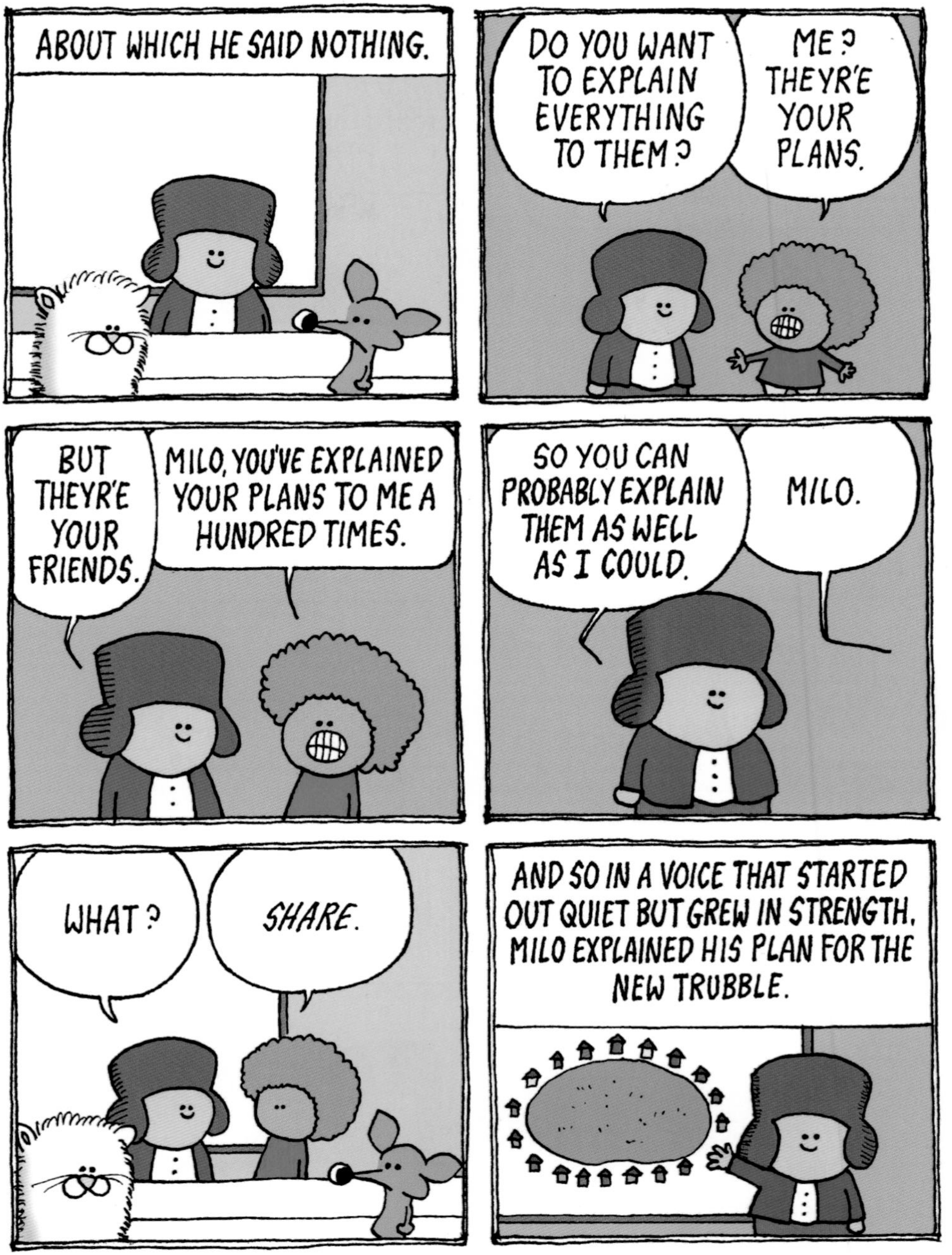
ABOUT WHICH HE SAID NOTHING.
DO YOU WANT TO EXPLAIN EVERYTHING TO THEM?
ME? THEYR'E YOUR PLANS.
BUT THEYR'E YOUR FRIENDS.
MILO, YOU'VE EXPLAINED YOUR PLANS TO ME A HUNDRED TIMES.
SO YOU CAN PROBABLY EXPLAIN THEM AS WELL AS I COULD.
MILO.
WHAT?
SHARE.
AND SO IN A VOICE THAT STARTED OUT QUIET BUT GREW IN STRENGTH, MILO EXPLAINED HIS PLAN FOR THE NEW TRUBBLE.

AND WHEN HE WAS DONE, HE ASKED:

SO DO ANY OF YOU HAVE ANY CONSTRUCTION EXPERIENCE?

AT WHICH POINT THE CHIHUAHUA, WHO UP TO THAT POINT HAD SAID VERY LITTLE, SLID A RÉSUMÉ ACROSS THE LUNCH COUNTER.

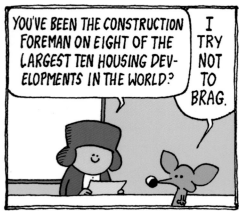

YOU'VE BEEN THE CONSTRUCTION FOREMAN ON EIGHT OF THE LARGEST TEN HOUSING DEVELOPMENTS IN THE WORLD?

I TRY NOT TO BRAG.

WHICH STRUCK SQUIRRELY McSQUIRREL AS BRAGGING. AND SO HE WROTE A BOAST OF HIS OWN ON THE BACK OF A POPOLO DOPOLO'S MENU.

I CAN GET YOU 5,000 SQUIRRELS WHO WILL WORK FOR PEANUTS.

AT WHICH POINT THE KITTY, NOT WANTING TO BE OUTDONE, HANDED ANOTHER NOTE TO MILO.

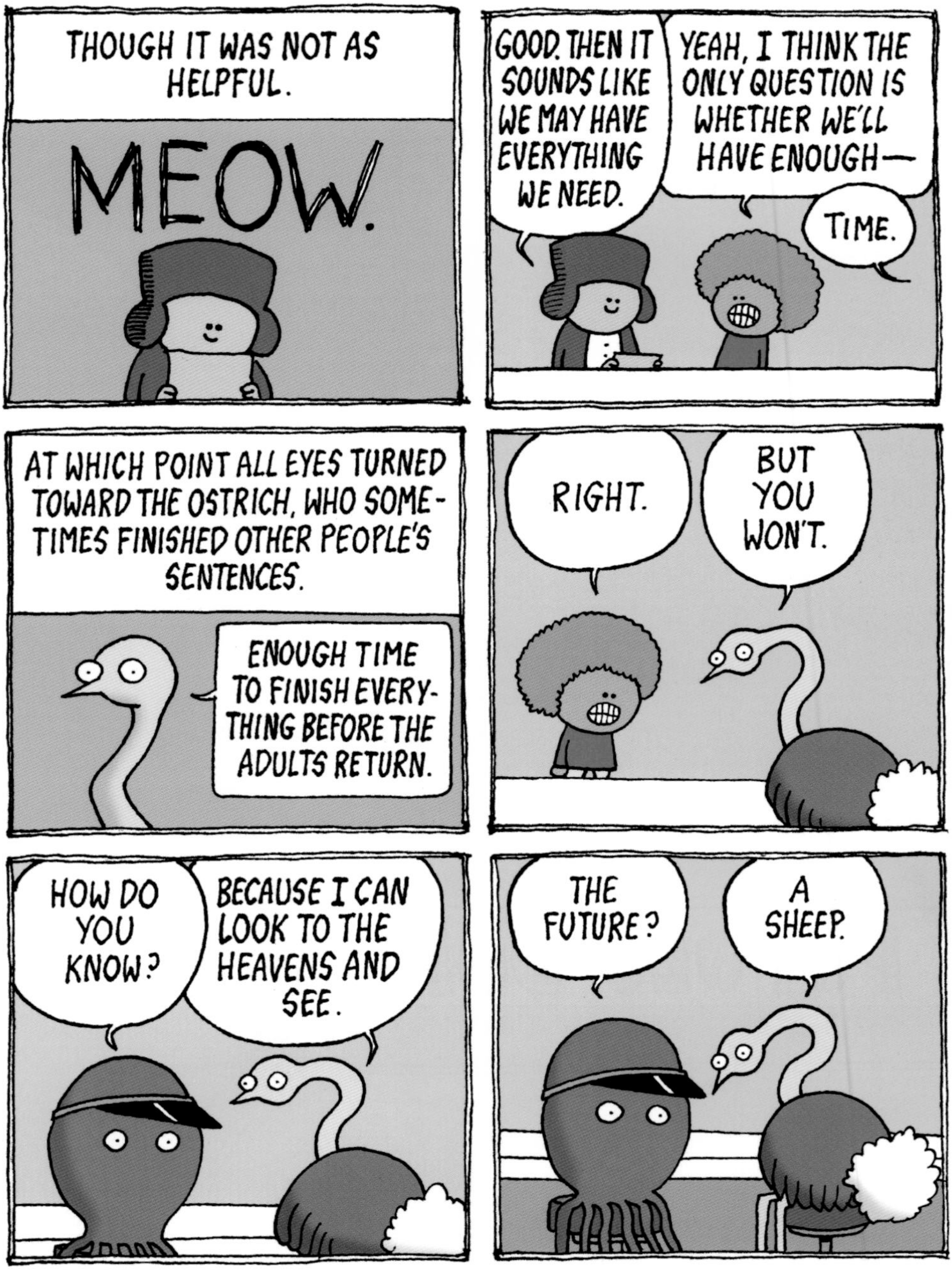
THOUGH IT WAS NOT AS HELPFUL.
MEOW.
GOOD. THEN IT SOUNDS LIKE WE MAY HAVE EVERYTHING WE NEED.
YEAH, I THINK THE ONLY QUESTION IS WHETHER WE'LL HAVE ENOUGH—
TIME.
AT WHICH POINT ALL EYES TURNED TOWARD THE OSTRICH, WHO SOMETIMES FINISHED OTHER PEOPLE'S SENTENCES.
ENOUGH TIME TO FINISH EVERYTHING BEFORE THE ADULTS RETURN.
RIGHT.
BUT YOU WON'T.
HOW DO YOU KNOW?
BECAUSE I CAN LOOK TO THE HEAVENS AND SEE.
THE FUTURE?
A SHEEP.

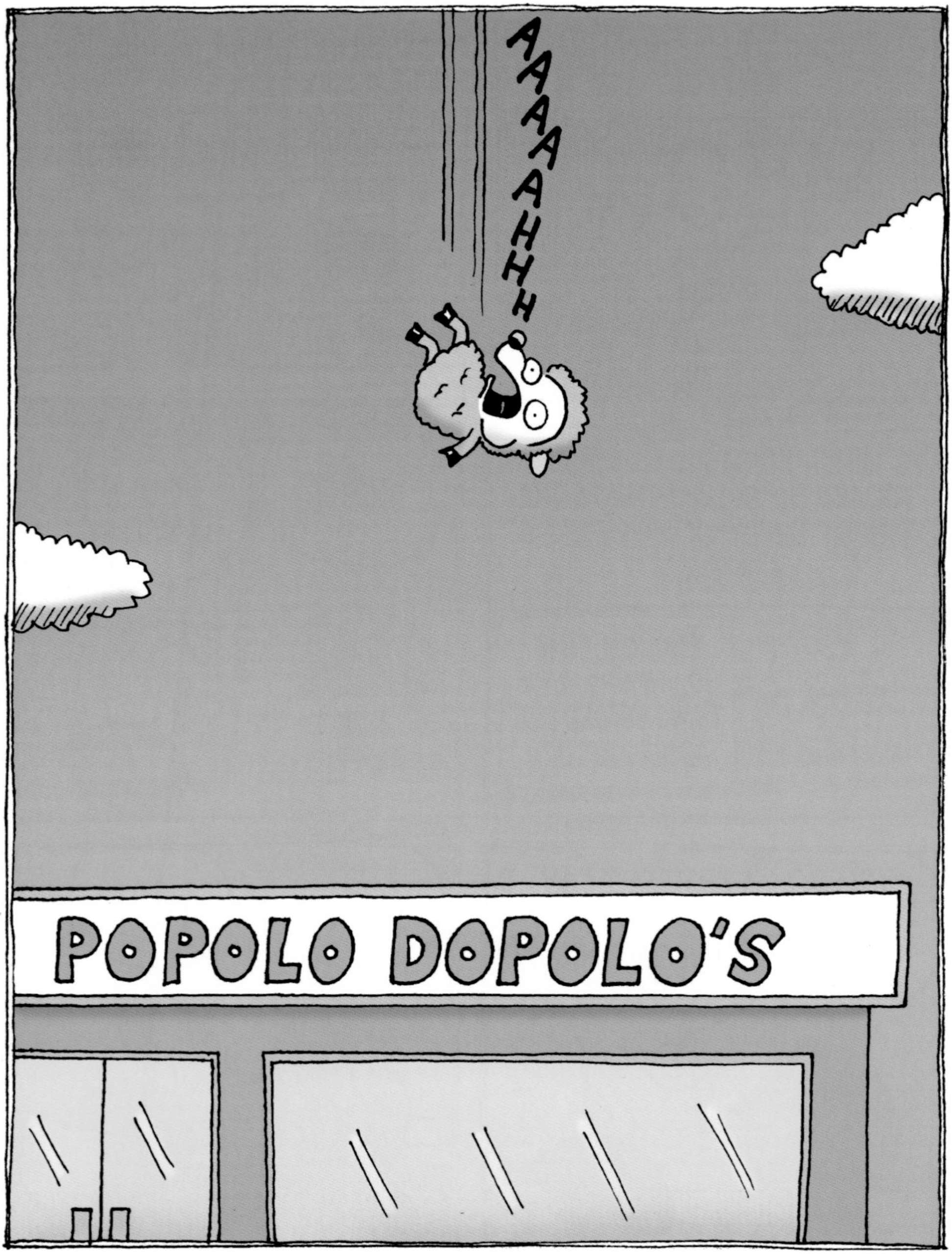
AAAAAAHHHH
POPOLO DOPOLO'S

CHAPTER LOOKOUT

IN WHICH...

YOU SHOULD COVER YOUR HEAD FOR PROTECTION

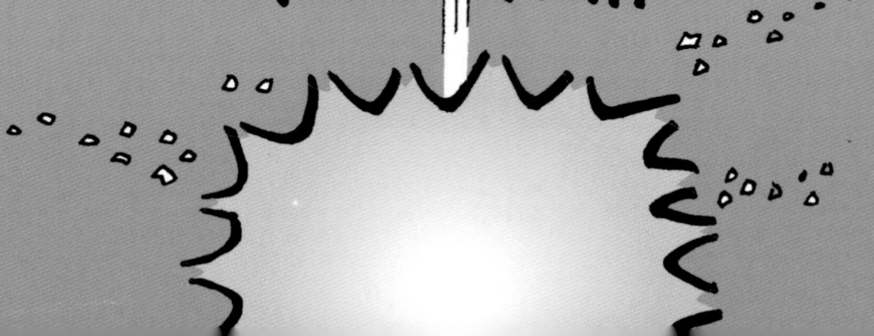
KSSHHHH

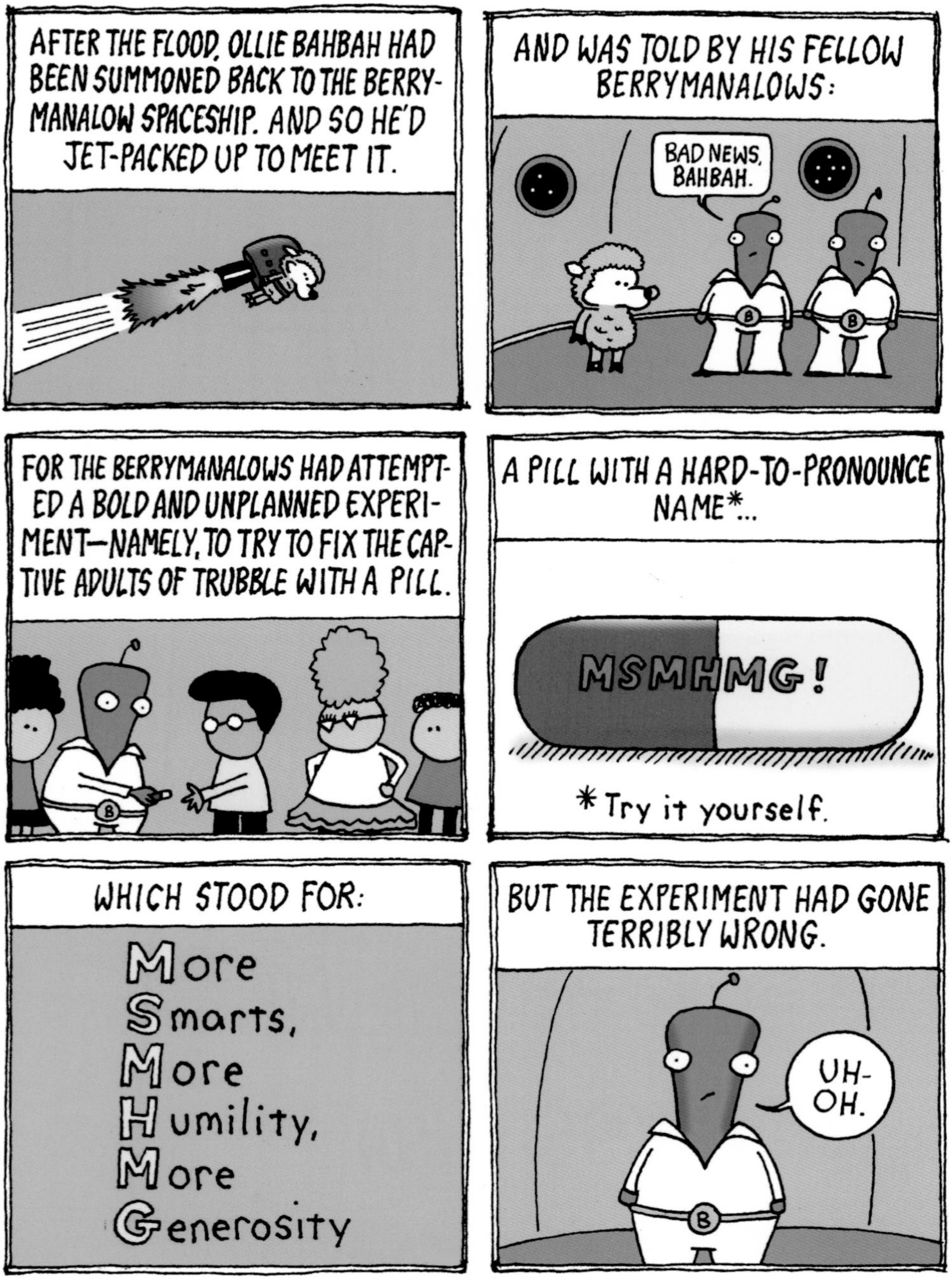
AFTER THE FLOOD, OLLIE BAHBAH HAD BEEN SUMMONED BACK TO THE BERRYMANALOW SPACESHIP. AND SO HE'D JET-PACKED UP TO MEET IT.
AND WAS TOLD BY HIS FELLOW BERRYMANALOWS:
BAD NEWS, BAHBAH.
FOR THE BERRYMANALOWS HAD ATTEMPTED A BOLD AND UNPLANNED EXPERIMENT—NAMELY, TO TRY TO FIX THE CAPTIVE ADULTS OF TRUBBLE WITH A PILL.
A PILL WITH A HARD-TO-PRONOUNCE NAME*...
MSMHMG!
* Try it yourself.
WHICH STOOD FOR:
More
Smarts,
More
Humility,
More
Generosity
BUT THE EXPERIMENT HAD GONE TERRIBLY WRONG.
UH-OH.

AND THE ADULTS HAD GOTTEN LESS SMART, LESS HUMBLE, AND LESS GENEROUS.

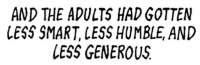

LET'S **CRASH** THE SPACESHIP FOR FUNZIES!!

SO MUCH SO THAT THE BERRY-MANALOWS COULD NO LONGER COEXIST WITH THEM ON THE SPACESHIP.

AAHHHHHHHHHH

AND SO THEY WOULD BE RETURNING TO TRUBBLE MUCH SOONER THAN EXPECTED. WHICH OLLIE BAHBAH PARACHUTED DOWN FROM THE HEAVENS TO TELL MILO.

UNTIL HIS PARACHUTE BROKE AND HE FELL THROUGH THE ROOF OF POPOLO DOPOLO'S.

I GUESS WE NOW HAVE A SKYLIGHT.

BUT OLLIE'S THICK WOOL SOFTENED THE FALL, AND WHEN HE RECOVERED, HE ASKED MILO AND WENDY TO FOLLOW HIM INTO POPOLO'S PRIVATE OFFICE.

PRIVATE

WHERE HE TOLD THEM...

I'VE GOT BAD NEWS AND MORE BAD NEWS. WHICH DO YOU WANT TO HEAR FIRST?

THE BAD NEWS.

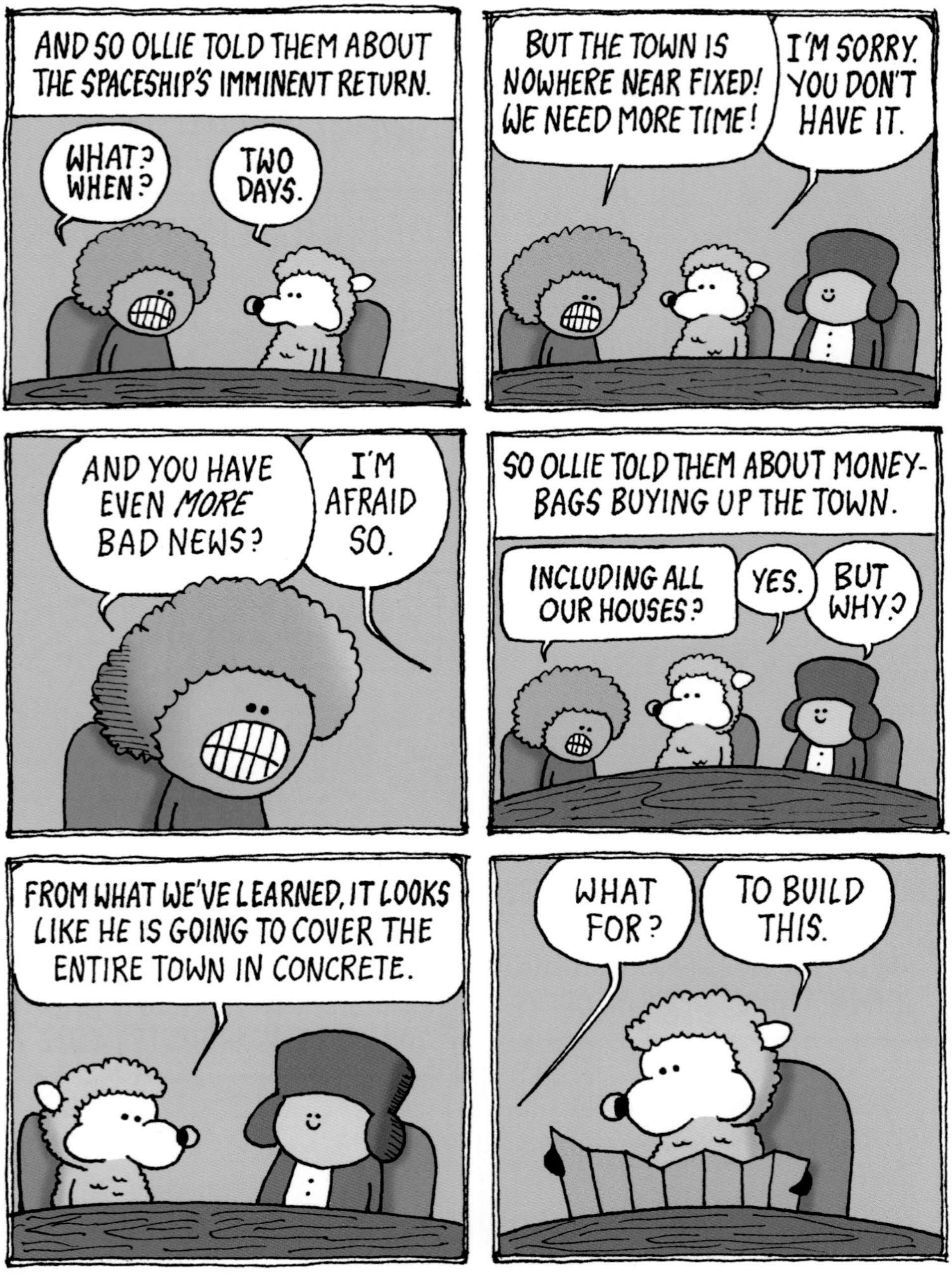
AND SO OLLIE TOLD THEM ABOUT THE SPACESHIP'S IMMINENT RETURN.
WHAT? WHEN?
TWO DAYS.
BUT THE TOWN IS NOWHERE NEAR FIXED! WE NEED MORE TIME!
I'M SORRY. YOU DON'T HAVE IT.
AND YOU HAVE EVEN *MORE* BAD NEWS?
I'M AFRAID SO.
SO OLLIE TOLD THEM ABOUT MONEY-BAGS BUYING UP THE TOWN.
INCLUDING ALL OUR HOUSES?
YES.
BUT WHY?
FROM WHAT WE'VE LEARNED, IT LOOKS LIKE HE IS GOING TO COVER THE ENTIRE TOWN IN CONCRETE.
WHAT FOR?
TO BUILD THIS.

OLLIE PINNED A BLUEPRINT ONTO POPOLO'S OFFICE WALL. IT SHOWED A HUGE DOLPHIN ATOP A BEACH BALL.

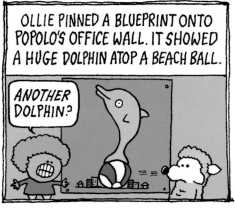

ANOTHER DOLPHIN?

YES, BUT THOUSANDS OF TIMES LARGER THAN THE "WHY-WHY." THERE WILL BE LITTLE ELSE LEFT IN TRUBBLE.

"OTHER THAN SCRIBBY'S 'GRAND BANANA,'" ADDED OLLIE. "WHICH IS NOW THE 'GRAND BANANA BANANA.'"

GRAND BANANA BANANA

MEANING THAT THERE WERE NOW SO MANY PROBLEMS THAT NO ONE KNEW QUITE WHERE TO START.

THOUGH WENDY TRIED.

THE SPACESHIP WILL NEED SOMEWHERE TO LAND IF IT'S GOING TO DROP OFF ALL THE ADULTS, RIGHT?

"OF COURSE," ANSWERED OLLIE. "ESPECIALLY AFTER I USED THE LAST PARACHUTE. AND YOU SAW HOW THAT WENT."

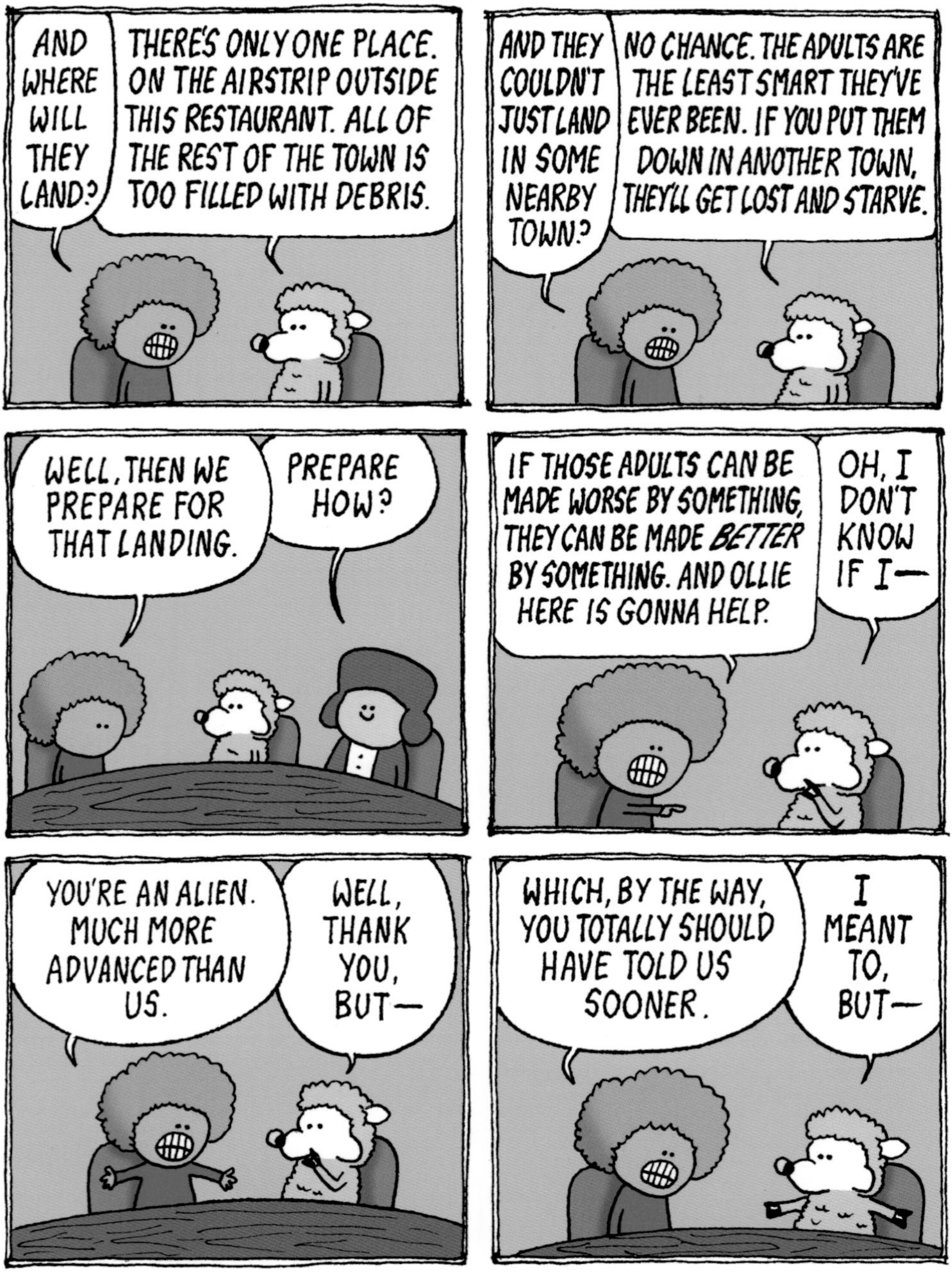
AND WHERE WILL THEY LAND?
THERE'S ONLY ONE PLACE. ON THE AIRSTRIP OUTSIDE THIS RESTAURANT. ALL OF THE REST OF THE TOWN IS TOO FILLED WITH DEBRIS.
AND THEY COULDN'T JUST LAND IN SOME NEARBY TOWN?
NO CHANCE. THE ADULTS ARE THE LEAST SMART THEY'VE EVER BEEN. IF YOU PUT THEM DOWN IN ANOTHER TOWN, THEY'LL GET LOST AND STARVE.
WELL, THEN WE PREPARE FOR THAT LANDING.
PREPARE HOW?
IF THOSE ADULTS CAN BE MADE WORSE BY SOMETHING, THEY CAN BE MADE *BETTER* BY SOMETHING. AND OLLIE HERE IS GONNA HELP.
OH, I DON'T KNOW IF I—
YOU'RE AN ALIEN. MUCH MORE ADVANCED THAN US.
WELL, THANK YOU, BUT—
WHICH, BY THE WAY, YOU TOTALLY SHOULD HAVE TOLD US SOONER.
I MEANT TO, BUT—

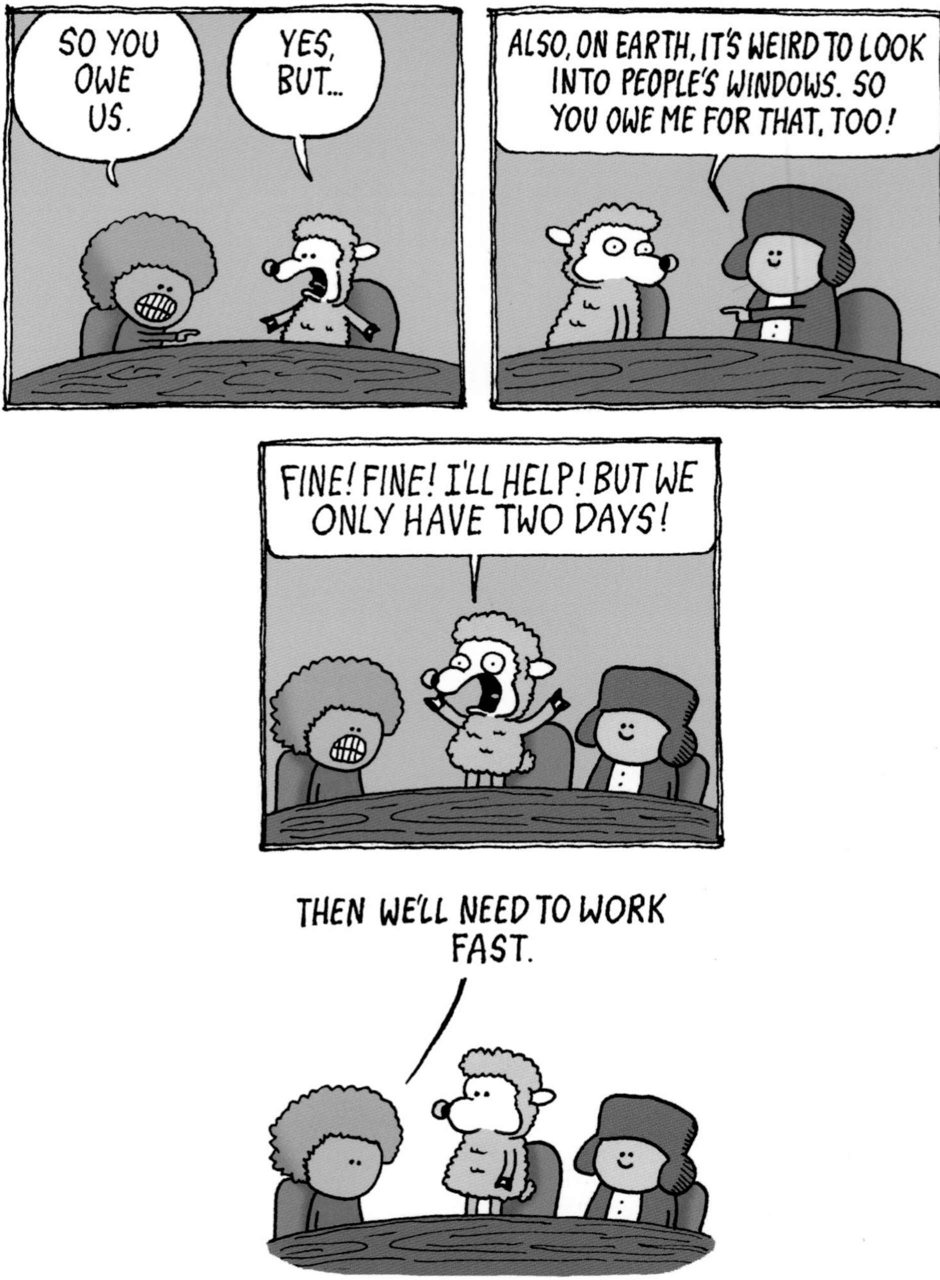
SO YOU OWE US.
YES, BUT...
ALSO, ON EARTH, IT'S WEIRD TO LOOK INTO PEOPLE'S WINDOWS. SO YOU OWE ME FOR THAT, TOO!
FINE! FINE! I'LL HELP! BUT WE ONLY HAVE TWO DAYS!
THEN WE'LL NEED TO WORK FAST.

CHAPTER NOBEL PRIZE

WHICH IS...

... WHAT WE SHOULD WIN FOR WRITING THIS BOOK.

WHAT NOBODY COULD HAVE FORESEEN WAS THAT ON THE DAY OF THE MEETING IN POPOLO'S OFFICE, MONEYBAGS WAS HUNGRY FOR GYROS.

Mmm, GYROS.

AND SO HE DECIDED TO LEAVE THE SAFETY OF HIS MANSION AND HEAD OUT TO POPOLO DOPOLO'S, WHICH HE KNEW FROM THE GIFT CERTIFICATE HE'D GIVEN TO MILO.

GIFT CERTIFICATE $2.75 REDEEMABLE AT POPOLO DOPOLO'S

THIS GENEROUS THING

AND THERE MONEYBAGS OVERHEARD THE CONVERSATION ABOUT THE RETURN OF THE UN-SMART ADULTS.

AND NEVER ONE TO MISS AN OPPORTUNITY, MONEYBAGS HATCHED A PLAN.

HE WOULD MODIFY HIS GIANT DOLPHIN STATUE BY PLACING A MASSIVE DINNER PLATE ATOP ITS NOSE.

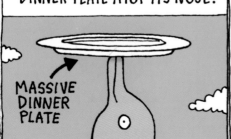

MASSIVE DINNER PLATE

A DINNER PLATE LARGE ENOUGH TO SERVE AS A LANDING PAD FOR THE BERRYMANALOW SPACESHIP. AND A SIGN MAKING THAT CLEAR.

Aliens, drop your humans off here.

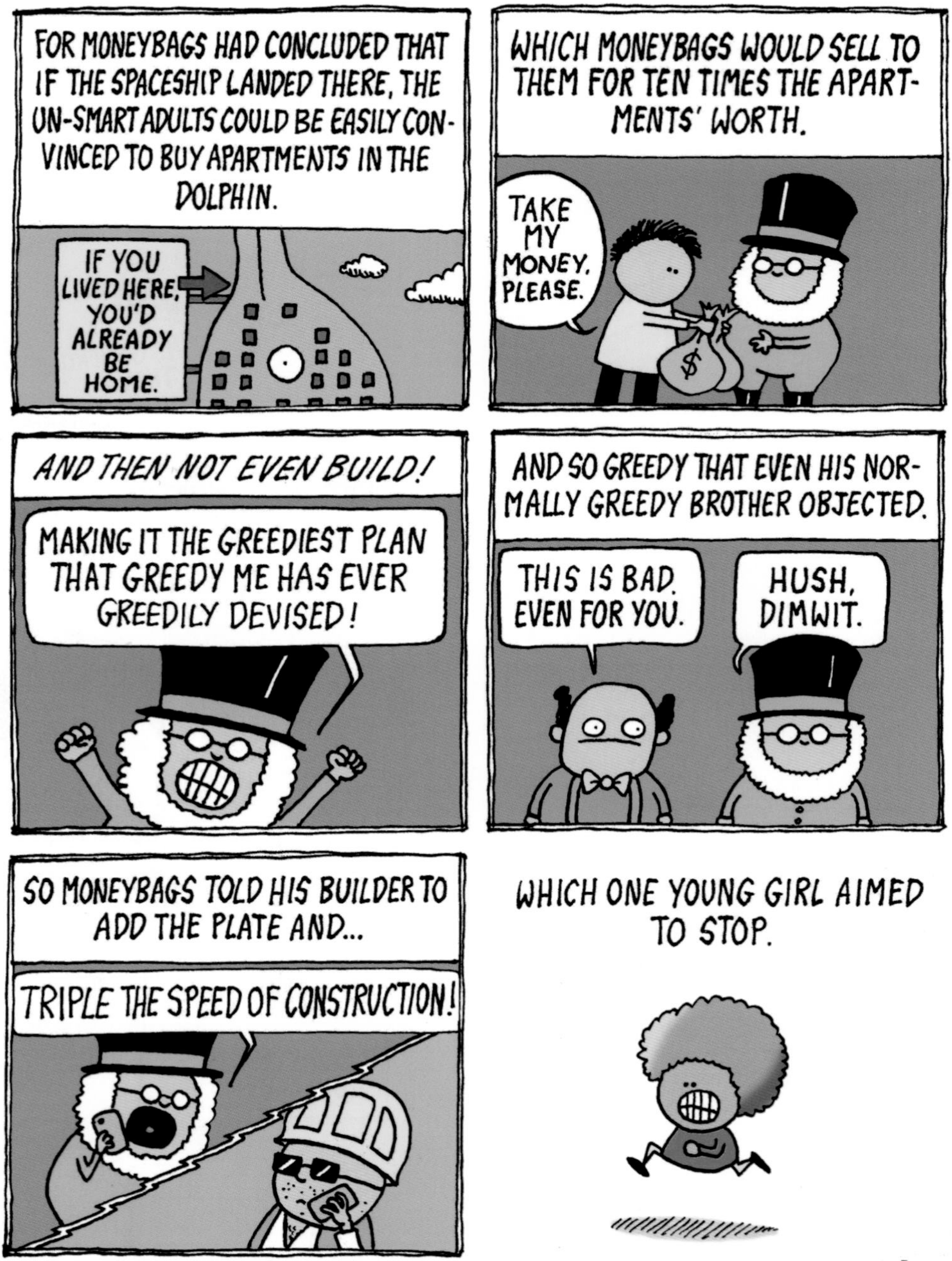
FOR MONEYBAGS HAD CONCLUDED THAT IF THE SPACESHIP LANDED THERE, THE UN-SMART ADULTS COULD BE EASILY CONVINCED TO BUY APARTMENTS IN THE DOLPHIN.
IF YOU LIVED HERE, YOU'D ALREADY BE HOME.
WHICH MONEYBAGS WOULD SELL TO THEM FOR TEN TIMES THE APARTMENTS' WORTH.
TAKE MY MONEY, PLEASE.
AND THEN NOT EVEN BUILD!
MAKING IT THE GREEDIEST PLAN THAT GREEDY ME HAS EVER GREEDILY DEVISED!
AND SO GREEDY THAT EVEN HIS NORMALLY GREEDY BROTHER OBJECTED.
THIS IS BAD. EVEN FOR YOU.
HUSH, DIMWIT.
SO MONEYBAGS TOLD HIS BUILDER TO ADD THE PLATE AND...
TRIPLE THE SPEED OF CONSTRUCTION!
WHICH ONE YOUNG GIRL AIMED TO STOP.

CHAPTER SHORT

WHICH IS....

SHORT

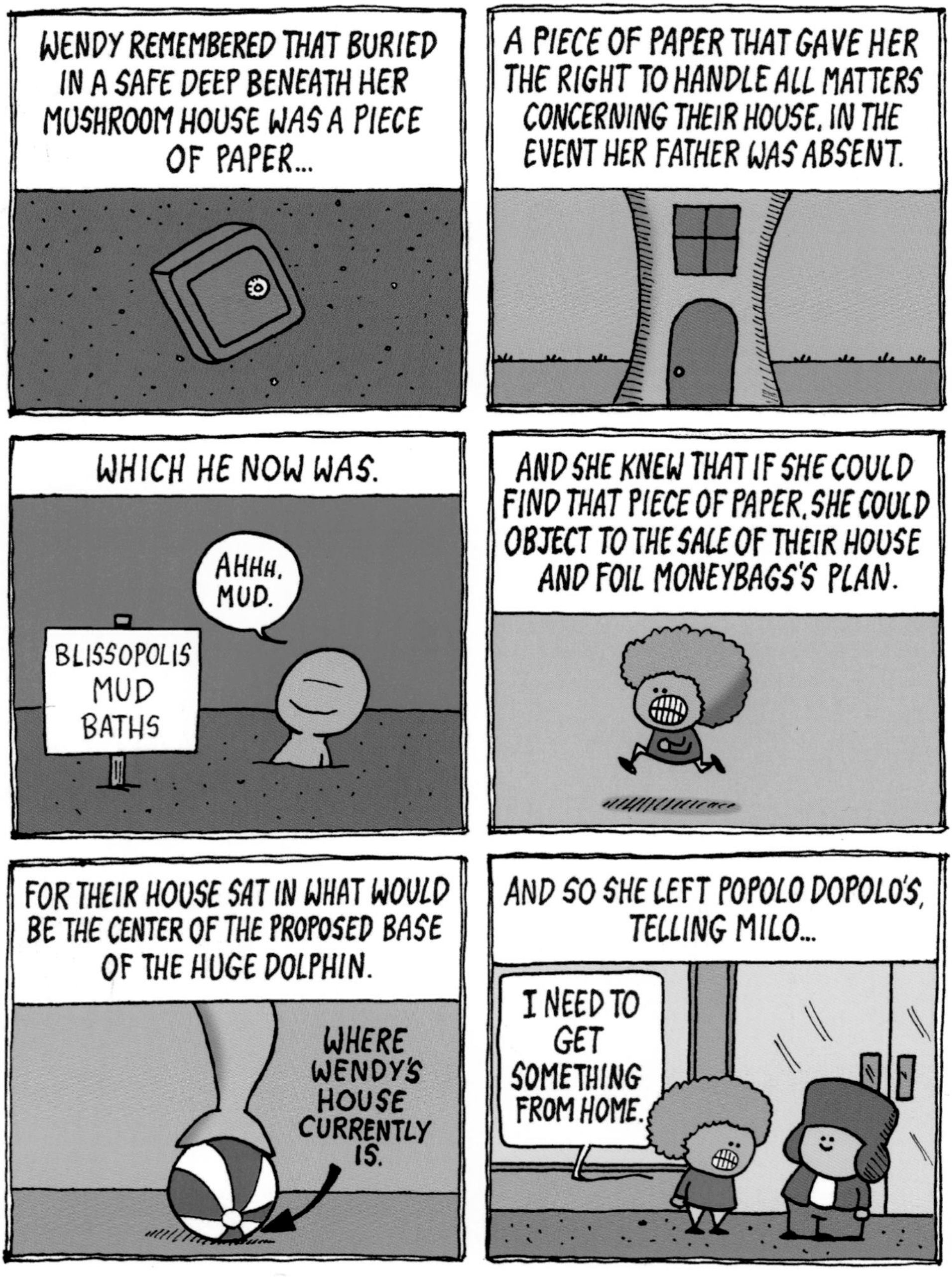
WENDY REMEMBERED THAT BURIED IN A SAFE DEEP BENEATH HER MUSHROOM HOUSE WAS A PIECE OF PAPER...
A PIECE OF PAPER THAT GAVE HER THE RIGHT TO HANDLE ALL MATTERS CONCERNING THEIR HOUSE, IN THE EVENT HER FATHER WAS ABSENT.
WHICH HE NOW WAS.
AHHH, MUD.
BLISSOPOLIS MUD BATHS
AND SHE KNEW THAT IF SHE COULD FIND THAT PIECE OF PAPER, SHE COULD OBJECT TO THE SALE OF THEIR HOUSE AND FOIL MONEYBAGS'S PLAN.
FOR THEIR HOUSE SAT IN WHAT WOULD BE THE CENTER OF THE PROPOSED BASE OF THE HUGE DOLPHIN.
WHERE WENDY'S HOUSE CURRENTLY IS.
AND SO SHE LEFT POPOLO DOPOLO'S, TELLING MILO...
I NEED TO GET SOMETHING FROM HOME.

TO WHICH MILO RESPONDED...

WHAT ABOUT THE LITTLE GIRL AND—

MILO, I THINK WE BOTH KNOW THAT PROBABLY DIDN'T HAPPEN. IT WAS A TOUGH DAY. YOU WERE STRESSED. IT'S NOTHING TO BE EMBARRASSED ABOUT.

WITH WHICH MILO AGREED.

YOU'RE PROBABLY RIGHT.

AND SO WENDY RAN OFF.

AS MILO AND OLLIE SAT DOWN TO CREATE THE THE DEVICE THAT WOULD SAVE THEIR TOWN...

THE "CATERPILLAR O' CHANGE."

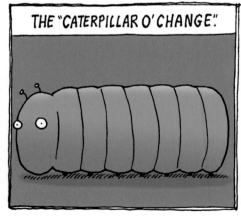

CHAPTER SIX

WHICH IS...

A
NUMBER
WE
DON'T
THINK
WE'VE
USED
YET

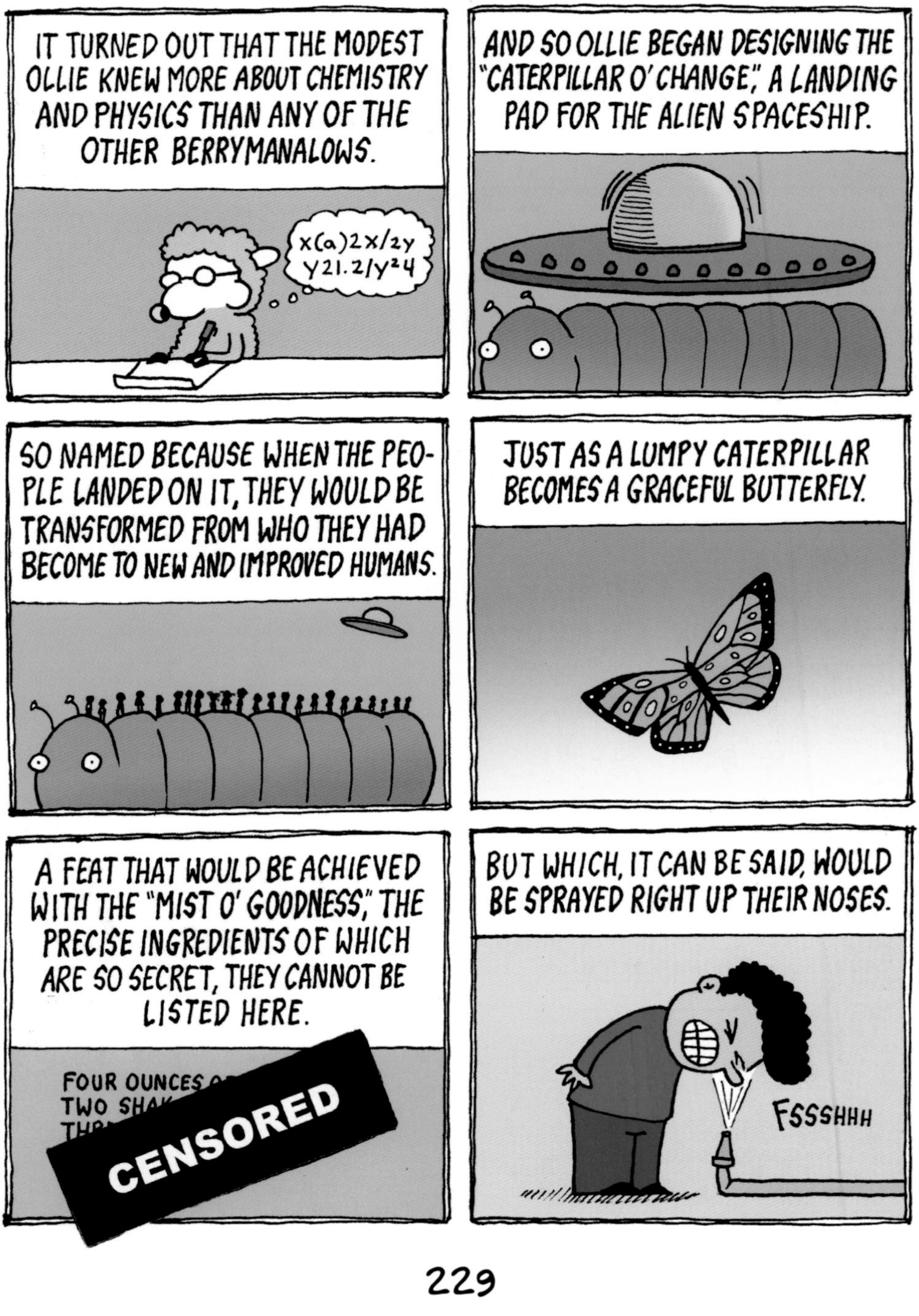
IT TURNED OUT THAT THE MODEST OLLIE KNEW MORE ABOUT CHEMISTRY AND PHYSICS THAN ANY OF THE OTHER BERRYMANALOWS.
$x(a)2x/2y$
$y21.2/y^{2}4$
AND SO OLLIE BEGAN DESIGNING THE "CATERPILLAR O' CHANGE," A LANDING PAD FOR THE ALIEN SPACESHIP.
SO NAMED BECAUSE WHEN THE PEOPLE LANDED ON IT, THEY WOULD BE TRANSFORMED FROM WHO THEY HAD BECOME TO NEW AND IMPROVED HUMANS.
JUST AS A LUMPY CATERPILLAR BECOMES A GRACEFUL BUTTERFLY.
A FEAT THAT WOULD BE ACHIEVED WITH THE "MIST O' GOODNESS," THE PRECISE INGREDIENTS OF WHICH ARE SO SECRET, THEY CANNOT BE LISTED HERE.
FOUR OUNCES [redacted]
TWO [redacted]
CENSORED
BUT WHICH, IT CAN BE SAID, WOULD BE SPRAYED RIGHT UP THEIR NOSES.
FSSSHHH

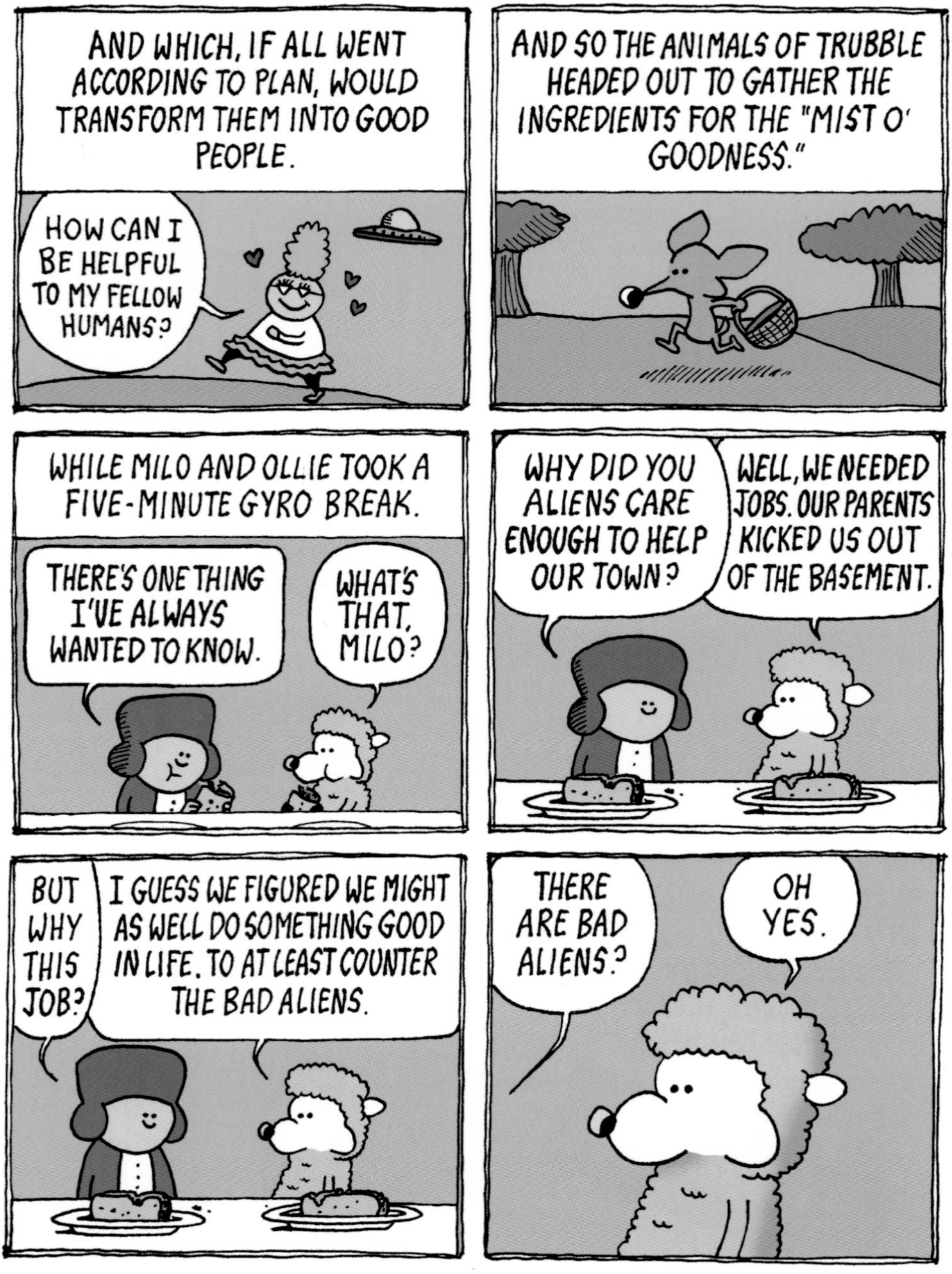
AND WHICH, IF ALL WENT ACCORDING TO PLAN, WOULD TRANSFORM THEM INTO GOOD PEOPLE.
HOW CAN I BE HELPFUL TO MY FELLOW HUMANS?
AND SO THE ANIMALS OF TRUBBLE HEADED OUT TO GATHER THE INGREDIENTS FOR THE "MIST O' GOODNESS."
WHILE MILO AND OLLIE TOOK A FIVE-MINUTE GYRO BREAK.
THERE'S ONE THING I'VE ALWAYS WANTED TO KNOW.
WHAT'S THAT, MILO?
WHY DID YOU ALIENS CARE ENOUGH TO HELP OUR TOWN?
WELL, WE NEEDED JOBS. OUR PARENTS KICKED US OUT OF THE BASEMENT.
BUT WHY THIS JOB?
I GUESS WE FIGURED WE MIGHT AS WELL DO SOMETHING GOOD IN LIFE. TO AT LEAST COUNTER THE BAD ALIENS.
THERE ARE BAD ALIENS?
OH YES.

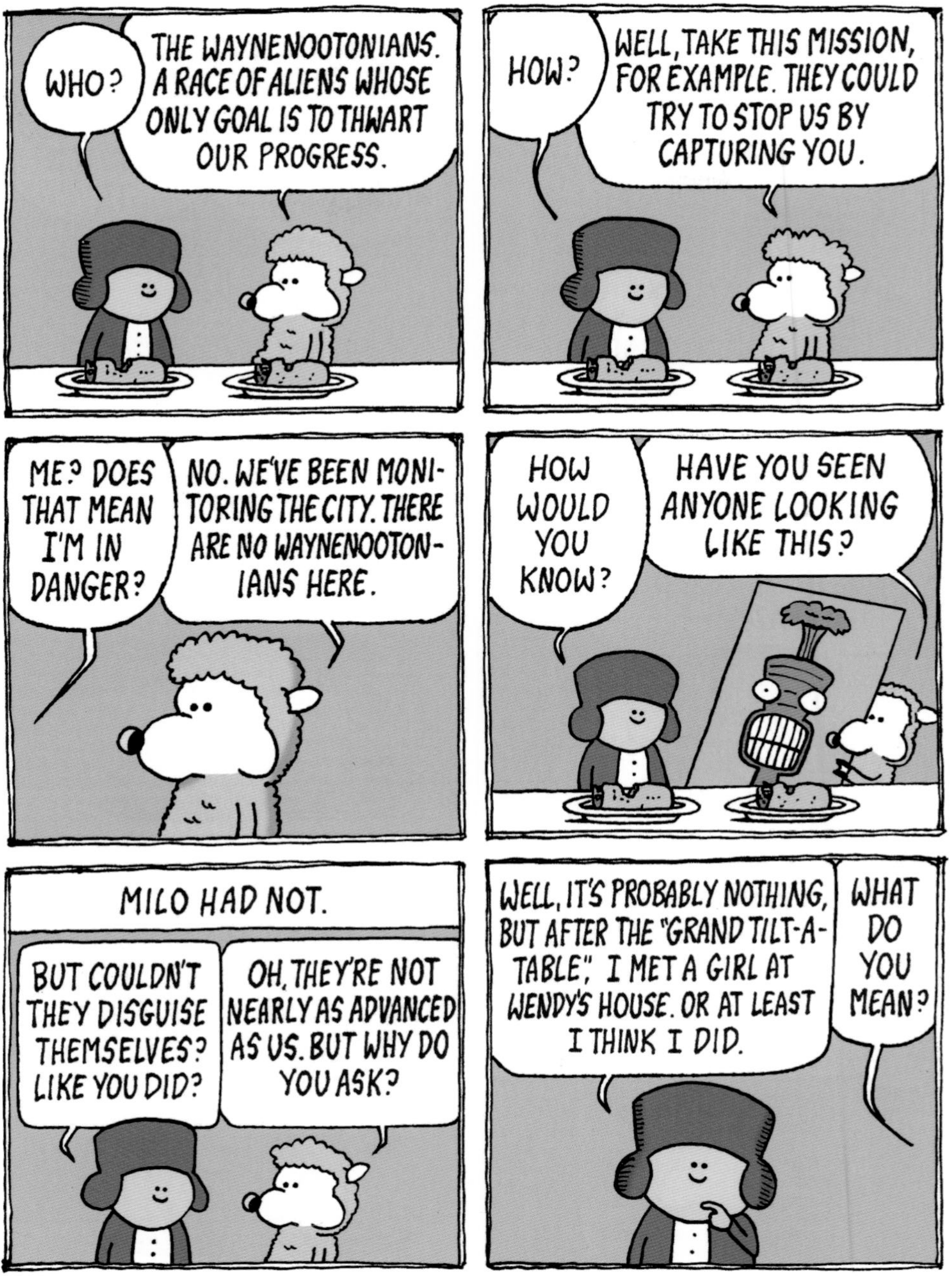
WHO?
THE WAYNENOOTONIANS. A RACE OF ALIENS WHOSE ONLY GOAL IS TO THWART OUR PROGRESS.
HOW?
WELL, TAKE THIS MISSION, FOR EXAMPLE. THEY COULD TRY TO STOP US BY CAPTURING YOU.
ME? DOES THAT MEAN I'M IN DANGER?
NO. WE'VE BEEN MONI-TORING THE CITY. THERE ARE NO WAYNENOOTON-IANS HERE.
HOW WOULD YOU KNOW?
HAVE YOU SEEN ANYONE LOOKING LIKE THIS?
MILO HAD NOT.
BUT COULDN'T THEY DISGUISE THEMSELVES? LIKE YOU DID?
OH, THEY'RE NOT NEARLY AS ADVANCED AS US. BUT WHY DO YOU ASK?
WELL, IT'S PROBABLY NOTHING, BUT AFTER THE "GRAND TILT-A-TABLE," I MET A GIRL AT WENDY'S HOUSE. OR AT LEAST I THINK I DID.
WHAT DO YOU MEAN?

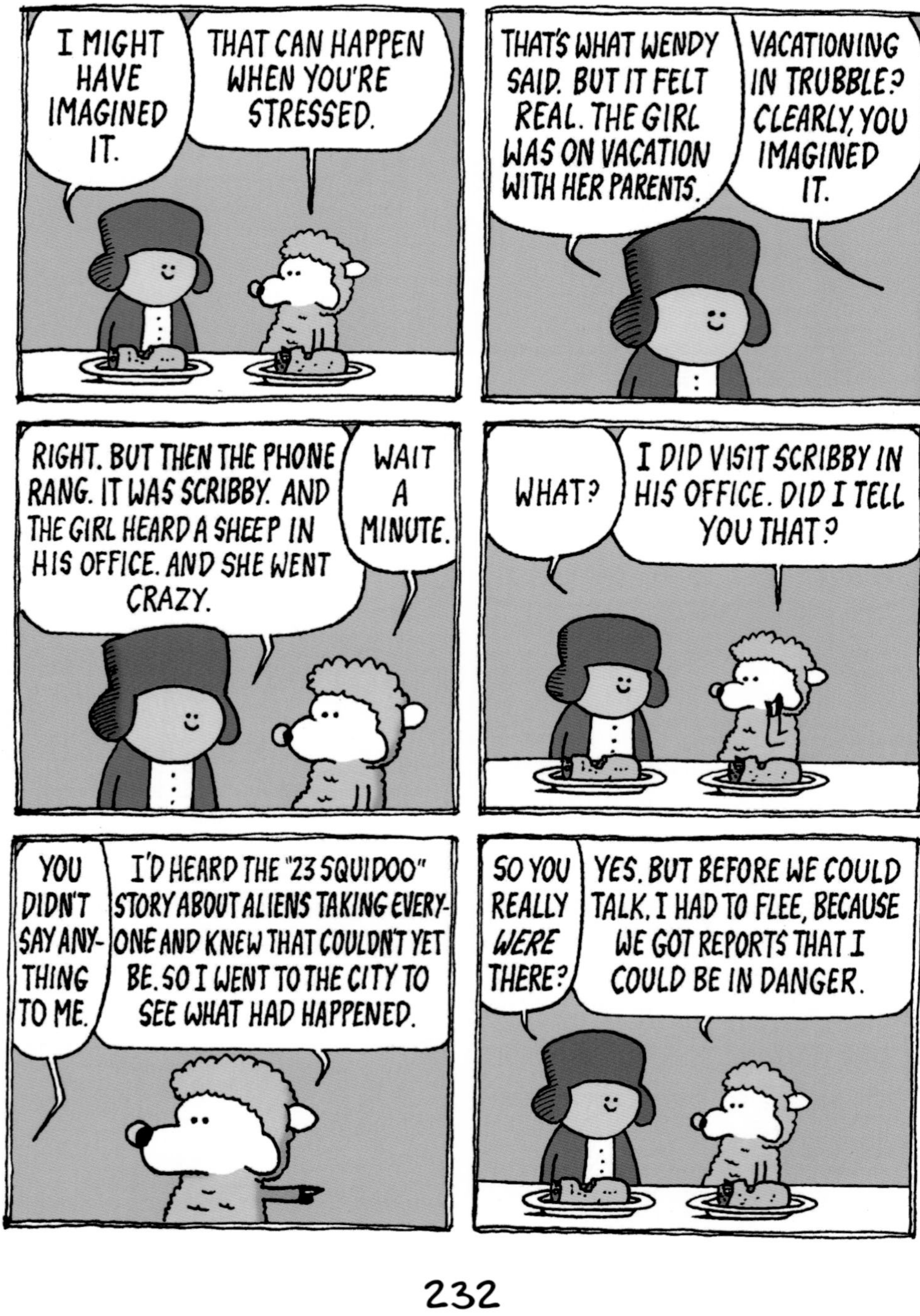
I MIGHT HAVE IMAGINED IT.
THAT CAN HAPPEN WHEN YOU'RE STRESSED.
THAT'S WHAT WENDY SAID. BUT IT FELT REAL. THE GIRL WAS ON VACATION WITH HER PARENTS.
VACATIONING IN TRUBBLE? CLEARLY, YOU IMAGINED IT.
RIGHT. BUT THEN THE PHONE RANG. IT WAS SCRIBBY. AND THE GIRL HEARD A SHEEP IN HIS OFFICE. AND SHE WENT CRAZY.
WAIT A MINUTE.
WHAT?
I DID VISIT SCRIBBY IN HIS OFFICE. DID I TELL YOU THAT?
YOU DIDN'T SAY ANY-THING TO ME.
I'D HEARD THE "23 SQUIDOO" STORY ABOUT ALIENS TAKING EVERY-ONE AND KNEW THAT COULDN'T YET BE. SO I WENT TO THE CITY TO SEE WHAT HAD HAPPENED.
SO YOU REALLY *WERE* THERE?
YES. BUT BEFORE WE COULD TALK, I HAD TO FLEE, BECAUSE WE GOT REPORTS THAT I COULD BE IN DANGER.

FROM WHAT? I'D RATHER NOT SAY. IT WILL ONLY SCARE YOU.

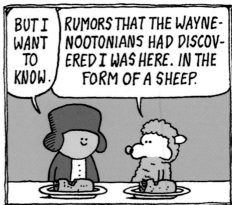

BUT I WANT TO KNOW. RUMORS THAT THE WAYNE-NOOTONIANS HAD DISCOVERED I WAS HERE. IN THE FORM OF A SHEEP.

AND? AND THEY WANTED TO GET ME. BUT THIS REALLY DOESN'T CONCERN YOU, MILO.

"GET" YOU HOW? BY HIRING ANIMALS TO EAT ME. I'M A SHEEP. IT'S NOT HARD.

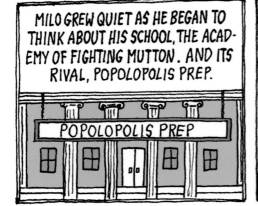

MILO GREW QUIET AS HE BEGAN TO THINK ABOUT HIS SCHOOL, THE ACADEMY OF FIGHTING MUTTON. AND ITS RIVAL, POPOLOPOLIS PREP.

POPOLOPOLIS PREP

WHO, TO SHOW THEIR DOMINANCE OVER THE FIGHTING MUTTON, HAD CHANGED THEIR MASCOT FROM THE "PLATOS" TO THE ANIMALS SHEEP FEARED MOST.

THE PLATOS

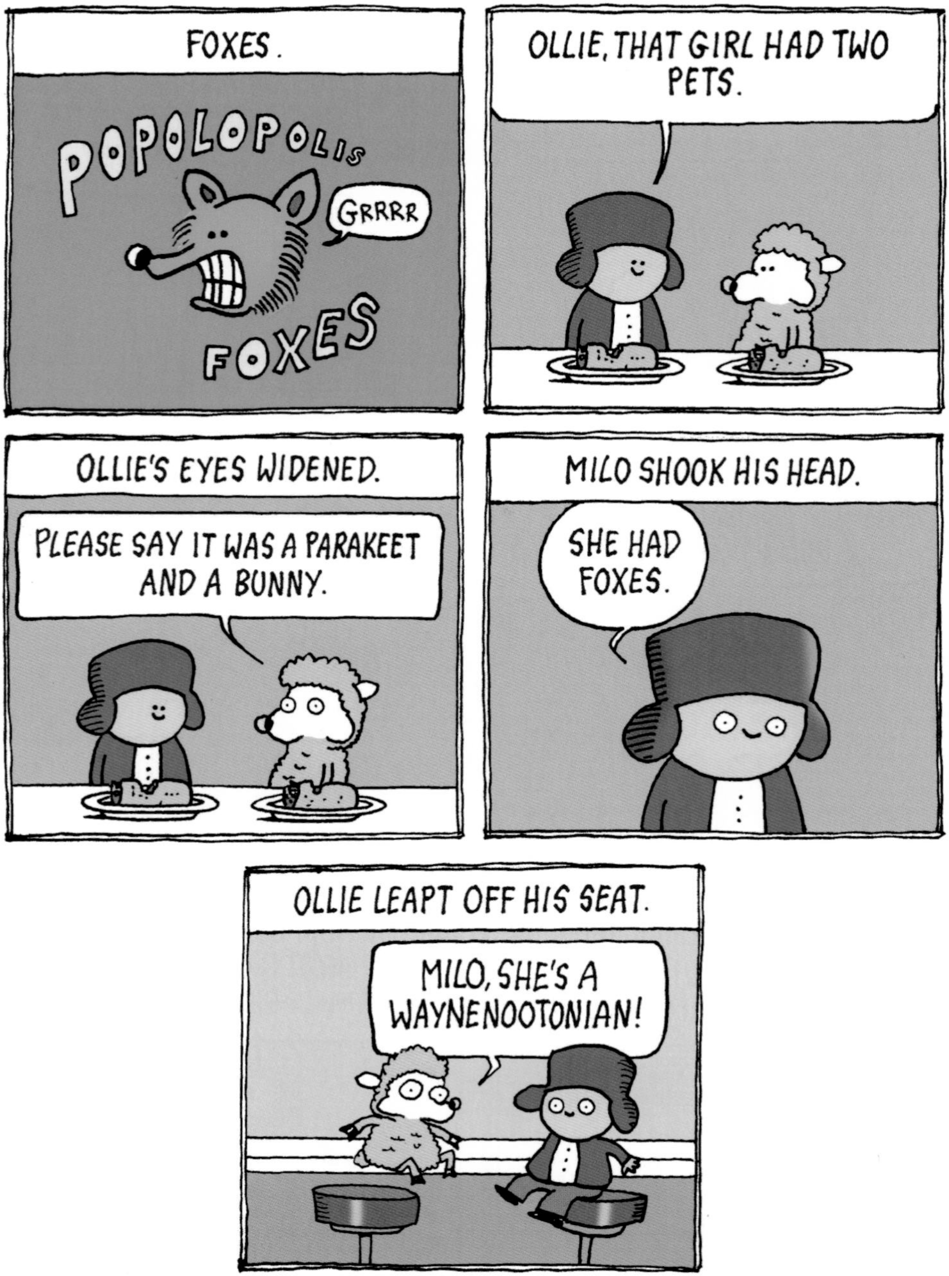
FOXES.
POPOLOPOLIS
GRRRR
FOXES
OLLIE, THAT GIRL HAD TWO PETS.
OLLIE'S EYES WIDENED.
PLEASE SAY IT WAS A PARAKEET AND A BUNNY.
MILO SHOOK HIS HEAD.
SHE HAD FOXES.
OLLIE LEAPT OFF HIS SEAT.
MILO, SHE'S A WAYNENOOTONIAN!

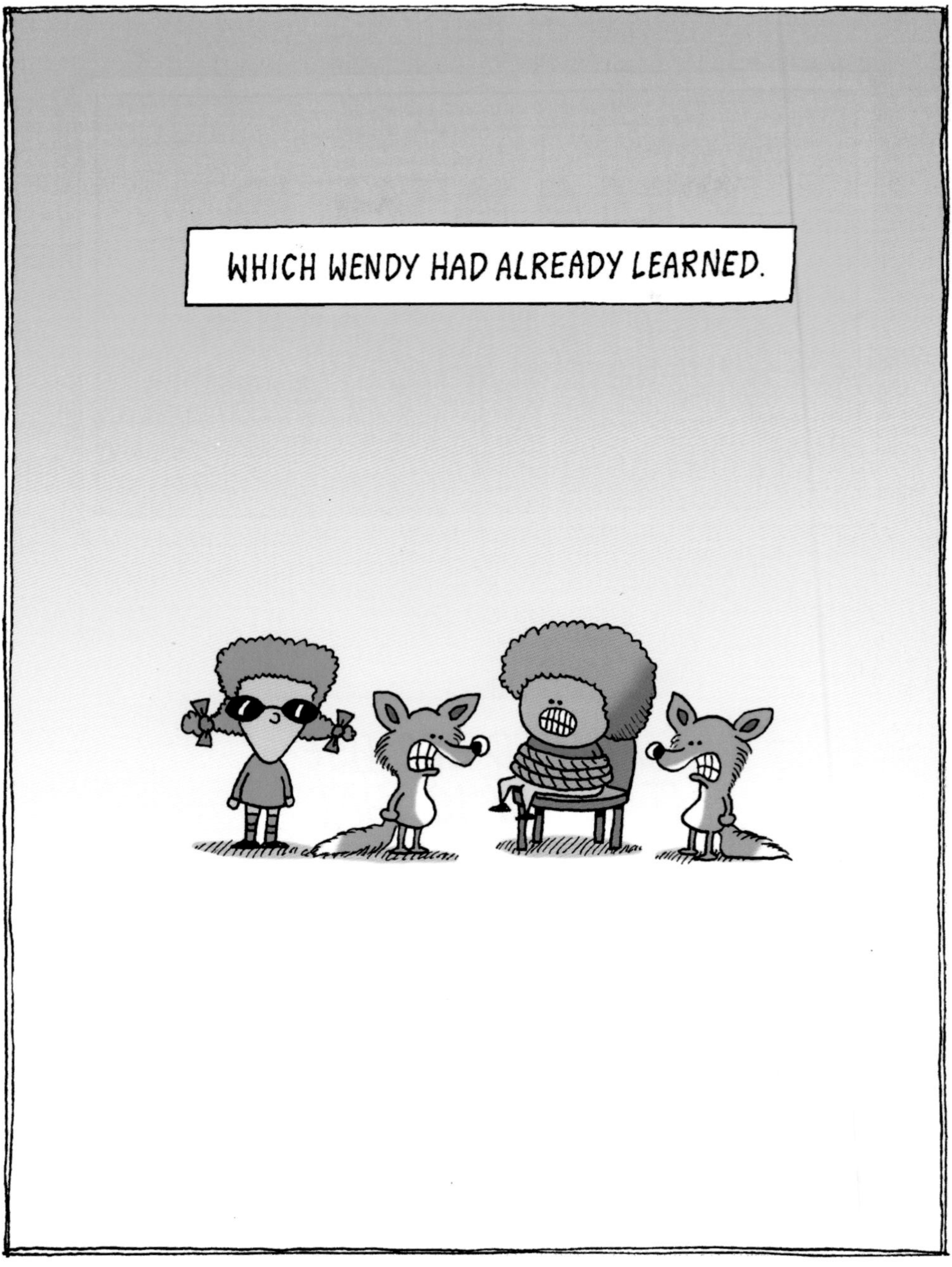
WHICH WENDY HAD ALREADY LEARNED.

CHAPTER STUPENDOUS

WHICH IS...

SO NAMED BECAUSE IT REALLY IS THAT GOOD!

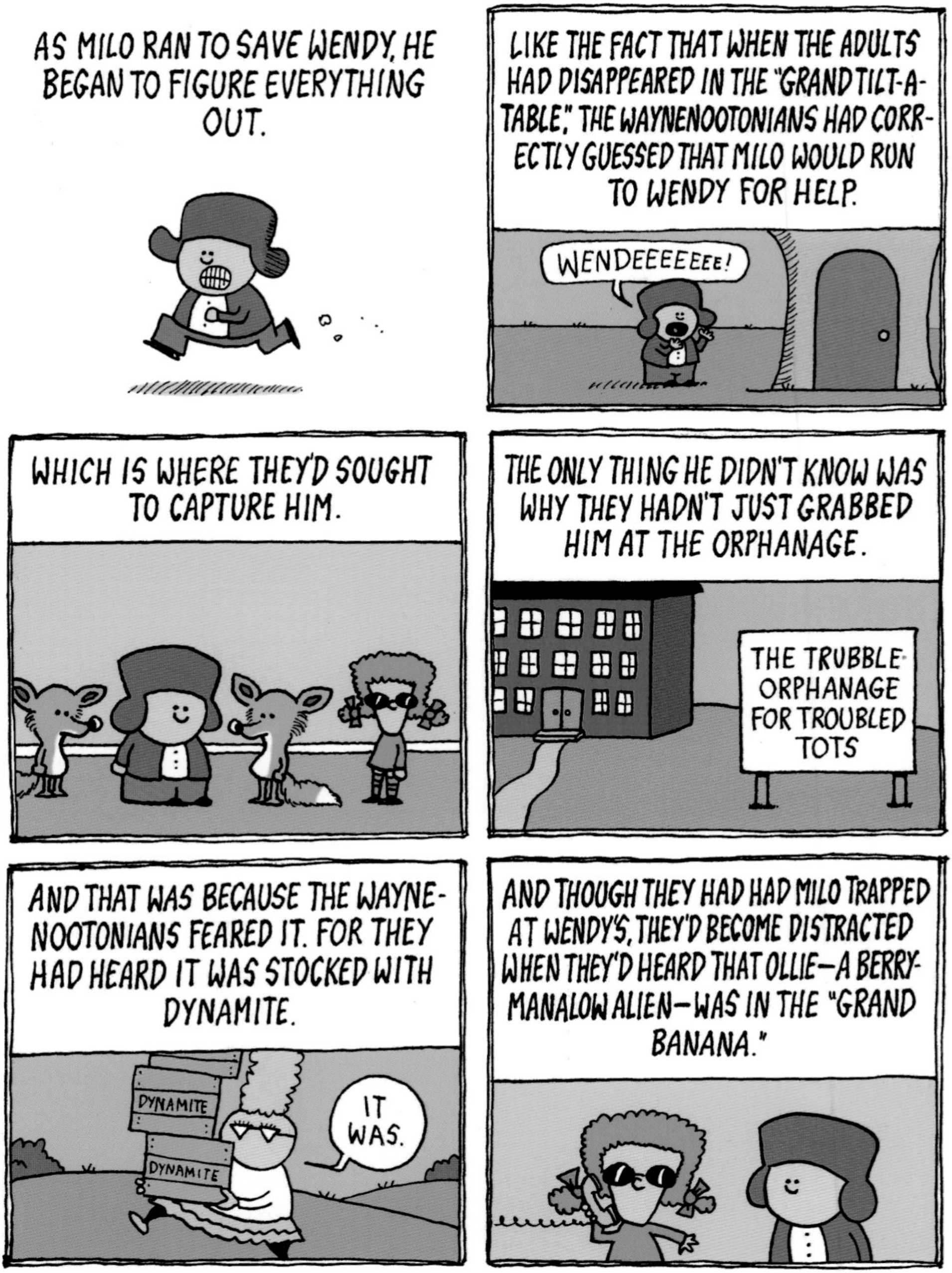
AS MILO RAN TO SAVE WENDY, HE BEGAN TO FIGURE EVERYTHING OUT.
LIKE THE FACT THAT WHEN THE ADULTS HAD DISAPPEARED IN THE "GRAND TILT-A-TABLE," THE WAYNENOOTONIANS HAD CORRECTLY GUESSED THAT MILO WOULD RUN TO WENDY FOR HELP.
WENDEEEEEEEE!
WHICH IS WHERE THEY'D SOUGHT TO CAPTURE HIM.
THE ONLY THING HE DIDN'T KNOW WAS WHY THEY HADN'T JUST GRABBED HIM AT THE ORPHANAGE.
THE TRUBBLE ORPHANAGE FOR TROUBLED TOTS
AND THAT WAS BECAUSE THE WAYNENOOTONIANS FEARED IT. FOR THEY HAD HEARD IT WAS STOCKED WITH DYNAMITE.
DYNAMITE
DYNAMITE
IT WAS.
AND THOUGH THEY HAD HAD MILO TRAPPED AT WENDY'S, THEY'D BECOME DISTRACTED WHEN THEY'D HEARD THAT OLLIE—A BERRYMANALOW ALIEN—WAS IN THE "GRAND BANANA."

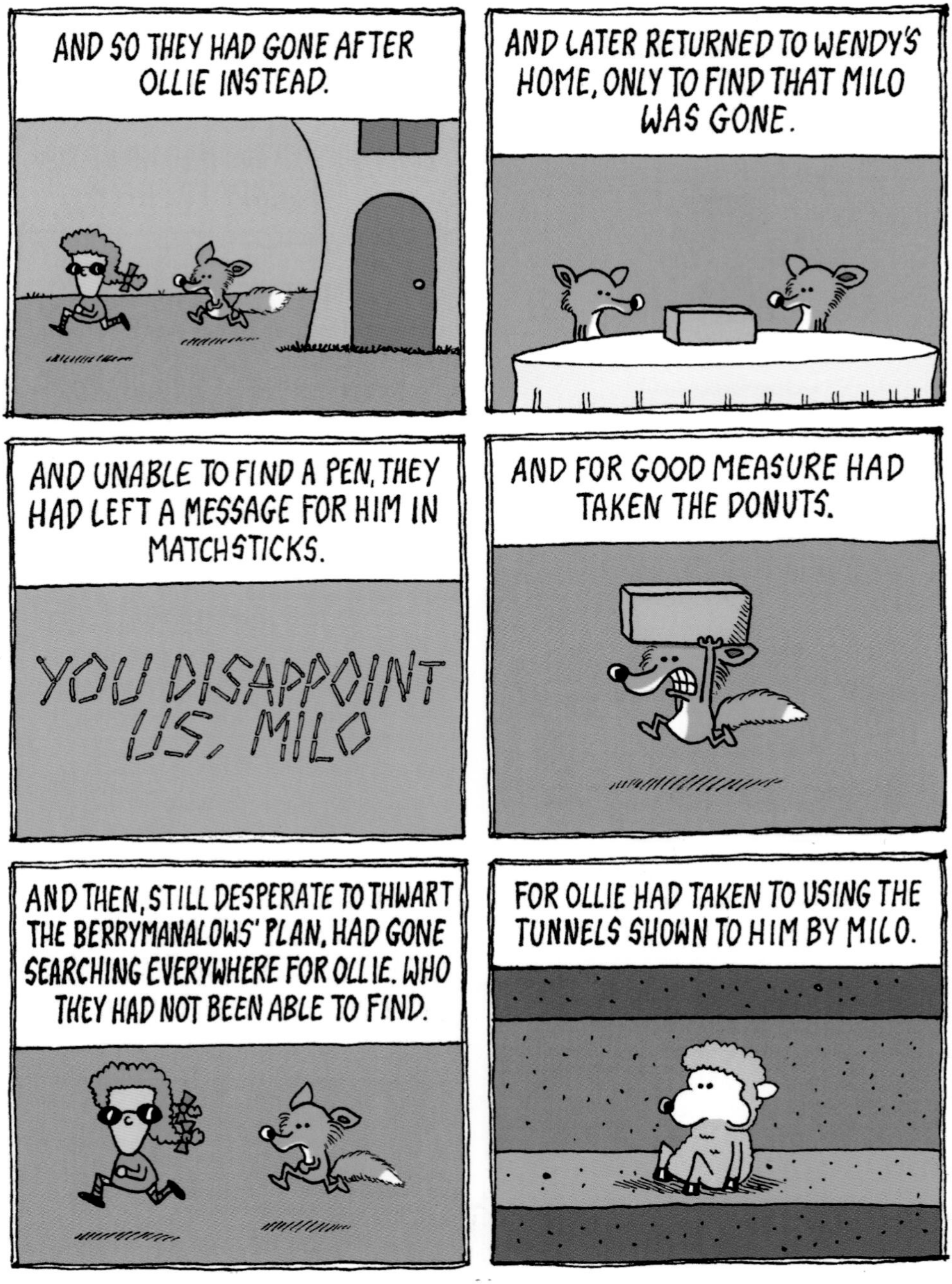
AND SO THEY HAD GONE AFTER OLLIE INSTEAD.
AND LATER RETURNED TO WENDY'S HOME, ONLY TO FIND THAT MILO WAS GONE.
AND UNABLE TO FIND A PEN, THEY HAD LEFT A MESSAGE FOR HIM IN MATCHSTICKS.
YOU DISAPPOINT US, MILO
AND FOR GOOD MEASURE HAD TAKEN THE DONUTS.
AND THEN, STILL DESPERATE TO THWART THE BERRYMANALOWS' PLAN, HAD GONE SEARCHING EVERYWHERE FOR OLLIE. WHO THEY HAD NOT BEEN ABLE TO FIND.
FOR OLLIE HAD TAKEN TO USING THE TUNNELS SHOWN TO HIM BY MILO.

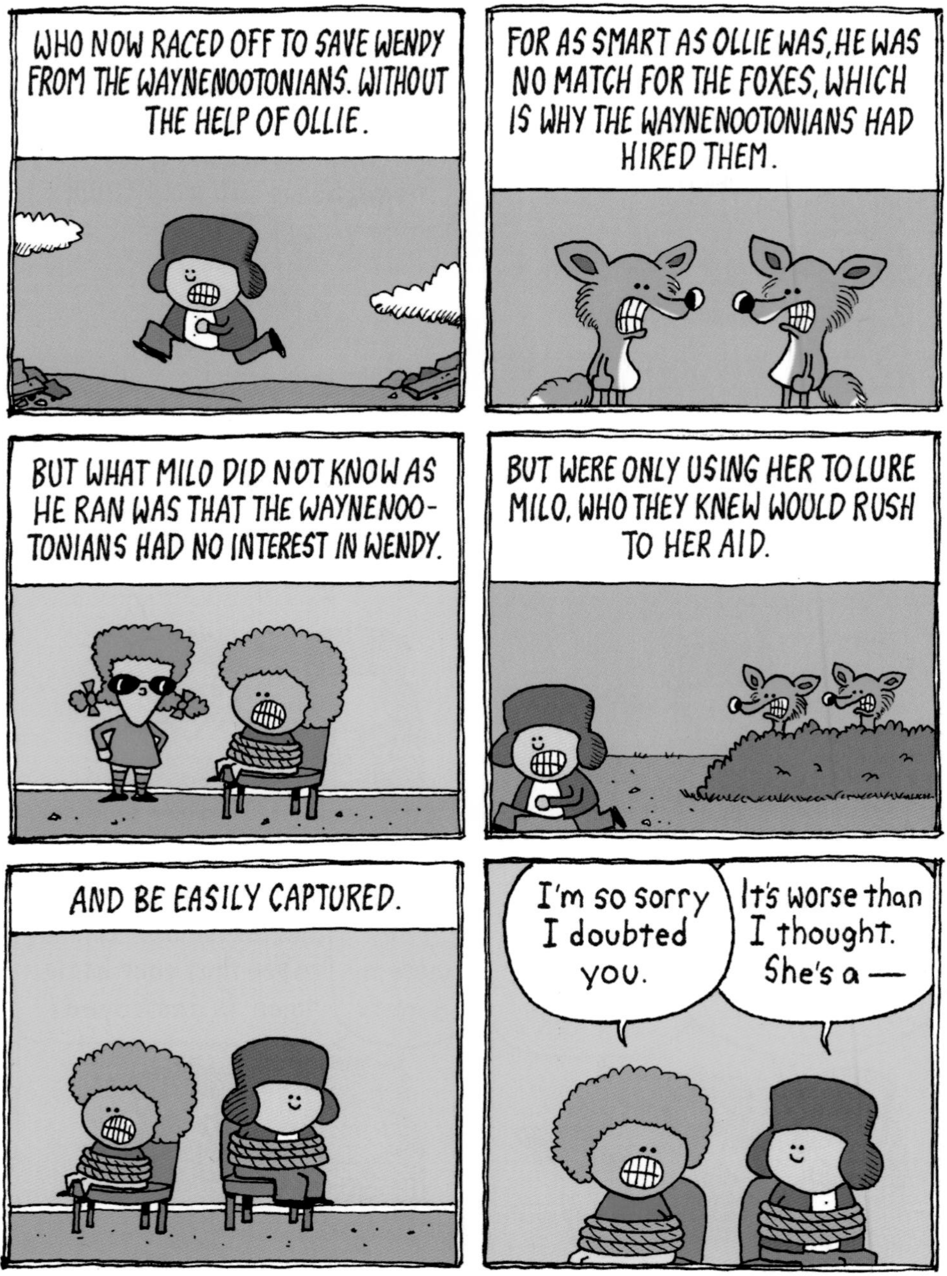

WHO NOW RACED OFF TO SAVE WENDY FROM THE WAYNENOOTONIANS. WITHOUT THE HELP OF OLLIE.
FOR AS SMART AS OLLIE WAS, HE WAS NO MATCH FOR THE FOXES, WHICH IS WHY THE WAYNENOOTONIANS HAD HIRED THEM.
BUT WHAT MILO DID NOT KNOW AS HE RAN WAS THAT THE WAYNENOO-TONIANS HAD NO INTEREST IN WENDY.
BUT WERE ONLY USING HER TO LURE MILO, WHO THEY KNEW WOULD RUSH TO HER AID.
AND BE EASILY CAPTURED.
I'm so sorry I doubted you.
It's worse than I thought. She's a —

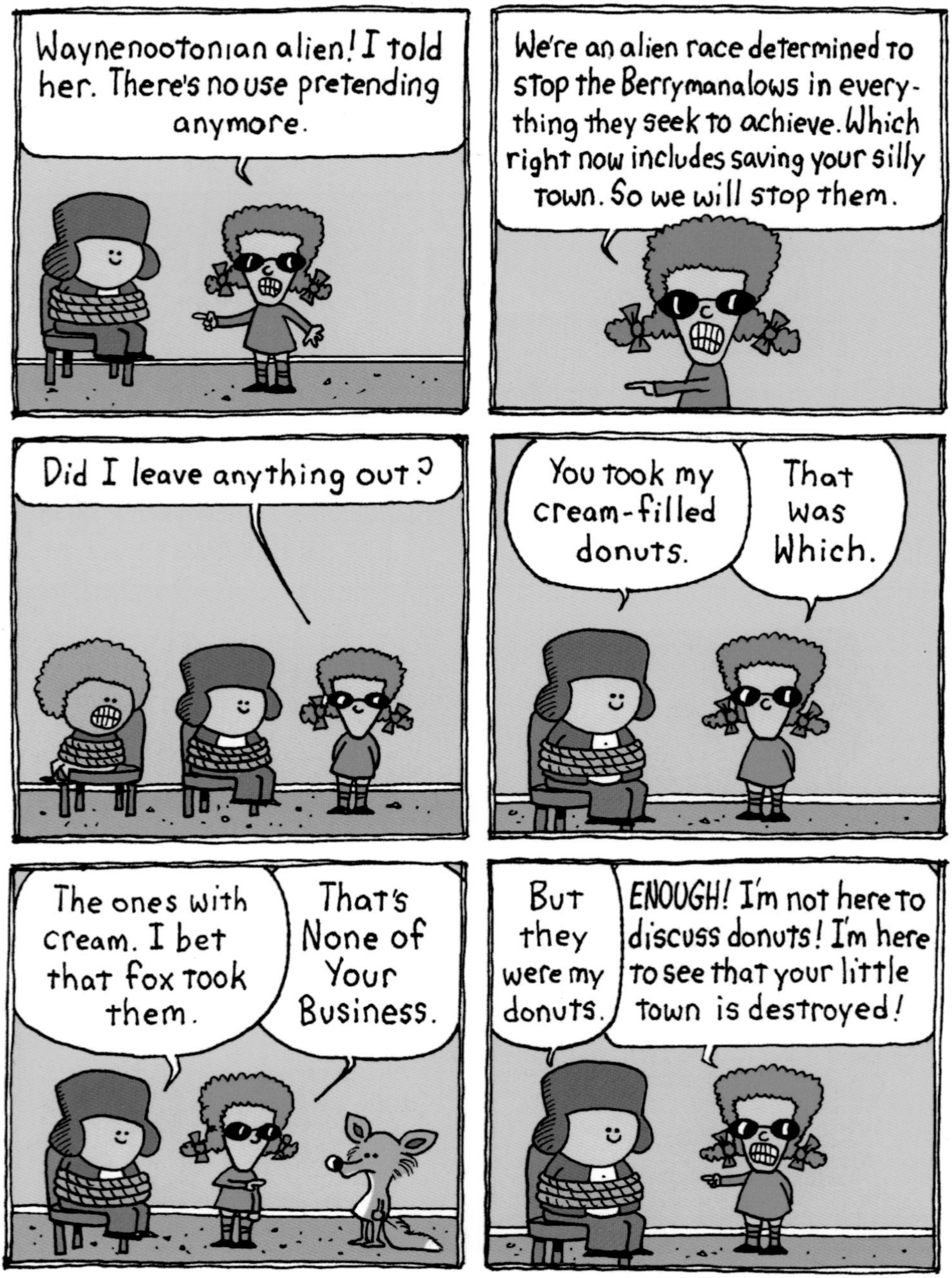
Waynenootonian alien! I told her. There's no use pretending anymore.
We're an alien race determined to stop the Berrymanalows in every-thing they seek to achieve. Which right now includes saving your silly town. So we will stop them.
Did I leave anything out?
You took my cream-filled donuts.
That was Which.
The ones with cream. I bet that fox took them.
That's None of Your Business.
But they were my donuts.
ENOUGH! I'm not here to discuss donuts! I'm here to see that your little town is destroyed!

AND SO WENDY SPOKE UP.

WHAT DIFFERENCE DOES IT MAKE TO YOU? YOU DON'T HAVE TO LIVE HERE. BUT WE DO.

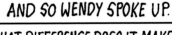

OH, YOU'RE SUCH A BORE. WHATEVER DOES MILO SEE IN YOU?

AND MILO DEFENDED HIS FRIEND.

SHE'S MY BEST FRIEND. AND SHE'S RIGHT. JUST LEAVE US ALONE. WE DON'T MATTER TO YOU.

OF COURSE YOU DON'T MATTER TO ME!

APOLOGIES FOR MY TEMPER. MS. PURPLE HAIR HAS LEFT ME IN A FOUL MOOD.

BUT THE POINT IS THAT YOU'RE CORRECT, MILO. THIS ISN'T ABOUT YOU. IT'S ABOUT THE BERRYMANALOWS. AND THEY *DO* MATTER TO US.

BUT WHY? THEY'RE JUST—

FORMER LOUNGE SINGERS! AND SO ARE WE! BUT THEY WERE GOOD ENOUGH TO GET GIGS! AT NIGHTCLUBS! AND WE NEVER WERE!

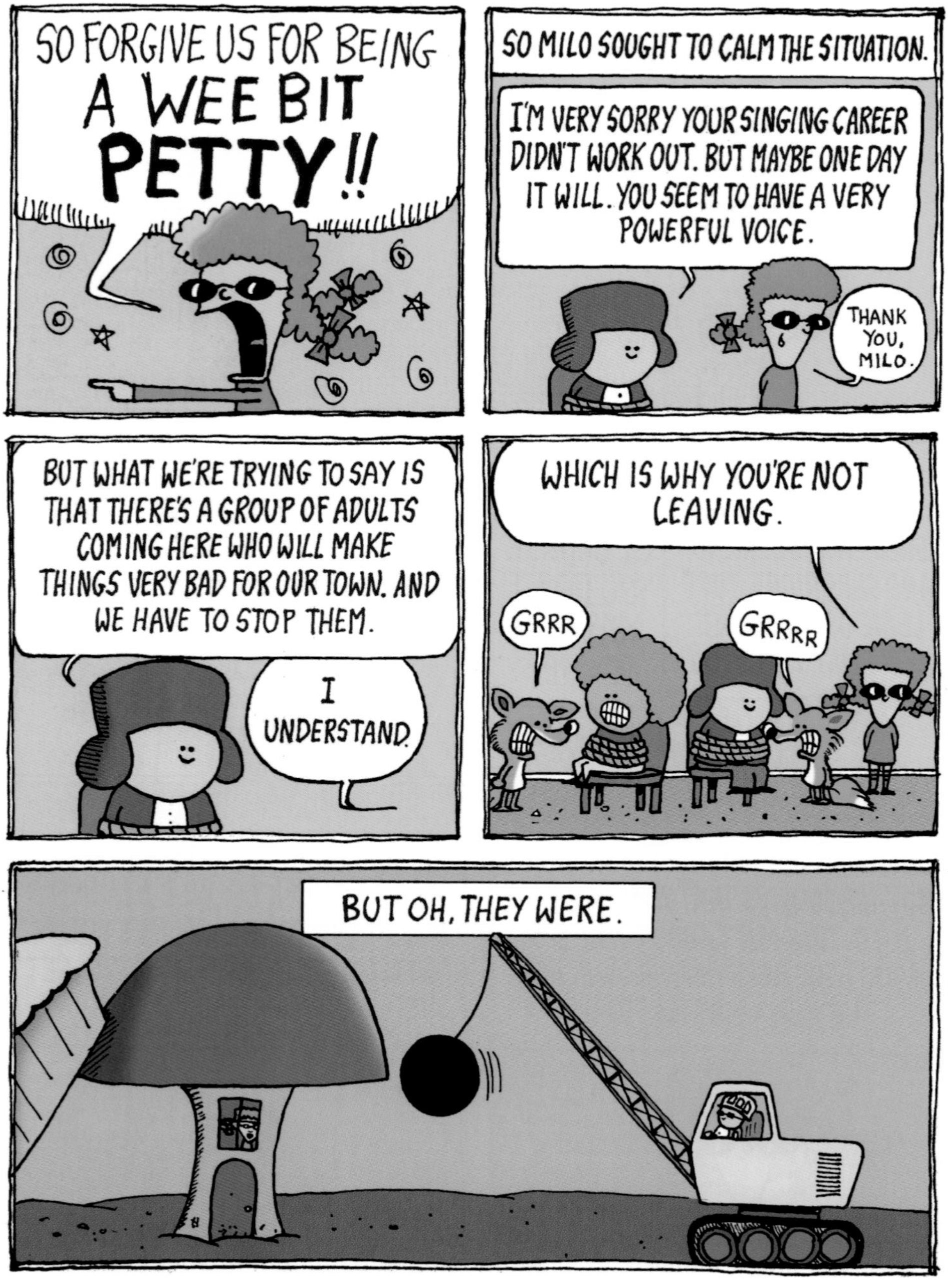
SO FORGIVE US FOR BEING A WEE BIT PETTY!!
SO MILO SOUGHT TO CALM THE SITUATION.
I'M VERY SORRY YOUR SINGING CAREER DIDN'T WORK OUT. BUT MAYBE ONE DAY IT WILL. YOU SEEM TO HAVE A VERY POWERFUL VOICE.
THANK YOU, MILO.
BUT WHAT WE'RE TRYING TO SAY IS THAT THERE'S A GROUP OF ADULTS COMING HERE WHO WILL MAKE THINGS VERY BAD FOR OUR TOWN. AND WE HAVE TO STOP THEM.
I UNDERSTAND.
WHICH IS WHY YOU'RE NOT LEAVING.
GRRR
GRRRR
BUT OH, THEY WERE.

CHAPTER KABLOOEY

IN WHICH...

THINGS GO...

KABLOOEY

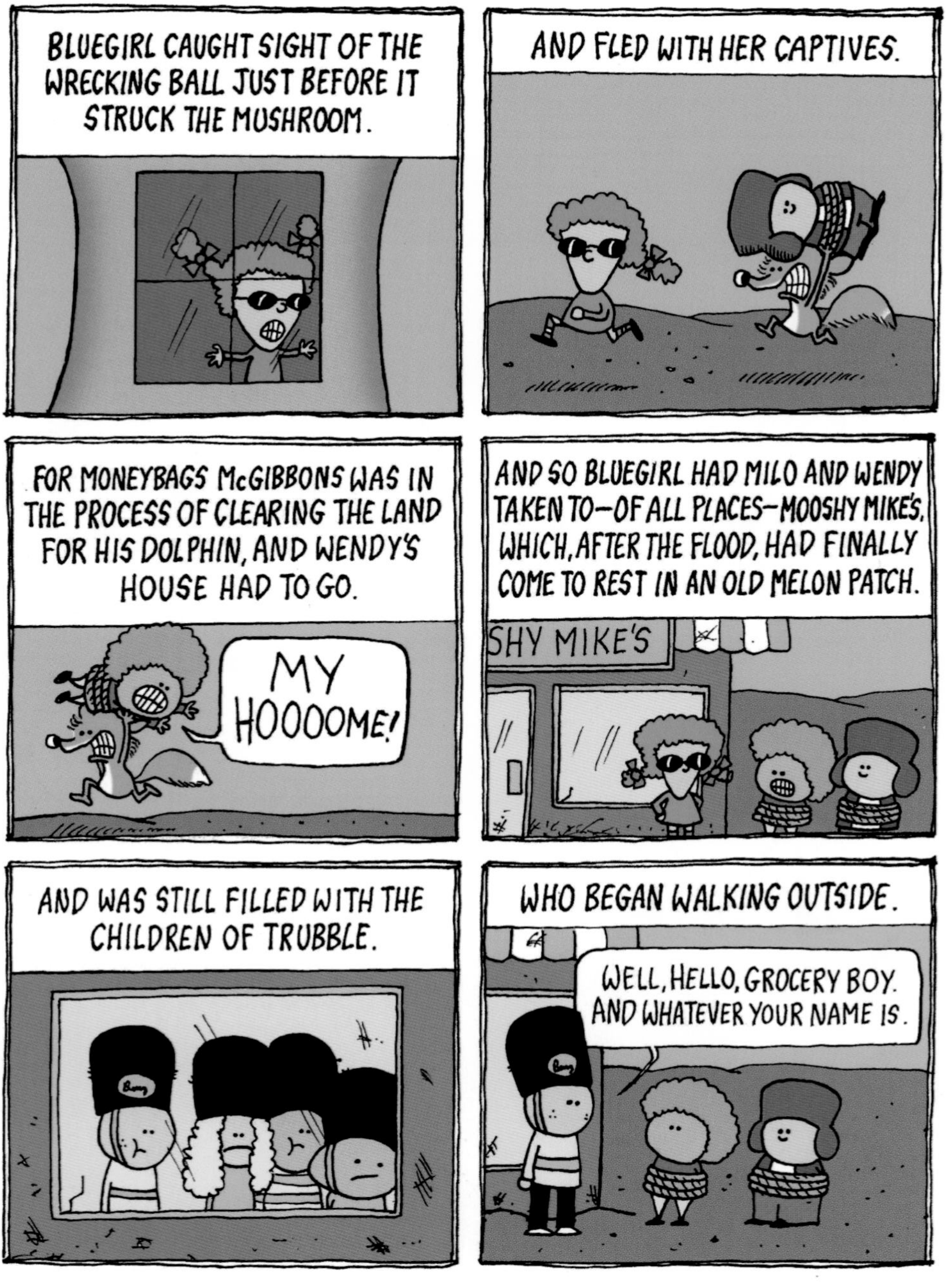
BLUEGIRL CAUGHT SIGHT OF THE WRECKING BALL JUST BEFORE IT STRUCK THE MUSHROOM.
AND FLED WITH HER CAPTIVES.
FOR MONEYBAGS McGIBBONS WAS IN THE PROCESS OF CLEARING THE LAND FOR HIS DOLPHIN, AND WENDY'S HOUSE HAD TO GO.
MY HOOOOME!
AND SO BLUEGIRL HAD MILO AND WENDY TAKEN TO—OF ALL PLACES—MOOSHY MIKE'S, WHICH, AFTER THE FLOOD, HAD FINALLY COME TO REST IN AN OLD MELON PATCH.
SHY MIKE'S
AND WAS STILL FILLED WITH THE CHILDREN OF TRUBBLE.
WHO BEGAN WALKING OUTSIDE.
WELL, HELLO, GROCERY BOY. AND WHATEVER YOUR NAME IS.

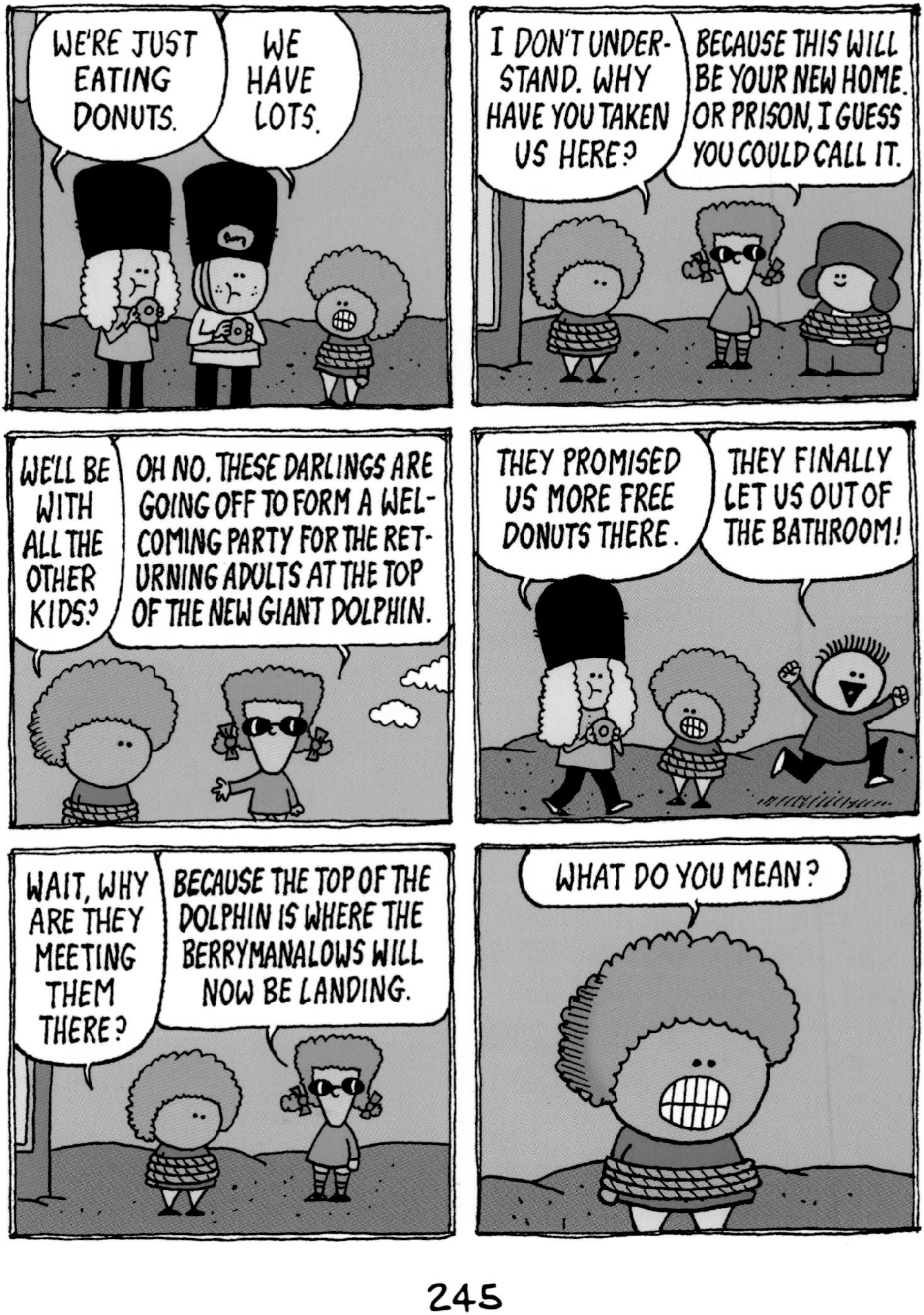
WE'RE JUST EATING DONUTS.
WE HAVE LOTS.
I DON'T UNDER-STAND. WHY HAVE YOU TAKEN US HERE?
BECAUSE THIS WILL BE YOUR NEW HOME. OR PRISON, I GUESS YOU COULD CALL IT.
WE'LL BE WITH ALL THE OTHER KIDS?
OH NO. THESE DARLINGS ARE GOING OFF TO FORM A WEL-COMING PARTY FOR THE RET-URNING ADULTS AT THE TOP OF THE NEW GIANT DOLPHIN.
THEY PROMISED US MORE FREE DONUTS THERE.
THEY FINALLY LET US OUT OF THE BATHROOM!
WAIT, WHY ARE THEY MEETING THEM THERE?
BECAUSE THE TOP OF THE DOLPHIN IS WHERE THE BERRYMANALOWS WILL NOW BE LANDING.
WHAT DO YOU MEAN?

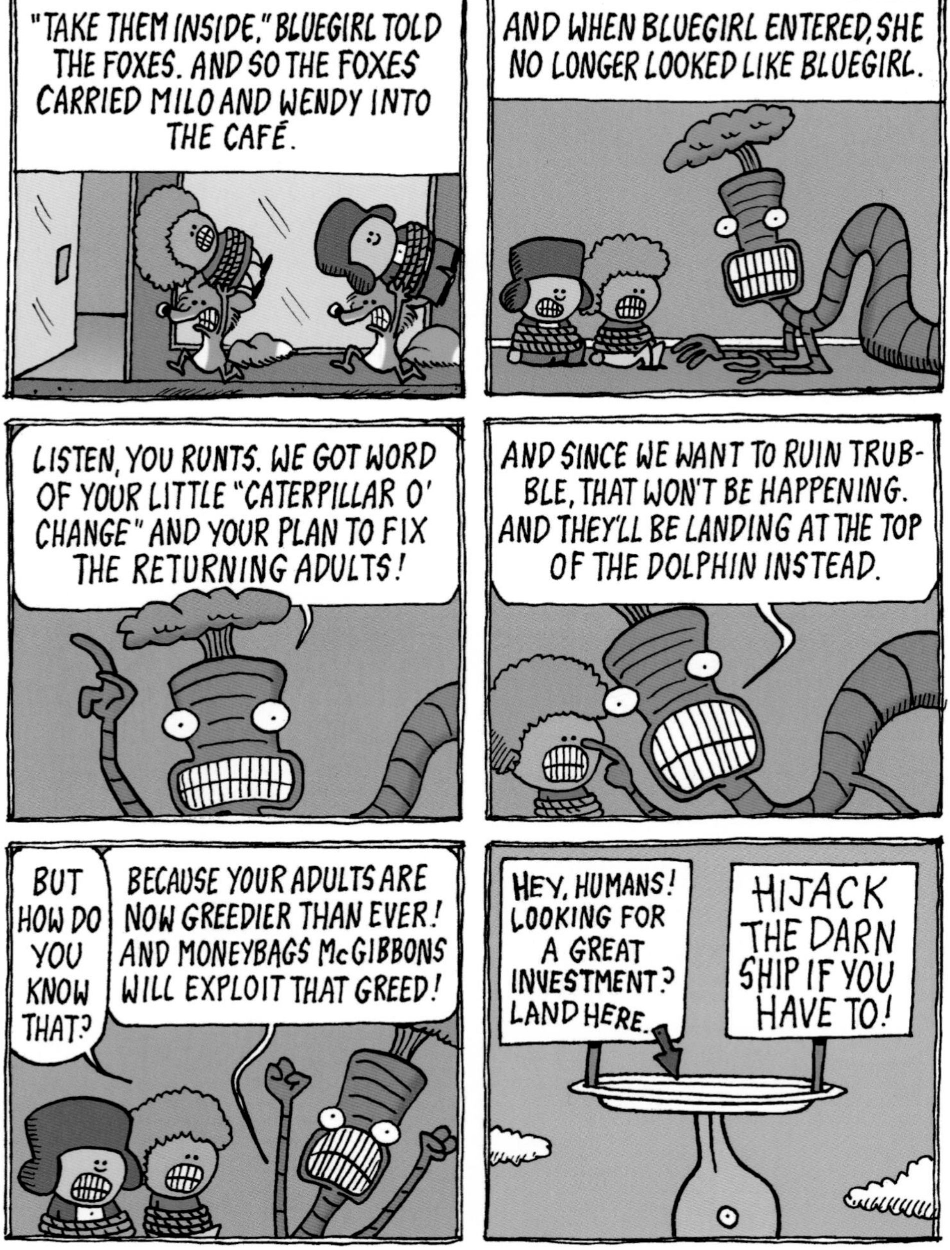
"TAKE THEM INSIDE," BLUEGIRL TOLD THE FOXES. AND SO THE FOXES CARRIED MILO AND WENDY INTO THE CAFÉ.
AND WHEN BLUEGIRL ENTERED, SHE NO LONGER LOOKED LIKE BLUEGIRL.
LISTEN, YOU RUNTS. WE GOT WORD OF YOUR LITTLE "CATERPILLAR O' CHANGE" AND YOUR PLAN TO FIX THE RETURNING ADULTS!
AND SINCE WE WANT TO RUIN TRUBBLE, THAT WON'T BE HAPPENING. AND THEY'LL BE LANDING AT THE TOP OF THE DOLPHIN INSTEAD.
BUT HOW DO YOU KNOW THAT?
BECAUSE YOUR ADULTS ARE NOW GREEDIER THAN EVER! AND MONEYBAGS McGIBBONS WILL EXPLOIT THAT GREED!
HEY, HUMANS! LOOKING FOR A GREAT INVESTMENT? LAND HERE.
HIJACK THE DARN SHIP IF YOU HAVE TO!

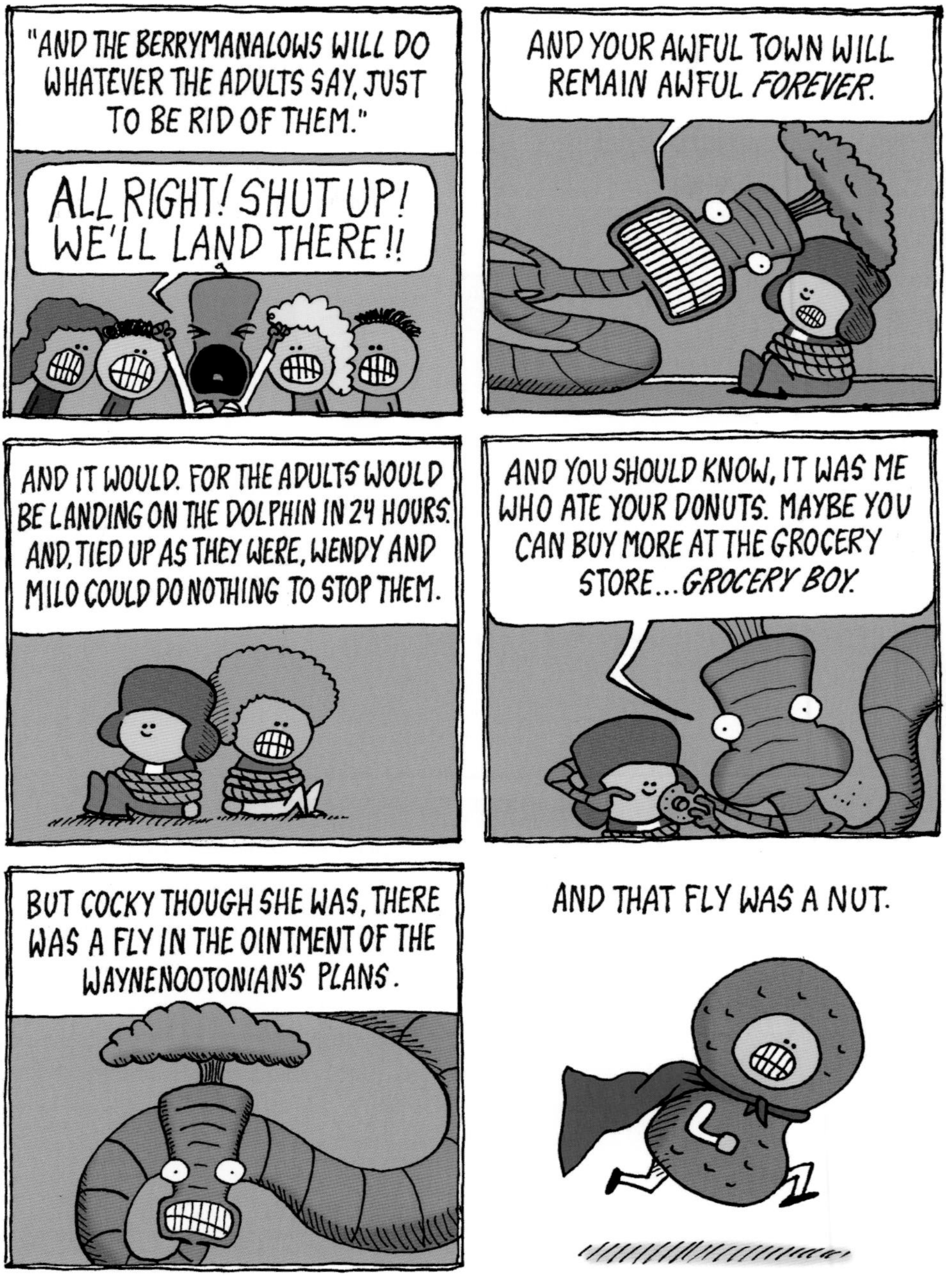
"AND THE BERRYMANALOWS WILL DO WHATEVER THE ADULTS SAY, JUST TO BE RID OF THEM."
ALL RIGHT! SHUT UP! WE'LL LAND THERE!!
AND YOUR AWFUL TOWN WILL REMAIN AWFUL FOREVER.
AND IT WOULD. FOR THE ADULTS WOULD BE LANDING ON THE DOLPHIN IN 24 HOURS. AND, TIED UP AS THEY WERE, WENDY AND MILO COULD DO NOTHING TO STOP THEM.
AND YOU SHOULD KNOW, IT WAS ME WHO ATE YOUR DONUTS. MAYBE YOU CAN BUY MORE AT THE GROCERY STORE... GROCERY BOY.
BUT COCKY THOUGH SHE WAS, THERE WAS A FLY IN THE OINTMENT OF THE WAYNENOOTONIAN'S PLANS.
AND THAT FLY WAS A NUT.

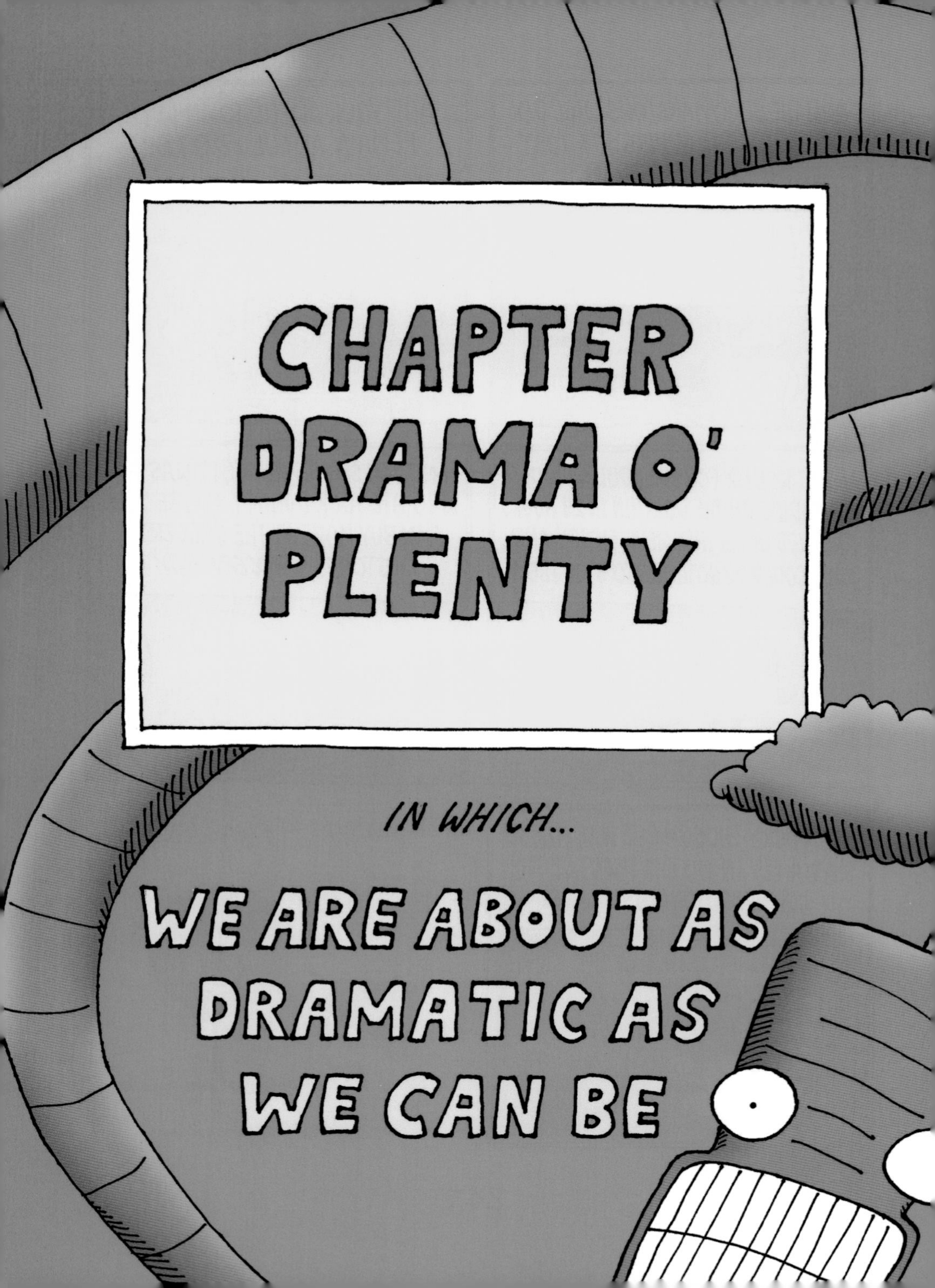
CHAPTER DRAMA O' PLENTY
IN WHICH...
WE ARE ABOUT AS DRAMATIC AS WE CAN BE

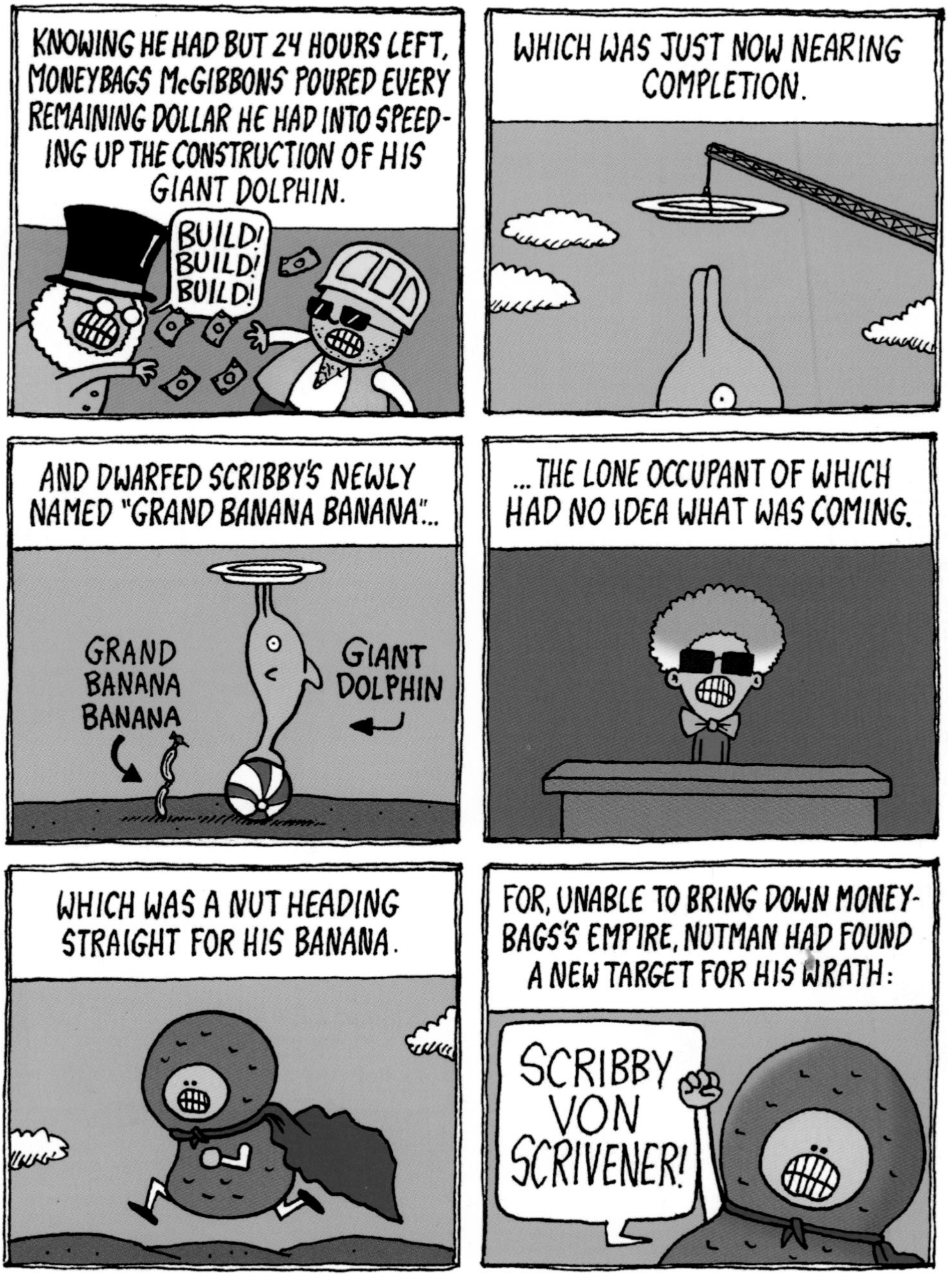
KNOWING HE HAD BUT 24 HOURS LEFT, MONEYBAGS McGIBBONS POURED EVERY REMAINING DOLLAR HE HAD INTO SPEEDING UP THE CONSTRUCTION OF HIS GIANT DOLPHIN.
BUILD! BUILD! BUILD!
WHICH WAS JUST NOW NEARING COMPLETION.
AND DWARFED SCRIBBY'S NEWLY NAMED "GRAND BANANA BANANA"...
GRAND BANANA BANANA
GIANT DOLPHIN
...THE LONE OCCUPANT OF WHICH HAD NO IDEA WHAT WAS COMING.
WHICH WAS A NUT HEADING STRAIGHT FOR HIS BANANA.
FOR, UNABLE TO BRING DOWN MONEYBAGS'S EMPIRE, NUTMAN HAD FOUND A NEW TARGET FOR HIS WRATH:
SCRIBBY VON SCRIVENER!

FOR THE LAID-OFF NUTMAN RESENTED THE FACT THAT SCRIBBY WAS THE LAST PAID EMPLOYEE OF TRUBBLE.

OH, DOES HE NOW?

AND SO HE RACED TOWARD SCRIBBY'S "GRAND BANANA BANANA" TO GET VENGEANCE...

AND UTILIZING A TRAMPOLINE HE KEPT FOR JUST THESE OCCASIONS, SPRUNG HIMSELF OVER THE BARBED WIRE SURROUNDING ITS BASE.

SPROING

AND RAMMED OPEN THE FRONT DOORS OF THE "GRAND BANANA BANANA" WITH HIS HARD PEANUT SHELL.

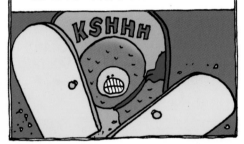

KSHHH

AND BOUNDED UP THE STAIRS TO SCRIBBY'S OFFICE.

WHERE HE CONFRONTED A FRIGHTENED SCRIBBY.

BEHOLD! I AM NUTMAN! FORMERLY SKIPPY VON TUBER OF THE DEPARTMENT OF WORDY THINGS!

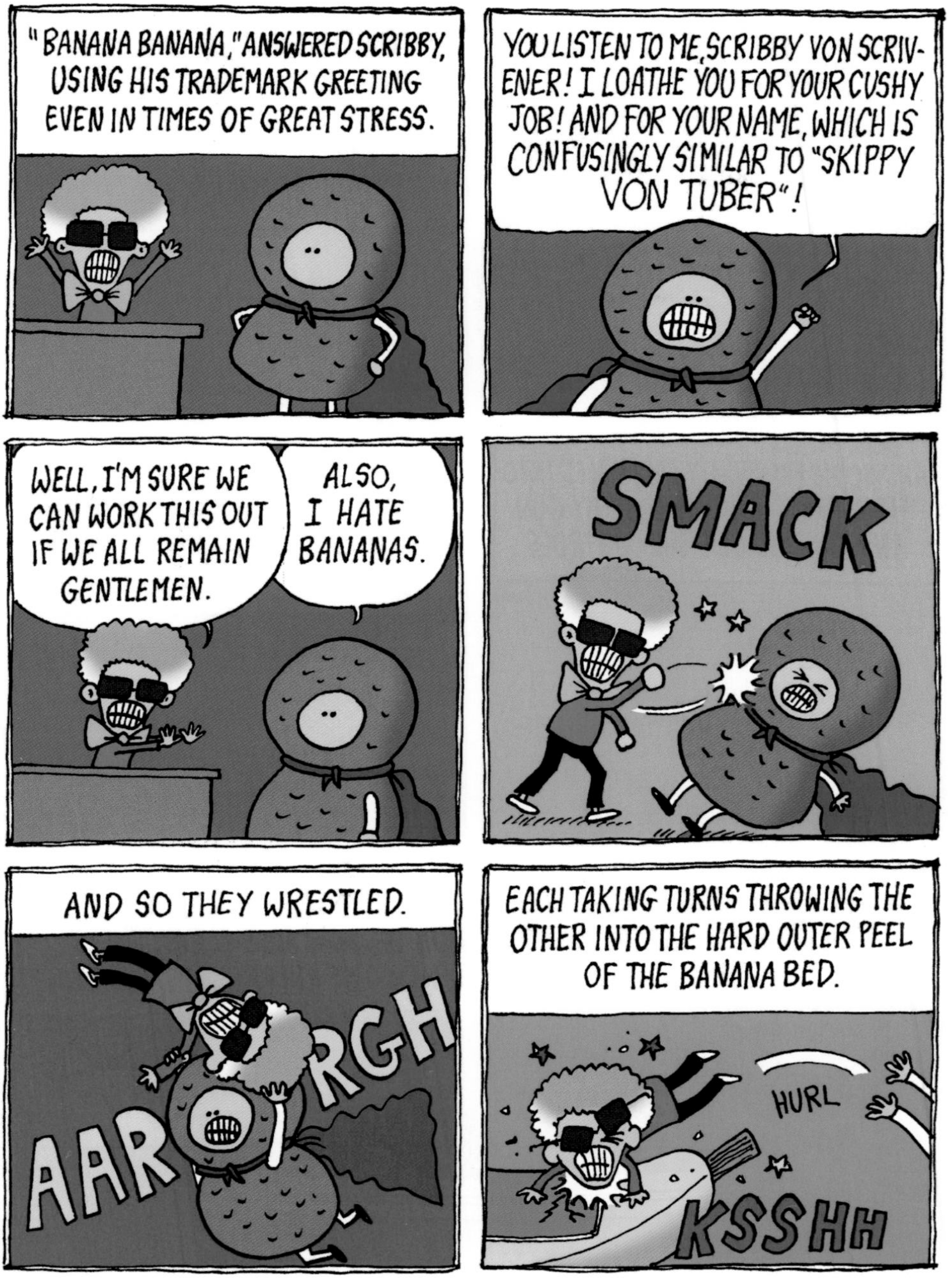
"BANANA BANANA," ANSWERED SCRIBBY, USING HIS TRADEMARK GREETING EVEN IN TIMES OF GREAT STRESS.
YOU LISTEN TO ME, SCRIBBY VON SCRIVENER! I LOATHE YOU FOR YOUR CUSHY JOB! AND FOR YOUR NAME, WHICH IS CONFUSINGLY SIMILAR TO "SKIPPY VON TUBER"!
WELL, I'M SURE WE CAN WORK THIS OUT IF WE ALL REMAIN GENTLEMEN.
ALSO, I HATE BANANAS.
SMACK
AND SO THEY WRESTLED.
AARRGH
EACH TAKING TURNS THROWING THE OTHER INTO THE HARD OUTER PEEL OF THE BANANA BED.
HURL
KSSHH

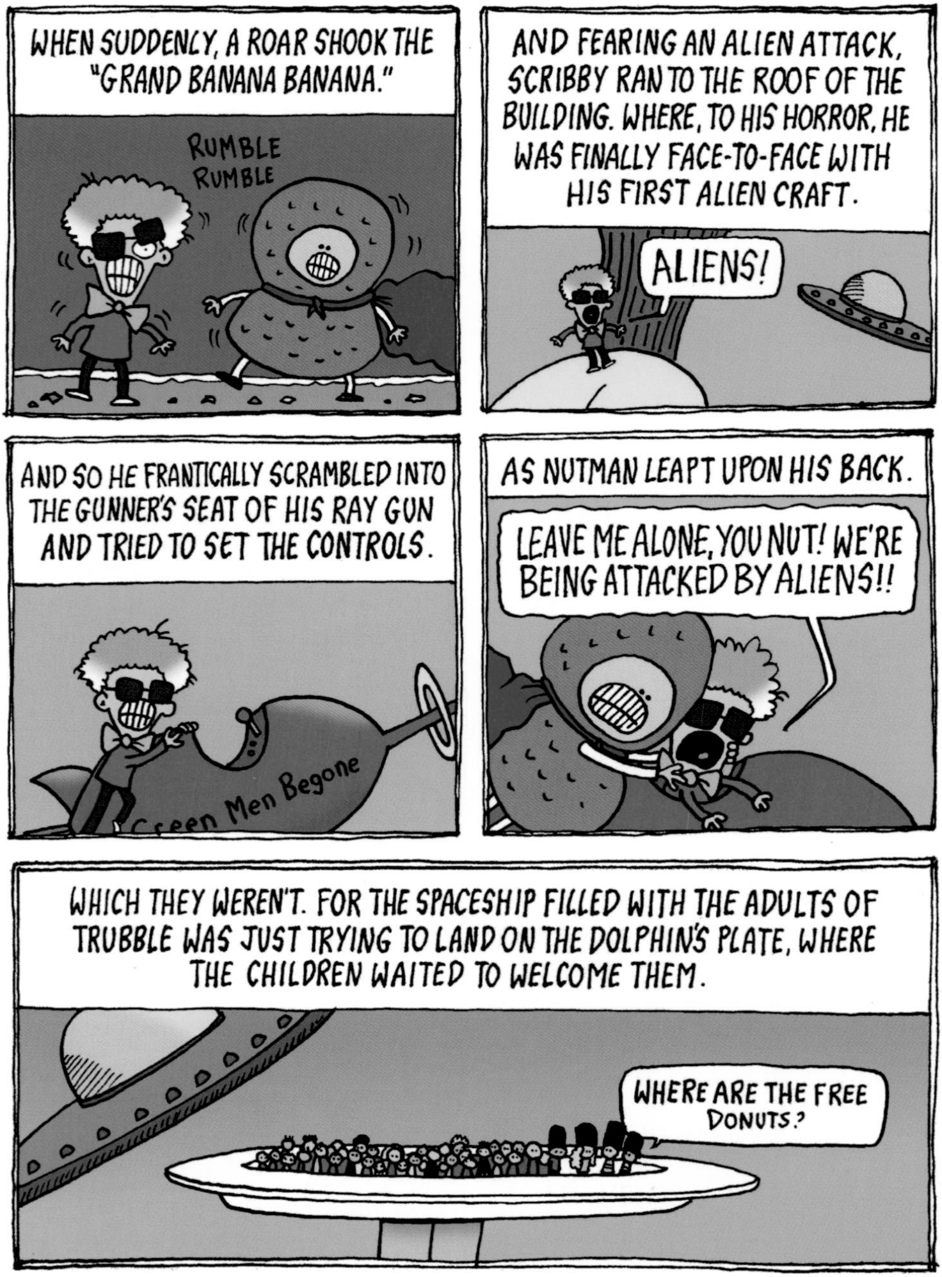
WHEN SUDDENLY, A ROAR SHOOK THE "GRAND BANANA BANANA."
RUMBLE RUMBLE
AND FEARING AN ALIEN ATTACK, SCRIBBY RAN TO THE ROOF OF THE BUILDING. WHERE, TO HIS HORROR, HE WAS FINALLY FACE-TO-FACE WITH HIS FIRST ALIEN CRAFT.
ALIENS!
AND SO HE FRANTICALLY SCRAMBLED INTO THE GUNNER'S SEAT OF HIS RAY GUN AND TRIED TO SET THE CONTROLS.
Green Men Begone
AS NUTMAN LEAPT UPON HIS BACK.
LEAVE ME ALONE, YOU NUT! WE'RE BEING ATTACKED BY ALIENS!!
WHICH THEY WEREN'T. FOR THE SPACESHIP FILLED WITH THE ADULTS OF TRUBBLE WAS JUST TRYING TO LAND ON THE DOLPHIN'S PLATE, WHERE THE CHILDREN WAITED TO WELCOME THEM.
WHERE ARE THE FREE DONUTS?

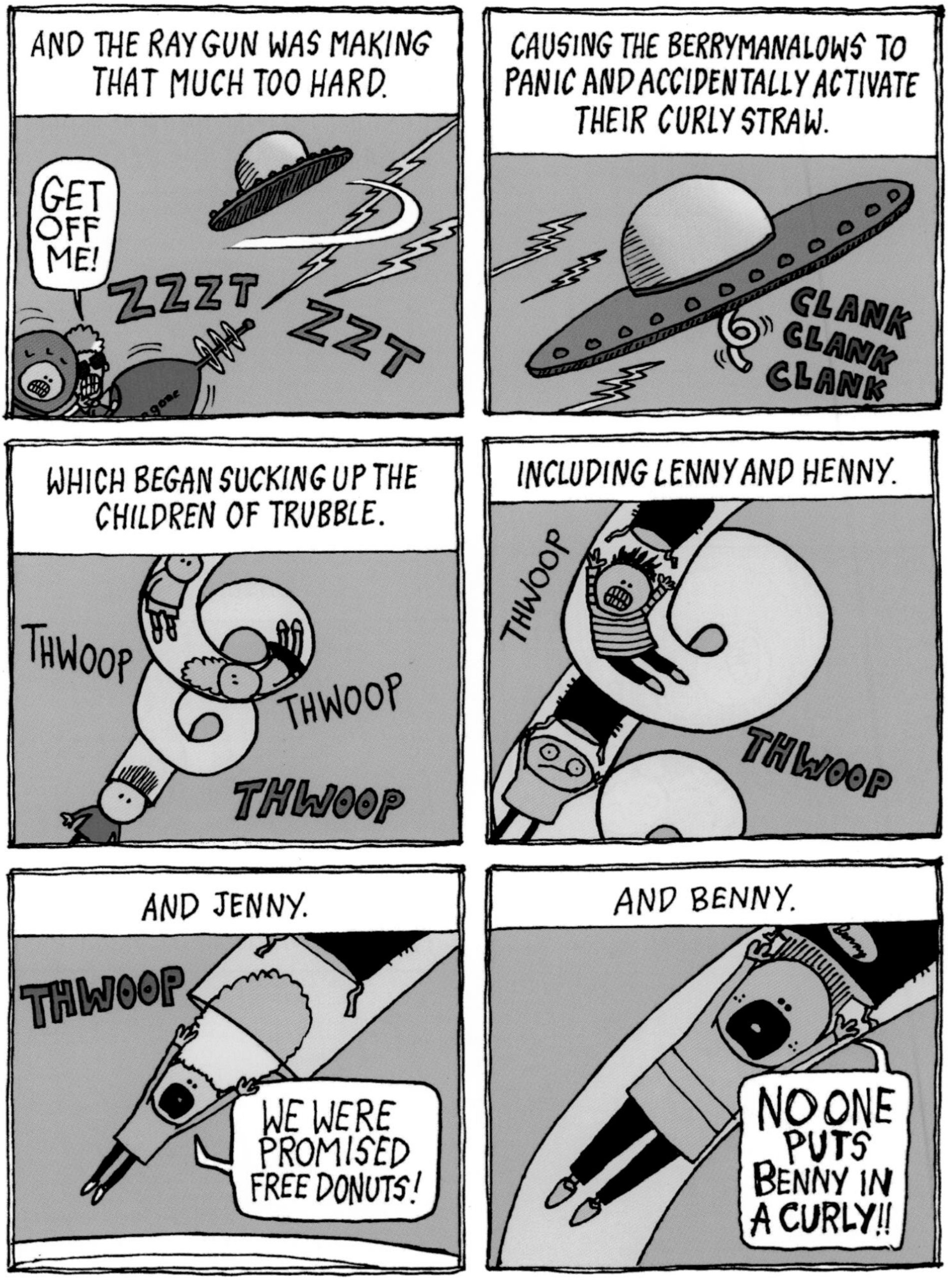
AND THE RAY GUN WAS MAKING THAT MUCH TOO HARD.
GET OFF ME!
ZZZT
ZZZT
CAUSING THE BERRYMANALOWS TO PANIC AND ACCIDENTALLY ACTIVATE THEIR CURLY STRAW.
CLANK
CLANK
CLANK
WHICH BEGAN SUCKING UP THE CHILDREN OF TRUBBLE.
THWOOP
THWOOP
THWOOP
INCLUDING LENNY AND HENNY.
THWOOP
THWOOP
AND JENNY.
THWOOP
WE WERE PROMISED FREE DONUTS!
AND BENNY.
NO ONE PUTS BENNY IN A CURLY!!

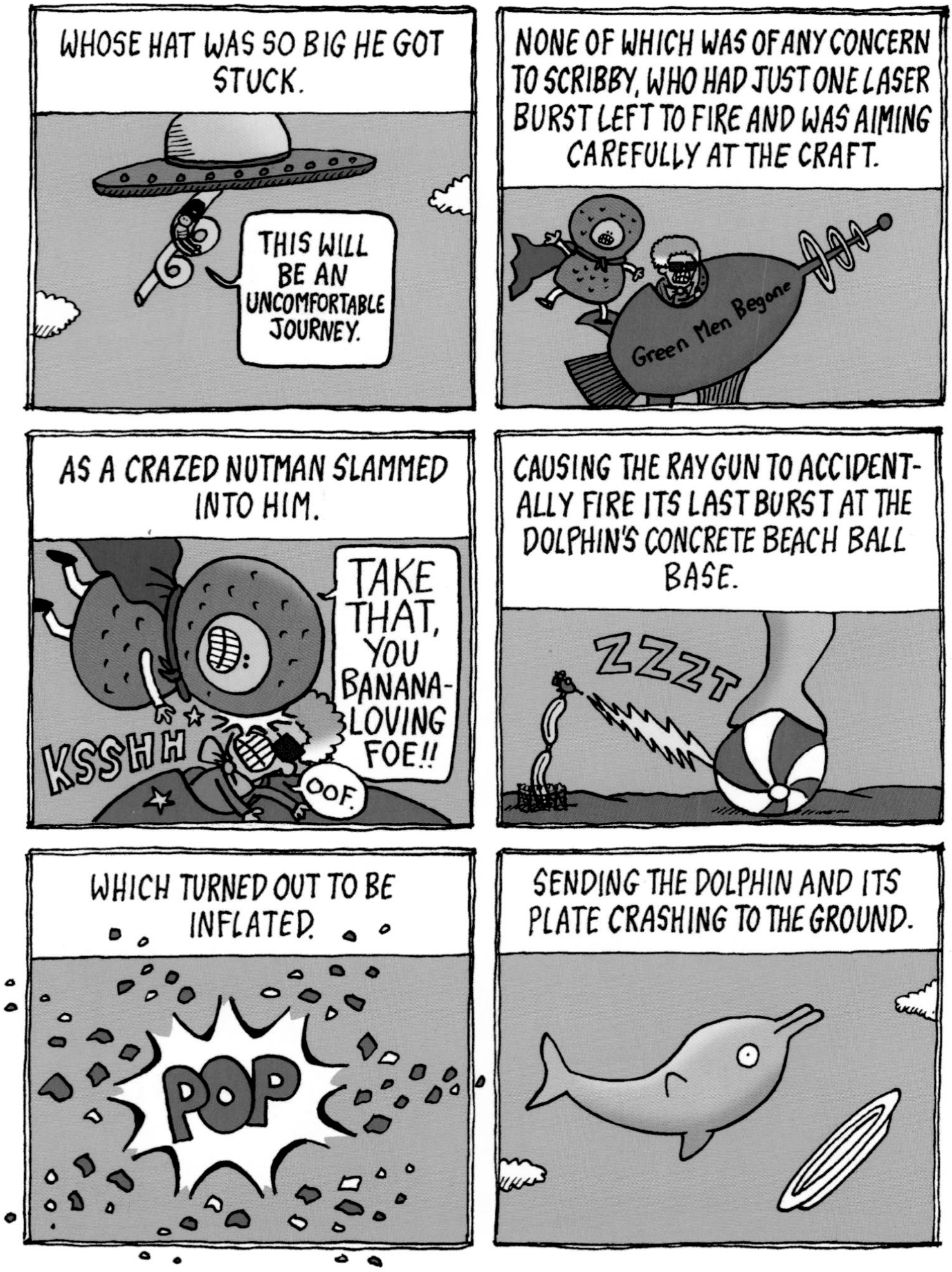
WHOSE HAT WAS SO BIG HE GOT STUCK.
THIS WILL BE AN UNCOMFORTABLE JOURNEY.
NONE OF WHICH WAS OF ANY CONCERN TO SCRIBBY, WHO HAD JUST ONE LASER BURST LEFT TO FIRE AND WAS AIMING CAREFULLY AT THE CRAFT.
Green Men Begone
AS A CRAZED NUTMAN SLAMMED INTO HIM.
TAKE THAT, YOU BANANA-LOVING FOE!!
KSSHH
OOF.
CAUSING THE RAY GUN TO ACCIDENTALLY FIRE ITS LAST BURST AT THE DOLPHIN'S CONCRETE BEACH BALL BASE.
ZZZT
WHICH TURNED OUT TO BE INFLATED.
POP
SENDING THE DOLPHIN AND ITS PLATE CRASHING TO THE GROUND.

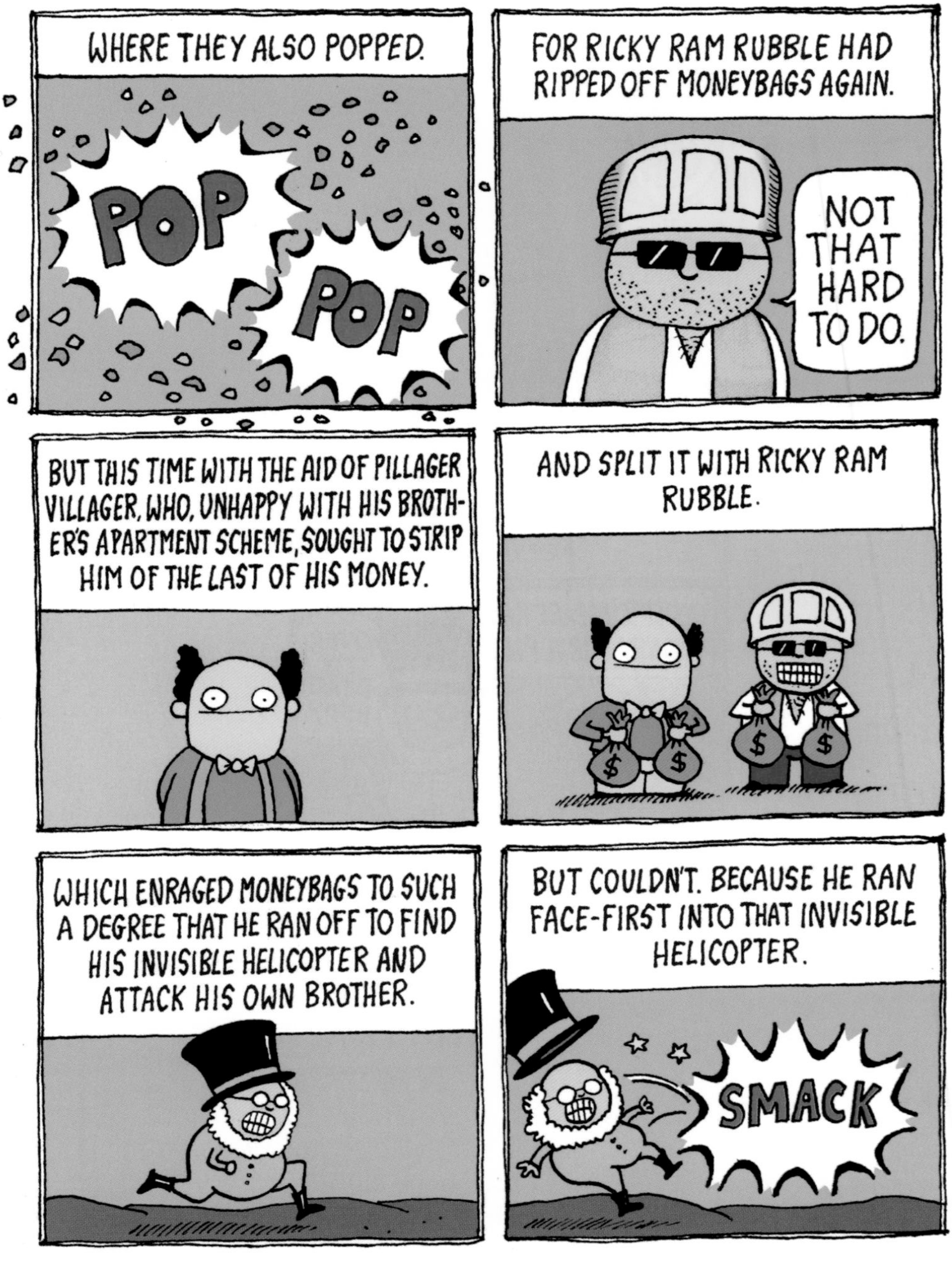
WHERE THEY ALSO POPPED.
POP
POP
FOR RICKY RAM RUBBLE HAD RIPPED OFF MONEYBAGS AGAIN.
NOT THAT HARD TO DO.
BUT THIS TIME WITH THE AID OF PILLAGER VILLAGER, WHO, UNHAPPY WITH HIS BROTHER'S APARTMENT SCHEME, SOUGHT TO STRIP HIM OF THE LAST OF HIS MONEY.
AND SPLIT IT WITH RICKY RAM RUBBLE.
WHICH ENRAGED MONEYBAGS TO SUCH A DEGREE THAT HE RAN OFF TO FIND HIS INVISIBLE HELICOPTER AND ATTACK HIS OWN BROTHER.
BUT COULDN'T. BECAUSE HE RAN FACE-FIRST INTO THAT INVISIBLE HELICOPTER.
SMACK

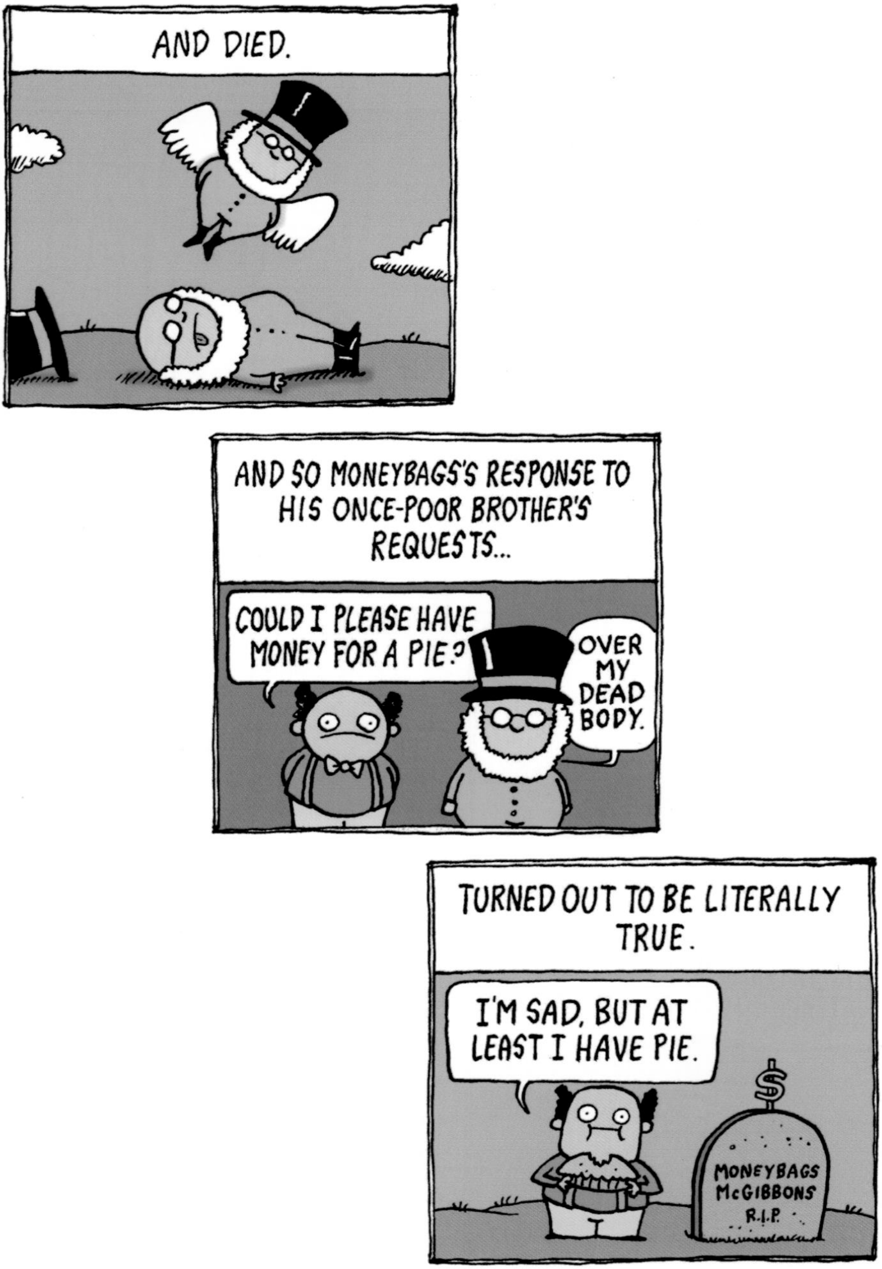
AND DIED.
AND SO MONEYBAGS'S RESPONSE TO HIS ONCE-POOR BROTHER'S REQUESTS...
COULD I PLEASE HAVE MONEY FOR A PIE?
OVER MY DEAD BODY.
TURNED OUT TO BE LITERALLY TRUE.
I'M SAD, BUT AT LEAST I HAVE PIE.
MONEYBAGS McGIBBONS R.I.P.

CHAPTER THIS JUST GETS BETTER AND BETTER

IN WHICH...

WE THROW ALL PRETENSE OF HUMILITY OUT THE WINDOW BECAUSE THIS CHAPTER REALLY IS THAT GOOD

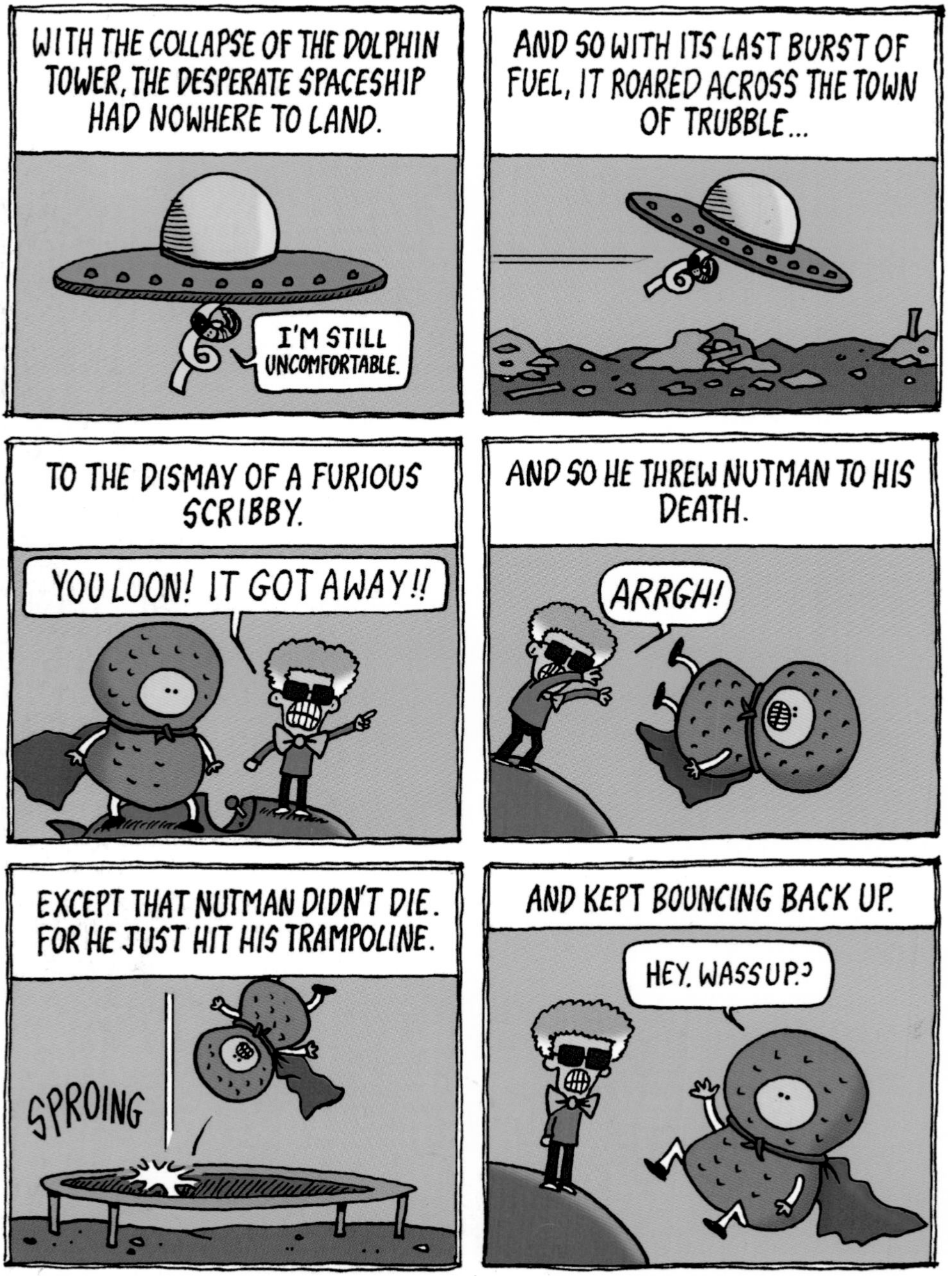

WITH THE COLLAPSE OF THE DOLPHIN TOWER, THE DESPERATE SPACESHIP HAD NOWHERE TO LAND.
I'M STILL UNCOMFORTABLE.
AND SO WITH ITS LAST BURST OF FUEL, IT ROARED ACROSS THE TOWN OF TRUBBLE...
TO THE DISMAY OF A FURIOUS SCRIBBY.
YOU LOON! IT GOT AWAY!!
AND SO HE THREW NUTMAN TO HIS DEATH.
ARRGH!
EXCEPT THAT NUTMAN DIDN'T DIE. FOR HE JUST HIT HIS TRAMPOLINE.
SPROING
AND KEPT BOUNCING BACK UP.
HEY. WASSUP?

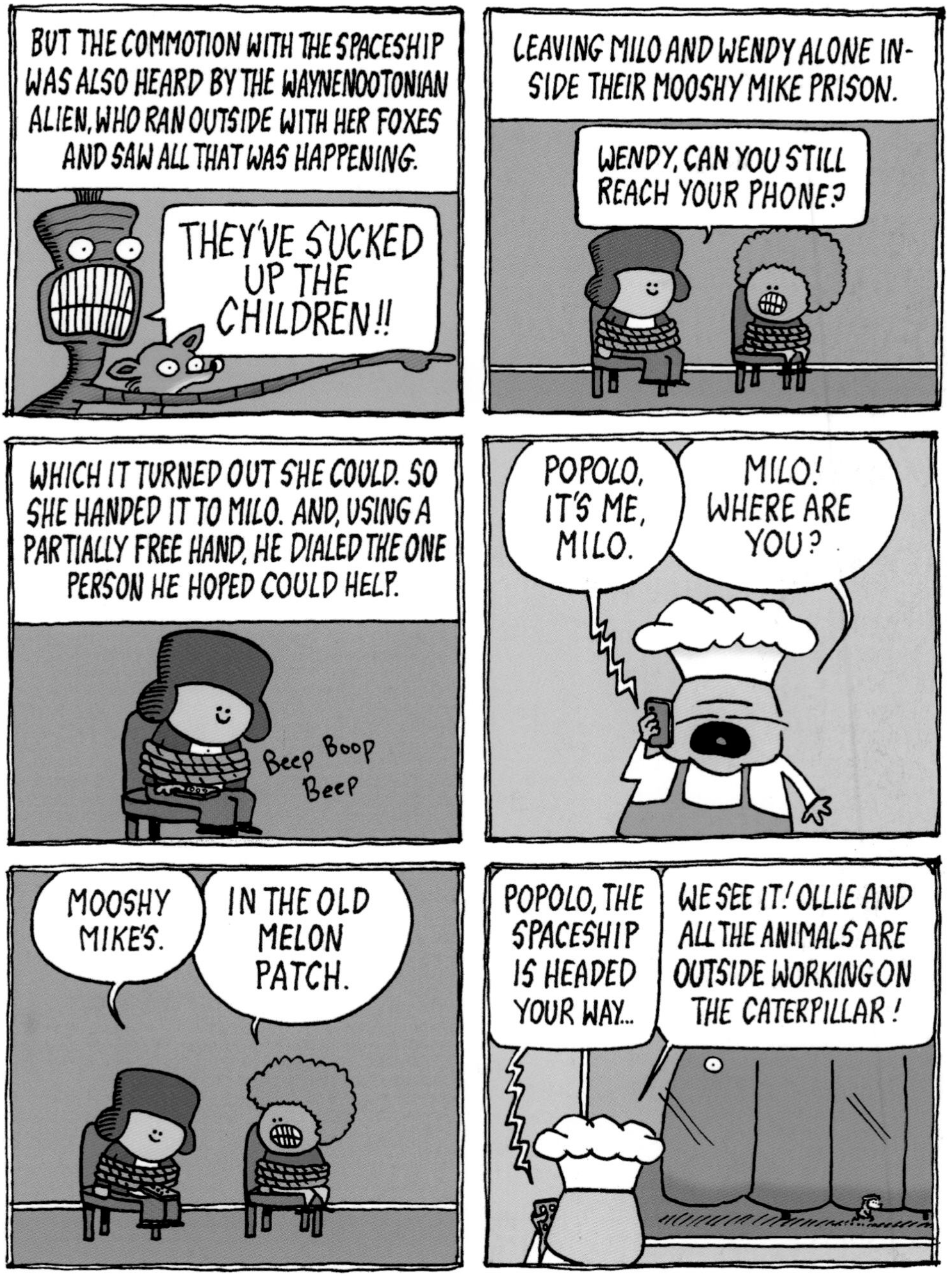
BUT THE COMMOTION WITH THE SPACESHIP WAS ALSO HEARD BY THE WAYNENOOTONIAN ALIEN, WHO RAN OUTSIDE WITH HER FOXES AND SAW ALL THAT WAS HAPPENING.
THEY'VE SUCKED UP THE CHILDREN!!
LEAVING MILO AND WENDY ALONE INSIDE THEIR MOOSHY MIKE PRISON.
WENDY, CAN YOU STILL REACH YOUR PHONE?
WHICH IT TURNED OUT SHE COULD. SO SHE HANDED IT TO MILO. AND, USING A PARTIALLY FREE HAND, HE DIALED THE ONE PERSON HE HOPED COULD HELP.
Beep Boop Beep
POPOLO, IT'S ME, MILO.
MILO! WHERE ARE YOU?
MOOSHY MIKE'S.
IN THE OLD MELON PATCH.
POPOLO, THE SPACESHIP IS HEADED YOUR WAY...
WE SEE IT! OLLIE AND ALL THE ANIMALS ARE OUTSIDE WORKING ON THE CATERPILLAR!

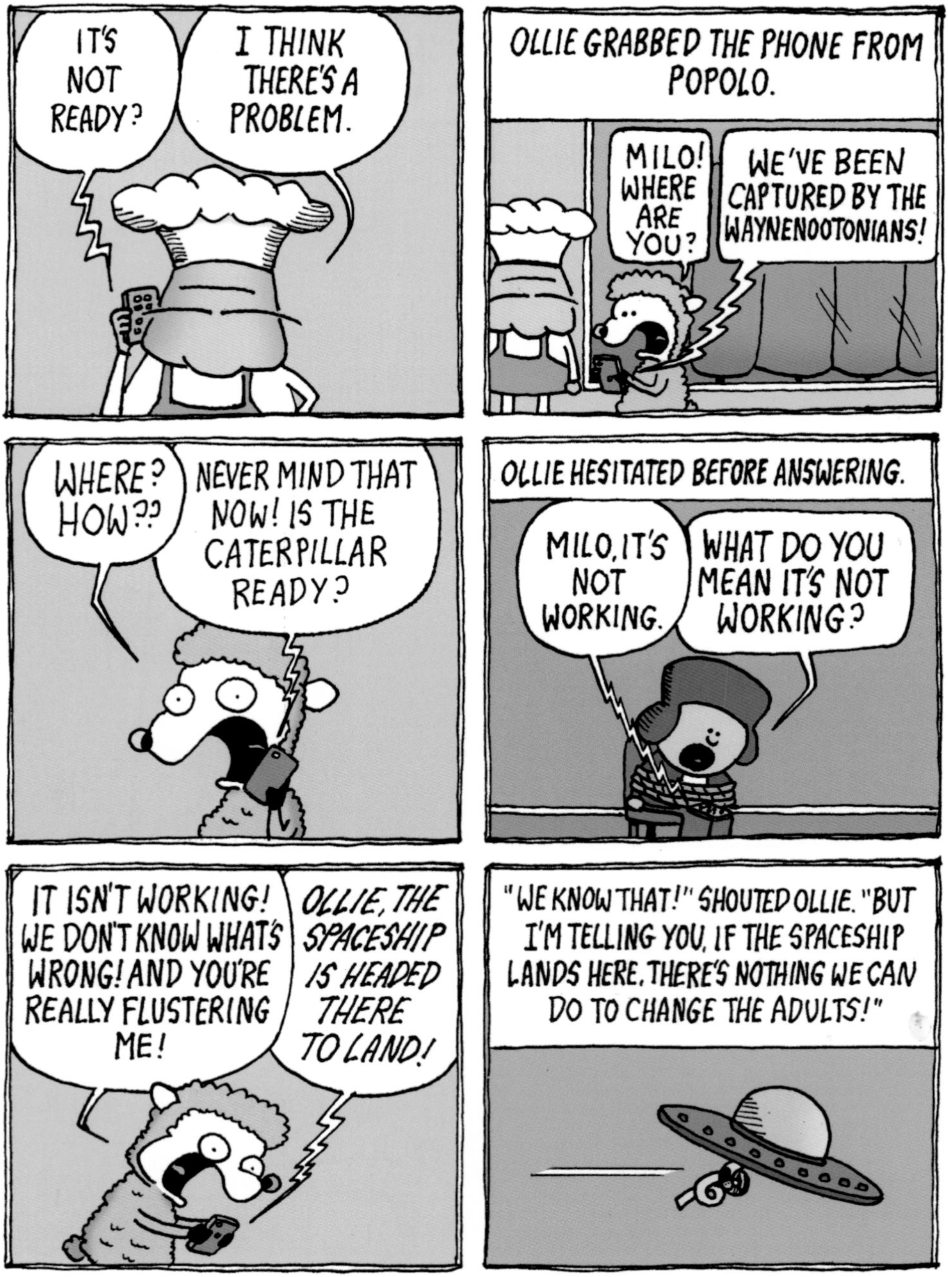
IT'S NOT READY?
I THINK THERE'S A PROBLEM.
OLLIE GRABBED THE PHONE FROM POPOLO.
MILO! WHERE ARE YOU?
WE'VE BEEN CAPTURED BY THE WAYNENOOTONIANS!
WHERE? HOW??
NEVER MIND THAT NOW! IS THE CATERPILLAR READY?
OLLIE HESITATED BEFORE ANSWERING.
MILO, IT'S NOT WORKING.
WHAT DO YOU MEAN IT'S NOT WORKING?
IT ISN'T WORKING! WE DON'T KNOW WHAT'S WRONG! AND YOU'RE REALLY FLUSTERING ME!
OLLIE, THE SPACESHIP IS HEADED THERE TO LAND!
"WE KNOW THAT!" SHOUTED OLLIE. "BUT I'M TELLING YOU, IF THE SPACESHIP LANDS HERE, THERE'S NOTHING WE CAN DO TO CHANGE THE ADULTS!"

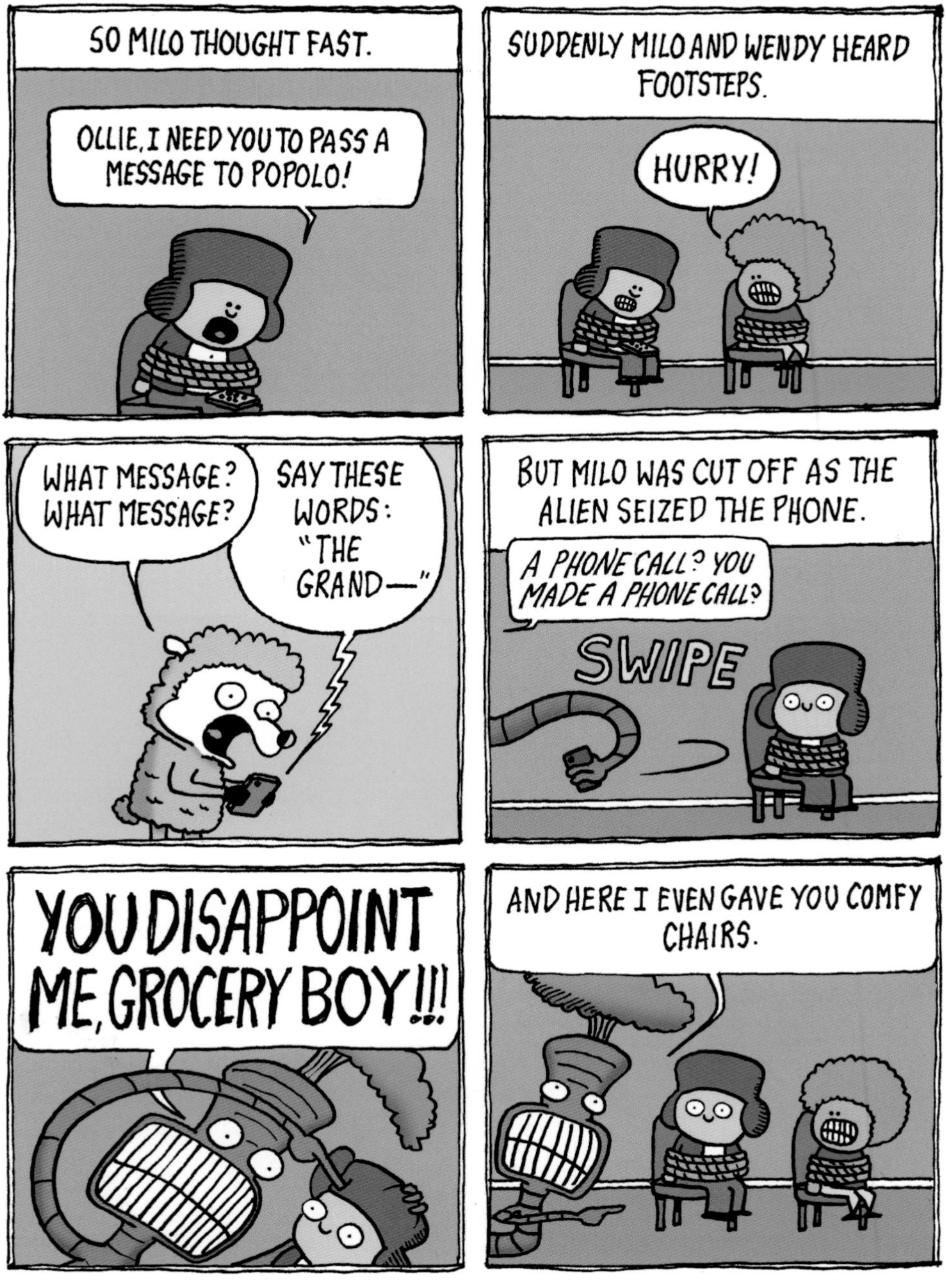
SO MILO THOUGHT FAST.
OLLIE, I NEED YOU TO PASS A MESSAGE TO POPOLO!
SUDDENLY MILO AND WENDY HEARD FOOTSTEPS.
HURRY!
WHAT MESSAGE? WHAT MESSAGE?
SAY THESE WORDS: "THE GRAND—"
BUT MILO WAS CUT OFF AS THE ALIEN SEIZED THE PHONE.
A PHONE CALL? YOU MADE A PHONE CALL?
SWIPE
YOU DISAPPOINT ME, GROCERY BOY!!!
AND HERE I EVEN GAVE YOU COMFY CHAIRS.

THE POINT IS THIS. I WAS JUST GOING TO KEEP YOU TWO HERE UNTIL AFTER THE SPACESHIP HAD LANDED AND THE ADULTS WERE LET LOOSE.

BECAUSE AFTER THAT, TRUBBLE WOULD BE RUINED. BUT NOW YOU'VE FORCED ME TO PUNISH YOU.

BUT WHY?

AND SO THE WAYNENOOTONIAN ALIEN CALLED OUT TO ONE OF HER FOXES.

None of Your Business!

WHICH CONFUSED EVERYONE.

SHE CAN BE VERY PRIVATE SOMETIMES.

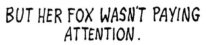

BUT HER FOX WASN'T PAYING ATTENTION.

FOR HE HAD SEEN LIGHTNING.

262

CHAPTER

SMALL

IN WHICH...

THE CHAPTER HEADING
STRAINS YOUR EYESIGHT

DURING THE BUILDING OF THE "CATER-PILLAR O' CHANGE", MILO HAD ASKED OLLIE AN OFFHANDED QUESTION:

WHAT IF THE SPACE-SHIP ISN'T ABLE TO LAND?

THAT WOULD BE BAD FOR THE ADULTS.

BAD HOW?

THE SHIP DOESN'T HAVE ENOUGH FUEL TO COME IN FOR A SECOND LANDING. THEY'D HAVE TO LET IT SLIP BACK INTO ORBIT.

SO?

SO THE ADULTS WOULD BE GONE FOR TWO YEARS, MINIMUM. BUT WHY ARE YOU ASKING?

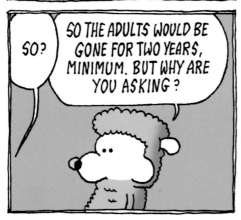

I DON'T KNOW. I GUESS IN CASE WE'RE NOT READY.

MILO, READY OR NOT, THEY'RE LANDING.

WHICH MILO UNDERSTOOD TO BE TRUE. UNTIL HE SAW POPOLO'S GYRO.

IT WAS A GYRO HUNDREDS OF TIMES THE SIZE OF THE RESTAURANT. AND THE PLACE WHERE POPOLO STUFFED ALL THE FOOD HE'D NEVER SOLD.

GYRO

POPOLO DOPOLO'S

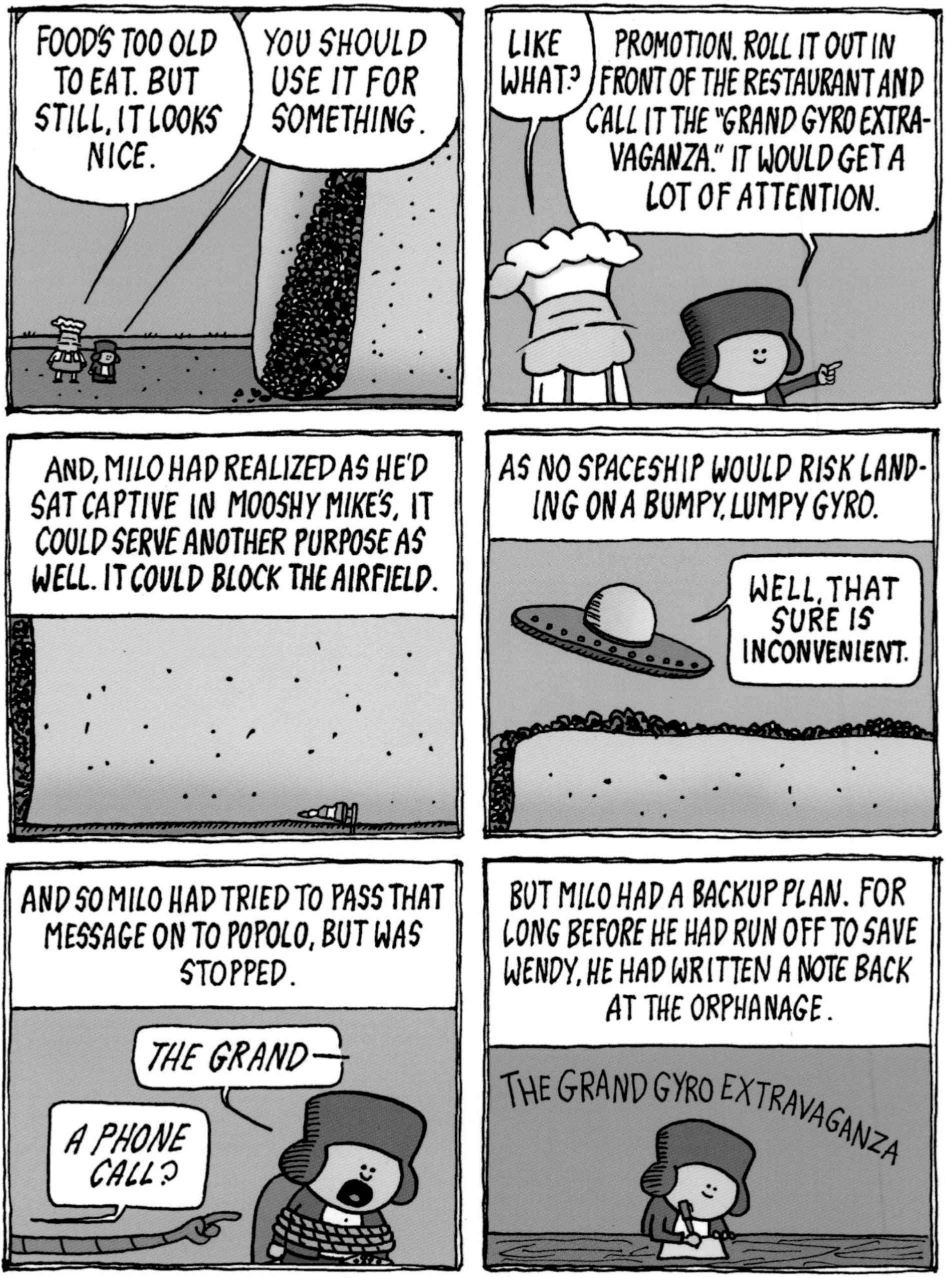
FOOD'S TOO OLD TO EAT. BUT STILL, IT LOOKS NICE.
YOU SHOULD USE IT FOR SOMETHING.
LIKE WHAT?
PROMOTION. ROLL IT OUT IN FRONT OF THE RESTAURANT AND CALL IT THE "GRAND GYRO EXTRAVAGANZA." IT WOULD GET A LOT OF ATTENTION.
AND, MILO HAD REALIZED AS HE'D SAT CAPTIVE IN MOOSHY MIKE'S, IT COULD SERVE ANOTHER PURPOSE AS WELL. IT COULD BLOCK THE AIRFIELD.
AS NO SPACESHIP WOULD RISK LANDING ON A BUMPY, LUMPY GYRO.
WELL, THAT SURE IS INCONVENIENT.
AND SO MILO HAD TRIED TO PASS THAT MESSAGE ON TO POPOLO, BUT WAS STOPPED.
THE GRAND—
A PHONE CALL?
BUT MILO HAD A BACKUP PLAN. FOR LONG BEFORE HE HAD RUN OFF TO SAVE WENDY, HE HAD WRITTEN A NOTE BACK AT THE ORPHANAGE.
THE GRAND GYRO EXTRAVAGANZA

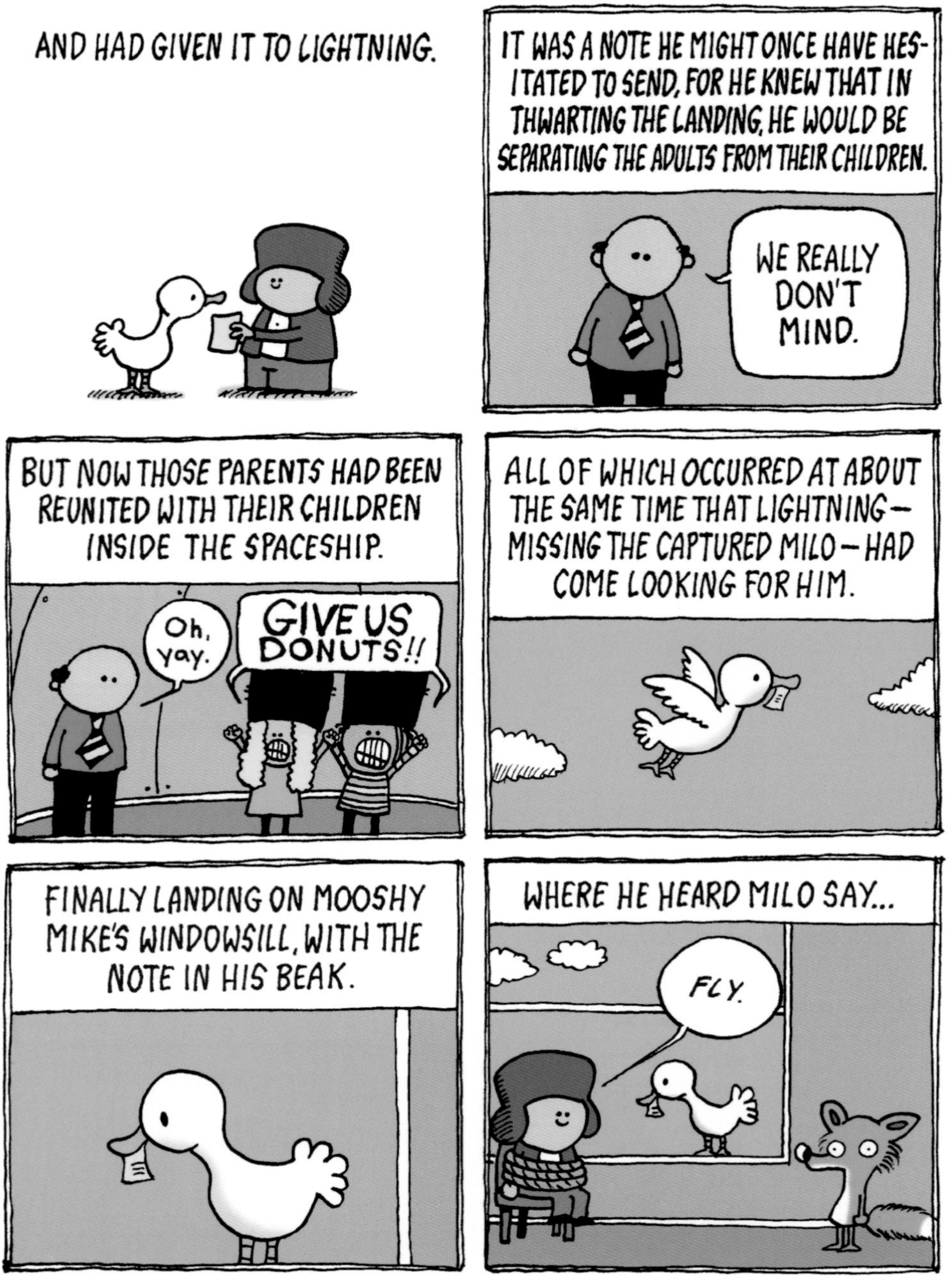
AND HAD GIVEN IT TO LIGHTNING.
IT WAS A NOTE HE MIGHT ONCE HAVE HES-ITATED TO SEND, FOR HE KNEW THAT IN THWARTING THE LANDING, HE WOULD BE SEPARATING THE ADULTS FROM THEIR CHILDREN.
WE REALLY DON'T MIND.
BUT NOW THOSE PARENTS HAD BEEN REUNITED WITH THEIR CHILDREN INSIDE THE SPACESHIP.
Oh, yay.
GIVE US DONUTS!!
ALL OF WHICH OCCURRED AT ABOUT THE SAME TIME THAT LIGHTNING—MISSING THE CAPTURED MILO—HAD COME LOOKING FOR HIM.
FINALLY LANDING ON MOOSHY MIKE'S WINDOWSILL, WITH THE NOTE IN HIS BEAK.
WHERE HE HEARD MILO SAY...
FLY.

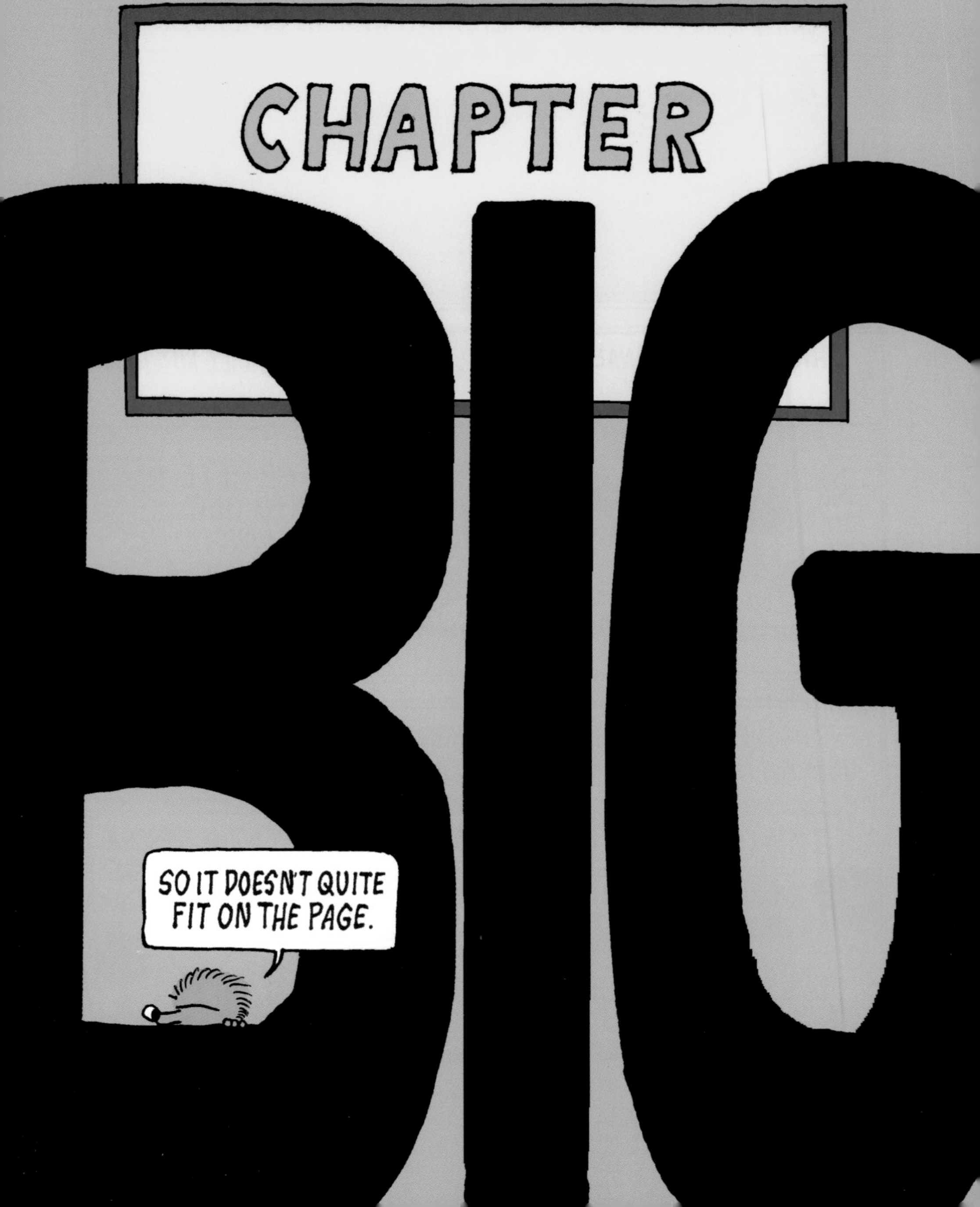
CHAPTER
BIG
SO IT DOESN'T QUITE FIT ON THE PAGE.

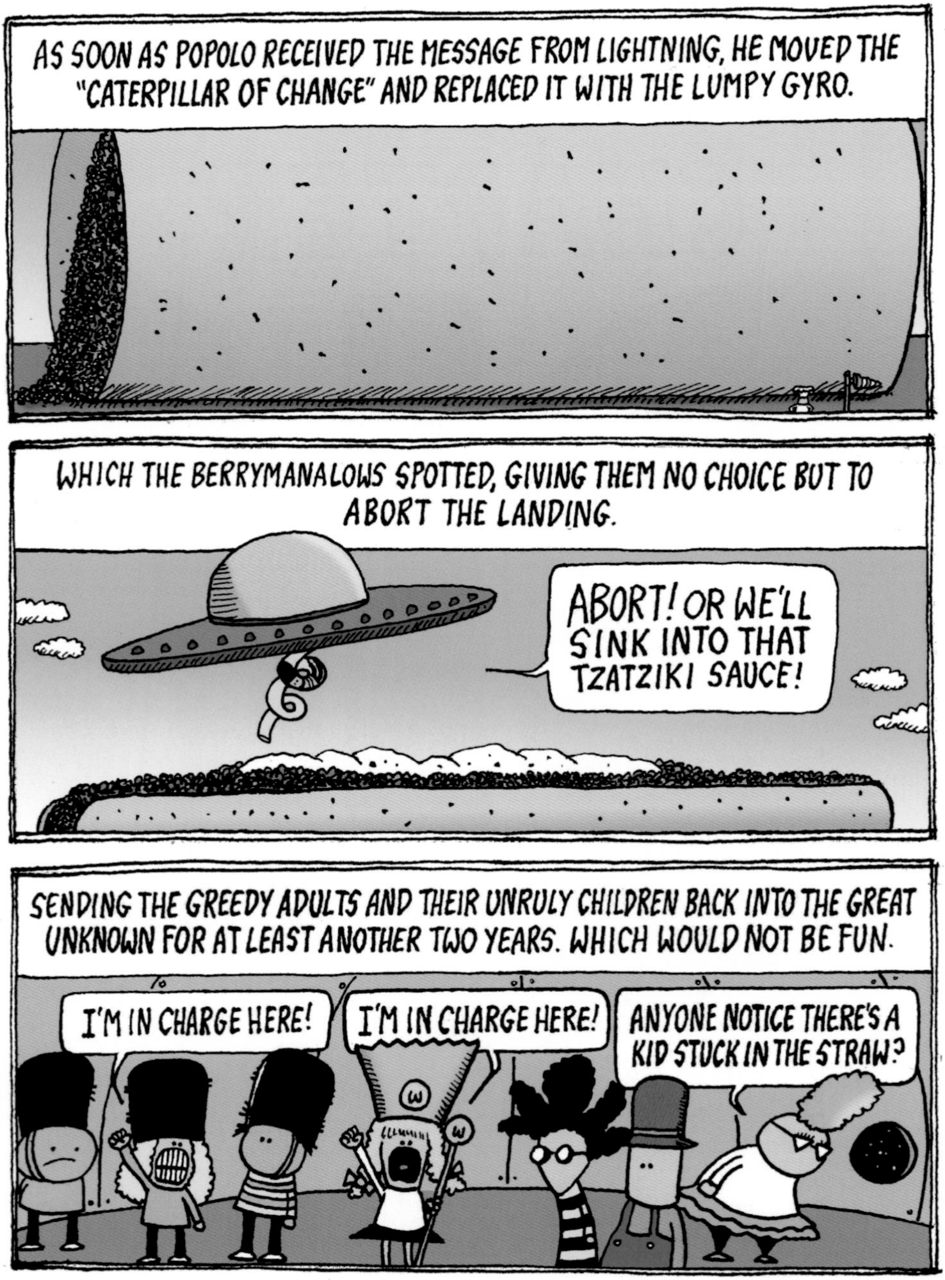
AS SOON AS POPOLO RECEIVED THE MESSAGE FROM LIGHTNING, HE MOVED THE "CATERPILLAR OF CHANGE" AND REPLACED IT WITH THE LUMPY GYRO.
WHICH THE BERRYMANALOWS SPOTTED, GIVING THEM NO CHOICE BUT TO ABORT THE LANDING.
ABORT! OR WE'LL SINK INTO THAT TZATZIKI SAUCE!
SENDING THE GREEDY ADULTS AND THEIR UNRULY CHILDREN BACK INTO THE GREAT UNKNOWN FOR AT LEAST ANOTHER TWO YEARS. WHICH WOULD NOT BE FUN.
I'M IN CHARGE HERE!
I'M IN CHARGE HERE!
ANYONE NOTICE THERE'S A KID STUCK IN THE STRAW?

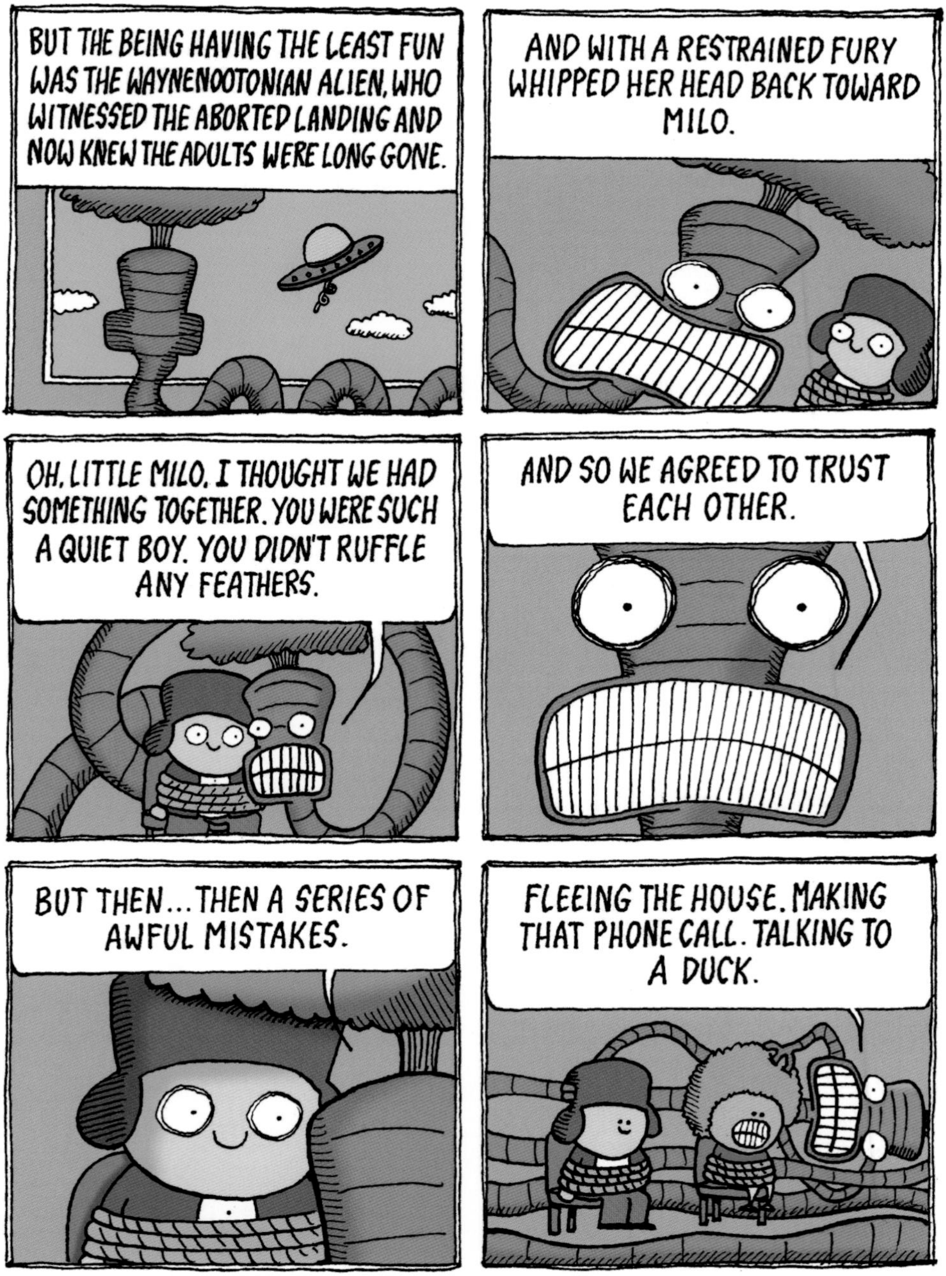
BUT THE BEING HAVING THE LEAST FUN WAS THE WAYNENOOTONIAN ALIEN, WHO WITNESSED THE ABORTED LANDING AND NOW KNEW THE ADULTS WERE LONG GONE.
AND WITH A RESTRAINED FURY WHIPPED HER HEAD BACK TOWARD MILO.
OH, LITTLE MILO. I THOUGHT WE HAD SOMETHING TOGETHER. YOU WERE SUCH A QUIET BOY. YOU DIDN'T RUFFLE ANY FEATHERS.
AND SO WE AGREED TO TRUST EACH OTHER.
BUT THEN... THEN A SERIES OF AWFUL MISTAKES.
FLEEING THE HOUSE. MAKING THAT PHONE CALL. TALKING TO A DUCK.

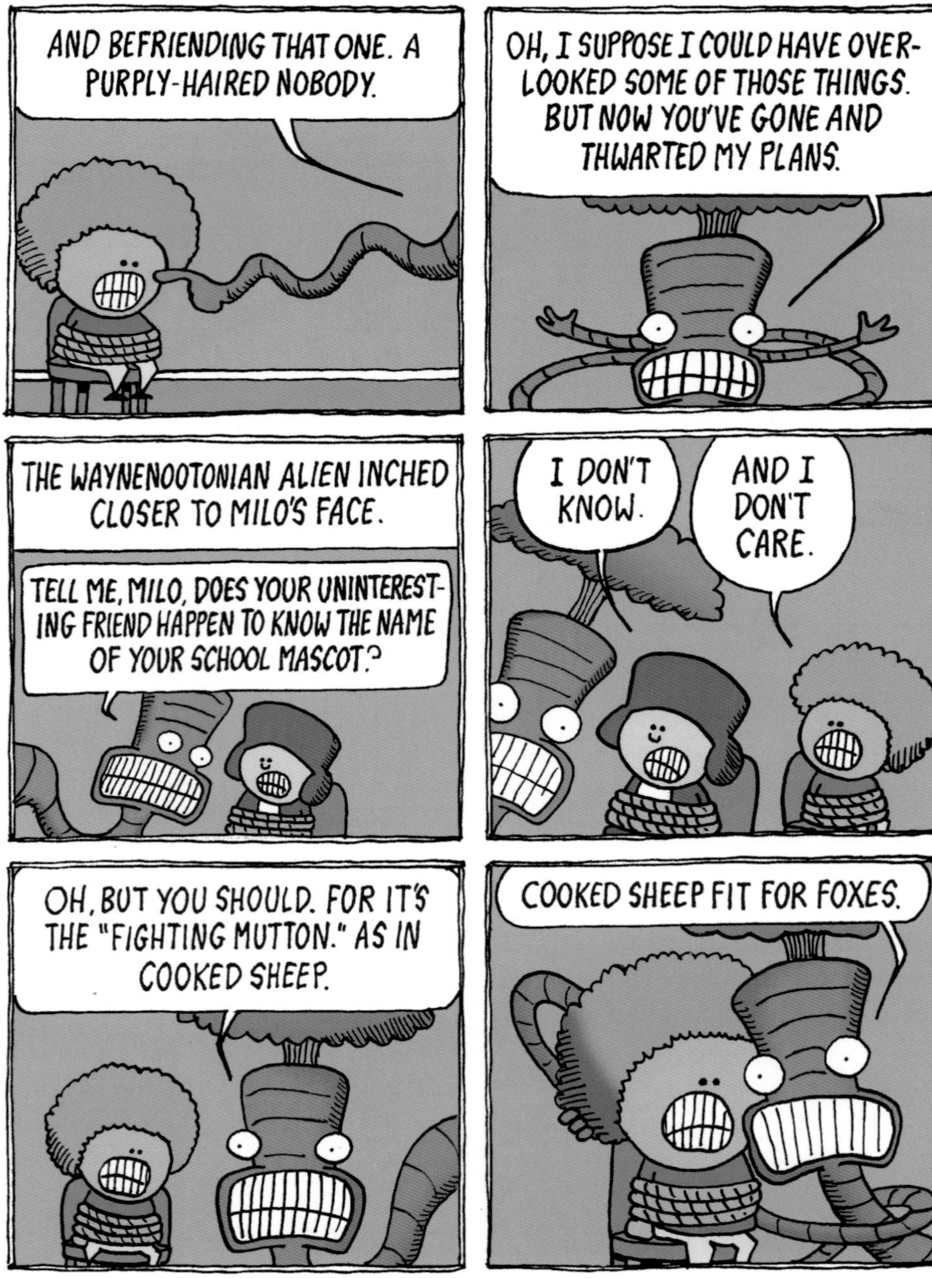
AND BEFRIENDING THAT ONE. A PURPLY-HAIRED NOBODY.
OH, I SUPPOSE I COULD HAVE OVER-LOOKED SOME OF THOSE THINGS. BUT NOW YOU'VE GONE AND THWARTED MY PLANS.
THE WAYNENOOTONIAN ALIEN INCHED CLOSER TO MILO'S FACE.
TELL ME, MILO, DOES YOUR UNINTEREST-ING FRIEND HAPPEN TO KNOW THE NAME OF YOUR SCHOOL MASCOT?
I DON'T KNOW.
AND I DON'T CARE.
OH, BUT YOU SHOULD. FOR IT'S THE "FIGHTING MUTTON." AS IN COOKED SHEEP.
COOKED SHEEP FIT FOR FOXES.

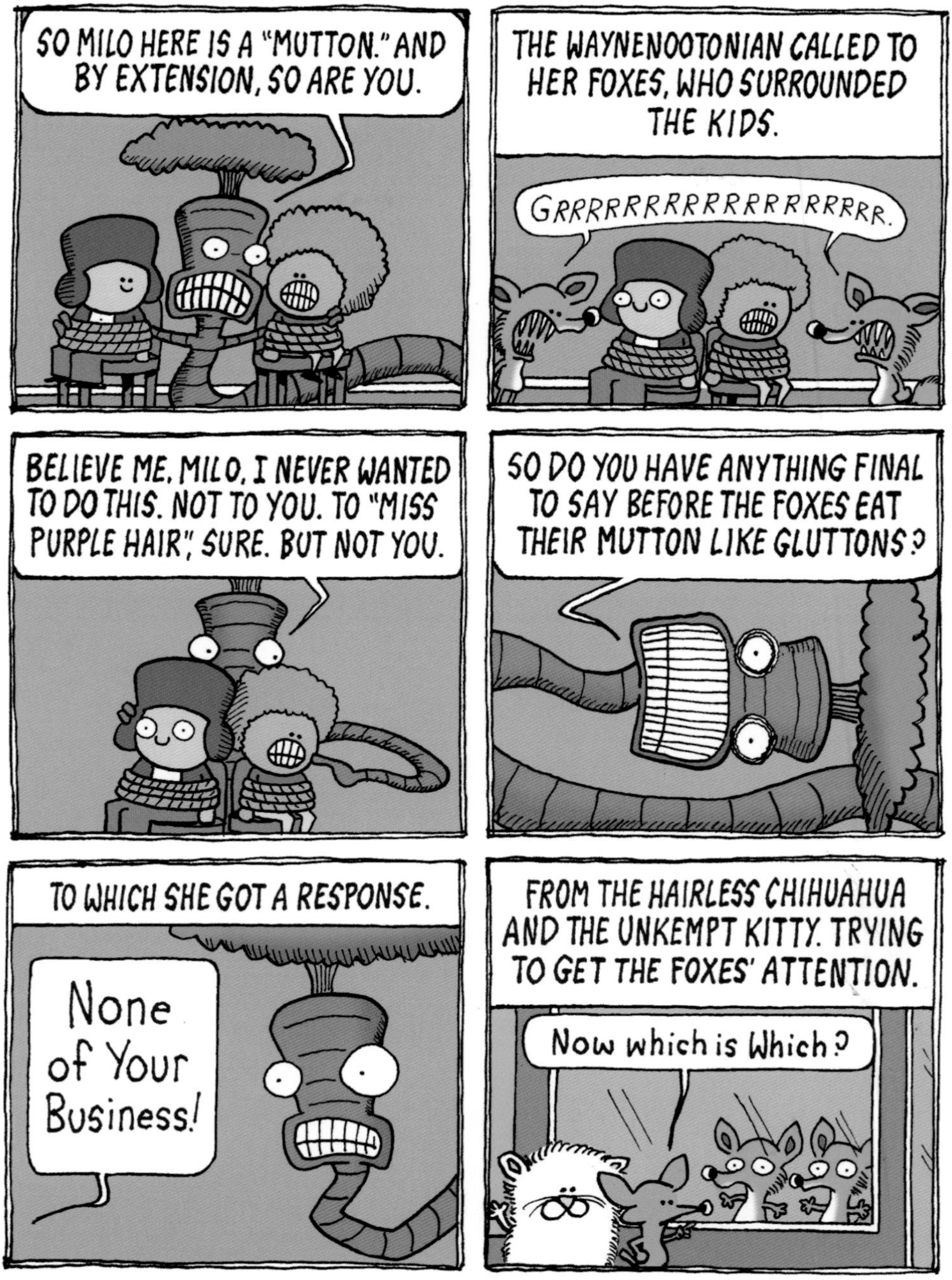
SO MILO HERE IS A "MUTTON." AND BY EXTENSION, SO ARE YOU.
THE WAYNENOOTONIAN CALLED TO HER FOXES, WHO SURROUNDED THE KIDS.
GRRRRRRRRRRRRRRRRRR.
BELIEVE ME, MILO, I NEVER WANTED TO DO THIS. NOT TO YOU. TO "MISS PURPLE HAIR", SURE. BUT NOT YOU.
SO DO YOU HAVE ANYTHING FINAL TO SAY BEFORE THE FOXES EAT THEIR MUTTON LIKE GLUTTONS?
TO WHICH SHE GOT A RESPONSE.
None of Your Business!
FROM THE HAIRLESS CHIHUAHUA AND THE UNKEMPT KITTY. TRYING TO GET THE FOXES' ATTENTION.
Now which is Which?

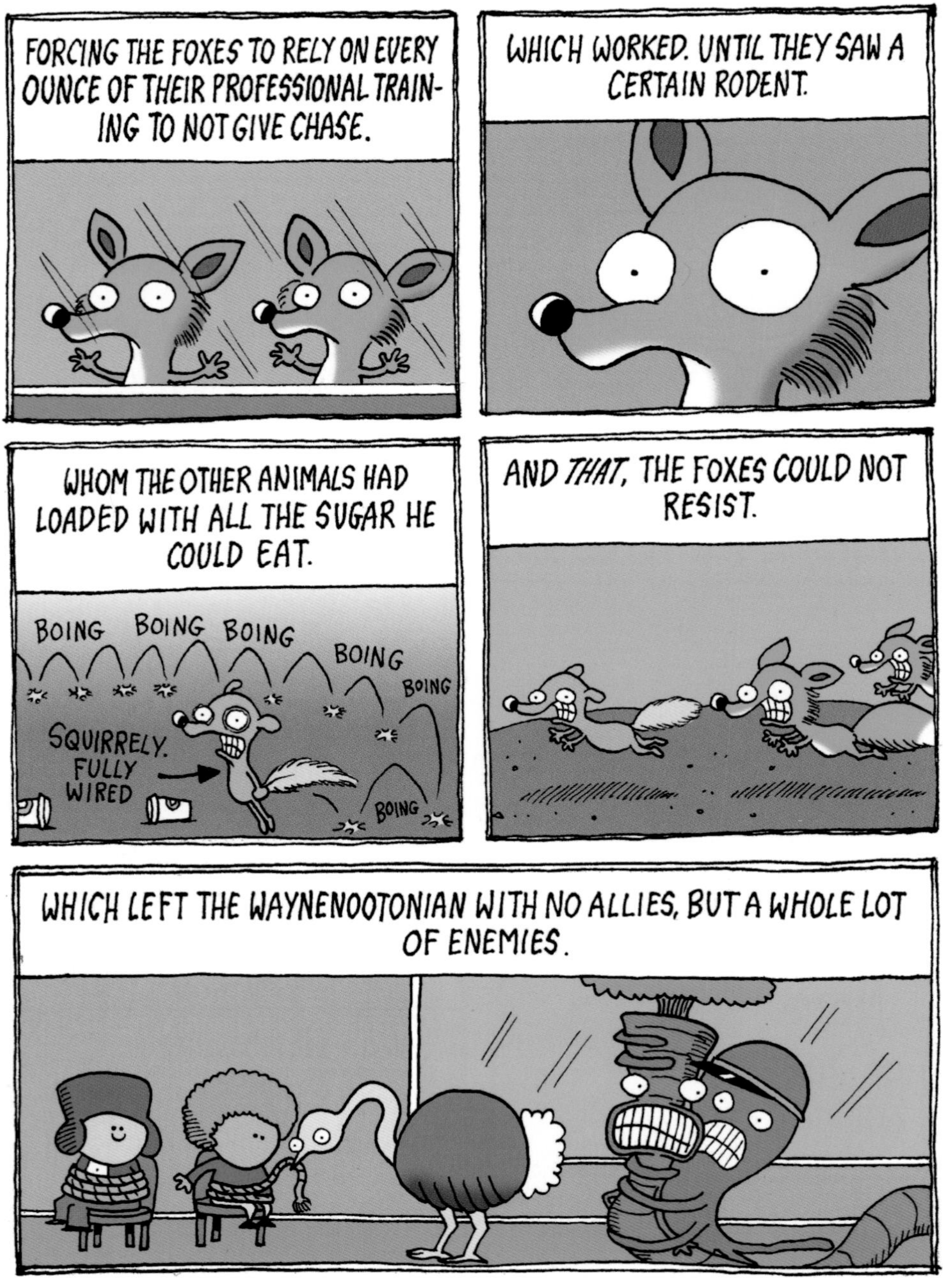
FORCING THE FOXES TO RELY ON EVERY OUNCE OF THEIR PROFESSIONAL TRAINING TO NOT GIVE CHASE.
WHICH WORKED. UNTIL THEY SAW A CERTAIN RODENT.
WHOM THE OTHER ANIMALS HAD LOADED WITH ALL THE SUGAR HE COULD EAT.
BOING BOING BOING BOING BOING BOING
SQUIRRELY. FULLY WIRED
AND *THAT*, THE FOXES COULD NOT RESIST.
WHICH LEFT THE WAYNENOOTONIAN WITH NO ALLIES, BUT A WHOLE LOT OF ENEMIES.

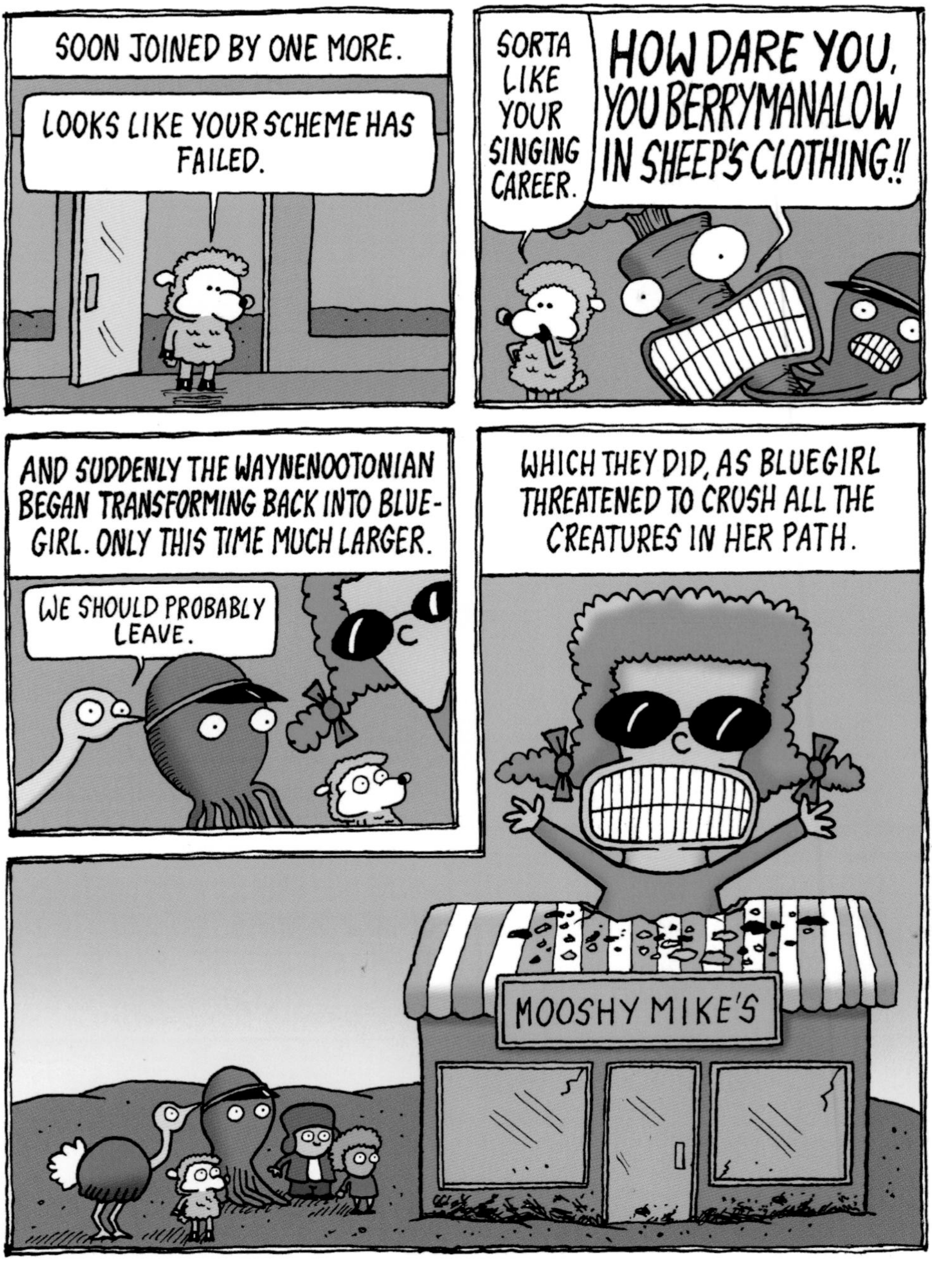
SOON JOINED BY ONE MORE.
LOOKS LIKE YOUR SCHEME HAS FAILED.
SORTA LIKE YOUR SINGING CAREER.
HOW DARE YOU, YOU BERRYMANALOW IN SHEEP'S CLOTHING!!
AND SUDDENLY THE WAYNENOOTONIAN BEGAN TRANSFORMING BACK INTO BLUE-GIRL. ONLY THIS TIME MUCH LARGER.
WE SHOULD PROBABLY LEAVE.
WHICH THEY DID, AS BLUEGIRL THREATENED TO CRUSH ALL THE CREATURES IN HER PATH.
MOOSHY MIKE'S

UNAWARE THAT THE ONES SHE SHOULD FEAR MOST WERE THE ONES SHE COULD NOT SEE.

REMEMBER US?

FOR WHEN THE "GREAT BATH WITHOUT BUBBLES" HAD STRUCK TRUBBLE, THE MOLES HAD BEEN TRAPPED IN THE RISING WATER.

AND HAD ONLY MANAGED TO SURVIVE BY VIRTUE OF THE FACT THAT THE RISING WATER LIFTED THEM LIKE BUOYS TO AN OPEN AIR VENT IN THE CEILING.

WHICH HAD LED DIRECTLY OUT OF THE JAIL.

AND SO WHEN THE WATER FINALLY DISSIPATED, THE FUGITIVE MOLES BURROWED THEIR WAY BACK UNDERGROUND.

WHERE THEY CREATED A VAST NETWORK OF *NEW* TUNNELS THAT COULD TAKE THEM ANYWHERE THEY WANTED TO GO.

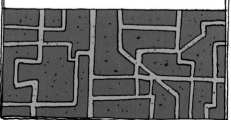

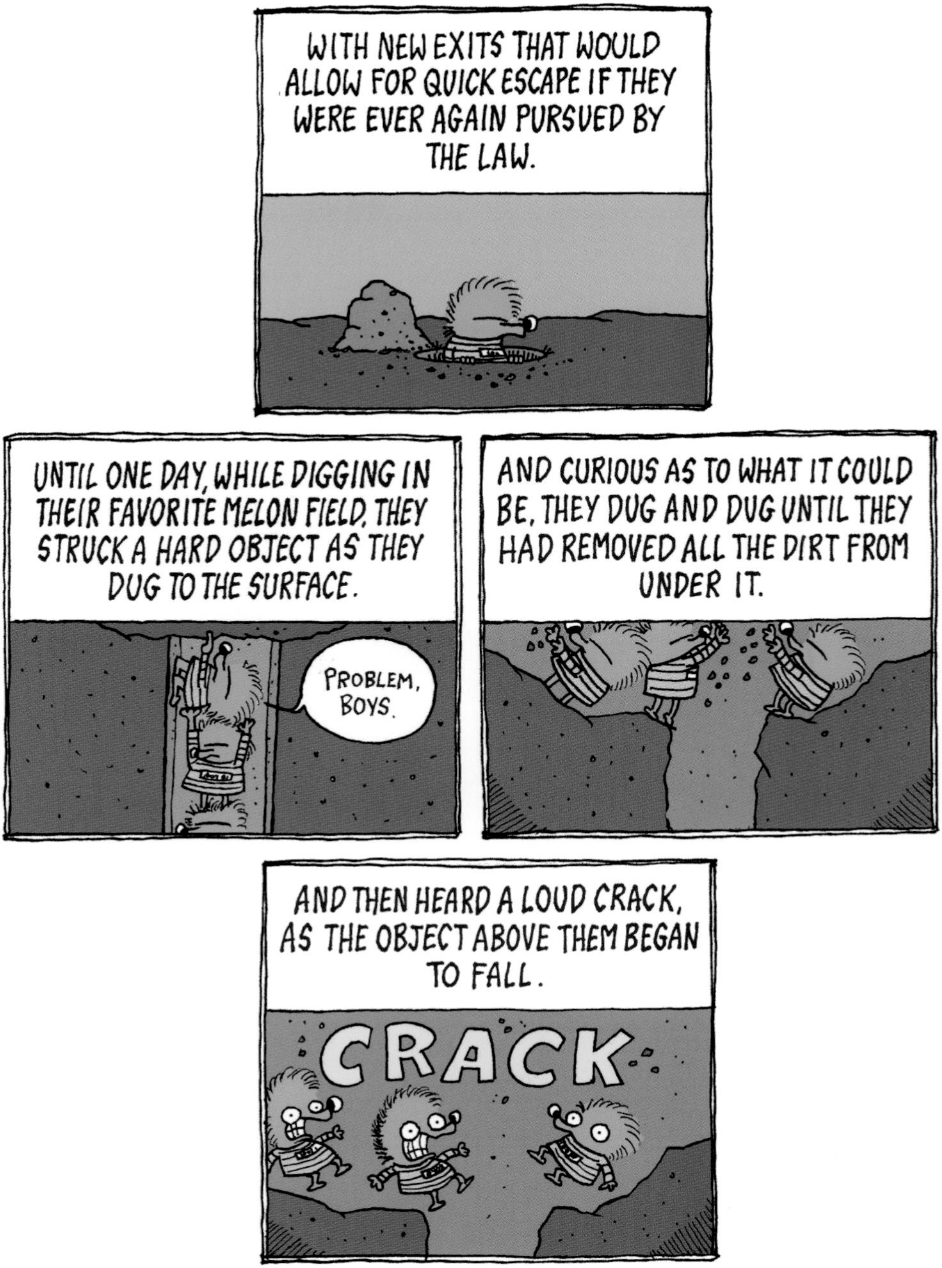
WITH NEW EXITS THAT WOULD ALLOW FOR QUICK ESCAPE IF THEY WERE EVER AGAIN PURSUED BY THE LAW.
UNTIL ONE DAY, WHILE DIGGING IN THEIR FAVORITE MELON FIELD, THEY STRUCK A HARD OBJECT AS THEY DUG TO THE SURFACE.
PROBLEM, BOYS.
AND CURIOUS AS TO WHAT IT COULD BE, THEY DUG AND DUG UNTIL THEY HAD REMOVED ALL THE DIRT FROM UNDER IT.
AND THEN HEARD A LOUD CRACK, AS THE OBJECT ABOVE THEM BEGAN TO FALL.
CRACK

WHICH MILO AND WENDY HEARD FROM ABOVE AS THE DIRT UNDER MOOSHY MIKE'S CAFÉ GAVE WAY.

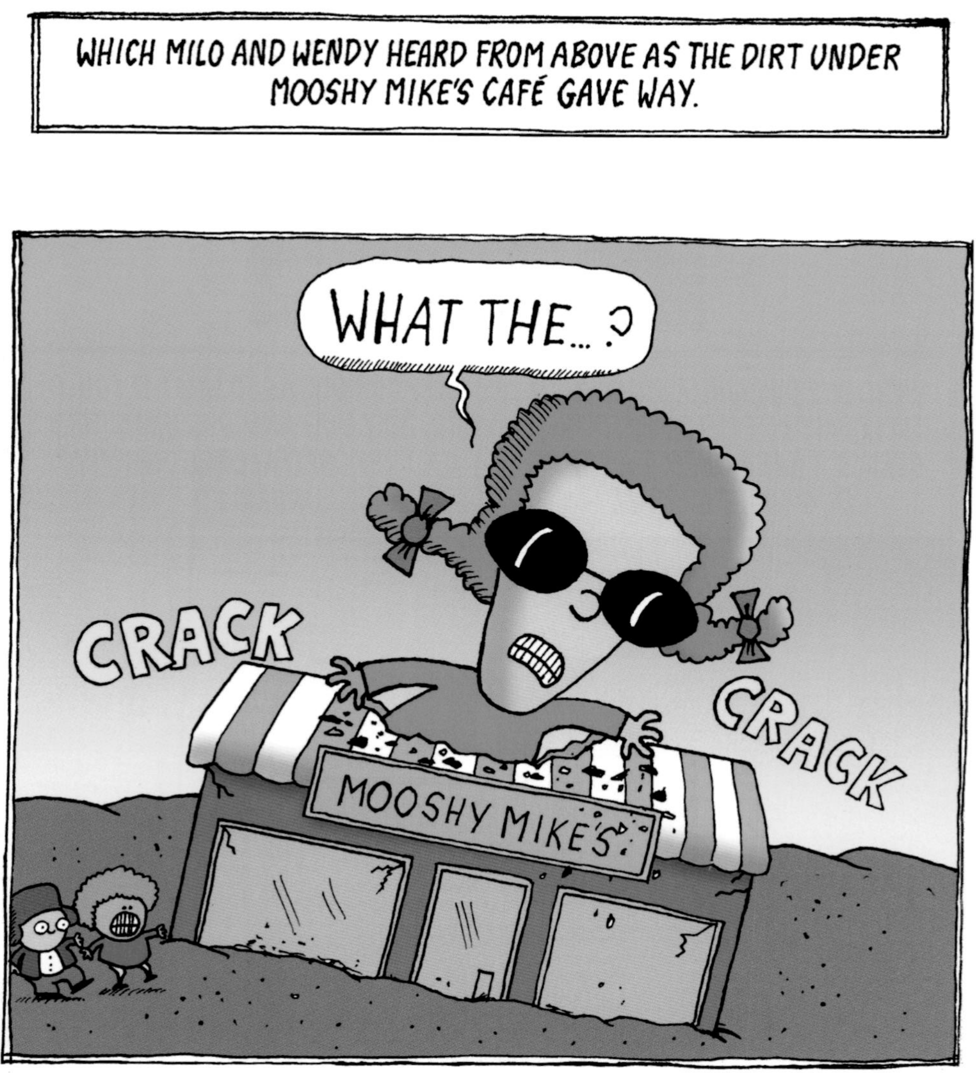
WHAT THE...?
CRACK
CRACK
MOOSHY MIKE'S

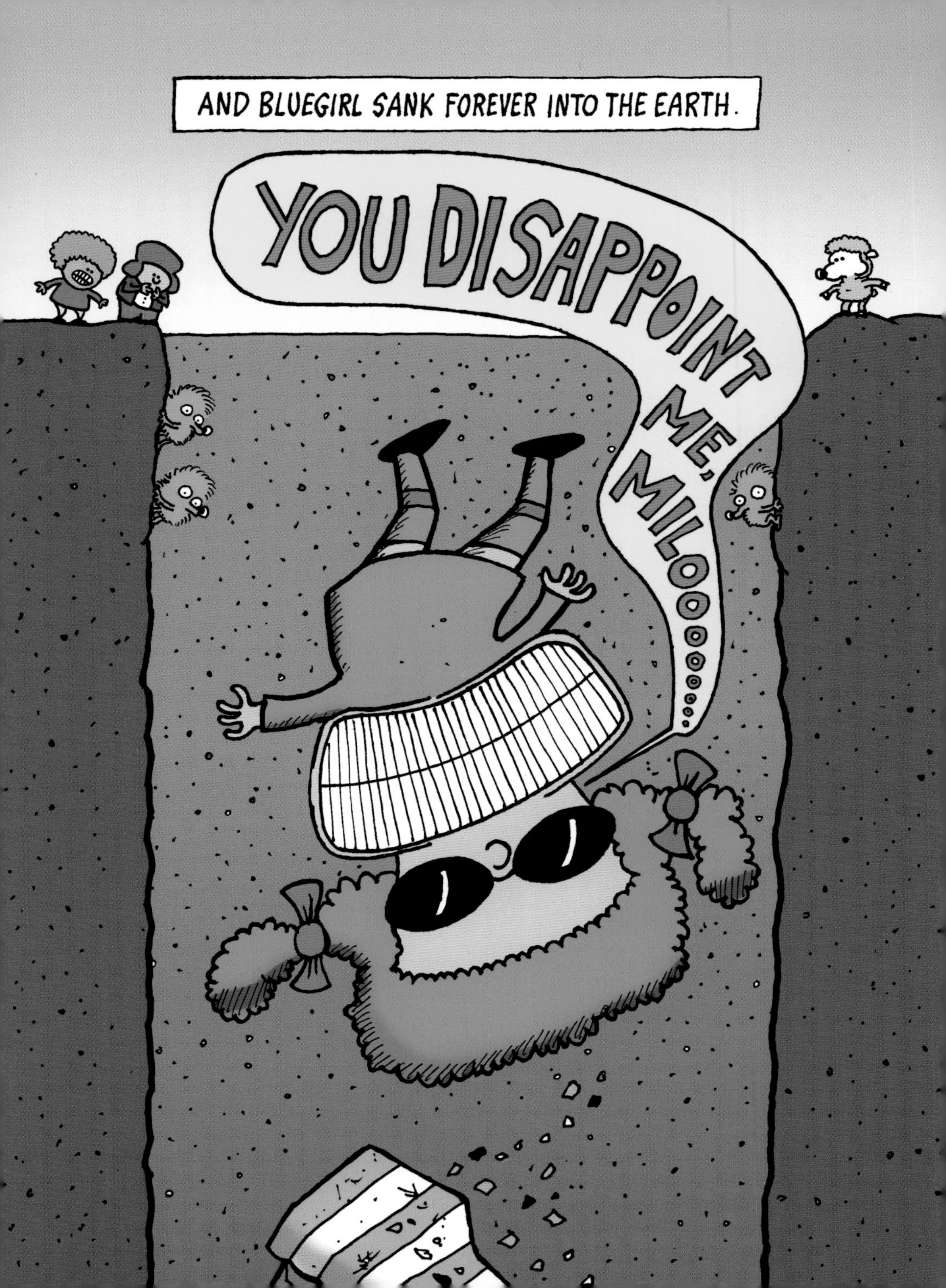
AND BLUEGIRL SANK FOREVER INTO THE EARTH.
YOU DISAPPOINT ME, MILOOOOOOOOO...

CHAPTER LAST FOR REAL

IN WHICH...

WE ARE NOT KIDDING AROUND

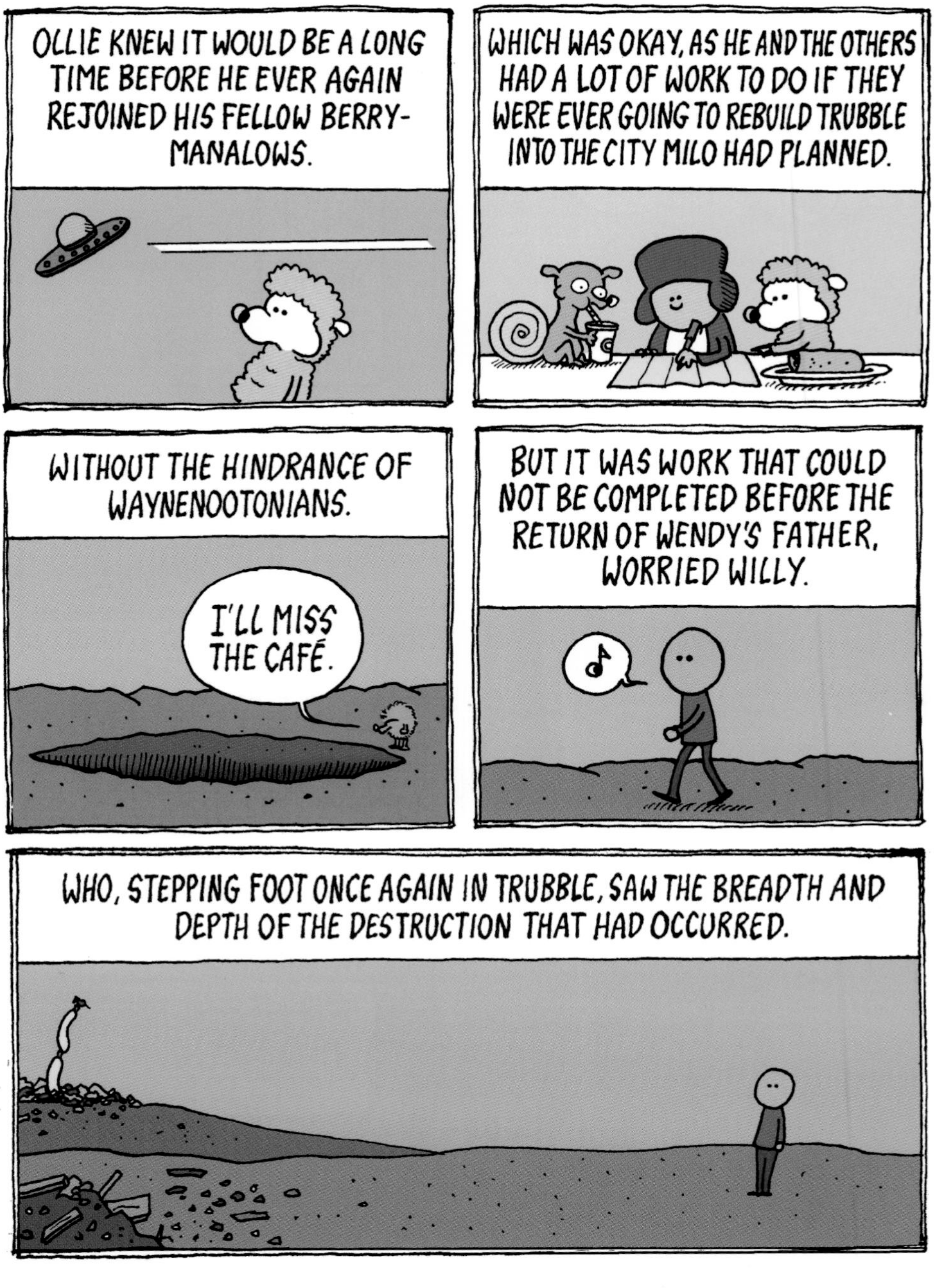
OLLIE KNEW IT WOULD BE A LONG TIME BEFORE HE EVER AGAIN REJOINED HIS FELLOW BERRY-MANALOWS.
WHICH WAS OKAY, AS HE AND THE OTHERS HAD A LOT OF WORK TO DO IF THEY WERE EVER GOING TO REBUILD TRUBBLE INTO THE CITY MILO HAD PLANNED.
WITHOUT THE HINDRANCE OF WAYNENOOTONIANS.
I'LL MISS THE CAFÉ.
BUT IT WAS WORK THAT COULD NOT BE COMPLETED BEFORE THE RETURN OF WENDY'S FATHER, WORRIED WILLY.
WHO, STEPPING FOOT ONCE AGAIN IN TRUBBLE, SAW THE BREADTH AND DEPTH OF THE DESTRUCTION THAT HAD OCCURRED.

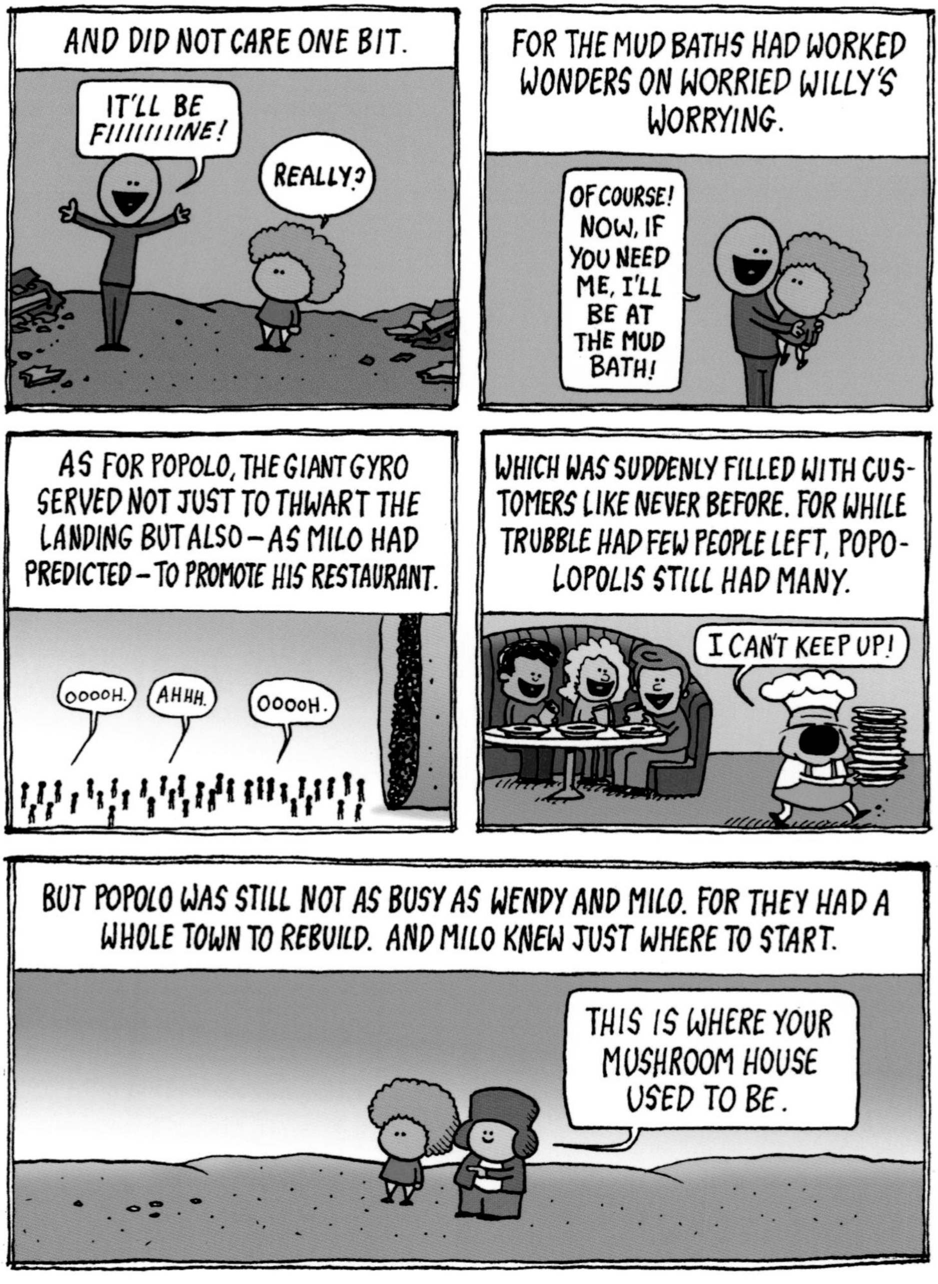
AND DID NOT CARE ONE BIT.
IT'LL BE FIIIIIIIINE!
REALLY?
FOR THE MUD BATHS HAD WORKED WONDERS ON WORRIED WILLY'S WORRYING.
OF COURSE! NOW, IF YOU NEED ME, I'LL BE AT THE MUD BATH!
AS FOR POPOLO, THE GIANT GYRO SERVED NOT JUST TO THWART THE LANDING BUT ALSO—AS MILO HAD PREDICTED—TO PROMOTE HIS RESTAURANT.
OOOOH.
AHHH.
OOOOH.
WHICH WAS SUDDENLY FILLED WITH CUSTOMERS LIKE NEVER BEFORE. FOR WHILE TRUBBLE HAD FEW PEOPLE LEFT, POPOLOPOLIS STILL HAD MANY.
I CAN'T KEEP UP!
BUT POPOLO WAS STILL NOT AS BUSY AS WENDY AND MILO. FOR THEY HAD A WHOLE TOWN TO REBUILD. AND MILO KNEW JUST WHERE TO START.
THIS IS WHERE YOUR MUSHROOM HOUSE USED TO BE.

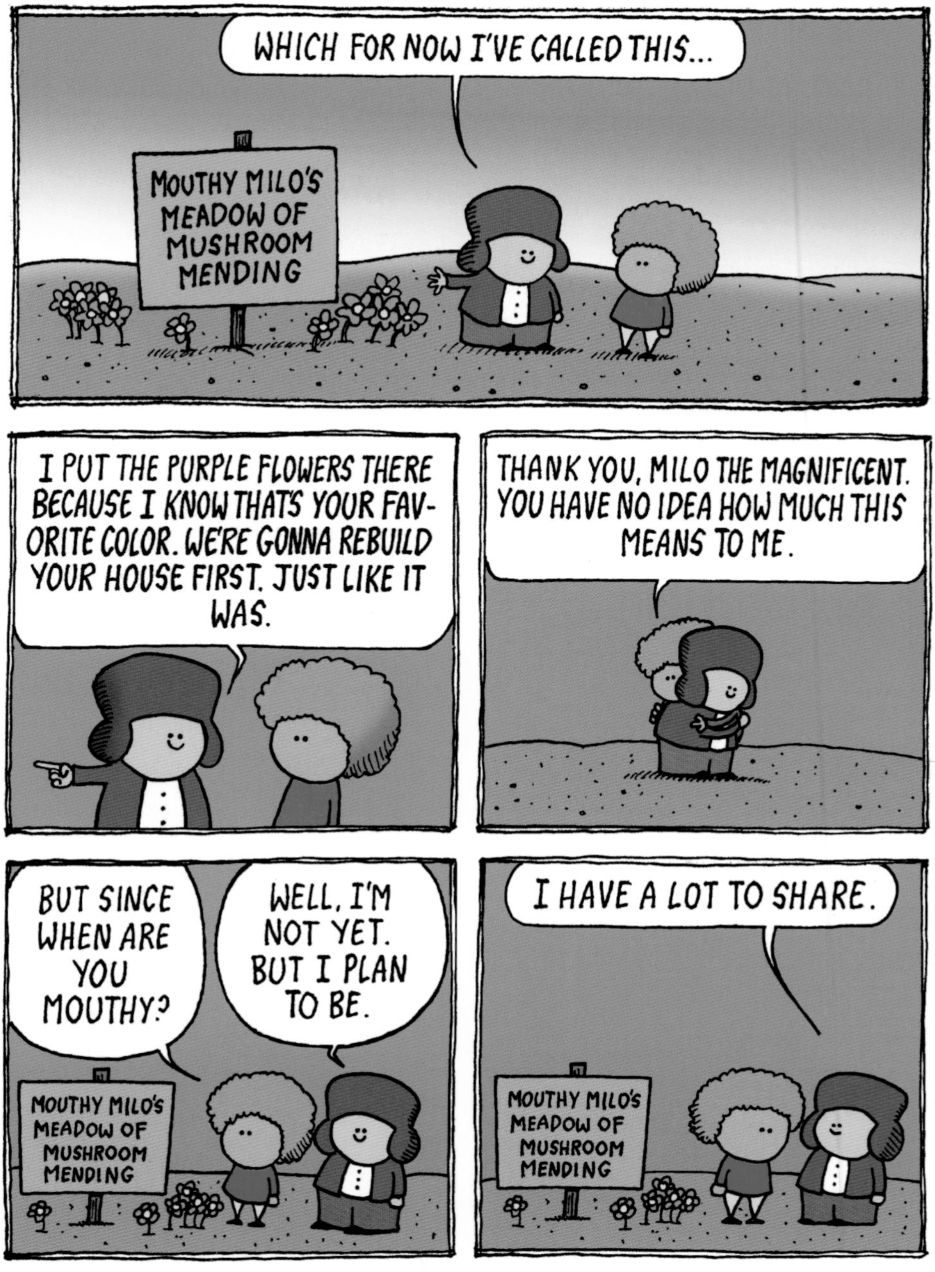
WHICH FOR NOW I'VE CALLED THIS...
MOUTHY MILO'S MEADOW OF MUSHROOM MENDING
I PUT THE PURPLE FLOWERS THERE BECAUSE I KNOW THAT'S YOUR FAVORITE COLOR. WE'RE GONNA REBUILD YOUR HOUSE FIRST. JUST LIKE IT WAS.
THANK YOU, MILO THE MAGNIFICENT. YOU HAVE NO IDEA HOW MUCH THIS MEANS TO ME.
BUT SINCE WHEN ARE YOU MOUTHY?
WELL, I'M NOT YET. BUT I PLAN TO BE.
MOUTHY MILO'S MEADOW OF MUSHROOM MENDING
I HAVE A LOT TO SHARE.
MOUTHY MILO'S MEADOW OF MUSHROOM MENDING

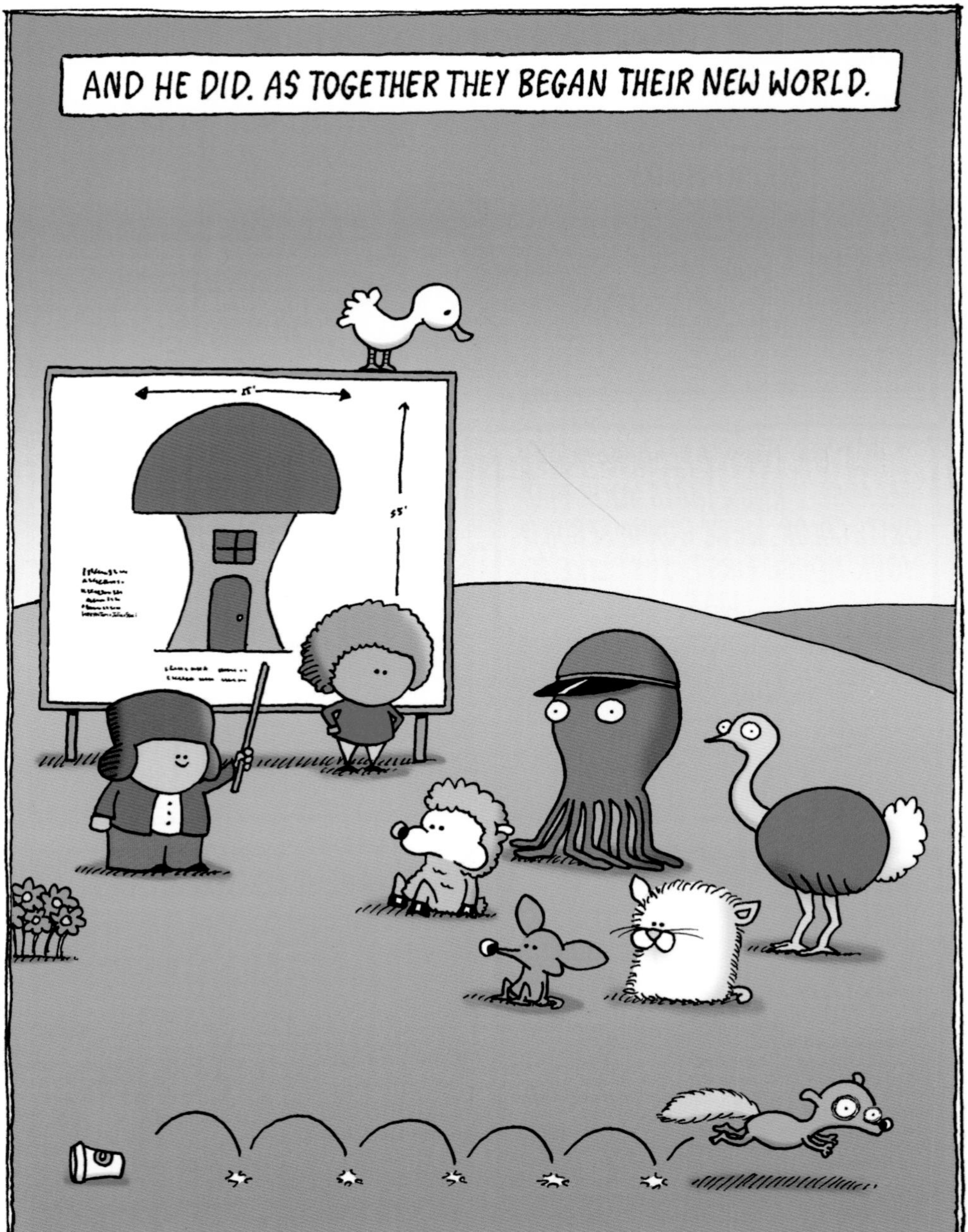
AND HE DID. AS TOGETHER THEY BEGAN THEIR NEW WORLD.
25'
55'

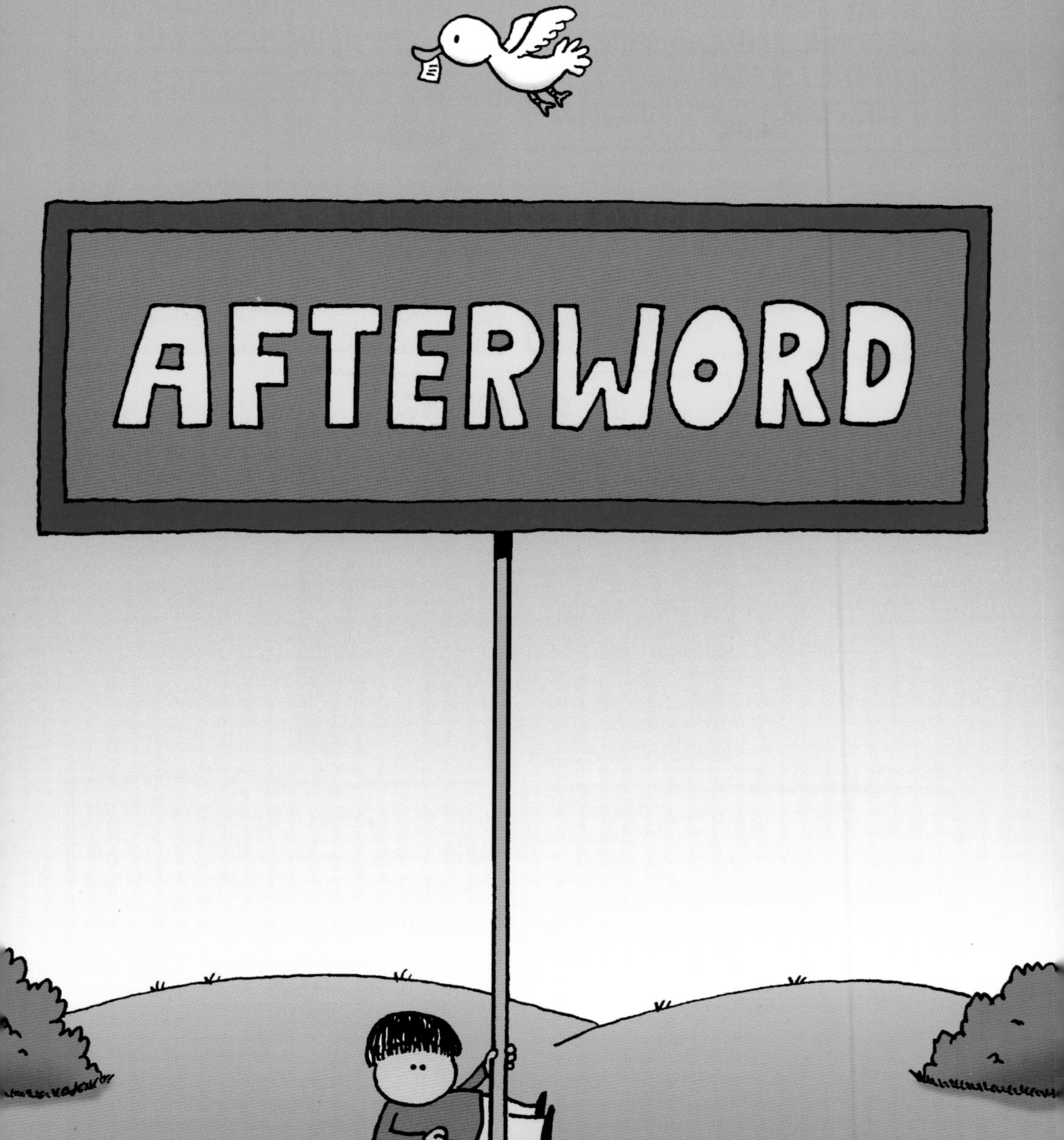
AFTERWORD

THE NEW TRUBBLE TOWN COUNCIL OF WENDY, MILO, AND OLLIE FINISHED THEIR FIRST MEETING AND ASKED IF THERE WAS ANY NEW BUSINESS.

AT WHICH POINT A STRANGE CREATURE CAME TO THE MICROPHONE.

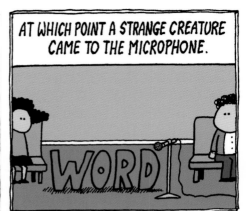

BUT SAID NOTHING.

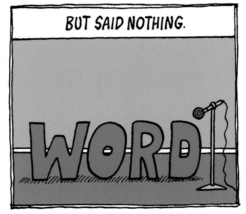

WELL, GIVEN THAT YOU APPEAR TO HAVE NOTHING TO SAY, IS THERE ANYONE ELSE WHO'D LIKE TO SPEAK?

WHICH WAS WHEN LITTLE RINGO SIMPKINS, WHO HAD SOMEHOW SURVIVED ALL THE TROUBLES OF TRUBBLE, STEPPED TO THE MIC AND MOVED THE "WORD" TO ONE SIDE.

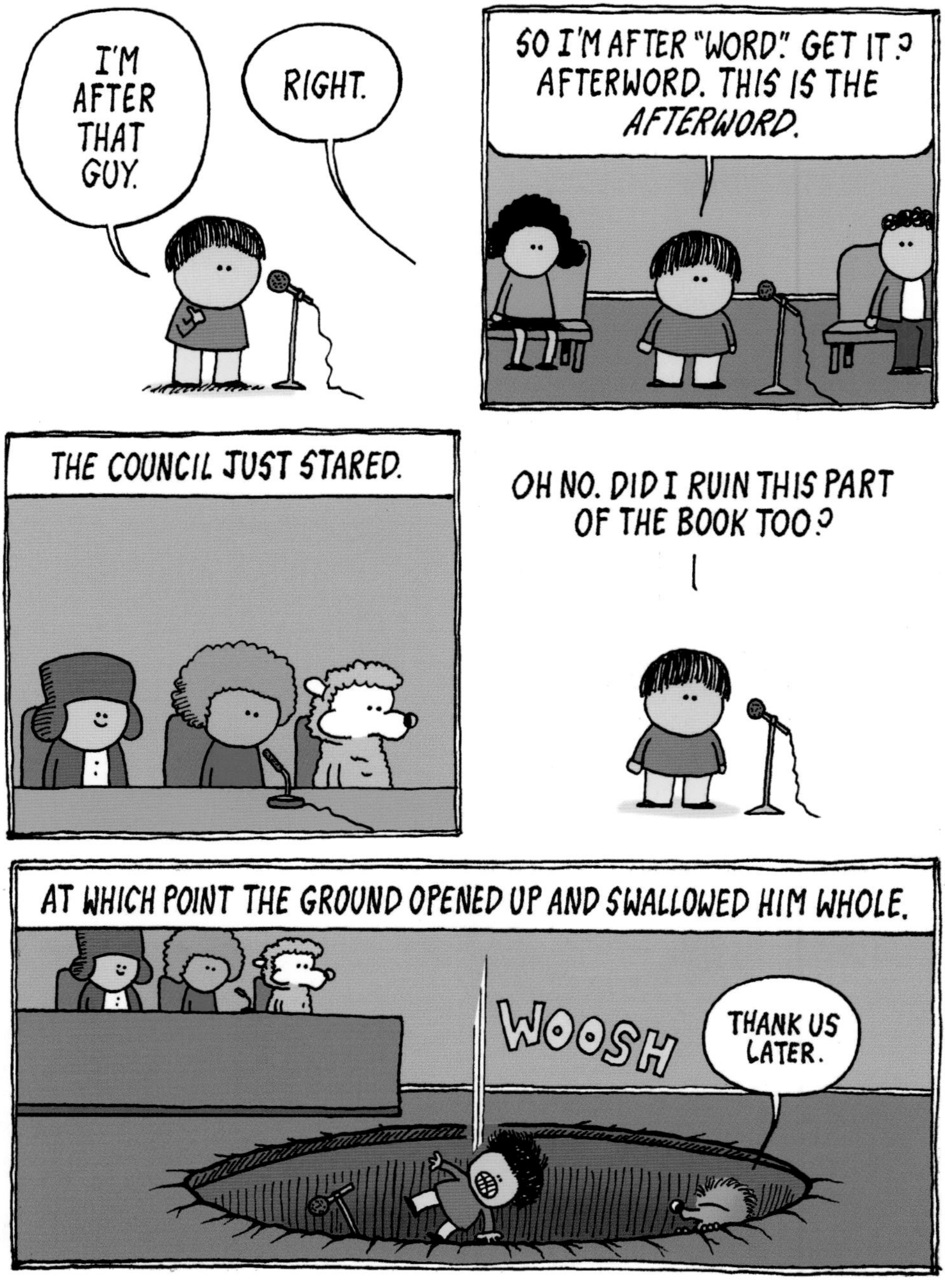
I'M AFTER THAT GUY.
RIGHT.
SO I'M AFTER "WORD." GET IT? AFTERWORD. THIS IS THE *AFTERWORD*.
THE COUNCIL JUST STARED.
OH NO. DID I RUIN THIS PART OF THE BOOK TOO?
AT WHICH POINT THE GROUND OPENED UP AND SWALLOWED HIM WHOLE.
WOOSH
THANK US LATER.

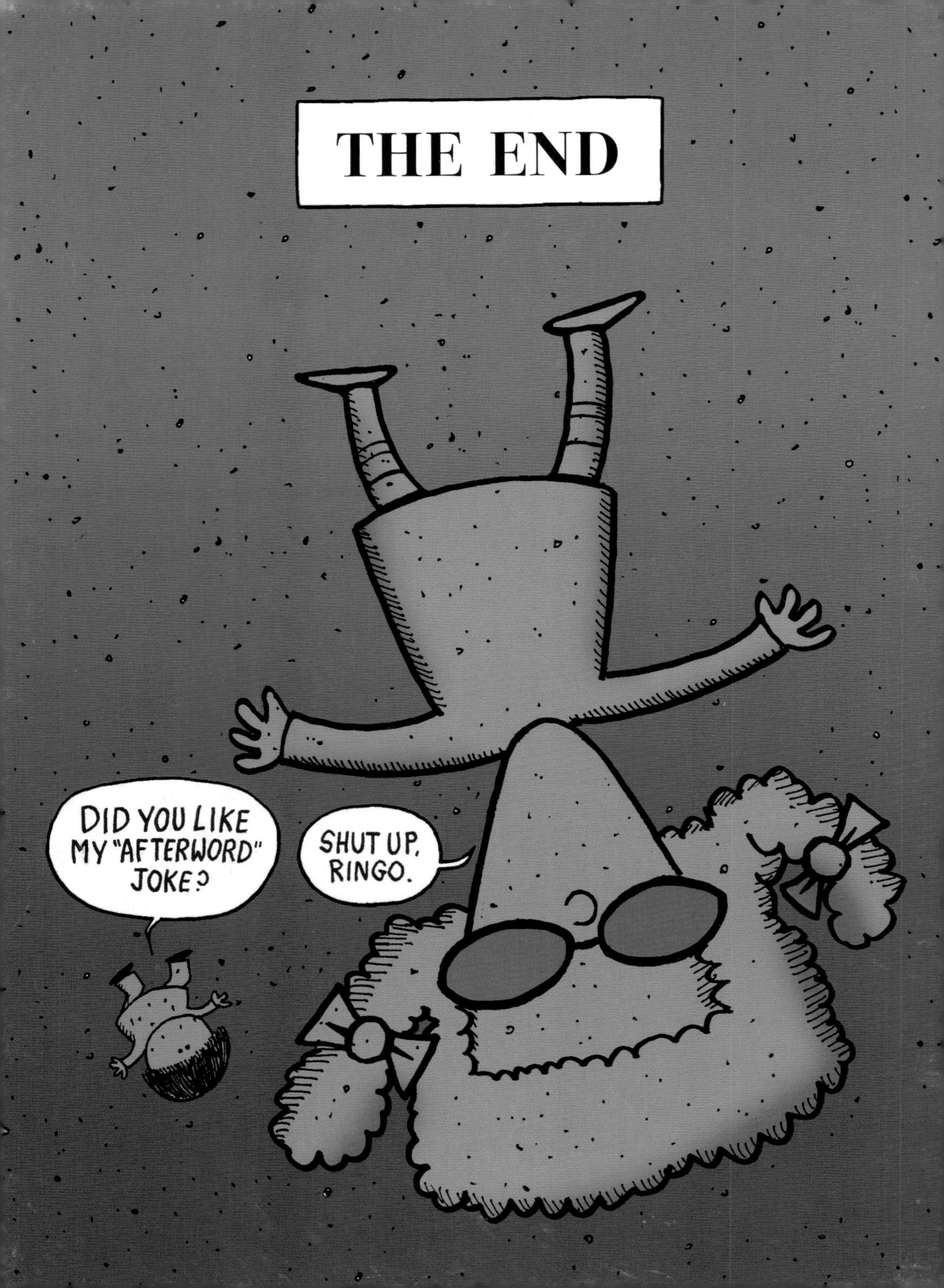
THE END
DID YOU LIKE MY "AFTERWORD" JOKE?
SHUT UP, RINGO.

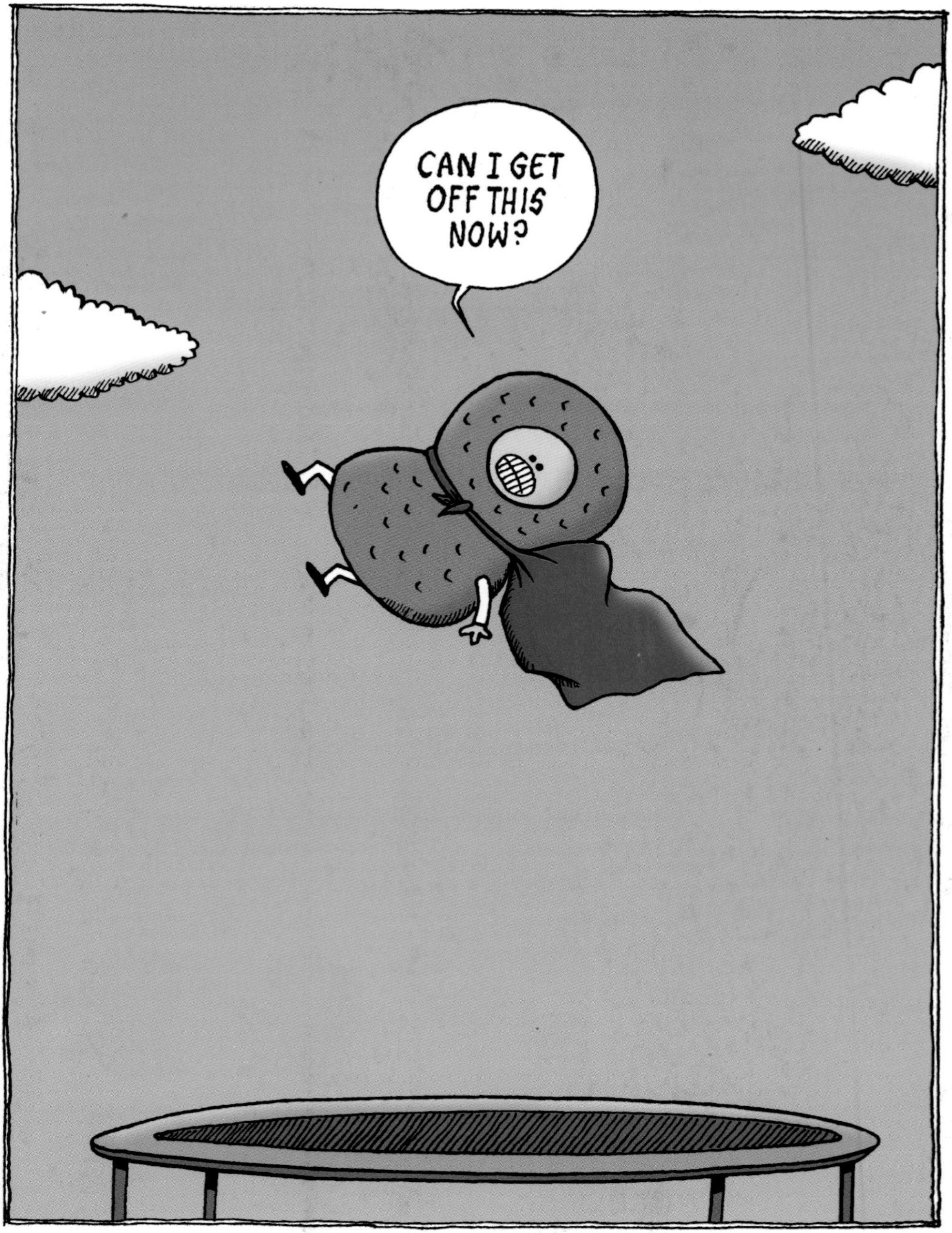
CAN I GET OFF THIS NOW?

ABOUT THE AUTHORS

The moles were due to report back to the Trubble town jail following the events described in the book.

They did not.

If you have information concerning their whereabouts, please contact local authorities.

This is their second published work.

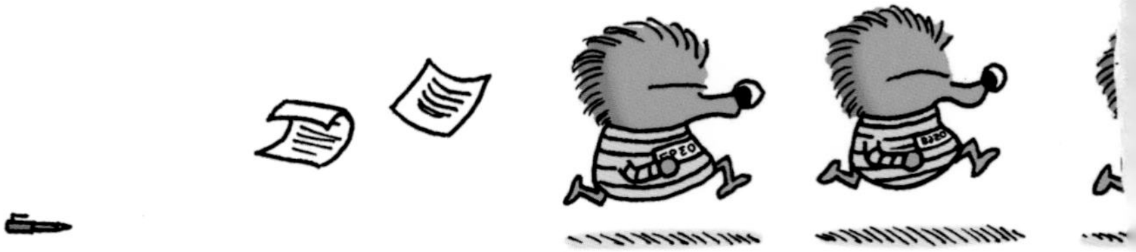